The Explorers

The Explorers

By

Kirsten Nimwey

ENGLISH EDITION

THE EXPLORERS
Copyright © 2014 by Kirsten Nimwey

ISBN: 150570152X
ISBN-13: 978-1505701524

Copyright covers all story, characters, and designs by the author.

Cover design: Kirsten Nimwey

All rights reserved.

No part of this book may be reproduced or transmitted in any form or by any means, electronic or mechanical, including photocopying, recording, or by any information storage and retrieval system without the written permission of the author, except where permitted by law.

1 PROLOGUE

Explorers, one of the groups of selected best fighters in the entire universe… who were called on and sworn to help restore and preserve what was left on the planet's surface and protect mankind from further devastation and chaos in hands of the invaders. This organization was divided into three subgroups by classes: the Ultimate Explorer (UE), which was the lowest class of the Explorers family. Second, the Extreme Ultimate Explorer (EUE), and lastly was the dream of most Explorer warriors which was the highest class of all… the Dragon Divinity Explorer (DDE). Their warriors were also called "Wielders".

According to people's belief, the Explorers were not just a group of warriors whose primary task was to defend and protect the world from annihilation against the invading forces. People believed that they were the guardians, servants, and warriors of the greatest king of all gods. Before a warrior became a part of the organization, he/she must overcome all the tests and obtain at least one missing power called the "Sacred Item" or the sacred stone. The chosen Explorer warrior (starting in the lowest class) would be rewarded and called as "Wielder". The "Sacred Item" had two types of stones: the Divine Stone and the Magic Stone. The Divine Stone held the power of an "element" that possessed strong power and elemental-based magics. This type of stone consisted of fourteen different types of elements: Holy, Earth, Time, Poison, Lightning, Deity, Fire, Darkness, Light, Trinity, Air, Ice, Water, and Gravity. The Magic Stone, was the second type of Sacred Item which held the power of a "magic". This type of stone consisted more than a hundred of its kind, but its power was limited and weaker than the Divine Stone. These two types of sacred stones were once possessed by the greatest king of the gods who released all of his powers and transformed into stones (Sacred Items).

Why thus the god released these powers and how did they all change as "Sacred Items"? Let us found out the course of history about the conquest of the gods and goddesses against their Greatest King; who was the sole master and the god of the universe whose name was King Jethro:

In ancient times, the former gods and goddesses, and even the animals and monsters were having a quarrel due to the unique power possessed by King Jethro, who was the predominant god of all whom they envied excessively. And even after the war, there was a lone monster who was furiously envied at King Jethro's power which was way beyond the universe. All of his powers consisted of fourteen elements and over a hundred of magics that became the main target of an obnoxious monster.

The lone monster thought of an evil plan and wished to seize the world, even all of the king's powers. He summoned the other gods and goddesses who were also jealous, and they secretly assembled to talk and draw an evil plan to topple the king. The lone monster said they had to conquer the kingdom of the Great King of all and take all of his priced possessions including his dignity.

"What? Are you going to conquer King Jethro's kingdom and steal all of his superpowers? Are you out of your mind?" asked one of a goddess.

"Yes, by all means! And I also want to rule the world," said the lone monster. "I want to become the Great King of the universe!" and he laughed.

"If your greed is the main reason why you seek help from us and even acquiring all of his powers, then we are not going to help you!" said the goddess. "Besides, what you only wished is for your own personal good!"

The lone monster felt angered.

"This is what we ever wanted and also want to become like him! But why you wanted to possess all of his powers and not even cared for the others?"

"No way, there's no point of helping you with your plans," said the other goddess.

The lone monster felt so angered once more, and he really wanted to possess all of King Jethro's powers. So he decided to make some excuses and device another plan to lure the goddess.

THE EXPLORERS

"Very well then, once we have conquered his kingdom and we got all of his powers, then there will be a power sharing where each and everyone of you will be rewarded. I will give each of you a free hand to choose which power do you prefer… unconditionally!" the monster with an evil smile on his face promised nothing but lies.

The gods and goddesses looked to each other as they nodding their heads thinking what they also wanted: to become the Great King and Queen of all. So, they immediately agreed to join the monster's plan.

King Jethro was so contented and happy to see his kingdom at peace. Everyone in the kingdom was living in prosperity and harmony. Not anyone, even the king himself knew nothing about the brewing danger posed in his kingdom. Though he had the best warriors and fighters in his arsenal, but the preparation to defend the kingdom was so relaxed except for some warriors patiently manning the area.

In the midst of the night, the monster's group finally arrived and lurking beyond the thick wall. Then they suddenly attacked King Jethro's kingdom with lightning speed. Caught unprepared, most of the king's warriors lost the fight against the powerful gods. Although most of the gods and goddesses' powers were weaker than of King Jethro, they still made to beat the king's warriors and the king himself. Majority of the warriors were annihilated instantly and what only left alive were the king and some survivors.

"Dear god," said the monster. "Now that we have you in our hands as a prisoner, you must surrender all your powers and we will spare your life. If not… you'll DIE!"

"Never! Over my dead body," the king replied. "You are a traitor and a ruthless monster!"

"A ruthless monster?" the monster laughed.

"Yes!"

"Why? Does a monster like me not deserve to become the Greatest King of all?"

"Never!"

The monster turned to a goddess present in the king's throne. "I give you the freedom to speak!"

The goddess responded in retorted way. "How about us? We are gods too, but we are not happy with the powers we possess… They are too weak and useless!"

scattered in all directions until they vanish in the wilderness. When they reached the human world, the powers transformed into just ordinary stones to cloak themselves against the eyes of known and unknown entities.

All of King Jethro's powers whether elements or magics were completely turned to stones, and they were now called as "Sacred Items" in mortal world.

The monster lost too much of his strength and energy. Frightened, as what the king might did to him. He wanted to escape but the king prevented him to run away.

"And because of your wickedness towards the gods, I will turn you to be the worst malevolent monster of the Darkness, and I will lock you in the underworld… forever!!!"

The lone monster screamed for help and with the snap of the king's finger, the monster quickly vanished in existence. He was nowhere to be found. The conquest was finally over, as a repercussion of what he did, King Jethro had lost everything. His powerful elements as well as his magics were all gone and scattered around the human world. He had no more powers left except his only one element that he never surrendered to the wicked monster during their encounter, which was the element of Holy Crusade.

The lost of blood from severe wounds in king's body made him weaker. He felt the poison in his wounds from the monster's sword slowly getting into his system. He had been thinking deeply of someone to whom he would give and entrust his only special power, and who would be the next one to inherit and rule his kingdom. He lived alone, away from his loyal servants.

Until, the king was getting more weaker due to the wounds. He summoned the Holy element and told his simple last request to the element itself…

"My Holy element, since that I ever have you in my possession… I never have made any request to you yet. Before I die, I want you to find me the perfect warriors to protect and take care of the other elements. Please bring me the right warriors to wield all of my powers. When you grant my dying wish, I will release you from my possession and give you the freedom to do what ever pleases you. Go away as fast as you can! Keep yourself for not being caught by evil."

King Jethro's palms shone. The element heard his first and last wish.

THE EXPLORERS

"Please find these warriors and flee!" and his voice echoed in the kingdom and slowly fading.

After three days, the king died and the divine element made its action to fulfill his master's dying request. The Holy element fled until it reached the human world and kept itself from any harm and danger. To avoid detection by the danger, the element transformed itself as an ordinary stone just like the other powers, and hid itself somewhere in the human world. Now, the Holy element was completely hidden beyond recognition along with the other powers.

More years had passed and the oblivion in King Jethro's kingdom was prevailed. New and modern world existed and a new empire was formed. In the Kingdom of the Gods, which was King Jethro's once ruled, a new gods and goddesses sprang to assert their powers. Zalan was now in charge of the entire kingdom. One night, someone paid visit to the kingdom unexpectedly. An unknown man, whose face was fully covered by a thick pure white hood and white robe. He told the gods that he was the soul of King Jethro. The gods were surprised on what they saw, but they all knelt in front of him as a sign of respect.

"Please take good care of my missing elements… As you are now the new king of all…" said the man in white robe.

"But how will I know that? I am not possessing any of your missing powers. They are vulnerable to danger."

"I know King Zalan," the man responded. "It's been too many years they have been kept hidden and unused for a very long period of time. They must be given to those who deserve and worthy of its power."

"How?"

"My powers are all turned into just sacred stones before they hid themselves in the human world. If they still remain hidden, their strengths are getting much weaker and weaker until such time their powers are no longer in use."

"What do you mean?"

"If an element that has the power of Earth is no longer used by a god for very long period of time, the element turns itself as a sacred stone and loses its power…"

"Do you think we can still recover this element even though it already transformed itself as an ordinary stone?"

"Yes and it's possible! We need to look for warriors who can find these missing elements and magics I once possessed. All of my powers!"

"How?"

"We need mutual and constant cooperation among the gods and goddesses. You need to look for the right people who can find my missing powers in the human world. Once they have gathered all these sacred stones, we have to turn the stones back to their true forms again as real 'elements' and 'magics'. And the right person who will be possessed by each of my powers will be the chosen Wielder. The human world will get very much affected if we fail to find all of my magics and elements sooner."

"Who will be the one to turn the stones into their true form? It seems too hard and impossible to do that right?"

"Only the deserving people I know who can do that or you Zalan, as the new ruler and king of our kingdom."

"I do not understand my lord… May I know how many elements are missing?"

"I have my fourteen elements that are now fully transformed into rare sacred stones called as Divine Stones and hid in the wilderness. But you also need to find all of my magics, though more than two hundred of them were gone too!"

The gods and goddesses surprised. They seemed to think that looking over a hundred powers were not easy to find and it was a tough job like looking for a needle in a bunch of hay. They did not even know the exact locations of each element that have been scattered around the human world, especially now they were all turned into just ordinary stones.

"Are you really uncertain about the exact location of your powers, my lord?"

"My apologies… I lost everything I had as well as my ability to track. I do not know exactly."

After a while, the white man slowly vanished into thin air as beautiful white feathers came out at the time he vanished. There was one feather that fell on the floor, and the beautiful goddess took it from the floor.

"Poor king… He suffered much before he died…"

King Zalan summoned the gods and goddesses, and even the angels, fairies, and other creatures to join their meeting.

"We need cooperation to find what is being told by king Jethro," said Zalan. "But how?"

"Do we think that we can find… these people that so called Wielders who can save King Jethro's powers that have been gone and missing for many years?"

"Yes."

"But we are all forbidden to go to the human world," said a fairy. "We are no humans, and we are not allowed to show ourselves to any human being."

"I know that. But there are other ways to cope with this."

The other fairy suddenly cut their conversation. "I know! I know the other way, my dear god. Why don't we all disguise ourselves as humans. I suppose, like ordinary people…"

The gods stared to each other, as if they knew there was still hope on how to reach the human world and save King Jethro's powers.

"The fairy of the stars is right! We can disguise ourselves as humans," the other fairy agreed. "You might forget that we fairies are capable to disguise and transform ourselves as humans! My lord, please allow us to enter in the human world and we will bring good news to you."

"You are right," Zalan agreed. "But how will you know in case that people might have…"

"Please do not worry too much, my lord," answered the fairy. "Fairies are very smart and wise, and we promise you that we will never fail!"

The fairies successfully entered the human world undetected. They mingled and showed themselves to the people as humans and it happened in a long period of time. People never noticed them as fairies because they were all completely disguised as humans. The fairies asked the people to help them search for the missing stones and they agreed to join on their search. But, they failed…

Another decade had passed and a new group of warriors formed called as "Explorers". The group was divided into three sub-groups to maintain the required qualifications of members and was also arranged according to their class. At first, most of the Explorer warriors were at the lowest class. But every year, some Explorer warriors were able to find sacred things like Magic Stones and were promoted to become Extreme Ultimate Explorer and Dragon Divinity Explorer, the highest class of Explorers.

A new breed of conquerors arrived and wanted to rule the world just like the evil monster did. One was a group of "Pioneer", the Explorers' most common nemesis. There was a time that the Pioneers entered the Explorers' bases and they battled. The Reminescence, another group of paladins also entered the bases and the war lasted long.

Meanwhile, a famous leader of Dragon Divinity Explorer felt deeply in love to a fairy named Isidra, unknown to him was completely disguised as a human. Isidra, conquered by her emotions was also felt deeply in love with the leader. They got married until the fairy gave birth to their eight children. Two of their children were twins while the youngest were triplets, but their three older children were taken and kidnapped by the Reminescence. The Explorers under the command of the leader of Dragon Divinity class thought of the welfare of his children and set aside the rivalry, so he decided to temporarily joint forces to the Pioneers to battle against Reminescence. The Pioneers agreed with the plan since Reminescence was also a pain in their ass and thought of evil plan in their mind. The Reminescence had no chance against the combined forces of the rival party, so they were easily defeated. But after a long period of time when the battle ended, the leader of Pioneer commandeered his warriors to kidnap all of Isidra's children. Four of her children was kidnapped by the warriors while the her remaining twin sons were able to kept inside their house to protect them. But suddenly, the Pioneer burst in the room. Her two older children were no longer to be found.

"Isidra, your four children are now under the grasp of our hands. If you're not going to tell your husband to surrender under my command... You will lose those twins you have left!"

"Please... We are a poor family..."

"What the hell do you mean by 'poor family'?" asked by Alexander, the leader of Pioneer. "How come that an Explorer's wife is a poor woman? This is unbelievable! Those Explorers are living in their mansions and they are very wealthy. You are a liar! Now tell him to surrender or else...."

"What are you going to do with my husband?"

"We Pioneers believe that he has the other elements... And we are going to get them from him. Am I right? I believe that he is the current leader of Dragon Divinity Explorer!"

"Y-Yes..." the fairy agreed. "But... I do not know where he is right now because he just left us here for our safety. He went somewhere, but he didn't tell me where he headed."

One of the members of Pioneer took one of Isidra's sleeping twins from a small bed sheet.

"Oh no! Please do not harm my child for this. I, uh… I'd say that I might know where my husband is… But I am not sure."

"All right," Alexander agreed. "Where is he?"

The fairy lied. "H-He is… In their… mansion!"

Alexander smirked. "What is he going to do in his rich home?"

The truth was, no one from the members of the first Dragon Divinity Explorers knew about the missing rare Divine Stones of element. They had found some of the sacred stones, but only "Magic Stones". They successfully turned the Magic Stones they got into their true forms as real magics. Then, the Explorers were chosen by the magics they saved to become their new Wielder and new master.

A member of the Pioneer returned her sleeping child in the bed sheet next to his twin brother. The Pioneers were about to leave, but they threatened Isidra before they left:

"When we go there and we fail to see your husband… I will kill your remaining twins. Oh and by the way, I just want to let you know that the rest of your children are already DEAD!" and then, Alexander laughed out loud.

"NO!"

"Hah, poor Isidra. How pity. Just remember this: if we fail to get those elements from your husband, your remaining twins will be the next!"

"No! The twins have nothing to do with this. Please let me… let me just die alone! You can kill me, but please not my innocent twins."

The Pioneers left Isidra with laughter. The pitiful fairy cried, but she was very clever and wise. She thought of a plan to escape and save her twins before the Pioneers returned. She placed the twins in a big basket and she went to a pier looking for a departing ship. There, she placed the basket and told her final words to her twins:

"Maximillian, Denver… my children… Please take good care of yourselves. Run away while you can and live alone among the others. You are brothers… Always remember that me and your father truly love you so much. There is nothing I can do to keep you away from harm and be together as family, but I need to do this for your own safety. This is the only way… Goodbye…"

Isidra cried as more of her tears fell to her cheeks while she kissed her twins' foreheads. And then, the ship began to leave. The fairy cried with a heavy heart as she was staring at the ship until it was completely gone to her sight.

2 THE BEGINNING

The ship departed as no one noticing that they were carrying the twins inside the basket. The basket was on the deck and the twins were asleep because the sea was calm and was sailing peacefully. It took few hours before they reached their destination called Dakar.

After five hours of travel, the ship arrived in Dakar. The passengers on board were preparing on getting their luggage. The ship was not yet anchored, but some of the passengers were getting excited to land when they jostled to each other.

"Please everyone… May I ask you to sit down for a while to avoid stampede?" said a ship crew politely.

The passengers listened and they sat. After fifteen minutes or so, the ship finally stopped. The passengers stood on their seats and they lined up properly. They brought their luggage with them while they were walking on a ramp.

When the exhausted passengers left the ship, a sailor inspected the ship if there were still any passengers left on board. As the crew was scouring the ship, the other sailor noticed the basket. He took the basket and started to search for someone who accidentally left the basket but no one returned to look for it. The sailor decided to go to their Captain to report about the abandoned basket.

"Captain, someone left the basket here!"

The sailor handed over the heavy basket to the Captain. But they both startled when they felt something was moving inside the basket. When the Captain opened it, he was surprised when the baby twins suddenly cried.

"Whose children are these?"

The Captain handed over the basket back to the sailor and ordered to find the owner of the two children. The sailor quickly ran while carrying the basket to find the twins' parents. He got off the ship and asked the passengers one by one, but no one seemed to be looking for the twins. No one told him that they were the twins' parents. Afraid and worried, he returned to his Captain.

"What?! Why you still have that basket with you?"

"Err, Captain… I asked them about it but no one told me that they own the twins."

"Huh, what do you think are we going to do with those two children?"

The sailor put down the basket and carried one of the twins. A small piece of paper fell from the child. He took a piece of paper and read what was written on it, but the only message said: "Maximillian Foster, son of Alex Foster of DDE…"

He also took a piece of paper from the other child in the basket and the message said the same thing, but in different name. "Denver Foster, son of Alex Foster of DDE…"

A sailor felt pity for the twins when no one was looking for them, so he decided to take the twins to his home. He posted a notice about the missing basket and waited all day long for any calls from anybody who might be looking for the twins. But the night came out as the sailor never received any report calls.

None. No one really looked for the twins. No one owned the twins. The sailor felt more pity to the twins so he finally decided that he was going to adopt them, and owned the twins as his sons. The sailor had no family, and he was overjoyed as the twins came to become a part of his life and not to be alone anymore.

"Is it true that these twins are the sons of a Dragon Divinity Explorer? But why did he abandon the twins? How pitiful!" he asked himself.

The sailor raised and cared the twins. After seven years, the two kids grew up as healthy twins. Though they were living in poverty because the sailor was not earning a lot, still, he managed to brought up the kids decently.

The twins grew up very industrious. They were helping their known father to look for food for their living. The sailor was very happy for his twins. And while he was at work, the two children could still guard their

THE EXPLORERS

home. Therefore, the sailor decided to call the twins with their name as "Kenji" and "Genji", instead of calling them with their real names.

The two children reached their seven years of age, but they were still unaware of their real existence: they were the sons of a Dragon Divinity Explorer and their mother was a fairy.

Night time fell when their stepfather returned home. The twins were very delighted when they saw their father brought home with money and foods.

"My children, I brought something for you," said their stepfather as he went inside their house happily.

"What is it dad?" Genji asked.

"Foods."

"What foods?"

"Seafoods. They're still raw but we are going to cook them now."

"What are seafoods?"

Genji was a playful and naughty child. That's the reason why he often fought with his brother Kenji, while Kenji was a loner and simple type of person.

"Well they are umm... fish, shrimps... like that..."

"Are there blood on them?"

"Of course, Genji! Why you ask?"

"I hate blood!"

Kenji shook his head. He wanted to talk to his twin brother but he couldn't.

"Eh... Why you ask then? I never drink blood!"

"So am I dad!" Genji answered with grimace. "I am not a 'monstah'."

Kenji laughed. "Of course brother, we are not 'monstah'. We are not going to drink blood. Its taste is real gross. But once they're already cooked, there will be no more blood."

"But how?" Genji was confused.

"I SAID WE ARE GOING TO COOK IT, YOU LISTENING TO ME!"

"Does blood gets dry? Oh yeah brother, if the blood dries... how? Blood is a liquid!"

"That will happen for sure, I just do not know how!"

"Weehhh... Maybe you are a monstah brother!"

"NO! I am a human."

"CURSE YOU OLD MAN!!!" then he raised his hand and stabbed the sailor with his sharp sword. Still unsatisfied for what he did to the old man, he stabbed the sailor five times in his abdomen… Until the poor man dropped dead and lying on his own blood!

Akira only closed his eyes in disbelief while the other members of Pioneer watched their leader killing the poor sailor. The boy slowly opened his eyes when he watched the pure blood flowing on the ground from the dead body of the sailor.

"My Pioneers, go and find those twins as fast as you can and bring them back to me, alive!"

"Yes sir," the Pioneers responded out loud.

"Failure is not an option, we will stick with our plans! We have to become superior among our enemies! First, we will finish the Explorers as soon as we can! You all got me?"

"Yes sir!"

"Good, let us leave this old man who had been useless to us!"

"Find the DDE twins!"

"And kill the Explorers!"

After they uproared, they finally left the house with a poor man's bloody corpse lying on the ground.

3 A NIGHTMARE

The twins fled from the Pioneers until they got very tired and rested for a while. They had been traveling all day long and passed through the forests, desert, and rivers only to ensure their safety. Though they were very exhausted and hungry, the twins continuously running for few more hours and got into another small forest where they rested.

"B-Brother, I am so thirsty…" said Genji in a hoarse voice.

Kenji did not answer. He looked very pale.

"Brother…"

Kenji still not answering Genji. He was too lazy to speak due to severe exhaustion.

"BROTHEEEERRR!!!"

"Yes, I know! I heard you. So am I brother, I am thirsty as well."

"Aww…"

"What? What are we going to do now? Don't lose hope. We're both suffering, we're in the same situation. Do not be a coward!"

"What coward are you talking about?"

"What I mean is, we need to be strong to overcome these hunger, tiredness, and this thirsty thing for a while okay?"

"I can't take it anymore!"

"I don't care! If you keep on asking, fine! But I can still suffer more!"

"Another thing is brother…" Genji continued with fear. "Where do we sleep? Where will we hide? If those evils will see us, maybe they will do what they did to us a week ago."

"I… I don't know!"

"WAAAHHHH!" Genji cried.

"Let's go brother, let's look for some place to sleep. The snow is coming."

The two traveled still with an empty stomach and dry throat. They walked three hours without stopping. The snow came, and it was a heavy snowstorm. The twins were both freezing badly.

"Brother... It's too cooooold!" Kenji was freezing.

The temperature was really cold so the twins hugged each other very tightly to kept themselves warm.

"B-Brother, do you think this also what happened to our mother when she was also in trouble?" Genji asked while freezing.

"M-Maybe brother... Ahhh..."

"W-Wait..." Genji whispered. "I-I see a glittering of lights from afar, there's a town over there!!!"

"W-Where?" asked Kenji in high hope. "I am chilling too much, and my vision is blurring. My whole body is getting weaker!"

Genji got more excited.

"Hahaha, hey brother it is really a town! Come on, let's go and hurry up. We can sleep there, my body's starting to numb!"

The twins walked in a hurry. "It is really a town! Hooray, maybe there are people living there to help us!"

But because of their hunger and exhaustion, the twins' bodies suddenly collapsed and fell on the snowy ground. Their bodies rolled over to the town and covered with snow.

There were some villagers passing by and they noticed the twins' unconscious bodies. But, they just ignored and pretended they saw nothing. They walked away calmly.

The town where the twins stumbled upon was called Damsville. Here in Damsville, the residents had no respect to each other. Majority of them were ill-mannered. Only few people were so kind to reach out other.

No Damsville resident managed to help the twins from the brink of death. They never cared about other people's well-being. What they only did was to just watch the twins who were still covered in dense snow and then they leave. As for the Damsville people, "mind your own business" was their law, and survival of the fittest was what they were.

A few minutes passed, Genji regained his consciousness and he slowly opened his eyes. He noticed his whole body and so his twin brother both

THE EXPLORERS

had been covered by snow like a mummy.

"Brother! Wake up. We cannot stay here, it's too dangerous!" Genji approached Kenji and he was removing away the snows all over his brother's body. Then, he pulled Kenji's arms going to a small cave to stay.

It's been a while before the snowstorm ended. Morning came when Kenji finally woke up.

"Where are we brother?" Kenji asked his twin brother.

"I don't know..."

"Ah!" Kenji quickly got up. "Is the snowstorm already gone? Come on and let's take a look for something to eat!"

"When you were still sleeping, I already did that. Look at my arm."

Genji showed his wounded arm with a trail of blood to Kenji.

"What happened to your arm?"

"I was begging for food from the residents here but I think they didn't feel pity on me."

"Oh? And then?"

"Look!" Genji suddenly cried. "Some rude man just beat me with a long wood of stick he was holding. He did not give any warning, and he just beat me to death so I protected myself, but my arm got hit... WAAHHH!"

Kenji hugged his brother to give comfort, while Genji's young face continued to cry.

"Who is this man who beat you?"

"I do not know, he just hit me that's all!"

"Where?"

"Over there!" Genji pointed to where he met the man.

"Come with me."

Genji stopped Kenji. "No brother! He will hurt you too!"

"You are my brother!"

Genji took Kenji to the man who beat him in the arm. When they reached the man's house, Kenji gently knocked and the door slowly opened. A huge man appeared!

The man was furious. "YOU AGAIN! What do you want from me?!"

Kenji responded very calm and polite. "I just want to ask food from you even just a little. I am begging you! We haven't eaten for more than a day..."

The huge man mistook that Kenji was the young boy whom he hit with his long wood earlier. "You might want to get hurt from me again kid?

Do you know how I hate naughty kids?!"

Kenji got pissed off. "Naughty? I am only begging with you for some foods to eat but then this is how you respond back to me?"

The man showed off his long wood of stick once again. "I say it again kid, I do not like naughty kids and I might hurt you again right now!" and then, the rude man slammed the wooden door very hard.

Kenji felt his eardrum popped. *How rude!* He told himself. So he knocked the door again out loud and when the man re-appeared, Kenji showed off his nerve!

"First of all, you don't have good manners! My brother and I were only begging for food because it's been more than a day we have not been eating! If you cannot help us, just tell it in a nice way! And oh, about what you did to my brother? I hope you would feel the same pain as what you did to him! You have NO respect and do not care at all towards others!"

"Hey you kid!"

"Yes, I am a kid. You don't need to tell me!"

"What am I gonna do? There's nothing for me to give to you, damn!"

"Well, that is okay! Just tell it in a nice way and we will just leave and ask someone, done! And stop hitting someone, YOU MONSTAH!!!"

And this time, Kenji slammed the door real hard which was stronger than the first monstah's slammed door.

"What are gonna do now brother?" asked Genji. "We still don't have food. There isn't somewhere for us to sleep either!"

"I know," Kenji replied. "Let's look for woods to build for ourselves."

"You mean… we will build our own house here?"

"Yeah, that is the only way."

"I'll help you brother!"

"Of course! Obviously you will help me in building our house…"

"What are we gonna do?"

"First, let's take a look for a safe place for us to build our own house."

"Let's build our house a li'l far away from those stupid residents! I LOVE the way they're treating us!"

"All right."

The twins looked for a safe place to stay in Damsville where they could build their own house. When they found the perfect spot, the twins started to look for woods. They found some, and the twins began to build their house. With no such experience in house construction, the result was terrible.

The twins stopped when they heard a continuous cries of a young boy and a girl in a distance. The twins ran fast to follow the voices.

"You bad kid! UMMM, a thief!!!"

When the twins reached the spot, they encountered a tall kid of the same age as them stealing foods from the two kids who were crying while trying to stop the thief.

Although the twins were still hungry, they showed their gallantry to help the two kids. From the speed of a flash, they reached the thief and took off the food he stole from the kids. After that, the twins returned the food to them.

"Ah, thank you... Thank you very much..." a boy said delightfully.

"We are thanking you both for helping us, you are brave!" said a girl.

"Wait, who are you anyway?" Genji asked.

"Ah, we are cousins. My name is Shiela and this is Aaron."

"Ahh..."

"And what about the other kid?" asked Kenji. "The thief? Who is he?"

"That's Claude," said Aaron. "He is our peer and also an orphan like us. We have been here staying for four years straight."

"You're orphans," said Genji sadly. "Me and my twin brother have been raised by a sailor without the presence of our real parents."

"You're fast," Shiela was impressed. "You guys made it to reach Claude even though he's taller and bigger than you."

"Yeah."

"You're awesome. So, where are you from? Where do you live? Hm?"

"Nothing."

"Nothing?"

"Why?"

"We got away from wicked people."

"You know what," Genji continued. "It's been a week that we got away from those mean people and until now, we haven't eaten anything just yet!" he was trying to let Shiela and Aaron hear what he really meant.

"Wow, you're strong! Why?"

"Long story..."

Shiela and Aaron took the twins to their house to take a break. Kenji told Shiela and Aaron about what happened before they reached Damsville.

"Hey! Why don't you guys stay with us? You see, we even grew up without the presence of our parents either. Only me and Aaron built our own house! Come on, join us, our house is small… But it's durable!"

"They're right brother," said Genji. "Let's stay with them for a while!"

"Don't worry, Shiela and I already cooked our food earlier, and there's still some food left. You can eat the rest so the leftovers will not be wasted."

"Thanks!"

"You're welcome," said Aaron.

While eating, they talked a lot until their next topics added some mischievousness. The four were having a good time until they bonded and became good friends.

After having a good meal and nice conversations with Shiela and Aaron, the twins took a rest in Shiela and Aaron's house. It was almost midnight when the twins slept very soundly.

But the twins seemed restless as they were both dreaming. They were dreaming about their horrible future. The dream was not pleasing. The twins' mysterious parents became their own nemesis and their parents warned that they would become their mortal enemy when they reached their adulthood!

Kenji saw his image in the future. He was an adult muscular warrior with an evil horn on his forehead!

Shiela and Aaron noticed the twins who were both moving, panting, and shaking constantly while sleeping. So they awoke the twins.

"Get up you guys!" said Aaron while they were shaking the twins' shoulder.

The twins suddenly woke up. "Why did you awake as well brother? Did you have a horrible dream as mine?" asked Genji to his brother.

"Yes… Our parents and my future image… I saw it!"

"M-Me too! I even saw my image in my dream brother, I will be very much handsome in the future!" Genji told a joke.

"No! Our parents… Their face looked very horrible and bad!"

"What? Was that your dream too?"

"Huh? Did you dream about it as well?"

The twins wondered. Was it true? Or was it just a nightmare?

4 THE YOUNG MORTAL

His name was Claude, a boy who had the same age as the twins and also an orphan. But unlike the twins, Claude was three years of age when he got separated from his parents.

He had a brother and sister and he was the eldest. His younger sister was the second and his brother was the youngest.

Claude was a son of a Skywalker, a group of rebels that was not seeking King Jethro's powers unlike Pioneer. His mother took him away because she did not want him to become a part of his father's group who was the leader.

Skywalkers were enemies and slaves of the first Reminescence. Before the mother fled her children, she told them this warning:

"Claude, never tell anyone that you are a son of a Skywalker! Don't reveal your true identity or you might be killed! You are their enemy. You must avoid them whenever you can!"

And now that he was a grown up kid, no one still knew that he was a son of a Skywalker.

Seven more years had passed and the twins grew up in Damsville. The twins were fourteen years of age while Aaron and Shiela were both eighteen years old. Because of Shiela and Aaron's help, the twins grew up more disciplined and more aware of new things in life.

Kenji and Genji had enough understandings to ponder in life and they both knew what was right and what was wrong. They were getting matured, so they say. The twins had found work to do enough to support their everyday needs. They still did not talk to any Damsville resident, though they had been living there for years.

Genji and Aaron were in charge in getting their food in the forest. They were also in charge in getting more firewoods, timber, bamboo, and dried woods for the renovation of their small house.

"Hey," Genji yelled and waving next to Aaron. "Leave this to us. Aaron and I will be hunting for food!"

"All right," said Shiela. "Kenji and I will be watching our house while you're gone."

"Okay," Aaron agreed.

The two were about to leave when Kenji said something to them. "Take care."

"Hehehe, thanks!"

The two left. What only left now were Shiela and Kenji.

"Kenji, it's been a long time that you and Genji stayed right here with us, isn't it?" Shiela asked.

"Yeah, why you ask?" Kenji asked.

"Nothing."

"It sounds like... you might want us to leave, is that correct?"

"No way! Me and Aaron are only embarrassed at you two because you help us a lot and there's nothing we can offer in return."

"It's okay. We're family here and we treated each other as brothers and sister. Like as one big family!"

Shiela smiled. "Thanks."

"Come on! There are a lot of things to do."

"By the way Kenji, how old are you now? And Genji?"

"14."

"14?"

"Yes, why?"

"So that means, Aaron and I are older than you two!"

The two kept busy working in their small home. After thirty minutes, the two rested for a while when suddenly they heard someone shouting:

"You filthy thief, when will you just... STOOOPPP AND LEAVVEEEEE!!!"

"What's that, Kenji?"

"I don't know. I'll check."

"Sure."

Kenji went outside and he followed the voice. He arrived at the bakery wherein he heard some shattering glass noises coming from the building. Kenji approached the bakery shop when a thief followed by a vendor came out with a broken bottle in his hand.

"You naughty thief, take this!" then the vendor threw out the bottle at the thief as hard as he could.

The bottle flew towards the thief and he got hit in the head very hard. The thief fell on the floor with a blood on his face. The vendor approached the fallen thief and pulled off his hair when Kenji noticed the culprit was Claude! Kenji was shocked and did not know what to do to help him. Then, the vendor pulled Claude's hair once again and faced over the residents and said:

"We all know that this kid is the number one thief in Damsville, right?" asked the vendor angrily. "What should we do now with this kid now?"

"Take him to the prison!" said a woman.

"Kill him!" said an old man.

"No, let's torture this kid first and then we will kill him, hahahaha!"

The vendor put down the bag full of fresh breads that Claude stole from the bakery. There were plentiful of breads inside the bag that almost got full by the naughty thief.

He pulled Claude again and Claude fell on the ground as his blood splattered on it. The residents took their beaters and whips while looking at the bloody thief. They were about to beat him when Kenji suddenly stopped them to protect the bloody thief.

"Hey! Are you one of his friends, eh? There might be lots of thieves here nesting in our town and you are one of them!"

"What are we waiting for?" a man said. "Let's beat them both."

The man tried to frighten Kenji by raising his hands with a long wood and was about to hit him, but Kenji stayed and did not dodge. He was staring closely at the man and the man stopped then he scoffed.

"You are brave kid! You didn't move to evade my first attack."

"Could you please just forgive this boy for what he did?" said Kenji in a nice way. "He is an orphan like me trying to live and survive in this world. We don't want to steal but hunger is pushing us to do it."

"We don't care if that's the reason! Why did he steal our belongings?! That's unfair! We're always working hard to look for a living!"

Kenji returned the food taken by Claude. "You already have what he got from you. Please let him go and I'll teach him a lesson!"

"What? You're funny kid! Do you think he'll listen to you? Are you a priest's son? You fool!"

"Let's beat 'em!"

The angry residents raised their hands again when Kenji closed his eyes while still protecting Claude.

"If you were the one got stolen by that kid, would you still want to forgive him, you fool? If you might be one of his friends then we will kill you both!"

The residents raised their hands higher with their beaters when Shiela suddenly came. The people stopped.

"He is nothing to do with that thief, please do not beat him!" cried Shiela.

"Hey Shiela, don't tell me that you're... Even working with these two thieves!"

"N-No... Oh," Shiela put out her 50 cents worth of coins from her pocket. "If you'd like... Here, you can take it!!!"

The residents looked at each other and slowly put away their beaters and whips. "We don't hurt little girls, especially teenagers! Let's leave people. At least we got our breads back!"

The Damsville residents agreed and they left when Kenji and Shiela looked at each other.

"Oh no Kenji, what are we going to do with this bad thief now? Maybe he'll beat us when he wakes up!"

"He's unconscious. Let's take him to our house!"

"What? Are you crazy, Kenji? You might have forgotten that... He's a THIEF!"

"I know."

"You know that! Then why should we have to take him home with us? The residents will surely think that he's exactly our friend!"

"Come on Shiela, I know what exactly I am going to do."

Shiela was forced to agree so the two took Claude to their home.

When they arrived home, they laid Claude down on their sheets while his head was still bleeding.

Shiela felt scared. "Kenji, you might've forgotten... It's been very long time since that demon kid stole everything from us here in Damsville, but then..."

"I know. I'll do something."

Genji and Aaron returned home with their food and other useful supplies for a living. Then the two was shocked when they saw Claude inside their house. They immediately took their beaters to beat the thief but Kenji stopped them.

"Stop this useless drama. I understand this boy, I'll do something to him."

"You're crazy brother!"

"Yes, I am TOO crazy!"

Genji felt angered towards Kenji. "You never realized how many times that this badass stole from us!"

"I know!"

Shiela stopped the commotion between the twins and they calmed themselves.

"All right brother, if he does something bad when he gets up… That will be your biggest fault!"

"Yes, I am responsible for this possible mistake!"

"I'll beat that kid later!"

"Then go ahead!"

"He'll see!"

Aaron and Genji waited for Claude to awake, but Claude was still unconscious. Until Genji, Aaron, and Shiela got tired of waiting:

"He is still unconscious until now," Genji said irritated. "I'm too tired of waiting!"

"Go and take a rest brother," said Kenji smiling.

"But where do we sleep if that badass is lying in our sheet?! Look, it got messy now because of his filthy blood!?"

"Yeah you're right," said Shiela. "I just washed it earlier… And I am sleepy as well!"

"Let's go Shiela," said Genji. "Let's sleep outside. It's still early… Afternoon."

"But we have not been eating yet, Genji."

"Oh… oh yeah!"

"Shiela," called Aaron. "Genji and I will help you cook our dinner, okay? I guess you'll need our help."

"Oh thank you Aaron. Okay, then cook outside. Did you get some woods?"

"Of course!"

Shiela faced Kenji. "We will go outside to cook for four of us. It's up to you if you still want to watch him, but we will call you when the dinner's ready, okay?"

Kenji nodded. "Okay."

Shiela went outside with Genji and Aaron. Kenji sat on the floor while looking at Claude's bloody face, but he felt a strange feeling that he did not know what it was.

"What's this sudden strange feeling I just felt now?.."

Kenji stood to get a wooden chair he made when he was still a kid, but the chair broke into pieces just as he sat on it. He smiled, realizing that he was getting older since the chair could no longer stand his weight.

So, Kenji sat on the floor. He had been waiting for Claude's first move when he awoke. The other three teenagers were cooking food outside when Kenji smelled the scent of a fried fish.

"Smells yummy..." he said to himself as his stomach started to crumble.

"Kenji, come here! Time to eat. Look how Genji just overcooked our fish! It's burned already," Shiela shouted from outside while laughing.

Kenji laughed. "That's okay hahaha, but that still smells good!"

"But the rest of the fishes are not overcooked. It's Aaron who cooked them."

"Okay, coming through."

"Is Claude still sleeping? Hope he never wakes up!" said Genji from outside.

"Hope so…"

Kenji was about to stand again when Claude opened his eyes and smelled the fried fish.

"What's that smell?" Claude asked.

Kenji answered in a snobbish way. "Nothing."

Shiela, Genji, and Aaron went in carrying their cooked foods when Claude's mouth drooled. He was about to snatch the foods when Kenji saw him and hit his hand.

"Claude, try to steal or this beater I am holding right now will hit your head once again," Kenji threatened Claude.

Claude was surprised of Kenji's threat and looked at him from head to toe. "Hello? Who the hell are you to talk to me like that?!"

THE EXPLORERS

Claude tried to snatch the food again.

"Go ahead, Claude… Or else your blood will flow down on the floor again!"

Claude gave up. "I-I'm sorry… I am starving now, can I have a piece of it please?"

"So you are starving as well. Then why you were trying to steal our food? You could just ask from us and we are gladly to give you some!"

Claude knelt down when he felt his wound in his left arm got pain. Then he cried.

"What the hell have I done?! I've been too shameful!!!"

The four wondered. They thought that Claude felt sorry and already realized his mistakes he had been doing for many years.

"Huhuhu… I've been a bad person! Moooommmm… please help meeee!" Claude sniffed.

Shiela heard Claude. "We've been living in the same situation, Claude. We are also hungry and starving. And we need to work hard in order to survive. We never tried to steal, because if we do… we might get hurt and killed. If your father is a thief, then try not to become like him!"

"Shiela, why?" asked Claude while still on his knees. "Do you know my father?"

"N-No why? Is he already dead?"

"No!" then he cried once again. "I know what I've been doing is wrong, but I was just doing it because I don't have money to buy for my own food!"

Aaron replied: "You know what Claude, if we only all worked together, then you would never walk alone. Look at Kenji and Genji, they were also hungry and suffering when they arrived here and met us… And yet, we worked together. Come to think of it, until now we are still living together happily without stealing anything and being beaten by someone else!"

Claude shook his head. "Is that mean… I could be with you all and accept me though I'm a thief?"

"Y-Yeah, if you're a good boy."

"How long have you been staying here?"

"It's been fifteen… Ah no, it's been fourteen years since Sheila and I stayed here. And for those years… we were also suffering in hunger and thirst but we never steal to live!"

Then Shiela continued. "So please never think that you are alone here, Claude. Remember, we are also living the same fate like you!"

Claude stared at the wounds as well as the bruises he got and seemed to have learned his lesson. He tried to stand on his own feet but his legs were quivering so he fell down again. His wounds were too painful and fresh.

"And if you never become a good kid, then nobody will love and care for you."

Kenji took a small fried fish on a banana leaf and he gave it to Claude. "Here take it."

Claude was surprised by Kenji's kindness even though he had been known for being a thief for years, and yet Kenji still showed his kindness to him. Claude shed tears, and he wanted to weep more when he forced himself to stand.

"What?" asked Kenji. "Take this and promise us that you will never do this mischief thing ever again, do you understand?"

Claude continued to weep. He did not want to take the dish from Kenji because he believed that showing mercy to the Skywalkers was a big shame to the group.

"I couldn't believe that... Despite of the things I've done to you, you all still care for me."

"Because we understand you, Claude. Oh here, why don't you take this now?"

"Thank you my friend, but please do not just simply give that to a person who doesn't deserve that blessing. I'm about to leave now..."

"Are you stupid? Where do you think you're going and later this afternoon the snow will fall again. It's too dangerous outside!"

"Please let me suffer too!"

"Don't be stupid, Claude!"

Kenji stopped the thief, but he knew Claude was not going to leave because he was weak due to the deep wounds he got. Kenji helped him.

"The king of the gods above will forgive you, Claude... Here, take it..."

"Kenji... Why?"

"C'mon, we understand you!"

"T-Thank you," then Claude hugged Kenji as he smiled.

Genji felt disappointed towards his twin brother when he gave their food to the thief. Claude accepted the food and he ate it as fast as he could! *Ummm, so yummy!*

A day had passed and the snow stopped but would return again soon. Sheila was already awake when Kenji woke up, but he noticed his twin brother was not around. Shiela quickly approached him.

"Kenji, your brother left earlier but he didn't tell me where he went."

"What? Since when?"

"I think… since dawn. And, the residents are outside. There is something written on the wall but I can't read it because they are blocking my view."

"I'll go take a look!"

"Wait… I'll go with you," said Claude with his forehead already wrapped in bandage.

The two rushed outside their home going to where the residents were looking at the wall. Kenji jumped higher to read the writing. It said:

"THE RESIDENTS OF DAKAR WERE AMBUSHED AND KILLED BY THE GROUP OF PIONEERS AND REMINESCENCE--"

"No, oh father! Is this the reason why my brother left as soon as he read this?" asked Kenji in shock. "'Coz… What they really wanted there were just me and my brother!!!"

"What do you mean by that?" asked Claude.

The people quickly turned around. They just noticed that the two were with them.

"That thief! Guess we're right, they're companions! Seize theeeemmm!!!"

"Claude, let's go back to Shiela and hide!"

The two dashed as fast as they could until they successfully reached back to their home and not being caught by those people.

"I do not understand Kenji, how could you become one of Pioneers?" asked Claude.

"You're wrong Claude," said Kenji while packing. "We are only their main purpose."

"Wait," Shiela interrupted the two. "What do you mean by that Kenji?"

"I'm going back in Dakar. I think my brother is there. We are going to save our dad. Are you coming with us?"

"I don't really understand Kenji, but where exactly is Dakar and what is it like there? Aaron and I can't just leave our house…"

"No more words Shiela, but remember this: since they're into us doesn't mean we are enemies. That's not it. The reason why they're looking for us is that we are sons of a DDE warrior!" then Kenji faced Shiela. "Forget it, I am leaving now," then he went outside. "I thank you and Aaron for everything. I promise I will be back here in Damsville!"

"Kenji… take care."

Kenji left their house carrying his belongings when the Damsville residents caught his attention.

"Hey, the other thief!"

Claude rushed outside just as he heard the residents' cries and helped Kenji to carry his bags and some foods. The people chased the two.

"Hey Kenji! We're now being chased by these people! Where will we hide?" asked Claude while they were both running fast.

"There's nothing else we can do Claude, but… to come with me going to Dakar!"

"Is it too far?"

"Not too far… But we can make it! My brother, I think he's already there. Why he didn't tell this to me?"

"O-Okay, I'm coming with you then Kenji," said Claude while running. "Well, there isn't anything more for me to do in Damsville since my record there is always bad!"

Many hours had passed when the two reached Dakar without resting and even taking a break to eat. Because of their perseverance and Kenji already knew where Dakar was, the two finally reached the said place in twelve hours!

The town of Dakar had changed a lot unlike before, and Kenji noticed that it was already abandoned. He saw something posted on a wall so he moved over it to read the writing: "RETURN THE TWINS TO US ALIVE AND UNSPOILED OR ELSE….MORE LIFE WILL BE LOST!!!"

"Is this Dakar?" Claude wondered as he was looking around.

"Yes, the place of torment!!!" answered Kenji crying!

5 THE JOURNEY

It was already too late when Kenji and Claude arrived in Dakar. Dead bodies were strewn all over the place. There were no more people living there and the whole town was completely abandoned. The small houses were dilapidated and were burned down to the ground.

"I wonder what happened to my father? And my brother… where is he?" Kenji asked Claude.

"I don't know!"

"C'mon Claude, let's take a look at the house where me and my brother lived before."

The two first went to the twins' former home seven years ago. When they reached the place, Kenji was surprised to see it was already demolished. Their house was completely gone and untraceable.

Kenji with a teary eyes, screamed out loud: "DAD! Where are you now? What just happened to this town?!" and then he cried.

There was a woman's voice responded in a distance. "Were you seeking an answer about that kid? Well, your stepfather has been dead a long time ago!"

Kenji was shocked as if the sky fell on his head when he learned what was happened. He looked around to find where the voice came from. "What are you talking about? Wait, who are you? Reveal yourself!"

A mysterious woman showed up from a high dead tree. "I am one of the Vanguards. Are you the son of a DDE warrior and a fairy?"

Kenji did not confirm nor deny the asking. "V-Vanguard? What are you doing here?"

"Nothing, we are one of the Explorers' enemy. We did not participate with Pioneers in destroying this place, and we do not intend to take you!"

"And my father?!"

"I do not know the name of your stepfather but I should tell you this: Pioneers were still looking and want to kill somebody here in this place!"

"Huh?!"

"Well, it's because Pioneers believe that Dakar is a cursed town. They know that there is a sacred object buried and hidden in this place which I do not know what it is. They are also looking for the twins of a DDE warrior, but your stepfather said nothing but lies… And then, BA-GOOM! They killed him!" then she laughed. "Your considered father was the first victim and who got killed by Pioneers when they couldn't find the twins. And then, every year they just keep on coming back only to look for the twins and kill the rest of the innocent residents one by one…"

"You mean, those Pioneers killed my father right after me and Genji ran away? That was already seven years ago!!!"

"Why?" asked the woman. "Do you still believe that he is still alive?"

"M-My father is already gone… THIS IS ALL MY FAULT!"

The woman teased Kenji. "Oh yeah, your fault… I'm sorry to hear that!"

Claude asked. "Kenji, what is the sacred object that woman was talking about? And your brother Genji… why he isn't here?"

"Oh by the way, there was another young boy who looked like you came here just lately. Maybe he is your twin brother. I was right… you are the twins they were searching for…"

Kenji ignored Claude's question earlier. "What? Where is he now?"

"Well… the Pioneers were here when he came."

"Then? Where is he now?"

"Now he's gone! Those Pioneers tortured and kidnapped him! Maybe he's also dead by now!"

Kenji felt a deep anger in his self. It seemed that he wanted to scream and destroy the world. Instead, he punched the ground repeatedly until his fist bled but he ignored it. The rain fell, and the droplets poured on Kenji's cheek.

"Come on Claude… My father's already gone… It's over…"

The woman touched her chin. "Hmmm, wait a minute. How about a little game? But be prepared for my attack if you don't want to get caught by Pioneers when they get back!"

"Kenji!" cried Claude. The woman began her first move by casting a black magic to Kenji. Kenji remained steady and did not evade the attack. He completely absorbed the full power cast on him until he suddenly lost his consciousness. And then, he collapsed on the ground!

"KENJI!" cried Claude, while trying to awake Kenji.

"It's a sleep-type magic where its victim will lose his consciousness and fell into the deep sleep for a long period of time or might be forever! But it only depends on its power that I cast on him. Wait, I wonder if he'll awake again? Hahaha, I have made my contribution on behalf of Vanguard! Ahahaha!!!" then she turned back. "Too bad that he wasn't prepared for my attack. Since he's already unconscious, maybe those Pioneers will see him here and take him just like his brother! Oh wait," the woman stopped and looked over Claude. "Skywalker…"

Claude's eyes grew bigger. "W-What? How did you know I'm a Skywalker?!"

"I noticed a scar on your chest that symbolizes Skywalker. Good! The Reminescence might return someday to take you too!"

"Just shut your filthy mouth, I've been hiding my true identity for a very long time!"

"Then you must come and follow me if you want to be safe…"

"No!"

"How rude. Well then, take this sleep magic and come with me!"

In a moment, Claude also lost his consciousness and the woman took him away from Kenji who was still lying on the cold and dirty ground. Asleep very deeply… Would it be forever?

The power of black magic was so strong that made Kenji remain unconscious for three years straight. It took a very long time since he fell in a deep sleep, until his friends were no longer at his side.

Until… a soft and warm lick by a stray cat on his right hand triggered his senses that made Kenji awake and return his consciousness in the real world.

The young man gently opened his eyes when the stray cat closely stared at him straight. He rose to where he lay down and lifted his hands but he appalled… as he noticed the big difference in his hands. It grew much bigger as well as its shape and when he touched his face, he also noticed the difference. He cried out loud when he also noticed his voice changed as well. Kenji was now a young man.

"I do not understand… I changed a lot. How long that I've been sleeping?"

The stray cat was still staring at him. Kenji asked the cat.

"How about you cat? Did you notice that I grew up like this?"

The cat was still staring at him. Kenji looked above in wonder. "Huh? Where am I? What happened?"

No response, Kenji bowed his head. "It's been a long time I'd been asleep… Ah, but why is it that my trousers got big as well? Agh, I don't remember anything!"

Kenji stood on his feet. His height was 5'7". "Oh, and I'm taller now!"

He hesitated for a while. "This is too confusing! I do not even remember what happened… What am I gonna do now? Why did I fall asleep?! Hey, was that mean I didn't eat anything that long?!"

The cat turned away as it seemed that someone was coming. Kenji heard some footsteps on the grassland and the cat went behind him.

"Who's there?" asked Kenji alerted.

The steps were approaching and the cat got frightened. Then it meowed.

An elderly woman appeared and Kenji thought it was an enemy. The woman was looking at him.

"What is it *lola*? Do you need anything?" asked Kenji.

"I have a question," asked by the elderly woman. "How come that you are still alive?"

"I… I don't understand *lola*."

"YOU'RE A LAZY YOUNG MAN!" answered the old woman. "Three years had passed and I never seen you awake. I even never seen you eating nor drinking! Imagine, within your three years of sleep without food 'til now… and what more surprising is… You're still alive?!"

Kenji had finally learned the reason. He had been sleeping for three years straight. Sleeping handsome!

"Umm… Well… I, ah…"

"What?"

"I had a curse that time…"

The old woman laughed. "What? A curse? Hahaha, what is this so called curse thing you are talking about? Did you mean that this place is cursed?!"

"N-No... I was cursed... W-Wasn't I?"

Kenji had no memory of what happened to him three years ago. "Wait *lola*, what is this place anyway?"

"What? You also don't know where you come from? You went here but you didn't know? What are you then, an alien? You lazy young man!"

Kenji got pissed off but he could not fight back the old woman out of respect. "N-No... I just lost some of my memories about my past that's all..."

"When you were sleeping, we were watching you. We assumed you were dead. We were about to bury you but we were wondering why you weren't rotting? My neighbors felt disgusted at you."

"What is this place?"

"This is Dakar, are you stupid?"

When the old woman mentioned the name of Dakar, a lightning memories suddenly entered Kenji's mind: his twin brother, and so on. He almost surprised the woman when he suddenly jumped for joy!

"Oh yes, I remember now! I remember what happened in the past."

The old woman wondered. "Hello, are you mad?"

"I actually remember anything now!"

"What on earth are you talking about?"

"*Lola*, I am a traveler... A son of a DDE warrior."

The cat meowed in interest, as if it wanted to go with the young man.

"Very well then," said the old woman. "I think I know what you meant earlier. Though I'm an old woman, I still believe in the curse. Come with me and eat first. I will let my colleagues know that you're finally awake, 'coz we were really mistaken that you're dead, or really that lazy!"

The old woman took Kenji in her small house when he began to reminisce his family: when he and his brother Genji were still together with their stepfather. A father who raised them, and in just a snap of a finger was killed by Pioneers... The old woman invited him to eat the meal.

While eating: "So lad, where do you think you're heading?" she asked.

"I will travel somewhere to seek answers..."

"I don't understand you."

Kenji wanted to ask the woman. "By the way, how long you've been living here?"

"Eh, we just moved here, two years ago!"

"Ah..."

"Well, before the Dakar was taken, the residents prepared to leave the place but it was too late. Many of them have died. But we preferred to move here because we continuously receive threats that our town would be the group's next target!"

"You mean the main reason why you moved here is because they are going to attack your place? Man, what's your town called?"

"It's too far from here," the old woman cried. "There's nothing else for us to stay so we decided to move here although we know it's still dangerous to stay. But if they come back again, we will just accept our fate… Well, I am from Bondore…"

"So the town of Bondore will be their next order of attack… What is their intention? Why do they keep on conquering?"

"I don't know! They said that they were searching for stones and we don't have any idea what they are. They had a lot of talks! Too annoying!"

"I know those things they were looking for, and only the group of Pioneers will be the ones to go there. They aim for greatness to be the leader of the universe and become the possessor of former Great King's powers. Yeah, as far as I remember, their leader told me about it when I was still a kid. But I will not tell you more about it… and I will not allow it to happen for sure!"

Kenji finished his meal by eating three scoops of rice. Wow, his belly grew bigger!

Feeling bloated, he decided to leave and say goodbye to the old woman who treated him nicely: "Thank you very much *lola*. I am leaving now and I will do my best to save Bondore from Pioneers!"

"Wait my boy," stopped the old woman. "Why don't you take some rest before you leave?"

"No, no, no need!" Kenji smiled. "I have rested for three years so I'm sure I gained enough energy in my body. Anyway, thank you very much for your kindness, *lola*!"

"Do your best my boy. Take care!"

Kenji walked aimlessly when the cat followed him. He noticed the animal behind him and felt pity on it.

He suddenly remembered that he had no idea where Bondore was, so he went back to the old woman just to ask its location. "By the way *lola*, where is the road leading to Bondore?"

"Oh, Bondore is in the northwest of Dakar, just across the huge river of Thales. Take care!"

Kenji left, but the cat was still following him so he wondered. "Why? Are you also alone like me? Hey, how about if you come with me so you're no longer alone?"

Kenji took the animal in his arm when the old woman quickly came out from her house and yelled.

"Hey, don't steal that cat! That is one of my neighbor's pet!"

"Oopppss... sorry!" Kenji blushed and he put down the cat gently and talked to it. "I thought you were stray. Someone owns you and I am glad to know that you are not alone..."   He petted the cat and then he left. The cat meowed as an answer when the young man was moving away.

Kenji was on his way to save Bondore, and to confront the Pioneers without fear! His first journey...

6 ISIDRA

Isidra was a fairy of love and emotion who had the power to feel all emotions as an energy coming out from any human beings living in the human world.

Perhaps she was the saddest living entity not only because she was alone, but also she was away from her own family. She lost all of her children as well as her beloved husband who was more concerned in all DDE missions as a leader of the Explorer organization. A type of leader who could sacrifice everything even his own life and family. She had no any news about what was happening with her family. In order to free herself from worrying, she went along with the goddess of love whom she cared so much. It had been many times she had been restless and uneasy while waiting for the return of her beloved husband and her children. And it had been years passed that all she had to do was to cry all day.

"Isidra, I've never seen a smile on your face... except those diamonds that keep on coming out from your eyes whenever you cry. Are you still hoping to see your family again?" asked one of the fairies who was Isidra's friend.

Isidra's tear fell once again on her cheek and it turned into a brilliant diamond. "Yes, I am still with high hope... My children are wise and smart. They can handle themselves in any danger they are facing, even in the hands of the enemies."

"But what if they will not return? What will you do then?"

"Don't speak like that! I-I have my twin sons and I took them in..."

"What did you say Isidra? Where?"

Isidra cried. "N-Nevermind! I am still hoping to be with my family again someday soon," then she mumbled to herself. "Reinhardt... you're my eldest son... I know you are all together now."

The fairy asked. "May I ask you something Isidra? When you were in the human world and married Alex, did he find out that you're a fairy? Answer me!"

"Why?"

"Well, maybe you've forgotten... Our lord forbids us to reveal our real identity to any humans that may compromise our kingdom. How much more if you are having a relationship with a mortal?!"

"I'm sorry... I tried to hide it but they already know...is it only today that you find out the truth?"

"How did that happen, Isidra? You were responsible for this!"

"Because when I gave birth to all of my children, there were two studs appeared in each of their body as a permanent mark symbolizing that the blood of a fairy is running in their veins... just like mine," then Isidra showed off her two studs pierced in her chest. "Alex noticed those studs and at first I lied about it. But soon after, there were marks coming out in each of my children's body. So, Alex forced me to reveal my true identity. For the love of my family, I finally admitted that I'm a fairy. All the while I thought every single fairies here already knew about it and that includes you."

"Those studs and marks were inherited by you, Isidra," said the fairy. "Do you think those are already permanent in their bodies?"

"Perhaps... maybe... though those marks on their foreheads can still be kept hidden... I think."

"Did you hide those marks when you were still in the human world, Isidra?"

"I was always trying. I was wearing long robes to keep them hidden."

"But you failed!"

"I know, the Explorers perceived when they noticed my children after I gave birth to them... But I didn't regret, because the Explorers understood about it, and they said that Alex was very lucky to marry a fairy like me. But I didn't tell them that I was not the only fairy who roamed in their world."

"When Lord Zalan learned such news, what did he do to you?"

"You really didn't have any idea about me, did you Skuld? When Lord

Zalan learned about what actually happened during my time in the human world, he forbade me for coming back in their world and interact with humans until he said so…"

"Now I know why you were not with us when we were searching for the Sacred Items. You were forbidden to go back in the human world without our lord's permission. In fact, those Explorers have gathered some of the Magic Stones but they have some difficulties in transforming the stones back in their true form as pure magics."

"I want to return the sacred stones I got when I was still in the human world, Skuld."

The fairy stepped back in shock. "What?! You've got some stones with you?"

"Yes! I got three Magic Stones but I didn't have the courage to give them yet because Lord Zalan is still angry at me…"

"How long you have those stones in your possession? Hey, were you stealing them?"

"Why would I steal the stones?"

"Then give those stones to Lord Zalan!"

"I'm scared… he might punish me even more if I tell him that I have these stones for so long."

"Lord Zalan will listen to you, Isidra. Come, I will accompany you to him."

"No, I can't!"

"Why? Are you guilty about this?!"

"No, just let me do this all by myself and tell about the stones…"

The fairy sighed as she shook her head. "Fine, I am leaving now. I noticed you've been restless, uneasy, and couldn't even talk to me seriously today…"

"Yeah… I'm sorry. I've been depressed for so long that's why."

"Goodbye…"

The fairy left Isidra alone in the room. She continued to think about what was happening to her family again.

"I've been suffering this pain in my heart… If only I didn't tell the truth, perhaps I am still happy until now. I truly miss my children so badly. Will they still able to hide their studs without me telling them? I hope so…"

She stood up, and then she looked at the clouds.

"I can't run away and betray our lord. But if I do, perhaps he will permanently remove my power as a fairy of love!"

Isidra continued to murmur alone as if she was talking to a blank wall. She was in constant motions back and forth restlessly while her eyes was looking around.

"Wait, my twins, I fled from our enemies they're... Oh yes! They're my Maximillian and Denver. I believe they're still alive! Reinhardt... yes, he is wise and very prayerful. How about the others? I wonder what are the names of my other children? Ahh, my two youngest daughters named Diana and Rebecca. Those little girls in tender years can live without me... Um, no! They were captured by our enemies along with their triplet brother! Uhuhuhu... Rohrer, my second son and Zoroaster, my third son... Where've... AHHH! Where are my eight children now? My worries are killing me. I've been drowning from this eternal despair!"

The other fairies heard Isidra's cries inside her room. They quickly entered the room to check, but the poor fairy of love suddenly collapsed due to excessive depression.

"Poor Isidra, it's been long years she has been living in depression..."

Isidra could no longer stand her worst sadness. Would there be a chance where she could see her family again?

7 BONDORE

Kenji was now on his way to Bondore in a collision course with the Pioneers who had been looking for him and his twin brother Genji. It took him only one and a half hours to reach Bondore from Dakar, with short rest.

But it was already too late when Kenji reached Bondore as the entire town was already destroyed, and what left now were some debris of stone walls and bloodied sands. Hundreds of houses were engulfed by a blazing fire. The trees were all dead and cut off down to the roots. The enemies never showed mercy to Bondore!

Kenji screamed out loud as he knelt down the ground and felt the deep anger to himself when he saw Bondore. He scoured the whole area and was hoping to catch and face the Pioneer to avenge the innocent villagers. Unable to catch anyone, out of anger; he pinched the soil, slapped his face, and then he screamed out loud once again.

After a long drama of the teenager came a young man whom he did not know. Kenji quickly stood on his feet and prepared himself for any danger. *An enemy!* He said to himself. The stranger saw him.

"Who are you? Are you a citizen of Bondore?" asked the stranger.

Kenji did not answer so the stranger asked again. "Why do you not answer? Are you a deaf young man?"

Kenji held his tongue in an angry look.

"Why are you looking me like that? Do I look bad? Do you know how to fight?"

Kenji finally answered but in question. "Are you the one who did this mess in Bondore? Who's with you? Pioneers?"

The stranger was surprised when Kenji mentioned the Pioneers. "Hey, where did you hear the Pioneers? What do you know about them?!"

"I know them enough! They are the ones who destroy this town and also the ones who killed my father!"

"How come you know them? Hey, who are you anyway?"

"You don't need to know my name, but there is something that Pioneers want aside from the stones… Me, me and my twin brother who are both sons of a DDE warrior!"

There was a flash of memories struck in the stranger's mind after hearing it from Kenji. He looked at Kenji's face very keenly and suddenly recognized the teenager's face, so he immediately took his long, sharp spear and pointed at him.

"Tell me lad… you are Maximillian, aren't you?" asked the stranger while he was pointing his sharp spear at Kenji's face. "Long time no see. You've grown gabby!"

"What are you talking about? Do I know you? Did I already seen you before?" How did you know my name?"

"Heh, how forgetful. I am Augustus Sawyer of Pioneer. Akira in short. Have you forgotten? Or is my gorgeous face seems unfamiliar to you?"

"Akira? Y-Yes, I remember you! We were just kids when we met. How did you come here? Were you the one who did this mess alone?"

"Oopppsss… Sorry wrong guess, my friend. Those Reminescence along with my fellow companions were the ones who did all of this. But I was not with them, and I was on a look out that the Explorers might arrived here… the likes of you who is the son of a DDE warrior!"

"Are your colleagues still here?"

"They already left and I just stayed here alone. I have a feeling that there is a sacred stone hidden somewhere in this place invisible to the eyes of my fool companions. Heh!"

Kenji got angry. "Do you think you can get me and take me to your father?"

"Of course, since you're still weak and useless! Come, let us fight and if I win, then I will offer your dead body to your real father! Perhaps the Explorers will finally give up on us. Hahahaha!"

Kenji tried to fight Akira though he was still inexperienced in real combat. For a very long time, he already forgotten what he had learned during his first training at the age of seven, while Akira was a great fighter as he was fully trained and the mastery of different types of offensive moves. So when the two fought, Kenji was being hit and the first one who fell on the ground. He lost the fight.

"You lost. How weak you really are, Maximillian! Get up before I kill you. I do not expect the son of a DDE warrior is weak! You should become a slave of Pioneer, GET UP!"

Kenji was forced to stand though he was wounded in his abdomen and his arms. He was about to stand when Akira quickly attacked him again and he tumbled on the ground.

Akira got irritated. "Such a boring creature you are! As if I was only fighting against a kid!"

Kenji stood once again but he got weak due to his wounds. Akira threatened him while pointing at his face. "I'll give you another chance to live and get prepared lad… The next time we will see each other again, you will have an opportunity to redeem yourself or else I will not spare your life! 'Till our next meeting!"

Akira left, leaving the wounded Kenji alone as he slumped on the ground. The poor young man wept, unable to avenge Bondore against a Pioneer.

"I-I'm a useless person," said Kenji sobbing. "I am nobody but a trying hard to become one… I only tried to be a hero who is not worthy to be a savior," and he sobbed again.

Kenji was unaware that there was man who had been watching him surreptitiously in a corner. He slowly closed his eyes and was about to lie down on the ground due to exhaustion when a man quickly approached him and caught his back.

"You're tired child," said the man looking concerned. "Are you hurt?"

Kenji slowly opened his eyes and stared at the man. "W-Who are you? Where's Akira?"

"Akira? A young man in red who beat you? Heh, he's a fool!"

"Why?"

"Well you see, he knows that you were weak and an inexperience fighter; simply an ordinary man! Why the hell did he have to deal with the likes of you?"

"I'm not just an ordinary man," said Kenji. "I am the son of a fairy and a DDE warrior."

THE EXPLORERS

"A fairy and a DDE warrior? Oh yeah, I heard it from you and Akira earlier. Wow, you know how well-known is the DDE around the globe. Sorry if I underestimated you…"

"Well, it is my objective… To become one of the highest class of the Explorers to see my real father."

"Does it mean you're a UE member?"

"N-No, not yet… I already heard about them from Pioneers."

"Hey, I learned from someone I met before that obtaining at least one sacred object is the only requirement for you to become an Explorer. But, that is not enough for you to become one. You must also be a great warrior in order to protect the Sacred Items from the enemies. As what I've seen earlier during your fight against Akira, it seems that you are inexperienced in battle."

"Yeah I know, you're right… I need to learn more of fighting techniques. Looks like I'll never get the chance to become at least one of the lowest class of the Explorers."

"Heh, I like you laddie!" said the man. "I am a master of martial arts that teach basic and standard fighting techniques to the likes of you. I travel around the world to search potential people and teach them how to fight. I teach both offensive and defensive in a martial arts school elsewhere. It's pretty far from here, but I have many students there."

Kenji's eyes grew bigger as he showed lots of interest. His adrenaline rush went haywire… in his mind he saw hope!

"R-Really? Please teach me then! R-Right now!"

"Well of course! Good thing I am currently searching for someone and I have found you! Your determination and enthusiasm will brought you there, and you've got potential!"

Kenji gaped. "What now?"

"It's your decision laddie. If you really want to come with me then I will take you there right now. I don't want to brag on you but do you know that some of my former students are now masters in their own? Though some of them already have their own families, the others are also mentoring now… Hmm, what about the others?"

The man continued to talk when Kenji interrupted him.

"My name is Kenji. What is your name?"

"Oh, my name is Rolando… It's a pleasure to meet you, Kenji."

"I want to train now. I am in a hurry!"

"I have my private plane with me. We will be riding there."

"A plane? Now I began to think how far your school really is!"

"Yeah, it is because it's in the other continent."

Kenji chuckled. "Wow, Mr. Rolando! You said you were just searching for potentials, but you even managed to get here in Bondore!"

The man's face turned red. "Well, yeah... Did I tell you that I was actually searching around the world?"

"Okay, as long as it is free... 'Coz I don't have any money to pay you in return!"

"I know, life is hard. Hey, you have some bags with you? Take them with you!"

Kenji put out his bag. "Yes, I have one."

"Then come with me now. I will inform my boss that I have found someone to mentor to. Let's go."

While walking away en route to the plane, Kenji felt severe pain and dismay in his heart when he failed to save Bondore from the hands of the Pioneers. "Forgive me, oh Bondore... I hate to leave you unsaved and it hurts my feelings too much..."

The two rode a truck driven by a man who was Rolando's colleague. Kenji thought Rolando was all alone. Inside a truck was another young man who would also be Rolando's new student. Kenji greeted the new student with a smile.

"Hello!"

"Hi!"

"Let us go. We will be leaving now," said Rolando.

Kenji wondered. "Um, I thought we will be boarding in an airplane?"

"Yes, we will Kenji. I left our plane in the other town. It's only twenty minutes drive by truck."

They traveled quietly. They passed through the forests, to the rivers, and so on. Just like days when the twins were traveling towards Damsville. Kenji was so quiet, and he was only listening to the various conversations between his companions.

"Where you from laddie?" asked Rolando to the new student. "Would you really like to learn how to fight?"

"Yes, even just basics... But I want to become a master," answered the student grinning.

"Excellent, then you will be facing Master Serge when you elevate to master level. 'Coz I will be no longer your mentor when you reach that level. You understand?"

Kenji interrupted the two. "What was that mean?"

"Well Kenji, if you already mastered the basic and standard techniques, then Master Serge will be your next mentor to teach you master techniques. However, he is temperamental and rigorous in training… That is why I warned Edgar."

"But you're still there, right?"

"Sometimes Master Serge and I are so busy teaching so we're not together, but often times we are together. There was also a time when me and him are both mentoring in the same room, but it only depends on our schedules."

"Do you think he'll force us to train very hard?"

"Don't worry Kenji, if your performance is great and if you can follow the instructions and learn the techniques in no time at all, then Master Serge will be pleased to you. Maybe one day he will help you reach your main objective right? The DDE? You know what Kenji, some of the Explorers were our former students. The others are now in DDE class! See? Maybe you will be the next DDE. Just always believe in yourself!"

After twenty-three minutes, they arrived in the other town where their airplane landed and they returned the truck to the owner who was Edgar's father. Edgar lived in the said town.

"Good luck on your training and train hard my son!" said Edgar's mother and she hugged her son.

Kenji felt jealous. What would it be like if his mother also did the same thing to him? He just watched Edgar's tearful mother because her son would be off to the other continent to train and become a new warrior. Edgar's mother moved aside to give way his husband to hug his son.

"Make your dreams come true to become a brave warrior someday soon my son. Good luck and do your best!" said Edgar's father.

After their long drama, the small airplane began its flight. The townspeople waved goodbye as the plane flew on its way to the other continent!

8 THE TRAINING

It took a long while when they traveled towards the other continent. Later on, Kenji began to think if he made a right decision to join with someone whom he just met. Were these people trustworthy? Or were they also one of the Pioneers' secret soldiers disguised as just somebody else? Kenji got worried thinking of what else could Rolando possibly do to him aside from to just mentoring him.

But Rolando seemed sincere and a trustworthy person. So Kenji smiled while looking at the airplane window. Later, he asked Rolando.

"By the way Rolando, how old are you now?"

Rolando turned to him. "Me? I'm thirty-five. Why do you ask? Want to know more about me?"

"Ah, so how long you've been teaching martial arts?"

"Well laddie, it's been 15 years. Because… I was in my early age when I finished and mastered my training."

"Wow," but Kenji's face seemed unfazed by Rolando's reply. "Do you have your own family now?"

"Oh yes laddie. I have three children. Why do you ask again?"

"Nothing. I just want to know that's all."

"Hmmm… sounds like you are getting pretty bored now, aren't you? Well don't worry, we're almost there. How about if we start right away as soon as we get there, hehehe!" asked Rolando jokingly.

"Sure, how about right now inside this plane? S-Shall we begin?!"

"Hahaha, Kenji! How funny!"

"I don't tell jokes a lot, do I?"

THE EXPLORERS

After an hour and a half, the airplane finally reached their destination. The flight was not that long because the country where they came from was close to their destination though it was in the other continent. The airplane landed and they went straight to the Training School.

Kenji saw a group of novice students who just started their first training in the school. Rolando took him to a vacant room where he could take a rest. Hey, this Kenji's new room was free of charge!

"I'll let you stay in this room to take some rest. You must be tired from our flight," said Rolando to Kenji smiling. "I will give you a whole day to take your full rest."

"I didn't walk through here. I'd been sitting in the airplane, but thank you anyway," thanked Kenji.

"Don't tell me you don't like this room I gave you?"

"It's not like that. I wasn't tired during the flight… I still have enough energy left."

"Even though you've got bruised by Akira's punches and his spear? Look at yourself, you got some wounds! What is that? Does it not matter to you, hm?"

"Because I do not want to show myself that I am a weak. You see, as a son of a DDE warrior I must show my strength and my power at all times."

Rolando nodded. "You're really such a brave person, Kenji… You are…"

Kenji nodded with a smile.

"So how about you Kenji? How old are you now?"

"I'm seventeen."

"Whew! You're still young. You know what, you are the second to the youngest student I've been mentoring in my entire life! But I have some students here who also have the same age as yours."

"Why is that? How old was he that time?"

"He was only sixteen laddie, but now he's married and have one child. It's been a long time when he was still my student. Now, he owns his own school and is also a mentor. He was one of my favorite and he'd been so useful to me… Huhuhu, I'm gonna cry 'coz I am missing him now…"

"I wanna start… right now! I will train hard… I will do my best!"

Rolando got hurt as the young man only ignored his story.

"Do whatever you want, Kenji. Just let me know if you need a break or if you feel any pain in your wounds. Now I know how stubborn you are, eh? Let's go."

Rolando gave Kenji a short tour inside the training school first before he would introduce him to the students. Kenji saw the trainees in the lawn and he watched every motion of their bodies as they were doing the martial arts such as Eskrima. The students' faces showed total concentration in every steps they were doing. Yeah, Rolando's right. Their age ranged from 23 to 25 but they were all looking matured for their age.

"So Kenji, for the start, just follow every bit of the movement and actions of my body. Like this," then Rolando showed off his moves to Kenji. But Rolando fumbled when he tripped short and felt embarrassed. Kenji only smiled at him as if nothing happened.

"Y-Yeah… I can follow you…" Kenji stooped down his head, still pretending that nothing happened wrong earlier.

"Before we begin the training, I firstly need to test the level of your strength as well as your immunity."

Kenji was surprised. "S-Sure why not… How?"

"I need to see your first warm ups, Kenji. First, you will run in the open field for one-hour without any pauses and nothing to drink."

"W-WHAT?!" Kenji was more surprised, gaping as he stepped back. "Is it difficult to do that?"

"Not much, this is because it's a part of your training. I will give you exercises on your first day as a warm up and you'll need to pass them at once before we begin your proper training. See? Now you're having a second thought of continuing the training. That is why I was giving you a whole day rest earlier!"

"Well? N-Nevermind the whole day rest, Rolando… I am really serious to start the activity now!"

Rolando patted Kenji's shoulder. "How stubborn you really are, laddie! Since this is your first time in this school, you better pay attention to whatever your teacher Rolando is saying! All ears nothing but me!"

Kenji put down his bag to begin his warm-up activities. They went to the other training grounds when he saw the other students who were also doing the same exercises. He smiled as he was watching them. "Well, at least I am not doing these activities alone."

Rolando showed Kenji the entire training field. It was huge and wide, and Master Serge was the owner of the training field. Kenji did not expect that Master Serge actually was the owner of the entire training school!

THE EXPLORERS

"Okay Kenji, you only need to run one hour straight in this field without stopping. If you get tired and exhausted, then you can walk as long as you want but still you are not allowed to make any pauses. But I'm afraid you can't make an hour straight since you've got some wounds in your body. Understand?"

Kenji was confident. "I can still do that no matter how many hours you can give me. I will pass it in no time at all."

"It's up to you Kenji," said Rolando and he shook his head. "How stubborn," then he looked at his stopwatch. "Go!"

Kenji ran and Rolando followed him. Whew, Rolando was impressed, since Kenji could run that fast despite of the wounds he got in his body. He measured Kenji's speed, and he seemed that the young man could pass his first activity. They ran together, but after a while, Kenji overran Rolando!

"You're very fast laddie! Akira will be a piece of cake if you train harder."

Kenji did not respond and he continued to run in the open field. He slowly raised his speed while the other trainees stopped their training to watch him. They were all impressed and admired the young man's dedication!

"Look, he is running very fast!"

"Yeah, he can run as fast as the speeding bullet!"

"Whoa, whoa, take it easy boys. He's just bragging and wants to impress us with his speed. Just watch if later he gets tired and falls on the ground. You might say there's nothing different between him and us. He was only an arrogant guy!"

The one-hour activity was completed. Rolando once again measured Kenji's speed and also his leg power. He noticed that Kenji never stopped his running and also never walked even for only at least a minute!

Rolando asked Kenji jokingly. "Kenji, are you really the son of a DDE? Guess your real father is a cheetah! You're too fast, and your fastest speed is 35 kilometers per hour! I never seen you walking for the whole hour!"

Though Kenji was panting, he still answered him with a smile. "Guess you're right, maybe I got this from my father who also runs that fast."

"Oh I see..." Rolando scratched his chin. "So, how about a break now? You just passed my first activity today."

"D-Don't worry, I can still do the next activity," said Kenji while still panting.

Rolando felt irritated but jokingly. "Hmpt! You're very, very, very stubborn, really! This will be your first time to get a bad record from me, eh?"

Kenji insisted. "Come on, I don't care! What important is to pass all of them in an earliest time. Please let me do the next activity right now…"

"Okay fine. Your next activity is to do the jumps in a jumping rope of ten million, err… I mean ten thousand times without stopping. That is all, just like you are doing the boxing training."

"Yes sir, I will…"

"Okay laddie, let's go!" then Rolando took the jumping rope and gave it to Kenji. "You and me will count together. Remember, you need to jump ten thousand times without stopping, okay? Do it now."

Kenji held the two handles of the jumping rope and he began to jump. They both counted as Kenji jumped, and Rolando could see the perseverance and determination of the young man to become a new warrior like him.

Fifteen minutes had passed when Kenji made 989 jumps. Rolando thought that this young fellow had shown enough great skill and speed that needed to improve more, a requirement to become a great warrior. *Pure energy*, so he said. This young man did not give up so easily in his warm-ups. The trainees were still watching Kenji with amazement and wonder. They could not believe what they saw. They remembered when they did the ten thousand jumps - they had a break and could not last that long. For them, Kenji's stamina was truly remarkable!

There was a student watching Kenji who seemed jealous and disgusted. He could not understand how Kenji did it without stopping.

"Hmpt, it looks like something suspicious is going on in here!" said the jealous student. "He'd been dashing long without stopping earlier and he passed. Then he immediately worked on the 10,000 jumps! No resting?! Gimme a break, I think he's trying to impress us and shows what he got, PWAH!" he spitted.

Thirty minutes had passed when Kenji made 5,000 jumps. The trainees were more impressed while he was still doing his successive jumps even though his body was already soaked in sweat.

"Hey you, dude! You can take a break if you want! You've been panting there and yet you're still showing your mastery there! That's arrogance!"

Forty minutes had passed when Kenji made 9,010 jumps, but this time his body finally faltered and collapsed due to exhaustion and starvation. The envied student suddenly laughed out loud next to his fellow trainees.

"Hahaha, that's already enough my friend. You're such a trying hard who wants to make some impressions! Look at yourself, lying on the ground full of dirt and sweat, poor boy... Hahaha!"

Rolando felt pity on Kenji since the young man was almost washed by his intense sweat when he collapsed. The trainees felt the same thing with their sad faces showing remorse and dismay, because he could almost complete the 10,000 jumps when he gave way. But Rolando understood and he already knew that Kenji could not make it since he lost a substantial amount of blood because of his inflicted wounds, and he never took a rest when they arrived in school. If Kenji rested first, maybe he could do the task with more than 11,000 jumps.

As for Rolando, he made his decision to let Kenji pass his second activity since the count difference was only small to the required target. The 9,010 counts was enough for him.

"Alright Kenji, you can take a rest now. And oopsss! Don't force yourself again to do the next activity, okay? Don't be hasty and too stubborn on me, understand?"

With not much energy left in his body, Kenji finally agreed to rest. He got up and walked back to his room alone like a drunken lad. Some trainee offered a hand but Kenji refused any help from them to take him in his room.

While Kenji was on his way to his room, he crossed upon an approaching young man who seemed familiar to his eyes. As the young man approached closer before him, he quickly called his attention and the young man stopped walking. The young man stared at the sweaty Kenji from head to toe in disgust. Kenji wiped his face first using a towel he was holding and the young man spoke.

"Excuse me, do you need anything from me?" asked the young man with the long band tied on his head.

"W-Wait, you... You seem so familiar to me," said Kenji. "Um, who was that again? 'Coz I think... you were with me before."

The young man only raised his one eyebrow. "Bro, I don't know what you're talking about, maybe that's a mistaken identity. I've been here for long and I'm also Rolando's student. You're new here right? Wow, if you only knew... we were all impressed at you earlier."

Kenji smiled sweetly at him even though they should not supposed to talk about it.

"Thank you," answered Kenji. "I came late here when you started your training. But honestly... you really seem so familiar to me."

"I see... Go ahead and look at my face."

"By the way, w-what is your name? Maybe later I can recall it..."

The young man pulled in his pocket and brought out a cigarette and a lighter. He lighted the cigarette first and he smoked.

"My name is Claude. Sounds familiar to you?"

Kenji slowly raised his face when he heard the young man's name. *C-Claude? Is that you? Oh yes, I remember! You were with me when we went to Dakar together. Oh, Claude... Claude? Long time no see! Have you forgotten me? I'm Kenji. Whoo-hoo, we meet again at last! Do you remember what happened in the past, Claude? You were a thief and we left Damsville to save my stepfather in Dakar. And then... I lost my consciousness when a Vanguard woman did something on me. I thought I would never see you again, but I am glad that you are safe and sound right before me, Claude...*

As for Claude, he was just looking straight at Kenji's face while still smoking. He was waiting for Kenji's reply. "Why didn't you answer? Is there something wrong with my name? Or does my face looks scary to you?"

"N-No, Claude," Kenji answered. "But I would like to ask if you can still remember what actually happened in your past."

Claude smoked. "Dude, do I look like a psychopath? Of course, I can still recall my past. Um, anyway... I am still on my break time. Maybe we will talk again sometime, 'coz I still have more training to do later. See ya!" then he walked away.

"Wait! How about Kenji? Does it sound familiar to you? Do you still remember anything about him?"

"Kenji?" said Claude as he scratched his chin. "Yes, I know him."

"Claude, That's me... Kenji. It's true, Claude! My name is Kenji from Dakar!"

Claude was shocked when he heard the young man's name. He suddenly hugged Kenji tightly and ignored the sweat all over his body. He was so excited to meet and see his long lost friend once again.

"Long time no see, my friend... Long time no see!" said Claude in a happy tone as they embraced. "You've grown a good-looking guy. I'm sorry if I didn't recognize you at once. I mistook you to just somebody else. It's a good thing you still recognize me, my friend!"

"So, how are you now? Do you still remember the woman who attacked on us? How did you manage to escape from her?" asked Kenji.

"Me?" asked Claude. "I'm alright, thanks. It's been too long that I underwent in the hands of Vanguard since that woman took me away from you. But because of Rolando's help, he rescued me from them. And then, he also took me here to learn the basics of combat. If you only knew how nice and truly kind Rolando is!"

"I didn't expect that Rolando would be the missing link and took both of us here, Claude. He is indeed the missing link and then we meet again. What a co-incidence!"

"Me neither Kenji, I wasn't expecting this would happen either."

The two hugged each other again while Claude was patting Kenji's dirty and sweaty back.

Afterwards: "Oh Kenji, you're full of dirt right now! Come, and clean yourself now."

Claude took Kenji in a vacant bathroom and the young man took a bath. He carefully wiped every part of his body including his wounds. Claude was just outside waiting for him to finish his bath. When he was done, Claude met him as he left the bathroom.

"Kenji, please forgive me for not able to rescue you from that woman in Dakar years ago. I was so disappointed that I even failed to just save myself from her. So Kenji…"

"Phew, what a silly apology! We were both in a same situation before so you don't need to ask me for forgiveness."

"Thank you Kenji," then Claude brought out another cigarette from his pocket and gave it to Kenji. "Would you like one?"

Kenji declined the young man's offer. "Claude, I am about to change my clothes. I'm also on my three-hour break. Oh and by the way, I do not smoke…"

Claude returned the lighter in his pocket and he smoked again.

"Claude, will you please excuse me for a minute? I'm sorry, I've been too exhausted today."

"It's okay. I'll see you later."

It took two hours when Kenji changed his clothes inside his own bedroom and rested. Then later, there was a knock on the door. It was Claude.

"Too-hoo, Claude!" called Kenji smiling.

"Kenji, I've just finished my training today. I've done it fast since the training wasn't that hard. Are you better now? My next training will be tomorrow."

"Yes, come inside."

"Thank you," then Claude went inside Kenji's room. He took a cigarette again from his pocket and offered it to Kenji. "How about a cigarette now?"

Kenji shook his head. "I said I do not smoke, Claude."

Claude returned the cigarette again. "Why not?"

"I don't want to get sick sooner. I still have my dreams to fulfill," he hinted.

Claude did not respond. Kenji confronted him directly on his face. "Claude, why is it that you smoke? I never ended up like that."

Claude puffed. "Nothing, it's only a habit. Or I presumed it just happened because of an influence."

Kenji combed his hair. "Influence? By whom? And since when? Ever since we split each other? Did you go with someone who influenced you to do the smoking?"

Claude changed the topic. "By the way Kenji, do you still have your training today?"

"I don't know Claude," said Kenji. "I took a bath even though I am still tired from the exercises. I hope the next exercise will be tomorrow."

"I'm sure he will let you do the next activity tomorrow. Rolando is far nicer than Master Serge."

"In fact... I never meet nor see Master Serge yet, Claude. Is he really that rugged?"

"My goodness Kenji, he became our teacher once when Rolando was away from school to do the special training lesson to a student alone. Tsk, he was very strict on us Kenji, but do you know the advantage of that old man?"

"What?"

"Though Master Serge is a curmudgeon, he could help us accelerate our training fast. That is why I am almost near in my master level of training."

Kenji also changed the topic. "Claude, I want to see my brother now…"

"You mean Genji?" asked Claude. "Yeah I remember him. Where do you think he is now?"

"And Claude… I would also like to become a DDE warrior."

Claude was surprised to hear about it, because he knew that Kenji was unaware of his real identity. He was a son of a Skywalker, and the rebel group was the former slaves of the first-generation Reminescence, who were also the enemies of Explorers.

"O-Oh yeah… Your father is the current leader of the DDE."

"Well, I promise myself that I will become one like them."

"I see…"

"What about you, Claude? Would you like to become a DDE too?"

When the three-hour break of Kenji was over, Rolando called Kenji to begin his next activity and Kenji waved Claude goodbye.

"I thought Rolando would give you the next activity tomorrow morning, Kenji," Claude whispered.

"No Claude, I was the one who told Rolando to continue my training today. Time is gold Claude, my time will be wasting if I only just lie down and sleep all day long."

"Well there's nothing else he could do to your stubbornness. You've been forcing yourself to practice a lot with not enough rest, and you will get sick far worse than taking a cigarette!"

"Nope Cloud," said Kenji and he hinted Claude. "If I get sick, I will get another disease other than lung cancer."

Claude laughed. "Whatever. Good luck!"

"Thank you for your time. See you later!" then Kenji left.

During his entire training with Rolando…

Kenji took seven months straight of his training schedule. During the seven months, he faced many trials and experiences such as running into the woods, jumping across the river, did the push-ups and countless warm-ups, and so on. After the warm-ups, he proceeded in learning defensive techniques and then the proper offensive techniques. Rolando taught him to learn and master the martial arts called Eskrima.

Next, Kenji learned the different usage of weapons as well as wearing protective armors. Because of their perseverance, he and Claude completed the full training together when they both mastered the basic and standard techniques imparted by Rolando.

Now, the two must deal with more things coming their way as they began their new chapter of being the new warriors.

9 SHINGUE

After their long period of rigid training and hardwork, the time had come for them to face the one whom the students feared the most... Master Serge, the master instructor for the master level of their training.

Claude caught Kenji's attention who seemed relaxed and whispered. "Hey Kenji, you seem so unafraid to our master instructor," and then he added jokingly. "Almost like it's just a cockroach who will be teaching you. You aren't afraid of him!"

One of the students was making his way out of the room who was actually the envied guy. He was accompanied by a blond guy with streaks of pink highlights on each side of his hair. The envied student said something on top of his voice where almost everyone could hear. "Dude, look at that Kenji guy. He is one hell of a trying hard who wants to impress us. Can you believe it, Shingue? He finally reached the master level at last. What a joke!" there was a hint of bitterness in his tone.

Kenji heard this and threw a dagger look towards the envied student's direction. He shrugged the student's remark off as he always did. And come to think of it, he never bothered to ask his name - until now. He did not even know the guy. Apart from Shingue, whose name he just heard for the first time now.

The envied student, together with Shingue went to where Claude and Kenji were standing and started talking to them.

"Hey dudes, I'd like you to meet Shingue. He's a good friend of mine and is not a 'trying hard dude' like someone here does, ya know," it was clear that the last remark was directed to Kenji. "Let's go dude. We have no more business here."

With that, the envied student walked away.

Kenji's rival dashed on, unaware that Shingue remained behind and whispered to Claude and Kenji. "Hello, I apologize for what Arthur said to you earlier. He's just a jealous nuts, that's all," so Arthur was the name of that student.

"Hm, I don't even bother to answer back to his taunting. He's been pissing me off for seven months already. You can ask Claude, have I ever done anything to that… that… Arturo guy before?" asked Kenji smirking.

Shingue went near them. "Does it mean, you've been here for long time? I wonder why it's only today we meet for the first time."

Kenji shook his head. "Huh? I've always seen you around, but you haven't seen me? Where've you been hanging around? I could still remember, you didn't have those pink highlights in your hair before."

"Ahhh…" Shingue replied. "I wonder? Ah, maybe it's because my training with Master Serge takes the whole day, That's why I never have a chance to see you."

"Why? Didn't you have any vacant time with Master Serge before?" asked Claude.

"N-Never…"

Silence. No one replied to what Shingue said. Later, Shingue asked the two. "Um, can I ask you a favor?"

Kenji wondered. "What is it?"

"Um, can I come with you two? 'Coz actually, I've been alone in this school for long and Arthur is really an unfriendly guy to be with. Well, you know what?" he whispered. "Do you know why Arthur always acts like that? Because he never got any friends here due to his bad attitudes. D-Don't tell it to him, okay? Because every time he meets someone, he'll criticize them! He is bullying every guy he wants."

"So Arthur is totally that crazy person, isn't he?" asked Claude. "Then why the hell he has to do that on us?"

"But I do understand him," said Shingue. "He revolted long ago after his parents split… In other words, he came from a broken family!"

While they were talking, they noticed Master Serge who was coming to their direction. He passed by in front of Kenji and the young lad saw his face in side ways. Kenji discreetly stared their instructor before he turned back to his friends and continued their talking.

THE EXPLORERS

"I think he seems so nice to me," said Kenji.

"Shingue! Shingue!" a voice calling Shingue from a distance.

"Ah, they're calling me guys. Hold on for a while," said Shingue and he left the two.

Claude waited for Shingue to move away from them when he asked Kenji. "Kenji, do you know that Shingue is an Explorer?"

Kenji quickly turned to Claude. "W-What? How did that happen? That ordinary young man? An Explorer?"

"Yes, because I heard rumors that he seemed to have found a sacred object that had been buried a long time ago. Maybe you're wondering how do I learn about those sacred things, eh? Now I know everything what you already know, Kenji. I know now what that Vanguard woman previously talked about with those so called Sacred Items."

"I see... So what is this Sacred Item he has, Claude?"

"I don't know, but I think his Sacred Item has something to do with... a chemical."

"Chemical? Of what?"

"Sshhhh ... not so loud, Kenji. I don't want this rumor to get spread like wildfire in the entire school, and later we find out that this rumor is all wrong."

"And where did you hear this rumor?"

"Well... I heard it from some of the students whom I talked with."

Kenji moved closer to Claude and he whispered. "In fact Claude... He doesn't look like fit enough to become an Explorer. Come to think of it, if he's an Explorer then he shouldn't do the training anymore! 'Coz I believe that Explorers are the anointed warriors who have mastered all combat techniques, am I right?"

Claude looked away from Kenji. "You're too boastful! You're not in the proper position to judge him and you're not even an Explorer. Or were you only jealous? At least, Shingue is a member of the Explorers although he's in the lowest class called UE."

"I'm sorry, Claude... Yeah, you're right, I-I'm only envy..."

Claude chuckled. "See? That's why you're underestimating Shingue like that. You're a loser, Kenji."

"Later, I will talk to Shingue, Claude..."

Claude's eyes wide-opened. "T-Talk?! Hell no, stop that! Did I tell you to shut up? I said I don't want this rumor to get spread. Did you get it? If

Shingue finds out that I did the gossiping, then the blame is on me!"

Meanwhile, Kenji was only staring at him as if he was playing innocent. He faltered. "Y-Yes, indeed... You are right."

Claude was surprised to Kenji's reaction. "I-Indeed? Hey Kenji, stop acting innocent and that you're, errr..."

Kenji smiled at him. "Claude..."

Shingue returned to them. "Hey guys, our training will resume tomorrow. Be prepared for your first meeting with Master Serge, hahaha!"

Kenji stretched his arms. "Good thing that the old man changed his schedule for today eh, Claude?"

Claude nodded. "Yeah, oh hey Kenji..." he pulled Kenji's arm and whispered. "Don't ya ever forget what I've told you earlier, okay? Or else... I will knock your head off!"

Kenji laughed. "Yeah... Yeah... I'm going to eat now."

"Wait Kenji, where the hell do you think you're going? Are you going to eat without me? It sounds like I am not your friend."

Okay, fine... Said Kenji to himself. "Come on, Claude. I have some business to do later."

The two went to the school canteen and they ordered their favorite Filipino foods: *sinangag, adobo, halu-halo, tapsilog,* and soups. When the foods were served, the two laid their meals on the table and sat on the two vacant chairs. They talked as they ate together.

After a few minutes, they saw Shingue who was looking for a vacant chair while he was holding the food tray. Kenji noticed more students inside the canteen and realized it was currently lunch time. He also noticed a vacant chair on their table, so he called Shingue. Then, Shingue placed the tray on their table and sat next to Claude.

"Shingue, it looks like you're already late for lunch," said Claude jokingly while eating. "And wow, you've got plenty of foods with you."

"Certainly," said Shingue in his red face. "I just love to eat Filipino foods that's why."

Kenji was just staring straight at Shingue and reluctant to ask what he wanted to know... even though Claude was there! But he couldn't... That Claude might got upset at him. But, he also could not resist his own curiosity, and he really wanted to ask Shingue about it!

"Guys," called Shingue smiling. "I would like to join with you! By the way, you are Kenji and Claude right? It's nice to meet you two."

"J-Join?" asked Kenji in wide-opened eyes and ignored Shingue's greeting. "What are you? Where are you going to sleep when I finish my full training? H-Hey, I have some business to do since I have been seeking an answer that needs to be answered soon!"

As for Claude, he was only listening to what the young man just said. He was only waiting for a hint that Kenji might say something that should not say.

Shingue noticed Kenji's unrelated response. "W-What answer?"

"It is because I really want to know something as soon as possible!" answered Kenji. "What I mean is, I-I have been dreaming to become an Explorer since my real father is a current DDE member! I would also like to know what is the secret behind those Sacred Items and what is their connection by becoming an Explorer, d-do I make sense to you?" Kenji clearly hinted that it was actually directed to Claude. Oooppss!

Because of this, Claude secretly stamped Kenji's foot under the table as a warning. Kenji felt that and he stopped, realizing that he could not gain control of his garrulity.

"Explorer you say eh, Kenji?" asked Shingue. "How come you are a son of a DDE member? Does it mean that you're a Dragon Divinity Explorer?!"

Claude could not stand his humiliation anymore and he feel ashamed, so he quickly laid down his head on his arms on the table.

"I don't know, Shingue. In fact, I still do not know the truth behind all of this! If I am really the son of a DDE, then I should belong to the DDE now, r-right?" answered Kenji in question while eating *adobo* (a chicken marinated in a sauce of vinegar, soy sauce, and garlic, browned in oil, and simmered in the marinade).

"Wait, wait, Kenji…" Shingue shook his head. "That doesn't make sense to me. If you're really a son of a DDE warrior, then they should be looking for you right now, am I correct? Anyway, who told you about them, huh?"

"My father might be looking for me ever since. I was still a child… when I heard it from the group of Pioneers."

Shingue quickly stood to where he was sitting on at the same time he banged his hands on the table. "PIONEERS! What do you know about them?"

"C'mon Shingue, please stop the drama… n-not right now," restrained

Kenji but in calm tone while Claude's head was still on his arms.

Shingue also calmed down his voice and he sat down again on his chair. "Okay, so what else did you hear from them?"

"They also said that my real father is the current leader of the entire Explorer organization. A DDE leader!"

Claude's head stooped more as if he was thinking whether to just leave the two or not. He really could not stand Kenji's continuous noise anymore!

Shingue almost spitted out what he was chewing due to excitement and quickly stood again. "A current leader of the DDE class! Hey, I know who their leader is... Nothing else but Alex Foster... no?"

Kenji was the next one to stand from his seat and was excited to know behind Shingue as an Explorer. "Yeah, that's him! Hey, how did you know his name, Shingue? My real father's name is Alex Foster and nothing else!"

"B-Because... I am one of the Explorers, Kenji."

Claude slowly raised his head on the table. He finally learned that the rumors were true. He calmed down and realized that he would no longer knock off Kenji's head anymore.

As for Kenji, he was gaping while his eyes was staring directly at Shingue. "You're an Explorer? Of what?"

"I am an Explorer but I belong in the lowest class, Kenji..." said Shingue. "When the Explorers found out that I possessed one of the Sacred Items, they want me to join with them. I was only a miner that time, and I accidentally discovered something glowing under the ground. It caught my eyes because of its unique beauty and color."

"What type of stone was that, Shingue?"

"It is a Divine Stone, Kenji... that was once a powerful element," then Shingue drank a glass of water. "There are more of them that have been missing like the stone I have now."

"Now I understand," said Kenji and he sat down. "Since when did you obtain that stone of yours?"

"Long time ago," said Shingue and he sat down as well. "Like... three years ago."

"And how old are you now, Shingue?" asked Claude.

"I'm seventeen, Claude..." answered Shingue.

"That means we're all in the same age," said Kenji while taking a sip of soup. "And you owned it, you're incredible!"

"Thank you," said Shingue. "Yes, good thing I got one. So, is there anything else you would like to know more?"

"No, no…" answered Kenji. "I've known enough. Thanks Shingue, now I have learned something today!"

Claude got bored. "Lads, I'm gettin' pretty bored in here now and I'm going out for a while. But I will be back later."

Kenji agreed and Claude left. "So Shingue, you done eating? O-Or are you going to eat more?!"

Shingue stooped his head. "Nope, I'm already stuffed…" then he leaned back on his chair.

"I'm going outside too," said Kenji. "I'll stay there to relax and smell the scent of fresh air since our training will resume tomorrow. See ya!" then he stood.

"Kenji, I wanna go with you!"

"Oh man Shingue," Kenji shook his head with his hands on his hips. "Mind your own business and don't go with me. Go somewhere that makes you happy. Goodbye!"

"Alright," Shingue smiled as he scratched his head. "Go somewhere that makes me happy, eh? He was right! As an Explorer, I must go along with my kind, a fellow Explorer!" he hinted.

Kenji left the canteen alone. He looked for Claude but he could not find the young man somewhere, so he went to the training grounds to relax and feel the breeze of air, while watching the male students who were doing their training lesson with Rolando.

He remembered the time when Rolando was still their instructor and he had been so nice and friendly towards them. Because of this, Kenji felt envy that he wanted to be Rolando's student once again.

The young man went to a tree to continue with his relaxation, until the envied student named Arthur reappeared again along with Shingue. He was holding a card, and he saw Kenji alone in the tree. Kenji noticed him but he looked away, but Arthur approached him so Shingue walked away.

"Dude, it seems like you didn't take your training for today, did you?" greeted Arthur with his hands on his hips.

"Are you out of your mind? Our next training will be tomorrow," answered Kenji annoyingly. "Anyway, I will not waste my time in here if it wasn't for the vacant time… 'Coz I get tired more if I only just rest here and do nothing! Oh bummer…"

Arthur felt angered and insulted, so he quickly pulled off Kenji's shirt.

"What the hell did you just say?! Hey, do you know whom you are talking to right now?!!"

Kenji answered in a calm tone though he was irritated. "Please Arthur, stop bothering me. I'm only relaxing here, just give me a break and stop messing up with me! Sorry, but I don't want any trouble here. Let's talk again later, okay? I'm not in the mood right now so please stop wasting my time!"

Without any warning, Arthur suddenly punched Kenji's face and he slumped on he ground "Why do you have to answer me like that?! The only reason why I hate you so much is because you've been a trying hard in this school and you've shown too much nonsense impression to our fellow trainees!!!"

The students turned to them, while Arthur was still in front of Kenji face-to-face. "What now asshole? I challenge you to fight me right now! If you only knew… I've been looking for a fight in here for a very, very long time!"

Kenji only smirked with anger as an answer while Arthur was still looking straight at him with his glaring eyes.

"Don't you just smile back at me you little jerk!" then Arthur punched Kenji's face once again. Kenji fell on the ground with his bleeding lips. He wanted to fight back, but he held his temper. Instead, he wiped the blood on his lips and the dirt in his shirt.

Arthur laughed out loud. "Show your high regard and respect to an Explorer, you coward!" and then he left off.

Kenji's eyes wide-opened and wondered to what Arthur just meant when he uttered "an Explorer". The students were all still looking at him, but he just smiled at them when he stood on his feet. Then, he walked away from them.

The young man went back to his room and continuously wiped out his face especially his bleeding lips in front of the mirror. After a while, Shingue came in and got surprised when he saw Kenji with a trail of blood on his lips.

"Hey, why did you bite your lips?" asked Shingue in surprise.

Kenji wondered. "Bite? I didn't bite it! That stupid Arthur was the one who did this!" then he washed his face with water.

"Did he punch you?"

"What else do you think he could do to me?"

Shingue scratched his chin. "Why? What happened?"

"It's such a nonsense and how very temperamental he is! I only ignored him when he suddenly punched me that's all… I've known that guy a lot!"

Shingue did not answer and was about to leave the room, but he heard Kenji murmuring in front of the mirror while washing his face. "Does he think I would show him respect with that kind of attitude?! Who else here that would give him such high respect? Does he deserve to be respected? Who does he think he is?! Some type of guy who is only pretending to be an Explorer though he's not? So boastful!"

Shingue got surprised once more when he heard the most surprising thing of what Kenji said. He stopped walking and quickly turned to his back directly to Kenji.

"A-Are you mad, Kenji? Didn't you know that Arthur is also an Explorer like me? He is one of my batch in the lowest class!"

Kenji was shocked and seemed like the entire sky would fall on his head. He slowly raised his head up facing in front of the mirror still could not believe what he heard from Shingue. A lot of questions were now scrambling in his head as he wiped his face with a clean towel.

10 THE IMPOSTOR

Kenji was open-mouthed in front of the mirror, and Shingue seemed worried thinking that Kenji might think he was siding with Arthur.

Kenji was confused and looked at Shingue's green eyes. "S-Shingue, I did not understand what you have said earlier…"

"Ah, look Kenji… Arthur and I have been friends for long since we were high school classmates. Like me, he also obtained a sacred stone but in different type. If I have a Divine Stone, then Arthur has a Magic Stone."

Kenji eyes looked intensely towards Shingue. "You certain about this? Tell me you're kidding right?"

"Kenji, we've been friends of Arthur and I am telling you that he is really one of us… though we both obtained different types of stone."

"What? And what kind of Magic Stone did Arthur get?"

"I am uncertain about it, Kenji… But it is a genuine Magic Stone."

"Oh? You're his friend, so you should know all about him. And I thought you're the only Explorer here in this school."

Shingue stooped down his head. "I'm sorry again, Kenji. Are you upset on me now?"

Kenji chuckled. "Why do I feel upset at you? That's okay!"

Shingue lifted his face. "Kenji, if you're really serious about becoming an Explorer then you need more perseverance and patience in life. You have to live and learn the real meaning of being a true warrior. In order to become one, you need to find and obtain at least one Sacred Item and then show it to the Explorers," then he whispered. "As for the tip, show them a little impressive stuff to get a higher chance of becoming one, because honestly I did the same thing and they recruited me. And then, they will give you tests to quantify your ability as their new warrior."

"Really? When they recruited you, what were the type of tests they gave you?"

Shingue sprang back in shock then he shouted. "What the hell, Kenji! Oh please… if I tell you everything I did during my tests that time then it takes me a week straight just to tell you my whole useless story!"

Kenji looked puzzled. "I don't understand Shingue, though you're in lowest class they'll still give you tests? Were they too hard for you?"

"Ah yes… But the other tests were so easy to pass, Kenji. And the other thing is, they're too funny. Sometimes the Explorers also ask you different things for an interview as if they are also hiring employees for work."

"So Shingue, how to get to the Explorer base? You shouldn't be here since you're one of them, nevertheless the Explorers ordered you to stay here for the training."

"Kenji listen, there are three classes of the Explorers' family. I am in the lowest class called Ultimate Explorers. Which means, their base is not only one but also three… Though the three classes are different from each other, and yet we belong in the same umbrella organization."

Kenji wiped his face again with a towel. "That's great," but there was no excitement shown on his face.

"Yeah, and you know what? The UE leader said that our team has the most number of warriors among the three sub-groups of the Explorers, because they have the most number of Sacred Items obtained than the two. As you elevate your class, their requirement becomes strict. The Dragon Divinity Explorer is the highest class of the Explorers family that makes them elite and only few members are in the list. This is because their members are the ONLY selected warriors by the gods to become the protectors and guardians of their artifacts, as well as the fourteen long-lost elements that are still remain hidden up to now. As for the sacred stone I already have, they are still uncertain if the stone is one of the missing elements or not. The bottom line is, obtaining a sacred stone is the key to become an Explorer and when they find out that you have one, they will recruit you to join the lowest class."

Kenji looked at his watch. "Shingue, it's already night time!"

"Oh I see," said Shingue wondering. "Okay, I'm about to go to my bed now. See you later."

"Wait Shingue," called Kenji and Shingue stopped from going out the door.

"Yes?"

"Shingue, in case I obtain a sacred object that the Explorers are also looking for, I'll go straight to you. 'Coz I need your help for this… okay?"

Shingue smiled. "Sure Kenji, we're friends from now on."

"Okay, thank you and good night," then Kenji wiped his face.

Shingue left the room and Kenji turned again in front of the mirror to observe his face. While facing the mirror, he had been thinking on what could possibly happen in case he would meet his parents and see his twin brother again. "My brother Genji, where are you now? I haven't seen you for a very long time, but I believe that you are still alive and well!"

And then, he went off to his bed to lay down until he fell asleep.

Meanwhile…

Genji was currently staying in a lucrative city hidden from the sun scorching heat. The place was so huge, beautiful, and exclusively designed for the rich and famous people. Since Kenji was staying in another country, Genji was now living in a capital city of Camoria called Camoria City.

Genji went in Camoria unwittingly after he left Damsville to travel from a distance to search for his real father. A wealthy woman found him in this rich city after she discovered that the young man was lost. Since the woman had no children of her own, she adopted Genji and took care of him as her own son. The woman's name was Madam Veronica, and she was married to an Explorer who belonged in the second class of the organization called EUE. Though the couple were wealthy and had an abundant life, the woman was barren and they were not blessed to have their own children.

And now that Genji also reached his seventeen years of age, he managed to live in his own life together with his known stepmother. However, Genji grew up with bad attitude influenced by his stepmother who treated him cruelly. With that, Genji lived all alone with no any friends to call on.

The young man was in his room when his personal butler came in whom he usually yelled at and being humiliated in front of his stepmother. "Master Grover, is there anything you would like to ask from me?" so Grover was what they called to Genji.

THE EXPLORERS

Genji stamped his foot showing annoyance to the butler. "Hey, how many times do I have to tell you not to come here unless I say so? Are you an idiot?!!"

The poor butler got hurt. "I-I was only concerned at you, my master... I thought you asked something from me and I didn't hear it clear."

"IDIOT!" shouted Genji. "I will call you whenever I need you so you better keep your ears clean. Get out!"

And then, the poor butler came out of the room hurriedly.

Genji suddenly became impatient. "I'm bored! I've been stuck in this city for too long. I want to go out and move to another country," then he stood up. "Hmmm, how long has it been since the last time I went to Damsville and Bondore? Those aren't too far from here as far as I know... W-Wait, I'll go outside!"

Genji went out of the room when he met Madam Veronica. "Son, it seems like you are going somewhere. Where will you go?"

Genji answered with his eyes closed. "Wandering. I'm going to use our own airplane."

"Where will you go I said?!"

"In Bondore. If you're going to ask me on what to do there, then that is none of your business."

"Bondore is too far from here and it is in another country! Tell me, is there someone there you are courting with?"

"N-No! That's not it. I just want to get out of here that's all!"

"I will let you go Grover, but assure me that you will return here before six o'clock at night. And I don't care how far you will go as long as you'll return home immediately!"

"Yes."

Genji moved off. He frowned while walking to reach their private jet. When he got into the airplane, he immediately left the country by his own.

After a few hours, the rugged young man had reached Bondore and he landed the airplane in a wide verdant lot. He came out in his jet when he heard a voice coming in the distance from the old woman whom Kenji met before.

"Kenji! Kenji!" called the old woman from afar.

Genji was surprised to hear the old woman as if the name itself was very familiar to him. He turned to where the voice came from and he saw the old woman approaching towards him. He thought the old woman mistakenly identified him, so to make sure, he pointed himself.

"Yes, you! There's no other Kenji I met in Dakar but only you right?"

Genji walked near towards the old woman. "In... Dakar? You met me before in Dakar? But this is Bondore, isn't it?"

The elder shook her head and sighed. "Yes and I know that I met you in Dakar. Ahem, perhaps you already forgotten me since we've never seen each other for months!" then she smiled. "Hm Kenji, I mean seriously... don't tell me that you're getting more forgetful than me now, eh?"

"Then why are you here if you're from Dakar?"

"W-Whaattt? Oh, and you already even forgot where I really come from! I belong here remember? I just thought to pay here for a visit since I heard the news that you failed to rescue this town. But it's okay to all, the residents knew that this would really happen. We've already accepted our fate, but we are still thankful for what you have done--"

"Oh yeah, whatever old woman," interrupted Genji as he turned his head to his side. "Why did you say that I failed to save this town?"

The elder did not respond for a while, and Genji seemed to understand what Kenji did when he was here just months ago. He found out the reason why the old woman said that thing to him, knowing that he was Kenji. He learned that his twin brother was already been here before, so he thought of something against his brother. He was going to ruin his twin brother's reputation... just for fun!

The old woman answered while Genji was looking at her wrinkled face. "They said you lost a fight against a Pioneer..."

"Ah yes," replied an impostor. "In fact, I never used my strength and never fought back at them. I actually gave up this town since I didn't have business here and this would not affect me. I could even win the fight with no sweat at all but I let them win because I realized that it was just a waste of time to fight with them unless I belong here. Well you know, none of my family were living here so why bother myself? That's why I decided to just give up this town to them and it's over. At least, I never got hurt and worst got killed."

The elder felt dismay and pain in her heart. "W-What? You really intended to only give up this town? But Kenji, I thought..."

Genji raised his voice towards the elder. "Shut up, you old woman! I changed my mind when I got here in Bondore because I only thought more of myself rather than to those people whom I actually don't know!"

THE EXPLORERS

"Just wait a minute you--"

Genji pointed the elder. "Stop talking old woman! You don't have a business to stop me! If you wanted to save Bondore against those Pioneers, then you should be the one who fought them and not me. You shouldn't depend your freedom to someone whom you think is a superhero! Why don't your old rheumatic body learn to do combat techniques along with all of the Bondore residents?! How shameful of you that you just sit there and rely on me. And I swear that you are a useless old woman along with the residents of this town!"

The elder's stooped down her head in shame and the tears ran down her face from Genji's rudely words, but still, she managed to answer him anyway.

"Kenji, was it you who actually said that you would save this town from any harm? So what's the meaning of all this… that you were all talk and promises?!"

"Why should I care in this town? There is nothing you could do to save Bondore anymore. As what I've said to you earlier, I already gave up this town to the hands of Pioneers, period!"

The elder quickly slapped Genji's smooth and white youthful cheek.

"I should have known this… that I trusted someone who just simply turned against us! I treated you like someone and I fed you in my house as one of us! But you're a liar… if only the residents will know this…"

"Fine then go!" answered Genji rudely. "Tell them what I've told you so they will also know what I did! And tell them to stop being too dependable! Didn't you ever know that the superheroes have their own weaknesses and get tired like you?"

"Tired?" asked the angry old woman. "How come you got tired if you never fought them and just gave up? How could a hero like you get tired by that? By sitting and doing nothing but prattling? And why did you say that we became so dependent on you though YOU were actually the one telling me that you would go in Bondore to deal with them?! Did I say anything to you like: *'Hey Kenji, can you go to Bondore and fight the Pioneers for us? We look forward to your success when you come back!!!'* Do you think we would stick ourselves to your garrulousness for nothing?! No! It is because we trusted you so much and you were the one who promised this foolishness! And oohhh… I was glad for believing your FAKE courage!"

Genji suddenly hesitated and realized what everything he said earlier seemed wrong. Perhaps his twin brother never did what he actually said, so he thought to himself. "Maybe my twin brother actually did what he told to her that time…"

The poor elder began to cry out loud. "You're a traitor! Now I finally know who you really are!"

Genji turned mad. "H-Hey you useless old woman, be careful of what you are saying! Stop your big mouth and just shut up okay!"

The elder was still sobbing when Genji spoke again rudely. "After all, this town has been destroyed and is already taken. It is useless now as you are! Go and spread what I've said to everyone in this town, goodbye!" then he walked away.

As Genji walked past to the elder, she turned her glance at the impostor's face and noticed something seemed different and strange.

"H-Hold on… Are you really Kenji?" she asked in doubt.

Genji wondered. "And what do you think who I am? Is there someone you know who is as handsome as me??!"

"You seemed to be different from what Kenji I met. I remember the two studs in his face… They are both in his chin, and not in the forehead!"

"O-Of course! I moved my two studs in my forehead for a change!"

"And… for what I know, he was a nice young boy. His gentle face, good attitude, and easy to get along with made everyone here trust him despite of his age… Wait, don't tell me that… that you're not Kenji?!"

"You're stubborn! That was a long time ago and I've already changed a lot!"

"NO!" the old woman quickly pointed Genji and glared at him. "You are not the Kenji I met! Though I am old but my sharp memory never lies. I still remember everything we talked. Those curses and magics! You… You are an enemy disguised as Kenji, an impostor!"

Genji felt deeply angered. "You're so annoying, you old woman! If it wasn't for your age then I already beat you!"

The old woman looked intensely at Genji with her sharp-looking eyes. "Let's see about that…"

The old woman stuck her glare at the impostor until her face slowly transformed into a witch-look. Then she came closer to him, as the impostor began to feel petrified when she was eyeing him suspiciously.

"I can see a dark side of you…" said the old woman as her voice slowly changed into low and creepy.

THE EXPLORERS

Genji recoiled in fear. "W-Who are you? Are you a witch??!"

The elder did not respond, which made Genji slowly move away from her in fear.

"How treacherous... Leave this town now or I shall give you the real taste of fear!"

Genji was stunned from what he saw. The old woman continued to speak.

"Run away and never return... and take this punishment I shall give to you!" and then, a flash of white light suddenly came out in her eyes at the same time she quickly raised both of her hands in the air.

The impostor appalled, and the whole scene was now completely covered in pure white.

11 WORRIES

The whole scene was still covered in pure white so Genji closed his eyes as he was dazzled by the shining light coming out from the old woman. And then, he cried.

Meanwhile at Kenji…

Kenji was currently sleeping when the marks in his forehead quickly reacted until it rankled so he awakened. He touched his forehead, and it was so painful as it was throbbing. He began to sweat.

"W-What is it that suddenly struck my forehead? What is the meaning of this?"

It was still dawn, but Kenji threw out the blanket and he got up from his bed while his forehead was still throbbing in intense pain. "Arrrgghhh! Why is my forehead hurting? Ahhh, it's too painful!"

Kenji went to the first-aid cabinet to take his rubbing oil and put small drops of it in his forehead. He rubbed it to ease the pain, but instead, it got worse as it rankled more. Kenji cried.

Good thing no one heard his cry. He went back to his bed and quickly closed his eyes, until he heard something whispering in his mind.

"I have been a sinful brother to you, Kenji… I slurred you behind your back… I maligned you!"

Kenji's eyes suddenly opened. He did not know where that voice come from and thought if he was the only one who heard it. Later, the mysterious whisper came out in his mind again: *"I have been a sinful brother to you, Kenji… I slurred you behind your back… I maligned you!"*

Something quickly entered his mind about the voice he just heard –

that voice belonged to no one else but only his twin brother Genji. "G-Genji... My twin brother is calling me!"

Kenji believed that his twin brother was in great danger and very much concerned towards him. "It seems that I am starting to feel my brother's presence... I wonder what is that mean?"

His forehead began to prickle once again so he slowly touched it with his fingers. He felt something oozing in his forehead. As soon as he took off his hand to take a look, he noticed his fingers with some drops of his blood!

Kenji did not get scared as he knew the possible meaning of his brother's call. Genji... he was in danger... because of this, he began to worry.

Morning came...

The students were all awake. Shingue and Claude were together, but they did not see Kenji. "Shingue, I know Kenji is already around during this particular morning, but I wonder why he isn't here?" asked Claude to Shingue.

"I dunno Claude, that's also what I know."

"I'm going to look for him in his bedroom. Maybe he's still asleep."

"Sure."

Claude walked away and left Shingue to check Kenji's room. When he arrived at the door of the young man's room, he knocked but no one answered.

"Hello? Kenji?" Claude knocked again, but still he did not hear any response.

Claude tried to turn the door knob and the door opened. He peered around to scour the room but Kenji was not there.

"Why did Kenji leave this room with the door unlocked? Where is he now?"

Claude returned to Shingue.

"So where is Kenji?"

"Kenji was not in his room, Shingue... But the door is open. Maybe he is just wandering around."

"Wandering? Kenji can't go somewhere because today is his training time!"

"Let's ask the students here. Maybe they know where he is."

"Why worry too much about him, Claude? Kenji is big enough to do what he wants to do even without our knowledge."

Claude nodded. "Okay…"

The two attended their breakfast and Kenji was still not around. "Geez Claude, it looks like Master Serge took Kenji somewhere to do his training alone, you think?" asked Shingue.

Claude mimicked Shingue's reply earlier. "I dunno…"

"Alright Claude, then I will go to his room and check on him. He can't just leave the door open as he left, can he? What if he's only hiding from us?"

Claude nodded again, and this time Shingue would be the next to go to Kenji's room. He opened the door. "Claude is right, the door is open," then he came in and also looked around in every corner of the room. "Kenji, are you there? Hello?"

No one answered to Shingue's call as he was still searching the room. "Kenji, you left the door open! Where are you now?" but still, no one answered.

Shingue walked around, until he noticed a few drops of blood in Kenji's bed sheet. He gasped in surprise and recoiled.

"Blimey! There's a blood in his bed… K-Kenji… what happened to Kenji! Oh no, I should let everyone knows about this. Wait, Master Serge!"

Shingue ran out of the room and he went straight to Master Serge and not to Claude. Good thing the master instructor's class had not yet started. Also, he noticed that Kenji was not with the instructor.

"Master Serge, Kenji is missing in his room right now! And I saw a few drops of blood in his bed sheet! Please go and take a look at it right now!"

Master Serge was so busy doing something that he did not listen to what the young man just said. Shingue was about to repeat it again when the master instructor spoke first. "What is it that you want from me, Shingue?"

"There is something I would like you to know master. I've just seen a few drops of blood in Kenji's bed when I came to his room. I was looking for him, and he was not there!"

"Perhaps it was his blood. Maybe he did something that injured himself."

"Did Kenji get badly injured? Wounded?"

"By judging from the drops of blood in his bed sheet, I would say yes."

Shingue rushed back to Claude to tell him what he just saw.

"Hey, what took you so long? Is Kenji there?" asked Claude boringly.

"He's not there... But I saw a blood in his bed."

After a long while of waiting, Kenji finally appeared before them and he suddenly collapsed. The other students nearby saw the young man and they quickly ran towards him.

"Kenji! Kenji! What happened? Why did you fall?" asked Claude while Kenji's head was on his arm and had difficulty to speak.

"Kenji can't speak well. Kenji, are those bloods in the bed yours?" asked Shingue.

The fallen Kenji responded hoarsely. "I... I had an intense headache and I didn't know why... My forehead, i-it was b-bleeding... as if it got wounded... I-It was too painful! And I c-can't even breathe well..."

"What? Your forehead was bleeding? Did you accidentally bump your head? Who did this to you? Let me see your wounds," said Claude.

"I-I don't have any w-wounds, Claude... But it was t-too painful..."

"How did that bleed if you are not injured?"

Kenji groaned in pain. "I-I don't know... My brother..." then he closed his eyes.

"His... his brother Genji... What does he mean by that?"

Shingue turned to Claude. "What's with his brother, Claude?"

"I don't understand him either, Shingue... But he just mentioned something regarding his twin brother."

"Oh? Kenji has a twin brother?"

"Yes, Shingue. His name is Genji."

Master Serge came to them and he was shocked to see the fallen young man. "What happened to him? Who did this?"

The students looked to each other and they did not know what actually happened to Kenji before.

"Hmpt, take this boy to our clinic right away! He must be checked and treated immediately. Go, quickly now!" he commanded.

The students along with Master Serge brought Kenji to the nearby clinic. Their clinic was so simple and yet it was huge.

"Thank you for taking him here. You may now go and proceed to your training," said Master Serge to the students.

"What about our training for today, Master Serge?" asked one of his student.

"I will be giving you a vacant time for a while, but I will return soon to resume our training."

"Thank you master," said the student and they left the clinic to rest.

As the students walked out the clinic, Master Serge looked over Kenji who was currently lying in bed with his eyes closed. Later, he moved his face closer to the young man and whispery asked. "Hey you, do you hear me?"

Kenji did not open his eyes.

"Kenji, can you hear me? Answer me..."

Kenji did not respond, until the doctor came in.

"Sir?"

Master Serge turned to the doctor. "I will be staying here for a while until he wakes up."

"No problem, but I need to check his condition first."

"Okay, okay... I understand."

Silence. After a few minutes...

"Sir, I think this boy seems to be okay. His condition is well and I did not see any problems at all," said the doctor.

"Really?"

"Yes, sir."

"What about his injury? Or... his blood problem?"

"I don't see any problems in his blood either sir, plus he has no any injury in his forehead as well as in his body."

"Good."

"Maybe this boy had pushed himself too much. He might be stressed from his continuous training that's why. But I can see that his condition is good right now, and no health problem."

"Good, but still I will be staying here until he wakes up."

And he did. Until the patient finally woke up...

Master Serge greeted the young man. "How are you now, Kenji? How's your feeling?"

Kenji's eyes were dilated and he slowly rose to bed with a pillow in his back.

"I'm okay now... I think I am feeling better."

"What happened to you earlier? Suddenly you just fell!"

"Yes sir, but I do not know why that happened. I had no idea what was going on. It just happened that I felt too dizzy until my head bled!"

"Your friend told me that it was your forehead that was actually bleeding and not your head."

"Y-Yes sir… Too late…"

"W-What did you just say?"

"I am getting too worried about my brother now… As I feel like something bad just happened to him. I need to look for him right now!"

"Huh?" Master Serge looked puzzled.

"M-Master, I would like to ask a favor from you if you may."

"What is it?"

"Please allow me to get out of this school to look for my brother alone… I can feel that he is in great danger and he needs my help!"

"But you have so much training to do today…"

"Do not worry master, I will return in this school as soon as possible!"

Silence. Master Serge could not grant the young man's request because of his safety, so Kenji raised his voice. "I need to go now and rescue my brother, please! I will not let him harmed and I will look after him. But I will return as I promise…"

Master Serge was tongue tied. Kenji could no longer stand his silence, so he immediately got up from the bed and quickly burst out the room. The young man just left the master instructor alone, but instead of getting angry, the instructor just smiled.

And then, Master Serge also left the clinic when he encountered Claude and Shingue at the door. The two stopped their running when they meet their instructor.

"Master, how is Kenji now?" asked Claude.

"Did he just go somewhere again?" asked Shingue.

Master Serge answered in question. "What's going on with your training now?"

"We were waiting for you to come back…"

"Really? Then let's continue the training. Let's go," then Master Serge walked away.

"S-Sir, wait a minute…. How is Kenji now?" asked Claude.

"Kenji's fine. He just left the clinic."

Claude and Shingue's eyes wide-opened and they dashed away. The master instructor only shook his head, but Shingue ran back and approached him again. "Where is he right now? Did he tell you where he went, sir?"

"What?! I'm busy right now! I don't know where that boy went, and you'll find that out soon!"

Then Shingue dashed away again.

Shingue thought that Claude was also looking for Kenji and he had to follow him fast. But instead, he saw Claude in the canteen and was eating his lunch rather than to look for Kenji!

Shingue shove Claude from his back while he was eating *chopsuey*. "How could you! I thought why you ran away from Master Serge earlier was to look for your frieeeedddnndddd!!!"

Claude played dumb. "Oh yeah? I-I forgot."

"WHAT ON EARTH DO YOU MEAN BY THAT?!" asked Shingue jokingly. "You're careless!"

"Shut up, Shingue. I'm sorry, I forgot about it because I've been starving since earlier."

"Whatever you say, Claude. Hey, you had your breakfast earlier!"

"Why Shingue? Do you think I know where he is right now? Do you?"

"No…"

"See? Why would I waste my time by looking for nothing though we both didn't have any idea where he went? It doesn't necessarily mean that I didn't care, but the truth is, I just don't want to get weary by only to look for him."

Shingue became silent.

"If this is about his brother Genji, then I already know what that is for!"

The martial arts school was not that pretty far to where Kenji went which was the forest. Since this was his first time to get out far in this country, the places were so unfamiliar to him and he was unaware to any danger he could possibly encounter.

Kenji wandered around. "Gosh… I don't feel the presence of my brother here…" this was because Kenji did not know that Genji was currently in Bondore. "Where will I see my brother? Darn… He's not here!"

His body was not yet fully recovered, but his forehead was no longer painful than before. He sat on the ground to relax for the meantime.

"I'm too worried about him. It's been years that we got separated from each other. Until now, I still don't hear any news about him. I wonder what he is doing right now?"

Kenji heard the sound of approaching steps in the grasses that seemed to be moving towards him. He turned to where the steps come from in his serious look. "What is that? An animal?"

A little girl appeared running from high grasses and she accidentally bumped Kenji and rebounded on the ground.

"Ah!" cried the child.

Kenji was surprised, but he reached his hand over the child to help her got up. "Hello, are you alright kid?"

The child did not answer.

"Are you hurt?"

The child stood on her feet. "No, I'm alright mister."

"Ah... So why were you running fast? Are you late in school?"

The child shook her head. "N-No... I was hiding."

"Hiding? Of hide-and seek? Are you playing with your friends?"

"No *kuya*..."

"Oh, then why is it that you're running that fast?"

"I am being pursued by someone."

"Who?"

"I don't know who they are..." then the little girl began to catch her breath.

"What do they look like?"

"They are all big men... They are many and big!"

Kenji felt agitated. "Do you think... they're all moving over here now?"

"They have not seen me... because I quickly ran away from them and I hid..."

"What is the reason why they're chasing you?"

The child pulled out something from her hand. "I just picked something that I don't understand what it is," then she showed an ordinary stone in perfectly round shape and had symbols engraved on its surface. "I was digging in the sand beach to build a sand castle when I accidentally discover this stone buried under the sand. It was so beautiful and it captivated my eyes and so I couldn't help not to take it. I took it, but then, there was a group of men in the beach who saw this stone in my hand. And then, they tried to steal it from me! Maybe it's because they were envy that I got this gorgeous stone first. But believe me, I was really the first one who'd found it. B-Believe me!"

"Can I borrow that thing in your hand and let me take a look at it? By the way, you can hide in here. I will accompany you. Do not worry, I am not with them."

The child's face looked concerned by uncertainty. "Well…"

Kenji moved his face towards her and smiled. "I promise you that I will never take that stone from you because you are its rightful owner. Plus, I am not with them and I don't have any intention of doing anything foolish behind your back, okay?" then he winked.

The child finally agreed so she lent her stone to Kenji.

"Thank you! Come, and let's sit together under this tree," said Kenji.

The two acquaintances sat under the tree when Kenji looked intensely at the stone's appearance. There were symbols carved on it and he turned to the child. "Wow, this stone was so beautiful to look at. You're good in--"

As he turned to the child, she was already asleep beside him due to extreme tiredness from running.

"She's is too tired. Now she's asleep…"

Kenji turned back his gaze to the stone. "It's impossible that this stone was only man-made and was just thrown away… or buried. It's shape is perfectly round though it is not much smooth. I wonder what these symbols are? Is this some sort of a treasure? AH!!!"

A flash of memories suddenly struck Kenji's head: the legendary powers that were transformed into just ordinary stones whether they were elements or magics… In other words, they were the sacred stones that Pioneers had been long searching for! With that, Kenji began to realize that this might be the possible reason why the group of men was chasing the little girl. Because they knew that the stone she got in the beach was actually a Sacred Item!

Kenji suddenly nonplussed, as if he wanted to take away the stone from the child and show it to Shingue to make sure it was also the one the Explorers were looking for. And this would be the perfect chance for him to become one like them!

Therefore, he became more concerned.

12 DIVINE STONE

The little girl was still sleeping beside Kenji while he was thinking intensely on what to do with the stone. "I want to take this stone from her and go back to Shingue, but..." and then he watched the sleeping child. "I just gave my word to her that I would not steal this stone. What if I go back in the school with her?"

Kenji stroked his chin. "Thus this kid will have a second thought if I take her there because of this stone. Or she might think that I am also one of those group of men who was chasing her. What should I tell her?"

Later on, Kenji heard another sound of footsteps on the grass and he alerted himself for the possible danger while watching the child. "I think it's them!"

The footsteps suddenly stopped and Kenji wondered. "Huh?"

He heard low voices talking in the distance. He sneaked towards the nearby voices to listen to their conversation.

"They are talking..." he said to himself.

"You guys are so completely idiotic! You couldn't even follow that kid! We need that kid!"

"We're truly sorry sir, but the child was too fast... She knows the different passages in this forest and could manage to get away from us that fast."

"How stupid! You guys are truly that dumbass! Why did I ever recruit you?! We don't need that kid, we need the one she got in her hand!"

Kenji shook his head. "I knew it! The thing what the kid got was not just an ordinary stone. Wait, where should I hide this kid?"

He moved away silently and carried the sleeping child in his arms, but there was another group of men standing in his path as he went out in the forest. His forehead began to prickle again. Annoyed what was happening in his forehead, still he managed to elude their attention. He turned back and ran in different direction but the other group prevented him in going any further.

"Hey you, why do you have that kid with you? Is she your daughter?!" asked a man.

"Yeah, give us the stone she got!" said another man.

Kenji answered calmly. "She is not my daughter… I am a friend. She said you were chasing her only because of the stone she got!"

"Blimey! That is a sacred object you asshole!"

"I hope you'll forgive this child… because she already gave the stone to me!" excused Kenji.

"W-What did you just say? What the hell are you?"

"Are you an idiot? I am a human!"

The man got irritated. "Hey lad! We are Humorians and you should respect us. How rude!!!"

Kenji became silent when he heard the name of that familiar group of Humorians who was also one of the Explorers' enemies. He felt sorry for them thinking they were just somebody else.

One of the Humorians laughed. "So, why did you become silent in all of the sudden? Are you afraid? Are you dumb? Probably you thought we're just some sort of bystanders wandering around in the forest, eh?"

Kenji felt embarrassed as his face blushed, but he did not show it to them. "I-I see… Yeah, I guess you were right. I mistook you for being some bystanders here. That's why I didn't give you my respect… Hehehe…"

"Now look who's talking! Don't tell us you are looking for a trouble, huh? F-Fine, if that is what you want and that's what you get!"

"Huh? I already admit that I really mistook you for somebody else and yet you're telling me that I was looking for a trouble? Hah, gimme a break!"

The Humorian posed himself for the fight. "Come on, let's fight!"

"Sir, don't you see that I am carrying a sleeping child? And please… I don't want any trouble… There's nothing for us to fight for."

"What? Are you a coward? Look, if you don't want any trouble, just give us the stone that kid is holding right now!"

THE EXPLORERS

Kenji put down the little girl on the grass when she woke up and saw a group of men who was chasing her.

"Ah... Those guys... Those are the bad guys I was talking to you about!" cried the child out loud while pointing at the men.

"Come on, you coward! Let's fight!"

"Geez, why should I fight you? I have the child with me!"

The Humorian got mad. "Grrr... take this you coward!" then he quickly punched Kenji. The young man caught unprepared for his first attack so he sprang back and the child cried.

"Oh no, *kuyahhhh*!"

"Hahaha, I thought you were a strong man," said the Humorian.

Kenji stroked his aching jaw and posed for the fight. "That is what you think!" then he retaliated using the moves he learned in seven months of training. The Humorians were astonished while Kenji was still doing his moves to his opponent. Then, he performed the somersault attack and the man flew away in short distance.

"What on earth..." said the Humorian in shock. "D-Do you think you can match my fighting skill?!"

The child jumped in amazement. "Yeahhhhh, *kuya* you're good with this!"

The opponent antagonized and he rushed in towards Kenji to do his next attack. But Kenji was able to dodge his attack. The child was amazed, but the Humorian followed his attack and Kenji got hit by his strong kick.

Next, Kenji followed his successive combos to the Humorian and the man absorbed all of his punches and kicks. He was terribly angered that make his face quickly turned red.

Kenji raised his feet and flipped back performing the somersault attack again and the enemy got hit in the chin. Then, he quickly fell on the ground.

"Yeaaaahhh!" yelled the overjoyed child. "*Kuya* just beat the bad guy!"

"Heh, i-is that the best you can do against the Humorian like m-me?" asked the man pretending to be unhurt by Kenji's attack.

"Why don't you just give up on me and leave us alone?" asked Kenji annoyingly.

"G-Give up?! You're son of a--! HUMORIANS!!!"

The man waved his hands calling his allies for help and the group hurriedly walked near him. "Hah, is there anyone here who would like to face this coward? Which one of you?"

His colleague approached him and moved to his side. "I will volunteer. Let me face this weakling and show him no mercy!"

The child got mad. "Don't call him a weakling you wicked man! Your friend just got beaten by *kuya* and I suppose you are the weakling… BLEEEHHHH!"

The Humorian volunteer ignored the child and he just turned directly to Kenji. "If you lose the fight against me then we will take the stone from the child, you understand?"

Kenji was still in his defensive pose. "Let's see about that!"

"Excellent," said the man. "This will be our deal!"

Kenji moved the child away from them to be safe when she spoke.

"*Kuya*, do your best okay? Later, I will tell something to you!"

Kenji stroked her hair and smiled. "Sure, I will do this for you. Just stay there and never come near to us."

The child nodded. "Okay!"

The Humorian got bored. "Hey, what are you waiting for? You've gotten too slow!"

Kenji moved away from the child to face his opponent and prepared for the next encounter. "I'm ready!"

The battle began. The Humorian dashed towards Kenji and performed his first attack, but Kenji evaded the attack. Their fight was fierce!

The child jumped again in amazement while cheering Kenji. The two were struggling to outwit each other as they were both performing their martial arts. The Humorian leaped forward and so as Kenji. The Humorian got hit by Kenji's quick attack.

The child was very delighted as she jumped in amazement. The Humorian who was far stronger than Kenji's first opponent got too much hits from Kenji's kicks and punches.

"You're really pretty good young man," said the Humorian. "But it doesn't mean that this fight ends here, urrryaaahhhh!!!" then he suddenly disappeared in front of Kenji.

Kenji's eyes wide-opened as he was surprised by the sudden move of his opponent. He looked around for his opponent in wonder. "W-Where is he? He just disappeared like bubbles before my eyes!"

The enemy suddenly emerged in his back and kicked him behind with full force. Kenji was pushed away in the distance and slumped on the ground when the Humorian followed the attack with his successive combos. Kenji was confused, he could not evade the attacks and the child was nonplussed with fear.

"Oh no... *Kuyaaahhh!*"

Kenji dashed away, and the opponent finally drew out his long sword. "Have the taste of my ruthless mercy and let me have your head as a prize, young man!" then he pointed the sword before Kenji.

Kenji seemed stunned, thinking on what to do to evade and dodge the attacking weapons which he was not yet fully mastered. Another thing was... Kenji was not even carrying any weapons in his hand!

Oh no... this looks bad, he got his weapon... He said to himself. *I am still a novice, dude. I-I am not in there yet!!!*

"*Kuya*, be careful!"

"Tsk, fine... Que sera, sera... Whatever it will be," said Kenji to himself. He would still try his best to face an experienced opponent with a sword in his hand.

The battle continued. As the Humorian slashed his sword at Kenji, the young man dashed away to save his life. He could not fight back, and all he could do at this point in time was to just ran away and dodge.

"What are you doing now, *kuya*? Why do you keep on dodging his attacks?!" the child was now concerned.

Kenji tried to fight back with only his bare hands when the enemy slowed down and got hit. As the opponent stroke his sword, Kenji would dodge again and then he would retaliate as fast as he could.

The child clapped her hands as a support and to cheer Kenji, and then the young man regained his chance to perform his combination of combos to the opponent.

As the two fought with each other, the Humorians seemed relaxed while they were watching the battle, knowing that Kenji's opponent was tough and well-experienced in combat. Kenji kicked again, but this time the Humorian quickly evaded his attack and once again he vanished. Kenji was shocked.

"What the..."

"*Kuya*, above you!!!"

Kenji quickly turned above. But just as he turned, he noticed the opponent's sword almost an inch away in his face. He quickly moved back in shock, but unfortunately the tip of the blade still reached his face and cut his nose bridge. He stumbled down and screamed in pain, as his nose bridge bled.

The child ran towards Kenji while he was still screaming in pain, as the blood flowed down his face.

"Now that I beat you... We are now going to take the stone from that kid. Give us the stone if you don't want her to get hurt!"

The child put her arms around Kenji's waist in fear. "K-*Kuya*, I'm scared!"

"No? Very well then..." with one stroke, the Humorian rushed towards them. "You're very tough... I will kill you now!!!"

The child screamed out loud. "AHHHH!"

Kenji had nothing else to do but to just close his eyes and wait for the blade to strike. As the sword with sharp blade was about to hit Kenji, Claude and Shingue came to the rescue and they prevented the attack by warding off with their own weapons in hand.

"Claude! Shingue!" called Kenji as he opened his eyes with hope. "It's good to see you!"

"And who are you?" the enemy was greatly surprised.

Claude answered. "We're your enemies!" then he attacked. But as he attacked, the Humorian's jet came above them and picked the Humorians up which made Claude missed the opponent and lost his balance.

"H-Hey! Why are you all fleeing? You cowaaaardddss!!!" he yelled.

The Humorians laughed from above. "Someone needs us now... 'Till we meet again!" then the jet zoomed away.

Claude and Shingue approached Kenji who was still sitting on the ground. "Kenji, where have you been? Good thing we immediately saw you and we came here on time! Why is your nose bleeding that bad?!" asked Claude.

Shingue was impressed. "Did you actually fight those guys all by yourself? How impressive!"

Claude noticed the little girl. "Wow, who is this cute little girl? Are you related to each other?"

Kenji shook his head. "N-No. I just met her here earlier... She will be coming with us."

"Why?"

Kenji turned to Shingue. "There is something I want to tell you, Shingue. M-Maybe later... after the doctor treats the wound in my nose."

"Go ahead, and I will take care of the kid. Come with me little girl," said Shingue and the girl looked at him.

"I-I don't want to, I just want to go with *kuya*!" said the child.

Kenji chuckled and he turned to Shingue again.

"Shingue… I need your help. You must come with me and we will talk about something important in my room… alone. J-Just you and me, okay?"

Claude asked. "You and Shingue alone? And what about me and the kid?"

Kenji smiled and he turned to the child. "Do you have a shelter of your own?"

The child smiled back at him and she nodded. "I can live somewhere elsewhere."

"Whoa, so that means you're homeless! So, why don't you come and just stay with us? Don't worry, I will take care of you. If someone is trying to bully you, just call my name okay?"

"By the way, what is your name *kuya*?"

"Oh yeah… My name is *kuya* Kenji!"

The two boys got impatient. "Hey, let's go home! You'll chat about that later," said Claude.

The three young men returned to their school along with the child. When they reached their dormitory, Kenji immediately told to Shingue the whole incident while his nose bridge was still in dried blood. The news reached to Master Serge, so the master instructor went straight to Kenji to talk about the incident.

"I believe what this young man said though I didn't see the actual incident. The cut in his nose bridge proved the veracity of his story," said Master Serge. "We will take you to the doctor now and you must be treated," he added.

The master instructor took Kenji along with Claude and Shingue to the clinic and the doctor treated the wound in Kenji's nose bridge. It took long after his wound was healed.

After a year passed, Kenji reached his eighteen years of age and as a mark of his battle against the Humorian, the wound in his nose bridge left a permanent scar. And for this year, Kenji, Claude, and Shingue finally completed their whole training and they fully mastered their martial arts skill. Graduation day came by and it was time for them to accept their medals as a recognition of their almost two years in training. While the little girl named Valerie, reached her eight years of age and she treated Kenji as her older brother. Brother and sister... as what they were.

During their graduation day, the three boys stood before the newly recruit trainees to receive their medals and certificates as official master warriors. The students applauded, then Rolando gifted them their new costumes as a remembrance and he announced their "class" to everyone that would determine what type of fighters they were.

"Kenji, since that you, Claude, and Shingue will finally start your own journey together, please take these three costumes as my gifts to you. I hope that you guys will like them!" then he wept. Now that the three boys had seen their primary costumes and they smiled.

"Thank you very much for this wonderful gift instructor," said Kenji with a smile. "Yes, I will absolutely wear mine during our journey. This would be my special gift from you."

Rolando took something and offered another gift to Kenji alone. "By the way, please take this special weapon as a gift to you from Master Serge. This will be very useful during any battle you will be facing. He said that this weapon must only be given to those who are brave and deserving fighters like you... The Kali."

"Oh my... such a wonderful gift it is! T-Thank you very much for this. I promise that I will fulfill my main objective and become an Explorer like those students you already mentored. I will make sure that this good news will reach to you and to Master Serge someday soon."

Note: Kenji's primary weapon is called Kali. It is a long staff that is forged by a very hard material with long sword inside. He can use the staff while the sword is inside or use the sword alone during the battle.

"Yes, I am looking forward to hear this good news from you someday my laddie," said Rolando and the two hugged each other.

After the long farewell, Kenji, Claude, and Shingue finally left their training school to begin their journey together, but they promised that they would come back again for a visit, in God's will. Before they graduated, they honestly confessed to each other that they had only one same goal to fulfill... To become a part of the Explorers' highest class called DDE. They would work together as a team, but the little girl Valerie would also be a part of their journey too.

After Shingue's careful observation, the four learned that the stone Valerie picked in the beach was indeed a Divine Stone. He said that the rare sacred stone was called "Divine Stone of Recovery", and he would accompany Kenji to the UE to help him become an Explorer. It was time for Kenji to test his strength when the right time came and also become King Jethro's new chosen warrior.

Kenji recalled what the sailor said when he and Genji were still living with him, whom they considered as their stepfather who was now gone in heaven:

"My boys, do you know that I have enough money now to take you to school?"

"What do you mean school, dad?"

"That means... I have enough money... I can now enroll you both to our school to study!"

"What is school dad?"

"School helps to educate a person to achieve his goal in order to become successful in life!"

As Kenji could still recall his loving stepfather, he began to wept while they were walking in their long path.

Claude noticed Kenji. "Kenji, why are you crying?"

Kenji tried to resist the deep pain in his heart about his stepfather's death but he couldn't.

Shingue did not get what that meant. "Maybe he still don't want to leave our school yet…"

"What's wrong, *kuya* Kenji?" asked Valerie with concern.

"Damn, how sensitive! A young man still cries like that!" said Claude. "A new warrior doesn't deserve to become a crybaby!"

Kenji sniffed. "I-I'm sorry guys… It's just that I remembered something… Something that I will never ever forget…"

Claude patted Kenji's shoulder. "Look, if you grow up like that, then it will slowly turns you into a weak man."

"Come, let us go!" shouted Shingue happily.

Kenji only nodded and smiled. And then, the four ran altogether very happily.

13 ENEMIES

A weird gathering of rival organization composed of different groups was held once in a lifetime. Though they were pierce competitors, still they found their ways to gather without bloodshed and set aside their differences. The groups present in this gathering were Pioneer, Mercury, Vanguard, Expland, Humorian, and Reminescence. Their gathering was called Rivalry Party, a once in a lifetime meeting of different organizations before their planned attack to the Explorers. Since they learned that their primary target was the same, they thought of having a gathering before they would go on their separate ways and become competitors again to a common enemies. Though the number of organizations were complete, not all of the members of each group had attended the gathering.

The party was held in an extravagant and luxurious palace of Reminescence. The Reminescence was a group of legendary paladins and the richest of all competitors. The Reminescence was not just all about wealth, but also the individuals behind the group because their warriors were all legendary and far more superior than the others. Unlike the Explorers and the rest of the organizations, the Reminescence was led by a monarch and some of the warriors were members of royal family.

The Rivalry Party theme was very formal. The women were wearing colorful Filipiniana gowns. The males were on their Barong Tagalog while the others were on their tuxedos. Though the costumes varied, they were still formal.

The king of Reminescence came in the beat of the drums and trumpets. The commotions stopped and all eyes were focused over the

THE EXPLORERS

king.

The king raised his hands and spoke with a grin. "All ears everyone, though we are all competitors in this field, we will still continue this joyful celebration for once in a lifetime before the war!" then he sat down on his throne as each of the group leaders were standing next to him.

The whole environment filled with deafening applause. The celebration continued as the members of each and everyone in the groups poured wine in their glasses and drank bottomless.

Alexander arrived, the leader of Pioneer and he approached the king of Reminescence while applauding.

"Wow, Your Majesty... at first we thought that you were stingy and mean. But you welcomed us here though we are all competitors," said Alexander frankly to the king.

"Don't you want a huge party like this?" asked the king.

"N-No, no, no it's not like that."

The noise continued.

"Your Majesty, why don't you please stand and drink wine with us? At least I could see the king of Reminescence drinking alcohol, hahaha!"

"Alright, I will be with you later," said the king.

The leaders around the king walked away when the king closed his eyes for a second and called a knight to command. "Go to Maximus' room and tell him I am calling him now. Tell him to get prepared for his piano number. Here's the key!"

The knight took the key from the king's hand and bowed before him in respect. "Yes, Your Majesty..."

A woman from Vanguard approached the king. She was very gorgeous to look at since she was wearing her fashionable golden gown. "Come and let us dance, Your Majesty!"

The king stood in his throne and asked the other knight to watch the throne.

Meanwhile, the knight reached the room and gently knocked on the locked door. "Prince Maximus, the king has summoned you now... You may now come out the room," then he used the key to open the door and came inside. He saw the lonely prince in the room who was now dressed and rehearsing in playing piano.

Prince Maximus was a genius in piano and once a cursed son of the king of Reminescence. During his four years of age, he was possessed by a strange spirit whose only intention was to use his body to kill his own father. As the king learned about it, he decided to shut Maximus in his room and the prince had been imprisoned there since childhood. The king forbade him to go out of the room in any given time, as long as the king did not say so.

But eventually, the mysterious spirit suddenly went out of the prince's body when the spirit was unable to fulfill the mission so he was healed, but the king was not fully aware that the prince was already healed. The king did not take any chances, so the poor prince was still remained in his room up to now.

As a result, Maximus grew up taciturn and unsociable as he never had a chance to meet acquaintances and talk to other people around. Instead, the king gave him an expensive grand piano to keep him busy in his imprisonment. Now, the prince had learned to use piano and he was well-experienced in playing music.

The prince stopped from playing his piano and slowly moved away. Then, he turned to his back. "What do you want?"

"Your father just called you, Your Highness. Please prepare yourself for your piano performance in honor to our guests."

Maximus turned back in playing piano again. The music he was playing was so beautiful but sad. So sad that the music came from his heart only to express his deep emotion for being locked up inside the sealed room for many years.

"My prince…"

Maximus moved his right hand as a gesture. The knight nodded and he left the prince alone in the room. He closed the door, but he could still hear the low sad music coming from inside.

"The guests will become emotional when they see and hear Prince Maximus' performance later," he said to himself.

The knight returned to the king and brought the key back in his hand.

"So what now?" asked the king.

"He will arrive soon, Sire. He is ready…"

"But where is he? Why didn't you take him out of the room with you? The other piano here is now ready. Here's the key again and ask him to go out now!"

"Y-Yes, Your Majesty…"

The knight hurriedly returned to Maximus' room as he heard the low sad music again from inside. He gulped and sighed first, then he gently knocked on the door.

"M-My prince, your father is commanding you to come out now and the other piano is now ready in the hall. The king has been waiting for you."

Maximus could not believe that his father gave him an opportunity to come out of the room and see the main hall of the kingdom he was longing for so many years. He gently stood in the piano bench without any reaction and adjusted the bow on his neck. Then, he came out of the room along with the knight and looked around to see what he missed during his long term of imprisonment.

The two went straight to the king's podium and the king motioned his hand to the guests and spoke. "Ladies and gentlemen, I am inviting you to listen to a happy tune performed by my dear son, Prince Maximus of Reminescence. This music is only dedicated to all of you for your enjoyment!" as the king paused, everyone in the entire hall yelled and applauded.

When the hall filled in silence, Maximus moved forward to formally sit on the grand piano bench.

"My gosh I can't wait! The king said that the prince will perform his piano number. I am getting so excited to hear the happy tune he's going to play," said a Vanguard smiling.

"Now that I see the king's son for the first time, I'd say that he was totally handsome!" said another Vanguard. "Happy tune, means happy face."

"He should," said a Humorian. "But that prince never smiles as soon as he enters the hall..."

The prince began to move his hands over the keys and started playing the tune the king was expecting. The music was stunning but very sad. The guests smiled at first, but when they heard the music playing, their facial expressions slowly changed into sadness. The other guests could not control their tears anymore so they began to weep!

"Y-Your Majesty," whispered the leader of Mercury to the king. "I thought the tune he would be playing for us was fun and happy to inspire everyone of us in this coming battle, but why he is playing the opposite? As if the music sounds like someone dies!"

The king did not answer back as his face blushed due to his sudden embarrassment towards his guests. Before the party, he already ordered Maximus to prepare a wonderful music for guests to hear but the prince played the opposite. *How shameless of you*, he said to himself as his hands clasped angrily. He just told to everyone that his son would be performing a happy tune to inspire everyone and they would enjoy his music.

"I-I don't know," answered the king. "His music is fun!"

Maximus intentionally played the sad music though he knew that he should play something happy and fun today. He only did that to express and release his true feelings he had been suffering from his long solitude!

"The music is good, but it changes the mood to our party because of its sad tune! Come on man, show us some fun music, will yah?!" said a Pioneer.

The music ended, but it was followed by another music that was more emotional than the first. Until there was a Humorian who seemed to get struck by his bitter memories when suddenly he cried out loud.

"Oh Fendir, why are you crying?" asked by the other Humorian.

"I-It's nothing my friend… I just remember my old friend, but what worse was when me and my ex-girlfriend split up."

"Hah, how sensitive! There's a lot of women out there whom you can be with in a lifetime!"

The music continued as more of the guests became tearful. The king hid his face with his big hands in shame and he got very mad. "How could you manage to humiliate me in front of our guests and I already gave you an order before the party! Damn you Maximus, let's see about that later!" said the king to himself.

The entirety of performance took thirty minutes straight with purely sad and emotional music. And for within thirty minutes, the guests never showed any smile on their faces but only pure tears and intense sadness. When the prince finished his performance, he quickly stood on the piano bench and walked out of the hall, leaving the grand piano and the guests alone.

Silence. No one applauded to the prince's performance even just one. The king's face turned red more from his humiliation since the prince never bowed his head and even said "thank you" before he left. Instead, the king walked before the guests and was forced to speak hesitantly.

"Ah… t-thank you very much for listening and watching my son's performance. H-His number was truly remarkable and I hope you all liked it!"

Silence. There was no any reaction coming from the guests as the king returned to his throne. Alexander seen no reactions from the guest, so he slowly clapped his hands signaling the other guest to follow. Later on, the noise and the commotions sprang back to life again as the party continued.

"Now where is that Mr. Lonely? I never seen him smiling during his performance earlier!" asked the leader of Expland. "Maybe he will turn older first than his father because of that, hah!"

"I saw Mr. Handsome just came out," answered the Vanguard.

The party still continued and the music was played by the grand orchestra. The males rushed to ask the female competitors for a dance in the grand ball. The other got their own partners, but the others were too bashful to dance.

"Okay fine!" said the Mercury jokingly. "There will be no such party like this next time and we will be enemies again. You might soon regret that you didn't take the chance to dance with the handsome guy like me!"

The grand ball continued at the hall. Alexander was only watching them and at the same time looking for Maximus. He was just standing next to the king. "Your Majesty, I do not see your son mingled with these people. Did you ask him to stay again in his room?"

"No," said the king in his serious look. "I decided to release him for the meantime to change his view. But later on, I will bring him back again in his room."

"But I liked his performance very much. I am truly amazed how he plays a grand piano professionally. Though his music was not that fun, I'd wish that he could only show his smile on us for even just a second..."

"My son is a cold person that's why..."

"C-Cold person?"

"He was still a child when I last seen him smiling until his four years of age. But when the time came he was being cursed--"

"C-Cursed?"

There was a Mercury who walked out of the palace and also looking for Maximus. He wandered around the garden when he saw the prince resting alone under the tree. He approached him and greeted him.

"Good evening!"

Maximus turned to him with no any facial expression. He just raised his eyebrow.

"We were very impressed with your performance earlier, Your Highness. You know that?"

The prince looked away. He did not answer back.

"Hey, don't you want to thank me for giving you such nice feedback?"

Finally, Maximus responded. "You are not my ally…"

"So you do can speak, eh? So what's the matter if I am not your ally?"

"I do not need anybody to talk to. Get away from me!"

The Mercury was surprised. "W-What, what? You want me to go away? I only greeted you and praised you with your music! Is that the effect of a person who has been imprisoned for a long time?"

The prince turned to him in serious look. "Why are you asking me about it as a person? Do you think I am a 'human' to talk to?" then he moved forward from the tree.

The Mercury offered him to shake hands. "I like you, Your Highness! We admired your melodious music. Congratulations!"

Maximus ignored the Mercury's hand and just walked away to return to the party, leaving the Mercury behind.

When the prince entered the palace, a group of Pioneers approached him and offered him a drink along with some foods to eat. Still, he rejected the offer and walked away. Next, he encountered an Expland who patted his shoulder. The prince only looked at the Expland's hand rested on his shoulder and raised his eyebrow as an answer, so the Expland withdrew his hand from the prince's shoulder.

"W-Why are you staring me like that, Your Highness? It seems that there is a monster in front of you, ahahaha!"

The Pioneers saw Maximus and they called him too. "Your Highness, come over here and have a drink with us just this night only!"

Maximus came near to the Pioneers. "Come here and sit with us and enjoy the night. Because tomorrow, all of us will be competitors again!"

One of the Pioneers grabbed a bottle of wine and poured in a glass. Then he offered it to Maximus. "Let us drink together, Your Highness! Cheers!"

The king suddenly came out behind them and quickly pulled Maximus away like a child.

"Maximus, you must come with me and we need to talk in my room!" said the king angrily while pulling Maximus hard.

"Oh come on, Your Majesty…" said the Pioneer who was tipsy. "We are still rejoicing with your loving son. Please give us more time to celebrate and have a toast together!"

The king was still pulling off Maximus away from them. The Pioneers could not do anything to stop him but to just let them go.

"Maxi, come back again later okay? We will all be waiting for you and save you a glass of wine!"

The father and son rushed into the room. As they entered, the king quickly slapped Maximus' cheek with full force. The unprepared son fell down on his knees.

"Shame on you, Maximus! Too shameful on you!!!" yelled the king as he walked in the room to and pro.

Maximus was about to stand on his feet when the king slapped his cheek again and quickly knelt down. His cheek immediately turned red.

"How could you manage to humiliate me in front of our guests? I didn't like your performance as you broke my order and ruined my party! Your music was too rubbish!!!"

Maximus did not answer and he just got up on his knees.

"Why are you not answering me, huh? Were you just trying to annoy me by that stupid performance of yours?!"

"Father... I would never humiliate you..."

"Stop lying, you fool! I told you before to perform a cheerful tune to everybody and not this some kind of stupid rubbish thing. Why did you do that for?!!"

Maximus stooped down his head. "I don't want to."

"See?" yelled the king. "If I only knew that you would really intend to play such garbage music of yours, then I shouldn't asked you to do the piano number and just stayed alone in your room!!!"

The king's slap left a scratch in Maximus's cheek brought about by the king's ring.

"So what do you intend to do now against me, Maximus? Will you just leave your father here bearing his humiliation you did? Maximus?!"

Maximus was silent.

"MAXIIIIMUUUSSSSSSSSS!!!"

"F-Father..." the prince faltered.

The king jabbed him with his finger. "Because of what you did, I am not going to release you again anymore! And this time, I will take you in the other room and will imprison there forever!"

"I'm already used to that…"

"Hah, really? Well let's see about that you fool! Get ready for this punishment I shall give you now!"

Maximus lifted his face for a second and stooped down again.

"I've been hating you so much Maximus since you were still young. I tried so many times to love you but I must admit that I never liked you though you are my son! Do not talk to me anymore… and I will never treat you again as my only son!"

"I do not understand you father…"

"BRONZE WARRIOOOORRSSS!!!"

The Reminescence's 3rd class warriors called Bronze, burst into the king's room and the king gave them an order against Maximus. "Take this fool to the other sealed room and let him suffer the hardship. Starve him until he crawls and begs for mercy!"

The 3rd class warriors were shocked to hear what the king ordered. "The… The prince you say, Your Majesty?"

"Yes, he humiliated me! That worthless, useless prince I called son! Aaarrgghhh… take him out of my sight!!!"

"But Sire… he is your son…"

"I DO NOT CARE WHO HE IS ANYMORE! Just take him there right now… Here's the key!"

The Bronze warriors were forced to follow what the king commanded in surprise. They quickly pulled Maximus and traversed into the darkness of the dungeon. This other sealed room was the prince's former prison when he was still a child, but the king felt pity on him when he saw the intense suffering of a young prince from heat and thin air.

"T-This room… again?" asked the prince in wide-eyed.

One of the Bronze class warriors opened the locked door as a cascading steam of heat suddenly moved out the room and touched their skin. The poor prince felt uncomfortable as his face expression suddenly changed.

"F-Father… why are you doing this to me? Why do you have to let me suffer with this kind of punishment?"

The Bronze class warrior answered him in concern. "My apologies Your Highness, but it was the king's will to suffer you like this… We can feel the intense heat of the room even in this distance."

"Fine… then do this request I will give you," said the prince. "I can

THE EXPLORERS

bear the suffering here as long as I have my old piano with me. Please bring forth the piano here and you may leave."

The warriors hated to see their prince suffer, but... they would be highly responsible if they disobeyed the king's order.

The poor prince entered the steamy room. It took less than five minutes when his body was already soaked in sweat. He was constantly panting as if he was now living in hell!

"P-Please... take my piano here in this room without my father's knowledge... This is my only request to you and I will ask no more... If not, I will do something foolish here if you disobey my simple request!"

The Reminescence Bronze warriors gaped and became silent to think that their prince might really did something "foolish" in his imprisonment.

14 TRAVELERS

The three young travelers ran at the verdant grassland together while playing chasing game with the little girl, Valerie. Enjoying what they were doing, the four were unaware they were too far away from the martial arts school they once lived with Rolando. And Kenji already forgotten of everything he recalled about his stepfather.

Kenji and Valerie were both laughing when they rolled over in thick grasses since the tip of the grasses tickled their bodies. As for Claude and Shingue, they were both resting under the tree.

"Shingue," called Claude. "I just realized that Kenji is quite childish, isn't he? Look how he still plays with a kid in his age."

"Don't be silly, Claude. It is because Valerie is the only kid among us. Kenji plays with her just to give her an entertainment that's all."

"Okay, so where is the stone now?" asked Claude.

"Oh dear, Claude…" Shingue raised his hands. "Do I have the stone in my hands right now?"

"Huh?"

"Of course, the stone might be either to those two!"

"Look how Kenji's face turned ugly now, Shin--"

"UGLY!"

"W-Wait Shingue!" stopped Claude. "What I mean is his nose. That long scar in his nose ruins his good-looking face!"

"Why? Does Kenji's face bothering you now?"

"Hell yeah! Whenever I look at his face, what I see is a sliced fish in a frying pan instead of his face! Hmmmmppptttt, so bawdy!!!"

Shingue laughed out loud. "I'll tell it to him!"

"Then tell him!"

The two were still busy playing in the grassland. When Kenji almost reached Valerie, the little girl suddenly screamed on top of her voice.

"Waaaaaaaahhh!"

"What was that!? That kid surely screams that loud," said Shingue.

"Eeeeeeee!"

"Haha, maybe a squeaking rat is following her from behind," answered Claude teasingly.

Shingue kicked Claude jokingly. "Shut up!"

When the two ran out of air, Kenji and Valerie went straight to Claude and Shingue to take a rest. Both were panting as they laid their tired backs on the grass with their eyes closed. Then they spontaneously laughed.

"Yo, how's the chasing game?" asked Claude to Kenji.

"Whew, Valerie and I are too exhausted now," answered Kenji panting.

"*Kuya*..." called Valerie to Kenji. "I am starving..."

Claude was surprised. "Well, we have a problem Houston. Kenji is not carrying enough money to buy you food!"

Shingue kicked Claude again. "Beeee quieeeettttt!"

Valerie turned to Kenji. "Um, *kuya* Kenji... What are we going to do? Do we have to just steal away foods somewhere so we can eat now?"

Kenji stroked Valerie's hair and shook his head. "That's not a good idea, Valerie... I never do that and that's bad."

"Oh yeah, *kuya* Kenji's right. Stealing is real bad!" said Shingue. Claude face suddenly blushed.

"I do not want to steal anything from others Valerie," said Kenji as he hinted Claude for being a thief once. "I never do that because my stepfather never raised me to become a bad kid though we were living in poverty. But still, I could live and stand on my own feet because I was using my mind to think of ways and strategies in order to survive... and without stealing of course. Do you get me?"

Valerie agreed. "Okay, I understand... But now... how are we going to think of strategies? You see, I cannot think for now because I'm really starving... How about you?"

"Well actually, I am also hungry now."

"So, let's rest first for a while *kuya*!"

The two rested when Claude saw something in the distance.

"Huh? It looks like there is a town over there!"

Kenji quickly got up on his back. "A town? Where?"

Claude quickly stood on his feet. "Over there! It's farther from here, though it's blurry but I can see it from here!"

"Well that is good then," said Kenji happily. "Why don't we go there later?"

"Hey, don't be arrogant Kenji. You're still exhausted from playing with this kid so you need to take a break for a moment. Recharge for more energy so you won't collapse when we get there!" said Claude with his hands on the hips. "Sit!"

"Maybe you will be the one to collapse Claude," answered Kenji jokingly. "So you sit!"

"Eh? Shingue and I just rested and my energy is already full."

"Okay, we'll go there later. How far do you think it is from here?"

"I can only see specks from the distance, maybe those are houses and other buildings."

"I'm afraid it is too far," said Shingue in sad face. "We need to ride a vehicle going that way."

"*Kuya*, do you think there are vehicles in there?" Valerie asked Kenji.

"I dunno!"

"I'm getting sleepy…" said Claude yawning.

Shingue glanced at Claude first then he turned in the distance. "It's still quite early so we still have more time to sleep and then we will go there… Before nighttime maybe, because it's no longer safe to stay here. Plus, it's scary!"

"Yeah, you're certainly right," Valerie agreed. "Maybe there are enemies lurking here in the dark."

"Okay, time to sleep guys!"

The four laid down their backs on the grass and went to sleep. The weather was cold and their bodies were dead tired which made them easily fall asleep. Later, Shingue moved over to the other spot as he felt itchy and was being tickled by the grass. He moved next to Claude, but still, his body kept moving back and forth and Claude had trouble sleeping with him. Claude felt uneasy with Shingue, so he moved next to Kenji. There, he firstly watched the young man's face as he leaned back and slowly closed his eyes. Until, he finally asleep…

THE EXPLORERS

Morning came. The four travelers were unaware that the sun was up and they were still sleeping when Valerie woke up first. There, she noticed the sunshine was scattered all over the forest and realized they had been sleeping long!

"Oh my, it's already morning!" she said in shock.

She quickly got up from her back and crawled to awake Kenji. "*Kuya! Kuya!* We forgot to look at the time and we've been sleeping the whole night! It's already morning. Remember what *kuya* Shingue said yesterday? We would be going to that town before nightfall. *Kuya!*"

Kenji just turned his back and did not awake. Valerie kept on awaking him, but Kenji was deeply asleep and did not mind Valerie.

Valerie gave up. She sat under the tree frowning. "Fine! I wonder how will you react when you wake up. I hope you won't get surprised!"

The child waited for the three young men to awake until passed seven o'clock in the morning. The young men were still sleeping deeply, and Valerie heard her growling stomach again and remembered she had been starving since yesterday.

"Geez, why does the stomach keeps on boiling all the time?" then she approached Kenji again to awake him. "*Kuya* Kenji…"

Valerie had done nothing but to look out for food and dried woods alone. She stood on her feet and began searching around. Good thing there was a clean river nearby. When she reached the river, her mouth suddenly drooled when the big fishes caught her attention. She was so eager to catch the big fish but there's only problem… she had no any fishing rod in her hand.

"Perhaps I am still able to catch a fish using only my bare hands. After all, I am a good swimmer!" said Valerie to herself.

She started to remove her slippers and then she waded into the shallow river. She swam, then she dived underwater to look for a big fish. There, she could see a school of big fish. She stretched her hands forward to catch one, but the fishes quickly swam away. She tried again, but once again she missed it!

Valerie swam faster with full speed. Luckily, as she swam perturbing the big fish, the school of fish nonplussed and they dispersed. There was a big fish, the breakaway from its group got trapped in a corner. This would be the chance for Valerie to catch her first fish. When she reached her hand for a grab, and viola! She successfully caught the fish.

Valerie swam up on the water surface going to the river bank to put the fish in the container. Then she smiled while watching the first catch she made in her lifetime.

Later, Valerie was inspired by her first catch so she dived under the water again to catch another fish. She lifted her hands and aiming for a grab but the fishes swam away faster than before. She swam forward and quickly swung her hands over them. The fishes dispersed again in all directions then Valerie managed to catch one but it slipped from her hand. She turned behind but the same thing happened. Until she could not hold her breath anymore so she swam back again towards the river bank.

The little girl pissed off from her failure to catch more fishes in the river. "Geez, those fishes are so quick and slippery! I'm so hungry now, ARRGGHHHH!"

Because of her extreme disappointment, Valerie could not help it but to just cry. She took the container with the fish and decided to come back to the young men who were still sleeping.

She sat down next to Kenji and put down the container next to her. The boys were still sleeping as she sobbed. After a while, she took the container again to just watch the fish.

Kenji heard Valerie crying so he awoke. But he was surprised to see that the sun was already up and the sky was colored blue. He quickly turned to the child.

"Hey Valerie, why are you crying? Did you have a bad dream?" he asked.

"No *kuya*," Valerie sobbed. "I had trouble catching fish for us to eat. I only caught one, see?" then she showed the fish inside the container. "I've been starving since yesterday, that's why I decided to find some food for our breakfast."

"Did you dive on your own? You're wet."

"Aha, I swam and dived to catch fish… but they were too fast and they did not want to get caught."

Kenji smiled at Valerie sobbing. "Well don't worry about us. We will catch one for our own. We're already grown up, so we'll forage for ourselves, okay?"

Valerie stopped crying and she sniffed. "How shameful I am, *kuya*…"

"What shameful are you talking about? You can eat your fish alone. Don't worry about us, we're not that hungry. We can still endure our empty

THE EXPLORERS

stomach."

Valerie was just about to leave to find some firewoods for cooking but Kenji grabbed her arm to stop her.

"No Val, I'll wake these two bums so we can get to that town as soon as possible. Man, we didn't notice the time last night and we're already deeply asleep. We planned to get there before nightfall. Look, it's already morning and we're still here."

"*Kuya*, I'm so hungry now... I feel like I'm gonna puke!"

"Okay, let's take a look for some firewoods so we can cook your fish now."

Valerie smiled. Kenji stood back to lead their way into the woodlands. Later, Claude was the next one to awake.

Claude yawned and stretched his numbed arms. "Huwaaahhh..." then he slowly opened his eyes and peered around. "What the--"

He quickly shook Shingue's shoulder to awake him. "Hey man, it's already morning. And it looks like the two have gone to that town and just left us here!"

Shingue groaned for a moment as he also stretched his arms while slowly opening his eyes. Then, he also noticed that the sun was already up and high!

"Oh-ho-hooo! They left us already, Claude!" he cried.

Claude scratched his head. "Geez, why those two did not awake us earlier and left us here? I'm pissed!"

After a while, Kenji and Valerie returned carrying some pack of firewoods and Kenji greeted the two boys. "Hey, Claude and Shingue. Good morning!"

Shingue quickly moved over to Kenji frowning. "Oh, we thought you'd already abandoned us here!" then he turned his head to his side. "Pfff... you guys are really not so easy to get along!"

"N-No, it is because Valerie has been starving for long. She can't help it anymore."

"Oh yeah? So how about now? It's already morning, what now?"

"Gosh!" said Kenji. "Then we'll still go there. That's no big deal."

Valerie gently pinched Kenji's arm. "*Kuya*..."

"We're about to cook Valerie's fish she just caught this morning. Look, she caught one here," then Kenji showed the big fish in the container to Claude and Shingue. "Imagine that in her very young age she knows how to think of ways to forage on her own? And this fish she caught looks big and fatty!"

Claude was amazed. "Wow, that's impressive."

The two put down the firewoods on the grass to start building fire. They piled them over when the child noticed something.

"B-By the way *kuya*, we don't have something to light up a fire... What are we gonna do now?"

Kenji smiled sweetly at the child. "Don't you worry, *kuya* Claude has a lighter in his pocket. You know him right? He's a smoker..."

Claude faltered. "Fine... Yeah, I have one," then he reached his pocket to pull out a lighter.

Valerie smiled. "We can just burn these woods until the fish is grilled... Though some part of its flesh might still be raw, but that's okay to me! Let's still cook it fast before the fire dies."

Kenji borrowed the lighter to Claude and he lighted the firewoods. Then he handed it back to Claude where he tucked the lighter in his pocket.

Fortunately, the fire grew big, big enough to easily cooked the fish. The fish was overcooked, leaving the burnt skin so its taste was bitter. The child was so hungry, so she just ignored its taste and devoured the whole flesh for only ten bites! The three young men were stunned by the girl's action. There's nothing they could do but to watch Valerie consuming the whole fish.

"K-*Kuya*," Valerie called Kenji in blushed face. "I'm still hungry..."

"But can you go with us to that town? Anyway, your stomach has been stuffed a little," asked Kenji in his face looking awkward. "D-Do you still feel sick?"

The child looked aimlessly to feel her stomach. "Not anymore, since my stomach is stuffed a little... Thank you."

Claude complained as he was pointing the child. "Well lucky for you since you've just had your breakfast already and we have not been eaten yet!"

Shingue raised his hand in boredom. "Come on guys, let's go to that town!"

The four travelers walked going to the town. They took thirty minutes to reach the said town when they get closer to the main gate. There, they stopped in front of it to look for its surroundings. The place looked nice and abundant as the people were living there with harmony. The environment was clean, exquisite, and they had discipline. This place they had seen yesterday thought to be a town, but it was actually a village called "Sierra Village".

"Wow, this place is so nice and clean," laughed Shingue.

"Yes, you're right Shingue," Claude agreed. "And it seems so peaceful. Good thing we found this place yesterday."

They walked near the main gate of Sierra Village to enter the village when an incoming gatekeeper stopped them. "Hey you, hold still!"

The four turned to a running gatekeeper and the gatekeeper moved over to them.

"Who are you four?" he asked.

Kenji answered. "Hello and good morning! We are all friendly travelers. My name is Kenji, and these are Claude, Shingue, and Valerie," then he bowed down his head.

"Um, so what is this place called anyway?" asked Claude in wonder. "It looks too peaceful to me and we like it here. It's so beautiful!" he added, impressed by what he saw!

"Ah thank you… You are in a peaceful village called Sierra. Why you ask?"

"Can we come in?" asked Kenji.

"Yes," answered the guard with a smile. "You are all welcome to enter."

"Thank you," said the four smiling and they entered the gate.

The four hesitated from walking when they looked around the peaceful village and noticed the happy faces of the villagers. They also noticed some *Kalesa* (horse drawn calash) moving around elsewhere which was the major transportation of the villagers. As for Valerie, her attention was caught by the children of her age playing outside. She smiled, as she was enjoying watching them as if she wanted to join with them.

Valerie asked permission to Kenji. "Hey *kuyas*, I wanna go there to play with them too!"

"But Valerie, we need to eat first and later we will go around to find something to stay here," said Kenji then he thought to himself. "Wait a minute… is there any accommodation here?"

"Sure there is, Kenji… Most villages have their own inns," answered Shingue. "Let's ask someone here where their inn is."

There was a little girl coming out from her house and she ran towards the other kids to play with them. But as soon as she was passing the four travelers, Claude restrained her.

"Hello!" greeted Claude at the little girl.

The child answered in surprise. "H-Hello to you too... Thanks."

"Do you know any inns or hotels maybe, offered in this place? We are travelers and we need some place to rest here. Is there any?"

The child quickly replied. "Yes sir! We have our inn here. It's over there, see? Just walk directly along this path and you will be there!" and then she ran away.

"Well, surely this village has their own inn, Claude!" said Shingue happily. "Let's go there and get us booked for even just a moment. Come on!"

"Hah, why are you such in a hurry? As if you have some money in your pocket for booking!" asked Claude.

"Um, well... Just a little..."

"What did the little girl said again, Claude?" asked Kenji.

"She said we'll just walk directly from here and then..."

The four noticed the child they asked earlier walking back pass to them and she was crying. They wondered.

"Oh, why are you crying?" asked Shingue.

"They don't want me to play with them," said the child sobbing.

Claude asked the child as if he did not care about what she just said. "Hey, can you show us the way to the inn instead? We need to take a break for a moment because we've been in a far away lands!"

The child was still crying. "H-Hold on for a moment..."

Valerie approached the child. "Hello!"

"Huh?" the little girl wiped her tears at first and then she turned to Valerie.

"Ahm... My name is Valerie, and you are?"

The child sobbed. "Agnes."

"Wow, nice name Agnes!"

Claude interrupted the two. "Hey girlie, so where is the inn here? Please help us to get there or we might get lost!"

"I don't think this village is not that big so you won't go astray," answered Agnes sobbing.

"Whatever, we still need your help to take us there!"

"J-Just a moment please, first I need to get something."

Agnes returned to her home and the four waited for her to come back.

"It looks like that little girl doesn't want to give us a quick tour to their inn," said Shingue while his eyes were focused at the child's house.

"No, she will take us there you will see!" said Valerie with confidence.

After a moment, a door burst open and Agnes went out from her house.

"Come with me!"

The five walked along with Agnes on the way to the inn.

"You see this path? You will just go straight to it until you reach our well-known bar," said Agnes to the four.

"A bar?" asked Claude. "We do not necessarily need to go to a bar. What we need is an inn. So, how much is the accommodation there per night?"

"I'm sorry sir, but I don't know…" replied Agnes. "But you can ask it to the innkeeper, they know everything you would like to know," then she continued to show them the way to the inn. "Then as you walk past to that bar, you will get to the mixed shops next. You know, like flea market, cafeteria, restaurants… Something like that."

"Wow, that's good to know then," said Kenji. "They have cafeteria here where we can eat our breakfast!"

The five continued to walk as they moved across the other path. The four travelers saw more of the stores nearby and there were *kalesas* passing on their way.

"We are almost near to the inn. Over there, that one big building that looks like a mini hotel!" Agnes pointed the inn in the distance.

"Oh, I see…" said the four.

"Certainly it is quite li'l big, isn't it?" said Agnes happily. "You will see and meet many terrorists there when you get inside."

"TERRORRRIIIIISSSSSTTTTTSSSS?!!" cried the four spontaneously as they quickly recoiled.

"A-Ah, no…" Agnes quickly shook her head and smiled in embarrassment. "What I mean was, y-you know those people who are from the other places or other countries. S-Something like that?"

"Y-You mean tourists right, A-Agnes?" said Kenji nervously while his hand was on his chest.

"Oh, y-yeah! So tourist is the right term for that… Apologies, I just forgot the right term, hehehe!"

"All right, let's get inside to that huge inn partners," said Shingue smiling.

"I am leaving you now guys. I told my mother that I would not be staying here for long."

"Okay, thank you for giving us a quick tour Agnes," said Kenji smiling. "Take care! I hope you will have your playmates sooner."

"Gotta go, bye!" then Agnes walked away.

Valerie watched Agnes running away from them to go back to her house. "*Kuya*, you know what? I actually want to play with Agnes because I feel like she doesn't have playmates in this village. Remember what she said that her neighbors didn't want to play with her?"

"Oh, so why don't you go to her house later and ask her to go play with you? There is nothing wrong with that. And the good thing is you will have a playmate of your age and also a girl... Not with us who are all boys and no longer in your age."

Valerie smiled. "Wait, what if I go there to her house now?"

"W-What? You're still a little hungry, and we will eat sooner when we're done booking our room!"

"Later *kuya*, don't worry I will return to you soon. Goodbye!" then Valerie dashed away from them.

"W-Wait, Valerie... Come back!" cried Kenji.

"My goodness Kenji, just let her go! She's only a child and she is really not supposed to be with us during our travels. We have our goal to do if it wasn't for that stupid stone!" said Claude. "Teenage boys don't need kids!"

"Come on man... Let's go inside now," said Shingue in a hurry.

The three boys went inside the inn. The inn was clean, spacious and simple. The heaters were set to warm temperature since the weather was cold. They reached the lobby, where the innkeeper was sitting in a front desk. She greeted the boys.

"Welcome to the Sierra Inn..." then the innkeeper smiled.

"Thank you," said Kenji and he walked over the counter. Claude and Shingue followed. "Um, do you still have an empty room available for us?"

"Ah, yes gentlemen," she answered. "There's still quite a number of them available."

"So how much is per night in here?" Kenji asked again.

"It's only cheap, sir. The cost is only five hundred pesos per night. Good for three persons per room."

THE EXPLORERS

"Waaa, that's expensive! D-Do you still have a much cheaper room available? O-Or do you offer some discounts here? Actually, we are four not three."

"I am truly sorry sir, but we do not have promo here so I'm afraid we cannot offer a discount for now," said the innkeeper sadly. "Besides, a five hundred pesos is actually inexpensive right?"

The three stooped their heads and became silent for a moment. The innkeeper smiled to them sweetly. "So what now, gentlemen?"

"Well... I'm still pondering about it. Because to us, a five hundred pesos is really expensive," said Kenji.

"We have a very tight budget, and we also need to buy some foods," said Shingue.

Kenji turned to Claude and Shingue. "Nevermind, that is not an excuse. Anyway, let's split our money to a hundred twenty-five pesos for each of us," then he turned back to the innkeeper. "Hold on miss..."

The three put out their money from their pocket and they combined it as they were counting the total amount. Then, they gave the payment to the innkeeper and she gave them the key in return. "Thank you for the payment, gentlemen. Please take this key of your room number 1908 which is at the fourth floor. Hope you'll enjoy your stay here."

"Thanks."

"Please make sure you do not lose this key or you will pay a penalty of another five hundred pesos. I apologize for this, but that is our company policy here."

"Okay, thanks for the reminder."

The three boys took the elevator going up to the fourth floor. The elevator door opened. They walked along the hallway while they were looking their room with number 1908. They looked at each doors one by one. When they found the said door, they immediately unlocked it using the key.

"So this is the room number 1908," said Claude while looking around the room. "This is crazy!"

Kenji and Shingue ignored Claude's reaction. They entered the room and they put down their bags on the floor covered in carpet. Then, Shingue rushed towards a bed to lay down. "Tan-tanan-tanannn... This bed is sooo soft!!!"

Kenji sat down on the edge of the bed. "So what now? Are we going to eat outside?"

"Of course, man! My stomach has been melted by its own acid!" answered Claude immediately.

"Let's go outside. I am feeling dizzy now…" then Kenji stood up to go out the room when suddenly he remembered something. "Oh, by the way. No one will watch our room here," then he turned to Shingue. "Um, Shingue?"

"What?"

"Claude and I will go outside to look for something to eat, so I am asking you to please watch our room. We won't be outside for long, okay?"

"Why don't we just lock this room instead since we have its key?"

"No way, and I'm afraid that we might lose it when we all go outside! Come to think of it, we don't have some extra money left in our pocket. Please…"

"Gosh, Kenji. Why don't you just put the key in your waist bag?"

"No, Shingue… I don't want to, just to make sure."

At first, Shingue was mum for a moment then he stooped his head. "That sucks, I will not be able to wander around the village."

Claude patted Shingue's shoulder. "Don't be sad, Shingue. Later when we're done eating, then you can go outside and walk around on your own. Then Kenji and I will be the next ones to watch the room while resting."

Shingue finally agreed. "Fine, so be it!"

Kenji nodded. "Thank you Shingue. I will leave you the key here. We will just look for some foods outside."

"Yes, go ahead. Scram!"

"Please give us your share before we leave. We will split up the amount again into three."

The poor Shingue pulled out his money left in his pocket which were two pieces of fifty pesos. "Here, a hundred pesos… Is this okay?"

"Great, so this means it will be Shingue's treat! Thank you very much for this, Shingue!" said Claude teasingly.

Shingue hurriedly took one fifty pesos back in his pocket. "Man! Here, just fifty pesos, this is the only money I got!"

"Thanks again for your parsimony, hahaha!" laughed Claude jokingly. "With that, we will add the rest."

"Fine, here's the other fifty pesos again! Damn you Claude, now go away!!!"

THE EXPLORERS

The two left the room laughing and Shingue would be staying alone to watch their room. They handed over the key to Shingue. Then, Claude slowly shut the door.

15 ESCAPE

The lonely Prince Maximus remained inside the very hot steamy room in his body full of sweat. The tuxedo suit he was still wearing had been soaked in sweat. He was in a corner with his head drooped in his arms, waiting for the grand piano he asked from the Bronze warriors.

Maximus got weakened, feeling roasted inside the oven. He could not breathe. He could not even move.

"Hah... Hah..." Maximus was panting while the intense heat was still steaming inside the sealed room. "W-Why does m-my father... h-has to do this t-to his own... s-son?"

The door opened. A Bronze warrior entered the room to look for the prince, with his face looking concerned as he felt pity on him.

"I'm afraid we cannot bring you the grand piano you requested, Your Highness. The king saw us, then he scolded and warned us. He said that the piano was forbidden to take in this room."

Maximus did not answer, but he heard the Bronze warrior.

"We apologize for this, Your Highness..."

The party of competitors continued inside the palace. The Pioneers were still waiting for the return of Prince Maximus. The prince's glass of wine was on their table and still not emptied yet.

The other Pioneers were already drunk. "Now where is *(hik!)*... our lonely Prince *(hik!)* Maximus go?" asked a drunk Pioneer. "We've been *(hik!)*... waiting for him *(hik!)*... that long! See this glass of wine that still *(hik!)*... not emptied yet *(hik!)*? We saved... this for him *(hik!)*!"

The other members of Mercury and Humorian were also drunk, so only few were left still dancing in the middle of the hall.

There was a drunk Humorian who was singing out loud along with the other Humorians who were also drunk. "*Ol ay wantid is so… Tu si… is nevir to pell… Ol da wi is hard bat ay tink dat it is so isi to porgit…*"

The other drunk Humorian continued the song of the duet. "*Du ay luk dat diserbing por yu por-ibir? Becoz ay em stil puling in lab wid yu su match…*"

A Mercury member got annoyed to their song. "Hey, your voice sounds like a squeaking door! It's too painful to our ears!!!"

The drunk Humorians ignored the Mercury. Instead, they still continued singing "rubbish".

"Hi Vane, it's been an all night long we're partying here, eh? The others are still energetic and they are really enjoying this unforgettable event," said a Vanguard to a Humorian.

"Yes, you are right. Good thing the king allowed us to have a party that long. The king have a good heart," agreed the Humorian.

"He really meant to extend the party because the next time we meet, we'll be competitors again."

"Oh, so that is why he is letting us extend the fun!"

"I am glad we all have the chance to meet each other. Because of this, it turned out pretty well as we've become friends for a short time… though we are still competitors."

As for the king, he was staying inside his room while easing the pain and resentment to his son. He had been there for long since he wanted to be alone for a while.

The king shouted in his room. "Maximus, the cursed son!" then he threw away the goblet he was holding.

"By the way," said the Humorian. "Where's the prince now?"

"I don't know! Haven't you forgotten that his father called him yesterday?!" answered the fellow Humorian.

"Man, that is getting longer than I expected. I am just missing his handsomeness that's all. I think that man could catch every woman's heart for sure."

"Damn! I am more good-looking than to that prince you'll see."

"Does that matter?"

"You see, those Pioneers had been also looking for him since the king called him. You know, that piano guy last night?"

"Why were they looking for him?"

"You know, to drink wine with them!"

"I see… Or maybe the prince just fled and hid from those idiots!"

"Heh, don't be a jerk *(hik!)*…"

The king still remained in his room. He felt fairly eased from his resentment. He was now relaxing in his bed when someone knocked on the door.

"Who's there?! I am not in the mood today to meet with someone right now!" he yelled.

Someone responded from outside. "Your Majesty, these are Erasmus and Alexander of Pioneer…"

"I don't want to get up right now just to open that door… Continue the fun and I will be there later!"

Alexander asked. "Um, so where is your son Prince Maximus right now, Your Majesty?"

"I don't care where he is right now… I will be there after a while. I am just giving myself a break since I am getting old and I need long time to rest. Tell Erasmus that he will be in-charge of the occasion since he is the second leader and Captain of Reminescence!"

"W-Well, please tell your son that we are still waiting for him. We are looking forward to see him again later."

The king did not answer. Then the two left the king's room.

Maximus was still inside the ferocious sealed room the king gave, he could not bear the heat anymore and felt that he was now going to die!

The weak prince was catching his deep breaths after the king ordered to add more heat inside the room with the temperature of more than fifty degrees Celsius. Why did the king have to punish his own son considerably by only doing what the prince needed to be done?

The poor prince wanted to escape inside the prison cell. He wanted to scream out loud. His shaking, weak body crawled on the ground trying to lift up his hand. "T-This is…"

Then he lifted his other hand as he was still struggling to escape. "…The… only way…"

Then, he forced himself to stand on his trembling feet. "…t-to… escape…"

Maximus weakly walked near the door, but there was a flash of light that suddenly lighted up in his chest and he recoiled. His eyes opened wide in amazement, then he noticed a thin mist engulfed the whole room and his body was gradually cooled down by the light in his chest.

"W-What is happening..." he surprisingly asked himself.

The light glowed more and so as the prince's body temperature dropped to make him feel cool and normalize his body temperature.

Later, the blinding light shone all over the entire room. The prince cried out loud by the dazzling glare that burned his eyes.

"AAAAH!"

Then, a huge influx of water suddenly burst from his body and poured all over the room. The water continuously flowing out from his body creating a massive flow of brine water.

Out of nowhere, the voice of a mysterious woman gently whispered in prince's ear. "Maximus... By the name of Water, you must be rescued... Come with us and follow the flow..."

Maximus was already under the high water and he could not speak.

"Maximus, you must grab the hand of the Water reaching you right now..."

Maximus was dilated underwater while looking for the hand of what the voice said, but he did not see it. He peered more.

After a second, a small spark of light at the bottom caught the prince's attention and he swam down as fast as he could. When he reached the light, he immediately touched it when the voice spoke again. "Do not be afraid, my prince... I will deliver you..."

In a moment, the prince gradually turned into water starting from his feet, the body, and up to the head. Then he vanished at the bottom leaving nothing to trace. The high water rushed out and slowly subsided inside the room.

A knight passing the hallway noticed the percolating water under the door of Maximus' prison cell. "W-What's this? It looks like the king's son is bathing inside his room. However, where did the prince get this water that..." then he touched the water on the floor. "This water is very cold! Where did the prince get this? In the refrigerator? No way, there are no any refrigerators in there but only heaters!"

The knight wanted to report this to their king immediately because the king only had its key and had the right to know what was happening, so he quickly ran towards the king's room. When he reached the room, he gently knocked on the door and called the king.

The king yelled. "How many times should I have to tell you that I do not have time to talk to someone right now?! I am not in a mood today!"

"King Maximus X," called the knight. "Your son... The prince..."

"What?" answered from the room. "I do not care if he is dead now!"

"T-There's a water coming out from inside the prison cell, Your Majesty..."

The king did not answer.

"Sire, with your permission... Can I borrow the key of that prison cell?"

The king was forced to open the door of his room and stamped his foot in annoyance.

"Here, take this key! But do not let him escape or else you will be responsible!"

"I will let you know about the prince's condition, Your Majesty..." said the knight and he took the key from the king's hand.

The king turned and slammed the door hard, then the knight left the king's room and walked in the hallway.

He returned to the sealed room and opened the door. There, he saw gallons of clean water still flowing out the long hallway that made the luxury golden carpet wet.

His eyes opened wide while staring at the flowing water. "W-Where does this water come from?! Prince Maximus!"

The knight burst into the room and he peered around looking for the prince. The entire room was completely soaked and he saw the heaters that were now totally broken. "The... The heaters, they are now broken!!!"

He also noticed something... The prince was nowhere to be found!

"The prince has escaped!"

The sentinel, secret weapon, and Captain of the Reminescence warriors, Erasmus arrived in the sealed room and surprised what he saw. "Oh? What is going on in here now?"

"Captain Erasmus," called the knight as he was approaching the secret weapon worriedly. "Prince Maximus... He just escaped from his imprisonment!"

Erasmus did not believe at first. "Hmm... It sounds like you are only drunk, Sir knight..."

"No Captain! Please come inside and see for yourself. The entire prison cell is now totally soaking wet by the cold water!"

Erasmus entered the room and noticed the broken heaters. "How amusing, even the heaters did not spare!"

"What are we going to do, Captain? The king will surely gets mad if he learns about this!"

"No, you have nothing to do with this and it is the prince whose to blame. We'll just let him go if he really escaped anyway!"

"C-Captain?"

"But command the other knights to find Prince Maximus immediately. Later, you will report this to the king. And oh, if he'll ask you something and he's not satisfied with your response, definitely you will be responsible!"

Erasmus left the room to return to his fellow Gold class warriors who were still guarding the party. As for the guests, they were now dead tired due to lack of sleep as they had been staying the palace for one night already. And none of them had left the palace to go back to their headquarters yet.

As for the knight, he was walking in a hurry to look for his fellow knights. He saw one, and he ordered the knight to find the prince. He also saw the others, and he ordered them the same thing.

"For now, no one of you will tell this to the king, is that clear?" instructed the knight to the fellow knights. "Now go and find the prince immediately!"

Meanwhile.

Unknown to Maximus, he was stranded in another dimension which was full of crystals and it was freezing cold. He was lying on the icy ground, but he was not freezing. He gently opened his eyes and he got up on his back. Then, he looked around to see the whole area.

"W-Where am I?" he wondered.

Maximus stood up and ran all over the place. The entire dimension was different from where he came and was so immense.

"Hello? Is there anybody here?"

No one answered. The prince thought that there must be an exit so he scoured the area within his reach but he failed to see one. "Where am I now? How did I get in here? I don't see any openings!"

Maximus ran in all directions while searching for an exit, but he noticed no matter how far he could go, it seemed like endless. Until he drained all of his energy and knelt on the ground.

The prince got pissed off. "What is going on in here? Did that mysterious voice just want to play games with me?!"

Maximus turned and looked in the distance when he saw an ajar door few meters away from where he was standing. He got surprised and asked himself. "I didn't notice that door earlier. I wonder if that door will lead me out of this mysterious place?"

He quickly ran towards the door he just saw in the distance, but he noticed that he could not come forth to the door as if it was still in the same distance from him. He stopped for a moment to catch his breath, but he tried to run again as fast as he could closer to it. Still, it was in the same distance.

Maximus got exhausted again and he fell on his knees panting.

"Tsk, you know? I would be more happy if you'd just take me back to my room instead of playing tricks on me here!" he yelled.

A female voice spoke. "Maximus... We cannot deceive the prince of Water and we give you respect."

"P-Prince of Water?" asked Maximus. "I do not have powers to become a prince of whatever!"

"Yes you have, Your Highness... That is why I saved you..."

"Saved? W-Wait, who are you anyway?"

"I am one of the former guardians of the Water element that is now turned to stone and is hidden in the human world..."

"Hidden?"

"Our lord King Jethro made his order to save you from your father's atrocity and you must live. The lord had already chose you to become a water bearer by the name of Water element..."

"That doesn't make sense to me! Does that King Jethro already knows who I am?"

"His soul is currently watching you from a distance, Maximus," said the mysterious voice. "The time has come for you to release your hidden power and bear its might under your control..."

"Hmpt, how funny!" reacted Maximus angrily. "Now what? What are you guardians going to do to me now? And what is this place by the way?"

"You are now in another dimension."

"Of what?"

"The Water and Ice," said the voice.

"Please just let me go," said Maximus. "I'd rather stay alone in my room than playing tricks on me. If you give me your respect, then you should do what I want… Now take me back in my palace right now!"

"I'm afraid I can not…"

"And why not?"

"Because the Water is needing you, my prince…"

All of a sudden, there was a shaking and grinding within the area. A strong quake felt all around and the huge ice appeared and sprouted all over the place. The temperature dropped more as a very cold air blew strong. Then, a huge shining crystal of variant colors suddenly emerged from the ground that imprisoned the prince. He was shocked to see that he was now trapped inside the huge crystal.

"W-What is this?! I knew it… You tricked me!" yelled the prince angrily while he was banging the crystal very hard.

"No, Maximus. By the order of King Jethro, I have to do this for your own good. It is the lord himself who will cleanse you inside and permanently remove away all your bitter past as a cursed son… that everybody still believes up to now!"

"Arrggghhh…" cried Maximus while he was struggling inside the crystal, and now he could not move his body anymore. His body got weak, while his muscles fibrillated and his eyes slowly shutting down… Until shortly, he lost his consciousness.

16 ROOM 1908

Shingue was still in the room alone holding the key of their room with number 1908. He was just lying on the bed wondering where the two boys were at now.

"Oh man... Those two had been longer outside than I expected," sighed Shingue boringly. "It seems they have deceived me. Oh bummer!"

Someone knocked the door. Shingue calmed down. "Yes, finally! Those two have just arrived..." then he got up the bed to open the door, but it was Valerie who knocked.

"Oh, how'd you find out our room number?" he asked the child.

"*Kuya* Kenji told me. I saw him and *kuya* Claude in a cafeteria buying food."

"Did they already buy our food?"

"Not yet."

"Oh, but you said--"

"Yes, they are in the cafeteria right now... but the queue line is way that long."

"WHAAAAAATTTTT??!"

"Yep."

"They've been there for too long! What is in the cafeteria anyway? Are there other cafeterias here somewhere that have short or no queue at all, Valerie?"

"There's a grill restaurant over there. But when *kuya* Claude tasted their offered free taste, he suddenly felt sick. They also gave *kuya* Kenji their free taste and he almost puked right after he tasted it!"

THE EXPLORERS

Shingue laughed. "M-Maybe it's because their food tastes terrible..."

"In other words... You are ABSOLUTELY right, *kuya* Shingue!"

"Okay..."

"By the way, that cafeteria is offering a huge discount promo today that is why they have lots of customers. We saw their dishes that are sooo yummy to eat. And oh, they also have free tastes!"

"Wow..."

"So when we saw their dishes, our mouths instantly drooled and we want to buy them in discounted price!"

"Okay, got it."

"They will be here sooner..."

"Good!"

The two starving travelers waited for Kenji and Claude to return. Half an hour had passed, still no shadows of two boys appeared in their room when Shingue looked at his watch. Then he got bored so he laid back again on the bed.

"Man, this will take us forever to just wait for those two..." he sighed.

"I'll go outside to check them," said Valerie.

"Nah, we'll just wait them here since you said they'll be here sooner."

"Ummm... I'll just go and tell them to come back soon."

"No, don't mind about it."

"Look what time it is now, *kuya* Shingue!"

"Don't be persistent. Why don't you watch a TV show instead?"

"And what will I watch?"

"You know obviously... Cartoons!"

"Okay, *kuya* Shingue. Turn the TV on."

"Man, and why should I be the one to turn on the TV?" then Shingue got up again to turn on the TV. He took the remote control to search any children shows in different stations, but he did not find any.

Shingue smiled while scratching his head. "Um, Valerie... how about the current news broadcast instead?"

Valerie was not interested to watch news broadcast. "I don't like that!"

Shingue turned off the TV. "Okay, how about that?"

"Eeeeee!"

"Um, well... what about if you just listen to a radio? Is that okay to you?"

"Okay, sure."

As for the cafeteria where Kenji and Claude were still at the queue line…

"Kenji," called Claude. "We've been here for almost an hour."

"I know. How annoying… You see, there are some customers here who are slipping in queue. Imagine how disrespectful they are?"

"Why don't you tell them?!"

"Eh…"

"My goodness, I am sure we've already finished our breakfast much earlier if it wasn't for this stupid queue! Though we've tasted the other cafeteria's free tastes and yet I'm still hungry!"

"Whatever. See this line, Claude? We're now in fifth! Which means we're almost near the counter. Do you think this is even better than we were in seventieth?"

"Errr… My stomach is hurting, I might get ulcer here."

"You're not the only one who's hungry, Claude. All of us!"

"Yeah, yeah, whatever… Damn this stupid queue!"

The first four customers were done giving their orders when Kenji and Claude would be the next to give their order. They had lots of orders listed in the paper and gave it to the cashier.

"Take out," said Claude to the cashier then he handed the money they computed as charge.

"Take out, sirs?" asked the cashier. "Please, hold this number and wait for your orders. Thank you," then she gave the number to the two.

Kenji took the number and they walked away to look for empty seats, but they did not find any. "Damn it, there are even no empty seats!" he complained.

Claude patted Kenji's shoulder. "I understand why this cafeteria gets too much dine-ins today. We will just stand there in a corner. After all, we're in take-out."

"And where will we stand and wait?"

Claude looked around and scratched his head. "Well… Outside?"

Kenji shook his head. "We cannot stay outside, Claude. They will not see our number, or maybe they will not hear us. This cafeteria is way too noisy!"

"Go ahead and stay here alone!"

"Oh yeah, I will! I am doing this for four of us, so I will be waiting here."

THE EXPLORERS

"I'm going outside."

"Then go outside!"

"N-Never mind... I'll stay here with you."

After a while, the waiter came looking around as if he was looking for a customer. He was carrying a large bag of foods while jostling through the queued customers. "Excuse me, number 12 please!!!"

Claude heard the waiter's cry and asked himself. "12?" then he looked at the number he was holding which was twelve. "Um, Kenji... I think our order has arrived."

Claude pointed the waiter to Kenji who was still looking for the customer with the number twelve.

"Hey, you there!" Kenji shouted. "We are number 12. HEEEEYYYY!!!"

The waiter did not hear Kenji's call due to the noise in the cafeteria. Claude got pissed so he just came over the waiter while Kenji was still in a corner.

"Hey, we've been calling you over there and we have the number 12!" said Claude annoyingly.

"O-Oh I see..." the waiter faltered. "I truly apologies sir, but I never heard your call because of the noise all around."

"Oh yeah? Hell no!" replied Claude. "The people here are very noisy and at the same time you are wearing earphones! How'd you be able to hear our goddamn call?!"

"A-Apologies," said the waiter with his head stooped and he gave the food to Claude. Then Claude returned to Kenji.

"Here's our order. Now I learn that the waiter is actually deaf."

Kenji gaped. "R-Really?"

"Come on, let's go back to the inn."

The two jostled over the long queue line to pass through outside the cafeteria. They returned to the inn and walked towards their room 1908. As they walked in the hallway, they heard a loud noise coming from their room. Kenji knocked on the door. And when Shingue opened the door, the two suddenly met a high pitch sound waves from the noise of the radio.

"It is Valerie's fault!" cried Shingue out loud while his hands were covering his ears. "She maximized the volume of the radio and plugged it in a thousand watts of speakeerrrr!!!" then he moved next to Kenji. "She plays the music waaayyy too loud!!!"

"Turn off the radio! TURN IT OOOFFFF!!!" shouted Kenji. "We're disturbing other people next door who might be sleeping!"

Valerie did not want to turn off the radio so Claude rushed over the power outlet and quickly unplugged it. The loud radio suddenly stopped.

Valerie cried. "WA-HA-HA-HAAA! Musiiiicccc!!!"

Claude got pissed off again. "Hey kid! Aren't you disturbing other people next to our room?!"

"WAAAAHHH!"

"Darn it, what a mischievous kid you are! You are causing trouble in this inn ya know that?"

"WAAAA-HAHAHAHAAAAA!!!"

Kenji turned to Shingue. "Shingue, why did you allow Valerie to play such loud music on the radio like that? Blimey…"

"W-Well because…" Shingue showed off his hand with bites that left a scratch on. "I stopped her at first, but… she kept on biting my hand!"

"Aha! So that is what a kid does when she has been hungry for years!" said Claude annoyingly. "She is becoming a biter!"

"Well, I'm really hungry now that's why…" said Valerie sobbing.

Kenji rebuked Valerie. "Now I learn that you are a music lover and that is okay, but please do not play music as if you are in a live concert."

"I don't want to listen to a poor music… It's boring…"

"You can listen out loud like that, but please not in here okay?"

Shingue interrupted the two. "Hey guys, what now? Shall we eat then?"

Kenji hesitated from his rebuke at Valerie. "Ah y-yeah… Go ahead."

Claude opened the paper bag of foods he was carrying and placed it on the table. The four smelt the delicious scent of the foods and their mouths instantly drooled in hungriness.

"Hmmm… These foods surely smell sooo good and yummy!" said Shingue.

Valerie did not move away her eyes at the dishes served by Kenji and Claude. The two was still preparing the foods on the table when Shingue could no longer control his greediness.

"Hey Kenji, please hurry up and I wanna eat now!"

"Why don't you just help us here instead?"

"Then I will help you."

"You should helped us earlier."

THE EXPLORERS

"Okay, here I come!"

The four worked together in preparing their meal. They separated the different dishes in each bowl as well as the soups. Then, the four prayed before the meal led by Shingue.

"IT'S EATING TIME!!!" cried the four happily. They began scrambling in getting the variety of dishes on the table. And since they had no spoons and forks available on the table, they were eating their foods with their bare hands.

Claude and Valerie were scrambling over the *bulalo* (Filipino beef marrow stew) in the middle of the meal. As Valerie wanted to eat all of the *bulalo*, Claude did not want her to have it as he was taking away the child's hand over the dish.

Valerie cried again out loud. "Ahhh… Waaaahhh!!!"

Claude got pissed off once more. "What a crap! This is why I really hate kids with us! I knew it, this girl shouldn't be here with us from the very beginning!!!"

"Just give her the *bulalo*, Claude. Please be too patient on her," weaned Kenji.

"Ehhh?! Why should I? I am not able to taste my favorite *bulalo* if I give that to her."

"Here, there are more foods to choose aside from your *bulalo*, see?"

"Darn, a pork stew? Hah, don't make me laugh. How really annoying!"

Kenji took the food over Claude. "Here, take this stew. Let the girl eat the *bulalo*."

"Well I was the one who ordered that! *Bulalo* is actually my most favorite and yet… I would just let her eat all of that?!"

"Do not be selfish, Claude!" said Kenji. "Your *bulalo* is not the only dish on the table. We ordered five!"

"Those foods came from our money!"

"I know, but this will serve as your little help for Valerie."

"Darn it really! If it wasn't for that stupid stone, we would never meet that kid and be with us 'till now!"

"Stop that you two, we're in front of foooooddsss for cryin' out loud!!!" stopped Shingue.

"Waaahhh!!!"

Claude was forced to just give his favorite dish to Valerie with resentment. "Here ya go. Dammit!"

Shingue laughed while chewing. "My goodness Claude, why do you have to vie with a kid especially a girl? Just let her eat all of them for goodness sake!"

"That is why I really don't like kids to go with us, goddammit!"

"SHUT UUUPPPPP!!!" cried Kenji in husky voice because his mouth was full.

They continued to eat again. Claude took the pork stew instead and ate it in one small bite with deep resentment towards Valerie.

Later, Claude noticed that perhaps Valerie could not able to consume all of his favorite dish since it had many meats. So he decided to wait for Valerie to just give him what would left to his *bulalo*. *Don't devour that* bulalo, *you greedy kid!* Said Claude to himself.

Kenji ate five quail eggs and fried pork he ordered while Shingue ate hot *pancit canton* (Filipino-style noodle). But as for Claude, his garlic rice and pork stew were still unconsumed yet!

The room became suddenly quiet since the cries and weeping seemed finally over. Claude was now contented with his dish so he began to eat but very slowly. The three had eaten much already except Claude, who was still waiting for Valerie if she would give him the *bulalo* leftovers that she was still eating.

You spare me even just a little, you stupid kid… I was the one who bought that and NOT you! Claude said again to himself.

They finished eating. Nothing had left even just a small amount of soup. The three were stuffed full, but Claude got piqued more when he noticed his *bulalo* was also gone. He never got a chance to have a taste of it even just one sip of its soup!

Claude was gaping in shock. "My *bulalo* is… now completely gone? It had lots of meats earlier!"

"Y-Yeah, Valerie ate all of them of course," answered Shingue gaping as well. "S-She even ate the rest of the meats!"

Claude gaped more as if he heard the worst compassionate thing happened throughout his life. "S-She ate all of the meats… and she never offered me at least one? T-T-The one I bought earlier!"

Claude's body was shaking in anger when Valerie turned to Kenji with a smile. Her stomach grew bigger for being full.

"Kuya Kenji, I am about to go outside again to play with Agnes, okay?" then she burped.

Kenji's face could not believe that the child could actually consume all of Claude's *bulalo*. He faltered. "S-Sure, no problem but…"

Valerie ignored Kenji's reaction when she dashed away from the boys and went out of the room. She quickly closed the door when Kenji continued talking though the child was already gone. "…please go back to this room later before nightfall…"

Later, Kenji again suddenly heard another huge sound wave from Claude's cry but in jokingly way. "AAAAHHHHH, DAMMIT! I ONLY WASTED MY OWN MONEY FOR THAT STUPID KID! Huhuhuhu…"

"C-Claude," restrained Kenji once again. "That is okay. You can buy your *bulalo* again next time."

"What the HELL do you mean by *that is okay*?! This would be my chance to eat my favorite dish again after I lastly ate it a very long time ago!"

"Um… I mean yeah. But at least you gave the child a treat right?"

"Excuse me? No way! She already had her breakfast earlier before we get in this village!"

"The cafeteria is still open if you want to buy it again…"

"SHUT UP!"

Kenji's face suddenly frowned. "Fine! How selfish you really are… You're stingy!" then he quickly turned over the table to clean it.

"And yet you still think I am that stingy, huh? She ate my entire *bulalo* and she never gave me at least one meat leftover!"

"Whatever you say. Go on with your life!"

"Hell yeah!"

Kenji and Shingue continued to fix their table until they were done. Claude laid on the bed giggling in deep resentment.

"Oh yeah…" said Shingue happily. "I finally finished fixing the table, which means this is my turn now to go outside freely! Yo-hoo, my chance to wander around Sierra Village!"

"Go ahead Shingue," answered Kenji.

"I am going outside now, Kenji and Claude okay? So you two will be the next ones to stay in this room. I'll just wander around the village while letting my stomach digests everything I ate," then he pulled out the key in his pocket. "Here Kenji, catch!" and he threw it to Kenji.

Kenji caught the key and he nodded.

Shingue walked over the door and he waved. "Okay, gonna leave now. But will return before nightfall. See ya guys later!"

"Please tell Valerie to come back sooner. Take care!" Kenji smiled sweetly.

Shingue slowly shut the door. What only left now was Kenji and Claude.

Silence all over the room. None of the two spoke nor even making any sound. It seemed like the two were waiting for each other who would break the ice.

Kenji walked over the window. There, he saw a mountain in a range as well as the small buildings in every area of the village. He took the chair and dragged it near the window. As he opened the window, the frigid air quickly entered the room. Then he closed his eyes to feel the cold air that touched his skin.

He sat on the chair, feeling the cool breeze of natural air touching his face that made him more relaxed in front of the window.

Finally, Claude could no longer stand the lengthy silence between them so he spoke first. "It looks like this room becomes silent in all of the sudden," then he rose from the bed and looked around. "What is going on?"

Kenji did not answer.

Claude turned to Kenji who was still facing the window. He asked hesitantly. "Kenji um… Did you get mad at me earlier?"

Kenji remained motionless. Playing deaf perhaps.

"Psstt… H-Hey!"

Kenji turned his head to Claude and answered. "A little," then he turned back over the window.

"I… I see… Well you know me, I am a temperamental person. I am sorry if I upset you for that."

"Why did you scold the kid for only just a simple dish? Didn't you realize that the kid is an orphan and no one to turn to except us, Claude?... Is *bulalo* really that BIG deal to you?"

"I am sorry, alright?"

"Don't say sorry to me, Claude. Tell it to Valerie."

Kenji was still looking at the window when Claude stooped down his head and paused for a moment. Then he lifted his face and sighed.

"By the way Kenji, I am also sorry for what everything I did to you

THE EXPLORERS

and to your twin brother Genji… Well, to Shiela and Aaron as well. I know I'd became a naughty kid to you guys. So, I realize that I do not deserve to be with you and Shingue to become an Explorer."

Kenji stood on the chair. "Hey Claude," then he approached Claude and sat on the bed next to him. "Why do you think about that anyway?"

"You see, I do not deserve to become one. I think of myself now as a bad person. I just treated someone so badly that I shouldn't."

"Whatever you say again Claude," Kenji turned his back to Claude. "Well as for me, I am really determined to become one and use it as a tool to see my real parents soon. Also, to help the king of the gods… I need to find and save the missing elements. I want to become an Explorer… that is my dream. And failure is not an option. I will never give up."

"You are really determined to your dreams, Kenji. Well… I'll try too if I can."

Kenji faced Claude again. "Do not just try it, you really have to do it! And swear that you will not fail."

Claude only stooped his head, thinking deeply of what would he become. He sighed once again in his serious face.

17 A FRIEND

Genji swiftly ran in a swamp to get away from the old woman's wrath. He fled just to make sure the old woman would not harm him and be safe.

Because of his extraordinary speed, the old woman did not notice Genji's sudden escape.

The old woman remained standstill, then she used her power to figure out where the impostor's current location. She closed her eyes and concentrated to read what was in Genji's mind. "My power can still hound that sinful impostor no matter where he goes… Let's see… AHA!"

Meanwhile, Genji was continuously running as fast as he could when suddenly he felt something strange in his body. He felt a flow of electricity creeping across his body. Then in all of the sudden, his lips began to pop!

"AW!"

A flow of electricity passed again in his body so he paralyzed and stumbled on the mud. His lips was now bleeding. "W-Who is responsible for this? That wicked witch?"

His skin in his arm also popped and a little blood squirted out. He cried in pain of his wounds.

"Ah! How can that woman still able to hurt me though I am already so far away from her? Is she…" then he looked around. "Is she following me behind my back?!"

It also followed by the sudden pop of the skin in his leg. This now made a hole in his fitted pants.

Genji ran again as fast as he could and felt agitated to the old woman. "I-I have to ran faster so she can no longer reach me anymore. Stupid witch!"

It was all in vein no matter what the best he could do to save himself from danger. His clothes were now full of holes, but the old woman was not finished in punishing the young man. Genji would stand, run, and then fall again on the ground like a drunk man. He looked around once again and praying that no one was there. Soon, he gave up.

Genji was afraid that he would no longer able to return home to his stepmother in elegant mansion. But it did not matter to him anymore since he decided not to stay in there forever. And he was certain that his stepmother would not look for him.

After his lengthy escape, Genji innocently reached a popular school of one of a well-known cities around the world. The name of the city was Hunsterdam, and its school name was Hunsterdam University.

The Hunsterdam University consisted of students that most of them were scholars, top-notchers, and valedictorians. The students were best of the best, but it was too expensive to study in the said university.

The university was a talk of the town and envied by other schools since its facilities were complete and powered by high-technologies. Like common schools and universities, they had laboratories, computer rooms, art galleries, theaters, and so on. According to the Hunsterdam University students, their university was a school of geniuses.

In addition, the Hunsterdam University was the only school around the world that offered Primary, Secondary, and Tertiary levels rolled in one university. But since the tuition fee was very much expensive, it happened that the other people could not afford to study even though they were living near it.

Genji leaned behind the thick wall of the big university building when he realized that the electricity had already stopped flowing throughout his body. He was panting in heavy exhaustion so he thought of resting there for a while to recover his strength. He was breathing deeply with his eyes closed. And then, he sat on the ground.

After a while, the young man did not realize he instantly fell asleep from exhaustion. He was sleeping deeply and it was hard to awake him easily, especially that the entire university was quiet and the students were still in their class.

A few minutes passed, the Hunsterdam students were still in their class. But there were some students coming out from the university.

Genji was still sleeping. Later, the university bell rang as dismissal time of the Primary level. The young students' parents were now in the entrance gate to get their children. There were also school buses waiting outside, while the other vehicles were in the parking lot.

The area outside the university became noisy, but Genji was still deeply asleep. Some young students were hanging out in waiting sheds while the others were looking for their parents to pick them up. The others were buying street foods in mini stores, and the others were just running around the huge university park.

Later, the bell rang signifying the end of the class for the Secondary level or high school. There, a group of teenage students came out of the building possessing different kinds of personalities. Some of the females were demure while some of the males were arrogant. Like the young students, some of the teenagers were also hanging out the waiting sheds while the others were also buying street foods.

The bell rang again for the third time signifying the end of the class for the Tertiary level or college. Here, a group of matured students was the last ones appeared outside the building. They were under the age of sixteen onwards.

The variety of students were now outside the university. The others were walking off to their homes in different directions. But others chose the short route behind the university building.

There was a teenage man who as the same age as Genji wearing round glasses, thinking of passing behind the building not because of the short route, but to hide from his fellow classmates who were always making fun out of him. He was not afraid of them, but rather to get away from being bullied by them. He was being teased and humiliated in front of their female classmates. He did not understand why his fellow classmates always had to treat him like that. Was it because he became one of the Valedictorians in the entire Hunsterdam University?

He sneaked behind the building when he noticed the two feet between the drums. He got frightened thinking that someone was killed behind the building and dumped. His heart beat fast and confused whether he should still pass through it or not. He was scared, but his thought dared him to go for it so he approached the sleeping Genji. He was shocked when he saw the young man's body bathe in few bloods and his clothes full of holes. He stepped back in fear and wanted to scream, ask for help or report it immediately to the police.

The teenage student's hands were shaking in fear, trying to reach Genji's hand to examine his pulse. Then, he smiled when he felt Genji's hand was warm and his pulse was throbbing.

"I will help this man," said the student. "It looks like he got hurt very badly. How pitiful!"

He wanted to take Genji in a safe place somewhere, so he slowly pulled Genji's hand up to his shoulder to help him walk. The student looked around to find a place when suddenly a snow began to fall.

"Oh no, the snow has just started," he said while looking at the sky.

The student helped Genji to walk. They reached another park on the other side of the university where he laid down Genji at the bench and would try to awake him. He bent his body closer to Genji to look at his face when he saw his bloody lips.

"Who did this to this poor young man? Man, he got many wounds in his body!"

A cold tiny snow flake fell on Genji's face when he suddenly awoke and quickly rose. But just as he rose, their heads banged with each other and they both cried in pain.

"Aw!" cried Genji. "What's wrong with you?! Have you got no manners?"

"Um, it's not like that..." said the teenage student. "I just wanted to help you because I saw you lying down behind our university. And you're bloody... See?"

Genji looked around. "Who are you?"

The student smiled sweetly. "Me? My name is Cyan Wilford, a student of Hunsterdam University. I am a Valedictorian," and he smiled again.

"V-Valedictorian?" asked Genji in amazement. "So that is why you are wearing big round glasses like that."

"Not really, perhaps I am a bookworm and I do a lot of online research and homeworks."

"Ah..."

"Hold on," said Cyan. "I wonder what happened to you, mister..."

"...Genji,"

"Okay, so what happened to you Mr. Genji?"

Genji snubbed Cyan. "You don't need to know. Why should you care?"

"Huh? Why?"

"It's nothing really!" Genji stood on the bench and wiped the dirt in his body. "So where am I now anyway? I feel like I don't want to go back home anymore…"

"Y-You're in Hunsterdam… Genji."

"Hunsterdam? What's that?"

"This place you just came in."

"How far is this from Camoria?"

Cyan's eyes opened wide. "Hello?! Hey mister, I think it is over ten kilometers away from here! Hah, don't tell me you came here from Camoria?"

Genji did not answer, gaping as he heard Cyan's answer.

"Now what mister?!"

"I-If you only knew… I actually traveled over ten kilometers by just running…"

Cyan sprang back in surprise. "Whaaaattt? Are you nuts? You came here all the way from Camoria by just running? Hah, gimme a break! Or perhaps…"

Genji looked at Cyan. "What?"

Cyan pulled back a little from Genji. "P-Perhaps you are a criminal or a convict running away from the police chasing you! Look at you, you got bloods in your body and you're a mess! Tell me, are you being chased by the police, huh? Please don't lie to me!"

"You're absolutely wrong Mister Valedictorian," said Genji. "I thought you are smart!"

"Whaaaattt?"

"You aren't good in logic…"

"Excuse me? I got 1.25 grade in that subject mister!"

"Alright Mr. Logic," revoked Genji. "You are smart."

"Yeah really! And please stop calling me with *mister*, okay? I have my nicknames, but all of them do not include *misters*!"

The two were still goofing to each other as they talk. But later on, Cyan pouted from their goofiness and he stood on the bench. "Well, I am going home now before the snow blows hard. If you don't need my help, then so be it. I'll go!"

Genji smirked. "It's okay, no problem."

"Fine, goodbye and nice meeting you!" then Cyan walked away.

THE EXPLORERS

Genji sat on the bench wondering if the electricity was still in his body. He waited for five to ten minutes, when he assured that it was gone for good so he stood again and left the park.

As for Mr. Valedictorian, he had already forgotten about his classmates whom he fled earlier. He was walking home when someone called his name. "Wilford! Wilford! Stop acting like a deaf!"

Cyan heard the cry of one of his college classmates as if they were still teasing him like a kid. He tried to ignore his classmate but said to himself: *Oh no... Here we go again...*

Cyan was about twenty meters away from them but he was still being called. He innocently walked away in a hurry, but then he noticed his classmate following him while still calling his attention. This time, he ran fast.

His classmate shouted and calling his name while chasing him from behind. "Hey Wilford, are you a coward??!"

Cyan stopped from running and his classmate approached him while pointing at him.

"Hey!" shouted his classmate. Their fellow classmates approached them as well. "I've been calling you and you keep on ignoring me. You aren't wearing earphones, are you? Or were you just playing deaf on me?!"

Cyan pretended that he did not hear any. "Ah... Were you calling me earlier?"

His classmate surprised. "What the--? What do you mean by that?"

"If I heard you calling me, then I would hear you and turn to you. But I really did not hear anything so I never stopped walking."

"Hey Wil--"

"Bleeehhh!" teased Cyan sticking out his tongue like a kid.

The other classmate shouted at them while pointing at Cyan. "You two! Are you both going home together? Oh Fred, I hope you absorb even half of what that Valedictorian learnt. I suppose you will be the Summa Cum Laude in our batch, hahaha!" then he spitted on the ground.

Fred turned to his classmate. "Yeah man, I too notice that this Valedictorian is always focusing on books even though he keeps on tripping on the ground! And look, he is even trying to play deaf on us. Very clumsy!" then he quickly tugged Cyan on his shoulder. "So this time, why don't you have a break and drink some beer with us, eh? After all, we have been bullying you for a very long time and we have changed. So from now on, we are friends!"

Cyan saw Fred's evil eyes looking at him, giving him an impression that his words were all lies. So he removed Fred's hands on his shoulder. "I already know your style, mister. You have deceived me once so there's no way you will fool me again!"

"What the--" Fred quickly pulled Cyan's shirt. "You should thank me and Chris for showing you our kindness. Otherwise… we will humiliate you again to our fellow classmates!"

Cyan quickly removed Fred's "devil hands" again and stared at him directly. "You are both jerks!" then he quickly turned to his back.

Fred got pissed off and was about to hit Cyan, but Cyan spoke to them in his low angry voice. "I am not looking for any trouble, Fred. And if you do start the fight, I will report this incident and will ask the faculty department to drop you out in the university!"

The two stepped back in their faces gaping in surprise. They would be getting a final grade of five (5.00) in all of their subjects and would instantly kick them out in the university if the incident report reached the dean's table!

"Goodbye," said Cyan. "See you two again tomorrow."

Cyan continued to walk on his way when he saw the sidewalk vendors with some students buying and hanging out around the university. This caught his attention so he pulled out his money to buy a street food. He approached one of the sidewalk vendors to buy *kalamares* (fried squid) and pay thirty pesos.

There were lots of students still hanging around the university though the snow was already falling. Cyan looked around to find some vacant seats in waiting sheds but all of them were occupied. So he decided to stand at the side of the street.

He was eating one of the three sticks of *kalamares* when he saw Genji who was also eating street food on the other side of the street. He noticed that the young man had already cleaned himself but his clothes were still full of holes, so he approached Genji and greeted him while chewing.

"Oh, I thought you're gone home now and should not stay here?" asked Genji.

"Sorry, but I'd like to eat *kalamares* first," said Cyan and he scratched his head.

Genji did not answer and he continued eating his bought street food.

THE EXPLORERS

Later, they talked again and started to know each other more.

"You know what Genji? I feel like, I like you," said Cyan.

Genji hesitated. "W-What?"

Cyan chuckled. "I'd like to make friends with you, mister…"

"M-Me?" Genji pointed himself. "Do I deserve to be your friend?"

"It is because I can see in your eyes that you also have no friends like me. You are a loner, mister… as I do. We are both in the same situation."

Genji tried to answer jokingly. "Wow, I'm impressed Mr. Valedictorian! You can even read my mind by looking at my eyes like a book!"

"I-I am serious, Genji. I often dream of having a good friend just like my fellow classmates. You know, a real friend… A partner… The one who will never deceive me and be with me thru thick and thin… And I know how so sad to be a loner for so long. That is what I am."

Genji suddenly became serious. He never expected that a new friend would come along in his life in a weird situation.

18 FAMOUS

Kenji and Claude were staying inside their room 1908 while Shingue and Valerie were still outside the inn. Claude was sleeping in bed while Kenji was sitting on the edge of his bed while watching TV in low volume.

"Today's news: A heavy snow storm is now brewing the country today. The snow storm will likely to hit the major towns and villages so we would like to inform the public to get prepared as the storm already enters the country's area of responsibility. Please remain to your homes and stay updated for more news. The possible areas the storm will hit are Sierra Village, Prancy Fontana, Ridge Village... *blah, blah, blah...*"

Kenji was currently watching news flash and he thought to himself. "A snow storm? Oh no, I'm afraid this will take us a few days more to stay in this village. And we rented this room for one night only!"

"I repeat: A powerful blizzard has been entered in our country today and we would like to inform everyone to be prepared and return to your homes. For those families living in low land areas and other dangerous places, please evacuate immediately to avoid the possible cause of avalanche..."

Kenji went back to the window. He opened it and looked afar. The sky was now getting darker. "It's true, but Shingue and Valerie are still outside."

His eyes looked around and searched the two, but he did not see them both. "Anyway, they're grown ups and they already know what to do in case the snow starts to fall."

Kenji closed the window and awoke Claude. "Claude, wake up. You must find Valerie and take her back in this room now."

THE EXPLORERS

Claude was so difficult to awake. He groaned as he stretched his arms. "Ummm... What?"

"Please find Valerie and take her here..."

Claude's face suddenly frowned. "That kid? Why don't you find her yourself?"

"Come on man, I am preparing something before the storm comes."

"W-What, what is it again?"

"There is a storm coming. A heavy one..."

Claude quickly regained his senses. "W-What... what? A storm?"

"Yes, that is why I am preparing now."

Claude closed his eyes and scratched his head in annoyance. "My goodness, stop worrying too much about that kid, man. She's a grown up and I am sure she will return here before the snow storm comes! 'Coz even if I ask her to come back here, she will never listen to me so--"

"Stop talking Claude," Kenji got pissed off. "Go back to sleep."

Claude quickly rose from the bed. "O-Okay fine, relax man. I was only kidding..."

"What do you mean kidding?! I am not playing with you, Claude!"

Claude got embarrassed. His face turned red. "O-Ohh... That hurts..."

Kenji pulled his coat in the bag which was also given by Rolando and wore it around his body. "I will take her here. Geez, why do you always keep on complaining about anything that doesn't need to complain? Whatever you say as always..."

"A-Alright Kenji, I am going outside now..."

Kenji was leaving. "Just go back to sleep and don't waste your time with this nonsense!" and then he shut the door.

Claude only smiled before he spoke. "His name is Kenji. A hardworking guy but also a temperamental like me..."

Kenji walked in a hurry to the small hallway when he sensed the cold temperature inside the inn. He walked towards the elevator, and saw the windows with few snow flakes already falling. "Oh no, the snow is coming..." then he went inside the elevator.

He coughed. Then, the elevator door opened and he went out the inn when he saw more snows falling on the ground. He lifted his pointing finger when a snow flake dropped on it and rubbed it with his thumb. "It's getting colder..." and he coughed again.

The villagers outside were also busy preparing for the incoming snow storm. They were closing their stores while some children stopped playing and rushed back to their homes. The young man soughed for Valerie.

He could not find Valerie and even Shingue. He went to the fountain which was in the central area of the village where children loved to hang out, but still he did not see the little girl.

"Valerie... Where are you now? Please go back to our room..." he said to himself.

Kenji heard some weeping and shouting of children in a distance. His eyes opened wide. "What's that? Valerie!!!" then he ran fast to follow the source of the children's voices. "Valerie, where are you?!!"

Kenji tried to look for the weeping and shouting of the children. As he was approaching fast, he heard their voices getting closer to where he was. The snow became stronger and more snows rained down.

Finally, Kenji found the source of children's voices. He saw a group of unruly children, and Valerie was with them crying because she was being mobbed by them.

Kenji also saw a little boy holding the Divine Stone of Valerie. He was with his fellow playmates who were all boys, while Valerie and Agnes were both in a group of girls. The boy lifted the stone and shouted out loud. "This stone is mine!"

Kenji came near over the unruly children when Valerie saw him and cried. "*Kuya, kuya!* That mean kid *(sob)*... He took my stone *(sob)*..." then she sniffed.

"Valerie what is going on?"

"That ugly, mean kid took my stone!"

"Why? This stone is mine from now on!" cried the chubby little boy.

Kenji approached the boy who had the stone. "Sir, can you please give back the stone to us? That stone has its owner already..."

"No way!" said the boy stamping his feet. "Why are you here? Who are you anyway?!"

Kenji tried to make fun with the boy, so he pretended that he was angry. He put his hands on his hips and lowered his voice like a big muscular man!

"AHEM, I AM THE FATHER OF THIS GIRL! Why did you take her *marble*, HA? YOU MADE HER CRY?"

"Ahhh!" the boy suddenly got frightened and he recoiled.

"YOU DON'T RESPECT ME, EH? WOULD YOU LIKE ME TO TAKE YOU TO THE POLICE? NOW GIVE BACK THAT STONE TO MY DAUGHTER BEFORE I WILL EAT YOU LIKE A BOILED PORK! RAAAARRR!!!"

The boy trembled in fear along with his fellow playmates. Valerie smiled and Kenji winked at her.

"AHHH!" cried the boy. "I-I am sorry, mister! H-Here's your daughter's stone now… Please take it…" then he forced to give the stone to Valerie while the group of girls was mocking towards him. "I am so sorry… I thought you were only a stranger to us! Huhuhu…"

"Give me that!" shouted Valerie as she quickly took the stone from the boy's hand. "You even tried to yell at my father, you disrespectful kid!"

"Huhuhuhu…" cried the boy and he called his playmates. "Let us go now," then they ran away while still crying.

"Goodbye," said the little girls waving goodbye at the little boys happily.

The group of boys was already gone when Agnes turned to Kenji and asked. "Is it true that Valerie is your daughter? I don't believe it, you are still young to have a child already!"

"Ah… No…" said Kenji blushing. "She is not my daughter and I don't have a child yet. I was just pretending to be her father so the boy would be forced to return the stone to Valerie."

"Is that mean… You're still single, aren't you?"

"Ahm, yes…"

"Wow, he is still single Agnes, Valerie!" said one of the girls. "My gosh, you look handsome *kuya*!"

Kenji blushed once more. "Hehehe, no kidding right…"

Valerie looked at her stone to carefully check if it got scratched or broken. "Nothing. Good thing…"

"The snow is getting stronger," said Agnes. "We have to go home now!"

"Yes, we must…" said Kenji. "I watched the news earlier that the storm will hit this village. It already entered the country. A heavy one indeed…"

"Alright prince charming," said a little girl smiling and seemed to have a crush on the young man. "Take care, okay?"

"Yes I will, thanks…" answered Kenji. "You too, take care."

A little girl walked away giggling along with her playmates. Agnes also left without saying goodbye, but Valerie understood about it since they were all in a hurry.

"Let's go back to our room, *kuya*..." said Valerie.

Kenji held Valerie's hand and they walked together back to the inn. While walking, he recalled something when he turned to the child.

"By the way Valerie, have you seen *kuya* Shingue today?"

"No, why?"

"'Coz he also left the inn to wander around the village."

"No, I never seen him anywhere."

"I see... Alright, it doesn't matter anyway. After all, he's all grown up."

"Good thing you came and saved me from those mean boys, *kuya*."

"Yeah, so how is your Divine Stone now?"

Valerie showed her stone to Kenji. "Here, it is safe and unscratched in my hands again!"

"Let me see," Kenji took the stone from Valerie's hand. "You're right, it is unbroken."

The two were still on their way to the inn while Kenji was looking at the stone. The snow was getting more heavier when the stone suddenly felt the very cold temperature. A large snow flake fell on the stone and it gently touched the surface. Because of that, the stone quickly reacted and it brilliantly burst out its light. The two were surprised to see as they gaped in amazement.

"*Kuya* Kenji, the stone has its power!" cried Valerie dazzling by the light of the stone.

"You're right," said Kenji while he was still holding the shining stone. "I'm dazzling! I wonder what this means?"

The light was so bright but its beam was cold. Then, there were two unusual auras suddenly appeared around the stone.

Valerie pointed the stone. "*Kuya*, something just suddenly appeared from that stone! Looks like it has two souls surrounding it!"

"What if I drop it? What do you think?" asked Kenji with his hands trembling in cold. "The stone is too cold! My fingers are freezing..."

"Go ahead *kuya*, drop the stone!"

Kenji tried, but he could not drop the stone since his hand was already freezing.

"I... I can't. But never mind, let's go back to our room now, Val."

The two quickly ran to go back to the inn. When they reached the front desk, Kenji covered the stone in his hand using his other hand. They passed over the counter when an innkeeper noticed the light emitting from Kenji's hand.

The innkeeper wondered. "Sir, what is that thing in your hand?"

"Ah… fireflies," Kenji faltered. "We were catching lots of snow fireflies outside…" then they hurried away.

"Snow fireflies?" asked the innkeeper in wonder. "How many are those?"

The two reached the elevator when Kenji could not even move his other hand that also covering the Divine Stone. He could not reach the button so he asked Valerie to press it.

"Valerie, press the button of the fourth floor."

"Got it, *kuya*!" then Valerie pressed the button.

The elevator moved up when the stone felt the decreasing temperature inside Kenji's hand, since the inn was now using heaters and the warmth coming out from Kenji's palm. Later, the two noticed the light slowly vanished in Kenji's hands.

"The light has stopped, Valerie."

"Yes, you're right."

"Perhaps the stone adjusted into warm temperature when we get inside the inn."

The elevator door opened and the two came out. Kenji tried to move his fingers when he found out that he could move them again normally. "T-There, I can freely move my hands again. They're no longer freezing!"

He slowly opened his hands to take a look at the Divine Stone when he noticed the stone change its form as well as its color. "What on earth--"

"K-*Kuya*, let us go to our room first. Quickly now!"

"I know, but I wonder why the stone suddenly changes its form? What is happening really?"

The two knocked on the door of their room and it opened. It was Claude who opened.

"Hey guys, the snow storm is getting heavier," said Claude.

Kenji noticed Shingue already inside of the room.

"Shingue, how long have you been here?" he asked.

"I arrived just now…" answered Shingue.

"I did not notice you came in this inn."

Claude's face suddenly frowned again when he saw his little nemesis next to Kenji. He spoke low and in serious tone. "Kenji, the storm overtook you both."

"Yes, quite."

"H-Hey, don't be mad at me anymore, huh? We're in good hands."

Kenji quickly faced Shingue and ignored what Claude said. "Shingue, look at this stone. It suddenly transformed itself and changed its color."

"Huh?' Shingue was amazed. "How did that happen?"

"Perhaps this is something to do with time and temperature."

"I… I guess so."

Kenji approached Shingue in serious look. "Shingue, I want the Explorers to know about this as soon as possible, so that I will see my real father and become one of you…"

"Well Kenji… First, there is something I want to say to you," said Shingue. "Actually, I got an emergency call from Rolando earlier. He told me that the UE called them and said they were looking for both me and Arthur…"

"Arthur you say?"

"Yes, Master Serge told UE that we already completed our full training. So…"

"S-So what then?" asked Kenji eagerly.

"So, Rolando informed me that the Explorers will call me tomorrow morning to pick me up…"

"Shingue, if ever you'll meet the Explorers tomorrow… Will you help me show this stone to them? They are also looking for this for sure, and I as well!"

"Yes, certainly!" answered Shingue smiling in thumbs-up.

"And I will be one of you finally! Oh, if you only knew how excited I am now, Shingue!"

Claude wondered. "Do you think the Explorers can still come in this village with this bad weather? I'm afraid they will not gonna make it to pick you up here, Shingue."

"They can Claude," answered Shingue. "They will use our aircraft. I will also take you with them and will help you too in everything I can."

Valerie became jealous. "And how about me?"

Kenji and Shingue stopped for a moment… They already forgot about the child who was not into their plan.

THE EXPLORERS

"Can I also come with you and ride in an airplane?"

Shingue did not know what to say. "Ah… I believe that the Explorers do not allow children to ride in their airplane. You see, all of them are warriors…"

Valerie quickly took the stone held by Kenji and showed it to Shingue herself.

"I can also become an Explorer because I was the one who discovered this stone right?" it was true that Valerie was the one who found the Divine Stone and not Kenji.

Kenji became quiet in all of the sudden. He began to think what if the little girl would not let him have the stone she got since he was not its rightful owner. Just as expected, he would be coming with Shingue and Valerie would remain in the village. But the child wanted to go with them, yet she was still a child and inexperienced in fighting. But she had one of the rare sacred stones the Explorers need.

"Um, listen Valerie… The Explorers is not for kids," said Kenji smiling uncertainly. "It is not that easy."

"Kenji means you cannot be an Explorer because you are still very young," continued Shingue.

Valerie objected. "But in order to become one is to have one of the stones they're looking for no matter what the age is, right? Then I can be an Explorer!"

"You don't understand Valerie," said Shingue. "You cannot become one…"

"Well if you do not want me to come with you, then how will *kuya* Kenji become an Explorer? Remember that the main requirement to become one is in my hands!"

Kenji became anxious. The little girl was right. What if the Explorers would ask for the Divine Stone before they would allow him to get on board? He felt like the child had no intention of giving him the stone.

"And Valerie, it's too tough for you when you get there and become a warrior. That's why we do not allow children at your age to come with us," excused Shingue.

"No way!" yelled Valerie. "I'll go with you! Who will be here with me if I stay alone in this village?"

Shingue and Kenji looked at each other.

"What? Who then?"

Shingue only scratched his head. "Stop retorting with us Valerie please… and mind your own business. We have issues here that don't need your presence."

Valerie got hurt, and Kenji felt pity towards her. He wanted to defend the child but then…

"V-Valerie, why don't you just listen to the radio again if you don't mind?" asked Kenji awkwardly.

Valerie's face suddenly frowned at them, as if she was about to cry.

"I'm sorry, Valerie…"

The child did not answer. She could no longer hold herself from being emotional. So she cried before them when she quickly walked out of the room and shut the door real hard.

"V-Valerie, come back here! Where are you going? There's a storm outside!" yelled Kenji.

"Tsk, that is why I really hate that kid to come with us wherever we go!" said Claude angrily. "She's very stubborn and more of a headache!"

Valerie was about to go straight to Agnes' house carrying the stone in her hand. As she was passing the counter, the innkeeper saw her and prevented her from coming out the inn, but the child did not listen as she still ran out the entrance.

"HEY, IT'S TOO DANGEROUS TO STAY OUTSIDE. COME BACK!!!" cried the innkeeper.

Back to room 1908.

"Oh no Kenji, what about now? That stupid kid has the stone you need," said Claude. "What are we going to do? The Explorers will be here tomorrow morning though it still stormy."

"I don't know."

"How will I tell the Explorers that you do indeed acquired the stone?" asked Shingue.

"I also don't know."

"Damn, why don't you just steal that stone from her? You can do that!" said Claude.

Kenji shook his head. "I can't, Claude. She was right, that is her stone and not mine."

"Hmmm… How about now?"

The three boys continued to think very seriously until the nightfall came and the storm was still blowing hard. Later, they waited for Valerie's

THE EXPLORERS

return until twelve in the midnight. The child did not return, so they decided to lay down on their beds to go to sleep thinking the little girl was now in Agnes house.

19 THE WELCOME

The snow storm blew so heavily in Sierra Village with occasional chunks of ice continuously banged in the windows causing a sudden, loud noises.

Tugu-dug!

It was already two o'clock dawn and the storm was still blowing the village non-stop. The temperature dropped and the weather outside indicated no sign of easing. Heaters were operated inside the inn to equalize the worsened condition of below zero degree Celsius temperature.

Claude and Shingue were sleeping together in one bed, while Kenji was unaware that he already fell from his own bed and still he was asleep on the floor. His bed was kiddie sized, that's the reason why he fell by even just a slight turn on the side.

There were some twigs and leaves blown by the wind that banged the window which also caused a sudden loud noises. *BAG! BAG! BAG!* Claude heard the noises that awake him.

"What's that?"

He rose from the bed, threw away the thick blanket, and then he got up on the bed. Later, he felt the super chill of his body by the weather.

"Nyiiihhh… It's way too cold…"

The lights were all turned off around the room 1908 and it was pretty dark. Claude was about to look where the loud *"BAG!"* sound came from when he accidentally stepped on Kenji and he tripped. Then, he stumbled.

"Aw! Man, I tripped by the pillow lying on the floor," he said.

He stooped to grope the thing he just stepped on the floor when he

THE EXPLORERS

touched Kenji's face and learned that it was him.

"Kenji?"

Claude stood up and gently stepped across the floor to turn on the fluorescent lamp. There, he watched Kenji's freezing body on the floor bent tightly to feel the warmth of his own body. He noticed the young man gave up himself by giving the small blanket to the two and let alone stand the cold. Claude felt pity, so he quickly took off his jacket and he put it on Kenji's body. Then he gently carried him back to his own bed like a baby.

It was five o'clock in the morning. Shingue's smartphone began to ring.

"*Ti-ngi-ning... Ti-ngi-ning...*" a song ringing by Shingue's smartphone. "*Hey, you have a caller...*"

The smartphone was still ringing out loud and he was still asleep.

"*Ti-ngi-ning... Hey, you have a caller...*"

Shingue awoke due to the vibration of his loud smartphone. "W-What the... Oh, the UE! They're calling me."

He immediately took his ringing smartphone and quickly answered.

"H-Hello? Yeah man, what's up? Aha, doing good as always! Certainly, the snow storm is also heavy here--"

After the *"his"* and *"hellos"*, they began to talk about their meeting place. "Ha? Yes! I am in Sierra Village right now. I am certain that you are familiar in this place, right? I have friends here to come along with me. Yes, sir!"

The storm was still blowing strong but not as strong as before. "Hey, I missed everyone of you. I am thankful that I completed my long training so I am ready to be with you all again. Ah, did you already take Arthur? Hahaha! Alright, I'll just wait for you here in this village."

Their conversation took long. He first spoke to his friends, then to their leader. "Oh okay, I will be here waiting for you. Take care on your safe trip. Goodbye!" then he ended the call.

Shingue got very excited, so he did not go back to sleep until morning. Instead, he packed all their belongings. Good thing the storm was now receded, but the thick snow already covered the entire village and still unsafe for children to go out and play.

At six o'clock in the morning, Shingue sighted the incoming three aircrafts from the window. He saw the Explorer emblem painted on each ultrasonic jets and cried.

"Oh my, the Explorers, they're here!"

He immediately awoke the two. It was good they packed their things ready to leave the village when the Explorers came. The villagers who were outside cheered and waved at them, since the Explorers were really well-known around the world and believed to be the saviors of the oppressed. The villagers welcomed the whole party.

"The Explorers! Hooray, they come here for a visit!" said a woman happily while shoveling away the snow in their roof.

The Explorer aircrafts smoothly landed near the main gate. More of the Sierra villagers went out in their homes to meet their visitors and they all shouted for joy.

Kenji quickly rose to his bed still wearing Claude's jacket. He turned to the window happily. "Shingue, Shingue, the Explorers… They're here!"

Claude also rose and peeked in the window. "Wow, they're stunning…"

"Let's go, we have to carry our bags and go down now. They're looking for me and they cannot stay here any longer," said Shingue in a hurry.

The three carried their belongings and left the room hurriedly. They rushed outside the inn to look for the innkeeper who was taking photographs of the Explorers. They gladly handed the key and thanked the innkeeper at the same time.

"Thank you very much!"

"No problem. And thank you also for staying at our inn," thanked the innkeeper smiling. "We never thought that you are also one of the Explorers."

"We liked your inn so much as if we were staying in a grand hotel!" said Shingue in a joke. "By the way, I am the only Explorer among us, but soon they will be."

"Goodbye, we are looking forward on your next visit in this village sometime soon."

The three scrambled over the villagers outside when Kenji recalled something. "W-Wait…" and he immediately looked around to look at someone he treated as his little sister. "I almost forgot about Valerie!" then he walked away from the two.

Claude and Shingue came near the Explorers who were all wearing their uniform and Shingue introduced Claude to them with a little impression. "Sir, um… may I introduce to you one of my close friends who will be coming with us. His name is Claude…"

Claude smiled in short. "Um, good morning sir… My name is Claude Aldrich, one of Shingue's friends," then he offered to shake hands with the UE leader.

The UE leader gladly shook Claude's hand. He was wearing his special uniform worn only by the leaders of each of the Explorers' classes.

"It is a big pleasure to meet you, Claude. Alright, we can't stay here any longer and we need to board the aircraft before the snow storm returns. It will blow again anytime soon according to the weather forecaster. Claude, please get on board this plane with Shingue. Quickly now."

Shingue signaled Claude to get inside of one of the Explorer aircrafts. "Come on, Claude. The Explorers are in a hurry, there's a lot of things to be done today before the snow returns. They just came here to take us and nothing else. Come on!"

The two were about to enter the aircraft along with the leader when Claude noticed something. "Hey, where's Kenji? He's not here with us. Where is he?"

"Oh yes you're right. I almost forgot about him Claude," said Shingue.

The UE warriors were already inside the aircrafts and they were ready for takeoff, but Shingue quickly stopped them from hovering the aircraft.

"H-Hold on for a moment! There is someone who will also be coming with us besides Claude."

A UE member wondered. "There's another one beside him? Who is he anyway?"

"His name is Kenji."

"Ah, so there are two men who will be coming with you, I see…"

"Yes. J-Just a moment, okay? K-Kenji!!!"

Shingue quickly descended from the plane to look for Kenji. The villagers were now moving back to their homes because of the storm when he saw Kenji. Valerie was with him, and Shingue noticed the two facing each other closely and were both shedding tears.

Shingue walked closer to the two. The young girls and other boys were also there watching the two sadly. Shingue already knew the time had finally come to go and say goodbye to each other.

Kenji was on his knees to wipe away the tears of Valerie's face. Then, he spoke first. "V-Valerie… We need to go on in our separate ways now. I am coming with the Explorers to see my real father, and the truths I've been seeking throughout my life…"

Valerie with a heavy heart could not utter even a single word.

"Valerie, listen to me. I've been treating you as my younger sister for so long and it's hard for me to leave you this way," Kenji sobbed. He pulled out the handkerchief in his pocket and wiped his teary eyes.

Valerie still could not answer, because she did not want her *kuya* to leave, but she tried.

"*Ku-Kuya?* I don't want you to leave… I will be missing you so badly… Please return if you leave. Huhuhu…"

"Of course, Valerie. *Kuya* Kenji will be seeing you again, promise!"

"*Kuya*, I will be alone here…"

Kenji sobbed again. "Don't you worry, Val. You will be staying here with Agnes. She and her mother already accepted you to be a part of their family, right? At least, you are not alone…"

"No *kuya*! I always wanna be with you no matter where you go."

"Little sister, I promise you that I will come back here again to see you someday. Then we'll play again in the grassland, catch and broil fishes, play chasing game again… and much more."

"W-When?"

"I do not know, Valerie… Only time will tell."

Valerie sobbed. "Please tell me that you will be here again when I wake up tomorrow first thing in the morning!"

"I-I do not know, Valerie… Maybe it will take many more months, or even years."

Valerie cried more, so Kenji carried her in his arms and stood on his feet. Then he hugged her tightly. "Valerie, I love you…"

"*Kuya*, I love you too… Please come back very soon… I will call your name right away whenever I am in danger. I will!" said Valerie then she hugged Kenji back.

The children all wept and so as Shingue.

Meanwhile, the stone of Valerie felt the freezing temperature so it reacted and cast again its own light. The children dazzled, as well as the Explorers.

"What is that light?" asked an Explorer. "It's like…"

"…Divine Stone…" added Claude. "That man has the Divine Stone that is why he is coming…"

THE EXPLORERS

"Divine Stone? Who?"

Valerie was also dazzled by the light coming out in her pocket, but Kenji only ignored it in silence. She pulled out the shining stone when Kenji spoke again.

"Valerie, I have to go now... The Explorers are in a hurry..."

"W-Wait, *kuya*!" stopped Valerie while holding the stone that was still shining bright.

"What is it, Valerie?"

Valerie took Kenji's left hand first when she gently put the stone in his palm. Kenji was surprised, so he asked the little girl.

"Valerie, what is this?"

Valerie smiled. "*Kuya*, I know you need this stone and it will lead you towards your dreams. So here, please take this with you on your journey. I decided to just give it you as a simple remembrance, just promise me that you will return here and see each other again!"

Kenji smiled hopefully. "Valerie... t-thank you very much for this."

Valerie sobbed again. "I will definitely wait for your safe return, and also *kuya* Claude and *kuya* Shingue! I am really looking forward to that day!"

Kenji nodded. "We will... We will return..."

Valerie cried again when she said her last words to her *kuya*. "Take care... G-Goodbye..."

The two hugged each other again while Kenji was holding the shining stone in his left hand.

"Goodbye, Valerie..."

Shingue finally intervened the two. "K-Kenji, we have to leave now. The Explorers are in a hurry, come on!"

Kenji gently put Valerie down on the snowy ground. "We are leaving..." then he touched Valerie's cheeks to wipe her tears and kissed her on the forehead. The little girls giggled to witness the moment.

Everyone was still watching when Kenji thanked Valerie again for the stone. "Thank you once again for this stone, Valerie. I really promise that I'll come back to see you again!"

Valerie only smiled in tears when Kenji also go on board in one of the Explorer aircrafts with Shingue and waved goodbye. The airships began to hover in the air slowly.

"Goodbye, and thank you Sierra Village!" cried Kenji, Shingue, and Claude.

The villagers waved back at them as the aircrafts were hovering up in the air. Valerie cried more, since her *kuya* would soon be gone to her sight. She kept on crying and crying in sadness.

After the farewell, the Explorer aircrafts flew away from the village. Until they were all completely gone in the eyes of Valerie, so she shouted very loud as her voice echoed in the air.

"*KUYA*, I WILL WAIT FOR YOUR SAFE RETURN SOONER!!!"

She knelt down crying. Agnes and her mom approached her to give comfort and also wipe her tears.

The "Explorer HawkEye", the name of the small aircrafts of the Explorers were now flying in the air in their full speed. Kenji stayed in one side covering his face with handkerchief because he did not want to show his crying face to the Explorers. He was still holding the stone.

Claude and Shingue saw Kenji alone when Claude approached him and gently patted his shoulder.

"Um, I am so sorry about that..." started Claude in his low voice.

"Ahh..."

Kenji was still covering his sad face with a handkerchief. The plane was flying very smoothly, and it was quiet inside.

"Don't worry Kenji, I know the feeling. Sooner or later, you will see Valerie again."

Kenji answered, though his face was still covered.

"Valerie... even though she is a kid, she became one of my inspirations in life because..."

"...Because she is the reason why you are here with the Explorers today. She gave you the stone as her special remembrance to you, am I right?"

Kenji sobbed. "You know, I finally realize how happy I am to have Valerie with us during our travels. I am really glad to make friends with her and it was fun despite her very young age..."

Claude only stooped his head seriously. "I do not know."

As for Shingue, he was just talking to his fellow Explorers when he showed the ordinary stone to them with pride. One of the Explorers was amazed to see the stone so he quickly took it from Shingue's hand.

"I love this stone baby!" said the Explorer whose name was Vamir.

Shingue laughed, jokingly. "You're a sucker, Vamir. This is fake obviously! This is just an ordinary stone I picked in Sierra Village!"

Vamir was embarrassed, so he threw away the stone in the aircraft's window. "Blimey! I hate this stone baby!!!"

Celeste came near them. "So where is the real Divine Stone that young man got, hm?"

"It's in his."

"Then ask that young man to give you the stone so we can determine the authenticity! We need to find out the type of stone he got."

As for Claude and Kenji...

Claude sat next to Kenji. "Guess I'll just sit here with you 'coz I don't know anyone here yet."

Kenji lifted his head and finally showed his face. His eye bags were now swelling.

"Claude, I made another promise to someone again who became a part of my life…"

"Yup, you are right."

Kenji with hoarse voice tried to speak again but Claude stopped him. "Please do not talk. I already know what you are going to say…"

The UE leader appeared and he approached the two. The two saw him coming so they quickly stood from where they were sitting on. Kenji tried to stop crying and quickly wiped his tears though he was still sobbing.

"We do not allow men for being so emotional here in this plane," said the UE leader in a joke. "But I understand what that means… how is too difficult to part ways with a best friend," then he stroked Kenji's hair.

Kenji tried to control his tears from falling when Claude answered.

"Well… though he's a grown up, he's still a crybaby perhaps," he said jokingly.

The UE leader laughed and he spread his arms. "Alright! Anyway, welcome to the Ultimate Explorer which is the lowest class of the Explorers organization. My name is Elijah Tylers, the leader of this class," then he offered his hand to shake hands with the two and told a joke. "I am twenty-five years old and still single in life, hehehe… I've been the leader of the class for three years."

"It's nice to meet you. My name is Kenji…" greeted Kenji.

Elijah turned straight to Kenji. "Kenji, huh? Your name sounds very unique and I like it. Anyway, I already know the name of this young man, Claude."

Claude smiled at him.

"Well Kenji, can I please take a look at the stone you are holding now? Maybe that is one of the sacred stones we have always been looking for."

Kenji asked. "How many do you all need?"

Elijah frowned scratching his chin. "Um, much more!"

"Is that mean we will be staying here with you?"

"If the stone you are holding reveals that it is a Divine Stone indeed, then I will recruit you to become an Explorer!"

Kenji smiled and he showed the stone to Elijah. "Here… Shingue already made an observation to this stone and he said that this is a Divine Stone of Recovery…"

"Tsk, great!" said Elijah. "You are very lucky of owning that kind of a rare Sacred Item. I will make you an Explorer if…" he first looked Kenji's appearance from head to toe. "If you are a good fighter as well…"

Claude chuckled and bragged. "Ah, Elijah… My friend has been ripped with experiences. He already fought some powerful warriors you ever know!"

"W-What do you mean?"

"You know the group of Humorian and Pioneer, right?"

"Yes?"

"Well, Kenji fought against them and beat all of them!"

Elijah was amazed in very wide-eyes. "Oh? How did that happen? Those warriors were powerful as you might've expect. Especially Pioneers!"

"I… I don't know…"

"K-Kenji, it is true what your friend just say? Huh, is it really true?"

Shingue shook his head, but Kenji nodded awkwardly. He faltered. "Y-Yes sir, that is true…"

Elijah was in disbelief and he scratched his chin again. "Ah well, maybe it's true indeed… I-It seems that you're good… I can tell it by your appearance…"

Kenji smiled when Elijah spoke again. The UE members approached them looking straight at them seriously.

"Well, first I want you to prove your story to us. I want to see exactly your moves you made when you fought those guys. But not for now… By tomorrow I will challenge you and Claude to take our tests to see and prove your worth, do you understand me?"

"And how about the stone?"

"Tonight we will begin to analyze and examine the stone you've got. I want proof."

Kenji nodded again. "Okay, go ahead."

"But for now, errr... I'll give you the time to take some rest first. And please wipe off your tears. You see, this class wants a happy team since we are more lenient than the two higher classes. When the time comes that you get to the DDE, which is the highest class of the Explorers organization, then I am certain that you will miss this team so bad. Hahaha!" said Elijah jokingly.

"He's right Kenji, and do your best! We are looking forward to you to become a part of our team!" agreed one of the UE members.

Kenji gave the stone to Elijah with care. "May I take this stone with me for now?" asked Elijah.

Kenji's face suddenly changed expression. "Now? But I thought you said tonight?"

"We will also try to begin the observation earlier than we expect. After all, our other colleagues don't have their assignment for now so I can just ask them to start the observation with me."

"M-Maybe later... Not now..."

Elijah stepped back in surprise. "What? What? Hey man, how come you are not following my first command?! That is strictly forbidden, especially that I am the leader of this class!"

Claude answered instead of Kenji. "Well sir, it is because that stone is a special gift to him by someone he cares. A remembrance, in other words."

"Remembrance to him? By whom?"

"By the little girl..."

"That little girl I saw crying before him earlier was the one who obtained this stone? I thought Kenji only asked her to keep the stone in her pocket and lend back to him before he left the village."

"Yes."

"Then that little girl should be the one who is coming along with Shingue here, am I right?"

Claude faced Shingue with regret. "Shingue, I thought that the child is not allowed to join in your group? Now I begin to regret that we should take Valerie with us earlier..."

"A young person with a same age as Valerie is allowed to join in our group, Claude. But Valerie is an inexperienced child when it comes in fighting so she cannot pass the tests. And also, she will be having difficulty to train herself to learn combat techniques since she is too demure."

Claude stooped his head unbelievably. "Demure? Really?"

A little boy suddenly appeared before them who was not wearing his Explorer uniform. Claude noticed the boy and he pointed at him in wonder.

"Oh, so there surely is a kid in this group," said Claude.

"Yeah, he's just a boy but he's a really good warrior. His name is Marion," introduced Shingue.

"Ha-yaaaahhhh!" cried the little boy while proudly demonstrating his martial arts to Claude and Kenji. "My name is Marion, a young Explorer. Ha-yaaahhh!!!" he was showing a nice intro, proving that he was an experienced warrior despite his very young age.

"Wow, how impressive…" Kenji was impressed. "How old are you now, Marion?"

"I am nine years old, ha-yaaaahhh!!!"

Kenji laughed and told a joke. "Hahaha, how come a nine-year old warrior becomes so arrogant? Hahaha!"

Marion got pissed off instantly. He hated being referred by someone as "arrogant". So as his answer, he quickly kicked Kenji's face as strong as he could, and the young man suddenly stumbled on the other side of the wall.

"Geez Marion, that's bad!" stopped Elijah and he gripped Marion's arms. "Don't you do that to our guest!"

"It is because he said that I am arrogant!" shouted Marion.

"Well… i-it is because h-he just slipped off his tongue--"

"Bleeehhh!" teased the naughty kid at Elijah and he struggled. "Whatever! Let me go and I will leave!"

Elijah took off his hands in Marion's arms. Then the naughty kid began to demonstrate his moves again arrogantly before them. "Ha-yaaahhh!" then he left.

Kenji was speechless about what happened and so as Claude. He touched his cheek that quickly flushed when Elijah approached him and sincerely apologized. "Um, I am so sorry about that, Kenji. Um, you see…" then he whispered. "That kid is the youngest and really the naughtiest Explorer in the entire group. I want to let you know that he really hated being referred by someone negatively and he will surely harm you. Actually, he already did that to some of our guests even to his fellow Explorers… so sometimes we're embarrassed to his mischievousness," then he sighed. "But despite of his mischievousness, Marion is one of our best Explorers in our organization!"

Kenji was silent. He was only gaping at Elijah while still touching his flushed cheek by the naughtiest Explorer kid!

20 THREE STONES

Meanwhile in the world of gods and goddesses called Kingdom of the Gods, the different creatures were all living together peacefully and in harmony.

Isidra still in distress remained in her room, but she often walked outside to wander around the kingdom. The other fairies transported again in the human world to look for other sacred objects. She was still being grounded by the new king of the gods to come along with her fellow fairies in the human world.

It's been too many years that Isidra had endured the pain and anguish. And she never seen her children yet as well as her beloved husband until now. She had been thinking what they were all doing now.

Isidra got sick often times due to her excessive depression. At present, she was recovering from fever and she needed more time to rest physically, mentally, and emotionally.

The day came when she could no longer endure her depression and the worries that killing her. She wanted to go back in the human world so badly!

Isidra pulled out the three stones from her chest that she secretly kept hidden in the eyes of every gods for a long time. "What if I show these stones to our lord and maybe, just maybe he will change his heart and allow me to go back in the human world?"

She thought of counting the years she kept the stone in her chest. It's been several years!

"I really want to go back in the human world. I am getting bored in here!" then she cried.

Isidra was still weak and not fully recovered from fever. She got up on her bed thinking of going over the king. "I am going to our lord and show these stones to him... I am ready with my answers, in case he will ask me..."

Isidra opened the door and went out the room. There were only few creatures seen outside and in the hallway. Feeling dizzy, she walked alone in the hallway leading to the king's throne. She was eager to see the king, and the king's throne was not too far from her room.

She walked slowly to Zalan's throne. From time to time, she paused for a moment to catch her breath. To guide her way to the king's throne, she needed to touch the brick walls as she was walking in the hallway. She was determined to show the stones she got to the king and thought this would might help her to change his mind and allow her to transport back to the human world.

When the fairy of love came close to the new king's home, she suddenly felt nervous and scared. She reached the high Gate of Heavens which was the entrance of King Zalan's home. First, she watched the high stairs going up to the high building and took a deep, deep breath.

"I-I can do this..."

Not from afar, a unique creature called unicorn was watching her when she reached the gate of heaven. The unicorn approached Isidra.

"Is there anything you need, dear fairy of love?" asked a unicorn to Isidra.

"Um, it's nothing..." answered Isidra smiling. "But I just want to see the king and talk to him personally..."

"For what reason?"

"About ummm...."

The unicorn spread and flapped its two wings in front of the fairy.

"We cannot allow somebody to enter the king's home since he is busy doing something important for now..." said the unicorn.

"But, I need to talk to the king and it's also important... To talk to him... Really important."

The unicorn closed its eyes and took a deep breath. "I do not know. I do not want to disobey the king's order not unless if the security of the kingdom is at stake...."

Isidra smiled. "Do not worry. I'll take care of this."

"What do you mean?"

Isidra smiled again when she lifted her hands to show the shining three stones to the unicorn. "I'll show these to him!"

The unicorn got dazzled by the sparking light emitted by the stones then he asked Isidra. "Are those... Magic Stones?!"

"Yes. So... Maybe you can allow me to see our king now because I am pretty sure he is interested to see these stones, isn't he?"

The unicorn just mouthed in surprise and it agreed. "Ah... Yes...Yes. You may now enter the gate."

By the unicorn's power, the Gate of Heavens slowly opened in front of Isidra when she smiled again sweetly. "I am going in this gate now. Thank you."

The unicorn nodded when Isidra entered the gate. She stepped on the high stairs, slowly ascending on every steps until she reached the king's home. There were many fairies and other creatures in there having their merry-gathering, but they were all surprised to see Isidra inside the building. The fairy of love only ignored them, while the creatures were following their sight on her as she walked alone in the middle of the hall.

"Isidra, what makes you bring here to our lord's home and you aren't still fully recovered? You're suppose to be in your room resting until you get yourself recovered from your high fever!" said a fairy.

Isidra stopped walking and turned to a fairy. "Yes, because... there is something important that I want to show to him."

"Show something important? What is it then?"

Isidra dared to show off the shining stones again as she lifted her hands up high.

"Ahhh!" everyone got dazzled as well by the strong light coming out from the three stones.

"So, will you let me go and see our king now?"

"O-Okay, go ahead..." said a fairy. The other fairies and creatures only nodded at Isidra as they agreed.

"Lord Zalan is in his throne... Over there!" said the other fairy then she pointed the direction towards the king's throne room. "Surely he will be amazed to see those stones you obtained, Isidra."

Isidra continued her way going to the throne room while everyone was still watching her walking alone in the hall silently.

She kept the three stones back in her chest and went out the hall.

THE EXPLORERS

When she entered the main realm of the gods, more creatures were stunned to see her entering alone despite of her illness. They all looked straight at the beautiful fairy of love.

"Look, it's Isidra. Why is she here? I believe she is still sick up to now…" whispered a creature to the other creature.

Everyone was murmuring to each other while Isidra was walking her way to the king's throne. At least this time she was lucky enough to have a close encounter with the king.

The fairy who was Isidra's friend saw her and she approached. "Isidra, why are you here? You still have a fever!"

"I want to show these stones to our lord now. And I am too desperate to go back in the human world to see my family again," said Isidra.

"You are talking about the stones you got a long time ago right?"

Isidra nodded. "Yes, is the king still busy?"

"I don't know, but he is all alone in his throne room right now."

"I will talk to him… But I am scared to face him."

"Don't worry," said the fairy. "I will accompany you there and assist you for a while."

The fairy took Isidra to the throne room of King Zalan. There, they saw the king sitting on his throne alone while resting. The variety of Sacred Items obtained by the fairies in the human world were hovering around him. Isidra was so eager to show the three stones to him.

Later, her fairy friend knelt before the king. "You have to kneel before him, Isidra."

Isidra also knelt when the fairy spoke to their lord. "King Zalan, I am sorry to interrupt you this time but my friend Isidra wants to talk something important to you."

The king slowly opened his eyes and answered in question. "What is it about then?"

The fairy turned to Isidra. "I am leaving now, Isidra. I have to leave this conversation between you and our lord."

Isidra smiled. "Thank you for bringing me here, Skuld."

"You're welcome. I hope everything will turn out to be good…"

The fairy stood back on her own feet and then she flew off the room. What only left now were Isidra and King Zalan.

After the short silence, King Zalan asked again. "What is it that we'll talk about Isidra?"

Isidra was nervous. "My lord... there is something I would like to show you... Something I know that you are also needing..."

"What is it then, Isidra?"

Isidra put her hand in her chest once again to pull out the three shining stones and she lifted them before the king. King Zalan was thoroughly amazed to see the stones that were still shining so bright in his eyes.

"The sacred stones... those are Magic Stones!"

"Yes, my lord... I obtained these stones."

"O-Obtained?" asked the king surprisingly. "And how did you obtain those stones even though I already forbid you to go in the human world? Did you manage to escape behind my back?!"

"I have to confess to you my, lord... These stones had been kept hidden by me when I was still in the human world. I already obtained them in their world before I came back here to our kingdom... Kept hidden for a long time ago."

"It means that you already have those stones for a very long time, Isidra. But why didn't you show them to me before? Why just now?"

"Because... I am afraid that you might get angry at me again and punish me, my lord... Since I already made my mistake before by revealing my real identity to the humans..."

"And why should I punish you? I should be glad that you have obtained those sacred stones because they are also the ones we need that should remain in our kingdom!"

Isidra began to weep. "Please... take these stones, my lord," then she gave the stones to the king.

"Thank you Isidra," said Zalan smiling. "In spite of the punishment I rendered to you, still you have been faithful to me. Very well then, since you've got three stones then a reward must be given to you."

Isidra opened her eyes wide. "A reward? What do you mean by a reward, my lord?"

"A reward that something I should give back to you in return, because you still showed your loyalty to me and to all... And I am very impressed that you obtained three stones in the world of men at the same time. Unlike the other fairies, they could not give me the number of stones as same as yours."

"Did they already obtain the lost elements of King Jethro, my lord?"

Zalan shook his head. "Well, they said that they still have difficulty in finding the elements of our supreme lord, King Jethro… and they believe that they are very impossible to find. The world of men is always affecting its natural balance if the Divine Stones do not return to their true forms such as the element of Air, Water, Earth, Fire, Light, and more…"

Isidra pointed the Sacred Items around the king that were not very important. "What about those sacred objects, my lord?"

"Ah… The fairies obtained them as soon as they entered the human world. They are not as powerful and important as the sacred stones, but they should also remain in our possession because they have a great influence in maintaining the balance of power in the human world as well as the entire universe."

Isidra in her sad face. "That means… still none of us have obtain at least one of the fourteen long-lost elements…"

"None… And the world of men is getting worse today."

Isidra bowed in silence when the king spoke again.

"Isidra, because of your loyalty… I am giving you the opportunity to have a reward of your choice…."

Isidra lifted her face. "My lord?"

"I will give you a chance to ask one request and I shall grant it."

Isidra's eyes widened, gaping in surprise. She immediately thought of asking to bring her back in the human world in order to find her family. *This is my chance…* She thought to herself.

"Now Isidra, what is it that you want?" asked Zalan.

Isidra was silent.

"What is it, Isidra? Speak. Or do you still feeling unwell?"

"N-No it's not, my lord… But I am only too scared to ask this to you."

"Why Isidra? What is it then? I would like to know."

Isidra's face blushed. "I… I have been wanting to go back to the human world to look for my family… I-I am begging you, my lord… It's been a long time I'm too desperate to go back there and be with them again…" then she burst out crying, while begging to the new king.

"And why do you ask me about that? Is there anything that you want to ask aside from that?"

"There is nothing more I would like to ask, my lord…"

Zalan stroked his chin. "Impossible! Did I already forbid you to transport back to their world at any time, didn't I? You have committed a grave mistake by revealing yourself and showed your real identity to the humans. You disobeyed our laws! Ask me anything and your wish will be granted."

"But my dear lord… I've been all alone here… I am so desperate to see my children again! Please have pity on me… I promise… W-When I get to the world of men, I will permanently change my true form so they will never recognize me anymore. From head to toe!"

"How will you do that? Everybody there already knows you!"

"Not all the people there already know me, my lord…" said Isidra still crying. "Please King Zalan, I swear I will never do that again. I am begging you… I've always been alone and so lonely!" then she pulled the king's coat and stood. "I am so worried for my family and really wanting to see them all again!"

Zalan did not know what to react whether he should feel pity towards Isidra or not. Because he knew that Isidra was the only living creature that always remained in their kingdom and completely alone.

Isidra spoke again. "I promise that I will change my identity again and will never speak to any humans that I do not know," then she came closer to Zalan and kissed his foot. The god was surprised, but this softened his heart when he realized that the fairy of love looked more pathetic, and he heard that the fairy had been suffering depression several times that caused her to get sick very often.

The fairy was still sobbing in her head stooped. "Please my lord… That is only my simple request I would like to ask from you and nothing else…"

The king only nodded his head and raised both of his hands. "Isidra, promise me again that you will never do the mistake you already did in the past. You understand me?"

Isidra quickly raised her head. "My lord?"

"You see, my heart hurts more everytime I see a fairy of love always depressed… You almost get bathed by your own tears, you always get sick, you rarely eat and sleep, and always being too emotional. Besides, I hate to see you crying right now and suddenly faint before me. And I don't want to let that happen to you…"

Isidra was silent.

"Fine, I will allow you again Isidra. But this time, there is someone here that I will ask to join and assist you during your travel in the human world. You hear me?"

Isidra's face slowly came alive. Her beautiful lips began to smile wider than before. "Re... Re-Really?"

"Pfff..." King Zalan only sighed with a smile. "Yes, your wish is now granted. So I will let you go again freely as before, my dear fairy of love."

Due to the fairy's overexcitement, she could not help it but to hug the king tightly and kissed his foot once again. "Oh, thank you very much for this King Zalan!" she said happily.

King Zalan let go of Isidra's hands. "I shall summon the two unicorns who will be assisting you on your search," then he summoned the unicorns. The two beautiful creatures appeared in the throne room and they approached Isidra. One unicorn, named Meru was a female unicorn, while the other unicorn, named Pegan was male. "Choose one of these unicorns that will guide you there, Isidra..." he instructed.

Isidra pointed one unicorn. "I will choose Meru."

"Alright! From now on, Meru will be your guard wherever you go in the human world, Isidra. Anyway, why don't you take some rest before moving?"

"W-Well, I am in a hurry King Zalan. Besides, I am feeling better now..."

"Then go freely again and leave. And Isidra... I thank you again for saving these three stones back to our kingdom!"

Isidra smiled sweetly. "You are always welcome, my lord."

"Take care and good luck."

Zalan cast a special magic on the floor that would bring the two to the world of men. A portal called "Human World Dimension Floor" appeared on the floor and it opened. Isidra mounted on Meru, and she was an experienced horse rider.

"Please get in this portal now and may King Jethro guide you on your safe journey," said Zalan.

"Nyeeehhh!!!" Meru whined and they entered down the Dimension Floor together. Then, the portal slowly vanished right after they left Zalan's throne room.

21 EXPLORERS

Elijah gave the two young men a small private cabin of the HawkEye where they could relax and rest while they were still in the middle of the trip. Elijah would not want Shingue to stay with the two, but Shingue refused as he wanted to join them. Vamir chuckled.

"Why Shingue? Don't tell me you're a gay, hahaha!" said Vamir jokingly. "You have your own personal cabin here, right? But why do you want to stay with them in their room?"

"Because they are my friends," answered Shingue.

"Oh really?"

"Yes."

Kenji and Claude stayed inside the cabin. Silence. Later, Kenji put the ice cubes in a small plastic bag that Shingue gave and then he put it on his flushed cheek. Claude noticed him and wondered.

"Kenji, I don't think the kick you've got is not that hard and besides you don't have mumps. You should not use ice bag. Hey, it's snowy day!"

Kenji was still holding the ice pack on his cheek and answered. "Mind your own business."

"Whoa!"

As for Shingue, he mingled with his fellow Explorers and close friends whom he met again after a long time and talked with them for some updates.

"By the way," Shingue peered around the aisle. "Where's Arthur?"

"He is already back home in our mansion. Eh, why didn't you guys go home together? Are you cool with each other?" asked one of UE in question.

"No," Shingue chuckled. "I just, you know... Um, let him go on his own..."

"Because Kenji and Claude are there?"

"Ah yes. I just want to help them."

"How kindly you are."

"Oh yes, I am!"

As for Claude and Kenji...

"Kenji, I can feel how strong and painful that naughty kid kicked on your face. Damn, that hurts!" said Claude staring closer at Kenji's face.

"Yes."

"Whoa, that kid is so aggressive! Maybe Valerie might also get kicked by that kid if she calls him 'arrogant' by mistake. But you know, you are right Kenji. Marion is so, so arrogant--"

"Shhh..." shushed Kenji.

"Now I begin to feel that I don't like that kid, Kenji..."

"Shhh... I said!"

Claude sat on the floor in Indian-sit. "Do you still have the stone in your hands?"

"Nope, I already gave it to Elijah."

"I think he is kind, isn't he?"

Kenji nodded. "Aha, he is... And also all of them..."

Claude moved closer to Kenji and teasingly watched his face when he was about to laugh. "Kenji, now I clearly see your face. Your eyes are not just swollen, but also your cheek! I can imagine your face being attacked by the swarm of bees!"

"Whatever you say, Claude..."

Claude covered his mouth trying not to laugh, still looking at Kenji's face. Kenji glared at him, but this time he could no longer hold his laughter anymore so he laughed out loud.

"I-I'm so sorry, Kenji... Ahahahahaha!!!"

Kenji felt embarrassed so he quickly pinched Claude's arm surreptitiously.

"Ouch! That's painful..." said Claude rubbing his arm.

"So just keep your mouth shut and mind your own business," said Kenji in his low voice.

"I-I am really so sorry... It's just that, um... I am getting hungry that's why!"

"Ahhh…"

Shingue came in their private cabin and waved at them happily. "Kenji, Claude, just a few minutes and we will reach our base. The Ultimate Explorer Mansion!"

Kenji was eager to see the base. "Just a few minutes, eh? I am getting excited!"

"Yes. Our estimated time of arrival to our destination is fifteen minutes, buddy! By the way, I already reserved a personal room for you two in the mansion."

"Aren't you staying with us in your requested reserved room, Shingue?" asked Claude.

"I have my own room there, Claude."

Kenji got excited again. "That means that you guys are really wealthy, aren't you?"

Shingue scratched his head smiling. "If you ask the Explorers, yes… But if you just ask me alone, well I am not wealthy…"

Kenji's face blushed. "Man, do you think Claude and I are too awkward when we get to your mansion? Y-You know, Claude and I were not born with a silver spoon. We are only poor, and we are not used to live in a mansion like you used to…"

"My goodness Kenji, stop saying that! We are not looking for a person's wealth; but only his potential, determination, and worth as a true warrior of Explorers."

Kenji smiled and nodded. "Thank you, Shingue…"

Shingue looked at his watch. "We are getting closer and closer. The Explorers raised each of the aircraft's speeds so we will arrive in the mansion earlier before the storm returns. It is better to safe than sorry…"

"Correct, and also to prevent any possible engine trouble!" said Claude.

Kenji prepared their bags ready when he suddenly felt nervous. "I am feeling awkward."

After fifteen minutes, the three Explorer HawkEyes had finally arrived in the mansion safely and none of the aircrafts encountered engine trouble. Kenji and Claude rushed over the cabin window to look at the huge mansion of Ultimate Explorer below. The two smiled in excitement but at the same time they were also feeling uncomfortable.

THE EXPLORERS

The three aircrafts made their safe landing when the other group of Ultimate Explorers came out of the mansion to meet the arriving party. Some of them were wearing their uniforms while others were on their casual outfits. Kenji was amazed to see that the UE warriors were really too many.

The aircrafts' exits slowly opened when the passengers descended on the ramps. Elijah came down first, followed by the UE members.

Shingue quickly pulled Kenji's arm who was feeling shy to come down the plane and meet the other Explorers.

"Come on, Kenji! We need to go down now and I'll introduce you two to the Explorers!"

"Just me and Claude, Shingue?"

"Ahhh, whatever... Isn't it obvious? Let's go down now!"

Kenji was still shy. "Ah Shingue, maybe we'll just go out later, a lot of Explorers are still outside the plane. Let us wait for them to go back to the mansion before we proceed..."

"No way, stop that! I'll leave you and Claude here instead if you don't want to go out in the plane."

"N-No, please don't do this to us, Shingue..."

Elijah came over the three and signaled them to go out the plane now. "Pssstt... What are you still doing here? Geez, There's no room for shyness in this mansion and you have to come down now!"

Claude spoke to Elijah jokingly. "Certainly, this is just our first time to set foot in a huge mansion like this.... And we should stand tall to show them our good-looking appearance!"

Kenji was still blushing. "I-I will try..."

Shingue quickly pulled Kenji's arm and pushed him hard out of the plane exit. "Nah, you don't just try... You actually have to do it!"

Shingue gave Kenji a strong push causing him to scamper over the ramp and get exposed. The UEs quickly turned their gaze at the young man as he came out.

"Wow, that guy is surely so cute and handsome!" said an Explorer who was gay. "A surprise gift for me that suddenly fell out in the sky..."

Kenji got blushed from what he just heard. He never expected a gay member in the Ultimate Explorer class.

Claude and Shingue also descended from a plane and walked on the ramp when Elijah spoke to the UE warriors.

"UE warriors your attention please. May I introduce to you the new neophytes who are dare to take our tests and become a part of our class! We took them in Sierra Village and Shingue was the one who meet them during their long training."

The UE applauded when the gay came closer to Elijah and asked in whisper. "Who is he, Elijah? The one handsome guy in white?"

Shingue answered instead of Elijah who was only next to Kenji and Claude. "Oh Margot, these are Kenji and Claude. My new friends."

The gay giggled. "Ah! So Kenji is the name of the cute guy I was asking. A gift from heaven!!!"

Kenji asked in wonder. "What gift?"

"I thank you guys for the gift by bringing this young beautiful man in front of me, since my birthday was just a day ago, yes? *Cha-ruuussshhh!*"

The UEs shook their heads in embarrassment over their fellow Explorer's actuations when Elijah apologized once again. "I am so sorry for his actions... Margot is only barefaced and he has been looking for someone he wants to, um… I think you already know what I mean, right?"

Kenji only nodded in hesitation as an answer.

Elijah also nodded. "Well, we're so sorry for you... You see, his birthday was just a day ago that's why he thinks that you are our special gift to him…"

"Y-Yes, I understand…" Kenji faltered.

"Well, just have fun with Margot and I tell you that he is a certified sincere lover. But you know what? Honestly he is absolutely an extraordinary warrior. Imagine, he had made a record of defeating a Pioneer in the past tournament?!"

Kenji nodded again in uncertainty.

Elijah patted Kenji's shoulder. "And always remember that this class is the friendliest among the Explorer classes!" then he whispered in a joke. "By a bit of my advice, just watch yourself to that gay or you might lose your freedom forever... Geez, he is falling in love with you in an instant and that is what we called, 'love at first sight'. Hahahaha!!!"

"Okay…" agreed Kenji by force. "Well, good luck to me then."

Elijah turned to the Explorers. "Let them come inside the mansion."

Shingue took the two to their mansion along with the other Explorers. Margot walked towards Kenji and the young man noticed the gay was approaching him. He frightened, as if he wanted to disappear in the midst now though he really did not want to!

Kenji moved straight over Claude and hid in his back.

"Claude, just ignore me and keep on walking," said Kenji in Claude's back.

Shingue chuckled. "Hahaha, don't you like Margot? He is gay, but a sweet true lover indeed."

Kenji answered still behind Claude. "It doesn't matter to me! How come he falls in love with me in an instant?!"

"Mister Kenji… Too-hoo… Where are you?" said Margot pretending that he did not see the young man in playful way.

Kenji whispered to Claude. "Claude, I do not understand what really is going on in this group. This is not what I expect from them. Yes, they are real Explorers, but look at them… They are acting like high school students! They do not get too serious in this group…"

Claude in his listless face. "Yeah, I even noticed that…"

Shingue heard the two. "Of course, don't be so serious. Have some fun as what Elijah said!"

"Shingue, what about my stone? Where is it now?"

"I have it. Elijah gave it to me first and later they will begin the observation."

"Just take good care of it, okay? That stone is very special to me."

"Kenji… Whoo-hoo… Where are youuuu??!"

Kenji was unaware of Claude's action by quickly pushing him out in order to get exposed once again so the gay saw him.

"Aha, there you are! I actually knew it, tee-hee… Now come with me!" said Margot pointing at Kenji and he approached.

"Ahhh!!!" cried Kenji, but he did not run. "N-No, I will be staying here with Shingue."

Claude refused as he was still pushing Kenji. "No, I don't want to be involved in this nonsense thing so take him now."

Kenji suddenly glared towards Claude. "Claude, what are you doing--"

Claude smiled at the gay. "Come on, Ms. Margot. Kenji is completely yours now. You can take him alone to your mansion and have fun…"

Kenji glared more at Claude while Margot was putting his arm around Kenji's shoulder and together they moved away.

When Kenji and Margot went away, Claude felt a guilt for what he had done. Now that Kenji was gone to his sight and what he had left next to him was Shingue.

"Damn... I-I realized that I shouldn't give Kenji to that gay..." said Claude in regret.

Shingue shook and scratched his head. "Geez, Claude! I know Margot so much... When he falls in love with Kenji, then he will never ever let him go and never bring him back to us!"

"Wha-What? Really? Why is that?"

"Can't you see the spark in Margot's eyes? He wants him so bad and wants him for life!"

"Does he really like males?"

"Isn't it too obvious?! What do you expect from a gay? Falling deeply in love with a woman?!"

"Is there no other man here that is also as cute as Kenji? Why don't he just fall in love with that guy instead?"

"There is one... but that guy also doesn't like Margot. Previously, he was Margot's crush and he was always being flirted by him. But, it happened one day when the guy could no longer hold his patience with Margot when he suddenly punched him directly on the face... He felt sorry for what he did, because he really did not mean to do it. It's just that... well, he got pissed at Margot's advances that's all..."

"Who is he then?"

"Nothing else but Rain! He was totally pissed at Margot that time since he was a serious type of guy. A guy who doesn't like to be flirted, no time for nonsense chitchat, and a loner!"

"Rain is the name of the guy you are talking about? Is that a man's name?!"

"Probably yes."

"But why the hell his name sounds too funny? Heh, I believe that guy might be gay too that is why!"

Shingue laughed out loud. "If he is here with us and he hears you, let's see what he is going to do to you next. Hahahaha!"

"Why Shingue? Are you scaring me over to that guy? I only said that because his name sounds not too masculine!"

"That is just his nickname, hahaha!!!"

"You know what, Shingue? You're only saying that he is not gay, but actually he really is. Come to think of it, like poles repel each other and so as the gays. Do you think that there is something in him that we do not know?"

Shingue burst into laugher. "Hahaha! He will tear your skin into pieces if he hears you right now, you'll see!"

Then after goofing around, the two continued to walk together leading to the UE mansion.

As for Kenji and Margot...

Margot toured Kenji inside the huge mansion. Margot showed the young man their laboratory, pool, computer room, activity area, and more. They also reached the long hallway, where big portraits of the past Explorers were mounted each on the walls.

The tour continued, while Margot's arm was still on Kenji's shoulder and Kenji wanted to just leave the gay alone. His face was pale, as if he was dipped in vinegar!

"Come," said the flirty gay. "Elijah said that I should show you your new room now."

"S-Sure," agreed Kenji and he gulped.

"Kenji, why is it that I am the only one putting my arm on your shoulder, hm? You suppose to be doing this to me, please!"

Kenji's face was still pale. "I can't Margot... I... I am getting lame actually!"

"Oh, are you injured? Come near me and I shall give you lots of love!"

"N-No, please! I don't want to, Margot... Thank you alright! J-Just... take me to our room now. Show it to me."

The flirty gay in his sad face. "All right... Um, but don't you still want to put your arm around my shoulder?"

"N-No!" Kenji quickly shook his head in hesitation.

The two went to another hallway when Margot showed Kenji the private room of Elijah, followed by Vamir's, Shingue's, and so on. Lastly, they reached a room where there was a tag name posted on its door: "MARGOT". Margot innocently opened the said door of his room when Kenji noticed the tag name on it.

"And this will be the new room of where you sleep, my Kenji..." said Margot smiling.

Kenji stepped back surprisingly. "W-What?! Wait a minute... This is your room, isn't it?"

The gay put his hands on his hip pretending he knew nothing. "Huh? How come that this room is mine? Elijah told me that this is your room."

"Look, up there!" Kenji pointed the tag name on the door. "You name has it. This room is officially yours not mine."

The gay screamed on top of his voice that would surely hurt Kenji's ears. "Eeeeee!!! I forgot to remove the tag, ohhhh..." then he quickly pulled away the tag and just threw it on the floor. "N-No Kenji, it's nothing... This is your new room now!"

Kenji began to glare towards Margot. "I said I don't want to, Margot... Anyway, thank you for the tour and I need to go back to my friends now. I will be joining them," then he turned away.

"But... Oh my dear sweet Kenji..."

Kenji was about to leave Margot and walked leading back to his friends when he met a man wearing his Explorer uniform. The man was tall, handsome, and well built. Margot caught his attention and fell in love again with the guy, but at the same time he was scared.

"H-Ha? It's my Rain... Ahhh!!!" Margot giggled at first seeing his long time crush then he moved away in flirty way, seducing the two to follow his back and chase him.

The two men remained standstill. Kenji smiled delightfully when the gay was already gone.

Silence. Rain spoke first.

"I can't quite imagine how Margot also does the same thing on you, doesn't he?"

Kenji scratched his head. "Certainly, hehe... Um, but why is he afraid at you?"

Rain smiled. "It is because that guy also likes me, but I really hate what he always does on me. One time, when I could no longer hold my temper because of his advances, I accidentally punched his face. You know because..."

"Well, it is because you are a very good-looking guy... He couldn't hold his self control. Ahm..."

"So you are the young man who obtained the stone of Recovery. Where did you get that?"

"Ahm... I-In..."

"Nevermind," said Rain and he offered his hand to Kenji to shake hands with him. "My name is Reinhardt, and not 'Rain'. That is just how my friends used to call me in short. I am Elijah's assistant leader and sometimes a spy. Explorers' one of the spies..."

"Hi Reinhardt..." greeted Kenji and they shook hands together. "My name is Kenji."

Reinhardt nodded. "Nice to meet you, Kenji. I am a twenty-two year old Explorer and a missionary as a sidejob."

"You're a missionary? Why? Do you plan of becoming a priest?"

"Not as in priesthood, but a missionary who spreads good words for all of us to be saved. I am used to read holy books whenever I have a chance to do so, and memorize the entire contents because I always have it since childhood... Which makes me want to live a simple and normal life, and I hate flirts like Margot always does... Or should we call him in his real name as Mark," then he altered the topic. "So, are you planning of becoming an Explorer and join our class?"

Kenji nodded. "If I am worthy enough to become one of you, then I'm on it."

"Perhaps they will recruit you. I can see the potential in you and I am sure that you can pass the challenges we will give you."

"W-Why? Aren't they too difficult to handle?"

Reinhardt caught his attention when he noticed something on Kenji and ignored the question.

"W-Wait a minute... Your chin... There are two studs pierced on your chin!" said Reinhardt as he was pointing Kenji's chin.

Kenji touched his chin. "Ah, yes indeed. My stepfather said that these studs were already in my chin since birth..."

Reinhardt quickly pulled Kenji's collar to move closer to him. "No way... Don't tell me... YOU!"

Kenji was startled and hesitated by Reinhardt's serious stare. The missionary moved his face closer to Kenji's chin to examine the two studs.

"R-Reinhardt, so what about if I have these two studs in my chin?"

Reinhardt answered in his sharp voice. "You... You are one of my missing brothers... The son of Isidra and Alex Foster!"

22 THE EXPERIMENT

Reinhardt was still pulling Kenji's shirt. His sharp eyes were looking directly at the studs as he gently touched both of them while examining.

Kenji was mum, gaping before Reinhardt. Confused on what he heard and he did not know what to do or say. He only gulped.

Reinhardt moved his face closer to Kenji's face, still touching both of the studs in the young man's chin gently. Kenji was still silent.

"So it is true… Our studs are really identical…" said Reinhardt in low voice.

Kenji gulped again in an awkward look. "Our studs? Do you also have the same studs as I have?"

Reinhardt quickly answered in his high tone. "Yes! Your studs are exactly the same as mine. Look!" then he showed his pair of studs that was pierced in his left arm. "These are the studs we inherited by our mother who is a fairy. These are the birthmark we all same have to attest that the blood in your vein is the same as mine!"

Kenji could not believe of what he had discovered and one of the plain truths he had been seeking throughout his life. He was still in shock and could not believe what was happening, but he could see in Reinhardt's face that the man was not lying… and there was an evidence that he just saw. Moreover, he learned that Reinhardt knew something that he also knew beforehand!

"Is that mean… that me and my brother Genji are not just the only sons of our parents?" asked Kenji.

Reinhardt answered calmly. "No, we are eight. And we were all fled by

THE EXPLORERS

our mother whose name is Isidra to save us from the hands of the invading enemies."

"W-What? Eight, you say?!"

"Yes, but… I do not remember your existence. I was very young at that time to know what was going on. By the way, we have two younger sisters, named Rebecca and Diana. But they are triplets as their other half is our brother."

Kenji shed tears with excitement. "I… I have a twin brother, Reinhardt. Genji… His name is Genji Foster!"

"Ah! So you are my younger brother who has a twin brother, but 'Kenji' is not your real name. I remember now, your real name is 'Maximillian' while your twin brother's name is 'Denver'… Anyway, where did you get those weird names, huh?"

Kenji could no longer hold his excitement when he suddenly hugged his long lost brother. Reinhardt did not even expect in his wild imagination of seeing one of his long-missing siblings again… Maximillian Foster.

The two let go of each other when Kenji answered. "Those names were given to us by our stepfather who adopted us and raised as what we are now today. He said that he found us in a basket on board the ship."

"And Denver? Where is your twin brother now?"

Kenji stooped his head sadly. "We parted our ways in Damsville… Long time ago."

"I know that place you mentioned and I'd been there before. The Explorers used to travel each and every part of the world just to look and search for those missing Sacred Items."

"Um, so who is older to us?"

"I am the eldest among eight Kenji, or Maximillian I should say… I am your older brother."

Kenji hugged his older brother once again. "*Kuya* Reinhardt… I thought I would be completely alone and would never see you forever…"

"That was what I even thought. I've been in UE for long, but up to now I am still looking for all of you and I never stop. But being a part of this class is not good enough for me; I have a main goal… to become a part of the DDE class so that I will see our father."

"Brother… From now on, I am with you in finding our brothers and sisters. I will not let the time come that you and I will be apart again."

"You are right… we will never let that happen anymore."

Silence. Later, Reinhardt spoke again. "Maximillian, you told me earlier that Denver was in Damsville. I just got my assignment today and will be off on the next day by aircraft. I will be wandering around in different places to look for more of what the Explorers need. Why don't you come with me and we will search together?"

"Are you coming back there?"

"No, Damsville is not my primary destination. But I might have time to get there if it's close and along our way, you know... might as well see your twin brother if he still stays there."

"Who else is coming with you?"

"I usually travel alone, 'coz I hate other UEs to join with me. They don't get too seriously on their assignments. They keep on goofing around. You know…"

"I would love to, and I really want to see my twin brother again!"

Shingue and Claude came in the hallway and saw the two. The two were surprised to see that Kenji and Reinhardt's arms were both over each other's shoulders like they knew each other already.

Claude got jealous. "Who is that guy with you, Kenji?"

Shingue answered pointing at Reinhardt. "That's him! That's the guy I told you earlier, Claude. He's Rain, the one who accidentally beat Margot before!"

Claude almost laughed to hear what Shingue just said.

"See? I am absolutely right, Shingue. He is indeed a gay so he did not like--"

"Damn, just shut your big mouth Claude!"

Reinhardt's blood pressure suddenly shoot out and he looked at Claude intensely. "What 'gay' are you talking about?! Wait… Who is this new naughty guy as naughty as Marion, are you two brothers?"

Kenji answered instead. "Brother… He is my childhood friend, Claude."

Claude also asked Kenji.

"And who is that new guy you are with, Kenji? Don't tell me you are a gay as well?"

Kenji smiled. "No, Claude. This is Reinhardt, one of my long-lost brothers I just learned today. He is the eldest among us…"

Shingue and Claude could not believe their eyes so Shingue asked Kenji. "Rain really? How come that he is your brother? Man, Reinhardt…

you never said anything about it, huh?"

Reinhardt showed his pair of studs in his left arm and the two were astonished. "Yes indeed! His studs are identical to Kenji's chin," said Claude.

"Shingue, I know that you are familiar with my last name, aren't you? But why you didn't notice it when you were with Kenji and heard his name?" asked Reinhardt.

"Ah… Eh… It's just that um… I-I only lost my mind about it, Rain. Got a mental block I think," joked Shingue.

"Well…" said Claude facing Kenji. "I thought you and Genji are the only sons of a DDE warrior. So how many are you all then?"

Reinhardt answered Claude. "We are eight siblings and I am the eldest. Oh, I remember now…" then he turned to Kenji. "You are fourth among the eight and Denver is the fifth. Our mother gave birth to our youngest triplets a month after she gave birth to the twins."

Shingue gaped unbelievably so he asked Reinhardt. "O-Only a month right after she gave birth to Kenji and his twin brother? Hey, that was so fast and sounds impossible! How did that happen?"

"Did I tell you already that our mother is a fairy? She is no human, Shingue."

Claude was silent when Shingue turned to Kenji still looking confused. "O-Okay, enough of that. Kenji, come with me. I will show you where your new room is. The UE wants us to rest first before we move on."

Kenji nodded. "Okay Shingue," then he turned to Reinhardt. "Brother, if I have free time to come with you then I will let you know immediately."

Reinhardt nodded. "Go ahead, I will be waiting."

"Are you leaving now? Like going somewhere today?"

"No, but I am going to read something in my room. Goodbye," then Reinhardt left the three.

Claude called Kenji. "Come on Kenji, I want to take a rest now. Let's go!"

Kenji frowned at Claude. "Ah, I see. Fine, you can go now and sleep there on your own! Man, why do you interrupt our conversation today? This is just our first meeting, you know?!"

Claude smiled and quickly dragged Kenji. "Tsk, cool down man, hold your temper… Lad, you're just starving that's all!"

The three walked going to the room that Elijah gave to Claude and Kenji. When they reached the room, Shingue immediately opened the door when they saw Margot inside. Kenji's face suddenly changed in disgust seeing the gay again and he walked before the two men.

"You, why are you here in our room?" asked Kenji to the gay.

Claude and Shingue chuckled behind Kenji when Margot answered. "I just want to… um, have a chitchat with you and go to sleep here that's all…"

Shingue spoke to Margot. "And why do you have to sleep in their room though you have your own?"

Margot scoffed. "Well it's because… I am getting tired staying in my rubbish room anymore. *Cha-roosssshhh*, is it okay to sleep here with you, my *papaloozas?*" then he winked in flirty way.

Shingue rebuffed. "No, this is their private room. Meaning no one else will stay in this room except them and besides three is a crowd here!"

Margot went over the bed where Claude and Kenji would sleep on and laid there. "Fine, then I will be sleeping here in this bed instead."

"Geez, Margot… Stop being too importunate!" said Shingue. "I will tell Elijah that you starting your naughtiness again, you'll see!"

"So will I!" said Margot as he rose and turned his back at Shingue. "I will also tell Elijah that you've been stalking me wherever I go though you're not my type!"

Shingue completely lost his temper and attempted to push Margot away in the room. "You freakin' son of a--"

Claude suddenly yelled outside the room and called Reinhardt. "Rain… Rain… Come over here. I think someone wants to get punched by you again!"

Kenji quickly turned to Claude. Again, Claude pretended to call Reinhardt outside the room jokingly. "Reinhardt, there is a gay here who keeps on driving your brother really mad!"

And so, Margot stopped and he quickly stared at the three boys as if looks could kill. "I hate you guys so much!" then he stood back on the floor and scoffed. "I'm just leaving… Hmpt!" and then he left the room.

When Margot was already gone in the room, the three boys chuckled together. This time, Vamir came in the room along with his friends. The three stopped their laughing.

"Kenji, Claude, Shingue… Elijah is calling you and he wants to start the examination of your stone now. Please proceed to the laboratory immediately," said Vamir to the three.

"We will be there later," said Shingue. "Just tell him we will be there on time."

"No, Shingue. Right now, you are all coming with us."

"All right, all right…" Shingue stooped his head sadly. "I am still showing them their room, see?"

"Forget about it for now."

The three walked in the hallway with Vamir's group. Kenji and Claude looked around to see the beautiful decorations around the mansion and more big portraits were mounted on the walls. The entire walls were covered by wallpapers and they noticed the big curtains hanging each of the windows. The mansion looked absolutely luxurious.

They reached the laboratory in no time. The UE lab was not huge-sized, but its equipment and other facilities were complete and top of the line. There, they saw Elijah inside with the other Explorers and they greeted each other. Then, they began to scrutinize Kenji's stone.

Claude was wondering during the observation when he whispered Kenji "Kenji, why do they still have to study that stone though they already know it is a stone of Recovery? Are they still looking for more proof whether your stone is fake or not?"

Kenji was serious. "I do not know, Claude. Perhaps…"

Elijah turned to Kenji and clapped his hand. "Kenji, congratulations! According to our data analysis, your stone is indeed one of the Divine Stones we are looking for… You are very lucky of having it since we believe this type of stone is very rare and not very easy to find unlike the Magic Stones."

Kenji nodded with a smile. "Thank you."

"The reason why I called you is because I would like to propose an offer. First I want to ask you if you can just give us this stone and be in our possession. Do you agree with that?"

"A what?" Kenji suddenly reacted in shock. "Ah… No way… I can't. That stone is my--"

"Fine, fine Kenji," Elijah nodded and he held the stone in his hand. "Can I ask you something? What do you intend to do with this stone? Are you going to just keep it like a memento? 'Coz if you do, this stone will be useless as a Divine Stone that its power should not be wasted or treated carelessly. You all know that we are hardly looking for this type of stone and now you have found it, so you should give this precious to us."

"Elijah... Because... Ummm..."

Elijah's commanding voice became strong and frank. "Only a warrior that belongs in the Explorers organization has the right to hold the sacred stone like this and you know that. And what makes you think to disagree with this? Who gives you the authority to disobey this rule? Are you an Explorer to have the right to possess this stone in your hands?!"

Kenji was puzzled and did not understand what Elijah wanted to say. He bowed his head silently in disappointment: *I don't understand. I thought... they would surely help me of becoming a UE member and the stone would still be mine. I really don't understand... It seems like... Seems unbelievable and too confusing!!!*

"So, what is your decision now, Kenji? This sacred stone must only belong to the Explorers and no one else. And, this is not suitable for an ordinary person like you so you must understand this!"

"But I want to become an Explorer, Elijah!"

Elijah stopped. Silence.

"I've always dreamed to become a part of your group because I want to help you and your crusade against the Pioneer. I've been wanting to see my real parents and be one of you. I believe that stone will help me a lot to fulfill my dreams. That is why I do not want merely to just give away that stone because without it, I am nothing!"

"As what I observed from you... You do not have enough knowledge with regards to the proper use and handling of the stone like this. Without such knowledge you will not be able to maximize its power to extreme. We Explorers are all skilled warriors and I'm afraid you might just left behind. So this made me think to ask this stone from you since I've already changed my mind... But as a reward, we will give you something in return because you helped us to find the stone and then we will bring you back to your home."

"B-But why?! After I traveled a long distance and exhausting all my time and effort to find you then this is the only advice you can give me in return?! Why do you have to judge me like that? You do not even know my capability nor what I can do. I do not need anything in return! I want that stone and I will do everything to become one of you and fulfill my dreams!"

"Are you certain you can be one of the UE warriors like us?"

Reinhardt answered in the distance as he was approaching towards them. "My brother can pass all the challenges we will give him, Elijah. There is a unique strength hidden in our race so I am sure Kenji can become a part of our group. Remember this Elijah, I am his brother and I am an Explorer!"

Elijah was surprised. "Reinhardt, so this young man is your brother? Kenji? How could that happen?"

"It's a long story Elijah, what more important now is we met today and never be separated again. Just look what I've got in my arms and look what he got in his chin... They came from our same mother."

Elijah moved closer to Kenji's face to observe his two studs in his chin. "Unbelievable... How unbelievable!"

"Guess he's right... If Rain could pass the tests previously then surely Kenji can! After all, the Fosters seem to be all very talented and powerful," said Exer who was also a UE member.

"Fine, have it your way then," said Elijah and he shook his head. "There is nothing more we could do if this man doesn't want to give up the stone to us. So be it..."

"Kenji listen," Reinhardt patted Kenji's shoulder. "Do your best to pass their tests and prove your worth. I have strong confidence in you."

Kenji's face blushed and smiled. "Yes brother... I know... I have enough capabilities and experiences. Unique experiences that will soon reveal the answers to the question in my life..."

"Okay, I agree now," said Elijah to Kenji smiling. "I will not force this issue to you anymore, but if you really want this stone to be with you then prove your worth and become an Explorer. If you are really too confident of becoming a part of the group, then I must ask you now when would you like to begin your tests then?"

The young man stooped his head in shyness. "Um, can I take a break for at least two days and after that I will begin to take the tests?"

Elijah quickly nodded. "Okay, your wish is my command, Kenji. We are looking forward to you to become a part of the group."

Kenji lifted his head and also nodded. "Yes sir! And you guys wait for the good news of the incoming new member of the group. A new member, a new ally, and a new friend who will embrace the ideology of the Explorers!"

Elijah chuckled. "Heh, really? Okay, go ahead. We will see about that at the result of your performance. You can take your rest here for two days.

Shingue, please take them to their room now," then he turned to Claude. "Claude..."

"Claude will also undergo rigid tests with me, Elijah," said Kenji smiling.

"No, you will take the tests first before Claude."

Claude pouted. "Man, tsktsktsk... Why do we have to take the test individually? We're not cheaters, trust me. Come on man, let me take the tests with him."

"No, I said. Kenji will take the tests first, then you're next. I do not know you both yet so I don't want to give my trust on you for now."

Claude pouted again when Elijah turned to Shingue. "Go ahead, Shingue. Please take these young men to their room so they get rested. I'm afraid that their knees might tremble once they'll get to their tests, hahaha!"

Kenji chuckled. "That will never happen for sure, Elijah."

The three went back to the room when they saw their next visitor inside. This time it was Marion, the naughty kid whose still not in his Explorer uniform (he truly hated wearing his uniform) and was sleeping alone in the bed.

"What is the meaning of this?! After Margot, then it will be Marion," said Shingue annoyingly. "Is this kid really sleeping? Or just pretending?"

"You know kids these days, Shingue. They are good pranksters..." said Claude.

"I'll check..." Shingue moved closer to Marion to look at his face. "Certainly, he's only pretending. He's not asleep!"

Marion rose quickly and intentionally bumped his head at Shingue's. Ouch!!!

"OOOUUUCCCHHHH!!!" cried Shingue out loud. "You naughty little kid. How could you!"

"Hahaha! I fooled you, eh? Bleeehhh!" laughed Marion and he teased. Yes, the kid just fooled them.

Claude got pissed off. "Hey! Why are you here? This is our room!"

Marion stroked his chin. "Are you nuts? *Kuya* Elijah gave me an order to go in this room."

"An order for what?"

"He ordered me to stay in this room and sleep with you both. See? I brought my pillow here, and this is mine only!"

"Is it really true what you've said, you kind-hearted little kid?!"

"Yes, he really asked me to do it!"

Elijah came to the room, went inside and smiled at the four. "Kenji, Claude... this will be my simple test I'd like to take you both as a practice. I asked Marion to sleep in this room with you within two days just to test your temper and patience on him, haha! I hope you both will be happy spending time with him for a while and you'll might as well miss him so badly. Goodbye!" then he went out of the room and gently closed the door. He left.

Later, Marion gone wild before the three after Elijah left their room. "Hahaha! So I am now your boss in this room! Let me be your new king and you shall be my slaves, gwahahahaha!!!"

Claude was upset and whispered to himself. "Whatever you say, you damn, stupid little kid! You're getting into my nerve!"

Marion pointed Kenji and Claude teasingly. "Let's see here if you can follow my command! Let me test your patience against me! If you lose it and get pissed off, then I feel sorry for your bad result. YOU WILL BOTH FAIL *KUYA* ELIJAH'S TESTS AND WILL NEVER BECOME EXPLORERS LIKE ME... AHAHAHAHAHA!!!"

"Certainly we will. We will both pass the test, you damn silly kid!" cried Claude.

A-da-da-da-da. A-do-do-do-do. Those were the continuous annoying noises coming out from the four noisy boys inside the room. Gosh, they were making lots of noises that would surely hurt our ears. Later, Shingue decided to just remain silent while the three were still arguing.

Kenji stopped Marion from his continuous prattle and spoke calmly. "Alright Marion, you win... We will follow whatever you wanna ask from us. Yes, from now on you will be our new king within this room and we'll respect you. Our dear king--"

"Yeah, yeah, whatever!" yelled Marion. "I am going to sleep now slaves!!!"

"Fine, go to sleep then you dumbass kid!" said Claude to himself as Marion laid down on the bed and closed his eyes.

Kenji and Claude followed the naughty kid when they also laid next to him. Marion suddenly felt his bed getting heavier so he quickly opened his eyes, seeing the two boys were already beside him. He quickly got up and yelled.

"Hey you two! Why are you both sleeping in the king's bed?! Get off in this bed and leave me be, you slaves!"

"P-Pardon?" asked Kenji in wonder. "But this is our only bed in this room, oh my dear King Marion…"

"You fools!" Marion quickly pointed at Kenji. "I will never allow you both to sleep here in my bed! Get off here and sleep over there on the floor! Under the bed! Except to *kuya* Shingue because he is a friend of your king… you understand me, you filth?!"

"But…"

"Sleep on the floor I said!!!" Marion also pointed the floor.

Shingue shook his head. "I am not sleeping in this room."

Claude was only silent trying to control his short temper towards Marion. He was very irritated, as if he wanted to just kill the kid and threw him out of the room!

But because of that, the two had nothing else to do to defend themselves against the kid. Instead, they got up from their bed where they should sleep on if Marion was not there. Claude was still very irritated. Then, the two crawled on the floor and slept under the naughty little king's bed!

23 THE RESTAURANT SERVERS

The two spent their time with Marion in their room for two days. Two days of their long patience and forbearance to a single kid. Until the day came for Kenji to take his first test, and yet the young man never felt any fear and foreboding to face it alone.

Morning came when Kenji met Vamir along with his colleagues in the hallway. Vamir waved his hand greeting the young man and the young man also greeted him back.

"Kenji, Elijah ordered me to tell you that you should take your breakfast first so you will have more energy in your body when you undergo the test. He kept on teasing you, saying that your knees might tremble while you are in a middle of your tests!" said Vamir to Kenji.

Kenji laughed. "Oh yeah? Well, let's see about the results later!"

"Hahaha! Alright, go ahead and Elijah is waiting for you."

Kenji left the group to look for Elijah. He saw the UE leader outside the mansion seemed to be waiting for someone so he called his attention and approached him. Then, they greeted each other a sweet "good morning" while waving.

"So Kenji, are you ready for the test now?" asked Elijah smiling. "Now that your long waiting is over and I'm certain that you have enough energy to begin your first test."

Kenji nodded with a smile. "Yes, I am ready."

"How's you and Claude's two days with Marion? I think you both could withstand the kid's mischievousness and never fought back at him."

"Y-Yes… though Claude and I could not sleep well because we slept under the bed while Marion was too boisterous in his sleep."

"Excellent! You passed my practice test. Because of that I will give you a big special treat in our luxurious 'five-star restaurant'! Do you know what a five-star restaurant is?"

"Ahhh…" Kenji scratched his head in ignorance. "A restaurant to have… five stars in the ceiling?"

"No, that's not it! It is an elegant and expensive-type of restaurant. The Explorers organization owns the five-star restaurant whether it is UE, EUE, or DDE. We simply built it as our small business, sort of cooperative."

"Wow," there was a spark in Kenji's eyes. "Now I learn that the Explorers also runs a business, don't they? What about your customers? What do they usually look like?"

"Since our restaurant belongs to a five-star type of business, our customers expect our restaurant to have expensive menus. So generally our customers are of course, wealthy… or someone to have an abundant life!"

"Wow!" Kenji's eyes shone in wonder. "But… What about me? I am not rich, and I do not have money with that huge amount. I cannot eat there."

"Don't worry, I'll take care of it young man! Remember what I've said that this is my big special treat for you? For now I will give you a chance to perk up your life before you suffer during the tests we will give you, okay?" teased Elijah.

"A-Are your tests really that hard?" Kenji was concerned.

"I do not know for your part, but I remember previously when me and Reinhardt took the tests together… I could tell in his actions that the entire tests were only a piece of cake for him! I was so impressed to your brother's big heart. He's an excellent, fast learner, and a strong warrior. And he was the quickest one to finish all the tests. And so, that's what I am expecting on you!"

Kenji stooped his head. "*Kuya* Reinhardt…"

"So, let us go now shall we? Let me bring you to our luxurious five-star restaurant and proudly show you what it can offer!"

Kenji smiled. "All right. I am getting excited to have a taste of your foods."

Elijah stepped forward and spoke. "We don't need a vehicle to get there, we will just walk since it is only a few blocks away. The DDE decided

THE EXPLORERS

to build the restaurant near the UE mansion, that is why we are the closest to the restaurant, but farthest to them."

Kenji nodded. "I see."

"You have to call Claude. The treat is for both of you so he must come with you too."

"Sure, and Shingue?"

"He will also be there later."

Kenji was about to call Claude when he saw Claude just went out the mansion and approached them. The newcomer waved at the two and Kenji only waved back at him.

"Are we leaving now, huh?" asked Claude and turned to Kenji. "Vamir told me that we will eat at a five-star restaurant. Man, those foods are surely too expensive!"

Kenji blushed. "I know, Claude... And I am getting embarrassed."

"My goodness, Kenji!" reacted Elijah in his low voice. "Stop being too bashful and I highly forbid that! Come on then, let us go."

The three walked together going to the luxurious restaurant owned by the Explorers. They hurriedly walked and in no time they reached the restaurant.

The Explorers' five-star restaurant building was massive and elegant indeed. Though the three were still at the entrance, Claude already had an idea judging by the facade what it looked like inside the building. It was because he had an experience before during his childhood age that he surreptitiously entered a three-star restaurant to steal foods, but the guards caught him and kicked him out until he reached Damsville and grew up there.

"Here, boys... This is the restaurant I am talking about and we are proudly present it to you. Welcome," said Elijah to the two. "We can now enter inside."

Kenji took a deep breath before they enter the building. The entrance door had a motion sensor which made it open by itself. Suddenly, the warm air coming inside the building's heater came out of the door and it touched their skin.

The three entered the restaurant. Fortunately, the restaurant did not have much customers eating on the tables because of the storm. The temperature inside was moderate. It was stunning, the decorations were all attractive, the tables and chairs were all formally arranged and covered by the golden-red colored covers.

"Say Kenji... What can you say now to our restaurant?" asked Elijah to Kenji smiling. "Did the restaurant exceed your expectations?"

"Why, yes!" answered Kenji happily as he was looking around the restaurant in amazement. "But you don't have much customers here right now."

"Well, obviously because of the storm. But despite of the storm, the restaurant is still open for the two of you."

"Welcome to the Explorers' five-star restaurant," greeted a waitress to the three visitors and she offered a table for four. "Please, have a sit."

Kenji and Claude sat on each chairs, but not Elijah. The two noticed him.

"Elijah... Have a sit with us as well," said Kenji to Elijah.

"Ah, don't worry about me!" said Elijah smiling. "I will not sit. I'm not going to eat anyway, so go ahead and have fun. *Bon appetit!*" then he turned away and called. "ISAGANI!!!"

A young man came before them dressed in his waiter uniform of grayish white and black. His height was only average but presentable. He firstly bowed at the two holding the menu books.

"Kenji, Claude... Let me introduce to you one of the most popular and busiest waiter here in our restaurant, Mister Isagani Pharell," introduced Elijah to the two.

Isagani faced the two and he bowed once again.

"Hello, welcome to the Explorers' five-star restaurant. My name is Isagani Pharell, a waiter of this restaurant. I have been serving here for three years and I'm..." he hesitated for a moment. "...I am seventeen years old."

"Oh," reacted Claude. "Then you are still very young!"

And Kenji added. "Certainly you are. Imagine, how come a seventeen-year old man becomes a waiter of the five-star restaurant?! It looks like this restaurant is not strict in hiring someone when it comes to age. Hahaha, you're amazing!"

Isagani's face blushed in a sudden. "Ah, yes. I-I am seventeen years of age..."

"Why do you sound like that?" asked Claude. "Do you feel ashamed at your age? You're suppose to be hanging around with your friends and enjoying your youth instead of working. Listen, I am also seventeen years old, but I am an unemployed man. So you should be happy working here especially if it is a five-star restaurant. In that case, you have the opportunity to help your parents in their needs!"

Kenji agreed. "He's right, so you should be proud of yourself despite of your age."

"Okay, okay, introduction is now over," stopped Elijah when he turned to Isagani. "Isagani, please give them the menu books so they can choose their orders. Do not charge them anything even a single peso, it's my special treat. Sky is the limit, so just give them what they want to eat and charge it to me. They will be taking the tests later. And Kenji?"

"Yes?"

"I will leave you both so you can enjoy your meal. I need to go back to the mansion. There is something I need to work on. I want both of you in the mansion as soon as you finish your meal."

"Of course, we will. We know the way back so no worries."

Elijah nodded with a smile. "Good. This restaurant serves 'eat-all-you-can' to our customers. You can take your orders whatever you want to eat or you can go to the display area where you can choose what you want to eat... Isagani, you'll take care of them."

Isagani nodded. "Yes, sir."

"I'm leaving now. See you guys in your first test later. Goodbye."

Elijah left the restaurant when the two became suddenly quiet while looking at Isagani. Again, Kenji looked around the entire restaurant awkwardly when Isagani gave the two menu books and spoke. "Um... this is the eat-all-you-can restaurant. So um, you may take your orders now anything you'd like..."

"Eat-all-you-can?" asked Kenji showing ignorance. "Seriously, does this mean... we will eat all the foods here as long as we can until our stomachs explode? Wait a minute, is this a part of our initial test?"

Isagani laughed out loud. "No, sir. I mean you can eat any foods we have here as you wish. If you'd like to eat more, just go ahead. But if you don't, then it's okay as well."

Kenji answered jokingly. "Really, huh? I thought you guys will kill us by bloating and puke our stomachs empty."

Isagani chuckled. "Please take your orders now, sir. After all, we will serve you anything you'd like so go ahead and choose which foods you would like to eat. For now, our buffet table is unavailable because of the storm and a few number of customers in attendance," then he cleared his throat. "So... we will just bring all your orders here in this table instead."

Kenji frowned in a silly way. "Then this shouldn't be called eat-all-you-can. It should be eat-what-I-want..."

Claude turned away. "Gosh, then I'll make my first orders now," then he opened the menu book and browsed the available foods for today. Then, his mouth suddenly drooled and he spoke. "It seems I would like to eat all of them..."

Kenji also opened the menu book he was holding and also drooled. "Ahhh..."

"So..." Isagani took his small notepad over and pulled a pen in his pocket. "Can I take your orders now, sirs?"

It took few minutes for the two to browse their menu books and think what type of foods should they want to eat. Claude could not choose even one yet because he wanted to taste all of it. The foods were all delightful to taste!

Finally, Claude had made his first orders when he raised his hand and spoke. "Okay, I have my orders now laddie..."

"Really?" asked Isagani when he lifted his pen and pad to prepare in taking down Claude's orders. "What are your orders then, sir?"

"You don't need to write down my orders, you are just wasting your time."

"Huh? Why is that? What are those orders, eh?"

Claude returned the menu book he was holding to Isagani. "I am returning this book to you because all of the available foods listed there will be my orders," then he quickly pointed at Isagani. "Ooopppss, do not OBJECT, okay?"

"WHAAAATTT?!!" shocked the two.

"You serious about this huh, Claude?" asked Kenji.

"Of course! Since this treat is all for free, isn't it? Come to think of it, we won't be eating in this restaurant again next time 'coz I can't afford to order their so expensive menus!"

"Oh, okay..." Isagani took the menu book from Claude then turned to Kenji. "How about you, sir?"

Kenji took more time to order and after few more minutes he was still puzzled on choosing the foods he wanted to eat that he never tasted before. Claude turned away again, because he got bored.

THE EXPLORERS

"What the hell is going on with this man? Geez, he's too slow to order, hmpt!" said Claude annoyingly, but Kenji turned his gaze on him in glare look. Claude suddenly smiled awkwardly at him.

A minute had passed when Kenji made his orders and Isagani wrote them down in the notepad. After the orders, Isagani moved away from the two and approached the attending chef. He gave the notepad to him.

"Hah, good thing the two had made their orders after a long time. Man, it took them long to just browse the menus as if they were reviewing for their practical exam!"

"Stop saying anything and please be quiet, Tyrone! They might hear your taunting!" restrained Isagani whispering. "They want to become Explorers…"

"R-Really? Why, that's good to hear then. We will be having new friends!"

"Shhh, be quiet I say. Here, their orders are listed here," Isagani pointed the pad of listed orders at Tyrone. "Hurry, hurry! Their foods must be served sooner since they will be taking their tests later today as what Elijah said."

"Oh? They will begin their tests today? With both of us? Hah, perhaps those two think they can win the tests. The tests are not that easy! I remember the day when we took our tests with Elijah and we faced lots of difficulties during the challenges. Anyway, it was actually fun!"

"Oh, come onnnnn nooowww! Move away and tell your fellow chefs to begin their cooking. Tyrone, you're talking gibberish!"

Tyrone was also a server working in the Explorers' five-star restaurant and a chef. He was born to his wealthy parents but his parents were living in another country to work. In his teen age, Tyrone decided to leave his family in order to help and cooperate with the Explorers in search of the sacred objects. Until the time came when the group recruited him and became an Explorer.

As for Isagani, like Tyrone, was also an Explorer aside from being a waiter in the restaurant. Both he and Tyrone obtained each of the Divine Stones of Light and they met in UE mansion when the Explorers recruited them at the same time. Therefore, they became close to each other and established a friendship.

Elijah, as the UE leader asked them to work in the five-star restaurant as servers if they did not have any special assignments to do as Explorers.

And up to now, the two were still together even at work as they became best friends and partners!

Tyrone had been watching the two as if he wanted to talk to them, while the two were mum while waiting for their orders. At first, he cleared his throat then he began to speak.

"Hello guys... My name is Tyrone Federlein of UE. An Explorer..." greeted Tyrone at Kenji and Claude who were still both silent. "Hey man, why are you so quiet? Cat got your tongue, eh?"

"Aw! O-Oh, are you talking to us?" asked Claude innocently. "W-What did you say to us?"

"Yes... I only introduced myself earlier."

"Of course, Tyrone. We heard you earlier. My friend was only joking at you. My name is Kenji and this is Claude..." introduced Kenji to Tyrone.

The foods of the two came. Almost twenty waiters and waitresses were bringing the trays of different types of food the two ordered (perhaps the more number of foods they were carrying were all for Claude). The two got very excited to see their free specialties and eagerly to have a taste of them!

"The foods are served! See? Our service here is fast and reliable so you won't get bored in waiting for your orders!" Tyrone boasted.

Claude answered Tyrone's boastfulness. "Hmpt, fast eh? It's just because you don't have lots of customers today which makes your service really fast..."

The waiters and waitresses put down the trays on the table when Kenji remembered the scene where they ate their ordered foods with Valerie in Sierra Village's Inn. *It was fun to think about that day*, he said to himself and he smiled.

Then, Kenji began to gape in surprise when he saw all of Claude's foods before them. Even Claude did not know whether he could devour all of his foods or not so he was only scratching his head.

"Well, Claude... Do you think you can eat those foods you ordered?" asked Kenji to Claude in an awkward look.

"Why, I-I don't know... We'll see. They said if we can't consume all of these foods then it's okay. Just as long as I could taste their special dishes here one by one. If my stomach could no longer hold my greediness, then that is not my problem!"

"The foods will be wasted, Claude. You should consume them all."

"Whatever, hmpt!"

The two began to eat. Kenji kept on glancing at Claude to see if his friend could eat all of the dishes he had or not. And as for Claude, he was only chewing quietly like a man of honor.

During the meal, Tyrone tried to move closer to the two and he wanted to talk to them again when he touched Claude's shoulder to call his attention.

"Dude, why?" asked Claude while eating.

"How's our specialties?" answered Tyrone in question. "Hmmm… Can you hardly imagine how lucky you are since Elijah took you here in this five-star restaurant for free? But if you look at it in a bigger picture, how can you perform well if you're bloated? As a matter of fact, you will get a lot of trouble when you two face your tests later."

Tyrone seemed trying to frighten the two in order to lose their high confidence during the tests. Claude answered. "Is that so? Yeah, your specialties taste yummier than I expected… But with regards to the tests, Kenji and I will prove our worth to you and to anyone who will witness our test. We will pass the tests together with flying colors!"

"I hope…"

"What the hell do you mean by that?!" Claude instantly got pissed off while Kenji was still eating. "Hey man, you don't know me and my friend here yet to judge like that. Kenji is a great warrior, and he already faced great challenges and strong opponents during his journey before he reached the Explorers organization!"

"Claude, please…" stopped Kenji. "We are in front of our foods, so please just shut your mouth and remain calm," then he suddenly remembered the day when Claude and Valerie were both scrambling for *bulalo* when they were eating in room 1908. He hesitated. "Um…"

Silence.

"Nevermind, just eat then," said Tyrone patting Claude's shoulder. "You're not eating much yet. Look at your friend, he already ate some."

Claude did not answer. He remained calm like a baby in her mother's arm.

It was almost half an hour passed when Kenji finally consumed all of the dishes he ordered when he wiped his lips using a table cloth. As for Claude, his face got sweaty despite of cold weather while trying to consume all of his foods this time. Kenji did not know what to do to his friend when he noticed a lot of leftovers in his table.

"C-Claude?" Kenji faltered awkwardly. "Would you like me to help you eat all of those, hm?"

Claude was busy chewing when he answered with his mouth full. "Great, go ahead! Pleashe help me 'cozh I cannot take it anymore… Here, help yourshelffff…" then he gave some of the leftovers to Kenji. "Pleashe conshume all of them for me!"

"T-Thanks…"

The two worked together just to consume the foods remaining on the table. But since Kenji was already full, he could no longer hold to eat more or he might got sick. There were more than five dishes remaining, and Claude kept on offering the leftovers to Kenji while Kenji was still trying to eat more than he could!

Claude gave another turn to Kenji when the young man raised his hand and quickly shook his head in rejection.

"Why?" asked Claude.

Kenji could not speak so he only rubbed his belly to show Claude that he was very much filled. He winked as an answer, when Claude understood that and nodded slowly.

"But… the leftovers will be wasted! I don't want that to happen."

"I-It's your fault, Claude. Those are your dishes, you must do your best to consume them all!"

Isagani came carrying a pitcher of ice tea and two glasses on the single tray when he put down the glasses on the table and poured ice tea on each.

"Time to drink eh, my brothers?" asked Isagani smiling. "Of course, after you eat freely with our eat-all-you-can service, this time we will give you a drink with our bottomless service!"

"H-Huh? W-What is bottomless then?" asked Kenji in an exhausted way.

"Which means you can have a drink as much as you can! You can pick any drinks you want and we will absolutely give them all to you unlimited!"

"Whaaaaaatttt??!" the two quickly reacted in shock. "No way! We are already stuffed even without drinks! Please, we can't drink them anymore!!!"

The restaurant servers laughed out loud altogether.

24 THE TESTS

The two had finished their free eat-all-you-can treat when Elijah gave them an hour to rest inside the restaurant. Since the two were still much full and the UE thought that they would not be able to move quickly during their tests.

An hour had passed when Kenji and Claude decided to go back to the UE mansion since the sky had turned dark as the storm would brew the area once again. The snowstorm had been blowing for days and the two got worried.

But as for Kenji, he was still very determined and had a high courage to face the tests and pass them all at once!

"Thank you for your hospitality and good services you provided today. The foods are so delicious and we really enjoyed eating in your restaurant," thanked Kenji to the restaurant servers. "Claude and I need to return to the mansion now."

"You are welcome," said Isagani smiling next to Tyrone. "We are closing this restaurant now since the storm is coming sooner. Plus, we don't have customers anymore."

"Yeah, I agree to that. You should close your restaurant now," agreed Claude. "So where will you go home anyway?"

"Oh, us?" Isagani pointed himself and Tyrone. "We are coming with you, Claude."

"Coming with us, why? We will return in the UE mansion, Isagani."

"Yes, certainly. Actually, we live there!"

"Really?" asked Kenji unbelievably. "Are all the servers in this restaurant also Explorers?!"

"Ah, no! Only me and Tyrone are Explorers so we will go there with you two."

Everyone went out the restaurant when Tyrone locked the building's main entrance door. The lights inside were completely turned off and everyone was waving each other goodbyes. Kenji, Claude, Isagani, and Tyrone were coming back to the UE mansion altogether.

"Hey, we have to walk fast before the storm blows strong again," said Isagani to the three.

The four walked in a hurry. "I thought Shingue would be coming in the restaurant earlier…" said Kenji sadly to the three. "Elijah told me that."

The four returned to the mansion safely. They quickly burst in the main hall when the UEs laughed at them since their bodies were slightly covered in snows.

Kenji and Claude went in their room to change their clothes when someone knocked on their door.

"I'll open the door, Kenji," said Claude and he opened the door. It was Shingue and Elijah who knocked and they greeted Claude.

"Kenji, Claude… Are you ready for this big challenge and an opportunity to become one of the Explorers?" asked Elijah to the two.

Kenji answered while dressed. "Ah, yes! We are well-prepared now, Elijah."

Elijah chuckled. "Alright, pals! You must be in a hurry so we will begin your tests sooner. Do you know that Isagani and Tyrone are also taking their tests with you two today?"

"Isagani and Tyrone will be also taking their tests with us? I thought they're Explorers already?"

"Yes they are, but their membership is not yet approved. They have not completed the three tests yet because they'd became busy working in the restaurant at the time of our tests. They took the second and final tests in our batch, but they did not complete. Because of this, the DDE only gave them their temporary license and they need to re-take the tests in order to obtain their real and full license," Elijah chuckled. "I remember the time when Isagani and Tyrone took their practice exam with Marion… Hahaha, Tyrone instantly lost his patience towards the kid in less than a minute!"

Kenji stooped his head. "I'll be taking the tests first right?"

Elijah shook his head. "No, I changed my mind. You four will be taking the tests together to finish them sooner. I have strong confidence in you as long as you will not do any cheap tricks behind my back, okay?"

"Yeeeaaahhhh!" cried the four like kids. "Many, many thanks to you, Elijah. We won't!"

"Okay, let's go boys!"

"Wait…" Kenji heard Tyrone and Isagani's cries when he looked around the room and just noticed the two behind Shingue and Elijah. "You guys, I didn't notice you came here."

"Yeah, we just heard your cries buddy!" laughed Claude.

"We're fast, aren't we? Even our service here is very fast but still reliable, of course!" said Tyrone jokingly.

"Pfff… There you go again…" said Claude to his mind.

The four were now dressed when some of the UEs approached them just to see them. Since the four would be taking the tests together, this raised their confidence more and felt more determined to face whatever challenges would be.

First, the four went to a vacant room with Elijah when the UE leader explained something to them.

"Boys… during your tests, there will be no Explorer who will be helping you nor distract you since they will all remain in the mansion, you understand me? You guys will be taking the tests in the midst of the storm."

Kenji and Claude looked at each other in wonder, but then they all replied. "Yes sir!"

Kenji pulled the stone given to him by Valerie from his pocket and slowly closed his eyes. "Divine Stone of Recovery…" he whispered. "Help me for whatever I will face for today's tests. Please help me pass them all and make me an Explorer!" then he kissed the stone.

"What else?" Elijah was thinking. "Well, I'd say to you next what are the rules throughout the tests, okay? One rule: you are allowed to use your weapons individually, but for this test teamwork is not allowed. Of course there will be a teamwork, but it only depends on the challenge I will give you later."

"We have skills and abilities," interrupted Tyrone. "So Elijah, I have a question… Can we also use our unique abilities during the tests besides weapons?"

"What do you mean by 'unique' abilities?"

"If we can also use our powers during the tests? After all, Isagani and I have the Divine Stones we obtained in our hands so… Can we use them too, Elijah?"

"Ah, I see what you mean by that," said Elijah. "Yes you can, but how will you use your Divine Stones' power if they have not returned to their true form yet?"

"O-Oh… You're right," said Tyrone sadly. "As long as they're still Divine Stones… they are useless as if they're just ordinary stones!"

"So, tsk… Do you have more questions? Ask me anything now what you want to know while we are still here because later… I will no longer entertain your questions anymore. Remember, during the course of test it will only be you and you alone can help yourself in order to survive the test. No one will come in aid of you, your will and determination are the keys to survive!"

Kenji and Claude did not understand what Tyrone and Elijah were talking about the Divine Stone. The four thought quietly of what to ask when Claude began to raise his hand and asked. "Um, can we start the tests now?"

The three nodded and answered together. "We are all ready."

"Hahaha," Elijah laughed. "Nice question, Claude. Okay, let's go challengers and we'll begin the tests now!"

The five went out the mansion since the tests would be taking place outside in the midst of the storm. Elijah opened the mansion's main gate while the storm was already blowing hard. Instantly, they felt chills in their bodies.

"Guys, can you stand this intense cold outside the mansion? Here?" asked Elijah wearing his thick outerwear while the four were only in their casual wear. "You will take your 'Endurance Test' in this spot."

The four were only listening while they were wrapping their body with their arms to feel the body heat and to endure the terrific and freezing blizzard storm. "Your first test is so easy, it's the endurance challenge. All you have to do is to only stay here and do nothing in half day. But… you are not allowed to eat nor sleep during this test, okay?"

"W-What? Easy, you say?" asked Claude in surprise. "L-Look, we're already freezing to death here though we're only standing here less than a minute! Nyiiihhh…"

"Well, there's nothing I can do to help you against the cold. You really should do this in order to stay in the game. Do not worry, because we've already been there too. But, we didn't take the first test during the snow... Instead, we were exposed under the intense heat of the sun. Our Endurance Test took place above the high mountain where the sun was fully set."

"I-Is that so?"

"Of course, if we can... then so as you!"

The four remained silent.

"I have to separate you four as you take your Endurance Test. Kenji, please go behind the mansion and stay there. Claude, to the front. Isagani and Tyrone, to either side of the mansion. Go ahead, quickly now!"

It was difficult for the four challengers to move fast because of the thick snow engulfing the area. They hardly moved their feet due to the strong wind that pushed them away in their position. Kenji was trying to move towards the back of the mansion even some part of his body were already covered in snow. While moving, his arms were wrapped around his body while covering his head being hit by the chunks of ice. Then, Elijah went back inside the mansion to watch the four.

The challengers reached their assigned spot and they stayed alone on each side of the mansion. Less than an hour had passed when Kenji and Isagani both caught their colds when their body resistance gradually dropped against cold temperature.

"T-The first test will take for twelve hours. W-We began the test this twelve noon and... will finish in twelve midnight... M-Man... it is way too long..." said Kenji to himself as he sniffed. "B-But I hope I can make it. I-I can do it!"

There were some of the UEs who were watching the four from the mansion since Elijah commanded them while he was away. There were night vision cameras in every corner of the mansion which made them visible in the monitor screens in the control room at all times.

The four were still on their feet. But after five hours (five o'clock in the afternoon), Isagani could no longer hold his freezing so his body suddenly collapsed on the snow ground. While as for Kenji, he had been sniffing by cold for long and still pushing himself to stand against his own body weight. He covered his mouth with his hands and tried to breathe a hot air to put warmth in his freezing body. The UE watchers saw Isagani who lost consciousness so they immediately dispatched a rescuer to take him inside the mansion for medical check-up and put him to rest. And as for Claude and Tyrone, the two seemed to be doing their own strategies that were against the rules.

The snow blew hard. The two cheaters were doing something surreptitiously behind the cameras watching over them. Claude was taking advantage to use fraud in order to warm himself when the camera was away from him and so as Tyrone.

As for Kenji. Because of his great desire to pass the challenge, he followed the rules and never cheated. But his body suffered a lot and seemed to be collapsing soon as well. He really felt that he was dying from hyperthermia and would like to enter the mansion this time and just give up the challenge. But he could not… He would never fulfill his dream if he did… *Wait, is there any other way I can do to save myself from dying?*

The freezing temperature was taking its toll as Kenji slowly losing his consciousness when the stone shone in his pocket, so he pulled it out and held hard. He suddenly remembered that he and Valerie already witnessed the shining stone before and the little girl told him that the stone had its "power".

"Kuya *Kenji, the stone has its power!*"

"T-This stone is shining again! W-What is that mean?" asked Kenji looking at the stone held by his freezing fingers.

The same thing happened again when he and Valerie saw the shining stone for the first time when it burst out its own dazzling light. There were two unusual auras emerged from the stone again as Kenji spoke to it lifting the stone up high in the air.

"T-This stone feels the natural cold temperature again… Oh Divine Stone, p-please… h-help m-me…"

Kenji was astonished when his Divine Stone quickly responded unexpectedly. Suddenly a soft voice was heard.

"Kenji… I am the stone of spirituality. I am thanking you for your tireless care on me and because of this, I will help you…"

Half of the young man's body was already covered in snows. He faltered. "T-The Divine Stone… It really has its power!"

"Yes… I previously owned by King Jethro, my former master. I possess the power of the element called 'Holy'. By paying you back as a favor for rescuing me, this stone will finally return to its true form completely as pure element… The 'Holy Crusade'! By the element's power, you will possess an inherent power, strength, and unique abilities."

THE EXPLORERS

The dazzling light burst stronger as the stone was gradually returning to its true form as an element. As the stone fully transformed itself, its bright light also gradually converted into warm light.

Kenji felt alive when he felt the warm air hovering his body coming out from the light of the element. He closed his eyes while still lifting the stone up in the air to avoid eye damage. "Ah, it's warm... Oh, thank you..." then he opened his eyes and wondered. "Wait a minute, how did this stone cast a warm light rather than cold?"

"My power can casts both warm and cold lights. This time, the warm light coming out is by the power of the elemental fire called, the 'Holy White Fire'."

Kenji was delighted hearing about this when the element spoke again. "The warm light will be helping you to ease your chill, but there is another elemental fire that is very vulnerable to use when cast. Only the chosen Holy Wielder can only unleash that power in his own and in the right way."

Kenji put down his hand holding the stone and stooped his head. "B-But... I am only an ordinary person and I can't do that."

"No Kenji, I know your mother who is a fairy named Isidra... So you're not an ordinary person. You should be my new possessor, and I would also like to thank the little girl who found me after my long years of obscurity."

"V-Valerie?"

The two were still talking, but the warm light emitted by the element was not enough to heat up the young man's body, so the element sensed his freezing body temperature.

"Do not worry, I will help you. Just as long as you do what I ask you to do. Kenji, listen..."

"W-Wait... Who are you by the way?" interrupted Kenji in wonder. "Is it really true that I should be your new possessor? Why is it then?"

"Yes," answered the element. "It is me, King Jethro you are spoken to!"

Kenji's eyes widened. "R-Really? But how'd..."

"You deserve this power I once possessed, Kenji. You are one of my chosen warriors to become its new master called Wielder. As a Holy Wielder, you will be the leader of all the Element Wielders I will choose. You must also find and rescue my other elements because they are all still at risk..."

"Yes, my lord…" then Kenji kissed the stone once again. "I promise that I will use your element in a right way, my lord. The element of Holy…"

"You must shut your eyes and concentrate well as I give you more warmth. I shall bestow my power to you and become the Holy Wielder completely."

"Yes, my lord!"

"When you have done your duty as Holy Wielder, I will bring you to our world to be with your beloved mother, the fairy of love…"

"Yes, my lord…"

"Accept this power of element!" commanded the voice of King Jethro and the stone slowly moved and hovering closer to Kenji's chest. Kenji closed his eyes and breathed deeply as he was sensing the next move of the element. The Holy Element slowly penetrated and successfully entered inside his heart. Later, Kenji felt something different in his body that seemed to be changing gradually. He opened his eyes, when he noticed the white fire (also called White Flame) covering all over his body and the snows were melting on it. The White Flame was not visible to the naked eye of an ordinary man but not to the Wielders. Though his body was wrapped in fire, it did not inflict any harm.

"Kenji, my power and my strength have merged inside you. Please use it well and take care of it as you took care when it was just a stone. From now on, I shall declare you now as the Holy Wielder and new master of the Holy element!"

"I feel I am getting strong," said Kenji as he was examining his body. "There is a white fire wrapping around my body right now but I am not burning… And the heat is only moderate."

"Yes, it is. Since the white fire has an ability to protect you and keep you warm against snow. But in order for you to unleash the other fire which is more dangerous than the white one is to do it on your own."

The young man began to wept in gladness while the white fire was still in his body. "Oh, thank you so much for this, my dear lord…" then he wept more.

"You are a Holy Wielder now, Kenji. I put marks in your arms symbolizing that you already have the power of my Holy element."

Kenji looked at his arms. There were tattoos in both of his arms symbolizing the Holy element's fire. Those were the tattoos that would prove him as the Holy element's new master.

"M-My arms got their cool tattoos... What are these?" wondered Kenji.

"You are right my son," said King Jethro's voice. "Those tattoos are the symbols of the Holy Fire. The white part of the tattoo is the 'White Flame', while the black part is the 'Black Flame'... The Black Flame is more dangerous type of elemental fire to use than the white one, which can even harm you if you mistakenly use it in wrong way."

"Yes, my lord. I understand..."

"So please be careful in using and handling the two Holy Fires especially the black one..."

"I understand."

"Go ahead. My Holy element will serve you and will help you to achieve your dreams. May the element will guide you no matter where you go and will protect you from harm. Goodbye..."

Kenji smiled as he answered. "Yes, my lord... It will... Thank you..." then he began to think to himself. "So I am a Element Wielder now. If so, then in no time... I can be a DDE right away!"

The young man was still on his feet while his whole body was still covered in white fire. "...So that I will get the chance to see my real father at last..."

While as for Claude and Tyrone...

The two were still busy doing their own tricks in order to survive in their ordeal. The camera were focusing straight at them, but the two remained standing on their own feet in the snow ground.

At twelve midnight, the storm was still blowing outside but not as hard as before. The three had finished their first test when Elijah, Shingue, and Reinhardt went to them to check if they made it overnight. Then, Elijah raised his hand and gladly signaled that the three had passed the first test.

"You guys cheated on me and we caught you in the camera! You used your powers that are illegal to my rules... O-Or whatever they are called man," said Elijah, but he was not angry.

"Who is using among us? I thought we can use our powers we already have, eh?" excused Tyrone. "You said that we could use our stone as long as we want because you believed they're still stones and useless... Or don't tell me you've changed your mind again!"

"Y-Yes, you can... But you shouldn't use your powers for too long.

It's cheating already. Plus, I never knew that you have some powers though you're not a Magic Wielder."

"I don't have one," said Claude. "I-It was only a lighter!"

"Hmp, you never mentioned about using the power for 'too long', Elijah. By the way, I don't have any powers… That was only a magic trick!"

"Yeah, yeah… magic trick, lighter, whatever you guys," said Elijah and he chuckled. "You guys passed the first test. Isagani has a high fever today, but you can now sit back and rest for an hour and we will proceed to the second test. Do you understand me?"

"I'm getting hungry again…" hinted Claude. "We never ate for half a day."

"As what I've told you yesterday, you are not allowed to eat nor sleep during the tests. That is our best challenge to you. But, you are allowed to have a drink."

Claude only mumbled in resentment when he drank a glass of water Elijah offered. Kenji and Tyrone also drank more than a glass of water in order to relieve their starvation.

"Oh yeeeeaaahhhh… Rest time now!" said Tyrone happily stretching his arms. "Well I need to visit Isagani and will stay there to rest with him," then he quickly preempted Elijah. "H-Hey, hey, I know what you're thinking, I will not go there to sleep okay?!"

Elijah did not answer. Then, he moved away with Tyrone when Shingue and Reinhardt came and approached Kenji and Claude.

"Kenji, Claude, congratulations!" Shingue congratulated the two with a smile.

Kenji smiled. "Thank you. Hey, we only have an hour to take a break before the second test!"

"That is not too long!"

"How is Isagani? Will Elijah have him pass the test instead?"

"I don't know, because Isagani's body is really weak against cold since he is a sickly person since childhood. His immune system is weak, which makes him get sick very often. Elijah did not know on what to decide for him."

Reinhardt had been wondering about Kenji's tattoos he just saw in his arms today and he was curious to ask about this. He remembered those tattoos were not in his brother's arms yet at the time they met and before the beginning of their first test.

THE EXPLORERS

"Um, so you're ready for your second test today?" asked Shingue to the two.

"Of course, guess I'm ready for that..." answered Claude in uncertainty.

"Alright, good luck then guys," Shingue smiled at them.

"Ahm, well..." interrupted Kenji as he faltered hesitantly. "There is something I want to tell you three about my..." he paused for a moment. "...W-Well, this is about my stone..."

"Your precious stone?" Claude wondered. "What is that? Did something just happened to your stunning stone? Did it get scratched? Or something?"

"No, Claude... Well it is, um..." Kenji showed his Holy Fire tattoos in both of his arms. "These tattoos symbolize Holy Fire that comes from the power of my stone."

"S-So, what then?" asked Claude innocently, even though he got surprised to see those tattoos for the first time in Kenji's arms. "Did you put tattoo in the middle of the test?!"

"My Divine Stone is no longer in my pocket. It housed inside my body to merge its power in me... In my heart..."

"Ah!" Claude quickly pointed Kenji in shock. "I know! You swallowed your stone in accident, didn't you? Man, what are we gonna do now to save-_"

"Please shut your mouth, Claude. I am serious!" yelled Kenji annoyingly. "Stop joking around, I am trying to tell to you guys what really transpired during the test!"

"What is it then? How did the stone go inside your heart, Kenji?" asked Shingue in concern.

Reinhardt remained silent but his face was showing curiosity. He had been waiting to know about his brother's tattoos they just saw today when Kenji spoke. "The elements that were transformed into Divine Stones were owned by King Jethro right? But the stone I had just went back to its true form as element and regained its real power again."

"What about it?" asked Claude seriously.

"I do not even understand, Claude. But, indeed... Therefore, the stone I had before was once King Jethro's power of an element... The Holy Crusade Element..." then he chuckled. "Do you guys understand what I actually mean? Besides, I think I am just the first person who brought back the stone to its true form and became the first Element Wielder."

"Is it because of your love and care to that stone?"

"Maybe, and King Jethro promised me that he will bring me to my mother in order to meet and see her in person…"

"Wait, wait…" interrupted Reinhardt when he heard about their mother and King Jethro. "Our mother, you say? Are you so sure that King Jethro really spoke to you? How did that happen?"

"Because King Jethro knows our mother who is the fairy of love, brother… And yes, he spoke to me and helped me turn back the stone to its true form."

"Does this mean… Since you are now an Element Wielder means you are eligible to promote to DDE, aren't you?" asked Shingue in jealousy. "That seems unfair to me because King Jethro helped you transform your Divine Stone back to its true form."

"He can not," answered Reinhardt. "According to the Explorers' superior leader, an Explorer of a lower class can not promote into DDE immediately as long as his rank does not raise from UE to EUE… Y-You know, as if you are studying in school and finish each of the school levels before you graduate…"

"Is that so? Though Kenji is an Element Wielder already?"

"Yes. So even if Kenji already has King Jethro's element doesn't mean he can be a DDE immediately. This highest class is very strict in raising an Explorer's class since they require something that needs to be done. In fact, I can now raise my class into EUE but the DDEs do not allow me for whatever reason they have. How annoying… Actually, there was a time I visited their mansion just to see my father, but the DDEs kept on telling me that he was not around. When I asked them where he went so I would look for him and they would not answer. That already happened many times everytime I was getting there just to see him. I never had a chance to meet him even once since he was always not around in the DDE mansion."

"Then tell them frankly that you are his son, Reinhardt," said Shingue as his opinion. "That should let you see your father after a very, very long time."

"I already told them about it, Shingue… But they would not want to believe me. I was getting pissed on telling them about it many times but still they would not believe. I had a hunch that my father was actually in the mansion and they were only telling me lies. So what I did was to only ask them to just force my father to come out of their mansion, but they said he was not in his mood to show himself to someone. Geez, I don't know… Even my father does not even want to see his son nor showing his interest towards me anymore!"

Kenji moved closer to Reinhardt in sad face and patted his shoulder. "When I finish all of our tests and become an Explorer, brother… Please accompany me to go to the DDE mansion and I will surely face them to see our father together!"

25 SECOND TEST PART 1

An hour of resting slipped away after the four had a long conversation during their break time. Now it's time for them to take their second test under the watchful eye of the UE.

It was one o'clock dawn when the snowstorm weakened. Kenji and Claude were now changing their clothes in their room.

"Kenji, did you get rested enough for only an hour today? Well physically yes, but my mouth has been exhausted just to have a chitchat with you earlier. Anyway, I enjoyed everything we've talked," said Claude.

"Aha," answered Kenji while brushing his teeth. "I am getting excshited for the shecond tesht and that ish okay with me. Why don't you shtop talking to me for now sho your mouth get reshted ash well? I'm brushing my teeth right now, shee?"

"But I've finished brushing my teeth. What I'm going to do next is to do the warm-up!"

Kenji rinsed his mouth. "You know what, I'm still stuffed. I ate so much foods in the restaurant yesterday. You see, it was a special treat for us!"

"W-Well, I'm feeling hungry again!"

Kenji began to think about what Reinhardt told them earlier. He thought to himself. "Why does my father not want to show himself to *kuya* Reinhardt though he is his son?" then he closed his eyes and sighed. "Does our father have no time for us anymore? Is he abandoning us? I have never seen him personally yet since me and *kuya* Genji were born, being fled by our mother, and up to now we're already grown up!"

THE EXPLORERS

Claude turned to Kenji after hearing him murmuring alone. "A-Are you saying something?"

"Nothing, that's none of your business."

There was a knock on the door. Claude opened the door when Margot quickly entered the room and he kissed Claude on the cheek.

"EHE-HE-HE-HEEEWWWW!!!" screamed Claude out loud.

"Eeeeee!!!" shrieked Margot in his blushing face. "Oh, I-I'm so sorry, cutie… I thought you were…"

Claude got instantly pissed off as he was wiping his cheek. "Blimey! You… Y-You, you--! What have you done to me? Why are you here anyway?"

"I only came to cheer my boyfriend, Kenji. I know today is his second test so I would like to give him my sweet kisses and my warm affection!"

"Oh man," Kenji covered his mouth in disgust. "Um, I do not need a cheer. I am fine, thanks anyway…." then he told a joke. "I am confident enough to pass the next test because I believe that I am far stronger now than Elijah's. Nah, I'm just kidding… N-Now if you don't mind, will you please just leave us alone?"

"Oh yeah?" said Margot. "I know you love me… And I know when's our anniversary, darlin'…"

"You, you flirt--!" said Claude annoyingly.

"No, Claude. Stop," stopped Kenji.

"See that? My Kenji is defending me from you! That's a sure sign of love. Thanks darlin'…" Margot winked.

"Come on, Claude. Let's walk outside now. Tyrone is waiting for us," said Kenji then he turned to Margot. "Ahem, thanks for the cheer, Margot."

The two went outside the room when they met Tyrone waving at them. "Kenji, Claude. Elijah is calling us now. Today is our second test!"

"Yeah, we know. Let us go," answered Kenji and they walked together going to Elijah.

Kenji spoke to his mind while his hand was next to his heart as he was walking. "Holy element… Please help me to exceed and pass the tests I will face today… So that I will become a part of the organization and see my father!"

"By the way, what about Isagani?" asked Claude to Tyrone. "What is Elijah going to do to him now?"

"Yes, we know. Isagani is forcing himself to finish the Endurance Test now but he doesn't know that he's suffering a high fever right now. His body temperature is too high, way above the normal!"

"Hah, gimme a break dude!"

"I am telling the truth…"

The three ran outside the mansion when they saw Elijah outside waiting for them again. He was still in his outerwear.

"Hello guys. Let's proceed to your second test now, shall we?" said Elijah smiling. "If the first test was only a piece of cake for you guys, then this time it will be quite challenging. Are you ready and up for this?"

The three remained mum while looking at Elijah's face.

"With regards to Isagani… I was not satisfied with his performance and he's unable to pass his first test yet, but instead I will give him a 'special test' to help him become a licensed Explorer."

Kenji stooped down his head sadly. "Poor Isagani…"

"Okay, so this is what your second test will be: there will be an Endurance and Skill Test once again. Each of you must fight and compete with an unknown creature which the Explorers called to as 'Vrandolon'."

There was a big question mark on Claude's head. "What is Vrandolon?"

"We dispatched strong Vrandolons in different locations where you will fight against each and everyone of them. A Vrandolon is a magical creature only summoned by the Wielder. One of the UEs has summoned three of his Vrandolons using his summoning ability thru the Magic Stone he obtained. He turned the said stone back to its true form which made him become a Magic Wielder and acquired a summoning ability."

"O-Oh, I see…" Claude faltered in amazement.

"So, since you already know the rules… I have changed one rule for you: If you're really possessing powers and magics, then you have all the time to use it anytime you like. But you should beat the Vrandolon you will be facing during the test. You will find them in their specific spots."

Kenji was nervous. "Perhaps… those monsters are strong. And you intentionally assigned them in different locations so we can take them one-on-one… Gosh!"

Elijah took three small scrolled papers in his belt bag and he showed them to the three. "Here, to be fair. Please pick one and you should follow what is listed here. The Vrandolon is waiting for you there. Do you get me?"

THE EXPLORERS

"Heh, I wish the Vrandolon I will face with is just a piece of cake," whispered Tyrone to himself. "Good luck to me then!"

"Come on, pick one now you guys!"

The three quickly picked one of each small papers in Elijah's hand. Claude picked first, while Kenji and Tyrone were both clashing with the same paper.

"Geez, man! There's another one here!" Claude pointed a small paper. "What has left will be yours, Kenji!"

The three had picked their small paper when Elijah spoke again. "Excellent! Now you can open the paper you have picked. You will be taking this test individually and spontaneously. Which means you are all alone in the wilderness during the test and nothing to call on for help."

Kenji asked Elijah while unrolling the small paper. "Hey Elijah, I thought we would be having a test as a team?"

Elijah turned to his back. "Yes, there would be. But not for now."

Claude was surprised seeing what was written in his paper. He was about to read it. "What the! Mine is in--"

"Shhh! Don't you tell it to them, Claude. This is confidential, but you should tell it to me."

Claude would be taking the test inside the cave located in one of the mountain cliffs. Tyrone would be taking under the huge sinkhole at the forest, while Kenji would take underwater at the sea. Their assigned location should be kept secret to their fellow challengers, so they whispered their location one by one to Elijah's curious ear.

"You may proceed and begin your test now, guys. All you have to do is find the unknown creature hidden at your pre- assigned place and retrieve the three flags. I don't care how will you taking care of the creature but I want you to extract at least ten scales from their body. I know its not easy for them to just give up the fight and you can have their scales. The scales are their armor protecting their sensitive body so you are really obliged to beat them first before they will give you the 'reward'. When you finish the test, return here immediately carrying the three flags and the ten scales of the Vrandolon. Do I make myself clear?"

The three answered at the same time. "Yes, sir!"

"Okay buddies, go now and I'm expecting each and everyone of you to win the fight and pass the test... Good luck!"

The three swiftly ran together away from the mansion, but later on they dispersed to their assigned spot in different locations. Elijah went back to the mansion and there he called for the UEs to give them order.

"Vamir, Shingue, and Marion. Please watch the three challengers and never show your presence to them. Monitor their moves, their individual skills, and the time involved after finishing the test. They are unaware that somebody will be watching them."

"Who will I watch?" asked Shingue.

"Shingue, you'll watch Claude. Marion, you'll watch *kuya* Tyrone. And Vamir, you'll watch--"

"I WILL watch my husband, Kenji!" a voice of Margot from nowhere was suddenly heard as he was approaching them. "He said something to me earlier that I would be cheering him during the test so, here..." he showed off the white towel he was holding to the four boys. Then, he was starting with his drama again. "If ever he gets wounded... oh... I will go near him to wipe his face and hug him very tightly... Oho-ho-ho! Oh my, Kenji... I will be there for you to give you lots of love. And then, we will--"

"Come on, Vamir. You'll be watching Kenji. Just hide and never try to show yourself to him," said Elijah to Vamir as he was ignoring Margot.

Margot got annoyed. "Hey, you ugly little buddy! Stop saying that! I said I would be watching my husband myself. He needs me!"

"Pfff... it's up to you Margot," said Elijah feeling embarrassed. "Go and watch your Kenji, but you will be going there with Vamir," then he pinched the gay's lips. "Please remain silent there and control your gibberish mouth! Just watch your husband there and NEVER try to make a move by showing yourself to him! I already know you much... that noisy, prattle mouth of yours!!!" then he pinched it harder.

Marion and Shingue were getting dressed when Margot asked Elijah. "Buy why should I go there with this ugly young man, Elijah? Shingue and Marion will be watching on their own alone. Come on, cutie... let me watch Kenji alone, I can take good care of him."

"Geez! Just shut up Margot," said Elijah annoyingly but in jokingly way. "Why don't you remain here instead? You keep on complaining and wasting our time!"

"A-Alright then... How annoying really... I will go with Vamir then. I will never be noisy there."

"That is very good to hear indeed! Keep your mouth shut because they do not know that somebody will watch them. Okay, here are your

THE EXPLORERS

smartphones now. Just call me for any updates, okay?" said Elijah and he gave the four communication gadgets to the watchers. "Take care."

The four were about to leave the mansion now when Elijah called Margot. "Margot?"

Margot turned to Elijah. "What?"

Elijah was doing a gesture by pinching his own lips when Margot understood what the leader wanted to tell him.

"Yeah, yeah... I know that already, you handsome jerk!"

"What the--! How could you, Margot. You're being so disrespectful towards your UE LEADER!!!"

Kenji was the first one to reach his assigned destination because of his unique speed that he inherited from his father. He jumped to a small tree, where he sighted the sea.

"So there's the sea... But it looks like I will be having trouble looking for the monster in this huge sea. Man, that sucks."

Kenji looked around the sea in the distance. "Hmm... And where will I find those three flags either? Perhaps they are hidden in the corals or in the sands. But it's dark... and it's still dawn!"

Later, the young man stepped on the white sand of the beach still looking for something. "Where is the starting point here? Where exactly the sea creature is lurking? Hey, the sea is too big!"

Tyrone was the next one to reach his destination. Claude seemed to be lost while trying to search for the cave in one of the mountain cliffs.

"Heeeyyy! There are many mountains here. Which of these has a cave? Oh, merciful heavens..." said Claude panting while making his own drama.

Back to Kenji.

Kenji was still having trouble in looking for the flags and the unknown creature. He did not know where to start.

"Another thing is, the water is very cold! How am I going to dive underwater in this temperature? Wait, I know!" Kenji touched his arm with the tattoo. "This Holy Fire can help me withstand the cold temperature and it can give warmth to my body. So, at least I have my defense against cold!"

He looked around once again. "Okay, I'm gonna start now," he said smiling. "Um, should I take off my upper wear? I don't mind with my pants and it's okay for me to get wet."

Kenji took off his jacket as well as his fitted shirt. He also took off his headband, the accessories in his arms, and his pair of boots. What only left in his body now was his pants. He would bring his Kali.

He placed his upper clothes, accessories, and boots in the sand. "Surely no one will take my belongings here."

Kenji began to wade in the cold water. The other parts of the sea became icy because of the storm earlier. "Wooohhh, it's too cold!"

Silence. Kenji stopped from wading in the water. "Man, it's too tough for me to dive underwater. Elijah shouldn't give this test in this location. Probably Claude and Tyrone are now battling with their monster. I think the heat of the Holy Fire is not enough to warmth my whole body and I might still chilling underwater. Ahhh... Anyway, that's not an excuse!"

Claude was still lost on his way in the mountains. He knew that he was in the right mountains, but which of the cliffs had its cave?

Claude cried out loud annoyingly. "Hey, you damn cave! Where are you right now? I really can't find you, goddammit!" and he ran. "Come on man, show yourself!"

He tried to run along the cliff, but he got exhausted when he passed the first mountain leading to the second mountain. Later, he heard a loud thunder coming out from the sky. "Man, guess the rain will fall next."

The snowstorm ended for now, but the rain would be the next to fall. Therefore, Claude hurriedly ran on his way. "No time to complain. I need to see the cave right away before I get wet by the incoming stupid rain!"

Claude was not the only one who was in a hurry, but also the four watchers who did not even expect that it would rain. They were also running in pursuit to their assigned challengers, but later they called Elijah by their phones because they forgot to ask the current locations of the three challengers before they left the mansion. Elijah answered. When they ended the call, the watchers immediately went in different directions and got separated.

"Oh dear Vamir, we must hurry! Elijah said that my husband is at the sea right now! It will rain soon and he will get wet, but good thing I bring this towel with me!" said Margot to Vamir in a hurry.

"Are you nuts? Kenji will really get soaked because he will dive under the sea! Besides, he doesn't need you anyway!"

The gay slapped Vamir. "Why are you saying that to me? Do you have a crush on me? Or are you only jealous?"

Vamir got pissed off. "Curse this noisy gay! You freaking son of a monster!"

THE EXPLORERS

"Shhh, be quiet... He might hear you. You're getting noisy, ex-boyfriend."

"Whatever! For every man you see is already your ex-boyfriend. Aren't you forgetting that you're a man as well, you jerk?!"

"Shut up, cutie! I will tell Elijah you've been flirting with me, Vammy!"

"Go to hell, you impertinent gay!!!"

Marion had noticed the large hole in the thick forest where Tyrone went by. He was the first watcher to reach his destination.

"Okay, here comes the king of Ultimate Explorer named Marion! Not *kuya* Elijah but only me... the future king of the DDE sooner!" he said arrogantly.

Silence. Later, the naughty kid began to think in wonder. He looked around. "So where will I hide?"

Claude finally found the cave. The cave was just behind the first mountain cliff. He was only looking at the front side of the mountains that gobbled lots of his time. Good thing he thought of going to the other side of the mountain cliff that had a cave.

Shingue was the next watcher who arrived when he saw Claude in the cavern entrance. "I can see Claude from here with my binoculars," he brought the binoculars with him and not the umbrella.

The small drops of rain began to shower when Claude entered the cavern. He firstly noticed the first flag asked by Elijah that was no longer stuck in the ground and he immediately picked it up.

Claude was the first challenger who had found the first flag though he was the last one to arrive in his destination. "Thank goodness I found the first flag and at the same time I did not get caught by the rain. I never thought it was so easy to have the first flag."

He was unaware that Shingue was watching in his back quietly. Shingue was hiding in a big tree when he returned his binoculars inside its bag. He could see Claude in the distance and he was not making any move to avoid detection. He pulled out his smartphone to call Elijah. "Elijah, Claude has just found the first flag. He is now proceeding to the second flag," he said whispering.

"Great! But it won't be easy for him when he gets to the ten scales. The Vrandolon he will face is very tougher than he expects. Still, do not make any moves nor sounds, okay?"

"Okay!"

Tyrone was the second challenger who had found the first flag. The first flag was stuck behind a tree that was covered by vines. "Hah, there you are!" said Tyrone. "You think I wouldn't find you, would you?"

Tyrone brought out his bag to keep the required objects asked by Elijah. "Good thing I have this bag," he said smiling. "Then I should even show my fast service here so I don't get embarrassed to that Mr. Eyebrow (Claude)!" then he stroked his chin.

As for Marion, he seemed reluctant to come inside the large hole entered by Tyrone. He thought that he might create a noise just as he entered and Tyrone would discover his presence. The large hole had nothing much to hide and it did not have much trees except the orchids and grasses clinging on the sinkhole wall.

"I am not going to follow him," said Marion. "I'll wait for him to get away from here before I follow his back. Good thing I am smart," then he pulled out a very small gadget that looked like a toy. It was a tiny drone that was not easily seen by the human naked eye. "I am proud to use my gadget called, 'Marion Flying Hidden Camera'! This little baby can fly and I can control its movement. All I have to do is wear this headband with screen which will be my widescreen TV and bingo! I am able to see *kuya* Tyrone now!"

Marion's drone was once owned by Elijah but later on he gave it to Marion. The said gadget had its joystick controller which was used to control the drone. The headband had a built-in antennae, headset, and microphone that could be also used in communications. This gadget was designed and perfected by Professor Sergio, the famous inventor of the Explorers who was already passed away. Only few chosen Explorers had that gadget aside from spies who were doing the surveillance activities. Luckily, Elijah had it and he decided to give it to Marion as his special birthday gift.

The naughty kid knew the proper operation of his toy gadget. He pressed the small button in the controller first and it turned on. Then, he wore the headband on his head. The camera's vision appeared on the headband's screen worn by Marion. Now, he was able to see what the camera could see.

"I need to move my high-tech night vision camera inside this hole now," said Marion and he pressed the button of his remote controller. The tiny camera began to float in the air and then he tilted the controller joystick. The camera was now moving on its way.

The two Kenji's watchers were still fighting with each other up to now, thus making their way to the site was hampered by their nonsense arguments. It was raining cats and dogs, and the two were drenched. But still, they kept on quarreling with each other.

"Oh my Vamir, it's raining already. My darling is getting soaked by the rain…" said Margot doing the flirty drama. "Ohhh… Perhaps Kenji is now looking for me and I'm afraid he might catch a cold…"

Vamir did not answer. He was getting tired of quarreling with the noisy gay.

"Vamir, maybe he is having a fever now! Come on and let's hurry…"

"Do you think it will be easy for us to move faster with this muddy ground during the rain? If you want, you can move away now and go on your own. I don't need you anyway!"

"Alright! Then I am going to leave you now," said Margot arrogantly. "How can an ugly young man like you become so sluggish," then he moved away faster.

Margot was only meters away from Vamir when he suddenly heard a wolf cry and he quickly recoiled, but just as he recoiled he accidentally stepped on a quicksand. Margot was now slowly sinking, and Vamir saw what happened to him so he laughed out loud as his revenge!

"Eeeeeeee! Eeeeeeee! Oh dear, Vamir," screamed Margot on top of his voice while slowly sinking in quicksand. "I'm sinking. Vamir protect me… PROTECT MEEEE!!!"

"A-HA-HA-HA-HA!!!" Vamir laughed out loud. "Oh poor Margot. So that is what an ugly gay ends up when he becomes so arrogant and hasty. Look at yourself now, you're getting muddy!!!"

Margot was still screaming while Vamir was laughing as he was watching him sinking in the quicksand. When Vamir saw Margot's head was about to sink, he immediately rescued the paled friend.

After the rescue, Margot suddenly wept in embarrassment. "Huhuhu… Kenji, where are you now? If my Kenji knew what you have done. Huhuhu…"

"Can you just shut your muddy mouth now?" said Vamir smirking towards Margot with his hands on the hips.

Kenji had been diving underwater for long and he was now carrying the three flags in his hand. His body was covered by the White Fire, though the fire was underwater it did not quench since the Holy Fire was not the same as the real fire.

Kenji was the only challenger to take the toughest test because he was doing the test underwater. It was too tough for him to dive underwater and hold his breath for long. He admitted he could not swim if it wasn't for Rolando during his long training with him. But if not, he might be drowned to his death now!

Kenji immediately swam back to the seashore right after he found the three flags and he stuck it into the sand next to his clothes. He put out the White Fire around his body when he just noticed it was already raining heavily.

"That's sucks... The rain is heavy, and my clothes I left here have been soaked wet too. I was unaware of it since I was busy under the sea."

Kenji had nothing else to do but to wear his upper clothes again. "I don't want these wet clothes to become itchy by the sands when worn. Man..."

Silence. He thought to himself. "The next thing I need to do now is to get the ten scales of the unknown creature I will face according to Elijah's instruction. Based on the term 'ten scales,' it gives me an idea of what type of this monster is. Obviously a reptile with scales... A kind of crocs maybe?"

He stroked his chin as he turned to the three flags stuck in the sand. "These flags will serve as my sign so I will know my way back near the mansion."

Later, he felt the chill in his body so he cast the Holy Fire again. While bathing in the rain, the young man breathed deeply several times before he would go back to the sea again. "One *(inhale, exhale)*. Two *(inhale, exhale)*, three *(inhale, exhale)*, four *(inhale, exhale)*..."

Kenji was exhausted after swimming underwater for long. But he was very much determined to finish the test and quitting was not his cup of tea so they said. If he really wanted to become an Explorer then he should pass this test and win it. And so, he prayed.

He rested for fifteen minutes while praying. Praying that he would find the unknown creature, defeating it, and acquiring the ten scales.

Later on, Kenji discovered something about the flaws of Holy Fire in his body. He noticed his body was gradually losing its energy after the prolonged use of the said fire. He learned that the stronger he was using the

Holy Fire was the same it was absorbing his human energy. Now, he was feeling weak.

"Now I learn that I shouldn't use this power for so long… I can only use it once my body has enough energy to consume. It looks like… I am the Holy Fire's battery in order for it to work perfectly!"

26 SECOND TEST PART 2

Good thing the two Kenji's watchers had finally reached their destination. Vamir's face was now showing the hardship he was dealing with Margot as he got much scratches and bruises in his cheeks by the number of slaps and pinches of him. While as for Margot, he was relaxed, feeling insensitive for what he had been doing with his colleague as he never got tired of slapping Vamir's innocent face!

The two were now in the seashore when Vamir noticed the three flags stuck in the white sand. "Those three flags of Kenji… he got them all!" then he quickly called Elijah by the phone to tell about the update. "Elijah! Kenji has taken the three flags. He is proceeding to the ten scales. He left the flags here in the seashore."

Elijah answered on the line. After the conversation, Vamir ended the call.

"Oh my Kenji! He's gonna catch cold… Poor darling. You see, he has been diving under the sea for long, and then… This rain will soak his body and I'm afraid he'll get a high fever! He's needing me!!!"

"A-Are you saying something, Margot?"

"N-Nothing. I wasn't talking to you, idiot."

"Oh, I guess I only heard an ant or a bee maybe. My apologies…"

"Are you simply saying that I was the one you've heard? Are you really feeling jealous at Kenji?"

Vamir did not answer. He was only controlling his temper towards the gay. Margot moved closer to the flags.

"Those three flags surely smell sweet as Kenji," said Margot and he took the flags. "I'll keep this so they will not lose. Kenji, you're so amazing!"

"Stop that, Margot! Put those flags back or later Kenji will find out that there's someone here when he gets back. Put them back now!" said Vamir annoyingly.

"Awww..." Margot stuck the flags back into the white sand in flirty way. "That sucks..."

"Do not ever do that again, you stupid gay! Your actions can reveal Kenji's suspicions... Think first before you act, damn you!!!" said Vamir angrily.

"It's okay if Kenji finds out that I am here. What if he'll ask me to swim with him together, and then later..." Margot began to do the drama act again while Vamir was losing his temper once more. "...maybe later we will do something very romantic under the sea... Ohhh my!"

"That's totally absurd! He will never ever need you, jerk!" shouted Vamir.

And then, their long fight started again...

The three challengers had completed in getting the three flags and they were now proceeding to their battle against the "unknown creature". Tyrone was taking the test under the huge sinkhole, where the area was dark and small. He was assuming that the creature was hiding in the dark, lurking behind the boulders while waiting for the suspected prey.

The three were still oblivious to their watchers who were still watching them surreptitiously. But as for Tyrone, he seemed to have a strong hunch that someone was following his back. He turned to his back, then to his sides, and elsewhere.

"I have a feeling that someone is watching me... Is that a Vrandolon?" he asked.

Since he was there all alone, knowing that no one else was following his footsteps but only the Vrandolon. The fact remained obscure that it was actually the flying camera that was following him.

Marion also entered the mouth of a big hole then he moved over the boulder to hide. "Yeah, *kuya* Tyrone is totally awesome!"

Claude was also on his way towards the Vrandolon's haven when the cave inside was getting darker as he moved forward. Sometimes he tripped off by the small rocks he was stepping on, and he was getting pissed by the flying bat that zooming right before his innocent face. But despite of this, he suddenly thought about the current condition of his friend, Kenji... Or in his true name as "Maximillian".

Their second test was tough. The place was unknown to them. They had no compass nor map that they could use to lead them in the right direction. What worst, they needed to look for the Vrandolon which was also unknown to them and they had to fight with them before they get the ten scales... Although they had not been eating yet!

Claude suddenly tripped again and got on his knees. He did not see another rock he just stepped on because it was almost pitch dark inside the cave. He fumbled on the ground, while still thinking about Kenji's situation.

He was uncertain about this strange feeling he suddenly felt today during the midst of the test. He did not understand why did Kenji just cross in his mind giving him mysterious thought on what could possibly might happen to him. Kenji was his childhood friend... Since he met him with his twin brother Genji in the town of Damsville.

Kenji's image suddenly appeared in Claude's mind. From being a young boy until he grew up to a young man. He remembered Kenji's advices and encouragements not to lose hope in life, for being so determined to follow his dreams and become a good person. He did not understand why he began to reminisce those things in all of a sudden. He even noticed the big difference in their behavior. Kenji had no vices and he had one. Kenji was long-tempered and he was the opposite. He had a strange feeling that Kenji might be in great danger during the course of his test!

"W-What is this eerie feeling I just felt right now? Seems strange... There's something keeps on bothering my mind that demoralizing me now..."

Claude walked slowly while Kenji was still in his mind. Later, he realized that he should make some new changes in his life from now on.

Claude tried to focus himself back in finding the Vrandolon again. His actions became agile while his troubling thoughts slowly faded away. He was still unaware of Shingue's presence, who even kept on tripping off the ground by the small rocks he was stepping on. But, he kept himself to be quiet and unseen. Until, he noticed Claude's motion was not normal.

"Elijah, I can see Claude walking restless today. It looks like he's getting more exhausted. I'm afraid he might not gonna make it to reach the Vrandolon," said Shingue to Elijah by the phone.

THE EXPLORERS

"Oh yeah? Just watch that kid carefully. Call me again for more updates," said Elijah on the line.

Claude became slow once again in his serious face. "How is Kenji right now I wonder? Kenji..."

Back to the sea.

Two hours had passed and the full moon was up. Kenji still could not find the unknown creature underwater. He kept on diving, swimming back to the water surface to catch his breath, then diving back again to continue his search. He limited his use of Holy Fire to save his energy, but he could not help it whenever he felt the intense chill by the very cold water. He did not realize that he was now getting farther from the seashore where the three flags were stuck.

Later, Kenji stopped his use of White Fire when he felt that he was losing his energy again. But after a few seconds, he was freezing again although he swam back to the water surface. "I already lose much of my energy and still I haven't seen this Vrandolon yet," he said.

Kenji forced himself to dive back to the bottom of the sea. If he passed out and losing his last breaths underwater then there's nothing else he could do. At least he did his "very best", and never gave up. He had left so many promises to those people he once encountered during his journey and he did not want to disappoint them. Rolando and Master Serge, Valerie and Agnes, as well as the old woman whom he met in Dakar.

He must be strong... He must be determined... He needed strength and power to pass this second test!

I do not want to fail... I do not want to break all my promises and turn into nothing... I need to succeed!

Kenji had a hard time to dive this time since he lost much of his energy by the Holy Fire. *If I do not succeed... I will never get the chance to see my real father, my mother... as well as my brothers and sisters... especially* kuya *Genji!*

Suddenly, the young man heard a huge whale-like cry from afar. This regained his confident back with full of hope because he knew surely it was the unknown creature. He immediately thought of going up towards the sea surface again to catch his breath and breathe deeply. He scoured the bottom of the sea from above to follow the source of the monster's cry. He would wait for the sea creature to come closer and when it did, he would catch his long breath on the surface... And then, he would dive back again to face that Vrandolon for the very first time!

"Claude is getting weaker, sir!" said Shingue when he called Elijah again worriedly. His eyes were staring straight at Claude. "It seems there is a problem!"

Claude was feeling demoralized. Chilling and exhausted as Kenji and Tyrone. But as for Tyrone, he was still showing his arrogance despite of exhaustion!

Shingue noticed Claude stopped for a moment to lay his back on the ground. The watcher's face was now looking concerned. "Poor guys… But do not worry, we'd even been there before so I believe you can also make it!"

Claude was lying on the ground in the midst of the dark cave. Only his glimmering eyes were visible in the darkness.

Silence.

"I think he was just resting. After all, this test is not a racing challenge…" said Shingue to himself.

Claude stood up again. He wanted to sleep for a moment to regain some energy but it was against the rules. He could only relax, but not too long.

He rested for five minutes to catch his breath, and he did not know that he was getting closer to the Vrandolon. He was relaxed, thinking that he needed more steps to take in order to reach the dread monster.

It was 3:30am when Tyrone felt the ground shaking all over the place, followed by the thunder coming from afar. He knew that the big monster was lurking under his feet and might attacked him at any given time. He prepared himself for any eventuality at the expense of the unknown monster. A huge shaking and deafening thunder was filled the sinkhole when he finally found the monster after it quickly emerged under the mud to do its first attack. Good thing he quickly dodged its attack. The Vrandolon was a giant worm overlaid by its colorful scales. It had eight pointed fangs and numerous sharp small fangs in its big mouth. Its tail had a pointed-like spear which could mutilate Tyrone's body in one strike.

"The Vrandolon!" cried Tyrone as he rattled in shock. The ground was shaking strong and he startled when he noticed that the huge monster had no eyes. Then, he smiled. "Ah, so that's where you were hiding, blind monster. Very well, then this is the end of our fight now! I will send you back to where you are perfectly belong… Underground!"

He drew out his weapon and pointed the monster. "I will show you what I can do to get your scales and defeat you instantly!"

The Vrandolon roared out loud when Tyrone began his first attack. The monster was so strong and was too quick for his size. Tyrone tried to attack the monster but the monster was good in dodging attacks despite the fact that it was completely blind. He also noticed that wherever he went, the Vrandolon could easily detect his presence and the giant worm could only attack offensively in the darkness. He could not figure out how he could defeat such wise and smart monster if this worm had a high anticipation in every breath and in every move he made.

Later, Tyrone learned that the monster had a high sense of touch to compensate his blindness. The worm was perfectly adopted to his surroundings, the absence of lights, and the serenity in which a faint sound of movement could be a loud noise to him. Tyrone also realized that the best way to come closer to the Vrandolon to wage an attack was not to make any sounds nor crackle that might have caught the worm's attention.

The two fought with each other under the dark when Tyrone's Divine Stone unexpectedly cast a strong light and the giant worm got dazzled so it recoiled. Tyrone stopped in doing his sets of attacks when he noticed the monster crawled back in fear. Now he learned that this Vrandolon's weakness was light.

Kenji successfully followed the source of the whale-like cry. He found it at the southwest side and it was indeed Vrandolon. "Glad I caught you…" Kenji said to himself.

He quickly swam upwards towards the surface to catch his long breath, but the Vrandolon felt his presence and even smelt his scent. He turned to the young man when he saw him swimming up to the surface.

"That Vrandolon surely is big and ugly! It is a giant blue squid with big eyes and ten tentacles," said Kenji to himself while still swimming upwards. "What is that? A squid with blue scales? I thought it was some sort of a fish."

The giant monster quickly moved over the young man who was unaware of his approach. He used his one long tentacle to reach Kenji's right foot and quickly pulled it. Kenji was shocked to see that he was being caught by this monster!

"Blimey! He caught me. I'm not yet ready… What am I gonna do?!" he said to himself.

The Vrandolon pulled his tentacle down over him as the young man groaned in pain by the strong kink of its tentacle. But Kenji immediately saw the scales in the tentacle that was coiling his foot. "The scales..."

Since the tentacle was full of scales, he tried to just take them by his hand and swam away. He was about to reach in the scale when the giant monster quickly slapped his hand with its another tentacle. Then, the Vrandolon pulled him again closer to its wide opened mouth!

"What am I gonna do now? I can't hold my breath anymore!" cried Kenji to his mind.

He knocked the tentacle with his left foot, but it did not let go of his right foot. The monster kinked his right foot harder which made Kenji screamed in pain. He knocked harder, but the tentacle was still in his right foot.

Kenji was getting nearer of losing his breath so he knocked the tentacle by his left foot as hard as he could. Unfortunately, the other tentacle also caught his left foot.

I... I don't wanna die...

Kenji tried to hold his breath again as long as he could when the monster's another tentacle entwined his body. The other tentacles grasped his waist as well as they were all pulling him down over the monster's mouth. His body was now wrapped by the tentacles, except his upper torso and his arms.

The young man thought of a quick plan when he turned his gaze over his right arm. "Wait... What is the use of my weapon if I do nothing and just let myself get eaten?!"

He quickly pulled his long Kali weapon in his back with his right hand. Its sword was already sharpened before he began the test. He quickly pulled the staff's body to draw out its sword, then he quickly swung the sword to cut off the tentacles. The squid cried in pain swimming away and released Kenji from his tentacles. Kenji quickly swam upwards back to the sea surface and quickly breathe deeply.

Claude was the third challenger who successfully found the Vrandolon. It was four o'clock dawn when he found it. The unknown creature was a huge type of crocs that also covered by the attractive green scales. It had two long tails covered with pointed spikes that could mutilate Claude's fragile body. The monster could be seen under the moonlight due to its glistening armored scales. It had a powerful jaw and six feet designed for quick movements both in land and water. Claude was attracted to its

THE EXPLORERS

nice scales.

"Wow, those scales are nice… but its possessor is, um… looks hideous!" he joked.

The Vrandolon was a great biter and was also aggressive as Tyrone's opponent. It even had strong sense of smell as Kenji's opponent, but it was weak and slow on defense due to its immense body.

Claude lifted his right fist wearing his primary weapon which was a glove and an arm brace. His arm brace was forged by a hard dense metal alloys and was only worn in his right arm. At the time of his long training, Master Serge taught him Karate and Judo martial arts techniques.

Their battle began. Claude was the luckiest challenger because he would be facing the weakest and dumbest monster among the three. Claude positioned himself in front of the croc to gauge the speed of its attack. The reptile advanced forward and swung its long spiky tail followed by a quick bite to the lad. Claude evaded the attack and he rolled over the muddy sands to prepare himself for the kill. Good thing he could easily take advantage the monster's stupidity by giving it his chain of strong blows. The young man thought that he could easily beat this dumb monster.

The monster took all the blows and pounds by Claude when it opened its mouth wide to do the attack. Then, it quickly dashed over Claude to bite his arm. Luckily, Claude dodged its attack.

"You are such the most nonsense opponent I've ever faced throughout my life. Take this and I'm gonna kick your ass!!!" shouted Claude and then he did the strong uppercut to the monster's jaw. BOINK!

The Vrandolon was not easy to knock out because of its huge size and weight. Claude followed his chain of combos while his high spirit was regaining to raise his good mood.

"Ha-oooweeee! Take that, and that, and that, you BIG ASSHOLE!!!"

The monster could not retaliate from Claude's combos as he was still being kicked and punched continuously. He roared when Claude stopped for a moment to watch his move and give his turn to attack. The large crocodile slowly attacked with his mouth when a green slimy liquid spurted and caught Claude by surprise. The slime was so thick that made Claude unable to move. The croc saw the prey stumbled on the ground and he opened his mouth for the big bite. Claude saw the chances, did his next strong uppercut again and the monster's head lifted up. The dumb Vrandolon stumbled and fell on the ground. It created a huge quake causing the stalactites to fell on the crocs' tail making the monster immovable.

"You're too boring!" said Claude boringly while watching the downed monster and then he dashed over it. "I shall put an end to this battle now. TAKE THIS, YOU FREAKIN' DEVIL!!!"

Claude would have made his finishing blow when the Vrandolon suddenly spoke. "Please do not kill me, young man… I surrender now."

The young man was surprised to hear that this dumb monster could actually speak.

Claude goggled at the Vrandolon in disbelief. "So you can speak… But why didn't you fight much with me earlier? Man, I was gettin' excited. I thought my fight with you was really that tough."

The monster felt embarrassed, but instead, he just made an excuse. "I see… Well it is because I'm already too old to fight and still getting older in each day. I am done with fighting and exhausted to kill someone."

Claude again in disbelief. "R-Really? M-Me too… I've been exhausted too and I'm sleepy!"

Shingue was shocked. His face gaped at the two. "O-Our Vrandolon just gave up the fight? B-But why did he do that?"

"I knew that someone would be coming here to fight me according to my master. You are small… but you're very strong!"

"Yeah, sure! Now that I beat you today and spare your life, then you should give me your ten beautiful scales as a favor. How about that?"

Shingue looked at his watch. "What? It's only 4:15am. Is that mean that they only fought for fifteen minutes? Why did our Vrandolon really just give up this exciting fight? Tsktsktsk…" then he took out his phone and he dialed the number. "Hello? Hey Elijah, Claude has just finished his second test today. He has the ten scales now!"

"Why, I can't believe it! Did he really defeat our powerful monster in the cave? How did that happen?" asked Elijah on the line.

"Well I do not understand what happened to your so called 'powerful monster', Elijah. You just said he was powerful, but look what he actually did… Your powerful Vrandolon just surrendered the fight!"

"S-Surrendered?"

"And that was FAST and totally EASY! You see, Claude fought with him for ONLY fifteen minutes! How ridiculous, hahahaha!!!"

Elijah stopped for the moment, but later on he cried jokingly while his

THE EXPLORERS

voice was breaking up on the line. "W-AT A US-L-SS MON-TER IT –S!!!"

"Now his test is done Elijah, period! That Vrandolon just broke your high expectation. Anyway, should I show myself to Claude now so we can go home together to the mansion?"

"You're only coward!"

"No, I'm not! What do you mean by that response? Are you still asking me to hide my presence and watch him while he gets home? And then I will still call you and say: *Elijah, Claude is going home now. He is moving across the--*"

"Geez, shut your mouth there, Shingue! Your voice is getting loud. Claude might hear you!"

Shingue was unaware that Claude was already standing behind him since he was already done in getting the scales of the Vrandolon. Claude did not hear his voice, but he saw him talking on the phone next to the boulder as he was passing over the cave exit. Shingue was still talking with Elijah on the phone when Claude put his hands on his hips while shaking his head in wonder. The conversation continued, until Claude got bored so he tapped Shingue's shoulder to get his attention.

"Hey you, what are you doing here?" asked Claude to Shingue. Shingue suddenly appalled and stopped talking, then he slowly turned to his back when he just saw Claude already standing behind him!

"Yaaaayyy, i-it's Claude!" cried Shingue when he suddenly dropped his smartphone and it fell on the ground.

"Hello, Shingue? Hello? Just--"

Claude gently picked up the smartphone on the ground and then he put it to his left ear to hear Elijah's voice on the line. Shingue stooped down his head while covering his ears in shame. His face was totally blushed!

"Shingue, still keep your presence hidden from Claude alright? Follow him and watch him going back here!"

Claude tried to make fun at Elijah by answering his order while his right hand was on his hip. "Excuse me? I'm afraid you dialed a wrong number, mister. There is no Shingue nor Vrandolon in here… because you are ACTUALLY SPEAKING TO CLAUDE RIGHT NOOOOWWWW!!!"

Elijah also suddenly stopped on the other line when Shingue quickly grabbed his phone from Claude's hand. Then, Claude asked Shingue in wonder. "Hey, but why are you also here, Shingue? Were you supposed to even take the test with me? Or were we supposed to work together as a team?"

Shingue's face was still blushing and he ignored Claude's question. He put his phone back to his ear again and spoke. He hesitated.

"Elijah, um… listen to me…"

"Goddamn it, Shingue! You're being caught by Claude already. You failed your stealth mission!" yelled Elijah jokingly when his voice broke up on the line once again. "YO-RE A HOP-L-SS EX-RER W-TCHER!!!"

The giant worm's body was irritated from the heat emitted by the Divine Stone of Tyrone since it was the first time that the monster was subjected to the direct burst of lights. Tyrone saw that he had a vantage point so he quickly attacked the confused worm. He was continuously pounding the irritated body of the Vrandolon causing the worm to lose much of his energy and create deep wounds in the soft tissues exposed to the lights. The worm could no longer hold the huge blows he received by Tyrone's attacks. He could not even retaliate because he was dazzling by the light cast by Tyrone's Divine Stone. It was 4:30am and the sun would rise soon. The watchers also got some scratches in their arms and legs by the spiky bushes, trees, and other things that could wound their skin. It was the price they got from spying the challengers. But among them, Vamir had the most number of wounds in his body… Thanks to Margot.

Tyrone was wearing his primary weapon in his arms called "arm daggers". Knowing that the monster was not in his comfort zone, Tyrone pulled out his dagger and stabbed the monster repeatedly into the abdomen and into the neck. The Vrandolon only roared in pain as the sharp daggers was cutting his body all over. Later, Tyrone stopped and watched his opponent, who was now twitching his body while groaning in pain.

"I thought you are strong, ugly monster…" Tyrone said.

To end the fight, Tyrone had made his "finishing move" to the Vrandolon when the Divine Stone cast its stronger light. The monster roared in dazzlement, unaware that Tyrone was already standing on the boulder that was hanging above his head. Then, Tyrone quickly stabbed the monster's head when his green blood suddenly squirted all over.

The Vrandolon was getting weakened and Tyrone was certain that it would no longer able to do the next attack and would no longer inflict any harm against him. He did not want to kill the monster, thinking that he already won the fight. So he decided to go on with his mission and took a

THE EXPLORERS

total of not ten but fifty scales. "These ten are for Elijah and I will save these forty for me as a living testament, that I was once defeated a dreaded monster and of course a souvenir!" he said.

Tyrone victoriously went out of the big sinkhole still unaware of Marion's presence. The rascal kid was very glad to see Tyrone back in the forest again in one piece. "*Kuya* Tyrone is totally awesome! I'm so, so impressed to him for being as great as me. He just finished his second test, huraaayyy!!!" he said happily when he controlled his tiny camera again and it returned to its spot.

He kept the camera and controller headband inside his bag and then he pulled out his phone to call Elijah. "*Kuya* Elijah, are you there? *Kuya* Tyrone has just finished his second test and he is now on his way back to the mansion. He's full of dirt!"

"Okay, so did he catch you?" asked Elijah on the line in his snobbish voice.

"What? No way! You know me, I'm a professional spy. I never cheated on you, *kuya* Elijah!"

"Do not be a liar. I know who you are!"

"I promise, *kuya*! He'd never seen me. I was only hiding in the shadows next to the hole opening. In the trees… I tried to go into the hole for a while but I went back outside thinking that *kuya* Tyrone might see me. So what I did was to use the flying camera you gave me and captured every action and every moment that *kuya* Tyrone did with the Vrandolon. That's that!"

"Very well then! Now go back home immediately. By the way, your *kuya* Shingue has already caught by *kuya* Claude!" said Elijah then the call ended.

It was five o'clock in the morning when the rain had stopped. Claude and Tyrone had returned to the mansion as well as their watchers still following their backs secretly (except Shingue). The two handed over each of their flags as well as the scales to Elijah, and the UEs applauded admirably when Elijah announced that they passed the second test.

"Hey man, we passed the test… I never thought we were both the same. Hahaha!" said Tyrone arrogantly to Claude while patting his shoulder.

"Yeah, I never thought of it either. Thank you…" answered Claude in his listless voice.

Elijah admitted to the two that they were actually being watched by someone when they took their second test. Claude did not make any reaction since he already knew about it.

"Shingue, later I will fire you out in this organization when I finish my work today!" said Elijah to Shingue jokingly and the Explorers laughed altogether. Then, he turned to Claude and Tyrone. "Alright, I am now giving you both a whole day to take your full rest before you proceed to your final test, understand?"

"Wait a minute… Does this mean that Kenji is also being watched by a UE right now?" asked Claude in wonder.

"Oh yes, and I dispatched two UEs to watch him there: Vamir and Mark."

One of the UEs spoke in concern. "But look what time is it now… Those three aren't still returning to this mansion yet 'til now. I think the Vrandolons we sent off to you are not that tough so we're certain that you can beat them easily."

Claude just noticed Kenji that was not around the mansion. He peered around. "Oh yeah? W-Wait a minute… Where is Kenji taking the test right now?"

"At the bottom of the sea. That is what he picked," answered Elijah.

Claude's face turned restless and worried. Unbelievable to what he just heard from Elijah. "A-At the bottom of the sea? Why in there? Maybe he's…"

27 REST

The two challengers had the pleasure to go to sleep for the whole day. Tyrone walked away from the group to go visit Isagani's room and check his condition.

"Elijah changed his mind again, Isagani…" said Tyrone to Isagani. "At first he said we were not allowed to go to sleep during the tests, but now he is giving us a whole day to take our full sleep."

Isagani was listening. He was lying on his bed.

"Really? Don't you want it? Now it's your chance to get recovered!"

"Nah, that's okay."

Isagani offered his hand over Tyrone to shake hands with him as his congratulatory greeting. "Congratulations to all of you… I am so proud of you."

The two shook their hands when Isagani added. "Do your best for the final test!"

"Of course I will! Hah, you know me right? I'm Tyrone!"

Isagani laughed. "Go ahead… Go to sleep, my friend."

Claude was now staying in his room seeming uncomfortable and restless. He was fluttering, walking back and forth while waiting for Kenji's return. There were lots of things started to trouble his worried mind again after learning that the young man was taking the test at the bottom of the sea. His face was looking concerned.

"Why Kenji's taking so long in his test? Is it hard to find the Vrandolon there? I hope he comes back sooner!" he said.

It was daybreak, 6:30 in the morning but Kenji was not returning still.

Claude tried to distract his troubling mind but he couldn't. "Man, what is happening to him right now?"

At seven o'clock in the morning, still, Kenji was not around. Claude could no longer wait anymore when he got up to his bed and scratched his head in annoyance. "DAMN! Vamir is still not calling Elijah until now. What if I go to Elijah and ask him to make a call to those two?! How I wish this test should have had its 'time limit' so when it ended, we would return in the mansion together."

Sleepy and exhausted, Claude ignored it. He walked out the room and went straight to Elijah.

Claude asked. "Elijah, could you please call those two?"

Elijah wondered. "Vamir and Mark? Why is that?"

"Well… because they aren't still calling yet. Look what time it is now! A-Aren't you noticing that?!"

"You're thinking about Kenji right, Claude? Don't you worry. He's fine. He will be here sooner. Go back to sleep now. You still have your final test tomorrow."

Claude was annoyed. His voice was getting sharp. "I want to know what is happening to him right now! Call them Elijah, please…"

Elijah was shocked to hear Claude's angry voice towards him even though he was the leader of UE class. He could see to Claude's eyes that the young man was disturbed.

"If you don't do that then I will not go to sleep," Claude threatened.

"Claude, you will lose in the final test. You will not be able to become an Explorer…"

"Geez, I do not care!!!"

Elijah was surprised, but he smiled and just followed Claude's request. "Fine, I will contact the two. Just wait here next to me and I want you to go to sleep after the call, okay?"

Claude nodded and answered in his calm voice. "Okay."

Elijah took his smartphone and he dialed Vamir's number and it rang. "I will turn on the loudspeaker so you can hear our conversation, okay?" he said.

"Okay."

The other line was still ringing… *Come on! Answer the damn call!* Said Claude to himself. *Vamir, please answer the call… I want to know how Kenji's doing now!*

THE EXPLORERS

Finally, someone answered the call. It was Margot. "Hello? Elijah, why are you calling us?"

Claude was only listening to their conversation. "My goodness, Mark! Why you didn't call me for some updates? Why didn't you answer the call sooner? I thought you were all dead!" said Elijah in a joke.

Claude was not interested to hear the two's condition, but the condition of Kenji. "Elijah, ask them about Kenji... I want to hear the news about him," he said to Elijah.

"Well it's because we still haven't seen my darlin' Kenji yet up to now. We waited for so long here and never saw him swimming back to the beach. The sun is already up. If you only knew, we already got bored and just slept here while waiting for him to come back. We're still here at the beach and we wanna go back home now."

"Y-You slept?! Hey there! What if Kenji already done with his mission and saw you both there?!!"

"Oh I mean, Vamir just took a nap for only a few minutes. But Kenji already took the three flags."

"I know it already, Mark..."

"Excuse me? Sir, please call me Miss Margot, not Mark!"

"Whatever you say, Miss Gay! Is there no other news besides that?!"

"Look, if there is one... then we should've had called you immediately since earlier... Right?"

Silence. Margot's right. They would surely make a call to Elijah immediately if they knew what Kenji had been doing during the test. But as what Margot said, it simply meant that even he and Vamir did not know what was happening to Kenji now.

"Alright Margot... Please call me immediately if you see Kenji out of the water, but still, do not show yourself to him, okay?"

"Yes, yes, I know that already. Goodbye."

The call ended when Elijah put down his phone on the desk and turned to Claude. "Claude... even Vamir and Mark have no idea what is going on to Kenji," then he looked concerned. "The sea is big and it's storming. I'm afraid that your friend might be carried by the huge sea waves and took him somewhere away from the shore--"

"Please stop saying that, Elijah!" shouted Claude angrily when he stripped off his clothes and wore thick outerwear. And then he took a *bolo* (a large single-edge knife) that was laid next to Elijah's phone on the desk.

"The heavy snowstorm will blow again later, and the water is very cold. I have a feeling that Kenji is in trouble right now. When I was still in the cave there were lots of things kept on troubling me. I knew it!" then he quickly ran away.

"Claude, wait! The sea is very huge. You do not know exactly where Kenji is at right now. Come back here, Claude!!!"

"I will look for those two and I will swim near them!"

"A-Are you serious?! You know the rules Claude. This is an individual test and no one will come to you nor to anybody for that matter to help. Otherwise, we will disqualify you and considered failing the mission," said Elijah in his commanding voice.

Claude stopped running and did not turn to Elijah. "I know the rules Elijah, and I am standing by the rules. Kenji is a great person and a brave warrior. I have a strong feeling that he has accomplished his test already. What gives me worry is that, Kenji is not a good swimmer specially underwater," he said.

"What if you find out he is still in the midst of his fight with the Vrandolon and he sees you?! What if your thoughts are wrong, Claude?"

"With such a long time, I don't think he is still okay!!!"

Claude hurriedly ran away again until he was completely gone to Elijah's sight. Then, Elijah cried out loud.

"CLAUDEEEEEEE!!!"

The weather was calm when Claude went out of the mansion. He knew where the sea was. "Kenji, I am coming!" he said to himself. He never thought of a possible danger he would encounter when he got to the sea by the freezing weather. He rushed towards the nearest beach from the mansion as fast as he could, ignoring the negative zero degree temperature, spikes by the vines, and bushes as he was passing through his way. He mowed the vines and other wild plants that were blocking his path with the *bolo*, then he jumped across the quicksand that was not covered by snow, and so on.

Claude's body got more of its cuts and scratches when he successfully reached the seashore. He immediately sought for Vamir and Margot but no one was there. He ran around the beach when he found the two and he moved over them. Vamir was already awake since he could not nap well and he turned to Claude in wonder. Claude saw the three flags next to them. He was panting before the two.

THE EXPLORERS

"Hello, Claude. How surprising, why are you here?" asked Vamir. "Are you done with your test?"

Claude ignored Vamir's question. Still panting before the two. "Where's Kenji? Didn't you see him yet still? What kind of spies are you?! You must know what everything happened to Kenji from the very beginning of this stupid test!"

"You mean… a-are you asking us to dive underwater just to watch him battling with the Vrandolon? Hey dude, it is not easy for us to swim there and stand the freezing water. We will both freeze to death not to mention that Kenji might see us!"

Claude was piqued by Vamir's answer. "And what about him? Do you think he is a cold-blooded amphibian that is not affected by hyperthermia? Didn't you ever think of his life before YOU Explorers took him here?! Were you all thinking that he was not immune in this freezing climate??!"

Vamir suddenly faltered thinking of what else to say to Claude. "C-Claude, look… It's all part of the rules. When you accept the challenge, you'll put your life on the line. Y-You know the risk and it's your choice not ours. Nobody forced all of you to accept the challenge and so, you have to pay the consequences if you're not taking care of yourself. W-We are concerned about the welfare of every challenger but what else can we do? We're just following orders."

Claude piqued more. "Are you out of your mind?! I don't think so!" then he moved away from the two and then he also attempted to swim in the sea. "I'm going to dive now!"

"You're going to look for him? What if he sees you?"

"You guys are all saying the same nonsense thing. Think before you say it, darn!"

"C-Claude, the water is very cold!"

Claude got away from them when he attempted to wade across the cold water. He swam away.

"CLAUDEEE!!!"

The seawater was still cold though some parts of it that were frozen were now melting by the sun. Claude forced himself to dive straight to the bottom, but sometimes he would swim upwards over the surface to catch his breath. And then, he would dive back again.

Claude patiently scoured the deep and searched for his friend until he noticed that he was getting farther from the two watchers. At the bottom, he found Kenji's Kali staff at the corals, but its sword was missing.

"Kenji... What now? Where is he?"

He took the long Kali staff and held it with his left hand. Then he looked around. "He is probably here somewhere. He left his staff here," he said to himself.

Next, Claude passed over the tentacles that were all cut and scattered underwater. He was disgusted to see the cut tentacles so he swam away. As he was passing through them he also found the corpse of a large squid monster. There, he saw the Kali's missing sword stabbed in its body. Now, Claude had learned what kind of Vrandolon that Kenji fought with. "So this is the unknown creature that Kenji fought today. B-But where is he?"

As Claude came closer to the Vrandolon, there was a hand under the corpse's body that suddenly caught his attention. It was Kenji's hand. Kenji was crushed by the monster right after he killed it with his sword. At first, the young man forcibly used his Holy White Fire while fighting with the Vrandolon that made him lose more of his energy, causing his body to falter before he made his finishing attack by stabbing the monster right in the heart by full force. With his weak body, he used his remaining energy to get away from the dead body. He managed to swim away from the fallen monster but its huge body had sucked and crushed him as the Vrandolon sunk deeper into the sea floor.

Claude quickly swam over the monster to push it as hard as he could with his peculiar strength. It was his unique ability, the ability coming from the inner strength of his body like Hercules. When the monster pushed aside, he slowly pulled Kenji and carried him in his back. He put the young man's arms over his shoulder and then he swam upwards. Claude was also a good swimmer since he was also mentored by Rolando.

Claude hated to go back to the two "bums" but he had to. When they returned, he gently laid Kenji in the white sand when Vamir and Margot quickly ran towards him.

"Claude... What happened to him?" asked Vamir.

"Kenji! Oh, my dear Kenji... My sweetheart..." said Margot flirtatiously.

Claude spoke as he was panting. "We must return to the mansion now. The snow is falling again. I will explain this to you later. Hurry!"

The three helped together to lift Kenji and they carried him back to the UE mansion hurriedly. When they returned:

THE EXPLORERS

"Claude? What happened to Kenji? Is he still alive?!" Elijah was shocked to see Kenji all wet and colored pale.

Claude answered angrily. "Don't ask me that! He is still alive! Why don't you check his pulse?!"

Elijah examined Kenji's pulse. "Yes, he is alive but he's drowned. Take him to the clinic right away and let the doctors do the rest. I'll give him oxygen. Poor Kenji…"

"ARE YOU INSANE?! If only you took him in the other safer location instead then he would never be like this!"

Elijah was greatly surprised.

"If I only knew that you took place his test in the sea then I would absolutely object it! The test in the sea was not that easy, especially when you were submerged against the freezing water underwater and fighting the monster while you were also holding your breath! He could die from drowning and even freeze to death! You put Kenji's life at risk, Elijah… You almost killed him!!!"

"Claude… Please don't yell at me…"

"You could even die in there if you dare to try, you'll see!"

"I see…"

Claude gently carried Kenji in his arms. His voice was calm now. "We're going to the clinic now… I'm sorry for what everything I just said to you…" and then he left.

Elijah did not answer. He only watched Claude walking away from him along with the other UEs who would be helping Kenji in the treatment. He did not intend to follow the two on their way going in the clinic and instead, he walked back to his office room.

Claude was only silent, watching the UE medics who were busy treating Kenji inside the clinic. They did the CPR first before putting the emergency oxygen tubes in Kenji's nose and brought him inside the anti-hyperthermia chamber. Though his body was still soaking wet, Claude's face was showing life.

Shingue came inside the clinic carrying a thick towel in his hand. He was also carrying a first-aid kit for Kenji's wounds.

After a half hour, the medics were all done with their treatment and they left the clinic. Shingue sat down on a chair next to Claude who was still anxious. They were next to Kenji who was laid down the bed now.

"How's Kenji now, Claude?" Shingue asked.

Claude answered in his low, weak voice. "He's okay now, but he is injured…"

"I-Injured? Where?" Shingue glanced at Kenji's torso that was covered and tied by white bandages. He was about to touch the young man's body but Claude quickly restrained him.

"Don't touch him," said Claude glaring at Shingue.

Shingue just noticed Claude was in his bad mood right now, but he already knew this bad-tempered person's natural personality. Claude was a hot-headed type of person and it was normal for him to lose his temper instantly.

But Shingue understood Claude since he had been exhausted for long and he needed to rest. They still had the final test tomorrow.

Kenji was deeply asleep in his bed when someone knocked on the clinic door. Claude's face's suddenly frowned when he heard a knock and Shingue saw him, so he stood in his chair to make his turn to open the door.

"How's Kenji?" Reinhardt was the one who knocked. "I only came just to see and check on him…"

"Oh, I see… Kenji's fine, over there!" answered Shingue in his low voice and he pointed his finger at Kenji. "But please do not make any sound, okay? Kenji is asleep. And Claude's… w-well, I think he is not in his good mood today…"

"Oh, I'm sorry… I just want to visit my brother, that's all. A-Anyway, I'm not coming inside then. I understand…"

"N-No, it's not that I don't want you to come inside. What I am only saying is that, just avoid making any sound…"

"Alright… Then I'm coming inside, Shingue."

Claude was in his bad mood this time which made the clinic very quiet. Due to overfatigue and exhaustion, Claude did not realize he already fell asleep.

It was twelve noon when the snow started again. Kenji's consciousness came back when he opened his eyes. And then, he asked Shingue and Reinhardt who were still in the clinic with him.

"Where am I?" asked Kenji dilated in his low, hoarse voice.

"You're safe now, Kenji. Your friend Claude saved you earlier. Over there, he is sleeping now," answered Shingue.

"He saved me? Where?"

THE EXPLORERS

Kenji had a trait of being forgetful. So when Shingue told him about it, he had already forgotten about it as well as what everything happened to him right before he became unconscious. But after a while, he would remember it.

"Oh, come on Kenji! Didn't you remember? You know, under the sea, of course! Claude said that the sea Vrandolon crushed you right after you killed him."

"Ah, yes I remember now! You're right, a huge sea creature who didn't want to give up his scales. It was very tough for me to take the test underwater," said Kenji and then he removed the oxygen tubes attached to his nose.

"Kenji, why?"

"I am breathing well now, Shingue. I don't need that anymore."

Reinhardt spoke. "Elijah said that he did not know if you completed your test because you took the three flags but you didn't take the ten--"

"Oh yeah!" said Kenji and he peered around to find his pants, because he noticed that he was only wearing underwear right now. The UE medics along with Claude stripped off his clothes earlier to treat him. "Shingue, the pants! Please give it to me."

Shingue took Kenji's pants that was hanging on the hook wall. It was still soaking wet when he gave it to Kenji. The young man seemed to be looking for something in his pants.

"What are you looking there in your pants, Kenji?" asked Shingue.

"Hold on... Ah! They're here..." said Kenji when he pulled off the beautiful scales in his pants.

"The scales... You got them, Kenji!"

"I kept these inside the pocket after I killed the giant squid. I was great, wasn't I?"

"Yeah! Go ahead, I will call Elijah immediately so he will see this, Kenji..."

Reinhardt restrained Shingue looking cautious towards Claude's mood. "Don't take Elijah here, Shingue. We will just go over him to give Kenji's scales because Claude is still sleeping... Let us give them more time and space to rest, and remember what you've said that he is in his bad mood today?"

Kenji slowly rose in the bed. "Go ahead brother. You can give these scales to Elijah for me. Please take this..."

Reinhardt took the scales in Kenji's hand and then he left the clinic with Shingue. Later, Claude awoke. He was shocked to see that Kenji was already awake.

"Kenji, you're finally awake. Where's the oxygen tubes in your nose?"

Kenji smiled at Claude. "I am breathing normally now, Claude. I removed it…"

Claude was just staring at Kenji. The young man noticed that.

"Claude, what's wrong?"

Claude shook his head. "N-Nothing…"

"I heard from Shingue that you saved me at the bottom of the sea… Thank you, I owe you my life."

Claude blushed and he scratched his head. "Hehehe… it's nothing! It's because I was thinking about you. You know that we've been friends for long, right?"

Kenji patted Claude's shoulder. "I am glad for having a friend like you, Claude… A person who always at your aid whenever you're in trouble… You know, like a bridge over troubled water!"

Claude was surprised to hear such compliments. "It is you who taught me on how to behave that way. Remember the time when the baker in Damsville caught me when I stole their bread? They almost killed me, but it was you who came by to protect me from sure harm. I will never forget that, Kenji."

Kenji chuckled and smiled. "That's nothing Claude, I only did what I had to do…" then the two shook hands and smiled at each other.

Claude suddenly remembered something. "Did you know that we were being watched by the UEs when we were taking our second test?"

Kenji frowned in disbelief. "Really? Who said that to you?"

"I caught Shingue by accident when I happened to walk past over him. He was talking on the phone with Elijah telling everything I did in the test."

Kenji laughed.

"What is so funny, Kenji?"

Kenji stopped laughing. "It's nothing… I was only surprised to hear what you've said. It was unbelievable really, because I'd never seen them when I was at the bottom of the sea. I mostly consumed my time underwater that's why. And Elijah never said anything about it to us."

Claude altered the topic of their conversation. "Kenji, was it hard for you to fight with this sea Vrandolon underwater? What did it feel like?"

THE EXPLORERS

"Why do you ask?"

Claude blushed again. He faltered. "Um... W-Well... it's nothing. I-I just want to know that's all... Because, I know how difficult for you to fight against the Vrandolon with that very cold water and holding your breath for long."

"Yes, Claude... You're right. If it wasn't for Rolando then maybe right now I'm already dead from drowning... P-Perhaps from the very beginning of our second test."

Claude suddenly frowned, feeling angered again towards Elijah. "There were lots of safer places to consider in taking the test but why in there at the sea?!"

"Elijah is not wise to consider about it? Why?"

"Kenji, Elijah put your life at risk. That was not a fair game and you almost got killed. Look at yourself, you've got more bruises and deep wounds than I have. You even drowned while looking and fighting with the Vrandolon!"

Claude was deeply angered when he suddenly punched the wall once with his fist and it got scratched. But, Kenji did not make a surprising reaction. Instead, he asked Claude as if he was acting dumb. "A-Are you saying something, Claude? What was it? Say it again please..."

Claude was shocked. "W-What? You didn't hear what I've just said to you? DAMMIT, DAMMIT, DAMMIIITTTT!!!" and then he punched the innocent wall again repeatedly with force until his fist bled a little.

Kenji did not surprise by Claude's reaction. Instead, he suddenly laughed out loud. Claude was shocked more, but he was no longer angry when he asked Kenji unbelievably.

"W-Why are you laughing, Kenji?"

Kenji stopped laughing. "It's nothing, Claude... I just want to laugh everytime I am feeling exhausted just to relax. And you know... I always love your company, Claude. You and I have been always together for long and I've known everything about you much... So in other words, I'm already used to your natural personality, hehehe..."

Claude moved next to Kenji. "Kenji, why don't you go back to rest again?"

"You want me to rest, Claude? I'm no longer sleepy. I'd been sleeping long under the sea remember? Hehehe..."

"J-Just do it for your friend's simple favor..."

Silence. After their long conversation, they finally went back to sleep to recover their strength for the final test.

28 THE FINAL TEST PART 1

The day had come for the three challengers to take their final test and become the new member of Explorers. The whole day of rest was fully enough to recover their strengths although the breakfast was not yet served by the Explorers.

Kenji and Claude were still sleeping together inside the clinic. Kenji was still in his bed while Claude's head was lying on the young man's bed. Kenji was sleeping to his side while his back was facing Claude only to avoid his injured body being hit by Claude's motions while sleeping.

Later, Claude awoke when someone knocked on the clinic's door. Reinhardt and Shingue came back again.

"Good morning to you both. You guys are now being called by… of course, Elijah! Goodluck to you guys!" greeted Shingue smiling.

"Please awake my brother right away. Tell him to get dressed," said Reinhardt also smiling.

"Okay…" answered Claude in his hoarse voice and he awoke Kenji. "Kenji… wake up now."

"We will wait for you outside. You know what? Though the temperature was cold, Tyrone still took his bath! The snow is pouring again, so get yourself prepared, okay?" said Shingue. "By the way, Elijah said that you must bring your weapons with you again. He will tell you later what your final test will be!"

Claude answered in annoyance. "Hmpt! Tell him to make consideration first or he will put Kenji's life in danger again, damn!"

"Yes, yes… Claude," said Shingue smiling. "I know that already!" then he left the clinic.

Reinhardt followed Shingue and he also left the clinic. Kenji awoke when he slowly opened his eyes. "Ahm, Claude? Where are we right now?"

"What? Have you forgotten again? We're in the clinic!"

"In the clinic?"

"Yeah, we slept here all day while they're nursing your wounds."

"Ah, yes… I remember now."

"You're still forgetful… Do you still remember your pasts?"

"Why, of course!"

"Okay. The reason why I awoke you is because that negligent Elijah is now calling us! Get yourself dressed and I'm going to change mine. By the way, you need to bring your Kali with you again."

"Okay."

The two wore their new clothes. Meanwhile, Elijah was waiting outside the mansion again while talking with the three Explorers that were unknown to Kenji and Claude from afar. The other UEs, like Vamir, Marion, and Margot were also outside waiting for the three challengers' arrival and they were all wearing their thick outerwear.

After Elijah finished his conversation with the three unknown Explorers, he asked them to move away from the mansion's entrance and hide in a secluded spot. Tyrone came first, while doing his fighting exhibition as an introduction to catch the Explorers' attention.

"Elijah, I am now ready for your final test!" cried Tyrone in his fighting pose.

"Yes, I know…" said Elijah without any reaction of amazement to Tyrone's exhibition.

"What do you know?"

"Nothing. So where are those two? Why they aren't still coming yet?"

"I even noticed that… My sweetheart is still inside," said Margot. "Why don't I fetch them, Elijah? Maybe they're still sleeping."

"Don't you dare, Mark! We already awoke them," said Shingue disgusted.

Marion approached Tyrone to give encouragement for the last test. "*Kuya*, do your best in this final test, okay? Be as great as me when I even did the test previously. I was good, wasn't I? I will support you and cheer you!"

Tyrone stroked his naughty little friend's hair. "You still haven't changed, Marion! Still an arrog... I-I mean, still a great Explorer kid among the universe, hahahaha!"

"Okay Claude, are you getting ready for this?" asked Kenji to Claude inside the clinic. They were now dressed.

"Of course I am, dude! I'm excitingly ready. Actually, I am only concerned at you... 'Coz you're injured..."

Kenji touched his injured body and he asked Claude to also touch it. His leg was also wrapped by bandage. "It is nothing. See? I'm not hurting. I am fine, believe me!"

Claude touched Kenji's torso gently looking serious. "Yes, I can feel it..."

"See? I don't feel any pain. I am fine!"

Claude gently pinched Kenji's torso and quickly closed his eyes feeling in pain. "Ouch, Kenji! I can feel its pain. I'm sorry..."

"Yup, me too... In fact, my body is throbbing right now... But a little. Let's go."

Claude was still looking concerned towards him. "You..."

Kenji lifted his right hand before Claude. "Let's do high five together, Claude. Come on," and then they did the high five.

Claude finally smiled. "Are you sure about this? Please take good care of yourself then."

The two went out the clinic and Claude locked the door since Shingue had its key. They talked as they walked, but Claude noticed Kenji was limping and he did not know if he had to assist Kenji in walking or not.

The two walked outside the mansion when the snow fell once again after the rainfall. The weather was capricious and unpredictable. More of the Explorers were outside, and they spontaneously laughed together by the weather's unpredictable change.

"Oh, oh... My husband is coming. Over there! Yoo-hoo, Kenji!" cried Margot while waving at Kenji.

Kenji and Claude ignored Margot silently and they walked straight to Elijah.

"Kenji, Claude, what took you so long? Why did you get dressed so slow? My goodness, we have been waiting for you that long!" said Elijah but he was not angry.

Kenji only scratched his head in embarrassment when Claude answered annoyingly. "Are you out of your mind, Elijah? Kenji is limping and he cannot walk that fast, so we're walking slowly."

Margot spoke. "Oh really? Perhaps you did something to my husband earlier?"

Claude got pissed. "H-Hell no! I was really helping him to walk."

"Okay, that's enough you guys!" interrupted Elijah when he clapped his hands. "Today is the beginning of your final test. By the way, are you ready for the last challenge?"

Claude scoffed annoyingly. "Tsk, then why are we here if we aren't ready?"

"Alright, our final challenge for you is easier than the second one. I'll explain the rules, okay?"

The three nodded in their serious face.

"Great! By the way, first I would like to introduce someone to you, guys."

"Introducing someone to us?" asked Claude in wonder.

"Yes, they are also Explorers belonged in UE. Tyrone knows who they are."

Tyrone's eyes goggled. "I know them? Who are they?"

"Of course, Tyrone. They are your friends. Those three just left here and stayed in the other country for a month to do their special training."

"Ah, yes I know them absolutely! Why? Are they related to your last challenge, eh? Did they return here already?"

"Yes, they've returned. I called them few days ago to come home in the mansion. Their training is done."

"I think Tyrone's right, Kenji…" whispered Claude to Kenji. "Perhaps those Explorers are related to our final test. Imagine, why would Elijah bother our time to just introducing those UEs to us, right?"

"Maybe you are right, Claude…" said Kenji and then he whispered to Tyrone who was only next to him. "Hey Tyrone, who are those UEs that Elijah's talking about? Can you please tell it to me?"

"Um, they are our colleagues. They left the mansion a month ago to train for the upcoming tournament. The reason behind this is because one of those three have obtained a Divine Stone that the Pioneer leader's son would want to take it from his hands. Therefore, the Pioneer leader's son had challenged him to battle with him in the tournament in an exchange for the Divine Stone's possession if he lost the fight. The other two Explorers also took their training and at the same time they were accompanying him.

THE EXPLORERS

The son's name is Augustus Sawyer and he will be our friend's opponent in the upcoming tournament! If Augustus will lose the fight, then our friend will take the strongest power he is possessing."

"I know him, Tyrone. He's Akira in short!" said Kenji in shock. "Will Akira really fight with one of those three?! What is his name? I want to know, Tyrone!"

Kenji stopped asking Tyrone when the three unknown Explorers appeared before them. The three challengers became silent.

"Hey, you guys! Welcome back to the mansion!" greeted a UE to the three Explorers. "Long time no see! How's the training abroad for a month?"

Elijah approached the three returnees when he introduced them to Kenji and Claude. "Kenji, Claude… these are the three Explorers I've mentioned to you earlier: Lucky Terrel, Jon Ethans, and Clio Raven. We took them in another country to do their special training, and the two accompanied Lucky before his upcoming one-on-one fight against Mister Sawyer in the tournament."

"Wait, Elijah… Which of them is Lucky? Nice name…" Kenji joked.

Elijah called Lucky and he came next to him. Then, Elijah put his arm over Lucky's shoulder. "Kenji, this is Lucky, he is my favorite gunner. He already held the number of titles won in the previous tournaments! His fight with Akira will happen next month!"

The three Explorers moved over Kenji and Claude. Lucky was the first one to introduce himself.

"Hello, guys. My name is Lucky Terrel of UE. I am eighteen years old and… simply one of the best!" he made a joke though the tone of his voice was serious.

"My name is Clio and I am sixteen years old," introduced Clio and he offered his hand to shake hands with the two.

"Hello… My name is Jon."

Kenji smiled while shaking hands with the three. "Nice to meet you, guys. My name is Kenji Foster and this is my friend, Claude Aldrich…"

After the introduction and shaking hands, they all stepped back to their position.

"Alright! So this is what your final test will be. It's fairly easy, all you have to do is to fight with these three and you must beat them!"

Claude whispered to Kenji again. "I told yah… What else can we do here but to just fight with them, right?"

Kenji firstly tried to do the warm-up awkwardly since his body was still injured. "Oh yes, that's fair enough. Go ahead, I'm ready!"

"BUT!" cried Elijah. The three challengers turned to him when he continued. "But your hands and feet have to be handcuffed, cast by my own power of magic. The handcuffs that I am talking to you must be demonstrated. Tyrone, come over here."

Tyrone pointed himself. "M-Me?"

"Yes."

Tyrone slowly walked closer to Elijah. Then, Elijah began casting a magic he called as "Heavy Chain" when a yellow electricity-like trail appeared around Tyrone's hands as he was moving his pointing finger all over the hands. Next, he also cast the same magic on Tyrone's feet. Then Tyrone suddenly felt a heavy weight in both of his arms and feet so he quickly fell on the snowy ground on his knees.

Tyrone was groaning while trying to lift his body back to his feet but he couldn't. He could not even crawl or move due to the weight of the handcuffs he was carrying.

Kenji and Claude were only watching Tyrone gaped in surprise. "T-Tyrone?" called Kenji to Tyrone looking anxious and nervous. "A-Are you okay? How's the feeling? Is Elijah really that serious that we should do that?"

"Yes! That is the only thing you can do for the last test. You must fight these three and beat them while you're heavily handcuffed. You are allowed to use anything you have in your possession. Think of possible strategies of winning the fight. Those are the simple rules. This last test is fairly easy."

Kenji was looking unbelievable to what he just heard from Elijah. "Whoa… Fairly easy, isn't it? You're really so serious with this!"

"So, I must handcuff you now and let the test begin!!" said Elijah to Kenji and Claude smiling and then he turned his fellow UEs. "Explorers, you have to go back to the mansion now so you will not disturb their test."

"Kenji, do your best okay?" said Margot to Kenji. "When you finish your test and return to the mansion, I will cook your favorite bacon! That's a promise!" and then he crossed his heart and made a flying kiss towards Kenji as he winked.

Kenji was forced to agree. "O-Okay, it's up to you…"

THE EXPLORERS

"Whoo-hoo, goodbye sweetie!"

The Explorers returned to the mansion. Kenji firstly watched Margot giggling as he was skipping away along with his fellow Explorers. Then, Elijah moved closer to him when the leader asked him to lift up his hands to get handcuffed. The same thing happened to Claude's when they both suddenly fell on their knees on the snowy ground with Tyrone.

"Holy cow! I-It's too heavy!!!" said Claude grunting irritably while on the ground. "Hey wait! Don't you think it's unfair? How can we use our weapons if we're into this?!"

"As what I've said, you have all the time in the world to do what pleases you. You are free to do anything during the last test. Why not think of any strategies that can be used and take it as an advantage to overcome your enemies. Don't be so concerned about the handcuffs. That thing is just robbing your focus and attention, which may be used against you to lose your concentration and consequently the fight. Like all the other magics, that kind of magic has its own weakness, only if you know how to look for it!" said Elijah.

The three were silent. Elijah turned to the three returnees when he patted Jon's shoulder. "Lucky, Clio, and Jon, you must choose which of these three will be your opponent. Jon, you are lucky number one."

"Alright!" Jon jumped in excitement. "Let's see… Well, I will choose Tyrone. After all, he is the only challenger here that I know and I am familiar with his moves," then he turned to Tyrone. "And, I'd also like to show you everything I've learned in Omania. Would that be okay to you huh, Tyrone?"

"F-Fine…" said Tyrone still struggling on his knees. "If you only knew how really heavy this thing in my hands and feet… I can't move my arm!"

"Clio, you are lucky number two!"

"I want to fight that guy with a, um… The guy with the red headband, short black hair… and with thick eyebrows!"

Claude frowned towards Clio. "Just go ahead kid. Keep on describing everything about me… Waste of time!"

"Okay, Clio. Claude is yours now. And Lucky, what has left will be yours, Kenji."

Lucky moved closer to Kenji. "Dude, you seem great. I like your looks!"

"Lucky," called Kenji while also struggling on his knees to move.

"You know Akira of Pioneer, right? I know him as well. Can you please tell me where he is now? As well as the Pioneers, where are they hiding now?"

"Hey dude, we are now in the middle of your final test. You need to concentrate more in the test rather than asking me about Akira. Okay, if you really want to know more about Akira and the Pioneer then you must beat me first and then I will tell you."

"Please… Even just a little information you can give me is highly appreciated, Lucky. I just want to avenge my considered father who was killed by those Pioneers, and that black-hearted Akira who destroyed the town of Bondore just a year ago! Please Lucky… Tell me when did you lastly seen him when you obtained your Divine Stone?"

"No more chit chat Kenji, let's do it now!"

"I am begging you, Lucky. When Akira and I met in Bondore, he issued a challenge and we would settle our issues only when we meet again."

"When?"

"I-I do not know. Maybe only time will tell… The day that I will not expect to meet him again."

"I don't care about your personal issues, just face me now and fight!"

Kenji got pissed at Lucky's last remark, but he controlled his temper. "So that's how an Explorer gunner behaves. To tell you frankly, the man before you and talking to is the new Wielder of King Jethro's Holy Element. The type of stone you have in your hands is the same as mine, but unfortunately you don't have the stone that holds the great king's ultimate power which is now in my possession!"

Lucky stopped in shock. "W-What did you say? You are the new Element Wielder of Holy element? O-Of King Jethro? How did that happen?!"

Kenji showed off his arm tattoos to Lucky, then he cast the Holy White Fire. The fire swept across his body for a moment and then he removed it.

Lucky knelt down on the snowy ground in his face looking greatly surprised. "You… You're right… You've already possessed the only element that me and Akira were fighting and scrambling for. Alright, alright, I shall tell this to you now… Akira also wants to take the Holy element and become its Wielder. When I obtained my Divine Stone and he learned about it, he assumed that the stone was possibly the Holy element so he planned to wrest it from me. Therefore, he challenged me to a fight in the upcoming tournament only for the sake of my stone. If he wins, he will take the Divine Stone from me, but if he loses... then I will take his strongest power!"

"But now you know that the element you've been scrambling for already belongs to me. How will you and Akira compete in the tournament if the great king himself has chosen me to become the Holy Wielder?! Both you and Akira's chances of becoming the Holy Wielder is already none!"

"I know... That means that we will be battling for nothing. NOTHING! How unlucky I am, dammit!!!"

"No Lucky... You are still blessed, because the stone you have is also one of King Jethro's long-lost element and you can transform it back to its true form. Which means, you will also become its new Element Wielder like me, Luck--"

"C-Can you please stop talking to me now?!" said Lucky annoyingly when he drew out his staff that was shorter than Kenji's Kali and had no sword. "Haven't you noticed that you and I still aren't starting the fight yet? Come on, let's start the test. I am getting bored by your blathering!"

29 THE FINAL TEST PART 2

Claude and Clio were now fighting with each other. Clio was one of the great Explorers whose primary weapon type were bows and bowguns. Though the magic handcuffs were weighty in their hands, the three challengers were struggling to lift up their hands with full force and do the attack to their opponent.

The three returnees were the chosen spies and sniper of Explorer organization due to their keen eyes. Their expertise was equally the same. They were the best in "target shooting" form of attack using any type of sharp throwable or projectile weapons to their target, in a distance with up to five hundred meters in great accuracy!

Their keen eyes' skill was trained and polished by Rolando and Master Serge as they also became their former students. A sniper rifle and revolver were normally used by Lucky which was his primary weapon. For any hand-to-hand combat and close attacks, then he would use his secondary weapon which was a staff. He named his staff, "Lucky Staff" because he believed that it was his only weapon that would bring him luck.

Bows and bowguns were Clio's primary type of weapon. Even if his target was far from him, he could still shoot an arrow precisely into the target!

As for Jon, he was still a kid when he loved to play darts. Even his mother's sewing tools were his toys when he tried to steal them without his mother's knowledge. Thus, this made him acquire a skill in handling darts until Master Serge discovered him with this such skill. The master instructor trained him once and gave him the same type of weapon he could use in battle. Jon's primary weapon were needles and blowguns. He usually targeted the victim's forehead, where he loved to blow his long, thin dart. The dart he was using on the target's forehead had its deadly poison, so the victim would lose his consciousness at first and then after just a few seconds, he would die instantly.

Jon could even throw a great number of darts and needles to the target with his bare hands. He would inject the needles to the body parts of his opponent during the fight like the "art of acupuncture", making the victim become stunned and paralyzed to death.

The three challengers fell on their knees again when they faltered due to the weighty handcuffs they were still carrying in their hands and feet, while Lucky's group was just doing their attacks on them.

Lucky kept on hitting Kenji's back with his staff as if he was enjoying it. Kenji screamed in pain.

"AHHHH!!!"

"Now what, Kenji? Why don't you get up? Come on, get up!" said Lucky and he repeatedly struck Kenji's back again.

Kenji screamed out loud again when Claude and Tyrone heard him. They quickly turned to the young man when they saw Lucky looking enjoyed in striking Kenji. With that, Claude got instantly mad!

"AHHHH!!!"

"Kenji!" shouted Claude. He even got angry more when he saw Lucky laughing while still hitting Kenji all over his body. He wanted to ask Elijah to stop this unmerciful game but Clio stopped him. At this instance, Claude got so angry and he forced himself to stand on his own feet and fight Clio.

"Could you please stop interfering me?! My friend is being hurt and beaten by your ruthless colleague and he cannot fight back! That's already an abuse. Take a look at my friend's condition! He is unable to move and so as we because of these stupid handcuffs! You must stop him now, my friend is still recovering from his injuries!!!"

Clio had stopped and answered Claude. "Well... it is in the final test's rules according to *kuya* Elijah. So which means we can do anything we want in this test freely against you, and this is a fair fight! Remember, you are even allowed to use your weapons and also fight freely with us!"

"Our fight would be 'fair' if we're not like this! This is the most nonsense, stupidest rule I've ever heard in my life. You guys are completely insane!!!"

"Hey *kuya*, in case you did not know... we were also subjected to that same situation when we took our final test. We took it seriously because of our desire to become Explorers! You guys are more fortunate because when me and *kuya* Elijah took this test together, we were not allowed to use our weapons while we're handcuffed. Imagine how many stripes and blows we got in our bodies that time? Good thing we were smart, and we found out the weakness of that handcuff magic so we passed the test!"

Claude stopped. He did not know if he should believe to what Clio had said or not.

"Anyway, don't you dare disturb what Lucky wants to do with your friend! Whether he is injured or not, he must find a way to escape from Lucky's attacks and retaliate the best he can!"

Claude's nerve reached to his wrath, and everytime he was extremely angry then he was losing his concentration, causing him to freak out again. He felt angered towards Elijah thinking that this leader did not consider Kenji's condition's first before taking him in this test. He shouted on top of his voice, and he wanted to protect Kenji but he couldn't... So he forced himself to stand and tried to remove the weighty handcuffs in all of his strength.

Clio was just watching him. He was not making any attacks towards Claude.

As for Tyrone and Jon, since the two knew each other, the fight between them seemed to be scripted and fraud now.

In the middle of their battle, Tyrone whispered to Jon slyly. "J-Jon, please don't beat me, okay? Let's make it appear that I can still beat you though I'm handcuffed. Do not make any serious attacks and also don't use your blowgun. You must understand that I cannot fight you squarely, and let's pretend that you lose the fight and I win the game, okay?"

Jon's face was looking anxious towards Tyrone. "B-But Tyrone... Do you think this is a clear cheat? This isn't in the rules!"

"Leave this to me, Jon! I am doing this only for today... Just do whatever I am asking you to do. You can attack me, but don't take it seriously... Just pretend!"

"I don't want to cheat, Tyrone... That's not my cup of tea, I'm worried."

"Just believe in someone who is older than you, Jon!"

Jon was forced to agree to Tyrone's illegal plan. He slowly shook his

THE EXPLORERS

head, and Tyrone grinned in gladness.

Kenji was surprised when Lucky took the Kali in his back and he placed it in his handcuffed hands. He could not believe that he was holding his weapon now.

"Lucky, what do you think you're doing? What does it mean?" asked Kenji to Lucky unbelievably.

"Um… it's nothing," said Lucky. "Anyway, I can see you cannot fight back on me and you cannot grab your weapon in your back. So I took it and gave it to you to be fair. Now that you have your long weapon in your hands, I think you can beat me now though you're still handcuffed, right?"

Kenji did not answer. He just closed his eyes and concentrated deeply. And then, he called his element in his mind. "Holy element… I am calling you… Come out and tell me the weakness of the magic that is handcuffing me right now…"

Kenji did not expect that King Jethro's image suddenly appeared in his mind. The king of all the gods called his name to his mind in whisper. "Kenji…"

"My dear lord," answered Kenji in his mind.

King Jethro spoke to Kenji in his soft voice. "Kenji, you cannot always rely your troubles to your Holy element all the time. Your element is so powerful only if you know how to use it. Sometimes there is a chance that your element will not obey your command, so you must learn to control and limit the use of its power. Use it and only if necessary."

"Please, my lord… Just one more favor… Can you help me out on how to remove these magical handcuffs in me?"

"Do you know that your Holy element already feel the power of the magic in you? Those handcuffs you have in your hands and feet are caused by the power of a magic that can be destroyed by the element. It is because the element's power is stronger and more powerful than the magic's power, so I am certain that your magical handcuffs can be destroyed by your element itself."

Kenji was impressed. "Really? How?"

"Kenji, you should not depend on me all the time. You should learn on how to use your element well even without my presence. Keep in mind that my element is always with you wherever you are. It will always help you even if I am not at your side."

Kenji did not answer.

"But for now I will guide you in everything you do temporarily. And when you become an Explorer, then you will no longer need my help anymore."

Kenji did not answer again.

"Now, in order for you to remove those handcuffs then you need to use the Black Fire. You must do this in caution, because this fire is so dangerous and wild especially to someone who will be casting it for the very first time. Your chances of being hurt and burned by this type of fire is very high. But this is the only way for you to get rid of this magic cast by the Magic Wielder! When you do so, you can move yourself again freely as normal and win the fight!!!"

Kenji quickly opened his eyes after he heard King Jethro's voice echoed. He noticed Lucky's face already gaped in surprise before him.

"W-What's wrong, Lucky?" asked Kenji.

Lucky stepped back in surprise. "Whaaaattt? You didn't know what was happening to you earlier, hm? Didn't you feel the strikes I just give you?"

"W-What strikes?"

"What the--! You're kidding me, right? Hey, take a look at your body. You have been covered by that weird looking white flame and then... I-I think you are invulnerable to my attacks, aren't you? Is that the Holy element you've told me earlier that is protecting you right now, huh?!"

Kenji was mum. He did not realize that the element had been protecting him while he was talking with King Jethro in his mind. Later, he hesitated. "O-Oh really? Well..."

"Hey, d-don't tell me that you didn't know what I've done to you earlier!"

"I-I know that, m-maybe..." Kenji smiled.

"Very well then... Are you ready now?"

Kenji answered with his serious smile. "Been ready..." then he spoke to his mind. "Hm... King Jethro said that I should use the Black Fire, but how can I release it?"

King Jethro answered to Kenji's mind again in his soft voice. "You need to close your eyes and concentrate deeply. In order for you to unleash the Black Flame is to memorize the correct sequence of your hand gesture. You can do it even though you are handcuffed."

"What are the gestures should I do, my lord?"

"While your eyes are closed, you must follow the movements of my hands that will appear in your dark vision, and eventually you must say 'Black Fire'! Right now you are invulnerable to your opponent's attacks since the White Fire is protecting you. Understand?"

"Yes."

"Keep your concentration steady and watch closely as I am doing my hand movements. Do it slowly but surely, but you need to be cautious and watch out for the harshness of the Black Fire that might surely harm you…"

Lucky began to pose himself for the attack. He dropped his staff to the ground and then he pulled out his revolver in the holster at the side of his hips. Kenji closed his eyes, waiting for the great king's hands to appear in his dark vision.

After a while, the image of King Jethro's hands suddenly appeared to his dark vision and they were also handcuffed. The god's fingers began to move, and Kenji imitated the gesture. Lucky noticed him.

"H-Hey, what are you doing?"

Kenji still doing the gesture while his eyes were still closed. He was doing it slowly but surely and in correct order!

Lucky could no longer wait for Kenji so he began his attack. Good thing, Kenji had finally ended his ceremony before he got attacked. So he quickly opened his eyes and screamed out loud. "BLACK FIRE!!!"

The sky went dark. Lucky, Claude, Clio, Tyrone, and Jon stopped their fight and they all looked up the sky. Kenji suddenly felt anxious thinking of what would happen next. He was panting nervously.

"W-What is going on?" he asked.

Suddenly, Kenji felt something heating up in his body, making his body temperature rapidly rose. Then, the Black Fire emerged from him and it quickly engulfed his whole body. The five were totally surprised when Kenji suddenly cried out loud in his strong painful feeling.

"AHHH! I'm burning!" he cried.

"KENJI!" cried Claude also.

"What on earth is that?" asked Clio in astonishment. "That's a weird looking wild fire!"

Everyone's attention was now to Kenji, watching him struggling while he was still burning.

"AHHHHRRRGGG!!!"

King Jethro spoke again to Kenji's mind. "Son, you need to suffer a little with the Black Fire around your body! This fire can eliminate any kind of magics in you so you can move freely again. Just a little more, Kenji!"

Kenji was still in his rage while screaming out loud. The five witnessed the agony in Kenji's face and they did not know on what to do to stop him.

"Kenji, suffer a little more… We're almost there, you can do it! Your handcuffs are getting nearly vaporized. Listen, majority of the magics' weakness is your Black Fire, but in order for the fire to eliminate them is for you to suffer the pain!"

Kenji opened his eyes. He was still in rage while freaking out. His brown hair fell down to his face and it covered.

"AAAHHHHH!!!

Claude could not help to watch Kenji anymore. He got mad towards Lucky, thinking that the gunner did the Black Fire on Kenji. He crawled as fast as he could towards Lucky who was still watching Kenji's struggle.

"You freakin' mad dog!!!" cried Claude to Lucky very angrily.

Lucky turned to Claude, but Claude quickly head-butted him in full force so he suddenly lost his consciousness. He fell on the ground, and he dropped the revolver he was holding.

The magical handcuffs in Kenji's hands and feet were now gradually vaporizing. The four (without Lucky) were all greatly surprised, until the handcuffs were all completely gone so Kenji was now free at last!

"T-The magical handcuffs, they're gone!" said Kenji unbelievably.

The Black Fire had quickly disappeared right after it destroyed Elijah's magical handcuff.

Lucky regained his consciousness again but Kenji did not wait for him to rise, so Kenji quickly walked over him and he strangled his neck using the body of his Kali.

Lucky was shocked. "K-Kenji! You're handcuffs, they're…"

"Oh yes, Lucky! Now that I am free again then you have no chance of defeating me!" said Kenji and then he pushed his Kali to Lucky's neck harder. "You will totally lose the fight with me…"

Elijah could not even believe his eyes to what he saw, but he could tell that Kenji was strong and smart. He had finally seen what he wanted to see to pass the test: the only strategy of removing his magical handcuffs and be free again.

Elijah had proven that Kenji was the true Element Wielder of Holy

THE EXPLORERS

since he already saw much proofs. To continue the test was no longer necessary and they might hurt each other if they would go on.

Yes... I should stop him now... You will lose, Lucky. I thought you would be our Holy Wielder. Akira does not know this either, but I am happy to know that the Holy element has already found its new possessor... Anyway, let's go back home... Don't you worry, I will give you a nice homecoming party, along with the new member of our family... Maximillian Foster!

He finally decided to stop the two when he called the gunner out loud. "LUCKY TERREL!!!"

Lucky could not turn to Elijah since he was now fighting with Kenji after Kenji let go of him. Their fight was aggressive!

"Stop fighting now, Lucky! Take a rest now, Kenji has passed our final test."

Everyone was surprised to Elijah's decision when Lucky moved away from Kenji and turned to Elijah. "What the--?! That doesn't make sense! Have you changed your mind again?! Remember the rules you explained?! The final test would only be over if these three have defeated us! And look, Kenji still haven't defeated me!"

Elijah closed his eyes and smiled. "I know, but have you forgotten that we're Ultimate Explorers? We are the most cheerful class of Explorers organization! We do not take our class very seriously because we want a happy team. Yes, I could still remember that our previous tests were even pretty tough, but the Explorers gave us much longer time to get recovered before moving on to our next tests. They fed us before our second and third tests, but not to these three... I gave them a whole day to rest, but that wasn't enough. The last time they ate was before they took their first test!" then he turned to Claude and Tyrone who were still fighting with their opponent. "Claude and Tyrone are still handcuffed until now, so their test continues."

"So what am I gonna do now?"

Jon was forced to do the act pretending that he was defeated by Tyrone. "Ah, Elijah... T-Tyrone has defeated me because... Ahhh..." then he tumbled, pretending that he was dizzy due to the continuous pounding of Tyrone and he lifted his shaking hand. "H-He did something weird on me that I failed to catch his quick attack until I suddenly felt weak. Ohhh, I-I'm getting weaker... I surrender now!" and he coughed.

Elijah's mouth gaped in wonder unbelievably. "J-Jon, you have your sharp eyes. But how come that you've missed Tyrone's quick attack on you?!"

Jon laid himself on the snowy ground when he secretly thrust himself with his own darts with no poison. Elijah came to him and moved his body upwards. There, he saw the darts that were stung in Jon's arm. Jon really had to harm himself intentionally just for Tyrone's test.

Elijah turned to Tyrone who was on his knees. "Tyrone, what did you do to Jon? How did the darts sting into Jon's arm?"

"Ah, yes!!!" lied Tyrone. "I did something more faster just to elude his sharp eyes. Through my mind, I could deflect the darts he blew on me. In other words, I have my psycho-kinesis ability! So even though I'm handcuffed, I could still beat him. Hahahaha!!!"

Jon instantly fell asleep, because the darts he pierced in his arms had sedative material. Elijah then thought that he lost his consciousness.

"Yes, you're tight. You defeated Jon though you're still handcuffed. Very well, you also passed the test. Congratulations!" said Elijah and he removed his magic in Tyrone's body. The handcuffs disappeared. "Congratulations that you beat Jon… t-though I did not see the actual thing you did to him…"

Kenji and Tyrone had passed the final test and they completed the three tests when Claude wept in despair, because he was the only person left who was still in the test. He fell on his knees.

Elijah looked at Claude in his sad face and he approached him. And then, he also removed the handcuffs in the young man's hands and feet. "Claude, I know how much you've suffered during your three tests with Kenji and Tyrone. I am sorry for what I have been treating you in the middle of these challenges. Forgive me if you feel that I have been torturing you and abusing you…"

Claude sniffed. "I-I failed the test, am I right?"

Elijah quickly shook his head. "Ah… no, no, no, Claude… Here's what I'm going to do to you in order for you to complete this final test. I will be giving you a special test instead, where you can only answer the questions like college exam! After all, you've already passed your two previous tests, right?"

"I don't want that…"

"D-Don't worry Claude, all you have to do is to answer the questions I will give you and… you will pass!"

"Are you saying that I am a weak person and I failed the physical exams I'd been going through?"

"N-Not really."

Claude did not answer while his tears still fell on his cheeks.

30 THE NEW EXPLORERS

The UE's in the mansion applauded spontaneously when they heard about Tyrone and Kenji's successful completion of their tests from Elijah. Reinhardt, Shingue, and Margot were the first ones who came over to Kenji to meet and greet him in the mansion hall. Kenji was now very weak, and he did not realize that he was now being carried by his older brother's arms. Reinhardt took the white towel from Margot to wipe his brother's dirty body.

"Elijah, I thought their final test would be over if they'd defeated our three returnees?" asked Reinhardt while carrying Kenji in his arms. "You're concerned. After all, they've passed their first and second tests."

"That is what I am thinking. They passed my tests, although Claude is short of passing the tests. But I'll just give him a special exam to complete his final test," answered Elijah.

"I see."

"Claude is also a great young man, Reinhardt. He is strong indeed."

"Certainly."

"However, he's being temperamental much so he is losing his own self-control all the time. That's the problem with Claude, that is his waterloo. He has a different type of attitude, that's why I want to test his intelligence in this special test under this condition."

"Go ahead. Anyway, I am going to take my brother to his room now. So when will you give their license?"

"I'll think about it, maybe tomorrow or today if all the requirements are completed and submitted for approval. I am glad for your younger

THE EXPLORERS

brother to become a part of our team now."

"Yeah, I gotta go. Goodbye."

Reinhardt walked, but after a few steps he stopped and turned to Margot. "Margot, by the way, thank you for the towel. Can you leave us alone for a moment so we can have a few minutes to talk?"

Margot stooped down his head with blushing face, but he agreed. "It's okay… Please tell Kenji I say hi for him."

"No problem, let's go Shingue," called Reinhardt and Shingue followed.

Claude was still weeping alone in a corner when Elijah approached him and patted his shoulder. "Claude, um… Come with me. You have to take your special exam now. Don't worry, it's easy."

Claude answered sniffing. "I'm sorry if I could not hold my feelings right now. It's just because I felt a big shame towards Kenji that he completed the tests and I left behind."

"What do you mean by 'left behind'? You mean--"

"Yes, indeed. I'm afraid to hear what Kenji might say to me…"

"He won't, Claude!" Elijah patted Claude's shoulder once again. "You also passed the exams, but I want a convincing result before I consider your test. However, you still haven't completed your final test so I will give you something different. Your special test doesn't require your strength, but only your mental ability."

"You told me about it earlier. Do you think I am a genius type of guy, eh? Just to remind you, I never attended school in my life!"

"Most of the UEs here did not attend nor finish their school either, but they still succeeded because of their skills and mental ability. Of course that's a plus factor if you have brains…"

"Well, I have no brains!"

Elijah stopped when he came to realize that Claude was in his bad temper again since he had been hungry and exhausted for long. Instead, he just smiled sweetly at Claude as an answer.

"You wanna come with me now, Claude?"

"W-Wait, what is your so called special exam is all about? Do I have to take a review first before moving on?!"

"No need."

"Later, okay? I am still very tired! I'm completely exhausted and my brains will not work perfectly. Do you understand?!!"

"Fine, I will give you an hour to take a rest but you're still not allowed to eat, okay? I just want to be fair for Kenji and Tyrone's final test."

"Whatever!"

"Go back to your room now and then after an hour please go to the laboratory. You can have a drink for a moment so you'll recover a bit of your strength. Tonight we will have a Welcome Party for Lucky, Clio, and Jon. And you will have a chance to be with them, then eat whatever you want to eat, Claude."

"Okay."

"You may now go to your room, Claude. We'll see each other again later."

As for the three returnees, the UE had planned to give them their Welcome Party, welcoming their return from Omania after a month of their special training. The party was also welcoming the new members who were now part of their team. The UE would also make an Explorer uniform for Kenji and Claude right away since Tyrone already had one.

Some of the UEs were now busy in placing luxurious decorations to the walls, windows, and facade, while the others were also busy in cooking delicious foods for the party. Most foods were all Filipino-style.

In most cases, only maids and butlers were doing their household tasks day-by-day. But for now, the UE warriors were helping them to make things faster. They had full coordination and cooperation.

Claude arrived in his room when he saw Reinhardt and Shingue inside who were both busy in taking care of Kenji. The young man had a fever aside from being weak.

"Kenji has a high fever right now, Claude…" said Shingue to Claude sadly.

"A fever?"

"Yes."

Claude came closer to Kenji and he gently touched the young man's forehead. His skin was hot so Claude shook his head in disappointment. "Tsk, tsk, tsk…"

"What's wrong, Claude?"

"I know how difficult it was to stay underwater for so long Shingue," Claude still had not forgotten their second test. "That is why I really hate Elijah…"

"But he's an Explorer now, Claude."

THE EXPLORERS

"I know, but he put Kenji's life at risk. Kenji was almost got killed when I saw him trapped underwater."

"But what could we do about it if that's what he chose?"

"That Elijah did not make consideration first!"

"Is that the only thing you want to say aside from that?"

"Much more."

Reinhardt interrupted the two. "Claude, Elijah had nothing to do about what happened to Kenji. We would really have to confront it and deal with it."

Claude tried to control his temper and answered. "Is that so?!"

Reinhardt nodded seriously.

"I'm going to sleep now," said Claude and then he went to his bed and laid there.

Lucky, Clio, and Jon knocked on the room's door and Shingue opened it. He noticed that Jon was already awake from the effect of the tranquilizer.

"Hey, you guys! Go ahead, come inside," said Shingue when he asked the three to come inside the room.

The three went inside the room when they saw Kenji and Claude lying in the bed. "Oh, so what's with these two new UEs?" asked Lucky. "It looks like they've suffered so much. They're very exhausted!"

"You're right…"

"I congratulate them, although we have not seen their first and second test but they looked great. And… we will be having new friends, hahaha!"

"Um," Jon gulped in guiltiness. "Tyrone is wise. He took advantage of my speed and he beat me. I like his psychic ability," then he smiled awkwardly since he knew they only cheated.

"Why, that's good to hear then."

"Where's Claude?" Clio was looking for Claude. "I want to see him. Imagine, that eyebrow guy prevented me from attacking him and then he was freakin' out! To tell you honestly, our fight was really that borin'!"

Claude heard Clio's remark and he quickly opened his eyes. He rose from the bed.

"What the hell did you just say?!" asked Claude in his sharp voice towards Clio.

"H-Hey Claude, CONGRATS!" said Clio to Claude teasingly in playful way. "Y-You were great in our fight earlier!"

Claude quickly came closer to Clio annoyingly, but Clio spoke first while his right hand was ready to shake hands with Claude. "Um... S-So you still have your pure energy... Hihihi, why don't you start your special test now?"

"I heard you earlier! I wasn't freakin' out, and to tell you honestly... Your stupid attacks were very, very TEDIOUS!" said Claude angrily.

"H-Hey! I was really telling the truth."

"Shut up!"

Lucky walked over between the two as he shook his head and pacified them. "Hey, hey, hey... relax fellas. We're outta here later."

The two had stopped when Lucky spoke again. "Fellas, we'll all meet at the Welcome Party later at ten o'clock in the evening. Kenji, Tyrone, and Claude need to attend the party because they will receive their Explorer license and badge. There will be a banquet later, so if I were you I would eat a light meal today before the party. And oh, we will have our special guests tonight from EUE and DDE. The DDEs will be the ones to award the license to our new members and they are all V.I.P!"

Reinhardt was shocked. "Wait a minute... The DDEs will be coming here tonight? Is that mean that my father will be here too? Well he really should come here tonight, so he will be surprised if he finds out that his other son is the new Explorer today!"

"Is your father not looking for you for a long time?" Lucky asked. "What kind of father is he?! We rarely see and meet those DDEs because they are elite and too rigorous!"

Reinhardt thought of asking. "What do you think? Will my father coming here too? You see, everytime I would go to them for a visit, my father did not want to show himself to me. The DDEs kept on telling me that he didn't want to meet somebody nor not in his mood to talk to anyone. Sometimes they even told me that he was not in the mansion, but I could feel that he was there."

Lucky only shook his head in uncertainty and decided to leave the boys now. "We're leaving now and we're going to help out everybody in the hall. We'll meet again at ten o'clock in the evening. Goodbye," then he walked outside the room with Jon and Clio and gently closed the door.

Claude laid down his back on the bed again and spoke sadly. "I just don't feel like of being an Explorer..."

Shingue heard Claude's calm voice this time so he answered. "Why is that? You should be proud of yourself today. You're an Explorer now."

THE EXPLORERS

Claude smiled. "If you only know what I mean, Shingue… Anyway, gotta sleep now."

Elijah made his call to the mansions of EUE and DDE as his invitation to attend the Welcome Party of the UE. He usually had a hard time to make his call to the DDE since this highest class was mostly busy with their assignments. They were usually ignoring the non-assignment related calls, even though the callers were their fellow Explorers in lower class. They had no time for anyone.

But good thing the DDEs were in their mood to talk with Elijah today. Elijah mentioned about his invitation to their party as well as the proper recognition of their new Explorers. "Please come to our mansion at nine o'clock in the evening to make preparation. This will also serve as our reunion party for all the members of the Explorers organization. The EUEs will come. Alright, we'll see each other tonight. You are our V.I.P for tonight's party, okay? That's all, goodbye."

Elijah ended the call when he put down the calling device on its base. Then, he turned to the fellow UEs who were still busy in making preparations for the party. "We must make haste. Maybe all of the DDEs will come here tonight."

Everyone was in a hurry. Later, Lucky came over to Elijah and asked the leader. Jon and Clio followed his back. "Elijah, is it really true that all of the DDEs will be coming tonight?"

Elijah stroked his chin in uncertainty. "I think so, why?"

"Do you think Alex Foster of DDE will also be here tonight?"

Elijah folded his arms across his breast. "I never heard about him for so long. Actually when I called the DDE, I asked them to relay my call to him, but they said he did not want to talk to me."

"Hopefully he'll come, right?"

"Lucky, Clio, Jon. Go and bathe yourselves now, and tell Kenji and Claude to wear formal attire like… You know, like tuxedo and Barong Tagalog… Or the one we usually wear during our formal parties. Okay anyway, I've changed my mind… We will all wear the same formal uniform for tonight."

"Oh man, that one again? That's the same thing we've always worn in every party. I'm sick of it anymore."

"You must understand this because that is our formal uniform. I want our party to look very formal."

"Can we change our formal uniform into its new style?"

"Come on, man… Go and tell them now so they get dressed sooner. We're running out of time."

"But I just came there."

"What a LAZYBONES you are, Lucky!" said Elijah jokingly.

"O-Okay, fine… Gotta go now."

Clio cut their conversation. "Hey, why don't you just announce it throughout the mansion? There are wall speakers around the mansion. It's a good thing that the UEs can also hear your announcement for the party."

Lucky agreed. "Yes, you're right Clio. What about that, Elijah?"

"Okay, fine!" Elijah stamped his foot jokingly. "You really are good-for-nothing. I am going to the booth for the announcement and I'll do it myself. Now go away from my sight!"

The three laughed. "Don't worry, you can give us the turn to make an announcement if you're too tired Elijah," said Jon.

"After all, you already know what to say, right? Okay then, go ahead. I still have more things to do for the upcoming party tonight. Tell to all the ladies to wear their red one."

And then, Elijah left the three. When Lucky, Clio, and Jon had reached the booth for the announcement, they stopped for a moment thinking of which among them should speak.

"It's your turn, Lucky. Since you have an attractive voice," joked Clio.

"Stop joking around, Clio. You cannot fool me that easily," Lucky scoffed.

"How did you know that, Lucky?"

"Know what?"

"That I am only joking?"

Lucky knocked off Clio's forehead but not that hard. "Pwah, don't tell me the reason why you're saying that is because you really want to speak, am I right?!"

Clio was feeling guilty. "A-Ah, n-no way!"

Lucky, Clio, and Jon were the type of Explorers who were witty and love to make jokes, especially Lucky. Lucky was the best among them to have a good sense of humor, and he always loved to make jokes even during their hard times too!

"How about you, Jon? Was it you who have won in a singing contest when you went out from your mother's womb? 'Coz you had a tenor voice when you sang... I mean, t-the loudest voice when you cried... W-Weren't you?"

Jon also knocked off Lucky's forehead but not that hard.

"I was just innocent when I was born. So just shut up, Lucky."

"Innocent?"

"How'd you know that I had the loudest voice among the babies born in my batch?"

Lucky stroked his chin. "Um, that's because I already met your ancestors before, Jon..."

"Whatever you say."

"Okay, therefore I shall speak now!" said Lucky as he was raising his right hand. "Give me the headset, Jonas!"

"See? Now we know who really wants to speak," Jon laughed.

"Come on, the headset. Give it to me!"

Jon gave the headset to Lucky and he gently put it on his head. They turned on the wall speakers that were mounted around the mansion walls. Then, Lucky made an intro. "Hello? Mic test... hello?"

"Go ahead, Lucky. Start the announcement," whispered Clio.

The announcement tone dinged. *Ting-ting-ting-ting!* Then it followed by Lucky's voice. "Announcement to all the beautiful and handsome UEs present here today. Our Welcome Party will begin at ten o'clock in the evening. All attendees should wear our formal uniform for tonight," then he made fun with the announcement. "To all the ladies... do the best you can to make yourself more attractive to the eyes of men present and wear sweet perfumes... By the way, Elijah mentioned that the ladies' formal attire should be, um... I don't know what it is called. The red one..."

Clio whispered. "It's a gown."

"Ah, so that's what it's called, a 'gown'! Dammit, what a stupid announcement I am making right now," said Lucky annoyingly but in a joke. His voice was echoing throughout the mansion. "We already know what we suppose to wear then why do I still have to announce it?! Nevermind the announcement. Goodbye and sweet dreams, little fellas!!!"

Ting-ting-ting-ting...

All of the UEs heard Lucky's announcement when they all laughed spontaneously right after the ding ended.

Kenji was already awake when Lucky made an announcement. Reinhardt and Shingue were still there in the room with him. Claude was still sleeping.

"We know that already, Lucky. Don't make the same announcement again ever!" said Shingue laughing. "We are used to wear that same uniform and I want to wear something new!"

Kenji spoke in low, weak voice. "What should we wear?"

Reinhardt answered. "Oh, don't worry about it, Kenji. I have an extra formal uniform for you. Tuxedo-like uniform for men and gown-like uniform for women are our most common formal attire during formal parties. Each of us has an extra. Shingue can give his extra to Claude."

Kenji nodded with a smile. "Thank you, *kuya* Reinhardt and Shingue."

"The party will be formal. Perhaps Claude will be done with his special test before the party starts. He can make it to get his license in time. All of the UEs must attend the party tonight."

"Will that uniform of yours fits well to me?"

"Yes, of course… Though I think it is slightly bigger to you when you wear it, but still it looks fine."

An hour had passed when Elijah called Claude to complete his final test by taking a special exam. The UEs began to groom themselves when Reinhardt and Shingue gave their extra tuxedo-like uniforms to Kenji and Claude before Claude went to the laboratory. Kenji was getting very excited after hearing from Reinhardt that the DDE would be in tonight's party… And this would be their big chance to see their father at last!

31 WELCOME PARTY

At seven o'clock in the evening.

Claude had finished his special exam given to him by the UE. He said that the test was okay and the degree of difficulty was equal according to the level of his intelligence. Elijah said he would announce the result of Claude's exam later.

As for Kenji, although he had a fever and injured, still he took his bath! He did not mind of his illness. He just wanted to be more presentable when going out and receiving his license at the party. He had a hard time of bathing himself due to his injury but he forced himself to get cleansed. He would be wearing his brother's extra uniform and it was very humiliating if he would wear it with his filthy body, and what more humiliating was for his real father to see him dirty and had a body odor during recognition!

The female UEs were quicker to move than males because of their lesser number. They were now on their beautiful red gowns and they were busy in putting face make-ups in the dressing room. The others were also busy in putting hair decorations and hairclips.

Clio and Marion were both grooming themselves in the same room. Clio wanted to help his adopted brother to groom himself.

"Hey bro, please put a lot of gel in your hair," asked Clio to his adopted brother while holding a small bottle of hair gel.

Marion still had his messy hair because he was too lazy to comb his hair. Due to his very young age, he was not as good-looking conscious as the other. But his attitude was the same as Claude since both of them were always bad-tempered.

"No way! That doesn't look good to me."

"Why don't you try it? If this doesn't look good to you then I wouldn't ask you to put a gel in your hair. Come on, put this on now."

"I do not know how to use that…"

"Fine! Then let me be the one to put this in your hair. Come closer."

"You? Please don't, *kuya*! Just comb my hair… Don't put that sticky gel on me. I don't want my hair looking electrified!"

"Ssssttt, stop complaining! Come here and I have to put this in your hair NOW. I know the best hair style I can apply on you, Marion. Trust *kuya* Clio and if not, I will knock your head off. Now move here or I'll come over you. The party will start soon."

Marion annoyingly stamped his foot as he was moving closer to Clio and frowned. "I hate being bullied by this stupid gel thing… I'm feeling embarrassed if my hair looks pretty bad!"

"I will not put this on you if you will look terribly bad and funny, okay?"

As for Kenji and Claude.

"Claude… how's your test?" asked Kenji to Claude in their room while also grooming themselves.

"It was okay."

"Was it too difficult?"

"Somewhat."

Kenji was about to put his black bowtie on his neck. He asked Claude to assist him in putting it to his neck. "Claude, it's Shingue's uniform you are wearing, right?" he asked.

"Yes, why? Do I look funny with this tuxedo?"

"I did not say anything."

"I'm sorry," Claude had finished putting on Kenji's bowtie to his neck. "Um, can you also help me on putting this bowtie to my neck, Kenji? Man, I wanna eat now. I'm so hungry. Imagine, we haven't eaten for days!" he complained.

Kenji was helping Claude in putting the bowtie when he complained more. "I'm feeling nauseating now, Kenji! Good thing my energy has one percent remaining!"

"Do not be noisy," Kenji chuckled, but he tightened up Claude's bowtie unintentionally.

"I-I'm strangling, Kenji! Loosen it a little."

THE EXPLORERS

It was still earlier than ten o'clock when the UEs had finally finished organizing everything for the evening party. The main hall where the party would be held was very well decorated. The UEs were all wearing the same formal attire now. The males were on their black tuxedo-like uniforms while the females were on their red gowns.

In front of the hall, there was a presidential table exclusively for the three UE returnees from Omania and also for the three new members of the Explorers organization. The UEs took Kenji, Claude, Tyrone, Lucky, Clio, and Jon to their special seats. Some of the UEs sat on their assigned chairs too, along with some of the EUEs who had arrived in the mansion first.

"The DDE said that they might arrive here pretty late," said Kenji to the five in his low voice. "But what I only want to do tonight is to see my real father, and he himself will pin my badge on to my lapel and give me my license."

The five nodded.

Tyrone looked at his watch. "It's almost ten o'clock. I have to go to Isagani first, perhaps he will think that I am forgetting him," and then he left the table.

Tyrone was already gone when Lucky spoke to his seatmates. "Guys, do you know that Tyrone is a… very unsociable type of person? You see, he's always sticking himself to Isagani, don't you think?"

"Just let him do what he wants," answered Clio. "Tyrone was raised by his parents for being pampered. His parents had been giving anything he wanted when he was still a child. A spoiled brat."

Claude was in disbelief. "Huh? His parents spoiled him all the time?"

"You see, they belong to a wealthy family!"

Claude stroked his chin. "I can see that…"

Kenji leaned his back to his chair and touched his forehead. "My head is aching and I'm feeling dizzy, but that's okay. I should have stayed here for a while," then he laid his head down on the table. "Geez, I feel awful… like I feel nauseous…"

Jon spoke to Kenji. "Claude said that you still took a bath even with fever. Now I can see how persistent and stubborn you are, hahaha!"

Kenji ignored Jon. His head was still on the table. "I want to eat now… Oh father…"

"Hey, hang in there. Wait a little more, dude. The party will start very soon!" Clio laughed.

The announcement tone dinged. "Ladies and gentlemen, the Welcome Party will start soon. It will begin at exactly ten o'clock tonight."

More of the EUE visitors had arrived in the UE mansion. Their appearance were noble-like since their formal attires were mostly designed like nobles in the Middle Ages, and they were wearing expensive jewelries.

"There comes another EUEs," said Jon as he turned to the newcomers. "I'm ashamed to come face-to-face with them."

"I know that, Jon. You didn't take a bath," Lucky joked.

Jon blushed. "H-Hey! The weather is very cold, but I'm still pleasantly smelled aromatic!"

The maids and butlers were in a hurry to serve the EUE newcomers by taking them to their seats. *What a dummy!* Said Claude to himself while watching the EUE visitors. *With this kind of snowy weather, they shouldn't use umbrellas. They're very inappropriate!*

"Look, more EUE visitors have arrived," said Claude still watching his so called, "inappropriate" EUEs.

"Man, now I am feeling awkward this time. Those EUEs look super formal for this party," said Kenji. "Father, where are you now? I want to see you."

More minutes had passed until nine o'clock in the evening, but the DDE had not arrived yet. Still more of the EUEs had arrived in the mansion.

"My goodness, those DDEs surely are so sluggish!" said Claude annoyingly. "Only an hour left before the party starts."

"They will come sooner," said Lucky.

"The remaining vacant seats are almost filled but they're still not here!"

"They will come, Claude. Don't worry, they have their reserved seats here."

"Maybe they just lied to us!"

There was a group of ten EUE warriors who came to the three UE returnees just to say hi to them and also to meet the new Explorers.

"Lucky, Clio, Jon! Long time no see," greeted by an EUE woman named Olympia, Vamir's ex-girlfriend.

"Hey, Olympia!" answered Jon. "How are you all doing now? It's been a long time since we lastly seen each other. By the way, Vamir is right over there. He's with his group with Margot. Why don't you come over him just to say hi too?"

"Of course, I will. I won't go back to our mansion without missing the chance to see him. I'll go there later. Guess he's still busy with his friends right now."

Lucky tried to tease Olympia over Vamir. "That's very sweet of you... Hopefully you two will be together again. Oh, by the way," he introduced Kenji and Claude to the EUEs. "These two are the new members of our group and this party is for them too as our welcome. Tyrone has finally completed his test so he will get his full license as well, but he's not here with us."

"Hey, congratulations!" greeted the ten EUE warriors and they offered their hands to shake hands with Kenji and Claude.

"So your name is Kenji and this one is Claude," said another female EUE named Georgia. "You know what? You are both good-looking!"

Kenji blushed. "Ah, thank you for that compliment. But I believe that my *kuya* Reinhardt is far more good-looking than me, though the UEs said we're simply look-alike."

The ten EUEs were surprised. "What did you say? You and Reinhardt are brothers?" asked a male EUE.

"Y-Yeah…"

"As a matter of fact, you actually look like him!"

"So you are the one that Elijah was mentioning about when he called us earlier," said Georgia while pointing at Kenji. "He said that the UE had recruited one of the new members who was a younger brother of my long-time crush!"

"Which means he's one of the Fosters," said another male EUE.

"I'm afraid that I might have mistaken you as Reinhardt sometimes!" joked by another male EUE.

Kenji blushed more. "Um, no… we're not perfectly alike. We're still the same… W-Wait, do I make sense right now?!"

"Alright, we're going back to our seats now. We just came here to say hi and meet you both. Gotta go!"

"Okay everyone, nice to meet you all."

"Nice to meet you too. We'll catch up again later!" then the ten EUEs left.

Silence. Later, the five continued their conversation.

"What a nice compliment you have there for being good-looking though you didn't sleep much, eh?" teased Lucky to Kenji and Claude.

"Don't tease us, Lucky. Claude and I have been starving for long 'til now."

Clio spoke. "Can you guys still wait a little longer 'till dinner?"

Claude quickly answered in his high tone. "Of course man! And at the same time we're getting an ulcer sooner!"

It was 9:45pm when Tyrone returned to the five. Still none of the DDEs had arrived in the UE mansion, not at least one.

"They're still aren't here," said Kenji boringly. "Only few minutes left before the party starts."

"Do not worry, man!" said Lucky confidently. "Elijah said earlier that they should come here because they are the party V.I.Ps. So surely we'll expect that they will arrive here before or during the party."

"What the heck! They are in the highest class of Explorers so they shouldn't come here very late. It's a shame if they 'arrive behind schedule' in attendance!" said Claude. "They're suppose to arrive here sooner than the EUE!"

Kenji agreed. "Claude's right, Lucky... They should arrive here sooner than the EUE."

"Don't ya worry I said, Kenji. If I said it, they'll come... Come on, stop worrying too much, will you?"

Later, they saw a group of Explorer HawkEye jets landed in front of the mansion. Some of the Explorer guests outside turned to them, as well as Kenji's group who were still waiting for the DDE's arrival.

"More of our visitors have arrived!" said Kenji delightfully. "Hahaha, I think it's my father now!" then he excitedly stood on his chair.

Lucky also stood. "Yes, I think the DDEs have finally arrived! Their HawkEyes look very different to ours."

The two along with Reinhardt waited for the newcomers to disembark, but a minute had passed they were still inside.

"What are you guys still doing in there?! Get out the plane now and show yourselves," said Reinhardt irritably.

The newcomers went out of the plane. Still, they were EUEs. "Oh... they're EUEs. I thought they're DDEs already," said Lucky in embarrassment.

More of the newcomers had arrived, but still they were also EUEs. Kenji was nearly losing his temper and he was getting bored of waiting for his father. He walked back to his seat while stamping his foot.

"What a bummer! My father is taking too long to come here and I'm getting tired of these EUE newcomers. What time it is now?! It's 9:55pm already but still none of the DDEs has arrived!"

Lucky answered Kenji in a joke. "D-Do not worry Kenji, later your stomach will be stuffed. You're just starving right now that's why!"

Kenji stood again to his chair to leave the four but Claude prevented him. Claude patted Kenji's shoulder so the young man sat down again.

"I want to tell Elijah to make his call to the DDE again to inform them about the party. They are the only ones who are still not around," said Kenji to Claude annoyingly. "I know they will come, but I don't want my father to be late in recognition of giving me my own license!"

"Do you give up now, Kenji?" Jon asked.

"N-No, it doesn't mean like that, Jon. However, I really want my father to give me my license personally and eat with me in tonight's special dinner. Imagine how wonderful it will be to eat dinner with him…"

"I agree with that."

The UE servers approached the six to give them bowls of soups right after they gave some to the guests. "Hello, handsome UEs, how about some hot soups to warm up your stomachs?" said one server and smiled. "Oh, would you like coffees too?"

"Thank you," answered the six boys smiling.

While still waiting, Kenji broke the stick he was holding in boredom. "Tsk, I really can't take it anymore!"

Silence. No one answered to what Kenji just said. They just drank their hot coffee.

Claude was the first one to fully consume his soup. It was obvious that he was really that hungry. He was also the first to empty his cup of coffee. "I want more…"

Lucky smiled. "You want some more, Claude? Hold on, I'll call the servers."

Claude felt shy so he stopped Lucky. "Maybe later… Not now. I am fine. I will eat whatever I want in tonight's banquet, so thanks anyway."

Kenji was the next one to fully consume his soup. And then, he laid down his head again on the table.

At last, the night Welcome Party had started. The host spoke to the guests with a smile on his face. "Ladies and gentlemen, Welcome to tonight's party. We are dedicating this party to the men who have successfully passed the test and elevated to become the newest member of the Explorers family. So without further ado, let me welcome you all and enjoy the night ahead of us. Good evening, Explorers!"

The music had started by the grand orchestra when Kenji looked around and spoke in concern. "Oh no, the party is starting… but the DDEs aren't still here yet. What's taking so long?"

Lucky was concerned too. "Yeah, they're taking too long…"

"This party is also for the three brave UEs whom we dispatched abroad to take their special training in the preparation of the upcoming fight against a Pioneer in the tournament. We also would like to dedicate this party to all of you," said a UE host. "Please let us give these brave Explorers a big hand!" then he applauded.

Everyone in the party applauded except Lucky's group. Kenji was looking around to his seat searching for DDEs while Lucky's head was stooped down, feeling ashamed and despair to himself of losing King Jethro's Holy element. He was feeling guilty of having this special party for them, because he already broke the Explorers' expectation of becoming the new Holy Wielder.

"Kenji," Lucky called Kenji in whisper. "The EUEs are still unaware of your Holy element. How will I tell to the EUEs that our special training in Omania was useless? Because you are a Holy Wielder now. Akira doesn't know this either, and he's still into my stone 'til now!"

Kenji did not answer. He was still looking around the hall.

Lucky stooped his head more. "It's too embarrassing really…"

"After our introduction to the new Explorers then we will give their badge and license during recognition. Our tonight's special guest who will award their license is the one but only our DDE superior leader--"

"But the DDEs aren't still here up to now!" said Reinhardt annoyingly to his seat. "I don't think they'll come anymore!"

"But before that, may we first listen to an Opening Speech by our honorable Ultimate Explorer leader, Mr. Elijah Tylers! Ladies and gentlemen, let's give him a big hand!"

Everyone applauded once again. Claude was wondering about the Opening Speech as if the party was like Graduation Ceremony. Elijah walked over the podium and he delivered his speech.

Kenji was about to lose hope to see his father anymore when the

THE EXPLORERS

Explorers sighted a group of ten Explorer jets approaching towards the mansion. The guests outside the hall stood on their seats while watching the incoming jets in the air that were about to make their landing.

One of the UE gatekeepers was passing through the visitors while making his way to the hall. "Please excuse me for a moment, the DDEs have finally arrived!"

Kenji quickly lifted his head when he stood on his chair and hurriedly ran off towards his brother. While Elijah was still in the middle of his speech, Kenji was passing through the guests just to reach Reinhardt. His face was now showing delightfulness and excitement!

Reinhardt stood on his chair as well. Kenji approached him and he grabbed his hand in excitement. They were now making their way to the entrance hurriedly while passing through the tables that were blocking their way. They wanted to meet the DDE leader right away!

Ahahaha! Do you hear that?! That's my father! Hahaha! Finally he's here… The only special person who will award my license to me. Yeaahhh!!!

The Explorer jets had landed when the DDEs were now getting off their planes. Their attires were all uniformed and looked very formal. Every DDE women had their own escorts. Not all of the DDE warriors had attended the party, and they remained in their mansion.

Kenji and Reinhardt had reached the mansion's main gate. The DDEs were all in the entrance while the two were both looking for their father.

One of the UE gatekeepers opened the main gate and the DDEs went inside. Kenji and Reinhardt moved over the garden for a clear look at the approaching visitors. They were staring at each newcomers' faces one-by-one, but Alex Foster was not with them.

"I think our father already went straight into the hall to surprise us. I didn't notice him that fast. What do you think?" asked Reinhardt to Kenji smiling. "I'm so sure that our father will be very, very surprised if he knows that one of the new Explorers is his son!"

"Hehehe… yeah, you're right, *kuya* Reinhardt. I am very excited to see and hear his reaction!" said Kenji smiling too.

"Certainly, b-but I really don't see him here… Do you?"

"Why don't we ask the DDEs? Let's ask them."

"Maybe not. Perhaps he's already inside. I am sure of it."

The DDEs were all gone in the entrance and they were now in the mansion. The two were still in the garden near the gate. The gatekeeper was only next to them.

"Wait a minute, Kenji… no one comes next. I told you he's already inside."

"You're right," Kenji was looking around the gate. "Wow, he's fast. We missed his way through here."

"Wanna go back inside the mansion now, Kenji?"

"All right."

The gatekeeper heard them and spoke. "Oh gentlemen, the DDE leader is not arriving yet. He will be here after a few minutes."

"Oh, is that so? Okay, we will just stay here and wait for him here. We thought we didn't see him," said Reinhardt.

The entire hall was filled with applauding noise again when Elijah had finished his Opening Speech. The two outside heard the applause. "Elijah's speech is finished," said Reinhardt and he chuckled. "Only few minutes left before you'll receive your badge and license, Kenji."

"Certainly. I hope our dad does not come here late," agreed Kenji.

"Next, now may we listen to the Inspirational Speech by the UE's assistant leader, Nemith. Please give her a big hand!"

The visitors applauded once again. "Oh, I thought the long speech was over. Nemith is the next one to make her speech," said Reinhardt.

The UE assistant leader's speech also took long while the two were still in the gate waiting for their father's arrival. When the next speech was over, the visitors applauded again.

Finally, the long wait had come! The gatekeeper sighted a single Explorer jet in the distance that was coming towards them. It was the DDE leader's private jet. "Our supreme leader of the Dragon Divinity Explorer has finally arrived!" he cried.

"This is it, *kuya*! He's finally here!" cried Kenji in excitement. "I can see his jet coming over here!"

Reinhardt was also excited. "I know, Kenji. I can see the jet too!"

The single DDE jet slowly stopped when it reached the main gate and it gently landed next to the other aircrafts.

"Kenji, that is really our father's plane! I actually know what it looks like," said Reinhardt.

"My goodness… I almost forgot that I am hungry!" said Kenji delightfully.

The jet's exit door opened when the aviator went out the plane first.

The two got more excited and were eager to see their father right away.

The aviator lifted his hand to grab hold the DDE leader's hand. The leader's foot appeared to the exit to get off the plane next... until he finally made his full appearance to the eyes of the two men!

The two had seen the DDE leader at last! But Reinhardt could not believe to what he saw. It seemed to what was happening was just a dream.

"Yoohoo! Our dad is here, HEY DAAAADDD!!!" cried Kenji in great excitement and he pulled his brother's hand. "Let's go to him, *kuya*. Look at him, he looks very great!"

Kenji was so desperate to come over to his known-father when Reinhardt quickly grabbed his hand and prevented him. Kenji stopped and turned to his brother, and he saw his brother's head was already stooped down with his face looking confused. Reinhardt was no longer looking at the leader of DDE.

"What's wrong, *kuya*? Come with me and we'll show ourselves to him."

"H-hold on, Kenji... I don't think he is our father..." said Reinhardt looking uncertain. "I know our father's face... Though it was a very long time ago. Or... maybe that man is not the DDE leader yet."

"You're only hungry, *kuya*!" Kenji answered in a joke. "You're hallucinating now, but I think he is the one!"

Reinhardt shook his head. "No, he's not! He's not our father. I have an old photo of him that was taken a long, long time ago. H-Here it is," then he showed off to his brother an old pocket-sized photograph of Alex Foster that was already faded and his face was very unclear. "T-This is our father, Kenji!" he said in his high voice.

"I never thought you have a picture of our father," said Kenji and he looked at the faded picture held by Reinhardt. "Where did you get this?"

"It was given to me by our mother, before she fled us when we're still very young!"

Kenji was surprised to hear that Reinhardt raised his voice towards him. He did not answer, until the DDE leader went inside the mansion.

Reinhardt annoyingly approached the gatekeeper. "Hey man, is Alex Foster the last man who has just arrived earlier? The DDE leader?!"

The gatekeeper faltered by Reinhardt's angry voice. "Um, sir... Yes, he is the leader of DDE... but he is not Alex Foster."

The two were shocked. "What did you say?! Then who is that man, anyway?!!"

Kenji turned to Reinhardt looking concerned. "*Kuya*, don't tell me…"

"Tsk, bummer! Come Kenji, let's ask somebody who knows that so called 'leader of DDE'!" said Reinhardt angrily and he grabbed Kenji's hand. They hurriedly went back inside the mansion.

The DDE leader was now sitting in his special seat when Reinhardt approached the personal bodyguard of the DDE leader. Kenji was only next to him still looking concerned, unaware to what was going on now.

In the middle of the Welcome Party, Reinhardt could not control his angriness anymore when he asked the personal bodyguard rudely without a greeting. "Sir, is he the current leader of the DDE class now?!!"

The bodyguard only raised his eyebrow as an answer to Reinhardt's question.

"Where is Alex Foster? Our father?!"

The bodyguard answered. "He is Mr. Spencer Briant who is the current leader of DDE for long. What do you two want from him then?"

"If our father is no longer our supreme leader then that is not a big deal for me! Now, where is Alex Foster?!"

The woman named Dianara who was the wife of Spencer Briant heard the commotion and answered angrily. She was sitting next to her husband. "What a rude Explorer you are, young man! My husband is the leader of DDE and no one else! How could you have that kind of attitude!"

Kenji slowly moved forward and answered calmly for his brother. "Um, I apologize for my brother's dealing with your bodyguard right now since he has been exhausted for working hard in today's assignments… We just want to know where our father whose name is Alex Foster at now…"

Dianara Briant laughed at loud before the two. "Why, I am glad that you have a better attitude unlike your older brother! And with regards to Alex Foster, didn't you hear the old news that Alex was already DEAD five years ago! He was brutally killed by Reminescence so my husband was the one who took his place as the new leader of DDE! Your father had been dead for long! Why? Do you think your father is still alive up to now? Hah, you two are SO pathetic… Too bad that you have missed the old news of him!"

The two were very shocked to hear it from the DDE leader's wife! They felt like the entire universe seemed to have fallen to their heads when they finally learned the full reality of their father!

32 THE TRUTH

The two could not believe what they had heard. They became so emotional not knowing that the tears from their eyes rolled down to their haggard face. This would be the big chance they had been waiting for so long in their entire life. Now that the opportunity came in their way, the chance to see their father personally was doomed.

But Kenji was the type of person who did not want to believe without any proof. Yes, he was a kindly man, but he was not that easy to be deceived. So he thought to himself, maybe that Dianara Briant's story was just a pure hoax.

Kenji's sensitive feelings was now excruciating, still wanting to hear from the DDE leader the real story itself. So he asked the personal bodyguard if he could talk to the DDE leader for at least just a few minutes. The bodyguard nodded, he went to the DDE leader and whispered to him the humbled request.

The DDE leader was obliged out of respect, knowing that the two brothers were the sons of the former DDE leader. He made himself excuse from the other guests and went out at the backstage to see the two brothers.

"Sir, I apologize to what just happened earlier, but I hate to believe the fact that my father is already dead! Tell me sir, tell me it was just a lie, right?! T-Tell me!" asked Reinhardt anxiously to Spencer. "I know who my father is! He is a great leader and a great warrior, but how come he was killed by Reminescence? HOW?!!"

Silence. Reinhardt continued. "Curse the DDEs! My father has been long gone but why did you just say this to me now?!!" he said angrily when he suddenly banged the backstage wall real hard causing a loud noise echoed in the main hall. The V.I.P guests and the crowd had stopped to what they were doing knowing that the DDE leader was at the backstage. The personal bodyguard rushed to the backstage to attend the DDE leader. Spencer Briant went to the stage and into the podium, then he spoke in front of the worried crowd.

"Ladies and gentlemen, may I have your attention please. Let me tell you a story and shed lights to the queries and humors, about the real story that transpired during the mission done by Alex Foster five years ago. But first, let me ask the forgiveness from the brave sons of the great warrior," he said as he was looking at the place where the brothers were standing. "It was five years ago when the Reminescence killed Alex Foster. They captured him during his secret infiltrate mission alone to their unknown territory and they brutally tortured him."

Kenji was no longer in his mood to speak. His body got weaker from exhaustion and at the same time, depression and despair. So he just knelt before them and shed more tears. Reinhardt was also shedding tears when Spencer continued the story. "During the torture, the Reminescence took all of his strength right they imprisoned him in their territory. Alex had been whipped, wounded, and pounded. He absorbed all the blows and the hardship only the strongest men could withstand. The Reminescence wanted to yield what Magic Stone Alex had, but he never gave up the precious stone even in life and in death. Alex Foster never feared for his life but he feared for the lives of the Explorer warriors so he made a deal to the Reminescence. He thought of giving up the Magic Stone he obtained called 'Magic of Strength' to the Reminescence in exchange, not for his freedom but for the lasting peace and assurance that the entire Explorers organization would not be harmed by the group. The greedy Reminescence accepted the offer and they finally made a covenant. When the Reminescence assured him that the covenant would be honored faithfully, Alex gave up the Magic Stone. Unknown to him, that the Reminescence being untrue to their words, wise and clever, that covenant was just a piece of trash paper and could be disposed at any given time. When the stone was handed over to the Reminescence, they took Alex to their cursed river, after placing a solid rounded cast iron both in his hands and feet. And then, they threw away his wounded body until he drowned to his death…"

THE EXPLORERS

"You're lying! That's not entirely true!!!"

"We all feared when we found out such news about his sudden death, since we were oblivious to his secret mission that time. We decided not to fight back with them to avenge him. We thought that we should not be carried away by anger and grudges, because we were afraid that the Reminescence might start a war and also took the other sacred objects we've already acquired. We strongly believed that they made Alex Foster's body as a bait to lure the Explorers to come forward and destroy us little by little. Therefore, we kept his death as a secret to all of the Explorers in EUE and UE… because we did not want to put your lives at risk against those very powerful group of paladins by only a single person's death!"

Kenji suddenly felt an intense depression until his vision quickly blurred and dimmed. He fainted, and his body collapsed on the floor.

"Kenji! Kenji" called Reinhardt while shaking his brother's shoulder. Then he turned back again to Spencer angrily. "So now I know the reason why my father didn't want to show himself to me everytime I visited your mansion… It is because he's already dead! Your stupid repetitive reasons were all lies!!!"

Claude quickly moved towards Kenji and he put his arms under Kenji's back. "Don't worry I'll take care of him, Reinhardt. Hey, gimme some hot water in here!" he yelled.

Elijah ordered to stop the party for a moment since he was also in his big disbelief. The UEs and EUEs were all shocked right after they learned what really happened to their former leader when Spencer had made his testimony tonight.

Silence all over the hall. Waiting for more stories might be told. Reinhardt still could not believe about his father's death five years ago. But later he accepted the truth. It was over anyway. His father had been gone for five years already, and it was also five years that he had been visiting the DDE mansion just for nothing.

He asked himself: *why did the DDEs have to hide Alex's death to us for so long? Why did they all lie to me?*

"That painful day, if you'd just sent more men to save my father from the hands of those ruthless Reminescence, then still, he should be alive today!" said Reinhardt very angrily while still crying. "Now I learn that the DDEs are all cowards!"

The DDEs were surprised and Dianara felt angered again towards

Reinhardt.

"What did you just say, you rude young man? You really are--"

The DDE leader signaled to stop his wife from her rant knowing what the brothers had gone thru.

Silence. Everyone's attention was now at the stage. Later, Elijah could no longer stand the long silence so he asked the Explorers who were in-charge of the orchestra to continue the party again. "Um, p-please start the music again. The party still continues," he whispered.

The formal music sprung to life once again, catching the guests' attentions back to the party so they turned away from the stage. The party continued. Then, Lucky came over to Claude carrying a bowl of hot water and a fan.

"Here's the hot water you asked Claude," said Lucky. "Is it really a hot water that should be given to an unconscious person?"

Claude was serious. "That is what I know. Go and please fan him!"

The other Explorer guests who were away from them were now at the party, but some other guests who were close to them were still in their attention. Some of the Explorers were fanning the unconscious young man when one of them moved closer to Kenji do the first-aid.

"Let us give way this man to do the first-aid and give Kenji an open air. He needs to breathe well," said Claude.

The guests followed and they moved away the tables and chairs to give Kenji a space and an open air. He was still unconscious, but he was breathing.

Reinhardt had lost his mood for the party anymore and thought that it was already "useless". He did not want to hear more of his father death, it was already over. No more regrets and disappointments, if that was really his father's fate.

Like Kenji, he was now feeling depressed as well. His cheeks had been soaked with his own tears, and it was too embarrassing for him to look like that in front of the DDEs. Dianara was still staring at him with her glaring eyes while waiting for his next action. So, he quickly turned away from her and walked out the hall going his own room alone.

"What a rude man he really is!" said Dianara angrily when Reinhardt left. "Go ahead, don't spoil the fun, let's continue the party!"

Everyone's attention went back to the party now, though the EUEs and UEs were still showing their sympathy towards Kenji and Reinhardt.

THE EXPLORERS

The noise all over the hall continued back to normal.

"I am going to take Kenji to the room now," said Claude while looking at Kenji's face. "I can carry him alone. He's just too tired and depressed about his father's death."

"Go ahead, Claude. By the way, the banquet is coming sooner," said Jon in his sad face. "You should be here before the dinner, so come back here immediately right after you take Kenji to your room. He'll miss his big moment of receiving his--"

"I'll give him his license and badge when the party ends."

"And oh yeah, he hasn't eating yet!"

"I will bring him food in the room later. Don't worry, Jon."

"Oh, okay then Claude..."

"All right, I need to go now... Actually, he still has a fever."

"Okay, Claude. See you again later."

Claude gently carried Kenji to his back and he walked away. Some of the guests were only watching them silently. Later, Claude met a DDE whose name was Zoroaster when he passed through the tables and chairs. Zoroaster was also a son of Alex Foster and Isidra who was also Kenji, Genji, and Reinhardt's brother... But, they all did not know about it.

"Poor lad," this was the first voice Claude just heard from Zoroaster while looking at Kenji in concern.

All of the DDEs, except Zoroaster knew about his identity as one of the sons of Alex Foster. Alex was already dead when Zoroaster became a DDE Explorer so he never had seen him personally. He was also very young when he got separated to his parents and to his siblings during the long battle of Explorers, Pioneer, and Reminescence. He grew up alone and lived all by himself. Until, he acquired a Divine Stone in his teen age and this sacred stone became an element of "Ice". Like Kenji, he also became an Element Wielder, and the Explorers recruited him to join their organization.

Zoroaster had reached his eighteen years of age when he left UE after he promoted to DDE. Spencer was already their leader when he moved to the DDE mansion, unaware to his unknown father's former leadership until to his death. Spencer had discovered Zoroaster's identity as one of Alex's son when he noticed the two studs in Zoroster's lower part of his navel, after he stripped off his sweaty shirt from doing the exercise.

"Where did you get those studs in the lower part of your navel, Zoroaster?" asked

Spencer to Zoroaster after Zoroaster stripped off his shirt soaked in sweat.

Zoroaster shook his head. "*I actually dunno, sir. I was wondering about these too ever since. I couldn't even take them off in my belly either. I already have them since I was still a child, so I think they're attached to my belly forever. But, these cool studs aren't painful!*"

Spencer did not answer and he ordered the other DDEs not to inform Zoroaster's real identity, and also his relationship to Reinhardt. So even Reinhardt had no knowledge that Zoroaster was also his missing brother whom he once became his long-time friend during Zoroaster's stay in UE.

What if time would reveal the truth that Kenji, Reinhardt, and Zoroaster were all brothers? What would be their reaction to each other?

"I know, that is why I am taking him to our room now to give him rest," answered Claude.

Zoroaster stopped for a moment when he noticed Kenji's studs in his chin. "W-Wait a minute… he has the same studs as mine, see?"

"W-What do you mean by that?"

Zoroaster blushed in hesitation. "N-Nevermind… His studs look cool either, and I like them too! A-Anyway, you can go now."

Claude simply ignored him. He looked away from Zoroaster and then he walked on his way.

Claude opened their personal room's door and came inside. He laid down Kenji to the bed and knelt before him. Again, he touched Kenji's neck when he shook his head. Kenji still had a high fever.

"Why did you still take a bath though you're feeling unwell and injured? Now look what happened to you…" said Claude and then he touched Kenji's forehead. "Later, I will bring you something to eat, okay? I'll be back again soon."

He stood back on his feet again, but before he closed the door he firstly turned his glance towards Kenji. And then, he shut the door very gently.

It was eleven o'clock in the evening when the time had come for the new Explorers to receive their license and badge. Claude was worried, looking very sad as if he wanted to stop the party now.

"Ladies and gentlemen, tonight is the time for the new members of Explorers organization to receive their license and badge to be given by our very special guest, Mr. Spencer Briant. Please give them a big hand!" said the Explorer host happily.

THE EXPLORERS

Everyone applauded again when the host spoke again. "May we call on the attention of our venerable Mr. Briant of DDE and the three new Explorers? Please come forward to the stage now."

Spencer stood on his chair, as well as Claude and Tyrone. They walked over the stage where they would receive their license and badge in front of the visitors. After the introduction by the inductee, Spencer firstly gave Tyrone's license and pinned his badge to his lapel when the guests applauded for him. Then, the two shook their hands and Tyrone walked behind the DDE leader.

Claude came next to Spencer when the DDE leader also handed him his license and pinned his badge to his lapel. They shook hands too when the guests applauded once again.

The applause continued when Spencer announced that the other recipient of the award was not able to come due to the high fever. Instead, he called on Claude to receive the award on Kenji's behalf. Then he moved closer to Claude's ear at the same time he handed over Kenji's license and badge. He whispered.

"Congratulations my boy, this is the license and badge of your friend. When he wakes up, tell him that it is not the DDE's fault about the loss of their father. They must learn to accept their father's fate. It can happen to anyone who upholds the mission and vision of the Explorers organization. They don't have their right to be mad at me anymore and I will not forgive their rudeness when it happen again. I have the power to revoke his and his brother's license... or to anyone who doesn't respect, follow, and uphold the covenant they cited during the ceremony. Do you get me? Do as I say since I am now your leader!"

Claude was surprised when he heard Spencer's unsolicited advice. He began to think that this DDE leader had a kind of worse attitude. *Excuse me? So that's how the DDE leader deals with us "very nicely". Giving me this nonsense threat because of their stupidity and cowardice! You're totally ridiculous!*

Claude was frowning and he did not answer. When he walked away from the stage, his eyes slyly glared at his side towards Spencer. Now he was feeling upset at him!

After the recognition, the host spoke to everyone about the banquet. Everyone got very excited and they prepared themselves for their formal meal.

Claude was very sad when he returned to his seat... He was upset by the attitude shown by Spencer. He felt so angry whenever he could see the beardy face of the DDE leader, Spencer Briant!

"Do you think someone will watch Kenji there?" asked Lucky when Claude sat next to him. "It's good to see you back, here, so you can eat as many as you like tonight!"

Claude just nodded.

"What about Kenji? How can he eat with us tonight?"

The UE servers came over the hall to serve the tray of foods to every guest's table. The meals were all delightful, but Claude seemed he already lost his appetite though he was very hungry.

Claude was the first person to take his meal. His food was already on the table when he pulled the server's sleeve and whispered. "Pssst! Can you also bring me more and then follow me. We will go over the room where my friend is staying in right now," he asked.

"How is he, sir? Is he okay now?" asked the male server. "No problem, I will bring much foods for him."

"And please bring us some hot milk too."

"Yes sir, I will bring out Mr. Foster's food here, hold on."

After the ten minutes of food serving, the guests took their meal. There were meats, seafoods, fruits, and vegetables for vegetarians. There were also appetizers served such as *buko salad* (young coconut in cream), *leche flan* (crème caramel), halu-halo (popular Filipino dessert), and much more.

"Time to eat!!!" cried Lucky, Clio, Jon, and Tyrone together and they quickly scooped their meals, except Claude. He was just sipping his hot soup first and then he stood on his seat. The four turned to Claude and wondered.

"What's wrong?" asked Jon. "Why don't you come and eat with us now?"

The two male servers came back to Claude while carrying each tray of foods in their hands. They signaled Claude in the distance and the young man walked over them.

"Do you know where our room is at?" asked Claude to the two servers.

"No sir, you are new to us."

Claude smiled. "Okay, anyway just follow me. I am bringing my own food. Follow me."

THE EXPLORERS

The four wondered again. "Hey, what's wrong? Where are you going again this time, Claude?" asked Clio.

"I'm going to eat in our room instead. No one is watching Kenji there. I think there's nothing else to do here, isn't it? I'll see ya later."

"But we have lots of servers here," said Lucky. "Why don't you just ask them to bring Kenji's food to his room? Plus, it's so much fun in here!"

"T-They do not know where our room is," excused Claude.

"Then tell them where. Come on, let me tell them. The second floor is too quiet and borin'."

Claude already ran out of excuses. "Ah, whatever! I'm going to eat upstairs. Come with me servers," then he left the four, carrying his own food along with the two servers.

Their room was not too far from the grand staircase when the three had reached the room in the second floor. "This is our room. I did not lock the door so we can just pull it easily," said Claude and then he pulled the bottom of the door with his foot to open it. "Please come inside."

They entered the room. They saw Kenji still lying in the bed. Claude walked over the small table where he put down his meal and called the servers. "You can put down those foods in this table. I'll move mine."

"Yes, sir."

The two servers moved over Claude and they put down the foods on the table. A pitcher of hot milk requested by Claude was there too.

"Thank you for your help... You may now leave our room," said Claude smiling to the servers.

The two servers bowed first before they left the room and gently closed the door.

Later, Lucky's group had seen the two servers walking down the grand staircase so they called them. "Hey, now where is that Claude? Is he coming down later?" asked Lucky.

"Well, we don't know sir..." answered a server. "He did not say anything to us when we left their room..."

"Those two are really good friends... There is no way we can separate them anymore," said Clio while drinking juice.

"Tell him to go back here after he finished his meal, we will have a grand ball next! It's going to be fun, dancing with some beautiful ladies here waiting for us," said Lucky.

"A-All right, do we tell it to him now?"

"Nah, later."

Everyone was enjoying their dinner and there were lots of foods served. There were ten big cakes displayed in front of the hall, since the number of Explorers who attended the party were more than a hundred.

"Wow, you've got lots of foods tonight for all of us!" said a DDE to a UE. "How about a take-out if I may? Hahaha!"

Claude had waited for Kenji to awake first before he would eat his meal, but his stomach was already craving for food so he began to eat to relieve his long hungriness. Then, he would help Kenji when he awoke later.

It was already dawn when the grand ball started. Everyone was in a hurry to finish their desserts to join the dance. Some of the visitors walked over the middle of the hall to dance with their found partners, while the others were still looking for their dance partner.

"It's grand ball time! Since this party is for the six of you, I'm expecting the new members should be here too," said Elijah to Lucky, Clio, and Jon smiling.

"We're really going to dance!" said Lucky. "But I don't think Kenji's gonna dance tonight. I'm not sure with Claude…"

Tyrone, Clio, and Jon were now looking for someone to dance with in the grand ball. The Welcome Party became very alive again with the happy orchestra. And the two DDE couple, Spencer and Dianara also walked over the middle of the hall to dance and enjoy the evening with the fellow Explorers.

33 THE VISIT

The Welcome Party would nearly come to an end. As expected by the group, Claude really never went back to the four to join the grand ball. Jon, Clio, and Tyrone had been enjoying themselves dancing with their found female partners in the middle of the hall.

"Man, that Claude is a party spoiler," said Lucky annoyingly while dancing with a female EUE. "He is missing his chance of seeing and meeting some beautiful women here tonight. Look, some of them are waiting for someone to dance with!"

"Correct Lucky, he's totally out of this world," said Tyrone while also dancing with his partner. "He should be like as barefaced as Isagani. Look, he still dares to join the dance here with us though he's not an Explorer yet!"

Meanwhile...

Maximus was stranded at the sea to where Kenji took his second test, after a few days of his imprisonment inside the large crystal. The mysterious woman took the prince to the sea intentionally for a reason...

The prince gained back his consciousness after he fainted inside the crystal. He gently opened his eyes, and he started to look around when he noticed that he was already out of the crystal and in a different place!

His eyes scoured the area trying to figure out where he was. He was lying in the shore when the small sea waves touched his skin. He could tell in the sky that it was dawn.

"W-Where am I?" asked Maximus when he slowly got up his back and wiped the sands that covering his body. "What is this place?"

A mysterious voice of a woman was echoed again to his ears while the cold breeze of air blew all over the seashore. "You are now in the world of men where a known element is staying close from here, Your Highness…"

"S-Staying?" Maximus was puzzled. "What an element is that?"

The mysterious voice answered differently. "As what I've told you before, we have saved you from your father's atrocity and you must live. Our great king of the gods has selected you to become one of the Wielders on his behalf. I was the one who took you here alone for your safety."

"I never asked any help from you and you know that!" said Maximus angrily. "I commanded you before to bring me back to my home rather than to just stay here in this place I do not know!"

"Aren't you glad of taking you here? Do you still prefer to die inside the fiery dungeon made by your own father?"

"NO!"

"So you should be here, Your Highness…"

"What am I going to do in here? It's so boring! How can I do what I love most? There's no piano in here!"

"I'll give you something to do in this world, Maximus. The reason why I brought you here is because I would like you to know that there is an element nearby that suits perfectly to your hidden power."

The prince laughed annoyingly. "Me? A hidden power? What are you talking about? You keep on telling me this nonsense thing. How come an ordinary prince like me has his own hidden power? Hah!" he scoffed.

The voice answered in her serious tone. "You will see, Your Highness…"

Maximus stopped.

"I have a feeling that the great king's ultimate power called Holy Crusade is here… It is close from this sea… I can feel it right now!"

Maximus was puzzled. "What are you talking about? And why should I care?"

The voice answered in a tone like she was up to something. "I am commanding you to look for the Holy element nearby and then you must bring it to me… Therefore, you will gain its great power and become the new Holy Wielder!"

"Wait, wait…" Maximus was confused when he heard something strange to this mysterious voice so he asked. "Who really are you? And who gives you the power to speak to me like that?"

"I am one of the goddesses who once joined the monster's group to conquer King Jethro's kingdom a long, long time ago. I survived from my death after the lone monster had betrayed us and King Jethro took away our strong powers as a punishment… as well as my power of being the Goddess of Water!"

Silence. The innocent prince was only listening although he was still confused.

The goddess spoke again with her evil voice. "So now I'll make my revenge by taking what is rightfully mine, the king's Holy element… to become the new Holy goddess! This is the reason why I took you in this world, Your Highness… Bring forth the Holy element to me and we will share its power together!"

"Go take it yourself," said Maximus annoyingly. "You are the only one who is needing it and not me. Now, take me back to my--"

"NO! You will bring the element to me and I will give you the lion share of its power. I am not trying to deceive you, Prince Maximus. Don't you want to become the new ruler of not just the world of men but also the whole universe?"

Maximus did not answer.

"The other reason why you're here is because I am not allowed to show myself in the human world but I have a plan to break that rule! I am going to enter to your body and use it so you will have an opportunity to utilize my one remaining power temporarily. I will do everything I can to protect you from any danger we will be facing!"

The innocent prince made his consideration first. "Is the Holy element a very powerful element?"

"It is not just a very powerful element, but also the most important element among the other elements!"

Therefore, the innocent prince immediately agreed to the goddess' evil plan of acquiring King Jethro's ultimate element. "Alright, I will help you!"

"Excellent, Your Highness! I have to go inside your body in order for me to enter this world and look for the Holy element with you."

"Alright, but how'd you know that the Holy element is just nearby?"

"Haven't you forgotten that I am a goddess, Your Highness?"

Maximus nodded. He did not want to prolong their conversation anymore although there were still things that he still did not understand.

"Let us start, Your Highness…"

Maximus' body slowly shone. A blinding lights were covering his whole body. The dirty tuxedo suit he was wearing was gradually evolved into something as well as his body. His body had slowly transformed into a muscular and fear-like warrior.

"What is this? My suit is changing!"

The prince's tuxedo suit was replaced by the male version of the goddess' iron clad armor suit and the warrior-like helm appeared in his head. He was now wearing a shining warrior-like armor suit, but it was not the same as the shining armors worn by Reminescence warriors.

The prince was now possessed by the Goddess of Water when she spoke. "I am the water goddess, Your Highness. All of my power of magics were all gone by King Jethro, and what I've only left in my possession is just the blue magic of Water… Although it is weaker than the Water element itself."

"What do you mean weaker?" asked Maximus.

"Always keep in mind that the only power I have is just a Water magic and not the Water element. King Jethro is the only god who can possess the fourteen elements, but after our war, he took them all in this world and lost his power. The fourteen elements are the most powerful type of King Jethro's powers… meaning that they are more powerful than the magics like the one we have here. Don't you remember that King Jethro already chose you to become the water bearer?"

Maximus just nodded at the same time he closed his eyes. He answered. "I see… I believe in you now. Let's find the Holy element then…"

Meanwhile in the Welcome Party…

Reinhardt was staying in his room, still did not intend to go down the hall to join the formal dance. The party had ended, the guests had gone and the entire hall became quiet in a sudden. Reinhardt was just lying in his bed, and there were tears still coming out from his eyes while mesmerizing the story told by the new DDE leader. He was in his distress.

Someone knocked at the door of his room. Reinhardt was not in his mood to stand just to open the door. He also did not want to talk to someone right now.

But the knock did not stop. With that, Reinhardt angrily shouted. "Stop knocking! I'm out of everybody, so go away!!!"

The knock had stopped, then someone answered very softly. "Brother... it's me, Kenji..."

"Oh," Reinhardt was surprised. He got up to his bed and quickly opened the door. Kenji was there, and Reinhardt noticed his brother's listless face before him.

"Hey, so you're awake now, Kenji. Come inside. I'm sorry for yelling at you--"

Kenji only smiled weakly while his head was stooped down. "It's okay..." then he went inside Reinhardt's room. "Someone told me that you still haven't eaten yet, *kuya*..."

"Yeah, how about you?"

"Yes, I'm already done eating. Claude brought me meals in our room earlier, then I drank a lot of milk. I have eaten much and now I'm stuffed..."

"That's good to hear then. That way, you're recovering fast."

"Yes. I have my clear vision too. I'm so full. By the way, Claude already gave me my license and badge, b-but..."

"But what?"

Kenji did not answer.

"What's wrong, Kenji? Do you feel any pain right now?"

"Yes I have, brother..."

"What then?"

Kenji touched his chest. "This one within me... My heart is hurting..."

"Kenji..."

Kenji was just quiet when Reinhardt spoke again. "Go back to your room and take a rest again, Kenji. Elijah said you have a high fever and you're still injured."

"You can take your dinner now, *kuya*. The party is over..."

"Really? Well that's a good news. Okay, I will eat later. I'm still not hungry much... and I've already lost my appetite right now."

"The other guests are gone back to their mansion. Why don't you go and eat now?"

Reinhardt was forced to agree. "Alright, I'm going to eat now. You can stay here in my room and get some rest. Wait for me here and I'll be back. I can't believe that the party ended very late this evening."

Kenji just nodded weakly.

"Gotta go. See you later."

Reinhardt was leaving when Kenji suddenly called him in his low voice. "*Kuya?*"

Reinhardt turned to Kenji. "What?"

"There is something I would like to talk with you later when you come back…"

Reinhardt was surprised, but whatever it was he only answered Kenji. "Okay…"

Reinhardt shut the room's door and he went down the grand staircase going to the hall. He saw some of the maids and butlers fixing everything that was left after the party. He was ignoring the Explorers who were crossing to his direction.

He reached the dining hall when he asked the servers in there to bring him some of the leftovers. When the food was served, he began to eat. Later, he just noticed Marion and Vamir in the other table sitting and talking to each other. They were not eating.

"Oh hey buddy," called Vamir to Reinhardt. "You never showed up again in the party earlier. We had an enjoying grand ball with the Explorer ladies. It was really fun!" he hinted.

Reinhardt was unshaken but he tried not to get noticed by the two. "Really?"

"Oh yes, *kuya* Reinhardt! You missed the cool banquet too. The party was totally noisy!" as usual, it was Marion. "We ate much, then lastly the party had changed into disco!"

"It's okay. There will be more parties coming next time," excused Reinhardt.

"But when? Maybe it will take long again!"

"I don't know."

Lucky, Jon, Clio, and Claude were all dead tired after the party and they were now sleeping in their own rooms. Claude was alone in the room since Kenji was in his brother's room.

Kenji gently leaned his back against the wall and sat on the floor, waiting for his brother's return after his dinner. Then he wept and sobbed again, thinking of what that new DDE leader said to him and to Reinhardt about their father's death five years ago.

Reinhardt was done eating and was about to go back to his room. He spoke to the two who were still having a chitchat to each other. "Why don't you guys go back to your bed now? It already morning, in case you didn't know."

"We know that!" said Vamir. "We're still very full, that's why we're still up this late."

Reinhardt did not answer so he just left the two.

He returned to his room and gently opened the door when Kenji turned to him. "Are you done?" Kenji asked.

Reinhardt answered. "Yes. So, um, what is it that we need to talk about? A-Anyway, why don't we just talk about it tomorrow instead? Let's go to sleep first. It's already morning."

Kenji chuckled. "I stayed here long just to wait for you... Let's talk about it now..."

"A-All right, if that is what you want. What is it about then?"

Kenji slowly stood on his feet. "Brother, don't you have any intention of going to the DDE mansion and talk to Sir Briant alone just to make sure? I am thinking of going there and speak to their leader. I don't think he was telling the truth, and considering the fact that you know our father of being the great warrior, right?"

"What?! Are you serious about this? Going to their mansion just to speak about the past! I-Is that the only thing you will intend to do there, Kenji?"

"Tomorrow I will be there. Oh wait, it's dawn already... So that means I will be there later and it's much better if you really have to come with me."

"You have a high fever, Kenji..."

"I don't care, brother!" Kenji cried again and got on his knees. "I'm still not convinced to what I have heard from them. I believe that our father is still alive!"

"Didn't you see their new leader now, did you?!"

"Maybe they're just hiding our father from us!"

Reinhardt did not answer.

"I am one of you now as an Explorer, brother... Which means that I have the right now to deal with my fellow Explorers. And if they make mistakes, then I also have the right to correct them!"

Reinhardt was confused. "What are you talking about?"

"In other words... I will force them to just tell me the truth, that's all!"

Reinhardt did not answer again.

"T-That is the only thing I want to say and I want you to come with me…" said Kenji in his calm voice. "Anyway, goodnight…"

Kenji would be off to the DDE base later this morning. He was so serious about his own plan when he told this to his older brother. Should Reinhardt have to stop his brother's plan?

It was eight o'clock in the morning. The sick young man took much of his breakfast first before he would start his visit to DDE today. He needed to ask permission to Elijah to go out of the mansion and borrow an available jet. Unfortunately, he did not know on how to pilot a jet.

He only cleansed his body in his room right after he finished eating and then he told Claude that he was about to leave. "I have to go for now, Claude…" he said to his long-time friend.

Claude wondered. "You're leaving? Where are you going?"

"I am just going somewhere for an important matter. I will ask Elijah's permission to let me leave the mansion."

"Where I said?"

"It's a secret…"

"You're going alone? You're still unwell, right?"

"I'm okay now… I do not know if *kuya* Reinhardt is coming with me today or not…"

Claude seemed to get the picture of Kenji's destination when he heard the name of the person whom he supposed to come along with. "I understand that, Kenji."

"Don't worry about me, I'm fine. I have to go to Elijah now. If my brother does not really want to come with me then I'll go on my own."

Kenji was about to leave the room when Claude called his attention and quickly approached. "Kenji, since Reinhardt does not want to come with you then I'll go with you instead. At least, you are not alone," said Claude.

"Oh yes, you're right. Then come with me! The UEs are also leaving the mansion to do their assignment. After all, Elijah is not giving us an assignment yet. Let's go, Claude."

Elijah was currently in the laboratory to examine the new set of Magic Stones acquired by the UEs. He was very serious in his analysis alone while the UEs were dispatched to their assigned destinations to do their daily tasks. Kenji and Claude went inside the laboratory and they told the UE leader that they were off to DDE mansion.

"Please excuse us for a moment, Elijah... But can we have your permission to let us go to DDE mansion and borrow a jet? Claude and I don't have our assignment yet for today," asked Kenji to Elijah who was busy.

Elijah already understood the reason of Kenji's main purpose of going to DDE mansion so he agreed immediately. "Alright, go ahead. By the way, each of the Explorers has their own assigned HawkEyes for use in their daily missions. And each of the HawkEyes only has a maximum capacity of five passengers. You can use the jet number 41T2, that is your brother's assigned aircraft."

"Thank you, Elijah!"

"By the way, please have Lucky, Clio, Tyrone, Jon, Isagani, and Shingue to come with you too for security reason since I also haven't given them their assignment yet for today. They already have their own assigned jets so they will not ride with you on your jet."

Good timing that the six came inside the laboratory. Elijah told them that they would be coming with Kenji and Claude and they did not refuse. They all wanted to travel!

Shingue tried to crack a joke while scratching his head. "Heh, maybe you would also like Margot and Marion to come with us too! Hahaha, just kidding..."

"Those two aren't here Shingue," answered Jon. "They're already off to their assignment, and I don't want them to come along with us!"

"I said I was just kidding, Jon! Do you think that I even want them to come with us? Hell no!"

They laughed together. Then, Kenji quickly raised his hand with his smiling face. "Let us go to DDE, everyone!"

The group were about to leave the laboratory when someone called his name in the distance. "Kenji!"

Kenji turned to his back to find out who called him. "Oh, it's *kuya* Reinhardt!"

Reinhardt moved closer to them and he smiled. "You're really into your plan of leaving, but who will pilot the plane without me, right?"

"*Kuya*, do you mean..."

"You're right, Kenji. I am also coming with you. What we have talked last night was reasonable. So what are we waiting for? Come on!"

The nine boys had left the laboratory to go straight to their assigned jets. When they reached the hangar, Kenji and Claude had seen their assigned HawkEye for the first time and Reinhardt smiled to them. Now, they were off to the DDE base to pay visit to their new DDE superior leader, Spencer Briant!

34 TWINS OF FATE

The three Explorer jets ridden by nine Explorers were now ready to takeoff. The jet engines were in full throttle and then they finally flew off the runway behind the UE mansion. Their introduction was amazing!

Reinhardt was the pilot of jet 41T2 while Lucky was for E47J and Shingue was for 14JK. Inside the jet 41T2, Kenji and Claude were both looking down the jet glass platform to view the scene below them. They were very high up in the sky with an altitude of 1,500 feet.

"Hey brother, when you have free time sometimes, can you teach me on how to pilot this jet? I'd also like to become an aviator like you!" said Kenji proudly.

"Sure, anytime when we're vacant sometimes," said Reinhardt.

"Yohoo!!!"

Claude asked. "Hey Reinhardt, how far is the DDE mansion from here?"

"Maybe our travel time is only four hours and a half, Claude."

"T-That's too far!" said Claude in disbelief. "Was that the reason why the DDEs came late to our party last night? Did they really travel that long, huh?"

"Did you notice their huge jet yesterday? It was carrying more DDE passengers but the DDE leader had his own jet. Maybe the leader wanted to go to our mansion alone."

"Hmpt, that makes me hate him more…"

Silence. Later, Kenji thought of touching the long scar on his nose. He suddenly remembered the little Valerie who was now in Sierra Village. He was starting to think how was that little girl doing now… Was she missing him so much already?

He also suddenly remembered his twin brother Genji, as well as Shiela and Aaron. But his twin brother was more in his mind so he turned to Reinhardt and asked in hesitation. "K-*Kuya*, when we're done in visiting DDE base… is it okay if we go to, um… Damsville too? F-For…"

"Damsville? The place we've previously lived before?" asked Claude immediately. "Damsville is too far! Why do we have to go there too? Didn't you forget how very good-hearted those villagers there?!"

"I just want to know if my twin brother is still there."

"I think he's no longer staying in there for long, Kenji. Maybe he already moved elsewhere."

"In Bondore?"

"I think he's not in there too!"

"Oh, come on. I am still going to find my twin brother, Claude. I've been wanting to see him so badly and I don't wanna let him be in great danger!"

Claude disagreed, but Reinhardt agreed.

"No problem, Kenji. I don't want to go back to the mansion yet right after our visit to DDE mansion," said Reinhardt.

Claude had nothing else to do to object Kenji's request so he also agreed. "F-Fine, so be it."

Kenji would also like to pay visit the old woman who treated him nicely in Dakar, and at the same time he would also want to apologize for his big failure in saving Bondore from Pioneer.

An hour had passed when they already passed over some places in the middle of their trip. They needed to travel more in few hours before they would reach the DDE base. The three HawkEyes were in the top of their speed!

"Brother," called Kenji to Reinhardt. "Is the DDE mansion based in another country? If so, that means you are passing through some of the countries everytime you are visiting the mansion… just to see our father…"

"Correct, now I already know that I've been visiting there and wasting my time for nothing!" said Reinhardt annoyingly.

"I feel sorry for you, brother… You're always expecting and hoping much to see our dad…"

"I'm so mad at the DDEs, Kenji. If they'd told me earlier before our father's death, maybe I should have had saved him from Reminescence!"

Someone spoke on the radio of their jet coming from Shingue's HawkEye 14JK. "Hello, fellas! How are you all doing? We are getting closer to another country!"

Lucky's group at HawkEye E47J answered on the other line. "We're all doing okay and we're still at the tail of jet 41T2. Hey Reinhardt, do you still know where the DDE mansion is?"

"Yes, I certainly know that, but I don't know exactly the name of their country although I've been there most of the time. I know the rich country called Camoria, and I believe that the DDE mansion is three hours long from there by plane. I-I'm not sure."

"So Camoria is the only country you know, um… W-Wait a minute, that's closest from our base, right?!"

Silence. Did you still remember the rich country of Camoria? That was the place where Genji stayed before he decided to pay visit Bondore and met the old woman.

Still during the travel, Jon pulled out a *pandesal* (salt bread) from a pouch he brought and he took a bite. Then, he offered some of it to his fellow Explorers. "How about some bread, guys? Would you like one?"

Tyrone took one *pandesal* from Jon's hand. "I want to have one, thanks. Good thing you brought some to fill our stomachs during this long trip."

They were now getting closer to the rich country of Camoria. Isagani spoke to the line of the two other jets. "Just five minutes left and we will pass over Camoria. The sky is getting darker."

Silence. Kenji and Claude did not know about Camoria for now so they remained mum.

"Get yourselves ready everyone," said Reinhardt as a warning. "We're now in the city of Hunsterdam and next to it is Camoria."

"Hunsterdam?" asked Isagani on the line. "I've heard that place before. Is that the city where a big university of genius' based? My mother studied and graduated in that university before."

Suddenly, there was something just hit below the jet 41T2 that came from Hunsterdam. The jet got badly damaged and was no longer controllable. Reinhardt thought that their jet got hit by a surface-to-air missile (SAM)!

"Ahhh! What's that?" cried Kenji. "Our jet just got hit by something!"

The HawkEye 41T2's tail was now on fire when Lucky's group were about to do the emergency rescue but their jet was also got hit. Good thing their jet was still under control since only one of its wing got slightly hit, and Lucky made a quick turn before their jet would be totally got hit.

The 41T2 jet was about to crash in Hunsterdam and Reinhardt was still trying to pull it up. He pulled the yoke as hard as he could but the plane was no longer moving up. They were about to crash at the bottom!

"AHHHH!!!" cried the two aboard the jet 41T2.

"Mayday, mayday our jet is out of control. We will have an emergency landing at the enemy's stronghold!" cried Reinhardt over the radio.

Shingue's group knew that they would be the next target of Hunsterdam, so Shingue moved their jet away from Lucky's jet. His two colleagues, Tyrone and Jon were both rattled in silence, but Jon quickly approached him and shouted. "Shingue, we will be their next target. Be careful!"

"I know!" shouted Shingue while trying his best to avoid the danger by climbing the jet to the safe altitude.

The 41T2's tail was flaming hot and just a few feet away before it would crash. Kenji suppressed his brother who was still insisting of saving the jet since they were almost near at the bottom!

"Brother, stop it now! Let's get outta here!!!" cried Kenji as he pulled Reinhardt's shoulder.

Reinhardt agreed and he immediately opened the jet's emergency exit. Claude moved over the exit and shouted. "Let's jump over here. QUICK!!!"

The three had jumped one by one to the exit, they opened their parachute until they reached the thick rainforest. Fortunately, the trees were big and the leaves were very thick delaying their bone breaking fall. Their parachute hanged on the branches and they sustained cuts and bruises all over their exposed body. They immediately cut the parachute and got loose all the way down to the ground.

The 41T2 jet had plunged to the ground and it exploded during the strong impact. Lucky and Shingue's group had seen the rapid spreading of fires at the grassy land and they became more cautious for the possible next attack. Shingue immediately radioed the home base for reinforcement and asked help to rescue the wreckage.

"Who is that badass responsible for this?" asked Reinhardt angrily. "Because of that, we've lost our jet! Darn it!!!"

"Let's go down and we'll go over that place!" said Kenji. "Let's find out who did the ambush and face them. We will avenge your jet, brother!"

The three had scoured the area for possible enemies who were hunting them down. Assuring that they were safe, they secretly went over near the main entrance of Hunsterdam.

They hid themselves in grasses and they took a peek around Hunsterdam's pandemonium. The citizens there were all gone in the city.

Later, the three had finally found the culprit… but the groups of Pioneer and Mercury! These two groups saw the three flying Explorer HawkEyes at the radar screen before they flew across Hunsterdam.

"There are three Explorer jets traversed in our air space!" cried a Mercury over the radio. "There is one downed jet, but the other two have escaped! Those pilots are very clever!"

Kenji's group was unaware that they were hiding in a wrong spot. There were Pioneers dispatched to look for the falling survivors and to also guard the area. The Mercuries were all in Hunsterdam while some of the Pioneers were outside the main city. The two groups were not together since they were also competitors.

"Explorers!" cried a Pioneer when he saw the three Explorers behind the grasses. "There are Explorers over here, seize them!"

"Damn," said Reinhardt in shock. "They caught us. Run!!!"

The three quickly ran away as fast as they could, but the other Pioneers suddenly appeared on their way. They stopped while their eyes were looking around nervously. Now they were being surrounded by the enemies.

The three drew out their weapons to defend themselves when a Pioneer shouted at them. "Drop your weapons on the ground and you're now being surrounded! Put your hands in the air so we can see them!"

"Where are the people here? And what do you want in this place?" said Kenji angrily.

"Oh… the Hunsterdam people?" asked another Pioneer. "They are now in our hands. The Hunsterdam belongs to us from now on! This time, we'll ask… where are the other two jets with you now? Why are you here? What are your mission?"

"We do not know, PWAH!" answered Kenji and he spitted the Pioneer's face.

"S-Shit! Goddamn this Explorer!!!"

The Pioneer slapped Kenji's face and they pointed their weapons at the three when Akira came along with his father, Alexander. Akira saw the three captured Explorers and he knew Reinhardt before. He also recognized his main rival, Kenji so he turned to him and stared intensely at him.

"Kenji! Or should I call you... Maximillian!" called Akira to Kenji. "Long time no see. Do you think I have forgotten you? I can still recognize your birthmarks... those studs in your chin!"

Alexander was surprised. "WHAT? Is he really Maximillian? Yes, he is the one! Now that he's with his older brother who is an Explorer too! The sons of Alex Foster we've been long looking for are here with us!"

Silence. Alexander laughed out loud. "HAHAHA, I can't believe what is happening. Look who's here with us right now, the sons of Alex Foster. What a twist of fate, I thought we will never see each other again."

Akira added. "Now that you're one of the Explorers, Kenji... Why don't you just come and join with us? I think you are a good warrior and I can feel its strong inside you!"

Kenji tried to brag Akira. "Not just a good, strong warrior and a UE Explorer... but I'm also King Jethro's chosen Holy Wielder now!"

"W-Whaaaaatttt??!" the Pioneers were all stepped back in shock when they heard Kenji's brag.

"That's too impossible! How did that happen? The element I've long wanted belongs to you now?! Go ahead, show me the evidence that you really are the new possessor of that element!" said Akira in shock.

The Pioneers grasped the two Explorer's arms when Kenji dared to show off his Holy Fire tattoos in both of his arms. Akira was totally surprised.

"I-I can't believe it..." said Akira as he was stepping back in surprise. "You're the new possessor of the Holy element. But how did that happen?! H-How??!" then he shouted out loud and he pointed at Kenji. "Ahhh! This is truly unacceptable. You do not deserve that element and it should only be mine!!!" and he slapped Kenji's face. "You are strong, but you're only a dork!" then he slapped Kenji again.

Claude tried to struggle and wished to help Kenji but the Pioneers were holding his arms very tightly. Later, he thought that the Pioneers could possibly harm Kenji if he tried to start a fight. They were only three against twelve Pioneers. Their other colleagues were not with them for help.

Akita pointed at the other direction. "Take them to our slaves, in the prison cell!"

Kenji jostled against a Pioneer but there was another Pioneer who kicked his legs and he quickly got on his knees. Just as he knelt, the Pioneer shot a tranquilizer to his back. Claude and Reinhardt were also shot by the tranquilizer, and the three instantly fell asleep.

"Bring these two in the prison along with the prisoners, but… take Kenji away from his two colleagues. You get me?" ordered Akira to the fellow Pioneers.

"Yes, sir!" said the Pioneers and they took the three UEs in Hunsterdam.

Lucky and Shingue's group were all safe when they successfully escaped from the ambush. The two HawkEyes landed in a distance away from Hunsterdam. Then the six Explorers went off their planes and they drew out their weapons. They were going to find their three colleagues and rescue them.

"I think those three are here," said Lucky hiding behind the grasses. "They are captured!"

"How can we get inside and pass through them undetected? Most of the Pioneers are here. The Mercuries are here too, and the other thing is… we aren't prepared!" said Clio looking anxious.

"Here's what we'll gonna do, my good-looking dudes. First we'll just hide and then…"

"…and then what?" asked Tyrone.

Lucky goofily ran away from them very fast and at the same time he cried. "Run!!!"

"Ahhh!!!" cried the five Explorers as they quickly ran behind Lucky. Lucky suddenly stopped running, and the five followed.

"Why do we stop?" asked Isagani in wonder.

"Hey man, don't take it very seriously. That was only a rehearsal!" said Lucky in a joke. "Come on man, be serious. You're catching the enemies' attentions by making gibberish sounds! I-I do not know on what to do either, see?"

"Pwah, whatever you say, Lucky!" cried Jon. Now they're starting goofing around rather than to seek for their three colleagues in Hunsterdam!

"Stop it, we're only wasting our golden time! Let's start the mission now," said Clio. "We should have started this since earlier."

The six Explorers sneaked across the spot that was not seen by the Pioneers and Mercuries. They peered around to see if someone was there or not. So they quickly moved across the other side towards a house.

The five Explorers were all behind an abandoned house while Clio was moving alone in a thick bush going to the prison cell. He was in–charge in making rescue mission while the other five would be watching for the incoming enemies.

Silence. Later, they saw a Mercury walking around who was also guarding the perimeter for the incoming enemies. He was not carrying any sharp weapons in his hand but just a gun. And… it was just an "ordinary" gun.

"Sssttt! Clio, shoot him with your bow!" whispered Jon to Clio to the other side. "Kill that bastard now!"

"No, don't!" stopped Lucky. "If he kills that then we will be responsible! Yes, I know they're our enemies too but they're not our main nemesis but only Pioneers. So we should only kill those Pioneers and not Mercuries!"

"But, what if…"

"Alright, if you're worrying too much then use your sleeping dart instead of killing him, Jon. He will never catch us anymore."

"He's right," Tyrone agreed. "You have your keen eyes, right? Do not kill him but just tranquilize him instead. Explorers do not always have to kill anybody."

"Okay," Jon nodded. "I'll do it."

"Hey Clio, nevermind the bow! Jon will be doing this for you instead!" called Lucky in whisper to Clio.

Jon pulled out a long needle with strong sedative material and whispered to himself. "Just a sting of this needle, tsk… you will get instantly fall asleep like a rock-a-bye baby in a cradle…"

Because of his sharp eyes and quick hands, the five Explorers did not immediately notice Jon's sudden move when the long needle quickly pierced the Mercury's neck. The Mercury felt a small ant-like bite in his neck until he instantly fell asleep.

"Now that this watcher is asleep, we can move forward towards the prisoners right away. If there are many Mercuries guarding inside, then we'll take care of them, okay?" said Shingue to his colleagues and the five nodded.

THE EXPLORERS

Claude and Reinhardt were together in the same prison and were still sleeping, but Kenji was in another prison. He was unaware that he was imprisoned there with someone whom he should not expecting to be with.

Kenji had regained his consciousness. He slowly opened his eyes when he noticed the prisoners' faces were all looking straight at him. He got up to his back and rubbed his eyes. He looked around in wonder, until his eyes moved across to a person that suddenly caught his attention… The person whom he had been long looking for… His twin brother Genji was also in the prison, along with Cyan!

Kenji's eyes suddenly opened wide when he saw his twin brother in a corner, and he was so sure that it was him when he saw the two studs in his forehead. As for Genji, his eyes were opened wide as well, and he also saw his twin brother's studs in his chin.

Kenji and Genji slowly crawled closer to each other while still looking straight to each of their eyes. They were both silent.

"B-Brother… i-is that really you?" Kenji asked Genji at first when they were now closer to each other.

Genji did not know on what to say to his found twin brother. His eyes began to shed tears and he could not believe of seeing his brother once again. He was speechless, while Cyan's face was in shock seeing his friend's sudden reaction towards Kenji.

Cyan moved next to Genji and looked at Kenji in amazement. "Hey, this man looks exactly just like you, Genji!"

Kenji heard the name mentioned by Cyan and found out that the man before him was really his long, lost twin brother. He could no longer hold his excitement anymore when he suddenly embraced Genji and cried. "*K-Kuya* Genji, it is really you!!!"

Genji was still speechless when he also embraced his twin brother tightly… He was in great disbelief.

Kenji's voice was hoarse when he spoke to his brother again while still embracing to each other. "H-How are you now, brother? I am missing you so badly after we've separated each other for so long… I… I love you, brother!"

Genji was still speechless, while looking at his brother's face constantly. He just sniffed and still weeping in gladness. The prisoners began to weep, carried away by the drama unfolding. Cyan wept too.

Despite of his big disbelief, Genji tried to answer in his hoarse voice.

"I… I love you too, brother. I've never seen you for so long and I am missing you so badly as well… I-I am so happy to see you again!"

"Why did you leave us in Damsville that time? What did you do when we got separated?" asked Kenji.

"I-I just wanted to avenge our stepfather that time, but…" Genji could not speak well.

The two let go of each other's embrace when Kenji spoke. "Brother… You know what? I am one of the Explorers now, and a chosen Wielder of the Holy element…"

"W-What? What Explorers?"

"I have lots of things I've discovered that you do not know, *kuya*. I am sure you will be surprised when I tell you those things. I have made much of my experiences while you are away from me… until I've become a Holy Wielder and an Explorer in the process."

"W-What are those?"

"I'll tell those things to you later, but for now I don't want you and me to get separated again… ever again!"

"Y-You've changed, *kuya*… It looks like you've already got too many experiences during your journey… And I'm…" Genji stooped down his head. "It looks like that I'm getting left behind… I'm sorry that I've become a useless brother to you, *kuya*!"

"What are you talking about? What you've said was not entirely true. Don't you worry, from now on I am here with you and I will help you to become one like me!" said Kenji as he was wiping his eyes and spoke again. "So as you, *kuya* Genji, you've change too. Maybe you've got some of your experiences too that I don't have, right?"

"Oh, yeah!" Genji turned to Cyan and called him, and then he introduced him to his twin brother. "By the way *kuya*, I would like you to meet my friend who is always here with me. His name is Cyan, a Valedictorian of Hunsterdam University. Do you know that I've learned a lot from him?"

"Oh wow, he's totally a smart guy!" said Kenji while looking at Cyan.

Cyan moved closer to Kenji and he introduced himself. "Hello mister! My name is Cyan Wilford, a college student of Hunsterdam University and a friend of your twin brother. I've learned much from him too and he a very good friend!" then he bowed down his head.

There was an urban legend believed by the fairies, gods, goddesses, and humans about the "Twins of Fate". According to the legend, when the Twins of Fate were together in the world's horizon at any given time, the world would be more imminent and vulnerable to destruction because of its cursed fate. But the legend also said otherwise if the Twins of Fate were not together in the horizon. It was because the twins had something to do with the world's destiny as well as the fate of all humans, but it was only believed to be a myth...

The fairies were all believed that Isidra's twins were the Twins of Fate when she gave birth to them. And now that the twins were together again, the question was... Was the legend true? Or was just a myth?

35 IN HUNSTERDAM

Claude and Reinhardt were now in the Pioneer's hands after their jet was shot down, and the Pioneers seized them along with Kenji. There were many citizens living in the said city thus lacking the enough number of prisons to lock them up, so what the Pioneers did was to take the two and the rest of the prisoners inside one of the classrooms of Hunsterdam University.

Claude and Reinhardt were both staying inside the university classroom along with the other citizens. The two men were both handcuffed facing the wall and were still unconscious.

Silence.

There were young ladies of Hunsterdam seemed to be falling in love with the two Explorers they were with in the same prison. "Hey, those two guys over there are so cute!" said a 2nd year female college student of Hunsterdam University. "Why don't we kiss them like a prince of Snow White so they'll awake?" said one of the young lady teasingly.

"What?! You're serious about this? A princess going to kiss her prince charming to awake him instead? That's too embarrassing!" said another female student who was her friend. "They're sleeping deeply. Don't do that!"

"What do you think, Flora? Are they still single? I can't help it because they're both cute."

Her friend shook her head. "I think they're already taken. Most of the cute guys like them are in their relationship already."

"Oh dear…" the female student felt disappointed. "That's too bad. I

THE EXPLORERS

wish one of them was my Mr. Right…"

A pregnant woman retorted the two students. "Hey, you two, could you please stop doing this nonsense idea since we do not know those guys yet. What if they're already married? Or they have pregnant wives as well?!"

"A-Anyway… Let's wait for these two to wake up. I really can't help it, they're so cute… Right, Eliza?"

The another female student nodded. "They are. Let's wait for them to wake up."

One hour had passed when a female student took out her smartphone to take pictures of the two Explorers who were still sleeping. The other girls followed her, as they also pulled out their smartphones and digital cameras they had in their bags.

"Come on, girls. Let's take pictures of them so we will have our remembrance from them!" said a female student holding a smartphone.

One of the male prisoners of the same age saw his fellow prisoners who were now taking pictures of the two Explorers in a corner. "Hey ladies, what are you doing there? Why wastin' your time with those guys and I am always here for you to take my pictures for free! Didn't you notice that I am more good-looking than to those two?! Besides, they do not belong here either!"

"Mind your own business!" said a female student while still taking pictures of the two Explorers. "You have no taste!"

The male prisoner got jealous. "I-I am more handsome than them. You girls are just wasting your time with them!"

The girls did not answer and ignored him. They were still busy in taking pictures in a corner.

Later, Reinhardt gently opened his eyes. He was blinded by the bright camera flashes before him and got dazzled. When he moved his body, the ladies shrieked out loud while giggling.

"Eeeee, he's so, so cute!!!"

The innocent Reinhardt were looking around in wonder. "W-What's this? W-Where am I?"

"You are here in a prison lad," answered an elderly woman. "We were all prisoners here."

The girls shrieked on top of their voice again which made Claude awake next. He quickly covered his ears and then he cried out loud as well. "What the--! It's too noisy!!!"

The girls suddenly stopped when one of them approached Claude and Reinhardt and introduced herself. "Hello cuties… My name is Lileta, a 2nd year college student of Hunsterdam University. What is your name?"

Reinhardt answered but different. "I-I'm sorry miss, but we have no time for this right now. We are both in a hurry!"

The female student felt embarrassed. "Don't you want to say your name to us?"

Claude answered next, "We need to get out of here now. We have a colleague who is also imprisoned in this place but we do not know where it is."

The male prisoner answered. "Hey strangers, there is another huge prison over there that is just behind this university. Next to mini barangay hall!"

"Well thanks about it bro," said Reinhardt to the male prisoner as he nodded. "We'll get rid those Pioneers and save you all and this place!"

Claude turned to Reinhardt when he just learned that their hands were handcuffed. "Rain, we're handcuffed… and it looks like the Pioneers took our weapons away from us when we're unconscious."

Reinhardt turned his head to his side. "You're right, Claude. And we're just the two of us here who are handcuffed."

"Damn, we're not gonna make it, are we?"

"Yes, we are. We're Explorers, remember that?"

The female students were silent while looking at the two Explorers. Claude and Reinhardt were both struggling in removing the handcuffs in their hands so they would bust out the prison and find Kenji immediately.

While as for Lucky's group…

Another hour had passed, but until now, Lucky's group were still hiding in the shadows and having a hard time in rescuing their three colleagues. Most of the enemies were guarding close to their spot and they were still figuring out how to pass through them without being caught.

"Jon, shoot him with your sleeping needle," Lucky whispered to Jon when he saw a Pioneer guarding the area close to them. "Or if you want… kill him!"

"No problem."

Jon began his attack by shooting a long needle to a Pioneer, but the Pioneers were all high-skilled and their reflexes were strong. So, the Pioneer immediately sensed the deadly needle as he turned to it and quickly dodged to his side. The deadly needle zoomed past to his forehead and it hit a tree. He picked the weapon.

"T-There is someone here who wants to kill me. The other Explorers, they're here!" cried the Pioneer and he dashed towards the fellow Pioneers. "The other Explorers are here!"

"The other Explorers?" asked his colleague.

The Pioneer showed the deadly needle to them angrily. "This is the evidence! This is their deadly weapon that almost killed me!"

Jon silently gulped and turned to the group. "Oh no, we're dead... The enemies know we're here. What about now?"

Isagani thought first. "What if we attack them? Maybe the six of us can neutralize them, you think? We've been staying here for long, and I'm afraid we may not gonna make it to save the three 'til nightfall if we don't make any move. We have no choice, Lucky!"

"No way," Lucky disagreed. "Those Pioneers are well-trained dreaded warriors Isagani, so do not underestimate them. And you know that!"

Shingue was impatient. "So are you saying that we'll just keep on hiding in here forever? Those Pioneers already know we're here, Lucky. Though we're outnumbered, we have nothing else to do but to fight back and save our friends!"

Lucky got pissed off. "You guys sound like you are not Explorers. Is this the result of your training? Remember what you've trained for. Don't be carried away by your emotions. But if you insist on your stupid thoughts, fine! Have it your way. Go on your own!" then he left the group.

"Hey, Lucky!" called Tyrone discreetly. "Where do you think you're going? Come back here!"

"It's up to you if you really want to show yourselves to them and get caught!" said Lucky annoyingly as he was still moving away from the five.

"Lucky! Come back here, Lucky!!!"

Lucky did not come back and walked away. The five were left behind the bushes. Lucky secretly moved beyond the wall, determined to save his three colleagues alone. He was prepared for any eventuality, and putting his life at stake.

Claude and Reinhardt were still struggling in removing their handcuffs to get themselves freed and get out of the prison immediately. Claude was pulling himself away from the wall as strong as he could, and Reinhardt did the same thing. They were not losing hope!

Later, Claude bit off his handcuff but it was too hard so he pulled himself away from the wall once again. They tried to slip off their hands but to no avail.

As for Kenji. Although his weapon was being taken by the Pioneers, he was still able to escape in his prison. The reason? With the help of his Holy element.

There was a novice Pioneer who was assigned to guard the prison cell alone where Kenji and Genji were imprisoned. When he went inside, Kenji quickly cast a Holy magic on him and he got hit. He did not get badly hurt, because Kenji did not intend of killing him.

"Why didn't you kill him?" asked Genji to his twin brother in wonder while looking at the downed Pioneer. "He's an enemy!"

"I don't want to kill… and I don't want to harm anybody. Like us, he's a human too with his right to live, brother…" said Kenji smiling to Genji.

"Yes, I know that brother, but this is different… He's one of our enemies and will have an intention to kill us soon!"

"No, he won't… We both have different perspectives, brother. However, the enemies can still change despite of being our nemesis. Don't worry about it."

Genji did not answer when Cyan asked. "So we're outta here now, right?"

"We will go out in this prison, just the three of us. It's very dangerous outside for the people if we let them go. We may be caught again if we do, so they should stay here," said Kenji.

"And what about this Pioneer?" asked Genji pointing at the downed Pioneer.

Kenji smiled. "We'll take him somewhere the Pioneers can't see him. I'll take care of him!" then he carried the Pioneer in his back. He placed the Pioneer in a room, tied his hands, and put a piece of cloth to his mouth, and he turned to Cyan. "By the way, Cyan… Are you so sure you really want to come with us?"

"Oh, yes! I want to go with you!"

"Well you do not know the dangers outside. We're going to hide when we get out of here, Cyan…" warned Kenji.

"Don't worry about me. I can take care of myself. Lemme come with you, please mister!"

"Okay, go ahead. Come with us, then."

THE EXPLORERS

"Yohoo!"

Cyan went behind Kenji when Kenji turned to the prisoners next. "You guys stay here, okay? We will help you get out of this prison sooner, I promise!" then, he moved away and the two followed his back.

Lucky was still hiding in the shadows and he was sneaking alone in his direction. He was able to penetrate the enemy line, not being caught by the Pioneers and Mercuries.

Kenji's group had reached behind the huge prison next to mini barangay hall. They saw some Mercuries guarding the area so they did not make any moves yet. Later, they heard someone talking to each other nearby. The two Mercuries were talking about the plan:

"Lorenz, do you know the place of Bondore that was recently attacked by the Pioneers? I think I've heard something that the Pioneers were into Bondore again."

"Really?"

Kenji was surprised, but Genji was more surprised. The old woman who attacked him before was currently staying in the said place. Kenji whispered to him. "Brother, the Pioneers are returning to Bondore once again! I remember my promise to an old woman there that I would save the town but I failed it. And then, they're into Bondore again!"

Genji was speechless when he heard it from his twin brother. He already knew what Kenji did everything in Bondore before. He failed the rescue attempt indeed, but he was unaware that Genji was been there too... And Genji made something to the old woman that hurt her feelings and ruin Kenji's reputation for fun... The impostor Kenji!"

"So what is the time of their attack in Bondore again?"

"It's already 11:30am, right? They will be there at exactly two o'clock in the afternoon."

Kenji was rattled. "Oh no, just a few hours left and the Pioneers will be in Bondore again... I-I must go there and save *lola* right away!"

Brother... that was... just an accident... Thought Genji to himself. *An accident I really did not mean to do something bad behind your back... In Bondore!!!*

Genji did not know if he should ever say it to his twin brother or not. If he would not say about it, maybe that old witch would be the one to say it to Kenji when he went there this afternoon. He did not want Kenji to find out about it anymore, and he wanted to stop him for going there!

"B-Brother, are you sure of going to Bondore today?" asked Genji hesitantly to his twin brother. "Is this a part of your plan?"

"For the mean time, yes… Why? I must hurry! My colleagues should all be with me before we go in Bondore. We will all going in Bondore together. We have no time!"

"But you failed to save Bondore before, right? That's what you've said earlier…"

"Yes, I failed it… But now I have my chance to redeem myself for that failure!"

"N-No, please don't!" Genji did not really want to.

Kenji was wondering. "W-Why is that? Don't you want to go to Bondore with me?"

"Um…" Genji was running out of excuses. "B-Because…"

Kenji looked at him directly to his eyes and still wondering.

"I-It's nothing… I just don't want to waste our time in going to that place since that town has been attacked by those Pioneers before. This is not a part of your plan, isn't it?!"

"No… I will fight for revenge. *Lola* was expecting this from me, *kuya*. Come on, let's save my colleagues!"

"W-Wait, how is Claude now? I haven't seen him for years too!"

Kenji was in a hurry. "I'll tell you later. Come on!" then he left hurriedly and the two followed.

Shingue's group was now hiding in a small garden of Hunsterdam when the three saw them and sneaked towards them. The group was so happy to see each other again safely, and the five were surprised to see Kenji along with Genji and Cyan.

"He looks exactly just like you, Kenji!" said Isagani in surprise when he saw Genji next to Kenji. "I-I never thought you have a twin brother…"

Kenji was still in a hurry. "Yeah, so where's Claude and *kuya* Reinhardt? Oh yeah," he turned to Genji. "We have our colleague here who is also our biological brother. His name is Reinhardt, but for now I don't want to waste our time with this," then he turned to Shingue's group again. "By the way, where's Lucky?"

"Well, he got upset on us and he left on his own," said Isagani sadly.

Tyrone's smartphone suddenly vibrated, there was a call. "Hey guys, it's Lucky!" then he answered. "Hello?"

"Turn on your phone's speaker so we can hear him too," requested by Jon. "Come on, we want to hear and talk to him also."

THE EXPLORERS

Tyrone turned on his phone's speaker in its low volume where anyone could hear. "Hey yah UEs, it's me Lucky. I just entered inside the university and saw Claude and Reinhardt in a classroom. They're safe now with me. Well many thanks to my sharp eyes and to my lucky charm (his short staff), hah! I burst in the university's Supply Room and took an ax to remove their handcuffs. We're coming out the building now."

"Excellent approach, Lucky!" answered Kenji happily. "Lucky, this is Kenji talking. We're out of the prison as well. Let's meet at the university entrance gate!"

"Gotcha, Lucky out!"

This time, the entire city was only guarded by the "weak" Mercuries and the Pioneers were not around. The Mercury was the weakest group of all the groups of warriors, which made the Pioneer and Reminescence treat them as their followers and always referred to as "weaklings".

The Pioneers were not around in Hunsterdam because they were all inside their large, modern airship, thinking that their captured Explorers would not be able to escape anymore in the hands of Mercury.

The two groups of Explorers met in the meeting place, and Kenji shortly introduced Genji and Cyan to Reinhardt, Claude, and Lucky. Claude and Genji were so happy to see each other again and they hugged each other.

Lucky returned each of their confiscated weapons he got in the Supply Room and they nodded to each other. And now they were complete:

"Kenji, do you still intend of going to DDE mansion now? We will travel across Camoria next," asked Reinhardt. "We don't have a jet anymore."

"Camoria? I know that place!" answered Genji very quickly. "I stranded to that place when me and *kuya* Kenji got separated, and I stayed there for long."

"Is that so? That means you know the way to the DDE base, huh?" asked Kenji.

Genji did not know anything about the Explorers much so he blushed. "Um… I've heard about the DDE already… I-I think it's too far from Camoria. But from here, we need to go through Camoria first before we get to their base. I'm sorry, 'coz I do not know them yet!"

"Blimey! Our father is a DDE leader, have you forgotten? But for now we will go to Bondore first. We don't have much time!"

"Oh yeah, I've heard that the Pioneers will be there this afternoon," said Claude. "It was a Mercury who said it to us!"

The group looked around the city to see if their way was clear and no one was guarding close to them. There were few, and those were all Mercuries.

"I know where Bondore is… but only from Dakar…" said Kenji sadly. "But from here…"

Okay, fine! I will tell to him that I've been in Bondore before, but I'm not going to tell him what everything happened when I was there! Thought Genji to himself. *You are really so importunate,* kuya *Kenji!*

"Forget about going in Bondore, Kenji…" said Tyrone. "That is not in our plan today, right?"

Kenji was annoyed. "No way! I need to go to Bondore right now and it's a part of our plan from now on! I'll fight for revenge, so we should arrive there earlier before the Pioneer comes!"

Genji spoke hesitantly after he could no longer hold his guilt of knowing the place of Bondore. "B-Brother… Actually, I know where Bondore is… I've been there before, right after I left Camoria…" finally he said it in his low voice.

Kenji was glad to hear this from his twin brother so he quickly moved closer to him. "Really? You know the way from here? Excellent then!"

"Yes, but it's too far if we go there by foot. I think it's over five to six kilometers away."

"That's okay! But I wonder what's your business there when you came, huh?"

"A-Ahhh…" Genji was nervous. "Ah… eh… ah…" his brain was functioning at great speed thinking of another reasons. "W-Well…"

"Nevermind, don't answer me anymore. I'm in a hurry. Come on then," stopped Kenji to Genji and then he turned around. "I know what you're going to say, you just passed through it."

Genji quickly agreed. "Y-Yes, that's it indeed! I just walked pass through it and came here. Good guess *(whew!)*!"

"Alright, now that we're all ready to face the Pioneers, let us go to Bondore!" said Kenji at the same time he lifted the Kali staff he was holding.

The group answered together. "TO BONDORE!!"

They were about to make their way to Bondore now before the group of Pioneer would come. But before they left Hunsterdam, they went back to the Supply Room of Hunsterdam University to get a weapon for Cyan. The Valedictorian was really eager to join their party and he was so glad to become a part of the group's mission. Then, they all went out the university successfully while the novice Pioneer guarding there was still unconscious.

36 JOURNEY TO BONDORE

The Pioneers were all inside their large airship still and relaxing along with Akira and his father who was their former leader, since Akira was now their new leader. They were so confident knowing that the Mercuries were all guarding the city and they did not know that the Explorers were already escaped.

The "negligent" Mercuries decided to left the city to return to their base and also left their fellow colleagues that were beaten by Kenji's group. The Pioneers were still not around, and even the novice Pioneer was still remained unconscious.

"Those Mercuries are all cowards, aren't they?" asked Clio laughing. "Now that they're gone, let's release the prisoners here and tell them to flee this city while the Pioneers are still unaware to what is going on now."

"Yup, and I have the keys!" Lucky boasted while his hand was on his hip. "Let's set the Hunsterdam people free!"

The enemies were gone around the city when the group successfully rescued the Hunsterdam citizens and they were free. "Take these keys and save the rest of the citizens," said Lucky to the escaped Hunsterdam citizens and he gestured a thumbs up.

"Thank you so much for rescuing us," said a Hunsterdam citizen. "May King Jethro bless you all, Explorers…"

Kenji smiled. "Thank you and you're always welcome."

The citizens nodded.

"Goodbye."

The Hunsterdam citizens quickly moved away from the group and they dispersed going to their safety. The group ensured that no more citizens left in the city before they would leave.

"They're all gone and free," said Reinhardt happily. "Next, we need to do our mission."

"Alright, let's go to Bondore!" said Cyan. "I can feel you guys are worrying about me joining the party but no worries! I am okay. I know how to fight, I promise!"

Isagani was incredulous. "Really? Maybe later you'll cry and turn back when we face our enemies there. You're a Valedictorian, so that means you're only good in academics. Hey, we are using weapons in battle, not books!"

"Ahm… no guys," good thing Genji defended Cyan. "You're wrong. Cyan is a great fighter too. I taught him how to fight, even a hand-to-hand combat. Hey, I am also proficient in battle so don't worry about me either!"

"So what now? Shall we go then? I'm so excited!" said Shingue. "I haven't been in Bondore yet so I want to see it. Come on, come on, come on!"

"Show us the way to Bondore from here *kuya* Genji," said Kenji looking at Genji.

"All right, you all follow me."

Good thing they still had one jet that was not damaged during the ambush earlier, Shingue's jet. Lucky's jet wing was slightly damaged, but the jet was still under control. Therefore, Shingue's jet had more passengers aboard.

Kenji, Genji, Reinhardt, Claude, Tyrone, Shingue, Cyan and Clio were in jet 14JK, while Isagani, Lucky, and Jon were in jet E47J.

The single HawkEye had only a maximum capacity of five passengers. The two survived jets began to hover in the air and they had successfully left Hunsterdam without the Pioneer's knowledge.

"Hey Genji, make sure that it's close to Hunsterdam since this jet is, um… ah…" Shingue could not tell the right words while piloting the jet. "This jet is overloaded, so I'm afraid this jet can't stand long in the air and we might crash! How far is it again?"

"Don't worry, just a minute my friend and we'll be there. I'm so sure of it. But if we go to Camoria from Hunsterdam, it's a little bit farther."

"Just a minute you say, eh?"

"Yes, I'm so sure about it. It's just over five to six kilometers away, remember?"

"Heh, then you went to Hunsterdam by foot! You're a good runner!"

Everyone was already gone in Hunsterdam when one of the Pioneers decided to check the prisoners but they were no longer to be found. "W-Where are the people here and the captured UEs?" he said while peering around. "One more thing… those Mercuries who are guarding here have gone as well!" then he ran back to his colleagues yelling. "Sir, the UEs and the prisoners have escaped!!!"

"What?" Akira was shocked. "They're all escaped? Where are the Mercuries? What are they doing now?!"

"They also left the city. I think those fools have left along with Explorers!"

"Those Mercuries betrayed us!" said Akira angrily. "They're very, very stupid!"

Alexander ordered the Pioneers. "Check around the entire city to see if there are people left! Hurry, we will all go to Bondore soon!"

The Pioneers rushed in different locations elsewhere when Akira spoke to his dad angrily. "The Mercuries are truly useless! They were easily get fooled by those Explorers and went away with them. They're all suckers!!!"

A Pioneer returned to them. "Sir Akira, none of the prisoners are here anymore!"

Another Pioneer also returned to them. "Their weapons are all gone too. They're no longer here either!"

Another Pioneer also returned. "Even those worthless Mercuries who were guarding the university were all gone for good! There is one Mercury we've found, but he's unconscious!"

"Nevermind those idiots! What more important is we already made a statement what we could do to those Explorers. We have downed an Explorer jet, and that gives them a warning to get prepared for our next attack. What I really need to see is nothing else but only Maximillian!" said Akira. "And take his Holy element!"

"Are we still going to Bondore today?" asked one of Pioneers. "What you only need there are those Divine Stones held by one of the Bondore residents, right?"

Akira gave a grimace on his face. "Yes, indeed. That is the only reason… The Divine Stones in the hands of an old witch. She knows I am

THE EXPLORERS

going there, and I have warned her that I would take those stones from her. After I get them all, I will also take the Holy element of Maximillian next! And lastly, I will make him bow before me and kill him... He knew that, because I already gave him a warning the next time we'll meet!"

"The Explorers have no knowledge that we will go to Bondore, haven't they? Hah, they will be totally surprised when they find out that we already owned the remaining Divine Stones from the hands of that old witch!"

"Come on, Pioneers! Let us go to Bondore!" shouted Akira to his fellow Pioneers. "Let's take the sacred stones from her hands!"

Kenji's group had finally arrived to Bondore and they saw the devastated town looking worse than before when Kenji lastly went here. The people were preparing again for their evacuation to a safe place before the return of Pioneers. They knew it would happen because the old woman had told them about the incoming danger with the help of her occult power. With her supernatural power, she had an ability to see the future of any human she knew. And because of her unique ability to track, she had finally recovered the buried stones with also the aid of her fellow entities. Now, the rest of the missing Divine Stones were finally saved and safe in her hands.

"The residents here are also preparing to evacuate!" said Jon while looking around the town. "That's good, they better leave the town before the Pioneer comes."

Claude and the other boys helped the residents to evacuate safely by leading them out to the town's exit. "Go, go, go, it's quite dangerous here and you must leave this town immediately! The Pioneers are coming. We'll take care of them!"

The boys were all busy in leading the Bondore residents to the exit. But as for Kenji, he was looking for the old woman whom he only knew in this town and gave her his promise to save the said town. "Come with me *kuya* Genji, let's find the old woman I met before in Dakar. I know she's here somewhere!"

"Um..." Genji hesitated. "W-Wait, I d-don't want--"

"Kenji!" a voice called Kenji in the distance. It was the voice of the old woman.

Genji heard the elder's voice when he rattled. *Oh no, here she comes...* He thought to himself.

Kenji was delighted when he heard the old woman's voice so he turned to where he heard the call. "*Lola!*"

The old woman suddenly emerged in front of him looking different. Kenji was looking surprised when he noticed her different appearance compared to the last time he saw her. She was on her beautiful white dress and her white hair was long. Plus, she looked a little bit younger than before!

"*L-Lola*, i-is that you? You look different…" said Kenji goggling at her.

The old woman embraced Kenji. "You're surprised to see my look now, aren't you? Yes, it's me. The one you met in Dakar. I admit that I am not human, but a fairy living in this world. I have the power to determine the future holds and I can also read the person's mind. Wow, I can see that you're a Holy Wielder and an Explorer now!"

The two were still embracing, while Genji's heart was throbbing fast. He was just watching the two, and later on he spoke to his mind as he glared towards the old woman. "Don't you dare tell to my brother what everything happened between you and me before! Don't try to humiliate me in front of him!"

Genji was shocked when the old woman stared at him still embracing Kenji. She heard Genji's thought to her and she answered to his mind. "I won't, impostor… We will keep this as a secret between you and me, and I hate to believe that you are his twin brother… You are my enemy… And I will get to know you more, remember that!"

Genji's face began to sweat when he heard the old woman's response to his mind. He stepped back in amazement and fear, he did not answer.

The elder spoke again to Genji's mind. "Always remember that, impostor. I hope that will teach you a lesson for what you did to me. You have your nerve to slur your twin brother behind his back. Your life is in my hands now, Genji!"

Genji stooped his head and answered to his mind. "I… I'm so sorry, I didn't mean to do that and I hope you'll forgive me now…"

The two had stopped their embrace when Kenji spoke to the old woman as his warning. "*Lola*, the Pioneers are going here today and we heard it from the Mercuries earlier. You should also leave this place immediately, and…" he stooped down his head in repentance. "…I want to say sorry that, um… that I failed to save Bondore before and broke my promise to you. B-But please don't you worry, today's my chance to fight for my revenge! I will do the best I can to bring back Bondore from the hands of Pioneers. I-I will!" then he gently took the old woman's hands. "I assure you that I will beat them, *lola*... I have my great power now..."

The old woman joyfully wept. "I know that, my lad... You still haven't changed. The Kenji I met before is still the same. Keep your heart as good as always and never change. With that, your kindness will always keep you away from harm and lead you to your dreams."

"Thank you," said Kenji and then he turned to his colleagues. "By the way *lola*, these are my friends. This one is Genji, my twin brother."

The old woman suddenly frowned towards Genji and glared at him slyly so Kenji would not notice. "O-Oh, your twin brother really? How nice to see that you two are exactly look alike!" then she quickly turned away.

"*Lola*, the Pioneers will be here sooner. You must leave now before they comes. It's too dangerous in here and everyone is already gone to safety!"

The sacred stones suddenly reacted in the elder's body as they shone in a short period of time. She felt their presence, so she turned to Kenji and spoke to him. "M-My boy, before I will leave this place... there is something I would like to give to all of you..."

Her chest began to shone before the boys when the seven Divine Stones she acquired went out from her body and they float around her. Reinhardt and Shingue were so shocked to see the rare stones before them and Shingue pointed at them.

"Those stones... They are all Divine Stones of elements!" he cried.

Tyrone was shocked as well. "What? The long-lost Divine Stones of King Jethro? But how'd..."

"Yes, my sons... These are the Divine Stones I got with the help of my fellow fairies who are also living in this world. These are what the Pioneers are up to. They will take these from me and use them in their own ways, but these stones will be a great help to all of you," then she smiled. "I think these stones seem to have chosen you to become their new master, because of your good deeds after I felt their reaction earlier. I can tell that they like you and you are trustworthy to be their possessors. Therefore, these sacred stones have finally chosen all of you to become King Jethro's new Element Wielders!"

The group could not believe what they have heard. The old woman continued. "I am not going to surrender these to Pioneers. They will just use the stones' powers to their evil ways and destroy the world's balance. The stones have given their trust on you… Please take good care of these and use their powers in a right way!"

They all nodded.

The old woman firstly approached Lucky and she gently handed his stone. With her help, the Divine Stone of Lucky returned to its true form as element and regained its strong power again. "This stone that you already obtained is an element of 'Time and Space', my boy. Now that it's finally returned to its true form, you are now its chosen Wielder. And you are now able to use its power under your command," then she gestured her hands when Lucky's element slowly entered inside his chest as he was closing his eyes.

She also did the same thing to Tyrone and Isagani who also both obtained each of their Divine Stones and returned to their true form as elements.

To Isagani: "You now have the element of 'Light and Blessings', my boy. Please take this element and become its new master…"

To Tyrone: "This element of 'Trinity' has chosen you, so you should take good care of it and handle its power rightfully."

Like Lucky and Kenji, the two elements also went inside Tyrone and Isagani's chest while their eyes were closed. Then, they looked at each other smiling.

Next, the old woman approached Claude and she gently handed over a Divine Stone that chose him and became an element again. "My boy, please accept this element of 'Earth' since it also chose you to become its new master. Congratulations," then the element of Earth slowly went inside Claude's chest as well.

Claude suddenly felt different right after the element went inside his heart. He felt like his inner strength became stronger than before, like real Hercules!

"Thank you very much for this, my lady…" said Claude gratefully and he nodded with a smile.

To Shingue: "Please take this element of 'Poison', young man. Use it well with care, because this type of element is more dangerous than to any liquid present in this world…"

To Genji. Although she still had her hard feeling towards him, she gave the stone to him. The sacred stone also chose him to become an Element Wielder. "This is the element of 'Lightning'… that is as sharp as your attitude. Take this and become its new master…" she hinted him.

To Jon: "This element of 'Fire' is yours, young man. But you must watch out to its power because it can even harm you when used without proper care. You must learn to handle this type of element well and keep its power under your control."

To Reinhardt: "You are the chosen Wielder of the element of 'Darkness'. With its power, you will become the grasper of the shadows and darkness."

To Clio: "For you, young one is the element of 'Gravity'. With that, you can now have an ability to control the gravity of the world."

And lastly, was to Cyan: "With your cleverness and being wise, you should have this element of 'Air'. Take it and use it well…"

Afterwards: "All of the seven missing elements I've got during my search in this world are now in your hands. Now that the Pioneers have nothing to take anything from me anymore, I can finally leave and return to where I come from. Please use the elements in rightful way and do not abuse it."

"Yes, we will assure you that these elements we have will only be used as needed for the common good," said Kenji as he nodded. "We're now ready to face the incoming enemies. We have the elements that will help us for the impending battle. We will win this fight for Bondore!"

The old woman nodded and smiled. "Very well… May the elements of King Jethro will guide you to your long journey… I know you will succeed! Goodbye…" then she slowly vanished like bubbles before the new Wielders' eyes.

"She is no human indeed. She just vanished before us with the help of her extraordinary power!" said Claude to the boys. "She's really a fairy!"

Genji laughed. "Hey guys, my Valedictorian friend just insisted to join the party without expecting anything, but look… he also acquired a power as a reward due to his good deed! How lucky he is, isn't he?"

"Yeah, you're right!" agreed Tyrone. "He's unaware that something is going to unfold and viola! He also become an Element Wielder like us, hah!"

Cyan shrugged his shoulder in ignorance but he answered. "Why? Genji just joined your party too, right? But he also become one like you!"

"Since we're all Element Wielders now… that means we Explorers are eligible to elevate to DDE immediately, right? B-But first and foremost, we must complete the UE and EUE since we can not accelerate. Oh man, that will take too long!" said Shingue sadly while he was scratching his head.

"Everyone in this town has evacuated safely and none of them have stayed. We should prepare ourselves now," said Kenji looking around. "While waiting for those Pioneers, why don't we familiarize ourselves in using our powers first? I am getting excited to see what your elements can do, fellas!"

"Alright!"

The eleven men trained themselves first. They were doing the fighting style they knew, and felt that they were getting stronger than before after they acquired the elements.

Kenji was even well-prepared to see and confront his rival, Akira. He knew that when they meet again, he would fight him and absolutely win the battle!

"Honesty Kenji," said Claude as he moved next to Kenji. "This is just our first time to have each of the elements. We do not know how to use them yet. What if later when we fight those Pioneers and we failed to cast our powers on them? It'll be too embarrassing, right?"

"I understand you concern, Claude… But why don't you try to cast it while there is time? Um, I mean… like doing a gesture and say something like I did in our final test?"

"What should I say?"

Kenji chuckled. "Why are you asking me? I am not a Wielder of your element, Claude. Although I was the first one to become an Element Wielder among us, yet I still don't know on how to maximize all of its powers."

"O-Okay… I will just make guesses then…"

"It's okay," said Kenji smiling. "Maybe you can cast out its power when you make a good guess, Claude. Go and try it!"

The Element Wielders had wasted no time, doing their warm-ups before they drew out their own weapons combining with their element's powers. They would try to make guesses in using their elements while the Pioneer was still not around. The funny thing was that, they did not know how to cast the elemental-based magics that they could use in an incoming battle.

THE EXPLORERS

Like Tyrone and Jon.

"All right, let's see what this Fire element can do right now," said Jon while his eyes were closed and he lifted both of his hands in the air. "I wonder what should I say? Oh, oh, I know! *Fireous Vonolamora!*" and then, there was no any *Fireous Vonolamora* magic cast.

Tyrone taunted Jon in funny way. "Waaaahhh! There's no fire coming out man," then he made a guess gesture. "Lemme try mine if I can cast my element's magic... Here we go, um... *Labasaceous Elementos Ng Trinitritos!*"

No magic was cast by Tyrone as well.

Jon laughed out loud teasingly. "Wahahahahahaha! He also failed so we're fair, nyaaaahhh!"

Tyrone felt embarrassed. "Well of course, this is just my first time and yet I don't know how to use it like you!"

The other Wielders also had their hard time in casting out their elemental-based magics and they were making different guess attempts. All of them were failed.

"Hopefully, my guess is right this time," said Cyan in his cute facial expression. "What are the words that are related to air? Oh! *Winda No Hanginin Ng Lumabasaki Ka Na!!!*"

Failed.

"How about this?" Genji was going a guess gesture. "Um... *Thundara Balabana... Mona...*"

Also failed.

Shingue was doing a funny guess. He had been saying long guesses in many times but he was just wasting his voice for nothing.

Yet, he insisted. "*...Poisonous... Dangerous... Poisonamita... Volteramos... Pultik... Mo... Mo-Mokonami...*"

No magic was cast.

"*Manami... Puteramosan... Itaronaminatox... Poison...* It's still not working! *Walaxinat... Poison...* Come on man, be fair with me. Please come out now!"

No magic was cast still.

"GRRR! *POSONATOCALOXIDAMUNITA! POISON NAMU TOXAMITIC!* AHHHHH!!!" Shingue cried.

The group heard Shingue's cry, so they all turned to him and they laughed out loud to his goofiness.

"HAHAHA!!!"

"*POISONAMOUS! PULTEXAMIX!* GEEZ, I GIVE UP NOOOWWW!!!" finally, Shingue gave up.

Like Shingue, the other Element Wielders were still doing their attempts in casting their magics. A few minutes had passed but still, everything was failed.

As for Claude: "*Mundomundo Vataxicus!*"

As for Genji: "*Thundara Lomotoma!*"

As for Clio: "*Oh my mind, oh mind… I mean… Gravity comma outta!*"

As for Lucky: "*Timenatix Motrix!*"

Kenji's ears were now hurting by the funny, gibberish guesses of his colleagues so he could not concentrate to what he was doing. He covered his ears with his hands, but yet he could not help not to laugh at their rubbish noises.

As for Tyrone: "*Trinitritos Ng Makah-Makah!*"

As for Reinhardt: "*Cloud of Darkness!*" nice serious guess.

As for Cyan: "*Tormadomos… Tornado Mokoh-Mokohhh…*"

"*Wanatoxan Mortixa!*"

"*Monocath Monocattthhh…*"

"*Doom of Darkness!*"

"*Heavenatic Magnetismmm!*"

"*Galacotic Forsia!*"

"Damn, still not working!"

"I am begging you, Element of Earth… Please come out now *(hik!)*!"

"*Magonte Tajajajajamamamanamo!*" whatever.

"Many guesses at once, but all were wrong!" said Kenji laughing. "Good thing I know at least one magic since King Jethro himself taught me on how to use it. Just the Holy Fire magic!"

Every guesses were all totally useless. A lot of precious time were wasted in doing their attempts to cast out the powers in their hands, but to no avail. Only a few hours had left, and later on, the Pioneer would be in Bondore!

37 THE PIONEER

Claude gave up to their nonsense guesses they were making and thought they were getting too stupid while the others still persisted. "I quit," said Claude while he was walking towards Kenji. "I am just wasting not only my voice, but also the time, Kenji!"

"Certainly."

"Ya know what? There is nothing for us to brag about to the Pioneers since our elements are useless for now. Maybe they won't even believe that we're Element Wielders, will they?"

"Don't care."

It was earlier than two o'clock in the afternoon when the Pioneer had come to Bondore. As they descended, they meant to land their huge airship to where Kenji's group was standing. The Wielders quickly moved away from the landing area in annoyance.

"Whoa! They have come here earlier than to what we're expecting," cried Shingue.

"Maybe it's because they got surprised when they saw none in Hunsterdam. Hah, they're fools!" said Tyrone.

The Pioneers got off their airship when Akira quickly got off first and saw the Wielders. "Explorers, w-why are you here???" he asked in wonder.

Cyan answered. "We have been waiting for you. What do you want in this place?"

"I knew it! Those Mercuries are totally useless! I know how wise you really are with this, Maximillian… You are!"

Kenji tried to antagonize Akira. "To say simply, I am far wiser than you!"

Akira laughed in annoyance and then he looked around, just as he noticed that no one was around the town anymore. "S-So where are the villagers here? Where is the old woman?"

"I'm sorry, Akira. We've already sent out the residents here earlier. We knew that you would come here. And with regards to *lola*... the things you want to take from her are already gone!" said Kenji.

"What? T-They're no longer with her anymore? Why? D-Do you know what we want from her, huh?!"

"Guys?" called Kenji to his ten colleagues and they showed off each of their tattoos in different parts of their bodies. "The Divine Stones you need from her belong to us now, Akira!" bragged Kenji. "We knew your only purpose of coming in this town. Sacrificing the lives of people here for the sake of Divine Stones that *lola* has.... So instead of giving up the stones to the evil likes of you, she gave all of them to us for the safe keeping. Now, please leave this town right now and never, ever come back again anymore!"

The Pioneers were shocked to hear about this so Akira got very, very angry. "And why the hell did she give those stones to all of you instead of me? She was not wise enough of choosing someone very worthy to own the king's power and become the new master! You are her enemies too, you power-grabber Explorers!!!"

"Shut up, Akira! Maybe YOU are not wise enough!!!" answered Kenji angrily. "You do not deserve all of this, you don't deserve the world!" and then he drew out his weapon. "A wicked, heartless person like you do not deserve such good blessings given by King Jethro. You all suffer for this!"

"Hmpt... We will take those elements from you, Wielders. You'll see!"

The two groups of warriors began to pose themselves for a fight. They drew out their weapons and pointed at each other's opponents. Explorers versus Pioneers.

"I'm gonna kill you, Maximillian!" shouted Akira at Kenji at the same time he was dashing towards him with his spear. "Take thiiiiisssss!!!"

The Pioneers followed Akira when they also rushed towards the Wielders and the battle began. Alexander faced Reinhardt for a fight.

Meanwhile, the other Pioneers were only staying in their airship. They were guarding any Explorers who would try to attempt in entering their airship.

The eleven Wielders were fighting against fifteen Pioneers without the aid of their Divine Stone's powers. They could easily defeat the enemy if they could use their powers.

Kenji did not expect that Akira also had his own power of magic and could also summon as Evoker (summoner of basic and weaker types of monsters and other creatures). Unlike the Element Wielder like Kenji, he could summon not just stronger Vrandolons (elemental-based monsters), but also stronger Eidolons (elemental-based gods/guardians related to a type of element).

For example, a Darkness Wielder could summon Cerberus (dark monster) as a Vrandolon and Hades (dark god) as an Eidolon. A Time and Space Wielder could summon Pegasus as a Vrandolon and Uranus as an Eidolon. The Element Wielders were good Summoners than Evokers like Akira.

Akira felt angered and envied because of the so called, "grabbers", who were always messing his life and preventing his dreams to become the new ruler of the universe… Especially Kenji, who was now being chosen by his most wanted element to become its new master and not him!

Why? What is it about them and why they're all eligible to become Element Wielders even though I am far stronger than them? They are just amateurs! They are still lacking experiences!!!

Due to his deep anger, Akira began to summon a creature who was a king phantom. "Cephei, I am summoning you to come out right now!" he cried.

The king creature appeared right after Akira summoned him. The group of Wielders was amazed to see the beauty of the said creature and they stopped.

"Wow! This beautiful phantom is a type of creature summoned by an ordinary Evoker!" said Lucky in amazement while looking at the creature. "I can't believe he can also summon though he's not a Wielder!"

"Let's see what your elements can do against me, Explorers!" said Akira in his angry voice. "Maybe those stones you have in your hand are just imitations, ESPECIALLY YOU MAXIMILLIAN! Show me what your Holy element can do!" then he quickly turned to the king phantom and pointed at the boys. "Cephei, attack them!!!"

Kenji quickly gestured his hands as his summoning command to his Vrandolon. "Here's mine, Apus of Paradise… I am summoning you now!"

he cried.

The Vrandolon, "Bird of Paradise" monster also appeared above Kenji. The monster had its white feathers on its body while its wings had their various colors. It was a huge Vrandolon!

Everyone was so amazed again to see another summoned creature before them. Now, there were two creatures that would join the battle.

The battle continued. Their fight was fierce as there were sounds of punches, kicks, and clashes of steel weapons during the fight. But the fight between Akira and Kenji was fiercer!

While Akira and Kenji were fighting ferociously, their summoned creatures were fighting above them as well. Akira would make his turn of slashing his spear to his opponent then Kenji would do the next turn. They were both swift in battle!

"Equuleus!" summoned Kenji to his another Vrandolon with his Holy element. The small, white horse appeared before him and he commanded next. "Equuleus, the Holy Attack!!!"

Equuleus rushed to Akira while evading the fireball released by the king phantom. Akira was confused, and the rushing Vrandolon quickly hit him with its magic. He yelled in pain.

"Ahhh!!!"

"Excellent, Equuleus! Now we're three against Akira and his phantom. Apus… attack him!"

Akira suddenly rattled when he turned his gaze at Kenji's Vrandolons. The others were still fighting with their opponents aggressively. Akira stepped back first, then he turned to Kenji angrily.

"Now taste this Black Flame, Akira!" shouted Kenji and he gestured again very quick. He yelled. "Holy Black Flame!"

The Black Flame quickly emerged and it moved towards Akira. Akira did not dodge sooner, so he quickly got hit and his body was now being engulfed by the black fire.

Claude was currently fighting with a female Pioneer named Cardin, which made him very defensive to her attack. He did not want to fight a female warrior, but Cardin was very importunate to face and fight him. With that, Claude had finally lost his temper and wanted to fight her back.

"Goddammit! You should be thankful that you're a woman, or if not… You're already a dead meat!" shouted Claude and he attacked.

But Cardin was a high-skilled warrior and she could defend herself without the aid of her allies. She quickly evaded Claude's attack and then she taunted.

Reinhardt cautiously attacked the skilled enemy, and he began to think of a monster that was related to his element. He knew one, it was the "three-headed monster" who was guarding the "main gate of the Underworld" called Cerberus!

He would attempt to summon Cerberus. Maybe the said Vrandolon would hear his call!

Alexander was just standing before Reinhardt still holding his weapon and he spoke to him. "Remain still, you old man… I'm gonna do something that will surprise you!" he taunted.

Reinhardt tried not to make any hand gestures and he just called his Vrandolon thru mental telepathy. Surprisingly, a huge burst of smoke engulfed before the two warriors and a deafening roar of the three-headed monster thundered. Everyone had stopped and were amazed again to see another Vrandolon of Reinhardt.

"Wow, another elemental-based monster!" Tyrone was impressed. "What dark monster is that?"

Akira was struggling to put away the Black Fire cast by Kenji on him. He was screaming in pain, while he kept on rolling on the ground as the black fire was burning him. But, Kenji was also affected when his Black Flame also burned his body. This was the sign that he still did not know on how to control the said fire. He was struggling to control his own element but it was failed.

"Curse you, Maximillian!!!" shouted Akira in pain as the Black Flame was still burning his body. "What is this thing you just did on me?!" then he still tried to command the king creature with all his might. "C-Cephei, blizzard!"

Kenji also commanded his Vrandolon while he was also burning. "A-Apus and Equuleus… You'll take care of Cephei. A-And I'll take care of Akira!"

The two Holy Vrandolons followed Kenji's command. Kenji also rolled on the ground and he was also screaming in intense pain by the Black Flame still burning him. "AHHH! Please stop it! I am commanding you to stoooopppp! AHHH, we're gonna lose the fight!!!"

A minute had passed and the battle continued. Most of the Explorers already neutralized their opponent and so as the Pioneers. As for Claude, although his opponent was a female warrior, he still defeated her.

Just as before, when Kenji ran out of his energy again then the Black Flame would slowly fade. He kept on asking the Black Fire to stop but it did not follow. The fire had consumed most of his energy before it finally ceased.

Kenji knew that this would really happen. He was not a Holy Master yet to control his powers perfectly. Akira was no longer burning and was immovable, since the Black Fire also consumed all of his energy while it was in his body. He was badly weakened, and his eyes were tightly closed. Cephei was also defeated.

The battle between the two groups had finally ended. Alexander saw his son lying on the ground still smoking hot. He hurriedly approached his son to awake him but he was no longer moving. He kept on shaking Akira's shoulder.

"Akira! Akira! My son… Akiraaaa!!!"

The Black Flame had an ability to consume the victim's energy and the victim would feel the intense burn in his body. The fire would not burn him physically, but it would consume a higher percentage of his energy in a short time than the White Flame. And, it would only put out when the victim's energy finally dissipated to 99.9%!

Kenji and Akira were both suffered the consequences. The Black Flame had devoured their human energy leaving them immovable. But Akira had suffered more since the Black Flame was focused on him.

"You will pay for what you have done to my son, Explorers!!!" yelled Alexander very angrily to the Wielders. "I will remember this day and you will pay heavy for this. You may have defeated us today, but not tomorrow!"

Lucky answered tauntingly. "Why not tomorrow? Heed what the great Confucius says: *'Don't put off until tomorrow what you can do today'*… Tomorrow maybe is already too late!"

"IDIOT! You took away all of my son's elements and shuttered all of his dreams, you grabbers!!!"

"No way!"

The Pioneers rode back to their huge airship and Alexander carried his unconscious son in his arms. The group of Wielders stepped back as the airship revved the engine.

"Hey, you cowards! Where are you going? Come back here, heeeyyy!!!"

said Tyrone.

"We will all meet again in our next fight, Explorers. We will beat you next time!" said Alexander angrily as he was moving back to their airship carrying his son.

"You said it wrong, you cowards!!!"

"See you again next time, Element Wielders!"

The Pioneer's airship slowly hovered in the air and then it flew away in Bondore. Later, Kenji slowly opened his eyes when he noticed that the Pioneers were all gone now. He looked around very weakly, as he was still lying on the ground.

"W-Where's Akira now? O-Our fight is not over yet..." he said hoarsely.

"They've already left. He said you're too fantastic so he did not want to fight you anymore," said Lucky jokingly.

"W-What? W-What does he mean by that? Did he give up already?"

"Yup."

"T-That's too impossible... They are highly trained with their special skills and they will not back out that easily, Lucky..."

"Yes, indeed. Your Black Fire consumed all of Akira's energy when you fought each other. You see, he couldn't even open his eyes... He was weakened very badly!"

"R-Really? I didn't know that," Kenji was in disbelief.

"We all saw him weakened. He's down and out!"

Isagani added in amazement. "But Kenji, you're amazing! You know how to use your power very well. You seem like a Holy Wielder Master now!"

"Correct!" agreed Shingue as he showed off his thumbs-up gesture.

Kenji blushed in shyness. "T-Thanks, but I was also got burned by own fire remember?"

Silence. The boys turned to Reinhardt next.

"Reinhardt, we thought you didn't know how to summon a Vrandolon... but you've called one successfully!" Jon was impressed.

Reinhardt smiled as he was scratching his head and answered. "I just remembered one monster who belongs in the Underworld, Jon. So I'm sure it's a dark monster... That's why."

The Wielders thought that the old woman had already left Bondore before the Pioneers came, but she remained in the town invisible after she vanished and hid herself away from battle. Then, she re-appeared before the boys.

"*LOLA!*"

"I was watching every bit of your actions with the Pioneers earlier, my sons…" said the old woman still in her true form. "I just hid myself and remained invisible to your eyes so the enemies would not feel my presence. Your skills and abilities, combined with your elements will be improved if you're going to read this book I am holding right now," then she showed off a very thick book about the elements, magics, and other powers before the boys. "This is the only book that will teach you the proper use of the element you are possessing: the Element Book. It explains everything about each of the elements' information, the right words you must say in summoning Vrandolons and Eidolons, the strengths and weaknesses of each element, and so on."

The Wielders moved closer to the old woman with their curious faces. They were eager to read it and find out what was in-stored for them. The characters written on it were small, and there were symbols and sketches portrayed on each pages.

"T-The letters are too small, and the words are all too deep!" said Clio and he joked. "Looks like I need to use a dictionary while reading it!"

The old woman smiled. "You're no longer needing it, lad. If you find it hard to understand the words written on it, then that's the secret made by King Jethro himself. You see, he made it that way to safeguard the sanctity of this book. No one will understand what is written on it specially if this book falls to the hand of an enemy. Only those people who deserve to have this book shall be given by King Jethro himself. The wisdom to understand every bit of known knowledge is written on this book, even the information about the known gods and goddesses in King Jethro's time are also inscribed."

Cyan was delighted. "That's good to hear then! So the next time we'll use our powers, we no longer need to make nonsense guesses anymore! That's totally great!"

"Yes, you are right there, son."

The boys were impressed. "Wooowww!"

The old woman approached Kenji who was now leaning his back on Claude's chest and she handed over the book to him. "The Holy Wielder should be the safekeeper of this book. I shall entrust to you this book and keep it safe the way it shall be treated. Please keep the book highly confidential to all non-Wielders."

Claude asked in wonder. "Um, *lola*... Why is it the Holy Wielder should be the only book keeper? Aren't we trustworthy enough to be the keeper of it sometimes? After all, we're Wielders too, right?"

Shingue agreed. "He's right, *lola*. Do we look untrustworthy to you even though the elements of King Jethro have chosen us?"

The old woman smiled sweetly. "It doesn't mean that I do not trust you, but it is because the Holy Wielder is the leader of all the Element Wielders..." then she nodded. "It is King Jethro himself who wrote this book and he wishes that way. Remember, he is the former possessor of your elements, so it is more appropriate to make the Holy Wielder the only keeper of this book. That is his rule. And to you as his chosen Element Wielders, you must use his book with an utmost respect."

The boys understood about it so they all nodded. Kenji was now holding their "Element Book" when he thanked the elder. "Anyway *lola*, thank you so much for this once again..." then he nodded with a smile.

Silence. Afterwards...

Everyone was back again to their jets. The two jets were zooming in the air at their high speeds freely while Kenji was reading the Element Book weakly by Reinhardt's request. "On guard before the gate sits Cerberus, the three-headed, dragon-tailed dog, who permits all the spirits to enter, but none to return..."

Reinhardt was currently piloting Shingue's 14JK jet still wondering where they should head next. "By the way, are we still going to DDE today? What do you think?"

"Still feeling energetic 'til now, guys?" asked Clio. "If ya gonna ask me, I still wanna travel more! I don't want to go back home yet!"

Everyone answered together. "Yeah!"

"Excellent! Good answer boys," said Reinhardt. "But we have a problem. Our jet is now running out of fuel. We're not gonna make it to reach DDE in a longer distance!"

His fellow UEs cried happily as if just kids. "Yeehaaaww! The jet is now running out of fuel..."

Everyone laughed.

"Hello Reiher (Reinhardt), we brought an extra fuel before we left the mansion!" joked Shingue. "Would you like me to bring it out right away then?"

"Okay, no problem," said Reinhardt while shaking his head. "We're still not gonna make it to reach the DDE base."

"And why again?!"

"Our jet is overloaded. It cannot hold our weight long enough to reach the said base."

The boys had already forgotten that their jet should only had a maximum number of five passengers. Yet, they still acted like innocents when they answered goofily. "Oh yeah, we thought we're just kids!!!"

They all laughed again. The sky went dark, signing that there would be a bad weather coming.

"Hey Genji, do you think we're getting closer to Camoria now? We need to move across the country first and travel in hours more before we'll reach the DDE base! Our jet is overloaded and it looks like the weather is getting bad. I'm afraid there's something that might happen to all of us here," said Tyrone to Genji.

Genji was unsure to answer. "O-Okay... I am not sure of it... If you think that the jet can't travel more then we'll go back home to our safety instead. Let us cancel our travel to the destination first. The other jet's wing is already damaged, so it is better to be safe than sorry!"

Cyan smiled at Genji. "Nice logical thinking, Genji!" he joked.

"Okay, let's cancel our flight to the DDE mansion right away," said Kenji as he was looking up the sky. "The sky is getting dark and we need to ensure the safety for each of us. Let's go back to the UE mansion!"

Everyone agreed. The line coming from the E47J jet answered. "Roger!"

"Firstly, let's read the book and learn on how we can adapt ourselves in using our powers properly. While we're still free from our assignments, let's try to summon the beast. So when we go back to the DDE base, we can show our powers to them so they will promote us to DDE class!" said Isagani on the other line.

The two aviators maximized the speed of the HawkEyes as they hurriedly flew back to UE base. It would rain strong sooner, and they needed to travel quite a distance before they would reach their base!

It was less than an hour when they had finally reached the sea where Kenji took his second test. "Yes, we're almost near to the UE mansion. I can see the open sea over there!" said Claude happily while looking down the jet window.

"Good thing we made it to go back home safely," said Isagani. "The rain is not falling in this area yet."

They were now traveling across the sea when the two HawkEyes suddenly began to malfunction. The cockpit control system had bagged down including the auto-pilot system… as if something was controlling them!

"Ah! What's that?" asked everyone in shock.

"Oh no! The jet seems to be malfunctioning. I can't control it anymore!" said Reinhardt in shock. "What's going on again this time?"

Lucky spoke on the other line. "Our jet is out of control! What happened to these jets? We're going down… We're going down!!!"

The two jets were about to crash. Everyone cried on the top of their voices. The two pilots tried to maneuver the jets to avoid the sudden impact in the water. The HawkEyes had made their final approach and they crashed into the water. Everyone on board got out of the jets and they scrambled together towards the shore. No one got wounded nor injured. Then, the lightning struck.

The Wielders had reached the shore. They were feeling dizzy after the crash. Their visions were spinning around and they were losing their balance. Isagani suddenly threw up after feeling nauseated.

"Geez, this is so bad! Why did the jets suddenly malfunction when we almost reached our base? We need to move fast, we have a long way to go," said Kenji annoyingly. "The rain is coming!"

Suddenly, they heard a laughter and an incoming footsteps in the distance. They turned away.

"W-Who's that?!" asked Jon.

A stranger in his shining armor appeared before the Wielders. Everyone was mum when he spoke to them in his serious voice. "I must admit that I was the one who did the incident, but please accept my apology…"

"Dammit, how rude you are!" shouted Claude at the stranger. "Are you simply saying that you have to crash our jets just to show and brag us your stunning shining armor? Yes, we like the costume, but you are SO rude! Who are you? What do you want from us?"

The armored stranger was staring intensely at them. "There is only one thing I need from one of you! My name is Prince Xandir Maximus with a task of taking the Holy element from you. Which among you is the Holy Wielder???"

38 PRINCE MAXIMUS

The group of Wielders was all facing the unknown man whom they just met today. They did not know the stranger's purpose, especially to Kenji… whom Maximus was the only one he was looking for.

"Which of you is the Holy Wielder?!" asked Maximus again. "Bring him forth to me, I need him right now!"

"What do you want from me, sir?" asked Kenji who moved before Maximus and faced him. "My name is Kenji, but my real name is Maximillian. I am the chosen Holy Wielder of King Jethro."

Maximus turned to him and said. "Ah, so you're the one… Maximillian, that name… I know a lot more about you."

Kenji's eyes wide-opened when Cyan asked. "So what do you really want from him?"

"Yield the Holy element and I will do no harm," answered Maximus.

Kenji was shocked. "And why? In the name of King Jethro, this element is mine and no one can take it away from me!"

The lightning struck and it hit the ground. The sky had dimmed and the strong rain began to fall. Maximus still did not want them to go.

"Do not force me to harm you!" said Maximus when he lifted his hand to cast his magic on the boys.

"Ah, wait, wait! What's wrong with you, Your Highness? What are you gonna do?!" asked Kenji nervously. "We are not looking for any trouble. We do not intend to fight you… H-Hold on!"

Maximus still cast his water magic and a huge burst of water came out in his hand. He released it in another direction when it hit a tree and it fell towards where the Wielders were standing. The group quickly avoided the falling tree and they turned to Maximus angrily.

"I knew it! You're a bastard type of a prince!" said Claude annoyingly. "If you're really looking for a fight, then we'll fight you right away!"

"Don't Claude," stopped Kenji as he turned to Claude. "We are not going to fight him! He is not our enemy, Claude," then he turned again to Maximus. "We will not fight you, Your Highness…"

Maximus smiled seriously. "Very well then, so you're going to give me your Holy element instead?"

"No… And we're not going to deal with you any longer. We're going home…"

Maximus got angry. "Stop! Or I will kill you!"

Kenji lifted his hands and he shook his head in disagreement. "W-We'll fight next time we meet again, sir. We need to go home now!"

"What??? I am still talking to you!" Maximus lifted his hand again while looking at Kenji angrily. "Don't turn your back on me when I'm talking to you! Very well then, face me… Aquarius!!!" he summoned. The blue Vrandolon suddenly appeared before them.

"Kenji, he's also a Wielder!" said Lucky surprisingly. "He can summon a Vrandolon too. Perhaps, he is a Wielder of the Water element!"

Kenji was surprised too. "I guess you're right! If he is, then why does he still want to take the Holy element from me?!"

"You're wrong," said Maximus. "This is just a power of magic and I am not a Wielder. That is why I am taking that element from you! AQUARIUS, strike them with your Gigantic Waves!" he commanded to his Vrandolon.

The Vrandolon followed, and a big volume of water splashed before them which made the group get washed away from the prince.

"Darn, why now?!" said Claude annoyingly.

Kenji wasted no time and he also summoned Apus again. The Vrandolon appeared, and the two monsters fought to each other.

"No more fancy moves Maximillian, it's just you and me… alone!" said the prince to the Wielders then he turned to Kenji. "Holy element is what I want from you. If you want to give up your life for the element, your wish is my command."

"No way!"

"Yaaahhh!!!" Maximus rushed towards Kenji and he attacked. Kenji quickly dodged his attack but Maximus followed the attack. He was fighting only with his bare hands thinking that Kenji was an inexperienced Wielder, but Kenji was attacking the prince with his Kali. The prince was attacking the young warrior very aggressively. He kept on pounding and kicking, followed by a sideway swat but Kenji kept on dodging his attacks while looking relaxed.

Kenji had made his turn to retaliate using his speed and agility so he knocked Maximus with his staff. Maximus felt embarrassed when he sprawled on the ground. He noticed Kenji turned to his back, so he saw the chances and quickly attacked him. Kenji evaded his attack very easily, but there was something seemed strange with Maximus… He was not quite as good and agile as Kenji. He was not even as tough as the Pioneers, because he already got too many hits from the Holy Wielder.

The group of Wielders noticed something wrong with the prince. They noticed the color of his eyes were not normal. His movements were so weird as if he was being controlled by someone. His actions were very strange. Kenji noticed that how many times he was knocking the poor prince down, the prince would stand on his feet and attack him again. Kenji could knock Maximus that easily.

Lucky was very serious in watching the fight between Kenji and Maximus, while Claude was laughing out loud at the prince as his taunt.

"A-HA-HA-HA-HA! What a weakling you are, dude! You dared yourself to fight Kenji alone, but I can tell that you're just a piece of cake for him!!!" teased Claude over Maximus.

"Claude… aren't you noticing something to Maximus?" asked Lucky to Claude seriously. "He is acting very strange…"

"Hah, no way! Maybe he's really that weakling, man!"

"Look at him… I can see in his face like he is being controlled by someone. Come to think of it, no one else wants to take the Holy element from Kenji but only Akira, right?"

"That is also the same thing I am observing to that man, Lucky…" said Reinhardt.

"Good thing you're noticing it too."

"Oh, come on guys!" said Claude in disbelief. "He's just a weakling really!"

"I don't think so."

Maximus was overwhelmed by Kenji as he fell down the ground with his bloody lips. While as for Kenji, he was standing right before him without any wounds and scratches in his body, except his right cheek. The Vrandolon Aquarius was also defeated by Apus.

"Y-You lost…" said Kenji looking concerned at Maximus who was sprawled on the white sand.

The Water goddess suddenly appeared when she went out from the prince' body. She rebuked the innocent prince very angrily while he was still sprawled. "You are a worthless prince! I should have known this, that you should still remain with your father and imprison there forever!"

Everyone was shocked to see the goddess looking very angry towards the innocent prince. "S-See? I told you, Claude… That prince is being possessed by someone, and that's her!" said Lucky to Claude. "Now you know, Claude…"

"You there… That means that this prince is not our enemy," said Kenji looking at the goddess. "But you!"

"How I wish that I didn't bring this cursed prince in this world if I knew how weakling he really was! Curse you, Maximus!!!" shouted the goddess as she was flying away from them but she stopped for a moment. She turned to Kenji in her glaring eyes. "I will take that Holy element from you sooner, you'll see!" then she disappeared into the Wielders' eyes.

"Hey, come back here!" cried Kenji.

The poor prince had lost his consciousness after the Water Goddess went out from his body. His body shone when his warrior-like armor suit returned to the dirty tuxedo suit he was once wearing. His real appearance returned.

"Poor prince," said Kenji looking at Maximus worriedly. "He's hurt…"

"You see, that mean, blue lady controlled him and put his life in danger. She's a wicked!" said Clio.

"Let's help this innocent prince. He's has nothing to do with our fight, but I hurt him very badly…" said Kenji looking at his colleagues.

"Are you saying that we're going to take him home with us, huh?" asked Shingue in wonder and he joked. "Oh no, we're putting his life worse than this, Kenji… Y-You know, the 'boyfriend hunter', Margot will see him there!"

"I'll take care of him," said Kenji smiling. "There is something I would like to know about him."

The group returned to the UE mansion and they reported what were transpired during their travel to DDE base. Then, they introduced Genji, Cyan, and Maximus who was still unconscious and Elijah was glad to meet the three.

The Explorer uniforms of Kenji and Claude were finally done. A UE handed over their new uniforms and asked them to wear it now.

The group took Maximus to the clinic. They gently laid the prince on the bed, and Kenji asked them to leave the clinic for a moment. The group went to the laboratory just to have a chitchat with Elijah. Later, the doctors were done in treating the prince and now he was resting.

"Margot is still not around yet and the others too. It is better to keep that man away from Margot," Elijah was referring to Maximus. "But I will inform everyone in this mansion that you're the chosen Element Wielders of King Jethro now. Congratulations!"

Kenji was patiently waited for Maximus to recover from the wounds and regained his consciousness again. He was curious and eager to know something behind this prince's mysterious personality. Later, he heard a voice calling him from outside the clinic. "Kenji, do you wanna eat now?"

Kenji shook his head. "Later…"

"Just come in the dining hall whenever you feel hungry, okay?"

Kenji did not answer. He was staring at the face of Maximus. "He's getting better now. I need to know about him."

The evening had come when Maximus finally regained his consciousness. The weather was still bad. He slowly opened his eyes and looked around the clinic. "Where am I?" he asked.

Kenji greeted the prince. "Good evening, you are in the UE mansion. We brought you here to help you. You know that? UE… Ultimate Explorer!"

Maximus was shocked to hear it from Kenji. 'W-What did you say? Explorer?"

"Yes, you're in UE mansion. Our base. We live here."

Maximus noticed Kenji's cheek with a bandage. "Was it me who did that to you?" he asked frowning in his low voice. "I-If I have done something that hurts you, my apologies."

Kenji pointed his cheek and smiled. "Oh, you mean this? Nah, that's okay. It's just a single scratch, Your Highness. You had nothing to do with our fight earlier."

The group of Element Wielders was now in the library to read the Element Book they borrowed from Kenji before they left the clinic. They were reading each of the book's contents one by one. They browsed and noted the "summoning commands" that they should say if they were summoning their Vrandolons during the battle.

"For a time she kept his birth secret from her father, but it became increasingly difficult to do so in the narrow limits of that bronze house and finally one day the little boy – his name was Perseus – was discovered by his grandfather," said Claude as he was reading about his Eidolon, Perseus in the Element Book. His fellow Element Wielders were just listening to him.

Meanwhile, at the clinic.

"May I ask you something weird, what is your name again aside from your real name as Maximillian?" asked the innocent prince to Kenji formally.

"Kenji."

"So Kenji, are you an Explorer now?" Maximus was not smiling.

"Yes."

"I would like to admit something to you… I am a former member of Reminescence…"

"Ah!" Kenji was very shocked to hear this from Maximus. "If so, then you are one of them who killed my father, Alex Foster!" he said in his high voice. "You imprisoned my father in your territory and tortured him brutally! You ruthlessly whipped him, wounded him, and even pounded him with your killing hands and then… you threw him away to the cursed river and let him drown to his death--"

"It was the Reminescence indeed who killed your father, but I was not with them."

"I don't believe you!"

Maximus glared at Kenji. "I don't want to go back in Reminescence anymore… Though I am the son of their leader. They are all merciless!"

"No way! You are one with those--"

"I SAID I AM NOT WITH THEM WHEN THEY KILLED YOUR FATHER!!!" shouted Maximus angrily to Kenji in his sharp looking eyes. "One day, you will learn more about me, Kendi, errr… Kenji!" he suddenly rattled when he mistakenly called Kenji's name. "I was able to escape from persecution at the hands of my own father, a king of Reminescence… With the help of the Water Goddess who possessed me."

"You escaped?"

"And therefore, I agreed to join the Water Goddess after she saved me from my father's atrocity and I was innocent to her wicked plan. She used me to get the Holy element from you, because she wanted to become the new ruler of this world and possess the ultimate power."

Kenji did not answer.

"D-Do you understand me?!"

Kenji only glanced at Maximus as his answer.

"Mister Kenji! I want to hear your answer. Do you understand? Answer me!"

"Yes, I understand you," answered Kenji in his calm voice.

"I have to admit that it was the Reminescence indeed who killed Alex Foster, but I was not with them that day… That is on the record! Now, if you want to find the Reminescence and take revenge, then I won't blame you. I am not going to stop you because I don't care about them anymore. Do you understand, Kenja, errr… Kenie… I mean, Kenji!"

Kenji just stooped down his head.

"Mister Kenji, I want to hear your answer!"

"Y-Yes, I understand, Your Highness… I understand!"

"Good. So what now?"

"There is something I want to know from you, Prince Maximus…"

"What is it?"

"When did you left your kingdom along with that Water Goddess?!"

Maximus turned away from Kenji and he shook his head. "I do not remember… Even my mind was controlled by that wicked goddess so I can't recall any. I'm sorry…"

Kenji stooped down his head again. "Well, it's okay. So, do you know anything about the Water element?"

Maximus turned back his gaze to Kenji and still frowning. "Yes, at least just a little."

"Maximus, I'm sorry that I accused you immediately about my father's death. I do not expect that the Reminescence prince has his guts to abandon his kingdom and forsake his own father."

"So what's the problem with that?"

Kenji lifted his head again and looked straight at Maximus. "W-Why don't you just come with us instead?"

Maximus was surprised.

"Its okay if you want to join with us! Besides, the Explorers are righteous warriors."

Maximus stroked his chin and looked at Kenji from head to toe. His voice was calm and he asked curiously. "What is the prime objective of the Explorers?"

"Um... well... We are the chosen keepers of all King Jethro's powers..."

"That's it?"

"Um... a lot more."

"What else?"

"We are also his guardians..."

"That's all?"

"Y-Yes..." Kenji faltered.

Silence. Kenji was the next one to ask. "Maximus, I've heard from you earlier that you know something about me. What are those? And, where did you hear those things, huh?"

"Oh, about that... I've learned it from your father before he was killed... As well as from the Reminescence."

Kenji nodded. "What did they say?"

"The Reminescence knows more about you than I do. It is because your name has something to do with the history of Reminescence and I have reached that history during my very young age," said Maximus and he stooped down his head. "Maximillian... that name, is the only one... the true king of Reminescence..."

Back to the Element Wielders.

The group of Element Wielders was still in the library, still reading the Element Book about the things they wanted to know with their elements and their powers.

"Hey Cyan, according to the book, who is your Eidolon?" asked Jon to Cyan.

"It's here. It's Ceres," answered Cyan.

"Who is she?"

"According to the book, Demeter is her name in Latin, while the other one is Ceres. She is the 'Goddess of Corn', who is the daughter of Cronus and Rhea. She has a twin brother, and his name is Dionysus. His another name is Bacchus, and he is the 'God of Wine'. By the way, which of you who has an Eidolon of Dionysus?"

Shingue raised his hand. "He is my Eidolon, and according to the book he is also the 'God of Fertility and Ecstasy'…"

"Wooowww…" they were all amazed.

Lucky's stomach suddenly growled, signing that he was getting hungry. "Hey guys, I'm getting hungry… How about you?"

Tyrone answered with pride. "Well don't you worry, Isagani and I can cook for you. After all, the weather is cold today so it's good to have a coffee too, right?"

"Alright, let's take our dinner now so we'll get back to our studies later," said Genji and he handed over the book to Claude gently. "Claude, please return this book to my brother in the clinic. I will help these guys and at the same time to have a tour in this mansion. I'm so excited to wander around your rich home!"

Claude took the book given by Genji and he nodded. "Alright, your twin brother and I will see you later. Have fun with the tour. Bye!"

"Thank you. See you later!" Genji left, along with his fellow Wielders.

The group had left the library when Claude walked back straight to the clinic to return the book to Kenji. He reached the clinic door when he heard a low conversation coming from the inside of the clinic.

"The innocent prince has finally awakened…" said Claude to himself. "Kenji is talking to him."

Claude gently knocked the door when the two heard his knock and they stopped talking for a moment.

"Knock, knock," said Claude while knocking. "May I come in for a while?"

"Oh, it's Claude," Kenji stood on his chair and he opened the door. He asked Claude to come inside the clinic. "What is it, Claude?"

"Um, here… We're returning the book to you now. By the way, we're going to take our dinner soon," said Claude and he handed over the book to Kenji.

"Oh, how soon? Right now?"

"Yes, Tyrone and Isagani are cooking our dinner now."

Kenji held the Element Book in his arm and then he turned to Maximus with a smile. "Maximus, thank you for telling me something about you. We're going to take our dinner right now and we'll bring you some foods here to eat, okay? We're starving actually…"

Maximus was feeling shy, but his face was still frowning. "Ah, don't mind me. I'm not hungry anyway, so please don't bother…"

"Don't be shy, Your Highness… You're not our enemy anymore. Help me avenge my father's death and bring him justice. An eye for an eye, a tooth for a tooth. Life is what they took and life is what they'll pay! Show me the way to your kingdom and we'll dare to face them personally!"

"But I don't want to return to our kingdom anymore. And Kenji, I do not know the way back to our palace. The Water Goddess took me astray in this world of yours! Do you understand me?"

Claude was mum. He wanted to say something to Maximus but he couldn't. Instead, he just asked Kenji to leave the clinic with him and left the innocent prince alone.

39 DEITY AND PEACE

The two left Prince Maximus alone in the clinic. Claude put his hand over Kenji's shoulder, then he led Kenji to his front going to their fellow Explorers.

Meanwhile in Pioneer…

The Pioneer did not expect that they would see and meet Isidra along their way. She was mounted on a unicorn named Meru, and they were both in their disguise. Good thing the Pioneers did not recognize her because of her different appearance.

The Pioneer lowered their airship and they immediately stopped an unknown woman. Isidra also saw them, and she turned quickly, rattled by their presence.

"The Pioneer!" cried Isidra looking anxious. "Our enemies who will kill my sons!"

The unicorn answered. "Do not worry, dear fairy. They will never identify you anymore because of your different appearance. They will never find out that you're Isidra."

Isidra was nodding while looking at the Pioneer. "T-They're calling us."

She was worried and nervous, but she asked the unicorn to come closer to the airship. Akira came out from the airship first, followed by the fellow Pioneers.

Akira was already recovered and seemed to have regained his energy again when he spoke to an unknown woman. "It looks like you're alone. What is your name?"

Isidra responded immediately. "Angeles, sir."

"Angeles?" asked Akira. "And where is Angeles from?"

Isidra responded once again. "From… I'm from Dakar, sir."

"Dakar?" asked Akira unbelievably. "That's too far from here? How'd you get here, Miss Angeles?"

"I ran away from there," answered Isidra then she stopped for a moment to look at Akira from head to toe. She noticed that Akira was already a young man, and she knew that he and her twin sons were in the same age. She thought to herself. "That means, my twins are grown-ups as well," she smiled.

"So why did you run away?" asked Akira to Isidra.

"To find the elemen--" Isidra accidentally slipped her tongue and the Pioneers heard her. The group was shocked.

"W-What?! Are you an element hunter?" asked Akira surprisingly. "Huh?"

"Ahm… W-Well…"

"Answer me, Angeles."

Isidra did not answer.

"Nevermind," Akira chuckled in mockingly way. "Do you know that there are no more elements here you can find in this world anymore? Because… they all have been taken already by those so called, Explorer grabbers! My elements-to-be!!!"

"Explorers?"

"Yes! Explorers, Angeles. And do you know that I just came in from a fight? I just finished a fight with Kenji Foster today! Do you know who that Kenji is? Maximillian? That idiot is my worst element-grabber ever! You see, my elements-to-be are in the hands of the Explorers already!"

"Maximillian Foster!" Isidra was surprised when she heard the name mentioned by Akira and thought to herself. "That means… my twins are still alive," then she smiled again and spoke to Akira in excitement. "The son--"

She accidentally slipped her tongue again. She was eager to ask Akira everything about her son, but she was afraid that the Pioneers might perceive her intention of asking.

Akira spoke in wonder. "Maximillian? The son of… He's the son of Alex Foster. That idiot!"

"Is he an Explorer?" asked Isidra and she could not control her eagerness again. "Maximillian... My son--"

Akira looked at her and became conscious after she kept on slipping her tongue many times, so he asked her in wonder. "Why do you ask about him? Do you know Maximillian Foster? Yes, he's an Explorer. And that idiot already took all the elements that should definitely be mine alone!" then he turned away and got mad. "I will take all those elements from him and become the new king of the universe!"

"No, don't!" Isidra quickly covered her mouth after stopping Akira by accident. "Um…"

Akira looked at her intensely. "And why don't you want me to do that?!"

"Um… Well… You should, um…" Isidra faltered while she was thinking fast on what to answer as an excuse.

Akira was still looking at her intensely and he came closer to her. "Tell me, are you siding with the Explorers, Angeles? Answer me!"

Isidra was scared to do another mistake again so she just shook her head and nervously spoke to Akira unrelated to his question. "Mister… errr…" she called. "Do not worry… I-I have found a long-missing element that I am carrying with me right now. G-Good thing your enemies have not yet found this element before…"

Meru was very surprised to hear what Isidra said that should be kept as their secret. The unicorn's eyes were wide-opened, but she did not show her surprising reaction to Akira.

Akira gaped in surprise. "What the--! You still have found an element here? Where did you get it? I can't believe that there's still an element left here that those idiots have not obtained yet! W-What is that element called?"

Isidra pulled out the last Divine Stone given to her by the fairy old woman (the elder Kenji met in Dakar) after they met elsewhere. The last long-missing Divine Stone was called, "Divine Stone of Highlord", which was almost the same as the Holy element. "I will give to you this stone I've found just as long as you will tell me the way to the Explorers' base. S-So you can also become a Wielder too just like them, right *(Please forgive me Lady Vanice… But I must do this for the sake of my sons. I am going to surrender the last stone to this Pioneer for a while, but later on I will recover it once that I have finally found my children!)*?"

Isidra handed the sacred stone to Akira when he quickly grabbed it from her hand. Then, he immediately agreed to her request due to his overexcitement. For a while, his attention was caught by the unexpected stone in his hand and never realized why she exchanged the stone for asking about the Explorers. "Thank you so much for this, Angeles! But why are you going to their base?" he asked while he was examining the stone carefully to see if it was real or not.

Isidra did not respond. Akira continued. "Alright, I know the way… but just the DDE base…"

Isidra quickly nodded. "Yes, that's okay *(I am really so sorry, Lady Vanice… Just for the sake of my family!)*!"

The Divine Stone suddenly reacted when it felt Akira's presence so it finally transformed itself to its true form as an element. It was the element of "Deity and Peace", and the element itself slowly entered inside Akira's chest that he did not expect.

"I can't believe that this element of King Jethro will choose this young man to become its new possessor," thought Isidra to herself. "Why did the element choose him despite of being the Explorers' nemesis?"

"Camoria is one of the closest countries from the DDE base. It's way too far from here by horse, even if from that rich country. You still need to travel in a long distance from Camoria before you get there."

"Well, about Kenji? Or Maximillian?" asked Isidra. "Is that man you're talking about staying in that base?"

Akira had already forgotten to find out the reason of Isidra's interest to Kenji because of his overexcitement by being another Element Wielder of King Jethro. He put his hands on his hips and gladly answered. "Oh… Kenji is a UE Explorer and not a DDE. I don't know the exact distance of getting there from here, but you can move straight along this path and you will be there. By the way, it is also far to get there by horse."

Isidra was very excited to see her sons again so she nodded. "That's okay! Thank you, mister…" then she stroked Meru's hair and spoke to her. "Let's go."

The unicorn whined out loud first and then they left the Pioneers. The horse ran swiftly away from them when Akira shouted out loud to thank Isidra once again. "Thank you very much for this, Angeles! I really mean it!!!"

The two already went away from them when Meru worriedly spoke to Isidra. "Isidra, what have you done?! Why did you give one of King Jethro's powers to those enemies after Lady Vanice entrusted you to keep it on her behalf? You are weak to such temptation! You broke her trust of keeping the last stone safe. You should never give it to others especially strangers!" she was referring to the old woman from Bondore who was now turned to a fairy.

"I know, I betrayed her and broke her trust, Meru… But I really can't help it… I only did that because I am so desperate to meet my family again!"

"That young man did not give you enough information that would lead you to your family! I can't believe you exchanged the last Divine Stone for nothing, Isidra. I am sure that King Zalan will be angry at you again and he'll forbid you to come back in this world forever! Perhaps he is watching us right now, and he is furious to what he just witnessed. With that, you will never get a chance to see your sons anymore!"

Isidra stooped down her head. She seemed to be aware of what would be King Zalan's next punishment to her this time. She felt guilty to what she had done but she was ready for any consequences. What more important was the moment that she had been waiting for which was now within her grasp.

"J-Just… Please don't get too noisy, Meru. Never tell to anyone what I have done today please… especially to Lord Zalan!"

"You can run but you cannot hide, Isidra. You have made another worst mistake again. The lord has caught you!"

Isidra became worried again. "N-Nevermind… Come on, let's go to the Explorers base now. My sons are still alive! Yes, they are all still alive!"

Meanwhile…

The Pioneers were all delighted to see their leader as the another chosen Wielder of Deity and Peace element. Akira was very glad when he lifted his hands and proudly announced. "I finally make my revenge. The karma has come! I am blessed with the last element that the Explorers have not yet obtained. I am one of the Element Wielders now!"

Alexander was happy for his son so he clapped his hands along with the Pioneers. "Excellent, Akira. I am so happy for you! Your strength and power is now equal to those idiots!" then he started to wonder about Isidra. "But I am wondering about that woman's purpose of going to the Explorers base, Akira. What do you think she wants from them?"

The weather was still bad and the rain was pouring. Akira only ignored his father and he cried out loud. "Angeles… THANK YOU VERY, VERY MUCH!!!"

Back to UE mansion.

The group of Element Wielders was now having their dinner when Elijah hurriedly approached them. "Hey guys, Margot, Marion, Vamir, and the others have just arrived home tonight! I don't want Margot to disturb your prince so you should keep him away, okay? You know how Margot really likes handsome guys!"

"Oh no… Kenji, your wife is here now!" said Shingue to Kenji in a jest.

Genji quickly reacted while he was eating. "Wait, is *kuya* Kenji already married? Wow, congratulations brother! So who is this lucky lady of yours, hm?"

Kenji suddenly choked as he was chewing his food after hearing it from his twin brother. "UMM… WATER… WATER PLEEEEAASSEEE!!!"

Claude quickly offered a glass of water to Kenji and Kenji took it. He was coughing while he was drinking it, and then later he spoke to Genji. "You know brother, it isn't true that I'm already married. Shingue just wanted to make fun of me that's all."

"Oh, so who is this person they were talking about as your wife? I thought you're already married."

Kenji took a bite of his waffle first then he answered. "It's nothing, brother really! His name is Margot. DID YOU HEAR THAT, BROTHER? HE?!"

Genji laughed. "O-Oh, I see… Okay!" then he ate.

"Oh no, Genji…" called Lucky to Genji. "You'd better watch out because he has a crush on your brother! Maybe he will fall in love with you next since you and Kenji are identical!"

"Hah, he's right dude!" Tyrone agreed teasingly. "I'm afraid you might lose your freedom when he sees you today!"

"Why is that? Is Margot really that dangerous?" asked Genji in wonder while drinking *lambanog* (coconut wine).

Reinhardt chuckled. "As in the most dangerous entity across the galaxy!"

Everyone laughed out loud and then they continued to eat. Silence.

"I'm not going to introduce you to Margot, brother…" said Kenji as he chuckled. "Oh, you too Cyan. You're new here too."

Cyan took a bite first and then he nodded in disagreement. "Hmpt, I'm not interested to meet that woman…"

Claude answered. "That is not a woman, mister! He's a man, but with a heart of a woman! When you see him for the first time, he is always wearing a makeup. But still, he looks like a real man!"

Everyone laughed again.

Later, Marion, Vamir and Margot came inside the dining room to take their dinner with their fellow Explorers. Margot was overjoyed to see the boys eating together and he was giggling so much!

"Oh dear, I see a lot of cute guys in here having their dinner tonight!" said Margot giggling and then he saw the two men that were just new to his eyes. "Whoa! And you even brought me home these new two cuties for me. How sweet of you!"

Shingue got easily mad to Margot's flirtatious actions again. "Please keep silence, Margot! Our dinner is over because of you."

Margot wondered. "You done eating now?"

"We're enjoying our food until you came in. But now, we suddenly lost our appetite!"

Elijah secretly winked at Kenji and he moved closer to him. "Kenji, the prince…" he whispered.

Kenji winked back at Elijah as his answer. "I know that… Thank you!"

"Boys?" called Shingue annoyingly while looking around the room since Margot was a total spoiler of his life. "I am feeling uncomfortable right now… I thought I am stuffed, but yet I'm still hungry! The whole environment is getting stinky after someone just came in tonight!" he hinted about Margot. "Anyway, let's go boys!"

The ten boys got the message. They looked at each other first and then they all agreed to leave. "Ah, yes… yes," they stood on their seats and took their meals. They were about to leave the dining room when the three newcomers wondered.

"H-Hey, where're you all going?" asked Vamir and Marion.

"You know, Vamir and Marion," Lucky turned to them carrying his own meal. "We'll move in the other room instead to continue our happy dinner. Somebody in here is messing up our bonding right now. Boys of the same feather flock together, right?"

Vamir and Marion looked at each other first and they smiled. "He's right, Marion. I'd love to have a dinner bond with them without an alien messing with me tonight!" said Vamir in tauntingly way since Margot was also a pain in his life ever since. "Alright, Marion and I will join you on your dinner too! Right, Marion?" and then he gestured a thumbs-up.

The naughty kid agreed and he nodded. "You're right there, *kuya* Vamir! We will join your dinner, *kuya* Lucky. 'Coz as far as we're concerned, we don't even want this jerk to come along with us in our dinner tonight!"

Margot got pissed off. "What did you just call me, you naughty little scumbag?!"

"Go ahead, Vamir and Marion. Take your meal now and we'll move along to the other room," said Claude to the two. "Let's go!"

Margot quickly turned to them with his hands on his hips. "So where will my husbands go right now?!"

"We will just continue our dinner elsewhere and leave you here alone," answered Clio. "We going to discuss something that is for boys company only, okay? Gotta go."

"B-Boys company?" Margot suddenly giggled while he was starting to imagine about him being surrounded by these boys who were killing each other in order to win his heart. Then he giggled once again. "Eeee! I love such topic. Please let me come with you, boyfriends!"

Claude answered in a mockingly way. "Heh, leave us alone. If not, we will ask Reinhardt to give you a hard punch on your face once again!"

Margot suddenly blushed and he turned his glance towards Reinhardt. Then, he turned away. "How about Kenji? Is he coming with you too?"

"Well he really is!"

Margot began to weep in jokingly way. "Huhuhu… I'm all alone… 'Coz I will always be… ALONE, WAHAHAHA!!!"

The group of boys had left the dining room leaving Margot alone. They did not even say "see you later" to him at least.

The boys were all outside the dining room with their meals when Genji spoke to them. "Geez, you're right. I can also tell that he's a dangerous Explorer," he laughed. "Anyway, so where are going to eat then?"

Kenji quickly made a decision. "I know where we should eat. Why don't we eat in the clinic so we can also include Prince Maximus in our dinner tonight?"

Shingue quickly agreed. "I agree! This is the best thing we can do in order to protect the prince against evil (Margot)!"

Isagani also agreed. "Alright, let's go to the clinic!"

Jon quickly pulled Kenji's shoulder. "But Kenji, that is a clinic and we should let Prince Maximus to get rested well. He is recovering right now, remember? Do you think aren't we disturbing him when we get there?"

Vamir was surprised, especially Marion. "Wait a minute, did I hear it right? Is there a prince in this mansion?" asked Vamir. "Is he cute?"

Marion was very much interested. "I heard it too! A new Explorer and a friend? A prince really?" he asked while eating *pandesal* (salt bread).

"Yes, really. Kenji fought him earlier and he was badly hurt," answered Clio.

Marion's eyes were now glittering towards Prince Maximus. "So that means he is very, very wealthy!" he said very happily. "I wanna see him and get to know him immediately! I'm sorry for my overexcitement… It's because I've been dreaming to see a real king in real life!"

"Just keep yourself quiet, okay? Especially to Margot. He doesn't know that we have a royal guest here," said Tyrone.

"Oh, o-okay… Shhhh… I will be quiet, I promise."

The group went straight to the clinic to visit the wounded prince of Reminescence. The prince who never smiled since childhood…

Claude whispered to Kenji when they reached the clinic's door and gestured his hand. "Kenji, knock the door."

Kenji gently knocked on the door and then he spoke in his low voice. "Um… good evening, Your Highness. Can we pay you a visit right now? We bring you your dinner here to eat with us."

There was no answer coming from the inside of the clinic.

"I guess he's asleep," said Reinhardt.

Kenji gently opened the door. There, they saw Maximus sleeping soundly in the bed. He spoke. "He's sleeping deeply… What if we just eat in the other room instead? Let's not disturb him for a moment."

Marion excitingly went inside the clinic and he watched the face of the sleeping prince. "He looks exhausted, but I am so much interested to know him. This is the BIG moment of my life!" then he turned to the boys. "Please *kuya* Kenji, I want to stay here. Come to think of it, who will be watching him while we're away? I'm afraid Margot will kidnap him and take him somewhere we don't know! I promise I will be quiet here."

Everyone had already forgotten about Margot and they answered together. "Oh yeah! That 'boyfriend hunter', Margot is here!!!"

"Are all the prince like him really hate noisy people? That's what I've heard before," asked Kenji wondering then he shook his head. "Anyway, let's keep our mouths shut, okay? Especially you, Marion…"

Marion freaked out again. "What do you mean by that'?! Maybe you're the noisy one not me!"

Claude got easily angry. He came closer to the child and retorted him. "I knew it! You never listen to your *kuya* Kenji, you naughty little brat! Just SHUT UP, okay?!!" his voice sounded very angry towards Marion now… The nerve!

"And why are you retorting me?!" asked Marion angrily to Claude as he turned to him. "I was only talking to *kuya* Kenji and no one else! You have no respect towards the Explorer king!"

"You freakin' son of a--!"

"COULD YOU PLEASE JUST SHUT UP?!!" cried Shingue, not realizing that they were now making noises inside the clinic. The naughty child was so persistent, until they did not notice that their noises suddenly awakened the prince. Maximus was distracted!

Everyone had stopped when they saw the prince of Reminescence rose to the bed. Kenji wanted him to go back to his sleep again but he shook his head.

Kenji moved closer to Maximus just to say sorry for disturbing his sleep. "We are so sorry, Maximus… Because of the noise we have here… Um…"

He waited for Maximus' respond. The prince looked at them intensely at first and then he asked. "Why are you all here? What's wrong?" he was serious but not angry.

Vamir was looking very much amazed, especially Marion after seeing the prince was finally awakened. Marion quickly approached Maximus and he dared to introduce himself to the prince. "Ahem," Marion cleared his throat first. "Good evening, Your Highness! My name is Marion and I am here to get to know you personally. Because, um… I-I have been dreaming to see a royal person in reality and become like you!"

Marion was very much delighted while his glittering wide-open eyes were looking intensely at Maximus. He continued. "I am nine years old by the way, Your Highness... How I really, really wish to become one like you... A prince, and a king! You make my dreams come true of seeing a future king, Your Highness... I... I..." he faltered.

The boys thought that Maximus would laugh at Marion's nonsense introduction so instead, Kenji spoke to him again in embarrassment. "Please forgive this child, Maximus. He just can't help himself of not seeing you tonight. He likes you so much. He's such an overjoyed child..."

Everyone laughed, except Marion and Maximus. Later the prince answered. "That's fine with me. It's so nice to meet him as well. I can possibly tell that this kid is a brave warrior too. Am I correct?"

Everyone was still laughing as they were mocking Marion's uncontrolled excitement towards Maximus, so the child's face quickly turned red in embarrassment. With that, Marion pulled Kenji's shirt annoyingly, but Kenji could not stop his laugh towards him.

"Okay, okay, fine!" said Marion to Kenji while he was still pulling the young man's shirt. "I hate you, *kuya*! You guys are so annoying!" then he quickly turned to Maximus and cleared his throat once again. "Mister prince... My name is Marion Raven. A nine-year old Explorer and the most handsome among the group! Sounds cool, doesn't it? I will be the king of this organization one day and I will kick these losers' asses when that time comes!"

"You're still a child, but you're in UE with that very young age," said Maximus seriously. "So which means the Explorers are not strict in recruiting their warriors when it comes to age, aren't they? Who is the UE leader?"

"It's Elijah Tylers," answered Shingue. "He's in our batch when the Explorers recruited us. He's nice and a great leader though."

"In fact, he has seen you already," said Lucky with a smile on his face.

Maximus stooped down his head. He altered the topic. "D-Do you have a grand piano here? I want to play a piano right now... It's been my fashion to play a music with piano."

"Oh, our grand piano is in the Music Room. Don't tell us you wanna take a walk just to get there and play a piano. You see, you're still recovering!" said Clio with a smile too. "What about next time instead, Your Highness?"

Maximus frowned more. He felt disappointed.

The Explorers were unaware that Akira was also an Element Wielder now. What would be Kenji's reaction when he found out that his mortal enemy was now a chosen Wielder as well?

Then, the boys continued their dinner along with Maximus inside the clinic.

40 WIELDERS

A few days had passed when Prince Maximus was getting better from the wounds he got by Kenji. He yearned for playing the piano again after he went away from Reminescence, so the UEs took him in the Music Room to grant his wish. The Explorers just learned how well Maximus could play a piano when they listened to his sweet, melodious music.

"Wow, he's very good in playing the piano!" Kenji complimented Maximus as he was listening to the music played by the prince. "Well as for me, I'm not good in playing the piano!"

"Yeah," said Lucky. "I can tell to his nice look that he is a great pianist. I like him!"

"And he plays professionally," added Reinhardt. "He's talented…"

"And look, guys!" Marion was pointing at Maximus' hands as he was pressing the piano keys professionally. "He is very skilled in pressing each of the keys! I wanna learn to play piano too. I should also be like him, whoo-hoo!!!"

Vamir just sighted. "Man, kids these days…"

The music played by Maximus was very pleasant-sounding to their ears which made Claude getting sleepy. The UEs thought that this prince could actually perform professionally in front of the huge crowd!

Kenji moved closer to Maximus who was still playing the piano and he closed his eyes to feel his sweet music. Later, he asked. "Maximus, what was your age when you learned in playing the piano?"

Maximus answered while still playing the piano. "I was just a child when I became interested in playing the piano. I think… I was only six."

"Really? You're incredible!"

Maximus did not answer. He continued in playing the piano.

"Who forced you to learn in playing the piano, Maximus?" asked Kenji again.

"No one. My father had a grand piano in our palace but he was not using it all the time. Then when I was imprisoned, he decided to give me his piano and I began playing it. Until, I had finally learned the basics by my own."

"You learned it all by yourself? Did no one teach you?"

"Well there was, but I quickly learned it well so my piano lessons did not take that very long."

Kenji smiled and he complimented Maximus again. "You're really incredible!"

Maximus did not respond again.

Kenji moved back to his colleagues. And later, a UE came to them in a hurry. "Hey guys, Elijah is calling you right now. Please go to the laboratory immediately."

Lucky nodded. "Okay, we will be on our way."

"You are going to make a report today except Marion and Vamir. So please come to the lab right away."

Kenji turned to Vamir. "Vamir, we need to make our report to Elijah today. I'll leave Prince Maximus to you, okay?"

Vamir nodded. "No problem."

Marion also answered in his high voice. "Well as for me, I am not going anywhere and I will just stay here! I'm still listening to his music. Plus, I will ask him to teach me how to play the piano!"

Kenji turned to Maximus. "We're leaving you for a while, Your Highness. We need to go to the lab first and make reports. We'll be back here later!"

Maximus did not respond again. He was still busy in playing the piano. The group had left the Music Room, and they all walked together onto the laboratory.

"Maximus is a very serious type of guy, isn't he?" said Genji while walking. "I wonder why?"

"You know," said Lucky. "He is just saving his voice since you were just talking nonsense to him!" he chuckled. "Man, I still want to listen to his music! Elijah, you're ruining my day!"

"I'll tell it to Elijah!" said Tyrone to Lucky in mockingly way.

"Then tell him!" Lucky laughed out loud.

In the laboratory...

"I didn't expect that you were all being chosen by the king to become the Element Wielders even though you're still in UE," said Elijah with a grin on his face. "There are two elements left that we still need to find. Once the fourteen elements are complete, then we are ready to present them to the DDE and make you a request of getting promoted."

Silence. Kenji and Reinhardt felt their disappointment again after Elijah mentioned the DDE.

"I am calling you today because I want you to make a report about the element type you have obtained. Oh, and by the way Kenji, I also would like to ask you if you want your twin brother and a Valedictorian to become a part of our team?"

Genji quickly answered Elijah's question instead of Kenji. "Why, of course! I want to become a UE too. My two brothers are Explorers so I must become a part of your team!"

"When do we start the tests?" asked Cyan.

Elijah closed his eyes and smiled. "Anytime you want will do. It's up to you."

"How about if we start the tests next week, Elijah?" asked Genji.

"Alright, next week then. It's a deal!" Elijah agreed.

Genji jumped with excitement. "Toohoo!!!"

"So now, please report to me the element type you have in your possession. One by one..." asked Elijah and then he turned to Kenji. "Kenji, you first."

"Alright," said Kenji and he took a deep breath first. "My element is called 'Holy Crusade'. This is the leading element among fourteen elements because this was once the ultimate power of King Jethro. So therefore, the Holy Wielder himself is the leader of the fourteen Element Wielders."

Claude was the next one to report. "My element is 'Mother Earth'. When the element chose me, I've acquired a skill of an inner powerful strength coming in my right fist. As the Earth Wielder, I am able to feel the vibration of the land surface and control the earth... According to the book I read, my element has its twin element called 'Gravity'. It is possessed by Clio."

"Okay," Elijah nodded. "On the other hand, your element is the other half of Clio's element of Gravity."

Clio answered. "Yes, and I am able to control the Earth's gravity and force."

Lucky reported next. "I possess the element of 'Time and Space', Elijah. For now, I am still unknowledgeable about my element's ability, but I know that my element is obviously related to time. That's all!"

Claude chuckled. "T-That's all?"

"Well, I do not know what else to say!"

"Okay, my element is called 'Poison'," reported Shingue to Elijah. "According to the Element Book I read, this type of element is one of the dangerous elements among the fourteen. B-But I am still learning more about it too for now…"

"I possess the element of 'Lightning'," said Genji next. "Of course, this element I have is not only concentrated to thunder and lightning. But it can also create the natural disasters in this world, just like storms!"

Jon's head was down when he made his report next. "Sometimes when I was training myself in using my own element, I was getting burned. It is because I possess the power of the 'Fire' element. According to the book, the Fire element is the wildest element of all fourteen elements of King Jethro. It is far too dangerous."

Reinhardt made his next turn to report to Elijah. "I possess the element of 'Darkness', Elijah. This is the only element that has an ability to hold the life and soul of an entity in the Underworld. This element can see unusual things that are not seen by the human naked eye, and it can also control the dark shadows. Because of its ability, the Darkness Wielder acquires the skill of 'six sense' and 'third eye'."

"Really?" asked Elijah in disbelief. "How?"

"I do not know yet. And I am still learning it along with these guys."

"Oh, okay! B-But why did King Jethro choose you to become the Darkness Wielder? You're a very kindly man!"

Reinhardt did not answer, so Isagani came closer to Elijah and made his report next. "My element is 'Light and Blessings', my friend. Because of the element's ability, I am now able to control the speed of light! I am still learning for more."

"And how about the Blessings?"

"I do not know yet, yahoooo!!!" Isagani had gone insane!

"Hah, relax dude. Don't get overexcited!" Tyrone laughed and then he turned to Elijah arrogantly. "Okay, now it's my turn, boys! You were all wrong about the unique abilities your elements could do because I... I, Tyrone Federlein of UE is the only Element Wielder that possesses the greatest element of all and should also be your only leader... I have the element of 'Trinity', that is as FAST and as WISE as I am. Hayaaahhh!" then he punched in the air arrogantly and he added. "Your elements have no match against my strongest element of Trinity!"

"Whatever..." said Cyan feeling strong disapproval towards Tyrone's boastfulness. "Anyway, here's my report. I am the chosen Element Wielder of 'Air', which can create strong wind disasters!"

"Like tornadoes and hurricanes?" asked Elijah.

"Yup, indeed. And one more thing, this element is the fastest element of all fourteen elements!" Cyan added happily. "It's great, isn't it?"

Tyrone quickly objected Cyan's last statement. "Hey, you are completely wrong about your element, Mr. Big Eyeglasses because it is just my element itself the fastest element of all and nothing else! Do you understand?!"

Cyan did not answer and was feeling hurt, but Kenji defended him as he spoke to Tyrone instead. "Tyrone, each of the elements that King Jethro gave us have their own unique strengths and abilities. So even if our elements aren't the same, still we're all equal. There is no strongest and weakest among us!"

"You're COMPLETELY wrong, Kenji!" Tyrone disagreed as he was pointing at Kenji. "Our elements aren't equal! The truth is that... I can greatly outweigh your Holy element!"

Kenji was also hurt. Everyone was looking at the two when Elijah stopped them and he turned to Tyrone. "Please stop this quarrel, especially you Tyrone! Your action is embarrassing to me."

The two had stopped. Elijah turned to the boys again and he continued. "I would like to let you know that the DDE member named Zoroaster has the element of 'Ice', according to DDE..."

"Do you know who Zoroaster is?" asked Lucky.

"...Not much, but the DDE said he is also one of the chosen Element Wielders. I don't know what's his element can do anyway," said Elijah then he turned back to Tyrone again. "Now Tyrone, you must stop this kind of attitude and you're still acting like a child. That is too humiliating! You are an Element Wielder just like your friends here so please act with utmost respect and be like one."

Kenji, Claude, Genji, and Cyan could not believe their eyes seeing Elijah scolding Tyrone before them like a child!

Tyrone seemed that he was embarrassed, but yet he answered Elijah in his sharp, angry voice. "I am a UE and also an Element Wielder! And you? Just a UE leader and a Magic Wielder who is now weaker than me, am I right??!"

Isagani stooped down his head in embarrassment over Tyrone's disrespectful dealing towards Elijah. "P-Please forgive him everyone. It is common for Tyrone to fight everyone here in this mansion. His insulting behavior towards everyone is natural for him. I'm sorry…"

Kenji, Claude, Genji, and Cyan were just mouthed before the two. "So that's his natural attitude when his temper flares!" said Cyan in wide-mouthed. "I think he is only looking for a fight!"

"Now you're starting this nonsense argument again, Tyrone!" said Elijah annoyingly to Tyrone. "Don't you dare retort me like that! You've been treating us with your ill-mannered attitude for so long and that isn't an Explorer should do to his fellow colleagues! A pride does not always help, instead, it will only ruin your relationship to us!"

"If then, then why were you stopping me earlier? Are you an Element Wielder to also DARE yourself to stop me like that, huh?!!"

Elijah got pissed off. The four were still mouthed before them and were all mum. "I said do not retort me, Tyrone! You don't have the authority to deal with me like that just because you're an Element Wielder now. I am the LEADER of this team, so I still have the power to kick your ass out of this organization! Do you think your pride and your power can scare me right now, eh Tyrone? I don't think so… 'Coz I will never, ever be afraid of you!!!"

Tyrone did not answer suddenly, realizing that Elijah was still their leader and could possibly kick him out of the UE if he still retorted back. So instead, he angrily stamped his foot and quickly walked out of the laboratory.

Then, Elijah turned to the boys again when Tyrone was already gone. Everyone was mouthed until now. "The report is over. You may now leave the lab," said Elijah.

Kenji slowly approached Elijah looking concerned. "Elijah, Tyrone has disrespected you earlier… I'm sorry…"

THE EXPLORERS

Elijah smiled to Kenji. "Nah, that's okay Kenji. We're already used to his behavior ever since because that's the way he is. He is always picking a quarrel, so all of the UEs here have become his enemies once. But with his such behavior like that he must be stopped at all cause… Even kicking him out in the organization if necessary!"

Claude could not believe to what Elijah said. "All of the UEs?"

Elijah chuckled. "Yes, everyone in this mansion, Claude! Even Lucky, Shingue, Clio, and Reinhardt were quarreling with him before. Except to Isagani, because Isagani is his best friend."

Claude was believed now. "So that means… you were not angry at him despite of what he had done to you?"

Elijah laughed at loud. "Of course not! I was not really that angry, Claude. I just pissed off once when I met him and quarreled with him for the first time. But now? Nah, it's all nothing. But sometimes, I need to show what I can do and so he'll think twice before he opens his big mouth again… Hahahaha!!!"

"Now I know… because when we looked at your face earlier, we could tell that you were really angry at him, Elijah! You scared me and Kenji!" Claude joked.

Elijah was laughing at loud and then he clapped his hands. "Hahaha! Alright… You are all dismissed!"

The boys went out the laboratory when Lucky spoke to the boys. "Now what? Should we return to Maximus again?"

"Why, of course!" answered Shingue. "We told him that we would come back later after the report, and we must protect him against the incoming evil force (Margot)… Hahaha!"

"Okay, back to Prince Maximus everyone!"

Maximus was still in the Music Room and playing his favorite tune in the piano. Marion was very much impressed to the prince who was still listening next to him. Kenji's group came over to the prince and they listened to his soft music too.

"You're back. How's the report going?" asked Vamir to the boys as they were listening to the music. "What were your reports?"

"There was a misunderstanding earlier. But it didn't end up to a real fight. Elijah and Tyrone were quarreling with each other," said Kenji to Vamir.

Vamir already knew Tyrone's personality so he nodded and answered.

"Oh, I see. Yes, that is Tyrone's natural behavior. So why did the two fight again?"

"Well it is because for such nonsense thing," said Cyan while he was shaking his head. "He was bragging about his element to us. He said that the fastest one among the elements only belonged to him," then he sighted.

Kenji moved closer to Maximus and he greeted the prince. "Hello! Our report is finished. I think you are having fun of playing the piano today, am I right?"

Marion turned to Kenji and he answered instead. "Be quiet! You are disturbing the prince!!!"

Kenji ignored Marion and he was still looking at the prince. "Maximus, don't you want to join with us? In UE?"

Maximus stopped in playing the piano. "Why?"

"W-Well... I just asked, Maximus..."

The prince quickly answered. "No."

"What do you mean 'no'?"

"I don't want to."

"You don't want to join the UE?"

"I don't want to."

"That's bad. If you only knew about our team..."

Maximus looked straight at Kenji in wonder. "Are you compelling me to join your organization?"

"Ah, no!" Kenji was insecure. "It's nothing... Um, you know... To also become our ally?"

Maximus resumed playing the piano again. "I'm sorry, but I don't want to join the Explorers."

"O-Okay," said Kenji in regret. "I will respect your decision, Your Highness. But this is your chance now to become a part of our team, right?"

Maximus stopped in playing the piano again.

"Ah... N-Nevermind, forget it then, Maximus!" said Kenji while he was shaking his head in dismay.

Maximus did not want to resume his music anymore. He stood on the piano bench and turned to his side.

"Why did you stop?" asked Kenji in wonder.

"I'm getting tired... I am still feeling sick," answered the snobbish prince. "Can I come back to the clinic again to rest? My head is starting to ache now…"

"Um, okay!" Kenji nodded. "Claude, please take him to the clinic. I need to take a shower right now…"

"Okay," Claude agreed then he turned to Maximus. "Come with me, prince Maximus…"

After the two went away and left the room, Kenji went straight to his room to get his clothes and his bathing stuffs in the cabinet. Then, he walked towards the public bathroom. The rain was still strong and the UEs could hear the splashes of the rain outside the mansion.

Kenji had reached the huge public bathroom when he saw Tyrone, Isagani, and Arthur (his other enemy he met in the Training School) inside talking to each other next to bathroom countertops. He walked straight pass through them as if he did not see them. He entered the vacant shower room and he took the shower.

While bathing, he heard the faint conversation between the three. But the conversation did not take too long, since they left the bathroom after seeing Kenji went inside alone.

Kenji's body was soaked in water. The weather was cold, and he wanted to bathe himself with lukewarm water. "There's a lot of things that are troubling in my mind right now…" said Kenji to himself. "And what more troubling is about that mysterious prince… I'm feeling strange about him…"

The water was still showering his body when he took a bar of soap and soaped his body. He closed his eyes, then he began to think about Tyrone next.

"You're COMPLETELY wrong, Kenji! Our elements aren't equal! The truth is that… I can greatly outweigh your Holy element!" said Tyrone to Kenji earlier.

Kenji just learned Tyrone's attitude today. He could not believe how he treated his fellow UEs as well as to their leader, Elijah. So that was Tyrone Federlein!

"P-Please forgive him everyone. It is common for Tyrone to fight everyone in this mansion. His insulting behavior towards everyone is natural for him. I'm sorry…" he even remembered what Isagani said to them earlier.

He also remembered Elijah's answer to Claude as he was laughing like nothing went wrong. *"Of course not! I was not really that angry, Claude. I just pissed off once when I met him and quarreled with him for the first time. But now? Nah, it's all nothing. But sometimes, I need to show what I can do and so he'll think twice before he opens his big mouth again… Hahahaha!!!"*

Yes, Elijah's right. We still do not know Tyrone yet that well. And I am expressing my sympathy for Cyan. But don't you worry Cyan, we will also get used to his behavior sometime soon, but not for now…

Kenji opened his eyes when he realized that the soap was already washed away in his body. He had been thinking for long and he needed to rinse his body now.

After he finished his shower, he took the towel that was hooked at the door of his bathroom and he wiped it throughout his wet body. He wore his clothes and then he went out the room.

"And one more thing… Prince Maximus do not want to join the Explorers. I know he is our enemy, but until when? He was a member of a group that killed my beloved father… I do not really know if I should believe in his story but… But it seems there is still something good in his heart!"

41 PERCY AND TADTEO

Kenji was done bathing and he was about to return to Maximus to ask him again about the Reminescence. He was walking over the clinic when Clio came approaching towards him. He was carrying a large box in his hands.

"Kenji! Kenji!" called Clio to Kenji as he was panting and Kenji stopped walking. "Kenji, the fairy old woman came here earlier and she would like to give you this box. This is quite heavy and it's warm!"

Kenji wondered while pointing himself. "For me?"

"Yes, she wanted to thank you for visiting Bondore and defeating the Pioneers. Actually, she was looking for you but Claude said you were in the bathroom!"

"Yes, I was… But how did she know our base?"

"I also asked her about it. She said that she was following us when we're going back to this mansion a few days ago!"

"I see. Um, so have you already seen what's inside that box?"

"Nope! This box is only for you, but it's heavy! Elijah met her at the lobby and they spoke to each other for a minute. And then, she left sooner. Oh, she said she would never, ever follow us anymore."

Clio handed over the large box to Kenji when he added. "Whatever that box is containing inside, then find it out by yourself. Maybe fragile…"

Kenji gaped in surprise. "F-Fragile?"

"Yes. Well look at the box. It says 'FRAGILE', so which means it is obviously fragile!"

"But why is it warm?"

Clio laughed. "Maybe that box has something inside that is warm. Like a hot coffee maybe or a newly baked cake?"

Kenji laughed at Clio's joke. "Hahaha, yeah! You're a joker, aren't you? Anyway, thanks! I'm feeling bad that I didn't have a chance to thank back *lola*."

"Honestly, Lucky and I were the ones to thank *lola* for you! Oh, I almost forgot… She said that you should call her *ninang* (godmother) the next time you meet her again. See you later, goodbye!" Clio left.

"Alright, thanks Clio!"

Kenji was walking back to his room to check what was inside the box given to him by Vanice. He was about to enter the room when someone suddenly spoke coming from the box. "Hey! Who are ya? Are ya Kenji Foshter now?"

Kenji suddenly appalled and he stopped walking. "Blimey! Someone is speaking inside the box. A hot coffee can speak nowadays!"

A voice coming from the inside of the box answered. "What ish thish hot coffee yar talking about? We are not coffeesh! Wait… are ya Kenji Foshter now?"

"Um… yes, I am…" Kenji faltered.

"Very well then, then let ush go out the boxsh now, birdie!" then the box opened up when the two animals emerged: a fat cat and an Adarna-like bird (a legendary type of bird with a long colorful feathers that can sing beautiful song). "Lady Vanicshe (Vanice) told ush to jusht go out the boxsh if the man named Kenji Foshter is now holding thish thing!" said the fat cat to Kenji.

"A-A cat and a bird?" Kenji was looking very much surprised. "But why did *lola* give you to me? As a gift?"

"No!" cried the cat. "Ya have a misshion to take good care of ush! Becaushe from now on, the bird and I will be yer new petsh!"

Kenji went inside the room carrying the two animals in the large box. Claude was sitting on the bed and wondered when he saw Kenji with the two animals.

"Huh? Why are you bringing a cat in here?" asked Claude.

The cat cried again. "Look mishter, I am not jusht an ordinary cat! I have a breed of a White Tiger, sho I am a crossh-breed cat!"

Claude was surprised. "What the hell, that cat can talk! How cute!"

"*Lola* gave me these two animals, Claude. I don't know why…" said

THE EXPLORERS

Kenji.

The cat cried again as it turned to Kenji. "I shaid yar going to take good care of ush, okay?!"

"O-Oh, okay then..." Kenji chuckled. "So, what is your name?"

The bird answered. "We don't have our name yet. You can give us our name that you like. It's up to you!"

It was already evening when the boys went inside Kenji and Claude's room for a visit. Kenji told them about the two animals. Maximus was also there, but he was standing away from them while leaning on the wall. Margot had finally learned about Maximus today, but he could not make a move to the prince yet because he was scared to his look. He thought that Maximus was a very snobbish type of guy... More serious and more snobbish than Reinhardt!

"Wow, they're so cute--" complimented Jon to the two animals when he noticed Maximus standing alone in a corner. "Maximus, look at these animals. They're too adorable! Come here and pet them!"

Maximus was looking uninterested. "I don't want to."

"Why?"

Maximus frowned towards Jon. "I don't like animals..."

"Why so?"

Maximus moved a little farther away from them. "I'm allergic to animals. I'm sorry," then he left the room.

"HEY!" yelled the cat when he scratched Kenji's face to catch his attention. "Pleahse give ush our namesh now, mashter!"

Kenji was hurt. "Ouch! I can't believe you can even do that to me. You have your sharp claws!"

"Hey, man. You should stop that," scolded Shingue to the cat. "That's bad!"

The cat stooped down his head. "I didn't mean to do that... I'm shorry..."

Margot came closer to the two animals to give them their first name. "All right, I will give you the names. You cat, should be named as 'Pussie' while you bird should be named as 'Birdie'! How's that? Teehee!"

"Margot!" called Reinhardt to Margot. "Please move away from them, okay?"

Margot suddenly blushed his face, turned to Reinhardt and he stared at him. He made a drama again. "Oh, my dear Reinhardt... Why are you moving me away from your heart? You hurt me!!!"

"Okay, how about 'Catmund' for the cat and 'Twitty' for the bird?" suggested Lucky as he was pointing at the two.

"How about 'Catty' for the cat?" suggested Jon.

"I am a male cat," said the cat. "And thish bird ish female."

"Well how about 'Kenny' for you, cat? Since that name rhymes with Kenji," said Claude.

"And for the bird should be 'Benjie'!" Genji added. "That name rhymes as well!"

"How 'bout ya, mashter?" asked the cat to Kenji. "Why don't cha give ush the names inshtead?"

"Oh, I know!" said Kenji as he clapped his hands. "I should name you as 'Percy' because that is the common name for cats. While you birdie, should be named as 'Tadteo' instead of Twitty! How about that? Now you have your names!"

"What ish my name again?" asked the cat.

"Your name is Percy, and she is Tadteo!"

"Percshy ish my name? Well, that makesh shense to me…"

"YESH! You're incredible PERCSHY, hahaha!" Kenji laughed. "What do you think?"

Percy was delighted in satisfaction. "Yesh! Yesh! I love the namesh… Percshy and Tadteo!"

Kenji noticed the two animals' belts with bells that were strapped in their neck. "Those two bells in your neck are cute. Did *lola* give you those bells before?" he asked with a smile.

"Yesh, mashter! She gave ush theshe beltsh when we were born," answered Percy. "The bellsh are too cute!"

"The belt will never be removed in our neck anymore," Tadteo added.

"Really? That's unbelievable."

"Yesh, mashter! She ish telling the truth," said Percy.

"Okay," said Kenji when he carried Percy in his hands and Tadteo perched over his shoulder. "So my only mission to the two of you is to take good care of you… No problem! From now on, you two will be my pets and I will be your master. How's that?"

"That'sh great! We would love ya to become our mashter from now on!"

Now it was time for everyone to sleep. Percy and Tadteo moved next to Kenji to sleep there. They were lying in the bed when Kenji asked the two animals. He was next to Claude.

"Percy, what is your breed again? You look very tame, despite of your strange look," he asked.

Tadteo answered instead of Percy. "Yes, he's a tame cat… But the only problem with him is that he's very talkative!"

"Hmpt," Percy scoffed. "For yer informatshion, even though I am a talkative cat, I am sho shmart!" then he turned to Kenji. "I already told you that master. I am a crossh-breed, mashter. Half-tiger and half-cat."

"Have you ever seen your parents before, Percy?" Kenji asked again.

Percy shook his head. "Not yet… shince birth!"

Claude whispered to Kenji. "Kenji, I don't think he is a cross-breed cat. I'm just curious… Um, you cannot mate the two animals in different species, right?"

Kenji nodded. "I dunno. Maybe the impossible becomes possible nowadays, Claude. I really don't know."

Claude pouted his lips looking unconvinced to Kenji's answer. "Nowadays really?"

Percy asked the two when he heard them talking. "What are ya two talking about right now?"

"Oh, it's nothing… Nevermind about it, Percy!" said Kenji smiling and he turned to Tadteo on Claude's lap. "Please keep your voice low because Tadteo is already sleeping. Go to sleep now, Percy. So when you wake up tomorrow, you will have a happy and pleasant morning, alright?"

Silence. Later, Percy spoke to Kenji. "Master, can I go to shleep on yer lap? I want a warm hug tonight…"

Kenji chuckled. "Go ahead. Come over here on my lap, and sleep soundly with me," then he patted his lap gently.

Percy moved towards to Kenji and laid himself on his master's lap. "Thank ya mashter. Pleashe forgive me if I am too heavy for you. Ya shee, *lola* Vanicshe cared me and Tadteo sho much ever shinche we were shtill a kitten and a chick. Until she took ush here in your bashe and got shcparated from her… I will be missing her sho much…"

Kenji gently stroked Percy's fur and he answered in his low voice. "Yes, Percy… I understand… Now close your eyes and go to sleep. Goodnight…"

The entire room became quiet in all of a sudden. Then, Claude also laid his back in the bed and Kenji followed. Until, they all slowly fell asleep soundly.

Morning came…

It was eight o'clock in the morning when Kenji and Claude woke up to get their morning exercise. It was their routinely habit of doing daily exercises every morning, but Claude was more active in doing exercise than Kenji. Sometimes, Kenji was skipping his exercise and he would immediately look for breakfast. Unlike Claude, he was only skipping his exercise if he needed to do something very important in the morning, otherwise, he would really have to exercise!

Kenji had a good mood today so he was doing his workout with Claude. Percy and Tadteo were still sleeping soundly in their room. Kenji and Claude went outside the mansion together to jog, then they would do push-ups in the mansion's gymnasium next. Because of the cold weather, the two never got soaking sweat in their body.

Clio's group saw Kenji and Claude doing exercises in the gym when they went inside and called them. "Hey, you're in a good mood today!" complimented Lucky. "Did you take your breakfast already?"

Kenji was doing the curl-up exercise. "Not yet. Maybe later."

"How about you, Claude?" asked Jon.

"Not yet either. Maybe later…" answered Claude while doing the weightlifting.

"Then we'll eat together later, okay?" said Shingue. "We will all go out the mansion and stay in the garden, and we will call you two later."

The boys had left the gym when Maximus entered inside next. He looked around the gym since the place was just new to his eyes.

"What's this?" asked the prince.

"Hello and good morning, Your Highness!" greeted Kenji to Maximus. "You're in gymnasium. Why do you ask?"

Maximus was frowning. "I know that. There is also a gymnasium in our palace, but I am not used to do exercises like that because I am imprisoned."

"Yeah, we know…" said Kenji. "You told me that already…"

"Maximus, did you take your breakfast already?" asked Claude. "Or would you like to eat with us?"

Maximus stooped down his head. "Not yet, and that's fine with me."

"Okay, we will call you later."

THE EXPLORERS

"H-Hold on," Maximus was looking for something. "I want to play the piano. Please let me play the piano again!"

Claude was thinking to himself as he was still weightlifting. "Oh boy, this prince's already looking for a piano first thing in the morning. That's the most expensive breakfast!"

But Claude understood him. The prince grew up in the presence of the piano and not his father! Poor Prince Maximus…

"The Music Room is always open for you, Maximus…" said Claude while he was still doing the weightlifting. "The piano is always there, waiting for your presence."

The prince quickly left the gym, going towards the Music Room alone. Kenji and Claude were left behind the gym along with the other UEs who were also doing their exercise.

"That prince is really so snobbish!" said Claude to Kenji. "He did not even say 'thank you' to me at least!"

"Claude," Kenji scoffed. "You know…"

"Fine, fine… But I hope he will change that kind of attitude, man. Is it only because he was born and raised as a very wealthy person too like Tyrone?!"

"Tyrone?" Kenji stopped doing the exercise. "Oh please Claude, don't you please compare Maximus to Tyrone again! My goodness…" then he resumed his exercise. "He is the same as Arthur!"

"Who? Maximus or Tyrone?"

"Tyrone, of course!"

Lucky and the others were now hanging out outside the mansion under the rain. They were all in the garden, and they were just having a good time though it was raining very lightly.

Maximus was now walking alone in the grand staircase going up. He was walking slow because of his slight injury by Kenji's attack. Some of the UEs came right across his way when they saw him and they wanted to assist him. The prince refused their help and he continued climbing the grand stairwell.

"By the way, that guy is our enemy, isn't he?" asked a UE who was being rejected by Maximus to assist him. "Elijah shouldn't allow him to stay in this mansion if he is!"

"They said he isn't our enemy," answered another UE to his fellow UE who was also being rejected by Maximus. "Do you know that his story is very touching according to our new Explorer members?"

"Oh, really? So what is the story of his life?"

"Ask Kenji yourself, he's not my close friend!"

Maximus reached the second floor when he saw Percy and Tadteo who were now awake. He tried to avoid the two because of his allergic to animals.

The prince steered clear of the two but Percy and Tadteo caught him. They seemed to be approaching him but still he was moving away from them. He walked away fast, pretending that he did not see them, but the two animals followed his back showing their interest to the prince.

"C-Can you please leave me alone? Get away from me!" said Maximus annoyingly while the two animals were still following his back. "I hate animals!"

"Ah... wait for ush, handshome!" cried Percy while running towards the prince. "We jusht want to talk to ya. Hold on for a minute, handshome!"

The prince began to ran fast despite of his injury and the two animals followed. They ended up chasing Maximus!

"Hey, what ish yer name, cuteboy?" asked Percy as he was running behind Maximus. "Tadteo and I want to talk to ya for a shecond... Hey, cute! Cute!"

The two were running around the second floor while Tadteo was flying in the air. They looked like they were now playing chase game!

"Geez, get away from me!" cried Maximus annoyingly.

"Why are you running away from us?" asked Tadteo. "We're not wild animals!"

"I don't care. Shooo!!!"

"Don't you like ush?"

"Ahhh! I hate animals. Now get away from me!"

The two animals looked at each other while they were still chasing the prince. "The man really don't want to make friends with us. I wonder why, Percy? Why does he hate us?" asked Tadteo to Percy while flying.

"Don't CHA worry! We will forcshe him to shtop hish running sho we can talk to him now!"

"And what are you planning to do then, Mister Half-breed Cat?!"

Percy smiled. "Watch yer eyes, birdie baby... I will do shomething that will absholutely shtop him!"

"Ah… okay!"

"Jusht watch the wildnessh of a crossh-breed cat who ish Percshy!!!" Percy quickened his running until he left Tadteo behind, but he was now getting closer to the running prince. "Hey, cute! We've been following yer back sho pleashe pay attentshion to ush!!!" then he jumped very high, reaching Maximus with his claws so he clawed at his back.

The prince was very shocked when he felt Percy's claws clutched in his back. The cat spoke to him as he was panting. "Do ya know we've been exshaushted in chashing ya just to know yer name??!"

Maximus cried out loud. "Ahhh! Get away in my back! Get awaaaayyyy!!!" then he sneezed.

Percy's sharp claws were still clutching in his back when he noticed Maximus sneezed again. "Oh? Why are ya shneezing? I jusht took a bath, huh?!"

Maximus ran back over the grand staircase to go down the first floor when some of the UEs heard his cry.

"MAXIMUUUUSSSS!!!" cried Vamir, Marion, Elijah, and the others.

"Get rid of this cat in my baaaaccckkk!!!" cried Maximus to the UEs.

"A-Ah, yeah! Hold on, we're coming!"

The UEs quickly moved towards Maximus when Elijah immediately removed Percy in Maximus' back. Then, he gently put down the cat on the floor.

Percy spoke to Maximus smiling while his tail was wiggling. "Ah, sho Maxshimush ish yer name. Okay, now we know… Why were you shcared to answer our queshtion? Do ya know we were loshing our energy jusht to know yer name? Hehehe!"

Maximus was annoyed, while Elijah and the other UEs were all laughing out loud. "I am NOT scared to the likes of you! I just really don't like animals, that's all!"

"Oh really, Maxshimush?" asked Percy and he drew near to Maximus intentionally.

"Tsk! Don't you dare come near me… cat!"

"My goodnessh! Why are ya sho shcared at me? It sheems that ya have sheen a large white tiger in front of ya, but look at me… I am jusht a shmall, cute, fat cat!"

"Dang, whatever!!!" cried Maximus and he walked away. The UEs laughed again out loud. Hahahaha!

42 EXPLAND

Breakfast time. Everyone was in the dining table. The UEs who witnessed what Percy did to Maximus were told to Kenji, Lucky and the others. Everyone was laughing out loud.

"Really?" asked Lucky laughing. "That was great!"

Elijah was telling the story.

"Yeah! Percy clawed himself at Maximus' back and then Maximus' cried at the top of his voice. He was running very fast!"

Laughter all over the dining room. Maximus' face suddenly frowned when he heard his name mentioned.

"I'm sorry if Percy did that to you, Your Highness…" Kenji was saying sorry to Maximus with his blushing face. "Cats are really that active in games, but Percy is a nice cat."

Maximus glared at Kenji. "Oh yeah? So that's why he clutched his claws in my back that almost scratched my skin… Is because he's a nice cat?"

Everyone was still laughing out loud except Kenji who was looking embarrassed for what Percy did to the prince.

"Maximus… it's because Percy and Tadteo do not know you yet and they want to make friends with you." said Kenji to Maximus still blushing. "Although I even just met them yesterday… But they're really very nice."

Maximus drank a glass of water. "Fine… But I was hoping that the fat cat should give me his respect. I am not that someone who is easy to get along with like you."

Kenji nodded. "Um, well… He didn't know yet that you're a prince."

THE EXPLORERS

The prince was calm now. "Very well, please tell the naughty cat who I am immediately."

Kenji nodded. And then they ate.

"Oh, by the way," Isagani was peering around the room. "Kenji, where is your cat and your bird?"

Kenji was chewing when he answered. "They're in our room. I'm feeding them there."

"Did they get their food already? Where did you get it?"

"Margot gave me the bird seeds because he also has a bird pet, while Baenard has the food for his cat pet," Kenji chewed again.

Everyone was in the middle of their breakfast when a UE came near to Elijah and whispered something. Elijah was surprised. "What did you say? All Explorers?"

"Yes, sir. Please proceed to the Conference Room right away because Sir Spencer Briant wants to talk to you. It's an emergency call."

Elijah stopped eating and he wondered. The UEs stopped as well after noticing their leader stood on his chair.

"Please excuse me for a minute, UEs. We have an emergency call from the DDE and I need to go to the Conference Room immediately. I will be back here later, okay? Don't worry, please continue your eating."

The Wielders were murmuring to each other. They were all wondering about the emergency call by the DDE.

"An emergency call coming from the DDE?" asked Tyrone. "I wonder what's it all about, huh?"

Shingue just shrugged his shoulders. "We dunno…"

"How about you, Reinhardt?" Tyrone turned to Reinhardt. "Do you know? Huh? Huh?"

Reinhardt shook his head. "I also don't know, Tyrone."

There was a question mark on Tyrone's head. "I wonder what that is?"

Everyone continued their breakfast when Claude asked everyone. "Um, why are you all wondering when there's an emergency call? What is that mean?"

Clio explained. "Well Claude, if there's an emergency call coming in this mansion means we have a new special assignment to do. You see, the DDEs is calling as an emergency, and this is about our special mission for today!" then he ate. "See for yourself, Claude."

Elijah returned to the dining room immediately and he moved straight to the UEs who were still eating. "Boys, please proceed to the Conference Room for the urgent meeting after you finish your meal. Especially to you, Element Wielders!"

"See?" said Clio to Claude. "I told ya!"

"What's the special mission about?" asked Lucky. "Say it now."

Elijah went back to his seat and then he gestured. "Boys, the DDEs have ordered everyone to go to their mansion immediately because the group of Expland has made a surprise attack on their base! They have captured some of the DDEs in the mansion and we need to be there to defend and help them. Priority level is very high."

"Now?" asked Claude.

"Why, of course! Now hurry up. The DDE base is way too far from here."

"Wait," Kenji raised his hand. "What is the group of Expland?"

"The Expland is another group of warriors and also our enemy, Kenji. Like Pioneers, they're also aiming to take all King Jethro's powers and rule the world. They have an ability to mimic everyone's appearance… Whether you're an Explorer or just somebody else," said Elijah to Kenji. "I think that's the reason why they've easily captured the DDE base although the base is heavily guarded."

"Where are they?"

"The Explands took the kidnapped DDEs to their base and the group is looking for all of us," said Elijah. "The EUE already heard the news today and they are now on their way to the DDE base."

Everyone became serious in all of a sudden. Elijah stood again. "I will ask the other UEs to get our main aircraft ready for our flight. Please hurry!"

"Roger!" everyone answered.

"We must hurry! The DDEs need our help," said Lucky to everyone. "We know that the DDEs are great warriors, but we still need to help them because they are our allies! Plus, the other sacred objects are in their mansion and they should have to be protected!"

"Yeah, we must protect all of the sacred objects we have already acquired from the very beginning!" added Isagani.

"Hurry!"

Everyone stood on their chairs and they went to their rooms to get prepared for their special mission. They took their weapons and other things that they could use in the possible battle. Some of them were on their Explorer uniform, but the group of Element Wielders, Marion, and Elijah were on their casual outfit.

"Claude, if we're going to attack our enemies today, what will you do?" asked Kenji to Claude in their room while taking their things ready for the mission.

"Of course, I will knock their asses out with my fist! And you know what, Kenji? I already have my knowledge to control my element. I am sure that I can finally use it in this special mission!"

"Really? That's good to hear."

"Sure, buddy!"

The two animals wondered.

"Mashter, where are ya two going and ya sheemed like in a hurry?" asked Percy while looking at his master.

Kenji was fixing his things. "Ahm, Percy... We will go somewhere related to our mission today. It is highly urgent. And, it is too far away from here..."

"A misshion?" asked Percy. "Tadteo and I will come with ya!"

"No, you can't Percy," Kenji refused. "It's too far away and also too dangerous. This is not a game."

"Where is that?" asked Tadteo.

"In another country, in another continent."

The animals were shocked. "Whaaaattt??!"

"You're not kidding, are you master?"

"Do you think that I'm joking, Tadteo?"

The two were silent. Kenji and Claude were done in preparing things.

"We need to leave you two for a while. This mission is urgent. Someone here will be watching you while we're away, okay?" said Kenji to the two.

The two animals nodded. "O-Okay..."

Kenji embraced the two. "We will be right back sooner. Don't fight to each other while we're away. If you get bored, go and ask the UEs here to play with you, okay? Anyway, Claude and I need to go now. Goodbye."

Kenji and Claude were about to leave the room now when Percy spoke. "Take care on your misshion, mashter..." then he licked Kenji's cheek and Tadteo pecked at his nose lightly.

"Thank you, goodbye..."

The group went to their meeting place which was the mansion basement, where their largest modern UE aircraft was stationed. Not all of the UEs would be coming in the said mission, but Elijah, Vamir, Margot, Marion, and the other UEs would be coming with the Element Wielders. A total number of thirty UEs would be sending off to the DDE base.

The large aircraft's engine was now roaring when Kenji and Claude arrived. Everyone was already inside the aircraft.

"Are we the only ones left you're waiting?" asked Kenji to Reinhardt who was standing in the airbridge with the UEs.

"No. Tyrone, Isagani, and Clio aren't here yet."

Claude saw Maximus alone who was sitting in a corner. He approached the prince and waved at him as a greeting. "Hey there, why are you here alone, Prince Maximus?" he asked.

Maximus answered in his low voice. "I just want to be alone right now."

"Don't you wanna join with the others over there?"

Maximus shook his head.

Tyrone came next, along with Isagani and Clio in the airbridge and they waved. "We're here now!"

"Excellent!" said Elijah. "We are now ready to leave. Make sure that everyone who's coming in this mission are already on board this aircraft now."

The UEs looked at each other and made a head count to check if everyone was already inside. The attendance was complete!

"Elijah, we're all here!" said a UE to Elijah.

"Very well then. Explorers, get ready for take-off!"

"Roger!"

The platform of the basement began to raise up high. The high-powered hangar moved outside the mansion and into the runway to let the large aircraft accelerate for take-off. After a few minutes, the UE aircraft had flown in the air.

"Okay guys, let us have our quick meeting about our mission first while we are in the middle of the flight," said Elijah to the twenty-nine colleagues. "Let's talk about the strategies we're going to do to save the DDEs in the hands of Expland. We all know that the said group is an excellent mimickers--"

"Wait," Kenji raised his hand to ask question. "Where did they take the DDEs? I mean, where is their base?"

Elijah stooped down his head. "I have not yet received such information about the exact location of their base, Kenji. The group is in the DDE base right now. We need to confront them."

Everyone was serious. Elijah spoke again. "Okay, so here's what we're going to do when we reach the base: We will divide our team into four main groups. The Element Wielders should be in two groups… while me, Vamir, and the rest of the UEs will be in the other two groups. Reinhardt will be the team leader of the first group and he will pick the Element Wielders to join in his group. Kenji will be the team leader of the other group and he will also pick his Wielders. Your mission is to find and rescue the kidnapped DDEs, while me and the rest of the groups will be guarding the mansion's perimeter from any Expland's reinforcement. For now I do not know what we're expecting when we get there, but it is far better if we have already made our groups just to make sure."

"I think they are up to something from us!" said Clio.

"Or they're want something from us!" added Tyrone.

"Maybe indeed, but we do not know what they really want from us yet," said Elijah seriously.

"Maybe… they're into our elements and nothing else!" said Genji. "But, are they Wielders too like us?"

"I don't know, Genji."

The meeting continued. Kenji suddenly began to miss Percy and Tadteo even though they were just new to his life. He spoke to Claude who was listening to the meeting. "I am missing the two already Claude," he said. "Good thing someone will be watching them there."

Claude answered differently.

"Hooray! I have learned on how to use my element now, Kenji! If there is a fight *(I hope so!)*, then I can finally show to those jerks the great power hidden inside my fist!"

Kenji just smiled as he was shaking his head. "Claude…"

"Kenji, I know I am not fully mastered yet, but at least I have an idea on how to control my element's power now!"

Kenji was still smiling sweetly. "Yes, Claude…"

Finally after the long flight, the UE aircraft had arrived in the DDE mansion when the UEs saw the large airship of Expland landed near the mansion gate. But as for Kenji, his attention was to the DDE mansion itself.

"So that is what the DDE mansion looks like," said Kenji while looking down the glassy platform through the DDE base. "Certainly... Their mansion is way too big!"

"Shhh... please remain silent," shushed Elijah and he turned to the UE aviators. "Pilots, please land the aircraft slowly. UE warriors, let's prepare ourselves to the possible fight with the Expland. Another thing, the Expland commonly has their unique ritual wherein they will offer the life of an eligible person to their Hydra Lord as a sacrifice. The group belongs to the Dark Mage class!"

"What? They are offering a person's life to their lord by killing him?" asked Claude in wonder.

"Yes, Claude... That is how evil they are!"

Claude got pissed off. "Dang it!"

There were Explands who were currently guarding the mansion gate when they saw the UE aircraft hovering above them and preparing to land. "The Ultimate Explorers, they're here!!!" cried an Expland as he was running inwards the mansion.

"Oh no, someone saw us!" said a worried Shingue.

"Don't worry guys, they will inflict no harm on us immediately. Maybe you have forgotten that they are needing something from us, right?" said Elijah.

Shingue raised his fist in anger. "If only I can poison those enemies right away..."

"Look guys," called Lucky to the colleagues as he was pointing at the another aircraft that was also landed near the gate. "The EUE aircraft is here too. They have been here ahead of us."

"Oh, yeah?" Jon noticed the EUE aircraft too. "I also just noticed!"

The UEs were all looking around when they suddenly heard a loud voice echoed coming from the mansion. The gate left ajar was now opening slowly. "Welcome Explorers. The gate is now open for you. You can now enter the mansion!"

"No doubt, that's him!" said Elijah annoyingly. "I know that voice... That is Neschar, the leader of Expland"

Everyone was mum when Elijah spoke again. "He is the loyal servant and guardian of their god, Hydra... who is hungered for a person's life! That's really him!"

THE EXPLORERS

A voice spoke again. "What the matter, Explorers? Why aren't you disembarking? Are you all afraid to show yourselves to us? Don't make any stupid moves or else you will lose all your allies' lives. Their lives are now in our hands, especially the life of your DDE leader!"

"Oh no, Sir Spencer Briant!" cried Tyrone and he turned to his colleagues. "Come on! Let's disembark now. The DDEs are in danger and they need our help now!"

The UE aircraft's bridge slowly opened when the voice spoke again. "Excellent. Now, get off the plane with your hands up in the air and get inside the mansion immediately. Quickly now!"

The UEs were cautiously disembarked the aircraft. The team separated themselves to their assigned groups first and then they entered inside the DDE mansion. When they reached the main hall, everyone was surprised to see that most of the Explands were inside, waiting for their arrival!

Elijah spoke as he was looking around the mansion. "The DDEs... Where are they? Where did you take them?!"

The black-haired leader of Expland showed himself to the Explorers. Elijah's right, it was Neschar.

"Elijah, long time no see..." said Neschar to Elijah as he turned to him. "It's been a very long time since we lastly seen each other. Don't worry, they are all still safe in our hands, but the life of Spencer Briant along with the seven DDEs are in grave danger!"

"Neschar..." called Elijah to Neschar while looking at him. "What do you want from us?"

"We have received news from the Pioneer that almost all of King Jethro's elements are now in your possession. We came here for one good reason, and that is to take the elements as well as the sacred stones from you. We mean no harm if you'll just surrender all what we need. And then... your supreme leader and the seven DDEs will be safe again back in this mansion with you!"

Hah, how lucky you are to just ask our elements in an exchange for the eight DDEs' life! Thought Kenji to himself. *We worked hard for these sacred objects for so long and now we will just give all of them to you that easily? You're mad!!!*

"In an exchange for--" said Elijah.

"Yes! That is all we want from you, Explorers..." said Neschar grinning. "What about that kind of deal? Don't worry my friend, once you give us all of your powers then we will leave this mansion immediately..."

Silence. No UE had made a sudden move towards the group. Later, Neschar looked at his watch and he spoke to the Explorers again.

"Very well then, I will give you one hour to decide. But the eight DDEs will still remain in our custody… And, we will all wait for your decision here in this mansion!" then he pointed at the Explorers.

"We made a promise to King Jethro that we will protect the elements at all cost, even in life and in death," said Kenji to Neschar. "He chose all of us to wield his powers… And we are being tasked to protect the human world against the evil, wicked likes of you!"

Neschar quickly turned to Kenji whom he just saw for the first time. "What did you say? Wait, who are you? Are you new to this group of so called, King Jethro's warriors?"

"My name is Kenji Foster of UE, a son of the former leader of DDE! My real name is Maximillian!"

"What did you say? Foster?" asked Neschar as if he had heard that name before. "You're the son of the former leader of DDE who is Alex Foster, huh??!"

Kenji answered. "Yes, I am his son! And I am also one of the chosen Wielders of King Jethro who is the possessor of his ultimate power… The Holy element!"

Neschar was surprised, but he did not answer anything to Kenji's remark. Instead, he intensely looked at Kenji from head to toe. With his unique ability, he could read Kenji's mind and learn everything about him like Vanice. He could see from the young man that he was the confirmed Wielder of the Holy element, but he also saw something seemed very strange from him… A face of an unknown man suddenly appeared in his mind for a second… He suddenly felt different… As if he felt a strong force that suddenly stopped him from analyzing Kenji's personality.

"Hmpt…" Neschar quickly turned back to the Explorers after he examined Kenji with his mind and power. "If you're still not going to give up your powers on us then you will instantly lose the lives of the eight DDEs--"

"But Neschar--"

"I will give you an hour to think about the deal while you are all imprisoned in this mansion. Especially you, Maximillian!" Neschar pointed at Kenji. "Now take these weasels in the prison!" he yelled.

The Explorers alerted themselves for the possible attack. They were now holding their weapons and posed for the fight.

"Do whatever that pleases you, but we will still never, ever surrender all of our powers to you!" said Elijah angrily to Neschar while he was pointing his *Sabre* (fencing-type of sword) at Neschar.

Neschar threatened the Explorers. "Go ahead, try to make a sudden move or the eight DDEs will all be dead! Try it!"

The UEs did not continue their attempt to attack. Instead, they lowered their weapons and Elijah dropped his sword to the ground.

Neschar quickly pointed his finger at the Explorers and shouted out loud. "Imprison them!"

A white gas suddenly appeared all over the hall to where the UEs were standing. They were all shocked.

"What's that?" asked Isagani.

"Damn, it's a sleeping gas. A trap!" shouted Maximus.

Neschar laughed. "Hahahaha! Fools, you are all being caught. Weaklings!"

"Cover your nose, everyone!" said Elijah to his colleagues and everyone followed, but sadly they could still inhale the gas.

"I can still inhale the gas, Elijah!" cried Shingue while his body was getting weakened by the gas. "My vision is blurring… I can't stand anymore…"

"A-HA-HA-HA-HA-HA-HA!!!" Neschar laughed at loud evilly. "Now who's the weakling? Come on, inhale more!"

"N-No… Holy…" said Kenji as he was getting weakened as well. His eyes became heavy. Until all of the Explorers instantly fell to their deep sleep.

Neschar moved closer to the downed Explorers and spoke to his colleagues. "Take them to the prison cell along with the other Explorers. But to Kenji… or Maximillian…" he was watching Kenji when he hesitated to speak for a moment. "Just leave him here. He is mine…"

"Yes, sir!" answered the Explands and they carried the downed Explorers in their arms going to the cells.

Neschar turned his gaze back to Kenji who was lying alone on the floor and watch him intensely. Then, he thought to himself and spoke in his low voice. "Maximillian Foster… The Holy Wielder and a son of the former DDE leader, Alex Foster… What was this strange power I just felt in you earlier? It was very strong… It was very powerful… A power of feeling that I've never felt before throughout my life! What are you? Is it you the only one we need to cure our lord since you have the Holy element of his mortal enemy, King Jethro?"

Then, he slowly carried Kenji in his arms while still looking at his face intensely. He grinned evilly. "Holy element... I need you... I am summoning you to be in my arms for a very, very important mission..." then, he chuckled.

43 THE HYDRA LORD

Noon time.

It was already noon when the UE, EUE, and DDE regained their consciousness after they fell on a trap by Expland. Margot was the first UE warrior who awoke, next was Clio… Until everybody followed.

"Clio…" called Margot to Clio in his weak voice. "We are in the dark DDE prison."

Clio rose to where he was laid down. He looked around the dark cell. "You're right. This is the mansion's prison. You see, almost everybody is here!" he said as he was pointing at the Explorer warriors. "They've dumped us in this place!"

Everyone was awakened when Marion put his hand on his head and he groaned. "Oh…" then he was shocked. "What in the world…"

Elijah quickly got up to where he was lying on.

"Damn… Those Explands tricked us by using their own stupid traps," said Elijah and then he turned to all the Explorers inside the same dark cell. "Guys… are you alright?"

The Explorers nodded. Elijah also nodded as an answer.

"Good thing nothing bad happened to us," said Lucky who was slumped on the floor.

Maximus also got up and then he touched his head. "W-Where am I again? This place is too dark!"

"We're in the DDE prison, Maximus…" answered Reinhardt to Maximus. "They imprisoned all of us in here."

Claude was noticing something.

"By the way," he said while peering around the cell then he quickly stood. "Where is Kenji? Kenji is not here with us!"

"Curse this sleeping gas!" said Tyrone annoyingly as he was kicking the bars forcibly. "I wanna get out in this prison. Release us!!!" and then he dragged the bars heavily.

"You're Wielders, right?" said Maximus while leaning in a corner. "What's the use of your elements if you're not gonna use it? Cast them on the bars. They might work to get out in this cell. The chance is here."

Claude was still peering around when Isagani jumped in excitement. "Oh yeah! I've been reviewing for long about my element, and now is my chance to use it for the first time, too-hooo!!!" and he jumped again.

"Okay, let's try it, Wielders!" said Lucky and he stood. "Let's get outta here and save Kenji and the rest!"

The Element Wielders tried to use their elements for the first time except Claude. He was still looking for his friend within the prison.

Finally, Tyrone had successfully cast his power of Trinity for the first time. The Trinity-based magic emerged before him, and Isagani clapped his hand as he was impressed to see Tyrone's successful attempt.

"Wow! Great attempt, Tyrone!" said Isagani delightfully.

Cyan also successfully cast his Air-based magic on the air, but unluckily the magic that came out was the strong whirlwind, causing each and everyone in the prison got all blown by the wind.

"CYAAANNN! STOP THAT, STOOOPPP THAAATTT!!!" cried everyone to Cyan out loud while they were hanging in the air.

Cyan was also in the air, but he did not know how to stop his own magic for being the first time Wielder. He was rattled, very shocked to what was going on right after he cast his own elemental-based magic. "H-How do I stop it? HOOOOWWW?!?"

Due to the strong blows by the whirlwind, the bars were blown away from the prison. Then, the whirlwind slowly stopped. But after it disappeared, everyone cried out loud again when they all suddenly fell down from the air. After they fell back to the floor, they laughed out loud instead of rebuking Cyan!

"Excellent, Cyan!" said Margot to Cyan as he was crawling over him in flirty way. "You should be my boyfriend!"

"Let's get outta here now," said Claude in his blushing face. "I must rescue Kenji. He is the leader of the Element Wielders!" then he left.

Elijah would have stopped Claude, but he was already too far away from them since he was in a hurry to save Kenji.

Kenji was now with the Explands in their main modern airship. He was still on Neschar's arms, and Neschar approached his colleagues to say his order to them. "We must fly back to our base now. I will leave the Explorers to the other Explands in this mansion. I need this young man so I want to take him with us."

"Yes, sir!" the Explands inside the airship answered.

The Expland base was located in the country of Burnham, which was close to the DDE base. The travel time was only thirty minutes from DDE base to Expland base by airship, and that was the reason why it seemed easy for these Dark Mages to travel to the DDE base anytime they wanted.

The large Expland airship began to hover in the air and was about to take-off. Claude had seen the escaping airship outside through the mansion window and he swiftly ran in the hall when the Explands caught him and blocked his way.

"The Explorers!" shouted an Expland angrily. "They have escaped! Catch them!"

Good thing the Explorers came behind Claude, and they all started their attack to help him.

"Take this... Fire!" cried Jon when he cast his Fire-based magic on the enemies and they got hit. But unfortunately, the said magic was weak enough so the enemies could still get rid of it in their bodies before the fire would spread.

Jon was shocked. "What the... O-Okay, fine! How about this one, idiots? Can you still survive with this?" he hurriedly pulled out his deadly darts and then he quickly threw them out towards the enemies' napes. The Explands did not dodge his splitting darts sooner, until their bodies had weakened and their skin color instantly changed to black. DEAD!

The mansion went into chaos. The other warriors were fighting with their weapons, while the others were using their magics to neutralize their respective opponents.

"KENJI!" cried Claude out loud while still looking at the escaping airship through the window. "Hey, Neschar! Where are you going?! Come back here!" and then he hurriedly ran fast going outside the mansion to chase the airship, but there were other Explands there who blocked his way again when he reached the mansion gate. "Goddamit!!!"

"HAHAHA!!!" Neschar's echoing laugh was heard in the air. "You are not able to reach us anymore. You will never, ever save your friend from our hands!" then he laughed again.

Claude was now scuffling with the Explands. He did not know on how to stop the hovering aircraft. "My element!" said Claude to himself and he strongly knocked off the Explands that were preventing him in going further. He hurriedly moved away from the mansion and then he lifted his right fist and cried out loud. "EARTHQUAKE!!!"

He punched the ground with his fist as strong as he could. The ground began to shake, but the escaping airship was unaffected by the strong quake since it was airborne. The airship was getting farther and farther from the mansion.

"Idiot!" shouted Neschar to Claude. "It's useless!"

The airship was now flying across the forest and Claude was still pursuing it as fast as he could. "The quake is useless… How do I stop these cowards? Damn!" he said as he was running very fast.

The airship was speeding away from him, until Claude was no longer able to reach the airship because of exhaustion so he fell on his knees. He was panting very heavily, while looking at the escaped airship already too far away from him. He angrily banged the ground real hard, until the quake had slowly stopped.

The airship was finally gone to his sight. He stooped down his head and he made a promise for Kenji as the sweat was rolling down to his face. "I promise to you, Kenji… I will find you wherever you are! I need to kick the Explands' asses first. Just hang in there and wait for us, we will be there sooner!"

He slowly stood on his feet again. He looked at the sky and he shouted out loud very angrily. "Curse you, Explands! Bring back Kenji to us!!!" then he ran back to the DDE mansion to help his allies who were still fighting with the Explands in the hall.

Neschar laughed out loud as he was looking at the airship window through the verdant forest. "Hahaha! See? The Explorer has failed in rescuing his sweet friend. What an idiot!" he was referring to Claude.

The battle in the hall continued. The new Wielders just witnessed how Margot was skillful in fighting the Explands alone. Cyan was looking at Margot unbelievably after he defeated his opponent. "Wow, that gay is too feminine to fight, but he can knock out his opponent that easily!" he teased.

"Oh, bummer!" said Lucky annoyingly while fighting an Expland. He was too cautious not to destroy the furniture inside the mansion. "We're damaging the mansion, maybe we should fight these imbeciles outside instead!"

Margot was still busy in fighting alone with his sword weapon called Jian. The gay would sometimes do his signature move of just slapping the opponent's face goofily, while Marion was using his bow weapon like his brother, Clio.

"Death!" cried Reinhardt when he summoned Death, the Reaper with his element to come out and join the fight. "Let's finish this fight. Death, slash your scythe to our enemies and take their souls to the world of Darkness!"

Claude was returned to the mansion hall. Only few remaining Explands were still fighting with the Explorers when he saw a downed Expland near the staircase. He approached the invader and strongly pulled his scarf. He asked the Expland in his glaring eyes. "You, monster! Where is your base located? Tell me!"

The downed Expland could not answer well to Claude's question. He hesitated to speak. "Ah… Uh… In, um…"

"WHAT?! Where are they taking my friend, I said??!"

"In… In Burnham… Our base is in that country…"

"Burnham? What are they going to do to Kenji, huh?!!"

The Expland was panting nervously, but Claude strangled his neck with his strong hands.

"O-Oh, okay fine! I will tell you… Once that Sir Neschar has taken someone like your friend, he is going to offer his body to our dragon lord statue as a sacrifice. It is our 'Hydra Lord'!"

"The Hydra?" Claude wondered. "So what Elijah said earlier was true…"

"Y-Yes, the Hydra is our lord. He turned to statue when he was punished by another god named Jethro. In order for him to return again to his true form, we must offer him the person's life who holds the king's ultimate power of Holy element. T-That's the reason why our leader is taking your friend with him. Your friend's fresh blood will be poured to the Hydra's statue along with his power as our lord's ultimate cure…"

"You mean… they're going to offer Kenji's life to your lord by killing him in order for the Hydra to return to his true form? Is that what is for?!"

"Yes… We learned about the new Holy Wielder who is an Explorer after hearing it from the Pioneer. We staged an attack on the DDE base in order for you to yield the Holy Wielder. Until, we have found him… Your friend… the Wielder of our lord's cure."

Claude strongly squeezed the neck of the downed Expland as he was glaring at him. He was angered more. "Tsk, I want you to come with us and bring us in Burnham! What about the other DDEs there?"

"Iggghhh… T-The eight DDEs? I-I do not know what Sir Neschar is going to do to them!"

Claude let go of his hands to the Expland's neck and he strongly dragged his arm. "Fine! Now take us to your base immediately and if not… I will put your life to an end with my own element!"

"N-No, please don't! I don't wanna die yet… I-I will take you to our base right now…"

Claude grabbed the Expland's arm again angrily. "Hurry up… Move!"

Thirty minutes had passed when the Expland airship had reached their base in Burnham. The airship gently landed on the ground and the Explands disembarked. Neschar came out of the airship next, carrying the sleeping Kenji in his arms and he walked across the ramp and into the Expland palace.

Inside the dark palace, Neschar walked straight to a room where the eight DDEs were imprisoned. There, he laid Kenji down the brick floor and then he turned to the DDEs and to Spencer Briant. "I'm here. I just brought the son of the former DDE leader who is Kenji or Maximillian Foster!" he said to the DDEs with his evil grin face.

"Kenji Foster?" asked Shiela, a female DDE when she heard Kenji's name and looked intensely at the young man. She was next to her husband who was Kato Brahms. "I know him for long. Aaron and I met him in Damsville and…"

"Yes," answered Neschar. "You are also one of the Fosters, am I correct?"

Shiela stooped down her head. "I can't believe that he is one of our cousins… and also his twin brother, Genji. When we were still young, we never knew that we four were actually cousins!"

Kato asked Shiela in wonder. "You were together in Damsville for long but you didn't know that you were all cousins?"

"Yes," said Shiela and she crawled towards Kenji. She smiled while looking at his sleeping face. "Oh, Kenji! I'm glad we meet again at last. How are you doing now? Aaron and I are missing you for so long," then she gently stroked Kenji's hair with a smile.

Aaron also crawled towards them and smiled when he saw Kenji. "Yes, you're right Shiela! He was the guy who lived with us in Damsville when we were young. I could still remember those two studs in his chin!"

"Stop that stupid drama! I have to leave him here for a while," said Neschar to the DDEs. "Later I will show him to our Hydra Lord, HAHAHAHA!!!" then he left the room and locked the metal door.

Spencer was very sick and he could not speak well. He was sitting in a corner next to his wife, Dianara and to the other two DDEs. Zoroaster was also with them, and he was sleeping on the other side of the room. Shiela and Aaron had no knowledge about their relationship to Zoroaster yet due to the DDE's secrecy to their kin.

Until, Kenji had finally regained his consciousness…

"Kenji!" called Aaron to Kenji happily when he saw Kenji's eyes slowly opened. "Remember me? It's me, Aaron! Your cousin from… From Damsville! Shiela and I are your cousins!"

Shiela gladly approached Kenji. "Hello, Kenji! Have you forgotten us? We lived together in Damsville before… Along with Claude, that Damsville's famous thief!"

Kenji was now wondering when he got up. "W-What is going on in here? Where am I? Uh…" then he turned to Shiela and Aaron who were both staring at him intensely with their smile. "And, um… who are you?"

"Oh, come on cousin. This is Shiela!" Shiela pinched Kenji's arm lightly. "Do you still remember when we lived together in our small house in Damsville and then we met Claude? The badass thief?"

"O-Oh!" Kenji remembered. "Oh, oh, oh, I know you two! Genji and I met you two in Damsville before and we stayed in your home for years, and…"

Shiela and Aaron were glad knowing that Kenji had finally remembered them. "Yey, you're right Kenji! Long time no see!" cried Shiela when she and Aaron hugged Kenji very tightly in excitement. "Aaron and I have been missing you so much because you never returned to Damsville again. Do you know that we are cousins?"

"Cousins?"

Shiela was ecstatically happy. "Yeah! I learned that I am a daughter of your father's brother, as well as Aaron."

Kenji smiled. "Really?"

"Yes, cousin!"

"Then… You and Aaron are both DDEs…" Kenji was overjoyed to what he just learned. "You're lucky…"

"Yeah… Aaron and I were promoted in an early time, Kenji. You know what? We have heard much about you! We learned that you and Claude are Explorers too, as well as your older brother (Reinhardt). We also heard that you're an Element Wielder now… Oh, by the way… We have an Element Wielder too in DDE, over there… His name is Zoroaster!" then Shiela pointed her finger at Zoroaster in a corner.

"Oh, I see. So what is his element?"

"He is an Element Wielder of Ice. He's a great warrior too!"

Kenji nodded. Then, Shiela pulled Kato's arm closer to her to introduce him to her cousin.

"Kenji, I would like you to meet my husband. His name is Kato. We got married just ten months ago."

Kato offered his hand to Kenji to shake hands with him. They shook hands.

"Wait a minute… I believe you're still young to get married, aren't you Shiela?" asked Kenji in wonder after they shook hands. "I'm eighteen… and what is your age now?"

"I am older than you, Kenji!" answered Shiela with her sweet smile. "I don't think I am still that too young for marriage anymore."

"Oh… Really?" Kenji scratched his head. "O-Oh yeah, I remember. You and Aaron are both older than me and Genji… Hehehe!"

Silence. Later, Aaron spoke to Kenji in his serious voice this time. "Kenji… The Expland is into you, d-do you know that?"

Kenji was surprised, but he did not answer to Aaron's question. Instead, he looked around the room in wonder. "Um, by the way Shiela and Aaron, where are we right now?" he asked. "This scary, dark room looks very unfamiliar to me…"

Aaron answered. "We're in Burnham, Kenji. The Expland used us as their bait in order for the Explorers to forcibly come here and take what they want from us. And do you know that you are the only one they really need? I just felt something very strong but strange in you, and that's maybe the reason why they also took you in this place with us."

THE EXPLORERS

"Huh?" there was a question mark on Kenji's head. "What do you mean by that strange strong feeling of yours?"

Shiela seriously spoke to Kenji. "Kenji listen, the Expland has their dragon-like lord called as the Hydra. He is one of the gods whom King Jethro punished long, long time ago and was turned to stone. In order for him to return to his true form is to pour your blood on him and suck the power of the king's Holy element from your body. The Expland believes that the Holy element is the Hydra's cure to restore his power and return to his true form again. And since that you're the chosen Holy Wielder of King Jethro…"

Kenji suddenly frowned in disappointment. "What a bummer! Why does everybody in this world want to take King Jethro's powers though they are not the chosen ones? That annoys me really!"

Aaron added. "In addition to that Kenji, the Expland will offer a person's life to their Hydra Lord as their common ritual, which means that they will kill you! They are all Dark Mages!"

"That will never gonna happen!"

"But what if they will kill you?"

"No they won't. The Holy element will never neglect me nor leave me on my side. It will not permit anything that will hurt me or if I'll die, the Expland will still never claim King Jethro's power from me!"

Shiela was amazed from what she heard from Kenji. She nodded. "You're brave, cousin… I am impressed to your courage."

Kenji's face was now looking very serious, but he felt more disappointed when he saw the Briant couple who were both asleep in one small bed inside the room. Their hands and feet were both chained. Later, he looked at his two cousins still in his serious face and then he closed his eyes. "King Jethro, I ask your guidance and protection. I know I can't do it all by myself but with your power vested in me, the Holy Element will protect me and help me to stop their evil ways. I swear to you, King Jethro that they will not be able to offer my dead body to their lord!" then he opened his eyes. A bright shining white halo suddenly glowed around his body for a second. "I can stop them alone… all at once!"

The two could not believe to what they had witnessed. They suddenly gaped in amazement by their cousin's power and courage in facing the incoming ritual by the Expland today!

44 SACRIFICE

The escaped Explorers of UE, EUE, and DDE were now on their way to Burnham using the UE's large aircraft. They brought some captured Explands who would lead their way to the Expland's base.

"Are you sure that this leads to Burnham?" asked Lucky to an Expland as he was pointing his revolver at him. "Remember, if we find out that you're lying… then you will never return to your base again… Alive!"

The Expland answered nervously. "Y-Yes! We're showing you the right way, we swear!"

Lucky tried to scare the Expland. "I can read your idiotic mind that you're lying! You see this gun? Do not force me to pull the trigger and put your life to an end today!"

"N-No!"

Lucky moved his revolver closer to the Expland's forehead. "I'll shoot you now!"

"N-NO, PLEASE! We are not lying, we really swear!!!"

The group of UEs along with Elijah was silent, while they were listening and watching Lucky's style of bullying to the Expland. Everyone looked very serious.

"Are we getting closer to Burnham now?" asked Genji to the Expland.

"Y-Yes! Close enough… I promise!!!"

Meanwhile in Expland's palace…

Neschar was now talking to their lord which was a giant Hydra statue in another dark sealed room. The Hydra learned that the Wielder of his cure was now in the palace, waiting for the right time to begin the ritual.

"He is the son of the former DDE leader whose name is Alex Foster, my lord. His name is Maximillian, and he is being chosen by the god to become the Wielder of his ultimate power. That same god who punished you and turned you to what you are right now," said Neschar while kneeling in front of the giant statue. "He's here, and he is ready for the offering."

The Hydra statue answered in his deep, monstrous-like voice to Neschar. 'WHERE IS HE?"

"I brought him in the prison along with his fellow Explorers we captured, my lord."

"I HAVE BEEN LONG DESIRING TO RETURN TO MY REAL FORM AGAIN, NESCHAR! DO NOT PUT THIS THINGS IN VAIN... AND I EXPECT YOU HAVE MADE THE RIGHT SELECTION TO THIS MAN SO WE CAN START THE RITUAL IMMEDIATELY!"

Neschar was still on his knees. "I won't... I will never, ever let you down, my lord... I am certain that I am bringing to you the right man who will bring you back to your true form again."

"VERY WELL THEN..." the stony eyes of the giant statue glowed in red. "BRING THIS MAN BEFORE ME NOW AND OFFER TO ME HIS LIFE IMMEDIATELY!"

"Yes, my lord!" answered Neschar and then he stood up before the Hydra.

"I WANT TO MOVE FREELY AGAIN! I'VE BEEN LONG WANTED TO RETURN TO MY FORM AGAAAAIIINNNN!!!"

There was a sudden earthquake around the room by the deep monstrous voice of the Hydra when he spoke to Neschar again. "NESCHAR, BRING ME THIS MAXIMILLIAN NOW!!!"

"Yes, my lord!" answered Neschar and then he left the room, leaving the giant statue alone.

"Oh, dear..." said Kenji as he was searching something in his back and waist. "They just took my weapon! Shiela, Aaron... Do you have your weapons with you?"

Shiela and Aaron shrugged their shoulders and shook their head. "We neither..." said Shiela.

"They already took our weapons when we were still in their airship," said Kato.

"Then..." added Aaron. "...when we arrived in this scary looking palace, the Explands mimicked our own appearances exactly from head to toe! They're good mimickers!"

"Then, what did you do next?"

"We could not fight them. We were all confused to who's who!" said Shiela who was still next to her husband. "After they mimicked us, they put us into their trap. We instantly fell to our sleep… Until they brought us here in this dark prison."

Kenji got mad. "Man, stupid amateurs…"

"The DDE mansion is in danger, Kenji. We were overran by these Dark Mages!" added Aaron in his angry voice. "We have no weapons in our hands now!"

"We can recover those weapons, Aaron. Don't worry about it."

"But, do you know where our weapons are, Kenji?"

"Don't worry about it!"

They suddenly heard a sound of the key clicking from outside the room. Then, the doorknob turned and the door opened. It was Neschar, along with the Explands!

"NESCHAR!" cried the Explorers.

Neschar pointed his finger at Kenji and he commanded the Explands next to him. "GET HIM!"

The Explands came inside the room and they quickly grabbed Kenji's arms to drag him out of the prison.

"Kenji!" cried Aaron.

"H-Hold on! What are you going to do to me now?" asked Kenji to the Explands looking confused.

"You will know when we get there, Maximillian…" said Neschar then he turned to the Explands. "Bring him to the Hydra Lord!"

"Oh no…" said Shiela looking worried. "Not that sacrifice please…"

Aaron ran towards the Explands to help Kenji but they strongly kicked his stomach away from them. They kept on dragging the young man out of the prison.

"Dang! Please do not hurt our cousin… KENJI!!!" cried Aaron as he was banging the brick floor real hard.

The Explands walked away from the room with Kenji and they locked the metal door. Aaron kept on banging the floor angrily while the seven DDEs were just watching him.

"Dammit! Dammit! Dammit!" said Aaron very angrily. "They are about to offer Kenji to their evil god now!" then he banged again. "They will bring havoc to this innocent world! We must do something to stop it before it happens!!!"

"Kenji..." said Shiela in her low voice while her hand was on her chest. "I hope that you can protect yourself... Please save yourself!"

The Explands took Kenji in another room. There, they shoved Kenji's back causing him to topple to the floor and tied his hands to his back. Then, they punched his face and kicked his stomach so he cried out loud in pain. The young man could not fight nor cast his magic since his hands were tied tightly. The Explands kept on assaulting the helpless Kenji cruelly, and then, they also tied his body so he could not move anymore.

"What, Maximillian? Does it feel good?" asked Neschar to downed Kenji as he was chuckling evilly. "Your Holy element is useless now! Go ahead Explands, show him the meaning of pain before he will die sooner!"

The assault continued in the room. The helpless young man had got many blows and kicks by the cruel Explands. He was screaming in pain, while Neschar seemed enjoying while watching Kenji crying in pain.

"G-Go to hell, Neschar!" cried Kenji in his hoarse voice to Neschar.

"Maximillian!" called Neschar to Kenji after he ignored Kenji's last remark. "Stand up! Prove to me that you really are King Jethro's warrior and is the son of Alex Foster! Stand up!!!"

The young man could not stand as he was groaning in pain. His body was bent on the floor after the blows. Neschar quickly moved closer to him and glared at him. "I said stand up, Maximillian! You really are the weakling!!!" then he slapped Kenji's bloody face.

"M-Maybe YOU are the weakling..." said Kenji in his weak, hoarse voice antagonizing Neschar.

"What did you say?!"

"U-Untie me and I will show you what a real man can do. Y-You're nothing but a cowardly leader hiding under the skirt of your lord Hydra and nothing else, am I right? S-So who's the weakling to us then? Me? Pwah... I-I don't think so!"

Neschar's blood quickly shot to his head upon hearing what Kenji said and instantly got mad, so he strongly kicked Kenji's cheek and his bloods splattered on to the floor. He pinched Kenji's cheek real hard, then he moved his face closer to him.

"GODDAMN YOU! You don't give me your respect, you witless

Wielder!" said Neschar angrily as he was still pinching Kenji's cheek harder. The young man cried out loud again. "If you only knew, Maximillian… It is your time now to say goodbye to those you love because today is the last day of your life!"

Kenji did not answer while Neschar was still pinching his bloody face. He knew what this Expland leader meant by that… The Hydra!

"We will bring your life to an end before him, but before we do that, first we're going to give you some pleasure… by being so disrespectful and insulting our lord!" said Neschar. "I like you, Maximillian… You're a nice toy to play with, do you know that?!" then he removed his hand from Kenji's cheek and moved away, but soon, he strongly kicked Kenji's stomach again.

"Arrgghhh…" Kenji was groaning in pain while his tied body was bent. His eyes were shedding tears by the intense pain he got from the Explands.

"Take off his clothes," commanded Neschar to his colleagues. "Untie him first!"

The Explands followed. They moved closer to Kenji to untie his body and his hands first before they took off his clothes and stripped him half naked.

"Tsk, tsk, tsk…" Kenji was shaking his head in disapproval. "W-What's the meaning of this? …Can't you even take off my clothes by yourself?" asked Kenji to Neschar in his harsh voice while glaring at him. "…Does this mean that you're the weakling than I am, indeed? Heh… How pathetic you really are… JERK!"

Neschar had completely lost his temper, so he quickly moved over Kenji again as he was jostling the Explands away from the young man. Then, he strongly hit Kenji with his sword's handle and stripped him again to almost naked.

"GODDAMN YOU, MAXIMILLIAN! YOU SHOULD GO TO HELL WHEN YOU'RE DEAD. YOU'RE TOTALLY THAT WORTHLESS!!!" then he pushed Kenji back to the floor in his naked, wounded body. "Look at yourself now. You've got too much bruises, wounds, and blood! You look more pathetic now than what you think, idiot!"

The assault continued. Neschar strongly kicked Kenji's hands so he would not be able to cast his Holy magic anymore. The helpless Holy

Wielder did nothing else but to just scream out loud in an intense pain.

Neschar ordered them to stop now by raising his right hand and spoke as he turned to his back. "We must stop the fun now. After all, let's give this Wielder a chance of taking his long deeper breaths for now because later he will breathe to his last breath!" then he quickly turned to Kenji and laughed out loud again. "Say goodbye now Maximillian, because today is your final day of your life. Take him to our lord now!!!"

A big, muscular Expland dragged Kenji in his arm and he carried him in his back. Neschar walked out the room along with his colleagues and they locked the metal door. Kenji's eyes were closed while his bloods were dropping to their path, but they were unaware that the group of Explorers had finally arrived in their palace. Neschar's group was currently on their way to their Hydra Lord, while the group of Explorers was now looking for the eight DDEs as well as Kenji inside the huge scary-looking palace.

"The Explorers!" cried an Expland when he saw the group of UEs in the hall. "Kill them all!"

"Now group ourselves into two!" said Elijah to his fellow UEs as his voice was echoing around the hall. "We'll take care of these. Element Wielders, you'll take care of Kenji! Please move fast, they will gonna kill him today!"

"Alright!" the Element Wielders followed and they left the hall, leaving Elijah and the other UEs fighting the Explands. As the Element Wielders were escaping the fight, Maximus followed them.

"Your friend will be gone too soon!" said an Expland to Margot as they were fighting with each other.

"You cahnnot dehceive meh, you stuphid looking mohron!" answered Margot as he was doing his martial arts moves to his opponent. "Mah husband Kenjih will nehver gihve up on you. Now take thiiiisssss!!!" then he suddenly kissed the Expland lips-to-lips!

"EEEE!!!" the Expland shrieked goofily as he was freaking out. His face was looking disgusted. "The gay just kissed me, too gross. AHHH!!!" then he ran away. Margot was delighted.

The group of Element Wielders was still searching for Kenji and the eight DDEs. "Hey, Explorers!" called Lucky out loud as his voice was also echoing in the hallway. "Where are you? We're here now to save all of you!"

The group of Explands suddenly appeared before them. Then they quickly mimicked the Wielders' appearance from head to toe. Even their weapons were also imitated except their powers. Everyone was shocked.

"What in the world…"

"Whoa!" Tyrone was amazed. "They just copied our exact appearances and also our weapons. That's totally amazing!"

"Yes, indeed! They really are good mimickers!" added Shingue.

The Explands suddenly rushed to attack them. The showdown between the two groups had started as their weapons were clashing to each other. The fight was fierce, long, and extreme!

Later, the fight had turned to disorder. Shingue accidentally attacked the real Isagani whom he mistakenly identified as an Expland mimicker.

"Stupid Expland!" shouted Shingue as he was doing his chain of combo attacks towards the real poor Isagani. "You have no originality! IMPERSONATORS, ha-yaahhh!" then he struck Isagani with his fist. "I am going to end this fight now, POISON POW--"

"S-Shingue…" called Isagani to Shingue looking hurt as he was limping before him. "I-It's me… Isagani Pharell of UE… I'm not your enemy… I-I belong to your side!"

Shingue was very surprised and he dropped his weapon to his side. Then he quickly approached Isagani in his blushing face and hugged him. "I-I am so sorry, Isagani. I assumed that you were fake, that's why!" he said to Isagani.

Despite of his injury he got from Shingue, the poor Isagani still managed to smile at him and laugh while everyone was still in the middle of the battle. "Understandable, okay!!!"

The battle was still in confusion. The mood of the fight was belligerent. Some of the Explorers were fighting with their own allies thinking that they were Expland mimics.

"Our fight is getting haywire!" cried Reinhardt as he stopped his attack to his opponent after realizing that their fight was getting out of control. "All of the UEs, please stand beside me and let us think of a way of finishing the fight without attacking our own allies. Quickly now!!!"

His allies stopped and they followed his command so they dashed towards him. Their opponents also banded together in a single line. The two groups were facing each other, but the Element Wielders did not realize that some of their allies in the line were Explands. Only the Explands knew who among them were their allies in their group and also in Reinhardt's group.

Silence. The two groups were still facing each other in their serious faces when Reinhardt spoke first. "We all know that your group is a great mimickers, but we UEs will still--"

Claude answered to Reinhardt who was in the other group, thinking that he was the fake one. "Heh! What is this UE you're blabbering about? You can even imitate the tone of our voices. What a joke!"

"Imitate?!" said Clio who was in Reinhardt's group. "Shut your trap, idiot! We can still defeat you today, it is much better to surrender the fight and take us to Kenji immediately... Rather than wasting our time with this boring fight!"

Some of the Explands were mum. They were just listening to the gibberish quarrel between the Element Wielders. They were grinning to their fellow Explands unnoticed to the Wielders' eyes. The other Explands wanted to make fun with the Wielders so they thought of joining the quarrel.

"We're real!" cried fake Maximus who was in Reinhardt's group. He was pointing at Jon. "You're the fake one!'

"I'm the real Jon!" answered Jon angrily.

The fake Jon teased Jon in mockingly way. "Hah, what a great impostor you are, cheater!"

"I said I'm the real Jon!"

"Fine!" said Maximus in his serious, angry voice. "Your talks are all too rubbish! I can perceive that the Explands are making fool out of us. Haven't you all noticed that?!"

The two groups fell suddenly silent for a moment. The quarrel had stopped. They looked at each other, realizing that maybe some of their fellow allies next to them were actually not the real ones. Some of them were Explands!

The fake Maximus who was in Reinhardt's group tried to deceive the real prince in the other group. "How about you? Can you even tell who among us is the real one and the fake one?"

The prince chuckled seriously. "Fool! Of course, we will only fight the same person who mimicked us. And, I am certain that these mimickers can not imitate the power of the elements. That's it, so we will have a clean, fair fight... Critical thinking!" then he pointed his forehead with his serious smile.

The Explands were mouthed. The prince supposedly had revealed the weakness of their mimicking tricks. Everyone looked at each other again, while the others were now looking intensely to their look-alikes.

"You're right, Maximus! Nice strategy. Good idea!" agreed Lucky and then he drew out his Lucky Staff. Then, he pointed his weapon at his look-alike. "Now Lucky number two, allow me face you alone and also kick your ass! Get ready for our fight!"

The other Explands were now defeated by Elijah's group and they finally told the Explorers where the eight DDEs and Kenji were at.

Meanwhile, the group of Neschar along with Kenji was now at the Hydra's room. Firstly, Neschar introduced the bloodied young man to their god while the young man's body was drooped over the shoulder of the big, muscular Expland.

"SO, IS THIS THE MAXIMILLIAN YOU WERE TALKING ABOUT, NESCHAR?" asked the Hydra to Neschar.

"Positive," answered Neschar grinning evilly. "He is the main Wielder of the god who punished you, my lord… The only one who will turn you back to your true form again."

The stony eyes of the Hydra statue lit up in excitement and joy. "IS HE ALREADY DEAD, NESCHAR?!"

"No, not yet. He refused to come with us, so we assaulted him first before we brought him here before you, my lord."

"WHAAATTT??!" the Hydra's deep, monstrous voice echoed, creating strong shake in the room again. "WHY IS TAKING SO LONG? I'VE BEEN WANTING TO MOVE FREELY AGAIN AS BEFORE SO I CAN TAKE MY REVENGE!!!"

"Do not worry, my lord. We will kill him right in front of you!" Neschar grinned again in his evil-looking face.

"I WOULD LOVE TO SEE THAT!" said the evil Hydra in excitement. "I DON'T WANT TO TAKE THIS ANY LONGER. NEVERMIND THE RITUAL… NOW KILL THAT MAN AND LET ME HAVE HIS ELEMENTAL POWER. MOVE!!!"

The big, muscular Expland laid Kenji down on the brick stand facing upwards when Neschar slowly lifted his long, four-edged sharp sword. He spoke to Kenji in his low voice as his eyes were looking at him. "Farewell, Maximillian…"

His sword was about to stab straight to Kenji's chest when something suddenly prevented him in killing the young man. He felt a strong force that pushed his hand in the air, which made him drop his sword and it clanged on the floor. And then, a speeding spear suddenly zoomed over them that came from above. Neschar avoided the incoming spear and he quickly turned above in his angry face. "Who is it? An Explorer? Show yourself, you coward!"

"I am not an Explorer and especially I am not a coward," a voice answered from above when a mysterious person appeared from the dark ceiling… It was Akira. "I am Augustus Sawyer of Pioneer, Maximillian's rival. I'm the new leader of our group."

"Sawyer? Leader of the Pioneer?" asked Neschar while looking above at Akira. The Hydra was feeling bored. "What do you want in here and why were you preventing me from killing him?! Would you also like to come with him to his death??!"

"You know, Pioneers… we are all unpredictable. Sometimes we can do things that even our friends think that we are not capable of doing it," then he jumped off from the top and faced the Explands. The Hydra was more in his boredom now. "I just came in the DDE mansion earlier because I was looking for a mysterious woman whose name was Angeles. She was the one who gave me an element of Deity and Peace. Since that day, the element of Deity and Peace was trying to control my well-being. I do not understand about it, but the element itself is sending me a message which is hard to comprehend. Sometimes, I am doing something that I don't usually do. So this raises my curiosity about her and the reason behind the need of something from Kenji!"

Neschar raised his eyebrow towards Akira looking puzzled. "And then?"

"I knew that she was in the DDE mansion because I told her the way to the base so I followed her. But when I came to the mansion, I held one of the guards there and he told me that there was no Angeles that came… And, he also said that Kenji was being caught by you," Akira was pointing at Kenji in his back. "I assumed that Angeles was here too… Anyway, it's doesn't matter when I come here without her presence. What more important is, I have found Kenji here in this dark, scary palace of yours!"

Neschar was now holding his sword again. "Now what do you need from him then? I don't care if you're the Wielder of Deity now. You're just interfering our ceremony today! Now go away and leave this place before I will kill you too!"

Akira did not answer. He was also holding his long cross-headed spear when later the Hydra spoke to Neschar. "NESCHAR, WHAT NOW?! I'M GETTING TOO IMPATIENT!!!"

"You have no right of killing Maximillian because I am the ONLY person who can kill him alone!" said Akira in his serious voice still facing Neschar. "He's mine... Mine only!"

"Mr. Sawyer, we are not enemy nor friends. Do not interrupt our business here. Leave at once or you will face our wrath!" said Neschar angrily. Little did they know, the Element Wielders were now on their way to the Hydra's room after their fight with Explands.

Neschar suddenly rushed to Akira and the two fought with each other. The Explands were surprised to the Pioneer's sudden move when Akira quickly gripped Neschar's body with his arms very tightly. The Deity element reacted when he felt Akira's strength in gripping Neschar, so it helped the Wielder to raise his gripping strength even more.

Akira quickly squeezed Neschar's neck after he toppled over the ground facing the floor. Neschar could not move and he could not even breathe well, so he called his fellow Explands in his angry, grunting voice. "H-Hurry... K-Kill the Holy W-Wielder for me... K-Kill that M-Maxim--"

"N-No, don't!" cried Akira as he was still strangling Neschar. "Don't kill him! He's mine only!!!"

"FAREWELL!" said the Explands next to Kenji as their weapons were about to strike, but...

"FIRE!

"AIR!"

"LIGHT!"

"WHAT THE--??!"

The group of Element Wielders had finally arrived in Hydra's room. Akira grinned seriously, as he was watching the Explands who were now burning by Jon's fire as he cast the Fire magic on them. The fire grew big with the help of Cyan's Air-based magic.

The Death appeared after Reinhardt summoned him and he slashed the burning Explands with his scythe. The Explands suddenly disappeared in thin air like bubbles, and their souls went straight to the Underworld by the Darkness element.

"Damn... I failed the offering!!!" shouted Neschar when Akira strongly punched his face and he toppled to the floor once again. The UE

Wielders (with Maximus) were appalled when Akira slowly walked closer to them and he glared at them. The Wielders moved one step backward from him, and they were all looking confused to what was going on.

"You lost, Neschar..." said Akira to Neschar as he was standing next to the Explorers. "Always remember, the good will always prevail over the evil!"

The boys were all gaped at Akira. They did not expect that Akira would say something like that, knowing that he was a ruthless, young warrior for so long.

Kenji slowly opened his eyes when Claude quickly approached him and smiled. "Kenji... we're finally here to save you... Don't worry, you're safe in our hands now..."

Kenji also smiled to Claude and answered weakly. "T-Thank you everyone... Thank you..." then he closed his eyes again.

"Don't worry, I am here now..."

"HOW COULD YOU INTERFERE WITH OUR CEREMONY TODAY, YOU WORTHLESS WIELDERS OF JETHRO?!!" cried the Hydra angrily when the room was shaking again by his deep voice. "I WILL END YOUR LIFE THEN BY MYSELF. BE GONE NOW!!!"

The Hydra's stony eyes glowed in red and a long beam of lasers suddenly came out from his eyes. The lasers were so hot and so powerful that anything they touched would be sliced into two. Since the Hydra was just a giant statue with limited movements, his laser attack would be his only offense and self-defense to the enemies.

The long beam of lasers crossed all over the room while the Wielders were all dodging them. Neschar joined the fight too as he was also dodging the lasers going straight to the Wielders. Akira had dodged a single beam when he swiftly dashed towards Neschar to give him the finishing touch with his spear. The god statue sensed the danger towards his loyal servant, so he threw a blinding beam straight to Akira for the kill. With his quick reflexes, Akira was able to reach the mirror hanging on the wall and he deflected the beam back to the statue. The Hydra was hit on his shoulder, and a piece of stone of his body fell down to the ground. The god statue was so upset and angry, so he threw more beams in all directions hoping somebody would be hit. The Wielders took refuge underneath the Hydra's feet, since the Hydra could not bow to reach them.

"Claude!" called Clio to Claude. "Since you and I are the Gravity and

Earth Wielders, why don't you use your strong fist to destroy that statue and I'll focus the gravity to the beams so I can lift them away from us?!"

"It's very easy for you to say, Clio… Yes, he cannot move freely, but he's a psychic monster! Do you know what I mean?"

"But we don't have a Wielder who can stop a psychic, Claude!"

"You're wrong, Clio! Haven't you noticed Akira right now?" asked Tyrone in the midst of chaos. "I think Akira is the only Wielder who can beat a psychic himself!!!"

"What do you mean by Akira?!"

"I can't believe my eyes, Clio… but I just found out that this Pioneer is one of us now! He's an Element Wielder too!"

"H-Huh?!"

"Listen, he is not just a Magic Wielder… but an Element Wielder of Deity and Peace!"

"R-Really? So how'd you find it out, Tyrone?"

"We have seen his actions since earlier! Haven't you noticed that?!"

Claude and Clio just noticed Akira's action of controlling the mind of the Hydra when the beams stopped appearing from his evil eyes. The two gaped in surprise.

Neschar and Maximus were now fighting with each other in mid-air. Behind his look as a snobbish, innocent man, and unskilled in combat, Maximus was actually a great fighter. Unknown to Explorers, he had his secret weapon in his hand. It was a flute made of real gold, a dual-function flute that could be used as an instrument and a weapon, since its end had its short sword that was hidden inside.

Kenji slowly stood with difficulty and he limped off in the middle of the fight. Akira stopped in his attack when he saw Kenji limping away. The Hydra saw him too, and he cried out loud. "MY ONLY CURE! COME BACK HERE!!!"

Upon hearing the monstrous voice of his lord, Neschar rushed after Kenji but the raging Explorers quickly blocked his way.

Still in the middle of the fight, Akira quickly came in aid to Kenji. Kenji's eyes were wide-opened, because he just learned that Akira was there too in the dark room.

Why is he here? What does this man want from me? Thought Kenji to himself. *A fight? Does he want to fight with me right now?*

"Kenji…" called Akira. "I'm here to…"

THE EXPLORERS

"A-Akira," called Kenji looking very surprised. "If you only came here just to fight with me today… then I'm ready. B-But… not for now…"

"I-I am here because…"

"Someone here wants to kill me, Akira…" added Kenji in his glaring eyes towards Akira. "I need to protect myself because--"

Akira gently lifted his hand to touch Kenji's chest and then he closed his eyes. Then, the two started to glow in white when Akira was uttering a "healing prayer" with his element, thus the wounded body of Kenji was slowly getting healed. Kenji was mum, but he was wondering to what Akira was actually doing to him right now.

After Akira healed the young man, Kenji could not help not to ask Akira about what he did to him while everyone was still in the middle of chaos. "Akira? Why did you heal me despite of our rivalry? What is this power you cast on me?"

"I just don't want others to kill you, Kenji… but only me alone," answered Akira in his serious voice.

"D-Don't tell me you're an Element Wielder now, aren't you?! What is it then?"

"Heh! I am holding the power of an element that is stronger than your Holy element, Kenji. It's a Deity and Peace element!"

Kenji was in great disbelief. "What? B-But… But where did you get it?!"

Akira smirked. "You will find it out someday. For now, you must live… Until the day will come that I will put your life to an end when we see each other again!"

Kenji was still looking very surprised.

"You should live, Kenji. For now I will help you kick the Expland's asses so their rubbish offering won't continue anymore. You understand me?"

Kenji just nodded, but still he was looking surprised. "Y-Yeah, you're right… I understand," then he posed. "Let's get rid of these enemies together for now, Akira…"

Akira did not answer. He watched Kenji from head to toe and noticed that he was fully naked without any weapons in his hand. So, he took off his coat and he gave it to Kenji. Next, he drew out his another spear in his back and also gave it to Kenji.

"Let's rock, dude!" said Akira to Kenji, and then the two joined the fight with the Explorers against the Explands.

At last, the group of Elijah had found the eight DDEs who were still imprisoned in the dark room. Spencer was still sick, and his wife ordered the Explorers to assist him in walking as they escaped the palace. Good thing that the group also found and recovered the weapons of Kenji and the eight DDEs in another room.

"I want to help the UEs over there!" said Aaron to Elijah's group. "Our cousin, Kenji is in danger and he needs me now!"

Elijah's group were mouthed. They just learned that Kenji, Genji, and Reinhardt had their cousin in DDE class.

"Gimme that Kenji's staff, quickly now!" said Aaron to the UEs as he snatched Kenji's Kali from Elijah's hand. "I will save him… I'll leave Mr. Briant to you. Keep an eye on him as you leave this place because he is sick and--"

Elijah refused to Aaron's request. "We will be the ones to save Kenji and you must go with the DDEs. This is our mission, so it is much better if you go back to your base and protect the mansion against the possible incoming enemies. Do not let the enemies overtake the base!"

"Just promise us that you will save Kenji and come back to the mansion with him," said Shiela to Elijah looking worried. "Thank you for saving us!"

"Give me that staff and go!" Elijah also took the Kali from Aaron's hand and he turned to the DDEs again. "You must leave here immediately and protect Sir Briant. Leave this mission to us. I am sure that Kenji is safe now. I'll give this weapon when I see him later."

The DDEs nodded when Kato answered. "Roger! We'll take care of Sir Briant as well as the sacred objects in the mansion… We've leaving now. Take care, UEs!"

The DDEs assisted Spencer in walking as they were now escaping the palace hurriedly. The seven DDEs had left the palace safely, but Zoroaster stayed behind with the UEs. Elijah noticed him, so he asked him in wonder. "Hey, why are you still here? You must come with your colleagues and assist our leader in going back to the mansion safely."

"The other EUEs and DDEs are currently in the mansion, so they're no longer need my help there," answered Zoroaster to Elijah in his serious voice.

"Oh, come on! You better go back to the mansion with them and help the Explorers in there!"

"I'm an Element Wielder, Elijah..." said Zoroaster seriously. "I'm a great help in neutralizing the enemies. Now it is my time to use my power along with you, Explorers!"

Elijah nodded and he smiled as he was staring at Zoroaster. "Alright then, let's complete this mission together. Follow us Zorro!" then the group ran together with Zoroaster towards the Hydra's room.

The long battle was still very ferocious. The Element Wielders were now able to summon their Vrandolons successfully. But the Hydra and Neschar were both protected by their "shield magic" so the Vrandolons could not destroy the giant statue. Claude gave a strong blow to the earth when the ground started to shake, but it was also ineffective.

As for Neschar, he was just standing in front of the Hydra within the shield magic. His face was looking confused, since they were now surrounded by the Explorers and Vrandolons who kept on attacking their shield. The Explorers could not figure it out how could they destroy the shield magic. Unfortunately, the another group of Explands suddenly came inside the room, causing the Explorers to lose their tempo from destroying the shield. They quickly turned their attention to the enemies, then they rushed again to start the fight leaving Neschar and the Hydra behind.

Akira and Kenji were close together in fighting the Explands as if they were partners. They were both casting their elemental-based magics to the enemies combined with their martial arts techniques.

Due to their ferocious, aggressive, and successive fights, the entire Hydra's room was getting destroyed. But later, Neschar decided to remove the shield magic to join the fight with them for a while. Then, he quickly went back to the Hydra again and mimicked Kenji from head to toe!

"UEs!" shouted Lucky as he stopped for a moment when he saw another Kenji next to the Hydra. "There's another Kenji over there!"

The UEs turned to where the second Kenji was standing, even Kenji had seen his self next to the Hydra.

Neschar secretly signaled his allies and the Explands changed their respective appearance into the same person as Kenji. Now they were all looking the same Kenji!

"What the--!"

The real Kenji was looking surprised to see his look-alikes all over the room. He was still next to Akira, but the disguised Neschar secretly teleported to his back and he cast a magic on him, causing him to be hypnotized by Neschar's magic. Neschar silently took Kenji away from Akira, then he hid the young man behind the group of fake Kenjis so the Wielders would not see him. Later, Akira noticed that Kenji was no longer at his side. He peered around to look for the Holy Wielder, and then, he cried to the Explorers. "Oh, no! They took away Kenji from here that fast! Geez, they're fleet-footed… I didn't notice their quick move next to me earlier!"

The group of Wielders with Akira gathered together to form a single line, while the group of Explands in their Kenji's appearance also gathered together before the Hydra statue. Neschar and real Kenji were actually just standing behind the Explands to hid themselves from the group of Wielders.

Silence. The two groups were facing each other and posing for the attack. In the middle of the silence, Neschar spoke to his allies in mind. "I'll leave these fools to you now and I'll take care of this Wielder alone. Do not allow these enemies to move close to our lord, you all get me?!"

The Explands answered spontaneously in Neschar's mind. "Yes, sir!"

Next, Neschar turned to the Hydra and also spoke to him in his mind. "My lord, allow me to move to another place with this Wielder so I can kill him alone without any interruptions. When I return, I will make sure that I will be bringing his dead body in front of you!"

"I AM LOOKING FORWARD TO THAT PLAN, NESCHAR!" answered the Hydra to Neschar's mind when he used his psychic power to transport the two to another place. The two suddenly disappeared like bubbles, and the Wielders did not see them since the fake Kenjis were all blocking them.

"Even if you hide Kenji from us, we will still know where he is!" said Reinhardt to the Explands. "Yes, you are all in his appearance, but you cannot mimic his powers. Now let's continue the fight again, you cheaters!"

The group of fake Kenjis spoke spontaneously to the group of Wielders. "We are Maximillian Foster. Which of us is real and which is not?"

Suddenly, a voice from far left shouted at them. "*Kuya* Reinhart it's me, Kenji!" then there was another voice followed from far right. "Claude it's me, Kenji!"

The Wielders posed themselves again for the fight while their eyes were peering at the mimickers. "Shut your filthy mouths! Return my brother to us, you devils!!!" shouted Genji.

The fake Kenjis also posed themselves for the fight. They spoke again simultaneously. "Get ready, Wielders… Maximillian's life will be over very soon. Near at hand!"

"I SAID SHUT UUUUUUPPPPP!!!"

The fierce fight continued…

As for Neschar and Kenji, they were teleported behind the palace right after the Hydra transported them with the use of his magic. No one was there, and Neschar laughed at loud while he was returning himself to his true form again, knowing that no one would interfere his plan of killing Kenji anymore.

"HAHAHA! Maximillian at last," laughed Neschar evilly while he was watching Kenji laid on the ground. He drew out his sword and he pointed it at the young man's face. "No one will me stop me now. So this is your last time to say your prayers… I AM SO EAGER TO KILL YOU, and the right time has finally come," then he lifted his sword up high and he shouted. "GOODBYE!!!"

When Neschar was about to stab Kenji, a sharp Sabre suddenly zoomed from the window and it hit Neschar's hand, causing him to drop his sword and he flinched back in pain. Elijah jumped off from the window above and he faced Neschar in his serious, angry face.

"AHHHRRGGGHHH!!!" Neschar cried out loud as a fresh blood was oozing down in his hand. "GODDAMN YOU, WHAT HAVE YOU DONE?!"

Elijah was standing before Neschar and he pulled his Sabre that was pierced into the ground. "You know what, Neschar? You are so predictable. You even failed in hiding yourself. What a moron you really are!" then he pointed his sword at Neschar.

Kenji regained the state of his consciousness again when the black magic cast on him slowly disappeared. He saw Elijah next to him, and he was alone. "Elijah?" he called.

"Kenji!" called Elijah to Kenji while his sword was still pointing at Neschar. "You're safe now. Marion, Vamir, and the others are now in the Hydra's room to help our colleagues. And I will help you kill this moron, okay?" then he handed over the recovered Kali back to Kenji. "Here's your weapon, I found it in one of the palace's room."

"My Kali!" said Kenji delightfully as he was holding his weapon again.

Elijah turned back his gaze to Neschar again. "You must accept your defeat now, Neschar… Because you are facing the two Explorers who will put your life to an end!"

Neschar did not answer. He took his dropped sword on the ground while the two Explorers were looking at him. Then, he suddenly rushed over the two Explorers who were shocked to his sudden, quick move. Neschar was also a great warrior and high skilled in fighting. Since he belonged to the Dark Mage class, he was possessing strong black types of magics that could give very strong blows to the two with just a single cast.

Neschar used his black magic, hitting the two Explorers and they flew away with its strong impact. The two retaliated immediately with their own weapons and their martial arts skill. Neschar cast his black magics on the two once again, but the two quickly dodged the magics and they struck again.

But after the long battle between them, the three were finally losing their strengths as if they were getting exhausted. The two Explorers were now looking weary and so as Neschar. They were all panting heavily, while their bloody faces were staring at each other with their glaring eyes. The fight continued.

"YAHHH!!!" shouted Neschar while he was attacking the two consecutively despite of his weariness. He did not want to be defeated by the two, but the two would also fight back immediately so Neschar would be hit by their strong blows.

Their aggressive, continuous fight took a lot of time, causing their bodies to finally ran out of strength by extreme weariness. Their wounded bodies were sprawled on the muddy ground. No one was moving. The three were all dead tired.

Silence.

Later, Neschar began to move. He slowly lifted his head first and then he weakly crawled towards Kenji who was still not moving. He weakly picked up his sword that was lying on the muddy ground and then he crawled again. He was seen by Elijah, who was lying few meters away from Kenji and he also crawled weakly to follow Neschar.

Neschar began to chuckle weakly as he was getting closer to Kenji who was still not moving. "Hahaha… It's now over… I-It's finally over!!!"

He chuckled again until he finally reached Kenji. Again, he lifted his sword up high when Elijah forced himself to stand and limped heavily as he moved towards Neschar. When Elijah reached Neschar, he quickly strangled him with his Sabre from behind.

"G-GET AWAY FROM ME!" cried Neschar as he was struggling himself to break free from Elijah's grip. They were next to Kenji, and Neschar bit off Elijah's arm so Elijah loosed his Sabre and he moved back in pain. Neschar was still holding his sword, but Elijah quickly strangled him again in his back. Finally, Kenji was the last man to rose, and he immediately saw the two who were both struggling right before him.

"Y-YOU'RE GETTING INTO MY NERVES!" cried Neschar as he was still being strangled by Elijah in his back. "T-THEN LET ME KILL YOU INSTEAD!"

Kenji's eyes quickly widened, and he cried out loud before the two. "NESCHAR, DON'T!!!"

Neschar made a quick, sudden move with his hands when Elijah suddenly loosed his neck and he quickly stabbed him with his sword in the chest. With such full force, Neschar's sword had penetrated Elijah's back!

"ELIJAAAAHHH!!!"

"Die now, you worthless Explorer! DIE!!!" cried Neschar and he stabbed Elijah again three times in the stomach.

Kenji was in great shock to see Elijah being stabbed by Neschar very badly. He wasted no time, so he quickly picked up his weapon and rushed to unmercifully stab Neschar in the chest. The young man was in his fury, as his eyes were now shedding tears of anger and he screamed very out loud!

"AAARRGGHHH!!!" Neschar cried in pain just as the Kali entered his muscular body. Elijah fell on the ground, bathing with his own blood from the wounds in his body. Neschar was the next one to fall on the ground, while the Kali's sword was stuck in his chest.

Elijah sacrificed his own life for the sake of his colleague and friend. He had shown gallantry and heroism in pursuing on King Jethro's promise of long lasting peace and stability in the universe.

Neschar was still alive gasping for air, but Elijah's condition was very critical now. He was catching his deep breaths while the blood was still flowing down throughout his body. He coughed badly, as the bloods also came out in his mouth.

Kenji gently lifted Elijah's head and he put it on his lap. He was preventing the rest of the bloods from coming out in Elijah's body. "No, Elijah… Please don't!" he said as he was tearing up the coat given to him by Akira to cover the wounds, but the blood did not stop from coming out. This time, Neschar had already lost his life… He was dead!

"Elijah… Elijah!" called Kenji to Elijah while weeping. Elijah's eyes were closed. "Please open your eyes… Elijah, hang on… Wake up! Our mission is complete now. The Explands are defeated. Elijah… Elijah!" then he hugged Elijah close to him very tightly.

Elijah slowly opened his eyes. He spoke to Kenji hesitantly in his weak, hoarse voice. "K-Kenji… You are right… I-It's over now…"

"Elijah, don't leave me," said Kenji while his face was already soaked by his own tears. "Maybe you have forgotten… we still have more missions that are needed to be done, right? You are the leader of UE… and we all need you so badly, Elijah…"

Elijah was now losing too much blood in his body. His body started to feel cold and numb. He did not answer. He slowly closed his eyes.

"Elijah?"

"K-Kenji… someday we will all be a part of the DDE… I promise…"

"Y-Yes…"

Until…

"Elijah? Elijah? N-No… Please don't leave us…"

Elijah's body already ran out of his own blood. He also lost his life as Neschar. Kenji kept on shaking Elijah's shoulder but he was no longer moving.

"Elijah, no… Please wake up… ELIJAAAAHHHH!!!"

Kenji embraced Elijah very tightly while he was screaming in grief. Elijah's bloodied face was leaning on his chest, and he kept on screaming on the top of his voice as he was still embracing Elijah.

"ELLLIIIJAAAAHHHH! NO… ELIJAAAAHHH, AAAAHHHHH!!"

The Explands sensed that their leader was defeated, so they decided to leave their palace immediately along with the Hydra. With the help of the Hydra's black magic, the group had suddenly disappeared like bubbles.

The Explands were all gone now when the Hydra's voice echoed all over the room. "WE WILL MEET AGAIN NEXT TIME! YOU WILL ALL PAY FOR WHAT YOU HAVE DONE TODAY! I SWEAR THAT I WILL RETURN INTO MY TRUE FORM AGAIN SOMEDAY

THE EXPLORERS

SOON! REMEMBER THIS!!!"

The boys were all mum as they were panting in exhaustion. It was already nighttime when the long battle ended. The lightning struck in the sky, until the rain began to fall strongly.

Kenji and Elijah were still outside the palace under the strong rain. Kenji was still embracing Elijah while still crying in grief. The rain waters mingled with his tears, as well as Elijah and Neschar's bloods that were flowing down the muddy ground...

The Expland palace was now completely ruined. Later, the Hydra used his unique magic to take Neschar's body with them as they were now fleeing away in the human world. Neschar's dead body had slowly disappeared before the eyes of Kenji, leaving the Kali sword and his blood to where he laid on. The rain was getting stronger, and Kenji screamed again on the top of his voice.

"ELIJAAAHHHH!!!"

His long, loud scream was heard by the Wielders who were still inside the palace. Claude quickly peered around to look for Kenji after he heard his scream echoing from the outside.

"H-Hey, that's Kenji!" said Claude to everyone.

"It came from outside the palace!" said Akira as he was pointing at the distance. "Come on, let's go over there!"

Everyone ran in a hurry to find and follow the source of Kenji's scream, thinking that the fight between him and Neschar was not yet over until now.

While running to the entrance: "Let's hurry up. Maybe Neschar will kill my brother immediately. I hope it's not too late yet!" cried Genji. "BROTHEEERRR!!!"

The palace's main door burst open and they ran outside the palace when they also got soaked by the strong rain. The lightning struck again, and the thunder was heard in the distance. They hurriedly went straight to the back of the palace when they reach Kenji and Elijah there.

Silence.

Shingue, Jon, and Claude were the first ones to approach the two who were still on the muddy ground. Kenji was still embracing Elijah while crying, and Elijah's bloodied head was still on Kenji's chest.

"What happened?" asked Shingue looking surprised. "What happened to Elijah, Kenji?"

Kenji did not answer. He was just sobbing. Everyone moved closer to the two when they saw Elijah in his body soaked by his own blood.

"K-Kenji... Don't tell me..."

Kenji slowly lifted his face and answered softly with his hoarse voice. "You're right, Shingue... It's already too late... Elijah's gone now," he sobbed, and then he spoke again in his angry voice. "It is all my fault why he died!"

Everyone was shocked to hear about Elijah's death. Because of this, some of them began to weep as well. Marion and Margot were the first to shed tears, as Marion cried out loud in grief so he quickly moved over Kenji and he looked at Elijah on Kenji's lap. He knelt on the ground, as the tears kept on falling from his eyes and he sobbed.

"*KUYA* ELIJAH! WAAAHHHH!!!" cried Marion as he was watching Elijah with his teary eyes. "I love *kuya* so much, I LOVE *KUYA* ELIJAH SO MUCH! Why did he die? WHYYY?!!" then he ran back to Margot to hug him while they were still crying in grief.

"IT'S ALL MY FAULT WHY HE'S GONE!!!" Kenji screamed again as he was sobbing. "Elijah, please forgive me! ELIJAAHHH!!!"

Genji and Claude approached Kenji, and they put their arms to each other's backs to comfort Kenji while their eyes were also shedding tears. Everyone was weeping now, except Maximus. As for Akira, despite of being the Pioneer, he seemed to get struck by everyone's intense sorrow as his eyes began to shed tears as well. He knew that he was not Elijah's close friend nor colleague, but why did he also felt a grief in his heart?

Then...

It was already late at night when everyone returned to the DDE mansion from Burnham. Akira was there, and the news about the incident happened during their special mission in Burnham was reached in the EUEs and DDEs who were left in the base. They were all in the main hall, and everyone in the mansion also wept after hearing about Elijah's death.

They were going to bury Elijah's remains in the DDE base, because it was the only Explorers base to have their own private cemetery for the deceased Explorers. From the very beginning, there were already few number of Explorers who have died during the battle because of their sacrifice for the sake of their allies, whom they deemed to be a part of their family. The large cemetery was found behind the DDE mansion. The burial ground was well-maintained, and each of the graves had a tombstone with a weapon pierced next to it. Those were the weapons of the deceased Explorers.

The Explorers wept more especially the UEs, when they were watching the group of DDEs now covering Elijah's body with a blanket. The UEs felt worried as they wept more, because their leader was gone now and their class had no one to lead and command anymore.

Each Explorers were calling Elijah's name while the DDEs were now carrying Elijah's remains to take him to another room. There would be a Requiem, a Mass for the repose of the soul of Elijah.

The funeral would occur immediately in the same day. All of Explorers were in the private cemetery after the Requiem, and they ignored the pouring rain outside the mansion. Everyone was on their Explorer uniform. Some of the DDEs were now burying Elijah's remains in his grave. The lightning struck, and everyone was still weeping in grief. The UEs were more affected, because they were the only Explorers who were closer to Elijah's heart than the EUEs and DDEs…

The burial of Elijah was so emotional. The UEs were grieving while saying goodbye to their UE leader, as the DDEs were now covering Elijah's body in the grave.

"Goodbye, Elijah!" it was the first voice heard by a UE who became Elijah's assistant leader once. "Always remember that we all love you so much! Thank you for everything, Elijah! We love you so much!!!"

As for Tyrone, he could no longer hold his guilt of what he had done to Elijah after he treated him much disrespectfully for a long time. He was apologizing to one of the mistakes he had made to Elijah when they quarreled with each other, a day before their special mission in Burnham. Now, he kept on saying sorry to Elijah as he moved closer to his grave. He was also grieving, along with the UEs behind him.

"I-I'm so sorry, Elijah! I'm so, so sorry for what I have done to you!!!" cried Tyrone while he was watching the DDEs covering Elijah's remains with the earth in his grave. He cried again, and he stuttered out loud where everyone could hear to reminisce the day he was quarreling with Elijah with his unforgiveable, sharp remark. "I-I am so sorry for what I have treated you for a long time we're together, Elijah. I-I know that I was wrong to give you that kind of rude remark, but the truth is that you are really our great leader, Elijah. I was just envied for your leadership… A-And I couldn't believe myself why I treated you and everyone like that despite of your kindness to me. I-I cannot forgive myself, Elijah... B-But I hope you can still forgive me..."

Tyrone kept on grieving for Elijah as he suddenly fell on his knees while sobbing. His fellow Element Wielders moved closer to his back, as Isagani gently put his hand over Tyrone's shoulder to give him comfort with his teary eyes.

"Tyrone... please stop now," said Isagani to Tyrone softly while also crying. "Elijah forgives you now, d-don't worry..." he faltered as he was also sobbing.

"Elijah..." said Tyrone. "I'm really so sorry for everything... I've disrespected you so much even though you are our leader, but despite for what everything I've done to you, you're still here to understand, love, and treat me as your brother..." he sobbed. "I thank you for everything we've shared together through thick and thin, for the love you gave to the UEs, and for heeding us... Thank you once again, Elijah... We will never, ever forget you because you always belong in our hearts. We love you always and forever!!!"

Silence.

Later, after the long silence and simultaneous sobbing, they suddenly heard a clap by an Explorer in the distance. There was another Explorer who followed the clap, until everyone also followed the clap. Everyone was now clapping, a long clap of grief.

"Let us all clap for Elijah, Explorers!" said Shingue to the Explorers while clapping with his teary eyes. "We should thank him for becoming a part of our lives... and also for becoming one of the heroes of the entire Explorers history!"

The clapping became louder all over the cemetery, and the Explorers were now calling Elijah's name as their joyful cheer for him. "ELIJAH! ELIJAH! ELIJAH!" they shouted. "ELIJAH! ELIJAH! ELIJAH!"

Kenji was now holding Elijah's Sabre when he came over to his grave. He slowly knelt on his knees before the grave and spoke in his hoarse, soft voice. "We promise to you, Elijah... we will continue your legacy for the future of the UE..." then he stooped down his head. "We will make sure that we will find the new UE leader who is the same as you. Once again, we thank you so much for everything... For your love, care, and your support. THANK YOU, ELIJAH!!!" then he pierced the Sabre next to Elijah's tomb. Everyone applauded once again, still with their teary eyes.

Morning came…

It was already morning when the UEs thought of returning home to their mansion after the burial. But after they would leave the DDE mansion, they thought of visiting Elijah's tomb first just to say goodbye to him. Then, they finally embarked to their aircraft again to go back to the UE mansion after the mission was accomplished. However, it was too painful for the UEs to go back home without Elijah this time… But the question was… would there be someone who would take Elijah's place to become the rightful new leader of the Ultimate Explorer? Who could that be?

45 NEW LEADER PART 1

One month had passed since Elijah's death and the bloody encounter between the Explorers against the Explands. The members of the UE were back to their old routine in their base, including the Element Wielders who were all already recovered from the savage attack by the evil Explands.

Kenji's Explorer uniform was already damaged so he took his uniform to a tailor. In the meantime, he was wearing the costume that Rolando gave to him before his graduation in the training school.

The UEs were morally devastated and mourned for a month due to untimely loss of their well-loved leader. Elijah was a great mentor and a leader. When he was still alive, everything was great in UE because he could handle his responsibilities well as their leader.

But now that Elijah's gone, who would do the responsibilities like Elijah did? Who would fill in the shoes he left? Who would rise up to the occasions when the needs called for it? Who deserved to be the next Elijah Tylers? Those were the huge questions that needed to be answered… and those questions were what the UEs had been talking about for a long time. Who would be their next leader? If there would be a new leader, what would also be their new system?

"What time do you think you can finish that?" Kenji asked while he scratched his chin. "Will that take longer?"

"Yes sir," answered the tailor while she was sewing. "I might take a week…"

"Week?"

"Yes... This takes a lot of process."

"Oh... okay..."

"You still have other clothes with you, right? That... that old one you are wearing."

"Yes."

"Oh, if that's the case, then just wait for it..."

"Thanks," and then he left.

As usual, back to normal. Almost all the UEs did nothing for now. The others were just hanging out at the stairs, rooms, the lobby, outside the mansion, and anywhere else while others were doing their exercise to stay fit. Clio was walking outside the mansion when Genji noticed something.

"Some of us are supposed to do their individual assignments now. It was like that almost every day, right?" said Genji and then he looked around. "But why is it that almost every one of us is doing nothing? How will they find the other sacred stones if we do nothing?"

"Because Genji, it's like this," said Tyrone. "Elijah's gone, right? Then what else are they going to do?"

"What? It's common sense. Whatever the assignments that Elijah usually gave them, they should still be doing it right now. And not like this, we're doing nothing..."

Cyan asked. "You, what is your task here?"

Genji scratched his head and laughed. "Um, well... it's, uh... I don't know!"

"Oh, you're no different."

Meanwhile, Reinhardt, Maximus, and Claude were at the gym exercising. Reinhardt was doing push-ups while Claude was weightlifting. As for Maximus, he was just leaning against the wall while reading a book.

The door to the gymnasium fell. Marion, Percy, and Tadteo entered the gym and chased each other. The concentration of the three broke because of the noises by the three who were playing chasing game.

"C'mon, Marion!" shouted Reinhardt. "Can you just play outside?" then he went back to do push-ups. "We three would like some quiet time."

"Here I come! I'm getting closhe to both of yah!!!" said Percy as he was chasing Marion and Tadteo. "If I catch ya both, watch out... Yer it!"

"You can't catch me cat, 'coz I'm fast!" said Marion arrogantly. "Maybe you'll chase Tadteo!"

"I have no patience chashing that bird anymore! She's-h a cheater! She flies-h!"

And the three still chased each other. Claude was shocked when the three jumped on him while he was lifting the barbell. Because of that, he dropped the barbell on his side just an inch away from his shoulder. He quickly got up, but he was not angry.

"Hey, you guys!" Claude pointed at the three who were still chasing each other. "Everyone... STOP!!!"

Marion stopped, but the two animals did not. When Percy saw Marion just standing there, he tagged him. "YER IT!"

"Hey! I just stopped because *kuya* Claude said so!" said Marion.

"What are ya shaying, ya kid?!" shouted Percy. "There's no *shtop, shtop, shtop!* Claude didn't shay anything!"

"C'mon," Claude stooped his head. Maximus just left the room carrying his book to get away from the annoying noises. "Percy... Earlier, I told you three to stop, alright? Look at your *kuya* Marion, he listened. We're busy here, ya know that?"

"NO!" shouted the cat. Marion and Tadteo were both silent. "We won't shtop because we prefer to play inshide thish gymnashium. Now shtop 'shtopping' ush 'cosh we're shtill playing. Shtop! Ya shtop dishturbing ush!!!"

"What the--! You even dare to argue with me even though I am right," Claude said jokingly while his hand was on his hip and he pretended to scold them. "Do you want me to tell your master Kenji so he can spank you?!"

"I don't want ya to tell on ush! Don't do that!"

Reinhardt laughed. "Dude, don't pick on them. Let them play. Look at Maximus, he already left."

"Yeehaw!!!" shouted the three. "It's good that *kuya* Reinhardt is here."

"Pff... Okay... Okay..." Claude said and he smiled. "Just don't make any noise, okay? ...Like shouting, you know?"

The three nodded at the same time. "Yes, sir!" and then they chased each other again.

Meanwhile, in the Conference Room.

Kenji and the UEs were talking. They were sitting in front of a conference table. The chandelier lights were on though it was still early. "I can't wait any longer," said Lucky. "We did nothing up until now..."

THE EXPLORERS

After a few minutes, the others arrived. Maximus was already inside the Conference Room with his "number one fan" Marion, who was sitting beside him. He was already finished playing chase with Percy and Tadteo. He idolized Prince Maximus so much and he really wanted to be his friend, more than ever because he was of royal blood.

"No one is leading the UE now..." said Clio sadly. "What about that? Do we need to find a new UE leader?"

"Of course," answered Cyan.

"But it's hard to find someone like Elijah. No one of us..."

Kenji asked. "How do we pick a leader here?"

Shingue answered. "Um... by voting, but you can't just vote. We will look at the person's qualifications and his experiences first. And then, he must convince us why we will pick him over the others as our new leader..."

"How will they introduce themselves?"

"Um, again... by whay of spheeecchh..." said Margot, who was sitting beside Isagani.

Kenji could not understand. "W-What? Say that again?"

"Spheeecchh..."

"W-What??!"

Tyrone shouted at their gay friend annoyingly. "You're even so flirty when you talk!" then he turned to Kenji. "Kenji, what he meant to say was speech. Those who will be running for leader will make a speech."

"Oh, so he means speech!"

"Here in Explorers, we should always have a leader," said Isagani. "It is highly urgent and top priority, so we need to have a new leader right here, right now. The DDE only considered our situation, so we can rest well while they repair their wrecked mansion."

"So, what now?" asked Jon. "It's hard to find someone like Elijah among us. For me, I want to be the leader here, but it can't be done. I'm not deserving..."

Genji was confused. "As in, right now? Do we all need to vote immediately? That may be kind of difficult."

"They won't allow it," said Lucky. "The DDE told us earlier that we should declare a new leader of UE right away. We should have a leader now."

Everyone was silent in the Conference Room, while Marion was trying hard to get the attention of Prince Maximus.

"Maxim! Please pay attention to the rightful leader of the UE here... none other than Marion Raven. The most handsome one in the entire Explorers history, and that's me!" and then he proudly pointed at his forehead. "The smartest and most handsome! You should be thankful that you were born good-looking like me!"

No one reacted to Marion's speech. Only the sound of cicada was heard.

After the lengthy silence, Lucky was the first one who talked. "Guys... as of now, um... First, let's find out who in this group will run for leader. After all, we already have known each other for long, right?"

"Then, afterwards?"

"Afterwards, the top three chosen with the highest votes will give their privilege speech. Then, we will vote again among the three. The one with the highest votes will be declared the new leader of UE. This should be a serious voting because this is for the sake of UE and Elijah. Let's choose the deserving one. So we can submit our report to the DDE immediately for their review and approval, and they will announce our new leader."

Everyone was serious. "What time will we start? After lunch?"

"Yes, that's it! It's still early. We have no choice. It's really urgent. Also, we can have more time to think and study the qualifications of our new leader."

"Okay. Let's vote seriously later!" said Shingue.

"Okay, dismissed."

Everyone stood on their chairs and left the room. They also informed the other UEs of what they talked about just then.

Kenji and the others nodded to each other and they walked in the hallway, while Maximus and Marion were still together. "Promise Maximus!" said Marion while he was following the prince. "I will vote you in the election and then you vote for me, okay? It's a deal, huh?"

Maximus did not answer as he walked with Kenji and the others. Lucky answered. "What's up with you, young king?! Maximus can't vote because he's not an Explorer, okay? You're the one who will vote, not him!"

"Huh?! That's unfair! He should vote. He can't vote me if that's the case."

"Oh, there's nothing unfair about that, Marion."

Marion sadly lowered his head. "That's too bad! Mr. Prince and I had an agreement!" he said as he still followed the prince. He looked at Maximus and spoke again. "Okay, how about this... I will vote for you, Maximus."

"You also can't vote Maximus because he is NOT AN EXPLORER, okay? Am I making sense now, Marion???"

Marion was ticked off. "What the heck! It looks like he can handle the life of a leader!"

"IT IS NOT ALLOWED! You're so annoying, geez..."

The group of Element Wielders went to the gym and informed Claude and Reinhardt about their meeting earlier. "Hey, friends," called Clio. "We'll see you in the Conference Room later after lunch. We will all vote for the one who deserves to be our new leader."

Reinhardt stopped from doing push-ups. "Why? Are the DDE looking for our report right away?"

"Yes, they said we should have a leader now. Hey, let's vote seriously later, okay?"

"Of course."

"Let's eat together so we can go there on time," Cyan suggested. "No one should be late."

"Okay," said Claude as he lifted the barbell. "Thank you for informing us."

"We'll see each other later. Bye," and everyone left. Claude and Reinhardt were left alongside Maximus.

"Hey, Maximus!" Reinhardt greeted the silent prince with a smile. "Come talk to us or your saliva might spoil... HAHAHAHAHA!" he joked.

The prince looked angered so Reinhardt stopped. "Oh, I was just joking. Pardon me... You're always not talking. Um, p-pardon me again. F-Forget what happened earlier, Your Highness..."

He and Claude were silent as they waited for the prince's answer. Maximus just looked at them and did not answer. Afterwards, the prince left them and got out of the gym.

Claude and Reinhardt looked at each other. "He's really not friendly isn't he, Reinhardt?" asked Claude.

"Always... as usual," answered Reinhardt and smiled.

It was not time for lunch yet, so the UEs had time to think who among them was the rightful leader. They scattered everywhere. Meanwhile, Kenji went back to the tailor. He was just going to check on his clothes while also thinking whom he should vote. The tailor was busy.

"Sir…" called the tailor at Kenji. "Is this okay?" then she showed the unfinished top to Kenji.

Kenji looked at the top. "Let me see… Yes, it looks great!"

The boys were talking about the meeting later. They were all outside as they walked by the garden in front of the mansion. "Every one of us!" announced Genji to everyone else outside the mansion. "It's also for our sake."

At first they were all serious, but later on they joked around. "If I were to vote, I would vote Lucky," said Tyrone. "Because I want his long-time dream of becoming the leader to come true!"

Lucky laughed. "Whatever! I never dreamed of becoming the leader, you idiot!"

"As for me, I'll vote for Margot!" said Isagani while touching his chin.

The boys were surprised. "Why?"

"Because he will be the first leader that we can punch and gang up on him in the whole Explorer history!"

Everyone laughed. After a short while, their laughter died down as they stopped walking. Because, they saw Akira coming towards them!

"Akira!" shouted everyone.

"Why are you here? How did you get in here?!" asked Lucky in wonder.

Akira scratched his head and did not answer Lucky's question. "I heard the news that you would all vote for your new UE leader today."

"Who told you?"

"An ordinary person…"

Tyrone laughed. "You're amazing, Akira! You're always updated to all the news around the world! You must be smart, right?!"

"Not really, I'm just a scholar…" Akira joked.

"SCHOLARRR!!!"

"Um, might I ask Akira," Shingue pointed at Akira looking wondered. "How did you get here and what are you doing here?"

"Hah, I got here by myself and I keep the reason as a secret. I already knew this place of yours for a long time."

"So, why are you really here?"

"I just want to give you all my tips about your election today..."

"T-Tips? But you're our enemy!" said Clio. "Why bother?"

Akira lowered his head. "Yes, I am your enemy... but I'm not like what I was before... fighting with you all everyday. That's because I learned that Maximillian Foster's a Holy Wielder and there's nothing for me to fight for anymore. Lucky, I'm not going to continue our fight in the upcoming tournament anymore. We're both winners, alright?"

Everyone did not understand. Akira spoke again.

"If I have the right to vote someone deserving to be the leader of UE, that'll be Maximillian Foster."

"K-Kenji? Really? Are you campaigning for Kenji?"

"Yes. Because in my opinion, he is far better than Elijah who was your previous leader. That's why I'll vote him!"

"Why do you think that *kuya* Kenji is deserving one?" asked Genji. "Why him?"

"Because Kenji always shows his best! He has strong determination, courage, sportsmanship, team player, and he even possesses his good and pleasant personality!" Akira said proudly. "He's always active in all your work and he doesn't give up that easily."

Clio and Shingue stroked their chin.

Akira suddenly changed the topic. "Might I ask... the guy I saw with you last time at the Expland's palace. The one with the long golden hair... Is he a member of UE? I mean that tall guy... 'Coz in my opinion, he would fit to be a prince in a stage play."

"Oh! I know who he is," a big bulb came out of Cyan's head. "Is Maximus the guy you're talking about?"

"Ah, I get it," said Genji. "Is it him? Why are you asking?"

"Because, when I saw him at Expland's palace, he looked like he could be on the same level as Kenji's. Now... Is he a UE member?"

Everyone shook their head. "Nope... He's not an Explorer."

"I see. What a shame," said Akira seriously. "But if the guy I'm talking about is an Explorer, I think I'll also vote for him..."

Akira kept on talking as he closed his eyes and leaned against the wall. Meanwhile, Lucky and the others whispered to each other because they suddenly thought why they chatted with their own enemy. And one more thing... They even talked as if they were great friends!

The boys thought that maybe Akira had changed a lot after he became an Element Wielder. That's why when they chatted with him, they felt that this Pioneer was not their enemy anymore, but a friend… A new found friend!

Even though Lucky and the others treated Akira as if he was not their enemy for a moment, they still could not give him their trust.

If Akira acted nice right now, you should never trust his angelic face. Look at his every move and action. Always put in your mind that he's still your enemy!

Everyone was still in their deep thought as Akira was still talking to them endlessly, without knowing if the boys were still listening to him or not. The Explorers just gawked.

"Wait… this new Element Wielder in front of us is our enemy, who possesses the element of Deity and Peace that is a brother of our elements. But wait, something's not right with the "Element Family". The elements we possess cannot be enemies!

But the bond of our powers won't be perfect if there's one missing. We can't lose this Deity and Peace. It is one of the sources of strength of our powers because it is also one of the primary elements of King Jethro aside from the Holy Crusade. So we must be complete!

Akira… What are you to us? Your power is an ally of our powers, but you're a Pioneer and we are Explorers… This is too confusing… Our powers cannot be enemies according to King Jethro's rule!!!

It was almost noon and the boys were all still in deep thought.

46 NEW LEADER PART 2

Ten minutes left before noon. The boys were still in deep thought, unaware that Akira was already done talking just a few moments ago. They all just gaped at him in silence!

Akira did not know if the people he was talking to listened or not. By looking at the boys' faces, it looked like their thoughts were in a different world.

"Those are all the 'tips' that I can share with you guys," said Akira to the boys. "Good luck on your election later… The Pioneer will learn such news from you immediately."

No one answered.

Akira was getting impatient. "T-That's all, Explorers."

Still, no one answered.

"G-Guys?!!"

Lucky and the others still gaped in silence.

"Guuuyyysss??!"

No one responded.

"EXPLORERS! CAN YOU HEAR ME?!!"

"AH!" there, everyone got back their senses again. "W-What? Say that again?"

"Did you understand what I said to all of you a while ago? It was long! Just my suggestions, you know?"

Honestly, no one of them even heard what Akira said earlier, but they did not make it obvious.

"Y-Yes! We understand," Lucky quickly answered but looking confused. "Thank you for your great and helpful tips *(What did he tell us earlier?)*!"

Akira was not leaning anymore. "Okay, I'll leave now. Remember that, Explorers!"

Everyone nodded and Akira waved goodbye. "Bye! See ya guys later!"

Akira already left the base when the boys asked each other with confusion. "D-Did Akira say something to us earlier?" asked Cyan. "Huh? Huh?"

"We really don't know. Hey Tyrone," called Genji. "What 'tips' did that Akira give us, huh? Tell us!'

"What? How should I know? I was thinking of something else earlier!"

Lunch time. Because of the large number of UE members, they had to separate the female UEs and the male UEs. They would still eat together, but the two groups would be separated in each of the long tables. There were many delicious foods already served on the tables. Everybody was already seated. First, there was a prayer led by Kenji:

"Thank you very much for all the blessings You gave to all of us today--"

After the prayer, the Explorers ate together in silence (which how it should be). The rice and other dishes were passed around.

Claude noticed that Maximus was not eating. The prince was just sitting next to him. "Maximus," Claude called to the silent prince in whisper. "Why aren't you eating? Go on and eat…"

Maximus shook his head. "I don't like this…"

"What do you mean? The food?"

"In Reminescence… whenever I eat, I'm always alone. I don't want to have company… it's too awkward for me… I'm not used to this!"

The look on Claude's face changed. *This guy is so picky*, he thought to himself! *He's really not friendly! Hey, you're not in Reminescence right now so do what the Explorers do!*

"You're not in Reminescence anymore," said Claude as he ate. "You should get used to it."

"I don't want to."

"Go eat now, Your Highness," answered Reinhardt. "Learn how to eat here with us."

Maximus still did not want to eat. Claude was forced to make a decision. "Okay fine. You can eat in your room instead, but think about it... You will feel bored in there!"

As for Maximus: "Don't worry, I won't."

"R-Really?"

"I won't."

A butler hurriedly took Maximus' food and accompanied him to his room.

"Don't yah worry yah guys!" said Tyrone as he raised his rock-signed hand proudly. "He'll get used to it little by little!"

When the lunch break was over, the Explorers rested for at least five to ten minutes only. Afterwards, they proceeded to the Conference Room. But there were some UEs who rested inside the Conference Room as they waited for the scheduled election.

As time passed by, there were more and more UEs arriving in the Conference Room. It was almost time to start.

Not four minutes later, the UEs who were going to vote had arrived, so it looked like they could start the voting now. Maximus was not included. He was in the Music Room. He was playing the violin alone, while Percy and Tadteo were both in front of him to watch his performance.

The two animals just listened to the sweet music played by Maximus. The prince was playing the violin seriously with his eyes closed. "The music of Prince Max is really soothing to the ears," Tadteo said as a compliment as she was watching Maximus. "Ohhh... Maximus, if I were a human, I think... You will be my prince charming!" then she fluttered with her blushing face. "I'm in love!"

"YER A FLIRT!" shouted Percy annoyingly. "The conchentrathion of Prinshce Maxshimush will be ruined! Be quiet!"

"But what can I do? I'm really in love with him!" said Tadteo while her wings were on her cheeks. "He's also cute!"

"Quiet, I shaid! He might kick ush out here!"

Tadteo did not answer anymore. She just stared at the prince as he was still playing the violin with his eyes closed.

"Yer jusht two yearsh old to fall in love!" Percy hissed. "Yer too young, birdie!"

"Is it time to start the voting here?" asked Vamir to all the UEs inside the Conference Room. "Has everyone here already signed the attendance?"

"Yes!"

"Okay, our voting will go like this," said Shingue. "You will vote one Explorer and your vote cannot repeat. The top three with the highest votes will introduce themselves to everyone, although we've already known each other, okay?"

Everyone nodded.

"For the top three chosen, you will tell us the reason why you deserve to be the new leader of UE *(speech time)*. Let's all be serious now! Meaning, no fooling around!"

Everyone nodded again. Kenji asked first. "Wait, if we are going to vote, why do we need the top three if there's someone with the highest vote?"

"Because that is how we vote here, Kenji… and just to be sure."

Kenji nodded with a doubt on his face. "O-Oh… I see…"

"After the speech, we will vote again. The one with the highest vote will be declared as the new leader of the Ultimate Explorer!" Shingue clapped. "Then, voting over! We will submit our new report to DDE afterwards!"

"Okay! Let's all begin."

It was time to vote. "The voting for the position of UE leader is now open!" started Shingue. "Just raise your hands and mention a name of the person you want to nominate."

Many UEs raised their hands. They wanted to mention a name of their choice. Shingue called a UE.

"I respectfully nominate Vamir Redfield for being the new leader of UE!"

Everyone clapped. Shingue wrote Vamir's name on the white board.

Everyone raised their hands again. It was Kenji who volunteered next. "I respectfully nominate Shingue Wilford for being the new leader of UE!" he mentioned the last name by mistake!

"M-Me?" Shingue was shocked. He did not expect that Kenji would choose him but many UEs applauded. Afterwards, he also wrote his name on the board. Cyan was confused because it was his last name that Kenji mentioned.

Again, everyone raised their hands. Claude was called next. "I respectfully nominate Kenji Foster for being the new leader of UE!"

"Wooh! Kenji, that's a good choice!" the UEs were impressed by the name mentioned and they applauded once again. Kenji's name was also written on the board.

Only fifteen minutes had passed but the board was already full because of the many names written there. The only thing missing was to write every names of the UEs included in the election!

"I respectfully nominate Lucky for--" said Reinhardt.

"I respectfully nominate Cyan for--" said one UE even though Cyan was not an Explorer yet.

"I respectfully nominate Francis for--" said Marion.

Twenty minutes had passed when they filled the space on the board with their names written tightly together. The first round was finished. "Okay, the voting for the position of UE leader is now closed!" Shingue spoke. "Now it's time to vote for our top three!"

Everyone applauded except for Marion. He was angry because none of the UEs picked him, not even one!

"Wait!" shouted the kid angrily. "Hey, what about me? My name is not on the board?!"

Everyone stopped. Silence.

"You're all unfair! You all don't know how to vote! What about me? I'm also deserving! All of you should have picked me!"

"Man… Here we go again," said Claude. "If we are with this naughty, li'l kid again…"

Kenji tried to be humble and answered Marion's question although he was already controlling his anger.

"Because… you're still very young to be the leader, my beloved king. Not every life in this world is just games. This is a serious election (some UEs were already disturbed because of Marion), that's why this job is for adults only, okay?"

"Whatever, but why were you chosen?"

"B-Because, that is how they think of me… They thinks that I am deserving to be your new leader…"

"Well, me too! I can even handle the responsibility as your leader of whatever!"

There were some UEs who felt angry towards Marion because of the delay while some really wanted to continue the election now. Even Kenji felt irritated towards Marion. His ears started to heat up! The nerve!

"Hey, why can't you answer anymore?!!" asked Marion on top of his voice.

"There is nothing to be answered in your question," answered Kenji. "We're just saying that you're not old enough to be--"

"YOU'RE WRONG! That's really unfair, especially to me!!!"

Blah, blah, blah... What kind of election was this now? It looked like it ended to a fight. *Blah, blah, blah...*

Marion spoke again. "What's wrong with all of you that you have no faith in me?! Even though I'm a king and still a kid... I'm great!"

Kenji answered. "What can we do if that is what they want to choose and they didn't choose you?!"

Marion spoke again. "They're wrong about me! A person who is nominated in the first round is good-for-nothing!"

"Nice mouth, kid! In your opinion, is there really a good-for-nothing person among the people we chose here?!"

"There is!"

"Okay! Then who, Marion??!" asked Kenji who was really, really irritated. "WHO?!!"

"YOU! YOU ARE, *KUYA* KENJI! YOU ARE A GOOD-FOR-NOTHING EXPLORER IN UE!!!"

Kenji felt a deep pain in his heart, but it was worthless for him. He did not answer anymore. Instead, he laughed in annoyance!

Lucky went close to Marion and scolded him annoyingly. "You naughty kid! You're making trouble again. Hey Clio, scold your brother here, will ya?!"

Clio also moved towards Marion and scolded him. "If you're just going to disrespect our voting like this then don't join us! I know we don't have parents anymore and I raised you alone... But I did not raise you to be disrespectful! Do you understand?!!"

Marion answered very angrily. "IF ONLY YOU KNEW THAT PRINCE MAXIMUS WAS THE ONE I WAS REALLY GOING TO VOTE!"

"Okay, vote for him, PERIOD! But even if you do, the Explorers here won't vote him because he's a Reminescence!"

Marion was already a grown up. He did not like being humiliated in front of everybody like that. The Explorers were angry at him now. He was ashamed. Because of what he had done, the UEs would not think of him as someone who deserved to be their new leader... But, they would still think of him as an annoying child!

"Marion, is that how you will treat us when you become our leader today? The leader who fights with his members? The leader who shouts? Does a person who shouts deserve to be the new leader of UE?" Lucky asked Marion face-to-face.

Marion was silent. He was depressed and ashamed to what he had done.

"What now, Marion? Why can't you answer?"

Marion lowered his head and sobbed.

"Marion! What?"

The "brave", naughty king cried instead. Clio noticed.

"M-Marion…"

"Hu… Hu… Hu…"

Now, the UEs looked like they felt pity towards him. Marion pulled out his handkerchief while he cried, as Clio put his arm on Marion's back to give comfort.

"Hu… Hu… Hu…"

Silence. But not long after, they resumed the election.

"Let's start the election now… o-or continue, I mean…" Shingue had forgotten that they already started the election. Marion was still crying next to Clio.

"Okay, let's continue so it'll be over!" everyone agreed.

The voting continued and Clio still scolded his brother.

"Please raise your hands in favor as I mention the name of a candidate for us to count your vote, okay?" said Lucky to the UEs. "Because of the number of names written on the board, I don't know what time we will finish the election!"

Everyone laughed and nodded at the same time.

"Okay, as I call the candidate's name… please raise your hands if you're in favor of him/her," said Lucky again.

"Okay, first name," Shingue pointed at the board. "Who will vote for Vamir?"

Some of the UEs raised their hands. Clio counted those who voted for Vamir after he scolded Marion, but he did not vote for Vamir.

"Only ten!" said Shingue with laughter.

"Ten?" asked a UE with his sad face because he was the one who picked Vamir earlier. "There is no hope! He cannot enter the top three!"

"Next is Elbert!" called Lucky.

The hands were raised again for those who voted for Elbert. Clio counted again. This time, the count was fewer!

"Dude, only five!" Clio laughed. "Vamir is higher! There is still hope, hahaha!!!"

"Next is Cyan!"

Only one UE raised his hand. The one who picked Cyan. Genji laughed out loud. "Hey dudes, he's a Valedictorian!" and he laughed again. "Raise more of your hands, dudes!"

Some UEs raised their hands, but only two. "Hah, just three!!!" counted Clio.

"How about you, Mister Genji?" called Cyan to Genji. "Why didn't you vote me?"

Genji scratched his head. "Sorry, but I'm going to vote for someone else!"

Because of the number of names, the counting process took a while longer. They would call for someone's name, and then they would count again. There were some candidates with only had two votes. Some even had just one.

Marion was still sobbing on one side. The naughty UE child was silent. His handkerchief was already wet as he was still wiping his face.

When counting was finished, the top three names with the highest votes emerged as the top candidates for the vacant position. Lucky, Shingue, and Clio were in-charge in counting the votes as the election officers.

"Hey," Jon was getting excited. "Tell us our top three!"

"Yes, yes, Explorers!" said Lucky in excitement. They were finished counting. "We are happy to tell you that our top three are all skilled and deserving to be our new leader today!"

"Okay, tell us," said Reinhardt.

Lucky held the paper with the list of top three UE candidates and he announced. "Ultimate Explorers, the top three who will give us a speech for today are Reinhardt, Kenji, and…"

The UEs were getting more excited. "And who?"

Lucky jumped. "ME! I'm in the top three! B-But why?!!"

"YAHOO!!!" the UEs gladly applauded. It seemed like they were satisfied with the results of the chosen top three.

THE EXPLORERS

"Wow, one of them will be our leader! Which of them will be?" asked Isagani in excitement. "I'm so excited!

"The top three who were called on, please stand up and proceed infront so everyone will see you."

Kenji and Reinhardt stood on their chairs. Lucky was already standing. "You three, please tell us why you deserve to be the new leader of Ultimate Explorer," said Shingue smiling.

The three went in front of everybody. "Who among you will be the first to make a speech?" asked Claude.

"I'll go first," said Lucky. "The Foster Brothers can go next."

Lucky stood straight in front of them as the UEs applauded again. Lucky made an intro first. "Ahem…"

Silence. Everyone was quiet when Lucky started his unprepared speech. Everyone was getting serious.

"First of all, I thank you all for choosing me as the top three candidate for the position of UE leader," said Lucky. "I am Lucky Terrel of UE, running for the position of UE leader because I believe that I have determination and guts to show everyone my… ah…" he lost himself for a moment. "…my worth as your new leader. I will do everything in my power to do my responsibilities and serve you all as your new leader… The Explorers, thank you very much for believing in me!"

Everyone applauded when Lucky's short speech was finished. Reinhardt was next. When he went in front of everyone, the female UEs shrieked for him. Margot was one of them.

"Eeeee!!!" the girls continued to shriek, but Margot was the loudest. Silence.

"Ahem," Reinhardt cleared his throat first that made the UE girls and Margot shrieked again. "Good noon to everyone. I am Reinhardt Foster of UE, a missionary and messenger of Ultimate Explorer running for leader. I believe that I can do everything that Elijah could do for being his assistant leader during his life. But I believe that I can do better (everyone was serious)… I promise you all that I will take care of our base and protect the Explorers until my last breath. And I will make sure our name prospers, ULTIMATE EXPLORERS! I will brag our group to everyone with high-spirit!" and then he raised his fist.

Everyone applauded. As Reinhardt's speech ended, Kenji suddenly became nervous. Because he was next.

Kenji went in front of everybody but nobody clapped yet. Everyone was very serious and all eyes were at Kenji.

Kenji took a deep breath first before he started his speech. He was about to speak when some UEs suddenly shouted at him, coming from the back of the room. "DON'T YOU DARE TO MAKE YOUR SPEECH NOW! THE RANK OF UE WILL FALL IF YOU BECOME OUR NEXT LEADER!!!"

Kenji was shocked. The others were shocked too. When they turned their heads, they saw a group of male UEs at the back and Arthur was with them!

Here we go again... Said Claude to himself and he spoke to the group of Arthur irritably. "Be quiet! Don't be too disrespectful! Okay?!"

Kenji got mad, but he kept his composure. He sighed to calm himself. He spoke, but Arthur interrupted.

"I am Kenji--"

"Yeah! Yeah! We already know you," said Arthur rudely. "Is your speech done?! Reinhardt will be the next leader of UE! Election is finished!!!"

Kenji got mad this time, even Claude was pissed off. He wanted to yell but he controlled himself. The other UEs were only silent. They were afraid that it would turn into a fist fight! Marion's moment was already finished, but this time it was Arthur's!

"You're not fit to be the leader of UE, Kenji," said Arthur. "I am telling you now, you are not worthy enough to be like Elijah!"

Kenji wanted to throw the table away to Arthur's group. His ears were now smoking hot! His blood was already boiling!

"Kenji is just a BIG, BIG LOSER!" Arthur added.

Kenji's patience ran out when he suddenly pushed the table and it fell towards the UEs with a bang. The UEs quickly stood and were concerned. They did not know if they should stop Kenji or not.

Kenji shouted in the Conference Room while everyone were silent.

"Arthur is a stupid person!" he yelled as he also threw a chair that was close to him. "Everybody's stupid! Everything they see in me makes no sense at all! Everything I've done is totally worthless! Okay, I'm a worthless person and a worthless UE in your eyes, but I have feelings and somehow I can feel all the pain and hardships done by you! Now, if you don't have faith in me, then why did you even pick me?" because of his rage, he said a lot of things that he did not actually mean to say. "You're all STUPID in choosing me! I am here in UE for a long time, and I have undergone a lot of experiences here that gave me a lesson to be strong and defend the idea which I believed in. BUT THIS ELECTION NOW IS JUST A BIG FOLLY, because everyone that you voted are worthless (everyone murmured to each other)! May it be Lucky, *kuya* Reinhardt, and especially me! For years that I have been here, your eyes see nothing that I have contributed anything in this group!" and then after, he kicked a chair. "From the time I got here, from the time that I received assignments from Elijah when he was still alive, and until I became an Element Wielder! If for you I am worthless in UE, for Elijah, it's the opposite of what you think! As you can see, Elijah believed in me! He had a full trust and confidence in me. So I'm thankful that there are some people here who still believe in me! I have beaten and killed a lot of monsters! I got the Holy Element of King Jethro! I passed the tests to become an Explorer! I followed all the assignments that Elijah made me do, and he didn't take that for granted! I loved being an Explorer because it became a part of my life! I defended the base from the invaders, putting my own life on the line, and yet..." he suddenly stopped.

Silence. Everyone was quiet. Kenji continued. "If only you knew everything I've experienced that almost put my life to an end. I'm still blessed in spite of that misfortune. I'm here in front of you alive and kicking with the hope that everything will be okay. I hold on to those experiences towards my victory! I love being an Explorer! I love being an Element Wielder! This is me! I'm sorry to disappoint you, but I can't change myself just to please all of you. You may love me or hate me but I will continue my way no matter what it takes. After all, I am just a worthless person to be your new leader, HOW UNFORTUNATE OF YOU! Sorry if the UE will be degraded because of me! BUT IT WILL BE EVERYONE'S FAULT IF THAT HAPPENS!!!"

Arthur was deeply angry because of Kenji's non-stop rant.

"You son of a--"

"RIGHT! AND WHAT ARE YOU, ARTHUR? We have been together here in UE for a long time, but if we compare ourselves to each other, I'm far better than you!"

Arthur quickly stood on his seat and acted as if he would rush over Kenji. He pointed at the young man. "HOW CAN YOU SAY THAT YOU

ARE FAR BETTER THAN ME, HUH??!"

"I'm stronger than you because I'm an Element Wielder now. I fight to prove my worth as an Explorer! Unlike you, from then until now… The only thing you can do is to bully everyone and fight with me again and again!"

"HELL, NO!"

"YES!"

"I SAID, NO!!!"

"One more thing, we are all chosen as the guardians and servants of King Jethro! YOU NEVER SHOWED YOUR LOVE AND RESPECT TO YOUR FRIENDS whom we all consider as ONE FAMILY! Is this family also worthless to you?!"

Arthur ran out of excuses when he suddenly changed the topic. "D-DISMISSED!"

"You can leave if you want to, Arthur and I don't care! After all, we are just wasting our time with this nonsense election! Full of negatives! Full of fights! Full of wrong efforts! Full of hatred! Anyway, I'm through here!!!"

When Kenji's long rant was finished, the UEs did not know what they would comment. Just look at the Conference Room now, the other tables and chairs… they were all broken!

No one applauded, but Shingue had the guts to talk even though the others were spaced out. "Kenji's right. I understand everything he said earlier. Yes, I agree with him!"

A UE followed Shingue's comment. "The UE will be stronger if he will be our new leader!"

The UEs whispered. Kenji was breathless and he was gasping for air. Claude went over him and gave him water. He remembered that the young man was still recovering from his sickness.

A while later, one of the UEs spoke. "I choose Kenji Foster for being the leader of Ultimate Explorer!"

The other UE agreed. "I also choose Kenji Foster for being the leader of Ultimate Explorer!"

And another UE again. "I vote for Kenji Foster for being the new leader of UE!"

Everyone applauded as they chanted Kenji's name in unison. Meanwhile, Arthur's group just walked out the room in annoyance. They did not want to join in the election anymore!

THE EXPLORERS

Everyone stood on their seats together as they still shouted for Kenji's name. As for Kenji, he was totally shocked because of the unexpected turn of events… Because of his endless ranting, it became enough to impress his fellow UEs!

Almost everyone in the room voted for Kenji, but Shingue asked them just to make sure. He smiled. "UE, who is our new UE leader again?"

"KENJI FOSTER!"

"WHO? I CAN'T HEAR YOU!!!"

"KENJI FOSTEEERRR!!!"

Because of the cries by the UEs coming from the Conference Room, Percy, Tadteo, and Maximus heard the loud noise.

Maximus stopped playing the violin and looked around. "It looks like the election is now finished…" he said.

"And it sheems that I already know who our new leader ish going to be, right Tadteo?" Percy asked Tadteo with a smile. "Ash I heard from their shouts, they all voted for our mashter!"

"Master Kenji is so awesome!" Tadteo answered as she jumped happily. "I really, really approve of all their vote!"

Kenji was still very shocked, but he realized that his endless rant gave much impression to the UEs because he was the new leader of the Ultimate Explorer from now on!

47 THE REPORT

It was afternoon when the election was finally over. Now it was time for election officers to submit their overall reports to DDE.

The butlers cleaned all the litters and messes that the UEs left in the Conference Room, while the Explorers already left.

Though the winner in just concluded election was not yet declared, they were going to transfer Kenji to Elijah's old room which was the exclusive room of the UE leader. Until now, the young man was still spaced out because of the fight earlier. He was not moving, as if he had a stroke or epilepsy… Later he spoke hesitantly. "I-I'm the leader of UE now…"

"Kenji's rant earlier was great, right?" asked a female UE to her fellow female UEs she was talking to. They were outside the mansion. "I knew it Flow! Kenji would replace Elijah!!!"

"You're right Flew! The DDE will be surprised if they find out this great news from us," agreed another female UE as she looked at her friends. "What about you, Flower? Do you agree with the choice of Kenji as our new leader now?"

"Of course!" answered a female UE.

"What about you Flown?" pointed another female UE at her friend. "Do you agree that Kenji is--"

"Yes! Yes! Yes!" a friend answered happily. "Of course, okay? I was one of those who voted for him! And while we were still thinking, he was the one I was really going to vote. His speech was really too impressive!"

THE EXPLORERS

Afterwards, the group of female UEs entered the mansion.

Kenji's group was now inside Elijah's old room, the "Leader's Private Room". They talked about the report for the day to be submitted right away.

"After we do the report, the election officers will sign it as a proof that the winner were already selected," Shingue said to Kenji who was still not in himself. "Before night, we will fax the report."

"Via facsimile?" Claude asked in wonder. "Don't we have to give the original copy and not just a copy by fax machine? Why? Do you also accept those?"

"It's okay!" Lucky answered. "When Elijah became the new leader, the report he passed was just a photocopy, hahaha!" he laughed out loud.

The UEs who were not in Elijah's time of becoming the new leader were all shocked. "R-Really?"

"Yes! Hah, you all don't want to believe me?!"

"What kind of report was that, huh?"

"The DDEs aren't really that strict," answered Shingue. "The DDEs are only looking for a simple report signed by the election officers, even just a simple handwriting. As long as there's a report that they can hold on."

Genji laughed. "Ah, okay... t-that's cool!"

"Yes, that's okay. At least, you won't have a hard time doing that report. You'll just tell them and click! You're a full-pledged leader blessed by the DDE!" answered Lucky proudly.

"Being a leader of Explorers is easy!" said Claude.

"Let's do the report later so we can fax it today," said Reinhardt and he stood on his seat. "Let's help my brother do the report for DDE."

"Okay, meeting is adjourned."

The boys also stood on their chairs as Jon and the others left Claude, Kenji, and Shingue in the room. "We're leaving," said Jon happily. "See you!" and then he walked behind the UEs as he closed the door.

Silence. When Jon and the others left the three, the first one who spoke was Claude. "Kenji, Shingue... um..."

Shingue looked at him. "Claude I know what you're going to say, maybe you're going to ask us how life is going to be from now on, am I right?"

Claude lowered his head. He felt embarrassed that Shingue had guessed what he had in mind.

Kenji was still in deep thought. He still felt a great grudge towards the UEs who fought with him earlier.

Later, Claude could not take Kenji's silence any longer. So he talked to him. "Um, Kenji… Don't think about it anymore. At least you still won, right?"

Finally, Kenji answered but not looking happy. "Thank you, I'm just getting too tired…"

"Rest here for a while. We'll just wait for you until later."

"I can't rest, Claude. I'm still thinking about…"

"About your responsibilities in UE?"

Kenji smiled. "Yes. About how will I handle the future of UE… And how will I do it just like how Elijah did for us. I think, I can't do it…"

Shingue's eyes looked around, as if he thought that maybe the two did not need him right now. He felt like he wanted to leave the room now.

Shingue stood on his chair, and the two stopped. "What's wrong, Shingue?" asked Claude to Shingue in wonder.

"I'll leave also. I'll just leave you two here," answered Shingue with a smile. "I need to do something. Also, Tyrone and the others are waiting for me outside."

"Oh, really?" said Claude. But in reality he really wanted to talk to Kenji alone for now. "Okay, it's up to you. The report is just a piece of cake, right?"

"Yes, really easy! It won't take a minute! When Elijah did the report, he did it for only thirty seconds!" Shingue joked.

"Even if we don't hasten our report?"

Shingue needed to go. "Even later! It'll only take twenty five seconds to finish. Promise!"

"Okay, thank you!"

Afterwards, Shingue left the two and gently closed the door of the room.

"Kenji, we're experiencing a new trial," Claude spoke quietly to Kenji and stooped down his head. "Now that you're our new leader, the whole UE relies on you on how you handle our group…"

Kenji was feeling discouraged because of the fight earlier. "I don't think I can do it, Claude…"

"Oh, come on man! Don't say that you can't handle being a leader because most UEs know that you deserve it! So don't tell me that you can't

THE EXPLORERS

do it. Because truthfully, you can even surpass Elijah!"

Kenji's doubt showed in his face.

"Kenji, listen. Do not doubt yourself. I know you. I know your capabilities. I know how strong you are. I know the whole UEs are behind you all the way that is why they voted for you. Kenji please, do not show them you're weak. The entire UEs and DDEs are looking up to you. Inspire those who believe in you. Show them your strength and they will follow you, but showing your weakness and everything will fall apart. Let your shine be seen among members who believe in you!"

"Claude, it's just…"

"Kenji, we're all here beside you. Of course, we can't depend all the work to our leader. We're all here, Kenji. Your friends and your brothers are always watching your back. Of course, unity and cooperation are the key words in order to survive in this world!"

"Why, Claude? Do you ever see in me that I really have the guts?"

"What the--!" Claude was shocked, as if he was asked the hardest question in his entire life! "Why, of course! Many times."

"Like what?"

"Come on, Kenji! How did you become an Explorer if you weren't brave and strong enough to overcome the obstacles hurled in you?"

Kenji pretended to be stupid. "What do you mean?" but he understood Claude.

"Damn, come on Kenji!" but Claude was not angry. "If I will enumerate it one by one then it might take us a whole day. You won't be able to do the report. For me, from the first time we've become companions, I have seen a lot from you. You have guts and you deserve to be our new leader!"

"Really, Claude?"

"Yes, yes, yes! So take away all the negative things that bothering your mind right now. Maybe that's why you're getting discouraged."

Both of them stopped when they heard someone knocking on the door. "Who's that?" said Kenji.

Someone answered from outside. "Mashter, it'sh Percshy and Tadteo…"

"Please come in."

The door opened. Percy and Tadteo knew how to open a door because they were taught by Kenji and could also speak.

"What do you need?"

Percy spoke hesitantly. "Tadteo and I jusht want to greet ya, um… CONGRATULASHIONSH, MASHTER!" and then he quickly jumped on Kenji and licked his face.

"Your cat is so sweet, Kenji," said Claude laughingly. "He's really, really fat."

"Shhh!" Kenji shushed Claude, and then he chuckled when Percy tickled him again.

At the Music Room.

The Element Wielders were hanging out the room while Maximus played the piano. He was next to his number one fan again, Marion. The kid's eyes were already swollen after he cried during election.

"I think Kenji has a good attitude towards UE," Lucky said happily to his friends. "I also think that he can surpass Elijah! You all get me?"

"We have the same thoughts, Lucky," Isagani agreed happily. "You're right, it looks like Kenji can surely surpass Elijah!"

"Just by his looks… he will make us do a lot of work! But don't judge the book by its cover. We might be wrong in our judgment."

"You're right," Cyan agreed.

Maximus stopped playing the piano when they all turned to the prince.

"Um… is Maximus an Explorer yet?" asked Tyrone in whisper.

"Oh yeah," Clio added. "I noticed that he has been with us for a long time. Isn't he a Reminescence anymore?"

"What will we do to him?" asked Genji.

Lucky smiled. "Kenji knows what to do with him. He'll take care of Maximus. Even both of you, Genji and Cyan."

Cyan's eyes widened. "Oh, yes! I remember. We're still not Explorers yet!"

"Um, guys?" Reinhardt called quietly. "It's better if we submit the report to DDE now. How about we tell him now?"

"Okay, we'll go to Kenji," said Jon. "Wait for us here in the Music Room," and then he turned to Isagani and Tyrone. "Hey, you two handsome guys! Accompany me to Kenji!"

"Okay," Isagani and Tyrone nodded and they accompanied Jon.

"Maximus," called Reinhardt to Maximus. "Let me just ask you. What's with you that you impressed us during our battle with the Explands? You're one of a kind, huh? You also have some cool hidden skills!"

Everyone waited for Maximus' reply, but his only answer was: "Nothing…"

"It's impossible that you don't have a hidden skill," answered Reinhardt. "Is it really true that you belong to a royal family?"

Maximus gave him a serious look, but still he answered. "Yes. I have the prince's blood and I'm a 'bearer'. I'm the only son of King Maximus X."

"So… you're really that super rich!" said Shingue as he laughed. "You're lucky, dude!"

"And he's not only that super rich!" Marion added with a sob. "He also has talents!"

"Ah, right! Speaking of talent, Maximus… What else can you play other than the piano and violin?" asked Reinhardt. "Do you know how to play the guitar?"

Maximus shook his head. "No, but I also know how to play the flute. The Reminescence said, from the time I was cursed I studied playing the flute. Because in our kingdom back then, each time I was worshipping the water, I played the flute.

"Wow."

"Because… I'm a water-bearer."

Lucky quickly pointed at Maximus. "That means, y-you're a Water Wielder!"

Maximus lowered his head. "I don't know. I had thought about it for a long time, but me being a water-bearer started when I was cursed…"

"If only you knew, Maximus… We don't have an Element Wielder that possesses the Water element yet!" said Cyan. "Maybe you're the last one missing from us. The last piece of puzzle we're looking for!"

"I thought the Water element is not the only thing you don't have?"

"We already found the other two elements. The Deity and Peace element belongs to Akira and the Ice element is with Zoroaster. So the only one missing is the Water element. Maybe, it could be you!"

Maximus did not answer anymore. He thought for a while. After some time, he was the one who asked them questions.

"Up to now, what do you all see in me? Still your enemy?"

Everyone wondered when the prince suddenly changed the topic.

"Not anymore," answered Reinhardt. "If you're not ever going to return to Reminescence then you're our ally now. Do you understand?"

Maximus nodded. "I'm never going back there, ever."

Reinhardt was surprised. "Really?"

"Yes."

"Does your father not looking for you at Reminescence?"

Maximus shook his head. "He doesn't see me as his son anymore. So, he's not looking for me."

Just then, Jon, Isagani, and Tyrone returned with Kenji and Claude.

"Hey, we're back!" Jon called out happily. "Kenji and the others said we should finish the report now! So we don't have to do anything later. Let's go!"

"Oh, let's help our new leader, Maximillian Foster to do his first report, yeah!!!" said Shingue happily as he raised his fist.

Everyone got their things ready. Lucky turned to Kenji and gave him instructions on how to do the formal report. "Listen Kenji, the DDE doesn't need a very formal letter. Just a simple one, but all the thoughts are there."

Kenji was serious. "So, Lucky this means… I'm just going to write a simple letter?!"

"Introduce yourself, then put your resolutions, and all the important things you wanna say. Just like that. As fast as that."

Kenji nodded. "Okay, I understand."

"Okay, let's start!"

"Wait, I'll get the paper that Elijah always used to write when he made reports!" said Clio happily with Jon next to him. "Just wait there," and he left.

"So Kenji, do you know what you're going to write there, hm?" asked Claude.

Kenji smiled. "Yes, of course. It's very easy."

The two returned. "Oh here, Kenji! We got one scratch and the clean paper," then they gave it to Kenji. "Also, here's your ballpen."

Kenji smiled. "Thank you."

"Oh, sit here!" Reinhardt offered Kenji a seat. "Come and I'll teach you."

Kenji moved closer to Reinhardt and sat beside him. Genji also sat beside his brothers. "Let me see, *kuya*."

Kenji held his paper and ballpen and quickly wrote. Claude noticed.

"Whoa! It's looks like he has some things ready to say now, huh?" he said.

"*Kuya* Reinhardt," Kenji called Reinhardt while writing. "Read this after for me, okay?"

"Okay, just keep on writing. It's okay if it's short."

While Kenji wrote his first report, Maximus played the piano again so they had a sweet music to listen to. Some were with Kenji, while the others were with Maximus to listen to his tune with their applause.

Claude was next to Maximus as he admired each movement of the prince's fingers as he stroked the keys of the piano. "It looks too difficult to learn! You have to memorize a lot and…"

Maximus was still playing the piano when Marion scolded Claude. "Keep quiet! Don't be noisy, *kuya* Claude. Can't you see he's concentrating? His concentration will be ruined! His music won't be that good anymore!"

"Wow, how skilled is Maximus for you, Marion?"

"Of course, *kuya* Claude… He's my idol."

"Wow!"

"Yes, *kuya* Claude!"

"If Maximus is really your favorite, you must also be that skilled in handling the piano."

"That's why I'll ask him to teach me."

"So why hasn't he taught you?"

"Because he's always busy."

"Ah, that's why!"

Kenji had written quite a lot when Reinhardt stopped him. "Oh, this is enough. Now, what we will do next is to proofread your work. We'll erase everything what we think is not that important."

Kenji wondered. "Oh, why will we erase? This is fine, at least it's a little long, right?"

But, Kenji gave the scratch paper to Reinhardt and he carefully read the report. "Hmmm…"

"Wait *kuya* Claude," Marion called Claude. "Do you feel jealous towards Prince Maximus?"

"Me? Jealous? Why?"

"Because he's skilled in playing the piano! He's very much amazing, right?"

"Yes, he's skilled. But I'm not jealous."

"But… I do feel jealous, *kuya* Claude."

"Ah, hehehe…"

"Maybe Kenji, um…" Reinhardt was thinking as he was reading the paper.

"Is it okay?"

"Yeah, it's okay. Your handwriting is even better than Elijah's! Ahahaha!!!"

"H-Hey, why are you looking at my handwriting? You even joked about it, *kuya*!"

"No, this is okay. If you like, we'll ask Lucky to double-check your work."

"Okay."

Kenji asked Lucky to read the letter and Lucky read it too. After a few seconds, Lucky quickly answered. "Yes! It's okay, Kenji. Great. Is this it?"

"Yes."

"This is great, Kenji. Promise! You can fax it now."

"This handwritten one?"

"NOOO! Of course, make it computerized!"

"Okay, I'll type. You and the others will fax it for me."

"No problem, man. Leave the rest to us!"

"Is really this easy to do a report here? Hah, piece of cake!" Kenji boasted. "I'll go to the Computer Lab."

"Don't forget to put your signature there, okay?" Lucky reminded.

"Of course!"

Kenji's draft report was finished, so he typed it himself. It only took less than thirty minutes including the time he printed it. Afterwards, Reinhardt and the others faxed the report and when they were done, they all rested.

48 THE NEW ALLY - 1

Kenji returned to his room to take a shower. He took a towel and other stuffs he needed. He was now staying in the leader's room. In that room he had his own bathroom so he no longer have to take a bath at the public bathrooms in the mansion.

The Element Wielders were outside the mansion again to hang out. They were always together like brothers. Maximus was with them.

"Where's *kuya* Kenji?" Genji looked for his twin. "He's the only one missing among us!"

"He told me that he'll take a shower first," Claude answered. "He'll catch up later."

"He's too much," Isagani said. "It's hard to wash clothes everyday!"

"He has a personal butler, Isagani," answered Jon. "He's the leader so he cannot wash his clothes by himself. Plus, we have laundry machines here!"

"Yeah! I was just joking."

"Look at the turn of events!" said Reinhardt to Maximus happily. "He became the leader of Explorers before me, but I became the Explorer before him. HAHAHAHA!!!"

"If that's the case," said Maximus. "He's more skilled than you."

Reinhardt scratched his head as he laughed. "Yeah! You see Maximus, he's also a Holy Wielder. As for me, though I'm a missionary of the Explorers, I got the Darkness element. One of a kind, hehehe... He's amazing!"

"Yes, I can't even believe it…"

Clio, Lucky, and the others were at the side of the mansion to shoot arrows.

"Your turn, Clio!" Shingue shouted towards Clio. "Don't be overexcited, or you might hit Lucky's butt and get fired!" he teased.

"Shut up man, just talk to your nose!" answered Lucky as he laughed.

"It's a good thing that Kenji knows how to write reports like that," said Tyrone. "I thought he would be needing my help, hehehe!"

While Clio was shooting the arrows, Cyan answered. "I even thought so… that he would ask for my help because I'm a Valedictorian…" and then, he lowered his head.

"You're arrogant!" Tyrone answered to Cyan quickly.

Back to Reinhardt.

"Maximus, how old are you now?"

"Um… Twenty. T-Twenty something?" Maximus was not sure.

"Since when you became a Reminescence?"

"When I was born, I was already a Reminescence."

"Ah… Right."

Akira suddenly surprised the boys because he showed himself in the UE base again. "UE!" he called with a loud clap. "Congratulations on your right decision!"

"Akira!" the boys were shocked seeing Akira inside their base again. "You're still here? How did you really get in here?!"

"Right," Akira answered as he walked closer to the boys. Still, he did not answer their question. "It's just right that Maximilian deserved to be the leader of UE and now we're equal!"

"Both of you?" asked Reinhardt. "So what will you do here?"

"Where is your new leader? I just want to greet him and shake hands with him."

"He's inside," Maximus answered. "Aren't you our enemy?"

"Hmpt, Mr. Golden Hair of Reminescence," Akira went closer to Maximus. "Just to remind you, mister… We're on the same situation. I'm a Pioneer and you're a Reminescence… You're also an enemy of Explorers."

"Not anymore."

"N-Not anymore? That means you're an Explorer now?"

"No."

Cyan asked Akira. "Hey, why don't you go back to your place and stop wasting our precious time?"

"Mr. Valedictorian, come on," Akira approached Cyan next. "It looks like you want me to go back to my base. Do you have any problem with me?" then he turned around to ignore Cyan.

Akira still waited for Kenji since he wanted to talk to him. When Kenji finished taking a bath, he went straight to the tailor to check on his uniform again.

"Is it finished?"

"Almost done sir," the tailor answered as she smiled.

"When can I wear it?"

"Maybe, in a day sir."

"Okay. I'm just checking," and then he took his almost finished uniform. "The stitches are really, really good... Yes, it's beautiful."

"Thank you, sir Kenji."

Kenji returned the uniform to the woman.

"Maybe... um," Kenji thought first. "I'll pick it up the day after tomorrow, okay? I really want to wear that sooner... the one I'm wearing is so itchy!" he joked. "I'll come back for it!"

"Yes, sir..." answered the woman. Then, Kenji left her.

It was almost night when Kenji went out of the mansion to go to his friends. The boys were still outside including Akira. Kenji was shocked when he saw Claude and the others talking to their enemy!

"UE!"

The boys looked at him. Kenji quickly went to them and came closer to Akira. Akira offered his hand to shake hands with him as he greeted. "Congratulations, Maximillian... I knew it, you are really my best rival ever!"

"Akira?"

"Yes, Maximillian. We're really alike and now we're equal!"

"L-Let's fight some other time, Akira..." Kenji said hesitantly and he continued. "By the way, thank you for healing me during our battle with the Expland and your help--"

"It's because I don't want others to kill you, Maximillian. I want it to be ME and no one else."

"Why are you here?"

"Nothing. I just dropped by to see all of you."

Kenji was still serious. The two of them were the only ones talking. Claude and the others just listened. "I am not looking for troubles with you again Explorers, because we Pioneers know how really good you are. And one more thing, I possess the other element that's an ally of your element and it makes me wonder… So I decided not to mess with you for a while."

Kenji was in disbelief. "Are you suggesting that you want to become our ally?"

"Like I said, it makes me wonder why I have the power just like you do that also makes me a guardian and servant of King Jethro. As an Element Wielder, I'm your ally. But as a Pioneer, I'm your enemy."

"So?"

"When we're done with our job for being the Wielders and when everything is clear to me, then we can fight again like before."

"Oh…"

"Hey, don't give me that damn answer! Why not we settle our issue here, or maybe you're scared!"

"S-Scared?! I'm not afraid of you, ever. We're equal!"

"That's right, but I'll become better than you."

"NEVER!"

"Hmpt, we'll see about that, Maximillian…"

Tyrone could not take it anymore, so he stopped the two with a smile. "Kenji, Akira… This is not the right time to argue! Not this time. Today is the special day for Kenji so please stop arguing!"

The two rivals still looked at each other. A few moments later, they moved away.

"So, Akira…" Kenji said seriously. "What is your plan for now?"

"I'm planning to join you for a while because we have the same primary mission. Also in seeking the truth why am I also chosen to become a Wielder. Maybe by joining you will help me to find out the pieces of the puzzle and know the truth."

"Do you think that you can fool us now? I know you!"

"Yes, ever since we met when we were still kids."

Kenji did not answer. Akira spoke again. "Hey, don't tell me you still do not understand me? Or you still can't believe that I'm also a Wielder now! You want me to beg on your knees?!"

Kenji just looked at him.

"Okay, Maximillian. I am not going back to Pioneer for a while…"

Everyone was shocked. "Whaaattt??!"

"Yes, I can do that. They don't look for me when I'm gone. But that doesn't mean that I'm turning my back on being a Pioneer... No, not that! I'm still a Pioneer in my heart. Believe me, it's just that, um... I only want the truth!"

"Even your father?" Clio's eyes opened wide. He stopped shooting arrows.

"Even my father doesn't look for me all the time!"

"Oh, gimme a break!"

Akira gently removed his red cap and scratched his head. "Okay, I'm not a spy or something. I just want to join with you while I'm seeking the truth. You can keep secrets among yourselves because I'm a Pioneer... That's okay, but let me join you for a while. I already told you that we're allies as Element Wielders and I am still a Pioneer in my heart..."

"Of course! We're not going to tell you our secrets, Akira," said Lucky. "Even if you bow down in front of us and kiss our feet, or hit your head on the floor--"

"I don't care about what you're hiding from us! Because we too, I admit... we are also hiding some secrets against you!"

"We don't care about that either..." Maximus answered in snobbish way.

"So, that's our deal. Believe me... We can't fight. Our elements are brothers and this is for King Jethro and not for anybody else.... Come on, you guys!" said Akira and then he turned his back on them. "No meddling, boys..."

The boys talked to each other. They talked about Akira's decision of joining their group.

"Wait, wait!" Kenji interrupted the boys. "I'll deal with you guys later," then he went to Akira, who had his back still turned to them. "Akira, look at me!"

"You're all so stubborn," answered Akira. "It's hard to convince you all!"

"Hey, look! What if one day you will betray us?"

"I told you that I won't betray you! Our elements aren't enemies!"

"Yes, we know that... That's written in the book that *ninang* Vanice gave us... The Element Book mentions a rule that the Element Wielders cannot become enemies... Elements should not fight against each other...

They should work together as allies."

"See?" Akira quickly turned to Kenji. "So, what now? You're the leader now so everyone's decision is up to you... You know, if you follow me and the book, your position as the leader won't be affected. We have a deal and I have another proof for you that I won't betray you... I saved you during the fight with Expland!"

"Ak--"

"When we return our elements to King Zalan and accomplish our mission one day, then we can become enemies again. And I will beat you!"

"That will never happen!" Kenji quickly answered. Later, he deeply thought about Akira's offer and then he sighed. "O-Okay, fine..."

"What do you mean by that?"

"Are you deaf? I said, okay. I agree."

"But Kenji..." Claude quickly moved next to Kenji. "Maybe you're forgetting--"

"I know that, Claude. Don't worry. Akira is right. We have all the elements and the Wielders cannot fight each other. It's in the law, because all of us are trusted by Lady Vanice and King Jethro!"

Claude stopped and looked angrily at Akira. Kenji turned to Akira. "Okay, Akira. Join us, but you can't stay here with us."

"Of course, I can't!"

"It's a deal!"

But as for Claude and the others, though the decision was unacceptable, the new leader had decided and there was nothing they could do about it. Claude wanted to destroy Akira, so he pulled Kenji slightly away from Akira and whispered. Akira noticed him because he saw the two looked at him as Claude was whispering to Kenji. So, he turned to his back again.

Meanwhile, Lucky and the others also looked at Akira with an uncomfortable look on their faces. Akira also noticed them, but his attention was now at the silent prince. Maximus was also looking at him so Akira went closer to them.

"Let me ask you Explorers, what was his reason that you let him join your group although he's also your enemy?" asked Akira after he stared at Maximus. "Was it because he's cute and handsome?"

"O-Of course not!" Clio answered quickly as he was shooting arrows. "You see, he has a story."

"A story? What story is that?"

"A story of his life."

Akira laughed. "What story of life is that, huh?"

Maximus answered. "I left from our place…"

"You left and afterwards you also became an Explorer?"

"No…"

"But how did you join them?"

"I told the Explorers to let him join, Akira," answered Kenji. "It was me."

"You? Why did you permit him to join?"

"I told you, I was the one who let him join."

Meanwhile, in Expland…

It was unfortunate to the Explorers that Neschar was still alive with the help of the Hydra's special power. The deep wounds in his body caused by Kenji's stabs were wrapped in clean cloth. He was laying down unconsciously in front of the Hydra. The Hydra healed him with his power which took a longer process before he got fully recovered.

The Explands were in the third dimension, a dimension of darkness where no human could enter except the Dark Mages like them and the living dead.

Later, the whole place suddenly shook when the Hydra shouted out loud because of the failed "offering". "MAAAAXXXIIMIIILLLIAAAAANNN!!!"

The Explands panicked and fear was all over the room. The Hydra shouted once again. "HOW DID THIS HAPPEN?! HOWWW?!!"

The whole place shook again, which made the small rocks fell from above. "I REALLY WANT TO MOVE! I REALLY WANT TO GO BACK TO MY TRUE FORM!!!"

The Explands ran away in fear but their lord saw them.

"YOU COWARDS! WHERE ARE YOU GOING?" shouted the Hydra. "DON'T BE STUPID! WE NEED TO DO THIS!!!" and then he released the flaming lasers coming from his stony eyes and hit a concrete post that fell down. Everyone panicked again.

The whole place was still shaking when Neschar slowly opened his eyes. He could not get up for now because of the deep stabs in his body. His vision was blurry. Afterwards, he slowly lifted his hands.

"W-What does this mean? I-I'm still alive… Ah…"

The Hydra stopped shooting lasers everywhere when he heard Neschar's low and husky voice.

"W-What happened…"

"NESCHAR!" called the Hydra angrily. "OUR PLAN HAS FAILED, DO YOU KNOW THAT?!"

"W-What p-plan, my lord?"

"IDIOT! THE DEAD BODY OF MAXIMILLIAN!!!"

Neschar was shocked when he remembered what the Hydra was talking about.

"I THOUGHT YOU COULD DO WHAT WE NEEDED TO DO, NESCAR! YOU FAILED!!!"

"M-My lord! I am…"

"NESCHAR, I TRUSTED YOU! I TREATED YOU LIKE MY OWN CHILD! WHY DID YOU FAIL ME?!?"

"Forgive me my lord, give me another chance and this time I will never fail you… Those Explorers just made their own trick against us!"

"WHEN WILL I BE ABLE TO MOVE FREELY AGAIN?!"

The whole place shook violently. Neschar's back was still laying down the floor and still weakened. His vision was still blurred.

"WHAT, NESCHAR? WHEN WILL YOU PROVE THAT YOU'RE WORTHY OF MY TRUST AND MORE SKILLED THAN THOSE WIELDERS, HUH?"

"I… I can prove it now, my lord!"

"WHAT DO YOU MEAN BY 'NOW'? LOOK AT YOURSELF! DO YOU THINK THAT YOU CAN BEAT MAXIMILLIAN AND GIVE ME HIS DEAD BODY LIKE THAT?!"

Neschar was shocked again.

"NESCHAR, I WILL GIVE YOU ANOTHER CHANCE FOR THIS! BY THE NEXT TIME YOU FAIL--"

Neschar did not wait for the Hydra to finish. "Yes, my lord!"

"WHAT DID YOU SAY, NESCHAR??!"

"I will do everything I can so we won't fail anymore!"

"THAT'S WHAT I REALLY WANT TO HEAR FROM YOU, NESCHAR!" said the Hydra as his deep voice calmed down. The quake weakened. "WHAT WILL YOU DO NOW, NESCHAR?"

"Let me recover from my wounds my lord. And when I am done, let my wrath be upon him! He will pay for this!!!"

The Hydra laughed evilly. "THAT'S RIGHT, NESCHAR! RELEASE ALL YOUR ANGER SO YOUR TRUE COLORS WILL SHOW UP AGAIN! KEEP THAT UP, MWAHAHAHAHA!!!"

The whole place shook again. The Explands ran away again to avoid the falling debris. The Hydra continued. "GO ON NESCHAR, BE FURIOUS… SO I CAN BE FREE FROM THIS PUNISHMENT SOONER!!!"

Neschar became so furious again when he remembered the day during his fight with the Explorers a month ago. The black aura came out of his body while he was furious. "Maximillian! I curse you! Get ready for your last breath the next time I see you! GET READY!!!" he shouted as the evil aura around his body became stronger than ever.

Afterwards, all of the Explands laughed together… Their laugh was heard all over the place… The laugh of evil!

Back to UE…

It was already nighttime when Akira decided to leave the mansion so he waved at the boys. "Boys, I'm leaving now. We're not enemies for the meantime, okay?" and he smiled. "Let's fulfill our missions together," then he walked away. "See ya all, Wielders. Bye!"

"Akira!" called Kenji with a smirk. "Get ready when we see each other again after we return our powers someday… You'll see, Akira!"

"Okay!"

Akira disappeared from their sight. Later, their stomachs began to grumble. The boys remembered that they did not have their snacks yet.

Grooowwwl…

"Friends," Shingue scratched his head. "It took us until night," and he laughed. "The last time we ate was lunch and we didn't have any snacks yet!"

"Boys," called Isagani with a smile. "What do you want me and Tyrone to cook now?"

"Ask Kenji. He's our leader now!" answered Jon and he laughed.

49 THE WILD BUTTERFLY

It was already evening when Akira returned to Pioneer. He discreetly avoided the guards in the UE base and headed to the main aircraft of Pioneer which was currently in the forest.

"I'm here, comrades," Akira quietly called out to his comrades and he was greeted by them. His father also greeted him.

"You've only returned to us now, Akira…" said a Pioneer. "Where have you been? We waited for you. We'll show you something."

Akira scratched his chin looking curious. "Show me something? What is it?"

"Earlier, we experimented when you left. You know the potion that Bert invented? We used it!"

"Where did you use that foolishness?"

"Go inside, so you'll know."

Akira was still curious, but unknown to the Pioneers that he just came back from UE base. He entered their aircraft.

They were inside the aircraft when Akira asked again about what his comrades would show him. "What will you show me now?"

A Pioneer took a large jar with a bee and a large butterfly inside. "Did you know that we mated these two different species earlier?" then he showed the two insects inside the container. "They've finished mating!"

Akira was shocked. "W-What? You managed to mate the two animals of different species?"

"Of course!"

Akira could not believe it. "R-Really? You saw them when they mated?"

"Of course! Before we paired them, we injected them first with the potion that Bert made. It was mixed with the saliva and blood of the monster that you killed long ago, Akira. Do you remember that monster? One of the wildest beasts in this world belonged in the Devourer class?"

Akira wanted to laugh. "In your opinion, what will be its result? The venom of that monster is too strong!"

"Earlier, before the two different species mated, we injected the potion in the female butterfly's womb so it will lay an egg within a short period of time. And possibly big too!"

Akira laughed. "Hah, stop your foolishness! Nothing will happen on your experimentation. It will only lead to nothing! Why did you think of doing that idiotic thing, huh?"

"Because Akira," the other Pioneer answered. "If we succeed, this will be our best weapon to beat the Explorers."

"W-What?"

"We're really sure that this will have a great result and you'll be surprised the results of this experiment. We only did this for the Explorers, and the offspring of these insects will also have its own powers…"

"How will the offspring of those insects have powers?"

"Don't ask… just watch and learn… you'll see. It's your fault, you left earlier. You didn't see what we did here…"

"When will the worm lay an egg?"

"After two days," said the Pioneer with a smirk. "This may be one of our best solutions to beat the Explorers!"

Two days had passed when the butterfly laid an egg. The egg was quite big compared to normal butterfly's egg. The color was bluish with a green slime all over it. It took only some few minutes when the egg suddenly hatched that fast. A new breed of insects crawled out of the shell with a pair of fangs just as sharp as blade. The creaking sounds from the fangs of a larvae could be heard indicating that the larvae was hungry. Then, it suddenly attacked the bee and the host butterfly to their death. The larvae devoured the parent insects into oblivion. When nothing was left, the larvae started to produce cocoon to undergo the metamorphosis. After a few more hours, a unique fully-formed wild butterfly came out of the cocoon and spread its wings yet colorful but sharp and deadly. It was looking strange. The crossbreed between two different species was so visible to the new breed of Wild Butterfly. It had big wings of different colors with pointed spikes protruded at the edges of the wings. Its head was a head of a bee with huge eyes and sharp bladed fangs. There was a stinger in its bee-like butt with two long tails, and there was one eye at the end of each tail which also had different colors. The butterfly was unique of its kind. He was too wild and he possessed hidden powers.

The newly born butterfly was in the big glass container with a tube connected to oxygen for breathing. The butterfly seemed to have his own mind. He crawled up the tube and used its sharp fangs to cut the plastic tube to his freedom. The Pioneers did not realize that the butterfly had escaped.

The Wild Butterfly had a hard time as he flew because of the size and length of both of his tails, but he still forced itself to fly faster. He had already gotten far away from the Pioneer aircraft when he saw a bird. He went closer to the bird and fanned the bird with his huge wings. The powder came out from his wings, but he did not blind the bird. Instead, it went to sleep. When the bird momentarily fell to sleep, the butterfly injected it. Later on, the bird had suddenly gone insane when it woke up!

The butterfly quickly recognized the messy "static" or "frequency" that he heard from the bird, and he knew what that meant. The bird was alive, but not in its usual behavior. The butterfly had discovered one of his unique powers and he wanted to discover for more.

A Pioneer suddenly panicked when he noticed that the glass container was already empty. "The butterfly and the bee… They're gone!"

The other Pioneers along with Akira rushed towards the room, and they immediately asked. "What happened, Boston?"

"I remember… Two days have already passed. The butterfly had already laid an egg!"

"What would that look like? And how did it escape?"

"I-I don't know, oh no! It might be anywhere!"

Akira was getting angry. "Right, you endangered us! Maybe it's a monster bee or something!" then he pointed at the empty, broken jar. "Would you look at that container? Isn't it obvious how too strong that creature might be??!"

The Pioneers had nothing to say now.

THE EXPLORERS

"The only way to do now is for us to quickly find that creature and bring it here before it's too late! It might cause a lot of trouble here!" said Akira as he quickly went into action.

The Pioneers went into the thick forest loaded with their weapons, but they had a hard time looking for the butterfly. "It must have gone far!" Akira said angrily to the Pioneers. "If you only knew how stupid you really are!"

"Maybe it won't do anything…"

"Stop talking!" Akira pointed at a Pioneer. "Who gave you the permission to recover the venom of the monster I killed? And you also did some foolish acts without asking for my permission!"

"Sorr--"

Akira left his comrades again. "Shut up and find that creature now!"

The wild butterfly heard a lot of frequencies coming from the people, animals, and even plants. He flew fast until he reached a small peaceful town and curiously watched the people from above. The people in the town worked energetically while the children played across the streets. Later, the children were still in the middle of their playtime when one of them noticed the strange looking butterfly. "Hey, friends look!" he called out to his playmates as he was pointing at the butterfly. "Look at the butterfly! It looks different!!!"

His playmates came closer to him and were surprised at what they saw. "And what kind of butterfly is that, Bryan?" asked another kid. "It's big and has two long tails!"

"Are you sure that's a butterfly, Bryan?" asked another kid. "It looks like a bee!"

"Come on!" shouted another kid. "Let's catch that butterfly!"

"Yeah!" the children agreed. "Then let's imprison it!"

The children quickly jumped to reach the butterfly that was flying in the air. "I can't reach it!" a kid shouted. "It's too high!"

"Let's get the net!" said a kid. "Chase it, I'll get the net!"

The children still forced themselves to reach the butterfly in the air, while the other kid looked for the net.

"Come down here!" said a kid as he was still chasing the butterfly in the air. "You don't want to be captured? We won't hurt you!"

The other kid found a butterfly and he went back to his playmates. "Here's the net!" he said and then he stroked the net again and again so he could catch the butterfly. "Come on! Let us catch you!!!"

The residents turned to the kids as they watched them catching a new creature to their eyes. Their mouths were gaped in disbelief seeing the strange creature for the first time.

"I'm coming!" said one of the kids who jumped high and caught one of the butterfly's tail. "Got you!"

"You're amazing, Nestor!" the kids shouted. "Okay, don't set him free!"

The Wild Butterfly forced himself to fly upward, but the kid was now pulling his tail. He got hurt as he was being pulled. With that, his eyes suddenly glowed and the kids were shocked. The butterfly was getting angry!

"W-What's that? Its eyes are glowing!!!"

"Maybe it's getting angry!" said Bryan and he was getting scared. "Nestor, l-let it go!"

"I don't want to!" said the kid. "I caught it. It's mine now!" and then he pulled the tail more. "I said, come here!"

"N-Nestor, don't!"

The kid was still pulling on one of the butterfly's tail when the butterfly looked directly at the kid. He gave the kid an evil look while his huge eyes glowed.

"What? Didn't we tell you that we wouldn't hurt you? Now, follow us or maybe you want me to cut off your tail!" said the kid as he was still pulling hard on the butterfly's tail.

The Wild Butterfly could not understand human language. But because of his unique abilities, the human language could be translated to the sound of frequency that he understood. So whenever a person talked, he would only hear frequency which he could understand.

"*(Static)* You want me to cut off your tail *(static)*…"

The butterfly became angrier, so he quickly pricked the kid's hand with his stinger. The kid got hurt that made him freed the tail. And then, the butterfly flew away.

"Nestor!" the children shouted when they went closer to the kid who was pricked by the butterfly. "You're so stubborn! We told you to stop! Are you okay?"

"Ah… O-Ouch," the kid could no longer move his hand in an instant. "My hand… it's getting numb… I can't move it…"

"Oh no," one of the kids panicked. "Maybe it has its venom!"

"Don't scare me!" the kid forced his hand to move, but he really could not move it.

"What now? How is it, Nestor?"

The kid did not answer because he suddenly felt hot and his hand became swollen. He felt the butterfly's venom spread throughout his body. So quickly, so fast!

"N-Nestor?"

The kid suddenly fell on his knees while his swollen hand became bigger. This time, he could not even move his whole body. He felt that the venom was spreading very quickly. He feared. "M-Mom... Mommy... I can't... move... D-Daddy..."

His playmates worried more when they asked the people for help. "*Mang* Ben! *Mang* Ben! It's Nestor, he can't move anymore!"

"Stay there, Nestor! We'll ask for help. Bear with us!"

All the children left the stiff kid when they asked for help. The kid sweated a lot when he started to cry. "H-Help, I-I'm scared!!!"

"It's Nestor!" called a vendor. "The kid can't move! Hurry, call an ambulance!" then she quickly rushed over the stiff kid. "Nestor... Come on..."

"*A-Aling* Berta... I can't move," said the kid as he sobbed. "I don't want to die yet... I want to play more..." then he started to shiver.

"Nestor, hang on! NESTOR!"

The butterfly's venom was too strong and it already spread throughout the boy's body. First, it flowed in the blood, until it spread throughout the whole body. Afterwards, the venom would thicken the blood, then the venom would kill the immune system. Then, it would flow towards the brain and the heart of the victim where all of the venom would be stored. Until, the brain and heart would swell... making them explode to the boy's death!

"My b-brain... My... he-heart..." the kid was now catching his deep breaths. "Like... Like..."

"Just bear it a little more. They already called a doctor!" said the panicked woman.

The venom had reached the kid's brain and heart, and now it was trying to stop his heart. The kid groaned as he laid down and he convulsed.

"No, please fight!"

A lot of blood suddenly came out of the kid's face: from his eyes, nose, ears, and mouth. The blood flow did not stop.

"Ahhh!!!" shouted the kid as a lot of blood continued to flow down on his whole face. "My heart and brain… T-They're like being squeezed so hard! AHHH! It hurts… MOMMYYYY!!!"

The ambulance arrived and the doctors hurriedly ran to the dying kid. They were just about to carry the kid but it was too late… The internal organs of the child, including his heart and brain had exploded so he passed away.

"Nestor! Nestor!" shouted the children when they noticed their playmate was dead. He died with his body stiff and his eyes wide open filled with blood. He was a little thin because of too much blood loss.

"NEESSSTOOOORRRR!!!"

"We're sorry but it's already too late," said the doctor sadly. "He is gone now…"

An elder went closer to them and noticed the dead kid on the ground. "What foolishness did you all do that you lost a playmate, huh?" he asked angrily. "That child is my grandson!"

The children cried. "We were trying to stop him earlier, but he was too stubborn! He was killed by the butterfly, *Mang* Elmer!"

The residents suddenly remembered the strange butterfly they saw a while ago.

"The butterfly with long tails that was pulled by that kid earlier!" shouted a guy.

The residents suddenly panicked and thought of many things.

"L-Let's get away from here! Those kind of insects might be living here! We will die early if we don't leave!!!"

The residents rattled in fear and quickly went home. By that time, the butterfly was already far away soaring high above the thick forest.

50 ATTACK

The UEs were unaware that the Wild Butterfly was in their mansion. They currently had a meeting and Kenji was speaking in front of everybody.

Kenji stated his mission and vision as the new leader of UE. One of his agendas was to officially recognize Genji and Cyan as their new members by continuing the test they already started. He also considered Maximus, because he noticed that the prince had been with them for a long time. Kenji asked Maximus if he also wanted to become a part of their organization, but the prince only answered as: "I don't want to…"

Kenji felt embarrassed and sad with the prince's short answer. He asked. "Why don't you want to? Don't you want to become an Explorer?"

Maximus only smiled as he shook his head.

Kenji lowered his head. "Um, how about that? You're still a Reminescence, but you're staying with us. In the eyes of Explorers, you're still an enemy."

Maximus looked straight at him. "W-Why? D-Don't you want me to be here with you?"

"Ah, no! No!" Kenji quickly answered as he laughed. "We're not like that. After all, you're nice to us!"

"Really?"

Meanwhile, the evil butterfly tried to listen to the UEs' conversation inside the mansion. There were guards outside, but they were also unaware of the creature's presence. The butterfly was lurking in a dark spot and was silent.

Meanwhile, the test continued as Genji and Cyan's faces were already filled with blood while both taking the tests. Their tests' schedule was delayed since the death of Elijah, and they were supposed to do it a long time ago. It was almost midnight when Kenji felt sleepy, while some of his friends watched the two challengers outside. The UE watchers pitied the two since they were exhausted much, but they could not do anything to stop them or change the rule. They even had experienced those tests previously, so they believed that the two could also win the said challenges!

"I'm getting too tired… My head hurts too much…" said Kenji while touching his forehead.

Claude noticed him. "Kenji, what's wrong?"

"My head hurts too much… I'm going to vomit…"

Claude knew how much Kenji worked hard all night in his tasks as the new leader and he had not rested well. He patted his friend's shoulder and nodded. "Okay, get some rest. We'll take care of the two, but don't worry… No tricks!"

"Hm? Why, are you going to do that?!" Kenji chuckled.

"Of course, not!" Clio answered. "We won't do that! You see, that's unfair!"

"Where's *kuya* Reinhardt?" Kenji's eyes looked for Reinhardt. "If you see him, please tell him that he'll stand as a leader for a while. After all, he's my assistant. Please, I haven't rested yet. I have a lot of assignments to do tomorrow…"

"Yeah, yeah… Okay, rest now Kenji," said Isagani with Lucky and they smiled at him. "We'll take care of things here for you," and they also patted the young man's shoulder. "No tricks, promise!"

"I haven't eaten yet…"

"Just leave everything to us. It's your fault, you're taking yourself as the new UE leader too seriously. You wanted everything to be finished right away," said Jon. "See, now you're stressed."

"Thanks a lot guys. Tell *kuya* that he's in charge here for a while, okay Lucky?"

"Leave this to us!" the boys said happily.

Kenji left. The boys were busy as they watched Genji and Cyan's current test. Kenji was going to take his late dinner. He had lost a lot of weight. Kenji reached the dining room, and he noticed that Maximus was already eating there. He sat next to him and greeted him nicely. "Hey, how are you?"

Maximus was almost done eating. "I'm fine, Maximillian…"

Meanwhile…

The guards outside never noticed that the butterfly got already inside their base, and in a few moments it could enter the UE mansion. As it came close to the mansion, different frequencies could be heard and they became louder. Noise of the UEs.

The butterfly looked up. There was a wide balcony above which was Kenji's room. He saw that the lights were on and it seemed like there were people in there. And by having the Devourer's blood and killer instinct, the butterfly looked for the next possible victim. He flew towards the balcony still unnoticed. When the creature reached the balcony, he looked through the window. Inside was Kenji's room. The lights were on but no one was inside. The butterfly's face was on the window, as his eyes were peering around to check. He looked for a minute, but still, no one was there.

The evil creature began to make his first action. Using the eye of his tail, he faced the eye on the window's glass and the eye glowed. The eye became incredibly hot and it melted a small part of the glass. The butterfly tried to enter, but due to his size he could not fit himself. Again, the butterfly melted the glass until the hole grew bigger and bigger. Afterwards, he successfully entered Kenji's room.

Kenji's room was quiet and the butterfly looked around once again. He never had seen this kind of room so grand. No one was still there. He waited for a first Explorer to come inside.

"I'm not used to eating a lot of food anymore…" said Kenji. He only ate biscuits and drank hot milk. "I'm full already…"

Maximus was still sitting on his side, even though he was already done eating. "If biscuits and hot milk are your appetite… Mine of course, is only half a snack. I eat less than you."

Kenji was in disbelief. "What?"

"That's our only diet, but it's not always like that. I also eat heavy foods if needed."

"But you're heavier than me, right?"

"Yes."

"But how did that happen?"

"Forget it, just eat," answered Maximus.

"But I want to know…"

"Later…"

"But I want to know now."

Maximus quickly stood on his chair in order to leave. The young man noticed him. "Wait… Are you leaving now?"

"I'm already done… and so you can rest," said the prince and then he moved away.

Kenji laughed. "Hmpt, I know your 'style'… You're just going to escape from me, because you don't want to answer my question!" then he ate another biscuit.

"N-No, not that…" said Maximus and he went back next to Kenji. "If we talk for long, you might not be able to get some rest."

"No…"

"I'm leaving. I'll join them… I'll watch the skills of your new Explorers," said Maximus and he walked away. Kenji was left all alone at the elegant dining table.

"Go, Genji and Cyan! GO!!!" Lucky and the others cheered the two challengers who were Genji and Cyan. "Your third test is so easy, hehehe! Why are you taking such a very long time?"

"Right!" shouted Tyrone. "Finish it all! Our leftover, *lechon baboy* (Philippine roast pig) for you was already eaten!"

Everyone laughed.

"Please, all of you be quiet!" said Cyan while both he and Genji concentrated on the test. "Just watch and learn!"

"Too bad, we also cooked *crispy pata* (Philippine dish made of deep fried pig knuckles) for you. Unfortunately, bones are all what's left for you too!" joked Clio.

The two still focused on their test while the boys disturbed them. They were just playing around, maybe just to give them entertainment.

Reinhardt was there. Isagani already told him about Kenji's request earlier. Now, he was just listening to the boys' pranks towards Genji and Cyan.

"Just, don't be noisy. What's up with you guys?" said Genji grunting with difficulty. "Our test is getting difficult!"

Fifteen minutes had passed after Kenji ate five plastics of biscuits and he planned to take another bath. He called the butlers and walked closer to them. "I'll leave this up to you," he said.

"Yes, sir."

Kenji left the dining room. He went straight to his room so he could take a bath in his own bathtub. He opened the door, unaware that there was a Wild Butterfly inside.

The evil butterfly hid as Kenji took off his clothes. The butterfly just watched him discreetly. The young man took off his top and went in the bathroom. The door was locked so no one could enter. The butterfly came out and heard the sounds of the shower. He even heard Kenji's voice. Kenji was humming a tune softly as he was taking a bath inside.

The butterfly looked around and did not want to leave. Since his first possible victim was already there.

"Wow, they're so skilled…" Maximus spoke seriously as he was standing next to Reinhardt. "So that's how you torture your UE companions…"

"Ugh!" Reinhardt was shocked and he almost spat out the coffee he was drinking. "Ahem, that's not called torture, Your Highness. But trials."

"Oh yeah? But you're just giving them a hard time with your trials."

"You're talking about something else. That's natural."

"I don't know about you…"

"Why? How do you give trials to your fellow Reminescence?"

"They just need to show their wit and tactics."

"That's also what we're looking for. Their wits and tactics."

"But not that brutal, look!"

Claude looked at him. "What do you mean by brutal? Is there anything brutal happening to them? Look at those two?! They're just sitting pretty!"

Reinhardt secretly pinched Claude. That moment, Claude realized that he was talking to a prince who was not used to his playful jests.

Suddenly, Claude smiled at Maximus… a smile that almost reached his ears!

When Kenji was done bathing, he dried himself using a towel as the butterfly thought of what to do if ever the young man would see and attack him. But as he was in the middle of his thoughts, the bathroom door opened. He panicked and hid again. There, under Kenji's bed.

Kenji was still unaware that someone was watching him. He then whistled.

Only his towel was wrapped around the lower half of his body and he dried himself off again with another towel. The evil butterfly was still watching him from under the bed while thinking of what to do. Kenji combed his long hair as he dried it with a hair blower.

"Wooohhh! So cold…"

It only took Kenji a few minutes to get ready before he went to sleep and the butterfly was still hiding under the bed. Afterwards, Kenji removed the towel. The only thing that was left of him was his fitted cycling shorts. He usually slept with only his short on so he could sleep comfortably.

The young man was almost naked when he laid down on the bed and turned off the lamp shade next to him. The heater was on and he wrapped himself with a thick blanket. He was about to close his eyes when he remembered something.

"Whoa, I haven't taken my medicine yet. And vitamin too!"

He rose up again, turned on the lamp shade, and then he threw away the blanket. Quickly, he took the medicine from the medicine cabinet and poured a glass of water. The butterfly was still watching him while he was now collecting all information he could see from the young man. He looked badly at Kenji, and he could no longer wait to do something evil against him.

Kenji drank a glass of water when the butterfly had the courage to show himself, but Kenji had his back turned. The butterfly slowly came out from under the bed and acted like he was going to attack the young man. But when Kenji finished taking his vitamins, the butterfly did not continue his first attack. He quickly returned beneath the bed again and Kenji did not see him.

The young man went back to his bed and was about to go to sleep. He prayed for a moment as the white aura appeared around his body whenever he prayed (as the Holy Wielder). After his evening prayer, he closed his eyes… when the lights were out.

It was very late at night when the butterfly felt frustrated because he could not wait anymore. He measured the possibility if Kenji was already in deep sleep or not, and then he went out of the bed. He looked at the young man who was asleep. He wanted to smell Kenji first.

His two antennas on his head served as his nose. He gently moved his antennas all over Kenji's face. He smelled the young man's blood and collected his personality. Moments later, Kenji suddenly moved and the butterfly quickly backed off with the thought that Kenji was awake, but no. Kenji only turned sideways.

THE EXPLORERS

Again, the butterfly went closer to Kenji and put his antennas on Kenji's cheek. Later on, the antennas reached the young man's forehead and neck.

The butterfly kept on smelling which made Kenji felt something ticklish. He wriggled and went back to sleep again. He laid on his other side this time.

The butterfly had finished smelling Kenji and he was familiar with the smell. He liked the smell of the young man's blood.

"I want to taste your flowing blood so I can duplicate the whole you, Explorer…" so the butterfly could talk.

The evil creature readied his killing stinger to initiate his first attack. Its eyes lit up.

A liquid flowed at the tip of the stinger making the skin of Kenji became numb. Then, he quickly injected his stinger on the lower part of Kenji's ear on his neck. Hence, he sucked the young man's blood like a mosquito. Kenji never felt the stinger embedded in his neck, and the butterfly sucked and sucked with laughter.

"GWA-HA-HA-HA, That's it…. That's it! Give me all your blood! GWA-HA-HA-HA!!!"

He already drank a lot of blood when Kenji wriggled again. The butterfly stopped and he quickly removed the stinger from the young man's neck. Just when the stinger was removed, Kenji suddenly felt an intense pain.

"Ouch!"

Kenji quickly got up and touched his neck. The butterfly was going to escape when Kenji saw him. The Wild Butterfly stopped, while Kenji's eyes were opened wide and was shocked at the sight of the strange creature.

"W-What kind of insect are you that pricked my neck?" asked Kenji while touching the part of his neck which had a small mark. "What kind of creature are you and how did you get in my room??!"

The two just stared at each other when Kenji found a rod to hit it with. "D-Do you have poison? I have never seen a strange insect like you! Are you a bee or a butterfly? Or something?!"

The butterfly spoke with his deep, monstrous-like voice. "There should be someone like you in Pioneer."

"WHAT?" Kenji could not understand. "How did you know about Pioneer?"

"I came from there, but thank you for your delicious, warm blood…"

"Whattt???" Kenji cried while he was still holding the rod.

Genji and Cyan's test was finished. The decision was up to Reinhardt. The half-moon was seen in the sky. The boys talked in the Conference Room with the two who just finished their tests.

"Goodbye!" and the butterfly flew away.

"Wait, stop!!!" cried Kenji and he quickly pulled one of the butterfly's tail. The butterfly could not move away anymore.

"Let go of me, Maximillian! If you don't want to die!"

"Selfish, animal! Pioneer's tool!"

The butterfly got irritated so he quickly pricked Kenji's hand. Hence, Kenji dropped his tail and he quickly flew away. He shattered the glass window in the terrace in order to get out of the room.

"Dammit!" Kenji said angrily as he touched his hand that was pricked by the butterfly. Suddenly, he felt fear that maybe the butterfly had deadly poison, but he felt nothing. His fist was not numb, but it also had a small mark.

He also touched his neck. That was another thing that he worried about. He needed to be checked by the doctor immediately before it's too late.

The UE had an Explorer medic so he went straight to the clinic. He went out of his room and ran into Claude. Claude was about to go to his room, but he noticed that Kenji seemed restless and was in a hurry.

"Oh, Kenji… I thought you are asleep now?" asked Claude to Kenji in wonder.

"Let's talk later, can we, Claude? It's an emergency…"

"Why? What's the problem, Kenji?"

Kenji's hand was still on his neck. "I'm going to the clinic. Bye…" and then he left Claude.

"K-Kenji…"

While the butterfly was flying away from the UE mansion, he quickly flew towards the forest. He knew that something would happen to him during the full moon. By having the Devourer's blood, the butterfly might suffer the same fate just like the beast that Akira killed long ago!

51 BIRTH OF EVIL

The Wild Butterfly was in the forest waiting for the full moon to appear. He looked for a hiding place especially now that he had Kenji's blood in his body. Their blood mixed. Later, he found a perfect spot and flew towards there.

Kenji was still restless inside the clinic as he waited for the result from the medic. He was laying down the bed when he saw Claude entered the clinic just to see him.

Kenji was still touching his neck when Claude asked.

"Kenji…" called Claude. "Are you okay?"

"Nope…"

"What happened to you? You've been touching your neck since earlier. What happened? Tell me."

At that moment, Percy and Tadteo also entered the clinic.

"I was unaware of a strange insect that got into my room. Afterwards, its stinger… it pricked my neck…" said Kenji.

"Oh no!" Percy was shocked. "Mashter! What did ya shay? What did it look like? Why didn't ya call me sho I could have crushed it?!"

"You can't take him on, Percy…" Kenji answered as he smiled. "I know you won't believe me, but its appearance was strange. And one more thing, it's from Pioneer's!"

"Pioneer?" asked Claude and Tadteo. "How did you know you that the strange creature is from Pioneer?"

"It told me," Kenji laughed.

"Whattt???" the three recoiled surprisingly. "It talked?"

Kenji laughed again. "I knew it, you won't easily believe in me! Hahaha!"

Percy and Tadteo joined the laughter, but Claude did not.

"I know you Kenji, so I believe you," said Claude.

Kenji stopped laughing. "Really?"

"Of course, Kenji you're my friend. You should have also called me earlier so I could have helped, right?"

"Right," said Tadteo. "Even us…"

The UE doctor entered when the four stopped. Kenji became worried again, though the doctor looked happy.

"D-Doc?" called Kenji nervously to the doctor.

"Well, Kenji…" said the doctor as he adjusted his eyeglasses. "I have good news for you. The result is negative. We didn't find any signs of venom flowing in your blood… Maybe because when you were pricked by that creature, the venom was not included…"

Kenji smiled. "R-Really?"

"Yes, because when we checked your neck, there was no change in the color of your skin. And look at your neck… Touch it, it should have greatly swelled, but no… It's just a rash."

Percy said. "Right, sheems like only an ant bit yer shkin, mashter…"

"If it had poison, the venom should already had killed you. Your neck should have been swollen by now, and the skin color would have turned violet. But no… It's just a small rash."

"Are you sure, doctor?"

Claude said. "Oh, so now you're the one who won't believe that easily…"

Kenji stooped down his head and said a prayer in gladness. "Thank you so much then if that's the case…"

"You're safe now, Mister Leader…" said the doctor happily. "You can go back to your room. You have nothing to worry about…"

Kenji shook the doctor's hand. "Thank you very much!"

Claude joked. "Doc, no charge right?"

The doctor even joined the joke. "Ah, no charge… Because if the result is positive, then I'll charge, hahaha!"

And they both laughed.

THE EXPLORERS

Meanwhile...

The Wild Butterfly was now completely hidden in a huge cocoon to shed his skin in preparation for his transformation. At twelve o'clock sharp, the full moon came out in the forest, and the evil butterfly laughed evilly for his upcoming metamorphosis. The cold wind blew around the cocoon to compliment the moon shine that shrouding the dark forest. "FINALLY! FINALLY! THE FULL MOON HAS COME OUT!" he said as he laughed.

The Wild Butterfly watched the full moon as it appeared in the sky. The lightning struck. "The moment that I acquire human's blood... my appearance will change during the full moon... And now... it will finally happen!"

The full moon was clearly seen in the sky. Then the lightning struck again followed by the loud thunder. "THIS IS IT... THIS IS ITTTT!!!"

The lightning struck again. A pale black light slowly shone around the butterfly's body. The creature began to transform. His body slowly changed. The transformation process was a little painful, causing him to groan in pain as his body transformed. But he could endure the pain that crawling all over his body. He would only experience much pain at first during the initial transformation. Hence, if he changed his form again, then he would not feel any pain anymore.

"HAHAHAHA!!!"

The butterfly slowly formed a human body and acquired two hands and feet. "Come on! RAAARRR... Even if its still too p-painful!"

His butterfly wings shrank and shrank until it completely disappeared in his back. Even his two antennas shrank in his forehead until it was gone. "Evil will be born!" he yelled.

Again, more black lights came out of the creature's body. His hair grew on his head and a lot more had changed in his appearance. His fangs appeared. The transformation was still painful. "Come on! I need to endure it... It's only in the beginning!!!"

His transformation was not yet finished when many bats suddenly appeared in the forest. The cocoon slowly ripped and a new creature fell on the grassy part of the forest. The bats saw the creature below them and they waited to suck some of his blood. The new creature looked like a person now, with no clothes on.

"GOOD-FOR-NOTHING!" the newly transformed creature cried

when he saw a colony of bats flying above him. "GET AWAY FROM HERE, ALL OF YOU!!!"

The bats were stubborn and they did not leave. The sweet smell coming from his body attracted the bats, making them more hungry. The bats swarmed the creature and they went all over him to quickly bite him. The new creature was shocked and groaned in pain as he instantly killed the bats that bit him and ate. The other bats did not come close and flew away out of fear. Since that happened, the bats' juices and venoms got mixed with his blood and became the part of his transformation. So, he grew two bat-like wings on his back as he still transformed.

"NOT ONLY GOOD-FOR-NOTHING BUT ALSO THAT STUPID!!!" cried the new creature and he laughed evilly. "Don't you know that this body of mine also drink blood like you?"

His transformation had finished. He slowly got up on his knees. The new creature started to walk. He had not seen his face yet so he thought of going to the river. When he reached the river, he immediately looked at his new appearance through his own reflection. Because of the blood that he got from Kenji, his whole appearance became look-alike... From head to toe!

"Whoa! Well, what do you know..." he said while he was still looking at his reflection in the clear river water. "Maximillian Foster of Explorers and I are a hundred percent the same..."

He gently touched his face and even his wings as he was still looking at himself in the water.

Later, he stood back on his feet again, and thought of an evil plan.

The newly transformed creature stretched his wings and started to fly as he laughed loudly. His eyes glowed red as a sign of evil. He did not care if people would see him flying around. He flew farther and farther until he felt hungry.

"I'M HUNGRY!!!" he shouted. "I WANT A LOT OF BLOOODDD!!!"

He flew as he looked for something to eat. Since he was a carnivore, he had his higher desire for meat and to drink a lot of blood. He looked for a town, because he knew there were a lot of people living in towns. Not only would he eat, but he would also get some clothes to wear. He had a strong sense of smell so he knew if he was near or far from people.

The full moon was still noticeable until he finally saw a town. There were a lot of people and they were all awake even though it was already midnight.

He stopped after seeing the familiar town and he chuckled. "Pitiful creatures…"

Unfortunately, the said town he saw was also the town he firstly visited when he was still a butterfly. The residents were now preparing to leave the town since the creature killed the kid named Nestor. He was watching them in the shadow. "Do you really think that you can leave here alive?"

The creature flew into the town when the residents saw him flying above them.

A woman was very afraid when she pointed at the evil creature. She cried. "AHHH! What is that?! Once there was a butterfly, now this time is a vampire!!!"

"Oh no, we'll die here early!"

Everyone looked up to where their so-called "vampire" was at. They all assembled in one place and pointed at the creature.

The new creature was overjoyed, while the residents were very afraid. He laughed aloud and told a warning. "If you don't want me to finish you all off, then leave now! BECAUSE I'M REALLY, REALLY HUNGRY NOW!!!"

"Runnnn!!!" shouted a guy. The people panicked.

The evil creature laughed out loud as he watched the panicked people running around the town below him.

"You're all so slow, GWAHAHAHA!!!" the creature continued to laugh. The panicked residents were still running around while the others stumbled in their panic.

"I don't want to die yet!" shouted a guy with shades on his head as he was running away from the creature.

The people shouted even more as the new creature started its assault. "Here I come! BWA-HA-HA-HA!!!"

The new creature flew fast above the screaming town folks as he was capturing his first meal. The residents were still running away. He got one.

"Got you!" he said as he captured an elderly woman and yanked her hair upward as he flew. "You're ancient oldie… You shouldn't have lived this long, hahaha!" and then he bit the elder on the neck while the elder just shouted. He drank all of her blood until nothing was left. The elder was dead when he tossed the skinny corpse on the ground.

"Delicious!" said the creature and he looked around. "Next!" he flew again.

Secondly, he then chased a girl with a ponytail who was running too gently. "Another one that wants to be my food!"

He also caught the girl and at the same time he drank all of her blood.

On the next day…

Morning came and the sun was up. There was no one in the town anymore and all that was left were the spilled bloods on the ground, along with the corpses with drained blood. Meanwhile, the creature was full and he already had his clothes on. There were marks of dried blood left on his face.

"Who said that I was a vampire? I'm not a vampire. I am just a butterfly…"

He looked around the town with evil laughter. "So much blood… So much meat… So satisfying! It's so great to be human! It's so great to be evil! GWAHAHAHA!!!"

There was a Hunter who was just passing by the town and he suddenly got frightened when he saw the whole place, even the new creature who did not see him. He nonplussed, and he quickly hid in the thick shrubs.

"O-Oh my…" said the Hunter as he was watching the creature who was now walking around the town. "I-I hope he won't feel my presence here…"

His body was shaking in fear as he moved towards the huge acacia tree. Again, he stared at the creature in his sweating face. "W-Who is he? A p-person with two wings and a long tail with a stinger…"

"I'm really, really full…" said the creature alone. "I still don't need breakfast, hmmm…"

"He looks like a vampire, but not really… Because if he's a vampire…"

"I still want to look around…" said the creature as he stopped walking. "I still want to find more happiness in this world…"

"Then he should be… Afraid of the sun…"

Silence. The Hunter spoke again quietly. "I-I need to know who he is, so I can report to the police right away!"

The creature continued to walk.

"I-I need to leave…"

The creature suddenly spoke. "Thank you for becoming Maximillian…

Because now, I am MAXIMILLIAN!!!"

The Hunter's eyes widened in shock when he heard a familiar name. He was still shaking with fear. "M-Maximillian? Hey, I-I know that guy! H-Him??!"

The creature began to spread his wings and he flew high above away from the town. Until, the creature was out of the Hunter's sight.

When the creature was already gone, the Hunter quickly came out of his hiding place. His legs gave away out of delight. "T-Thank you…" he said.

Later, he suddenly became petrified when he saw the whole town again. "It's all… disgusting!"

Then, he closed his eyes and spoke in disgust. "The smell is putrid!"

He coughed, and then he slowly opened his eyes. "Never mind… I've gathered information anyway! Now I know who you are, evil creature," he cried as he took out his rifle. "So you're the good-for-nothing Maximillian of the Explorers! I know you! With that, I'll report you to the police right away!"

He pointed the rifle at the sky and then he started shooting. "Be ready, you vermin! Look at the brutal things that you did! I really need to report this to the police now!" and then, he dashed away.

52 THE FALL GUY

7:00am at the UE mansion…

The boys were currently training outside the mansion in order to use their own elements. "Fire!" Jon shouted. They all knew how dangerous the fire really was and Jon had not yet mastered in wielding his element. With that, his Element Wielder companions kept their distance from him.

"Hey, Jon!" called Isagani. "Be careful, come on!"

Which Tyrone added. "Yeah, come on Jonas! You might burn down the whole mansion!"

Jon's body was engulfed in flames, but he paid attention to his companions.

"Don't worry," said Clio as he was also training. "Jon knows how to think. You see, he knows what he's doing…" and then, he began reading the Element Book he was holding. "Okay… in order for us to use our elements properly, we need to pronounce the commands correctly! Let me see…"

It was 7:15 in the morning and the boys were still training. Claude was not there. He was at the gym with Marion, Percy, Tadteo, Kenji, and the other UEs.

"I'm using the 10-kilogram barbell, see?" Claude said to Marion. "What do you expect? Can you do this?"

"Wah! That's not as heavy as you think," Marion said as he teased Claude. "*Kuya* Clio can lift a 45-kilogram barbell with only his one hand!"

Claude laughed while he was lifting the barbell. "That brother of yours... I have never seen him lifting a barbell. He can't even carry one plastic of rice! 'Coz if he does, he farts! Now you're bragging that he can carry a 45-kilogram barbell with one hand?! Whoa, gimme a break!"

Everyone laughed. Though it was a joke, Marion felt embarrassed. His face blushed. To ignore his embarrassment, he called Percy's attention instead.

"Percy," called Marion. "What's your breed?"

"Whoahhh... He changed the topic!" Claude laughed. "He has nothing to say anymore."

"I'm half-tiger and half-cat..." answered Percy as he cleaned himself.

Marion answered. "Oh okay, but why do you look more like a half-cat and half-fox... and not a tiger? Look at yourself, your ears are big. Fox ears are like that, right?"

Percy continued to lick his body. "Nope. Yer all mishtaken, playmate. My mother wash a tiger, while my father wash half-cat and half-foxsh... and maybe that'sh where I got my charm!"

"Whoah, that's cool!" Claude laughed. "You have a lot of breeds!"

"Wow, that's amazing!" Marion clapped happily. "The impossible becomes possible nowadays!"

Kenji was only listening to the conversation of the three as he warmed-up. He was a little tired, but he felt better. Whenever he heard the three laughed, he smiled.

Thirty minutes had passed when the boys got tired after releasing much of their powers so they rested for a while. "I'm getting weak," said Lucky as he laid down his back on the well-trimmed grass. "I consumed a lot of energy in my body..."

"Let's rest here in the garden," said Clio. "Natural air feels so good. You see, it's relaxing."

"So we mustn't waste the air's relief," Cyan added and he flew in the air. "Look at me, I can keep up with the wind without wings. I can fly!"

"Of course, you're an Air Wielder!"

The boys had not rested long enough when Akira came up to them. Reinhardt noticed him first. "Guys look, it's Akira!"

Genji quickly got up from the Bermuda grass to where he laid on. "What does he need from us now? And the gatekeepers let him in even though he's an enemy!"

"I wonder what he needs from us?" asked Shingue. "He's running towards us. It looks like something happened."

"UE! UE!" Akira called the boys as he was running towards them. He gasped for air.

"Hey, why such in a hurry? It seems you are being chased by a turtle?" asked Tyrone jokingly.

Akira was looking around while gasping heavily. "Boys, where's Kenji? I have something to tell you all."

"What is it?" asked Isagani.

Akira told them everything about the Wild Butterfly experiment. "My idiot companions just messed with things without my permission!"

"Where's the butterfly?" asked Maximus. "Is it gone?"

Akira touched his forehead. "The butterfly's gone. I'm telling you, that insect is evil and dangerous!"

"What now?" said Lucky. "Hurry! Tell it to Kenji now, hurry!"

The boys hurriedly took Akira to the gym and he also told the bad news to Kenji and Claude immediately.

"Your comrades are all stupid!" said Kenji irritably. "Did they really create that butterfly just for us, Akira??!"

"Yes, they told me that, but I did not agree with what they wanted!"

Kenji suddenly remembered something. "Wait, wait... Was that the butterfly that bit my neck last night?" he said as he showed his neck and hand with a smaller rash. "I was surprised to see that strange looking insect in my room, as if he had his own mind."

Claude was also irritated. "So he's that animal! Kenji panicked at the clinic because he thought that the butterfly had venom!"

"S-Sorry," said Akira and he lowered his head. "But I wasn't involved in the experiments and my companions' plan. I never thought that the pest would reach here... I told my comrades to find that insect right away, but they couldn't find it... e-even me."

Silence. The boys were now in deep thought.

"My worries are... what if that butterfly will cause much trouble anywhere? He's a monster because he came from the flesh and blood of a beast that I killed a long time ago. He's a Devourer. Maybe he already killed someone here!"

Lucky touched his chin. "You became nicer, Akira. I think..."

Akira was astonished by Lucky's unrelated remark, but he continued.

THE EXPLORERS

"Kenji, I'm telling you that this monster came from us, but I'm not involved in their evil plot even though they're my allies. Believe me!"

"Okay," Kenji's answered. "I believe you."

"So what do we do now? Where will we find it?" asked Isagani.

Silence. The boys were still in deep thought when they heard loud cries coming from the outside. A group of people was shouting from outside the main gate.

"What's that? I think there are people in front of the main gate," said Claude as he turned away.

"I don't know, and it looks like they're shouting," said Lucky.

A butler quickly burst into the gym and quickly called Kenji. "Forgive me sirs, but there are people outside who want to see Mister Kenji and it seems like they're angry!"

The boys wondered. "Angry?"

"Why angry?" asked Kenji. "Why do they want to see me and they're angry? What do they need from me?!"

"Um… I don't know, sir… They want to see you now. Just come out the mansion now…"

"Tough luck, they're interrupting us!" Kenji said angrily and he forcibly left the gym. "Just when we were talking about something important!" he added.

"What could it be?" asked Claude, and he also left the gym.

"Come on dudes, let's follow Claude," called Lucky and everyone went after him.

The boys went outside the mansion when they saw that the gatekeepers were stopping a group of people which was really angry towards Kenji. It seemed like they wanted to attack the young man. "YOU'RE SHAMELESS, MAXIMILLIAN! YOU'RE SHAMELESS!!!" they cried.

Kenji even did not know what was actually happening. He was wondering why these people were so angry at him. One of them threw something on Kenji and hit him in the head, causing him to fell down on the ground. The boys went beside him and they helped him to get up.

"What foolishness is this?" Reinhardt asked annoyingly. "Guards! Don't let them get inside!"

The people still shouted with their grief cries. "Kill Maximillian, let us have our justice!!!"

"J-Justice?" Kenji was confused. "What justice are you talking about? What did I do to make you all ask justice from me?!"

"YOU KILLED OUR FAMILY! YOU KILLED OUR CHILDREN! YOU KILLED OUR LOVED ONES!!!" they yelled.

"W-What???!" Claude laughed. "What the hell are you all talking about? Kenji didn't even leave the mansion in the past few days because he was sick!"

The people continued their cries. "KILL HIM! KILL HIM! KILL HIM!"

Claude felt angered. "And who's this liar that told you about this?!!"

"I did!" cried the Hunter, who quickly appeared before them with his right hand raised. "I saw the incident with my own eyes, that he killed and ate the people in a town earlier! He was so strong and he had giant wings!"

"Hah, you're amazing!" Kenji said angrily and he dashed towards the Hunter at the gate. "And how can you say that I was really the one who killed them?! I don't have giant wings!!!"

"He said that he was Maximillian!!!"

"What?" Kenji chuckled annoyingly as the people were still shouting at the gate. The police were also outside and they had guns all pointing at Kenji.

The annoying cries continued. Kenji forcefully pulled the Hunter's shirt towards him at the gate's spaces. "Do you think that I look like someone who eats people, huh?! LOOK AT THIS FACE!!!"

"Just admit to these people that it was you!" accused the Hunter. "ADMIT THAT YOU'RE RESPONSIBLE FOR WHAT HAPPENED AND I ALREADY REPORTED YOU TO THE POLICE! HOW SHAMEFUL OF YOU… YOU'RE CONSIDERED THE LEADER OF UE!!!"

Kenji body was shaking in anger so he tightly pulled the Hunter's shirt once more. And then, he strongly punched the Hunter in the face.

"HOW RUDE! No manners!" shouted Kenji as the Hunter fell on the ground. The boys stopped the young man.

"Why don't you admit it, Maximillian?" asked the Hunter as he was still sprawled on the ground. "What you're doing is wrong! You're a vampire!"

The shouts went louder all over the place. Due to the noise of the people, Kenji's ears quickly pulsed because of his severe anger. Thus, he could not control himself anymore.

"WHAT YOU ALL THINK IS WROONNGGG!!!" he screamed. Because of this, he cast the Black Fire with no control and accidentally burned the Hunter alive. The Hunter had gone wild due to his body being burned severely by the dangerous flames. He rolled over the dirt to put out the flame, but then, he died.

Suddenly, everything became silent. Everybody and even the boys could not believe what just happened.

Kenji's body was now engulfed in flames because of his deep anger. Everyone recoiled in fear when the young man had gone wild as he screamed. He was really, really enraged!

"THE PROBLEM WITH YOU ALL IS THAT YOU PUT BLAMES ON ME WITHOUT CERTAINTY!!!" he yelled as he burned the plants. The boys were just dodging the shooting flames, or they might also get hit by Kenji's power. "I HAVE NOTHING TO DO WITH THIS. I CAN'T DO THIS TO ALL OF YOU. I AM HERE TO PROTECT YOU AND NOT TO HARM YOU… PLEASE BELIEVE ME!!!"

Silence. Some of the plants and trees were already burned. The Hunter's burned body was attended by the medic and the Black Fire disappeared around him. Kenji was still in his rage as the Holy Flame was still surrounding his body. Because of his grave anger, his body slowly weakened. Claude noticed him so he took the courage to move closer to his friend and hugged him from behind. The Holy Fire also swept all over his body.

"Just let them be, Kenji…" Claude whispered to Kenji. "We'll take care of things here…"

"Get off me, Claude!" Kenji was still angry as he cried.

"Control yourself! Have you forgotten already? You've killed a man just now! A Wielder must not do this!"

The people recoiled in fear again and even the police, as they watched Kenji and Claude's body both on fire.

"H-He's scary…" said an old man. "H-He's a monster! A d-demon's child!"

Genji was about to reach the elder man when Clio stopped him. "Don't call my brother a demon! You blame too much!!!" he yelled.

The whole place was silent. Kenji gently touched his chest, and the Black Fire slowly disappeared from them both. He was quickly weakened because of the amount of energy consumed by the fire. So, he leaned on Claude.

"Claude… here I go again…" said Kenji in his harsh voice. His eyes were closed. "I'm getting weaker again… Claude…"

"Don't worry, Kenji… We'll take care of things here… I'll take you to your room."

Claude gently put Kenji's arm on his shoulder and they walked back to the mansion together. The gatekeeper slowly pushed the main gate and pacified the people. Moments later, the people began to shout again. This time, they forcefully dragged the gate so it would break and they could get in. They were going to attack Kenji.

"HEY! WHERE WILL YOU TAKE THAT DEMON?! WE'LL KILL HIM! WE'LL TORTURE HIM BEFORE WE KILL HIM!!!"

Claude stopped walking and Reinhardt answered. "Please shut up! It would be better if you all just leave. My brother did nothing against you!"

"Yeah!" Lucky added. "Kenji's a nice person and he doesn't kill people! He is here to serve and protect all of you, people!"

"Boys…" Claude called the boys seriously. "Take care of them…" and then, he and Kenji entered the mansion. The mansion's main door was about to close when the people strongly tried to wreck the gate.

The police at the gate held their guns and pointed them again at the boys. "Open this gate! If not, we'll arrest you all!"

"Oh no, oh no, oh no…" Akira shook his head in big disapproval. "Hold your temper, you don't know us yet!"

The people were still dragging the gate with their full force. "KILL HIM! KILL HIM! KILL HIM!"

"Please go home and we will find out who's the culprit. Do not force us to throw you out of the gate!" warned Shingue.

"WE'RE NOT AFRAID OF YOU! THERE ARE A LOT OF US HERE AND WE'LL TAKE YOU ON, YOU SONS OF DEMON!" cried the people.

The Wielders were surprised when the people called them as "the sons of demon" and not the sons of King Jethro. With that, they also barely lost their self-control this time.

"W-What did you all say?!" Lucky asked first. His voice sounded like he was getting in his rage as well.

An old woman answered. "Are you deaf? Why are you siding with that demon? Don't tell us you're even the sons of the demon, aren't you?!"

Silence. Yet, Lucky managed to hold his temper and faced the people in nice way. "Please, don't be carried away by your anger. I will assure you that Kenji has nothing to do with this. As your protector, we will find out who's behind this criminal act. You ask justice and we will bring justice to you. If we find out that Kenji was the person behind this mess, we will bring him to you and we will sentence him with full force of the law!"

The police were convinced to what Lucky had said. "You heard the man?" said a police. "Let's give them the presumption of innocence. Let us help them to bring the criminal in court. Give them enough space to work on so we can have justice for the victims!"

The people calmed down and were pleased with Lucky's promise and the police's request. After a few more consultation with each other, the people started to disperse and went home peacefully.

53 DARK BEAST

The boys returned inside the mansion. They were still puzzled by the reaction and clamor of the people earlier.

"I have a strange feeling that there's a semblance between Kenji and the criminal that made the town's folks so angry at Kenji, but I don't know what it is," Akira said as he scratched his chin. He did not realize that he was inside the Explorer mansion!

"Even me, I don't believe that Kenji was the one who did that," said Cyan. "Kenji never left the mansion for few days 'coz he's always sick!"

"Kenji hasn't given us assignments yet, but now I know the reason," added Tyrone. "'Coz he was sick!"

"Nonsense answer, hahaha!"

"Come on, let's visit Kenji again," said Jon. "He's angry almost everyday."

The Expland would start with their evil plan again. From another dimension, they returned to the human world in order to capture Kenji again, and Neschar made sure that he would not fail this time.

"Claude…" Kenji called, still weakened. "Why is it that almost every day I am having a bad day?" and then he touched his forehead. "And it's like this everyday, my blood boils in anger all the time and I easily lose my temper!"

Claude took a few moment before he answered. "T-That's nothing!" he looked like he was in deep thought.

Kenji stared at him in wonder. "What do you mean by nothing?"

"Um… Huh?! What?" Claude scratched his head. "F-Forgive me! Hehehe… I-I was just thinking about something!"

"What is it?"

Someone knocked on the door. "Sir Kenji?" a voice called Kenji from outside.

"Oh, come in."

The door opened. A Messenger.

"Oh, Borromeo… What's the matter?"

"Um sir, the DDE is calling you now over the phone. You have a new assignment today."

Claude quickly stood on the chair and raised his fist. "Yes! New assignment!"

Kenji also stood. "Tsk, damn… I'm not in the mood right now!"

The Messenger backed away after hearing Kenji's angry voice.

"G-Go to the hall now. The telephone is there. The DDE is on the line. They said that they will talk to you."

"Okay…"

The Messenger had left the room when the boys entered. Akira was with them.

"Oh no, I remember…" Akira quickly approached Kenji after realizing that he was inside the UE mansion now. "I only came here because of the butterfly. Kenji, what do you think we'll do now?"

Kenji hurriedly went out of the room. "Let's talk later. A call is waiting for me. It'll be quick. Wait for me here," and he closed the door.

"Call?" said Genji.

"Yes," said Claude. "The DDE is on the line right now and it looks like we're about to do something. I was thinking that maybe that butterfly has something to do with our mission. What do you think?"

Cyan sat on Kenji's bed. "It might be… Because…"

"Later, let's wait and see what Kenji has to say when he comes back," said Isagani. "Anyway, I'm getting impatient here."

Shingue and Clio sat beside Cyan. "I've already had a lot of training! Whoohh, I'm getting excited!" said Shingue. "Now, I really, really know how to use my powers!"

"Are we ready?" asked Reinhardt. "It might be an emergency again, right?"

"Well as for me, I already bathed!" said Tyrone.

"Hah, whatever!"

After a couple of minutes, Kenji went back to the room and he told the boys about their new assignment.

"Yo, bro! What did they say?" asked Genji.

Kenji's face was showing disappointment. "G-Guys, do you remember the Explands?"

Everyone answered. "Yes?"

"Because… The DDE received intelligence report that the Explands are going to attack their base again if we don't show ourselves to them immediately."

"Oh, now?"

"They found out that the Expland are here to wreak havoc again! So what we'll do now is to go to the DDE base since they have something for us to do against Expland."

"We'll fly there?"

"Yes… But the DDE will send a mobile for us. It runs fast so there will be no problem."

Everyone was serious when Kenji spoke again. "Here we go again… We must get ourselves ready while we're waiting for DDE's aerial vehicle to come."

Everyone nodded.

"A new mission… A new chapter of our battlefield…" said Kenji as his head was stooped down with his eyes closed. "I really don't understand what the Explands really need from us… It's so annoying!"

"They're only jealous with our powers that's all!" answered Claude.

Kenji opened his eyes. "I'm getting sick of those Explands! Because we have lost Elijah and… still they won't give up after they even lost their leader, Neschar!"

Meanwhile, the Pioneers did not expect that the evil creature was coming to them. When a Pioneer went out of their aircraft, he saw a blurry image of a creature shrouded by the thin mist of fog and was standing in a distance. He came across the unknown creature and he did not recognize its appearance because it transformed.

A Pioneer was astonished and the creature was looking at him. The creature approached him.

"W-Wait…" the Pioneer was looking concerned after seeing the creature's face closer. "I think I know him!"

The creature was almost near him when he called his comrades. "Comrades! Prepare yourselves, our enemy is here!"

"What did you say? Enemy?" said the other Pioneers and they hurriedly came out to see the creature near them. "Hey, that's Maximillian, right?"

"I knew it, he was familiar to me!" said a Pioneer and he drew out his weapon. "What do you need from us, Maximillian??"

The Pioneers stopped when the creature stood in front of them. Silence. The Pioneers quickly pointed their weapons at the creature, and the creature just raised an eyebrow.

"What, Maximillian? We're just a little busy right now, but it's okay since you are here... We can kill you now, HAHAHA!"

The creature answered. "Am I an enemy to you, huh? Pioneers?"

"Huh?!!" the Pioneers stepped back. "W-Why did you ask? Who are you?!"

The creature moved his serious face closer to a Pioneer's face and a Pioneer recoiled again. "W-Why? W-Why are you looking at me like that? Do you know me well?!" he asked angrily.

It was a sad thought for the creature that he was not recognized by the people who created him but that was understandable, since there was a huge transformation happened to him from being a butterfly to the new creature. He spoke. "Do you remember an insect that you created? What if you heard from me that the insect that left here from the jar came back again?"

It looked like the Pioneers had finally understood what the creature said. They lowered their weapons when they clearly observed the new look of the Wild Butterfly from head to toe. They noticed his long tail with a stinger that was almost similar to the Wild Butterfly. Again, they stared at the creature.

"W-Wait... Don't tell us..."

"You're right, I was the Wild Butterfly that has now changed form!" said the creature and he chuckled.

The Pioneers smiled uncertainly when they finally found what they long searched for. *You pest!* The Pioneers said to themselves. *For a long time we've been searching for you everywhere and now you've already changed form? Even Akira hasn't returned yet just to look for you!*

"And how did you copy Maximillian's looks?" asked a Pioneer. "Your presence, you're exactly like the dark version of Maximillian!"

The creature laughed. "Dark Maximillian?! The dark version of Maximillian… Hahaha, how naive…" then, he told the Pioneers everything that transpired when he left the Pioneers.

The Pioneers were silent. The creature spoke again. "It's amazing to have human and monster blood mixed together as one! I think I have a vampire attributes since I was bitten by a bat while I was in the middle of my transformation. Now, I feel like I want to eat flesh… and drink much blood!" and then he quickly opened his wings.

The Pioneers recoiled again. The creature noticed them. "Why did you suddenly back away from me?" he seriously asked.

"N-Nothing… We're just a little uncomfortable at you because…"

The creature closed his wings. "Don't be afraid of me because I won't hurt you! I'm your ally, aren't I?"

"Ah… Y-Yes."

"I just want to give you a reward for creating me. I did this because I want you to have someone like Maximillian… If you're all afraid of me and look at me differently then I don't care. I won't be nice to all of you, even if you created me or not!"

"W-What do you mean?"

"Because I have my own life now… And one day I will eat you all, AHAHAHAHA!!!" and afterwards, the creature left the Pioneers as he flew away.

"I knew it!" a Pioneer was angry. "Even if he said that he's our ally, we can't trust him! He's also might be our enemy from now on!"

"He looks strong," said another Pioneer. "The moment that he copied Maximillian, he can even copy his speed and strength!"

Back to UE…

The Explorers rode the DDE HawkEye and they were thinking if they should bring Akira in their trip or not. Later, Akira's phone rang. Quickly, he looked at his smartphone and his comrade was on the line!

"Wait a minute, Kenji…" said Akira and he immediately answered the call. "Yes, what's up?"

Meanwhile, the Explorers were silent. Akira sprang back in surprise. "What? The butterfly we're looking for has returned?"

"Wow, just as we thought!" said Cyan irritably. "Their stupid plan again!"

"What? He looks like Kenji now?!"

They all looked at Akira. "Akira, what happened?" asked Kenji. Akira was just listening to the other line.

"And then he left there? He transformed as Dark Maximillian, is that it?" Akira asked the other line.

"This means that Kenji really does have a look-alike now!" Reinhardt said angrily. "That's why those people kept on blaming him! They mistook him for Dark Maximillian!"

Akira put down his smartphone and spoke. "If that's the case, then that was the butterfly that sucked your blood, Kenji! He's Dark Maximillian."

Kenji thought deeply. "What now? I have a look-alike… If only the people knew the whole truth!"

"And a new enemy," said Maximus.

The aircraft was about to fly when Akira went down the plane.

"You're not coming with us, Akira?" asked Isagani.

Akira laughed. "I'm a Pioneer. But don't worry, I'll catch up on you… Element Wielders!" and he waved. "See you all guys later in your mission!" and then he left. Afterwards, the huge DDE Hawkeye flew freely in the air.

The Explorers were now in the middle of their trip. They never realized that the Explands were already in the human world. They planned to take the hidden Sacred Items in the DDE base, and also the other treasures found there. They were such a nuisance!

"Oh, man…" Kenji frowned. "Problems, problems, problems…"

Even his companions frowned. "Do you think that the Pioneer's creature is strong?" asked Jon with his lips puckered. "I can imagine him," then he lowered his head.

"Don't you ever think like that, Jonas!" said Tyrone annoyingly. "He's just weak. Even if he's human in shape, his strength is like that of a simple butterfly. Size is the only difference!"

Jon puckered his lips again. "What can I do? That's my insight, because I haven't seen him yet."

"Stop it!"

Jon puckered at Tyrone and gave him an angry look. He snapped his fingers and a small fire appeared on Tyrone's butt.

"OUCH! OUCH!" cried Tyrone as his butt was set on fire, though it was small. "Enough, Jonas! You're not funny anymore!!!" then he ran goofily in front of the boys.

"Stop that Jonas!" stopped Reinhardt as Tyrone was still running goofily. "Tyrone's getting hurt," and he laughed as he joked. "Wow, Tyrone can perform in a comedy circus!"

"ENOUGH, JON!" shouted Tyrone. "WATTEERRR!!!"

Maximus heard Tyrone's cry about asking water. Tyrone was still running around goofily.

"Water? Here you go!" Maximus gently gestured his hand when the burst of water suddenly appeared and showered everyone. Everything in the DDE HawkEye was dripping wet!

After five minutes…

All the boys were fully bathed inside the aircraft and they shivered by cold.

"Prince Maximus!" Clio laughed as he hugged himself. "M-Maybe… you really are our Water Wielder!"

Meanwhile, the prince who was also soaking wet was still serious. "I don't know…"

Moments later, they successfully reached the DDE base and their bodies were still all wet. The DDEs welcomed them from below. Afterwards, the DDE HawkEye landed. When the exit door opened, the remaining water poured out from inside the aircraft. Then, the boys came down the plane dripping with water. The DDEs were shocked!

"UEs!" called a DDE surprisingly. "What happened that you're all so wet?"

"Well, ah… I-It rained inside, hehehe!" Lucky joked.

"Kenji! Kenji!" Shiela and Aaron called as they came close to their cousin.

"How are you?" Shiela greeted Kenji while looking surprised to see him wet. "Seems like you have a lot of problems to handle right now, huh?"

"And you're all so wet!" Aaron laughed and he patted Kenji's wet shoulder. "Did it really rain inside?"

"Hmpt, don't believe Lucky," Kenji chuckled seriously as he coughed. "We just partied earlier inside your vehicle."

"P-Partied?" asked Aaron unbelievably.

"How did you party?" asked Shiela.

The DDEs led the boys inside their mansion, and their leader Spencer

THE EXPLORERS

Briant showed himself. His wife was not there. Now, the boys' bodies were wrapped in towels and yet they were still cold because of the air conditioners inside.

"Dammit, it's c-cold!" said Genji and Cyan together as they hugged each other.

The boys just sat on the floor. Kenji and Reinhardt's faces looked dim when they saw Spencer again. Spencer saw them, but he did not look for long.

"UE," Spencer's first call to the boys. "The reason why I called for you is because the mission for all Explorers has come… The Expland."

The Explorers (with Maximus) gathered in the main hall. Spencer spoke again. "To all the Element Wielders of this entire organization, we will leave the Explands to you… And, we'll take care of the Sacred Items here in the base. A-And…" he suddenly lowered his head.

The UEs turned to the DDE leader when Spencer spoke again. "…I have a bad news to all of you…"

"H-Huh?!" asked the UEs in wonder.

"We also found out that…"

Silence. Everyone was still silent.

"…that Neschar is still alive!"

The UEs were greatly shocked when they heard that kind of news. That cursed guy who killed their closest friend, Elijah just a month ago… They were all mum, while Kenji suddenly remembered that fate moment…

"Elijah… Elijah!" called Kenji to Elijah at that moment. "*Please open your eyes… Elijah, hang on… Wake up! Our mission is complete now. The Explands are defeated. Elijah… Elijah!*"

"*K-Kenji… You are right… I-It's over now…*"

"*Elijah, don't leave me. Maybe you have forgotten… we still have more missions that are needed to be done, right? You are the leader of UE… and we all need you so badly, Elijah…*"

"*K-Kenji… someday we will all be a part of the DDE… I promise…*"

"*Y-Yes…*"

Kenji and the UEs began to shed their tears (except Maximus) when they remembered Elijah. The young man poured out his feeling to the DDE leader as he cried. "How did you know that Neschar was still alive?!" and he sobbed. "How frustrating… THIS IS SO FRUSTRATING!!!"

"When we found out that the Explands returned, Neschar was the one leading them… Also their Hydra Lord. They're nearing us here…"

"This is so frustrating!!!" cried Lucky as he stomped on the floor in frustration. "This is so unfair! We can't accept that this cursed person is still alive while we've lost Elijah! THIS IS SO FRUSTRATING!!!"

"UE…" Spencer called the UEs and he decided to change the discussion now. "Let's all start to discuss our main plan. So everyone listen to me, is that clear?"

The UEs returned their gaze at Spencer with their teary eyes. Then, they listened to the plan they were going to do even though they still had deep disappointment in their hearts!

54 THE NEW ALLY - 2

Spencer was now explaining to the Explorers their strategies if the Explands came to their base. The explanation was so long that the UE boys became impatient. As Spencer talked, his vision came across to Maximus that suddenly prevented him from talking. The prince was next to Tyrone.

"W-Wait, Foster," said Spencer as he immediately pointed at Maximus. "Who is he? Is he a new UE?"

Kenji shook his head. "No, sir. He's a Reminescence, and he's been staying with us for a long time."

"What, a Reminescence?! And why did you let that boy stay with you if he's our enemy?! He's a member of the strongest group of paladins, isn't he?"

Reinhardt was the one who answered, his face was frowned towards Spencer. "Because we feel that he is our Water Wielder, Sir Briant…"

"W-What? Is he really? But why…"

"Let's just focus on our mission, Sir Briant," said Kenji in dismay. "Now that you have given us our tasks, can we start now? We will explain later about Maximus."

Silence. A little later, Spencer answered. "O-Okay. Let's all split up. The Explands are up to you, Element Wielders. We'll take care of things here. Any questions?"

"Did the Expland say anything about where they came from or anything else?" asked Clio.

"Nothing," answered Spencer. "When we heard the intelligence report, they just said that they would be here to attack again."

"Oh, so how will we know their location?" asked Isagani.

"You'll wait for them here," answered Spencer. "We'll stay inside the mansion while you all will be outside. Being the Element Wielders, you know exactly the reason behind. The Wielders who possess the elements are offensive type of warriors. And we, as the guardian Wielders of the sacred objects are defensive warriors."

That was the moment when the boys found out that the warriors of the Explorer Family had "offensive" and "defensive" types.

"And… by the way, please have this another Element Wielder to join your party who wields the element of 'Ice'. He's Zoroaster," and then, Spencer called Zoroaster.

Zoroaster came close to them and made an introductory salute towards the leader. "Yes, sir!"

"Go with them. I will let you also temporarily stay in the UE base."

"Huh??!" the Explorers were shocked at what Spencer said. Even Kenji and the UEs were in disbelief.

Zoroaster asked in wonder. "What do you mean by that, sir? Should I really have to join and stay with their base for a while?"

"Yes, and that's my order for you, Zoroaster. And Maximillian will be your temporary leader," said Spencer and he patted Zoroaster's shoulder. "Your forces will be stronger if the 'offensive warriors' are complete… Especially if you have joined strength, am I right?"

"I submit, sir… If that's what you want," answered Zoroaster.

"I just remembered…" said Reinhardt. "We still have one more Element Wielder, and that's him… The another chosen Wielder of King Jethro's Ice element."

Cyan smiled. "Heh, at least we have a new ally, right?"

Zoroaster also smiled and he approached the UE boys. "I'm glad to be with the UE warriors like you guys. I'm Zoroaster, and I grew up without the presence of my parents. Also, I'm a Mastersmith. You look like fun people to be with, right?"

"Is it true that after this mission, we'll coming back to the UE base with you?" Shingue asked. "You might get bored there! People there are all UEs."

"I'm not going to stay there for life, right?" Zoroaster laughed. "That

THE EXPLORERS

was Sir Briant's order so we can be complete. I'll be your ally and I'm glad to be with you guys in any mission that we will face."

"It looks like it's okay for him," Claude said hesitantly while looking at Zoroaster. "I'm afraid he might get bored there because he's a DDE and he'll go to the world of UE."

"Don't worry, Mr. Eyebrow," Zoroaster laughed. "Although I'm a DDE and you're all UE, we still have the same strengths as Element Wielders. And also, I am used to stay with the other Explorers there. I sometimes getting much bored in here because I have nothing much important to do except assignments!"

"Nothing… but make weapons for the Explorers, eh?" Genji laughed.

"Yeah, good answer… Hahaha!"

"Let's not make this any longer boys," called Kenji. "Let's go outside and welcome the Expland's arrival!"

The other DDEs returned to the mansion to stand guard inside. Meanwhile, the UEs along with Zoroaster went outside and stood guard. No one drew out their weapons yet.

Shiela and Aaron were in the main hall as they were assigned to guard there, while Spencer and the other DDEs were in a room where the Sacred Items were stored. "Don't ever let the Expland get inside here, Maximillian…" said Spencer in his low voice. "Now that Zoroaster is with you… The another son of Alex Foster who is also your brother…"

Outside the DDE mansion…

"Our group will be complete!" said Tyrone happily as he stood guard outside the mansion. "Akira is the only one missing here if Prince Maximus is really our Water Wielder, right?"

Kenji was deep in thought. But the Expland was not the only thing that he thought about, but also the butterfly that copied his appearance.

Problems… Problems…

"You're right about that, Tyrone!" Jon answered happily. "And we'll be a lot stronger!"

Zoroaster moved closer to Kenji because he noticed something on his face. "Hey, wait a minute… You also have those cool studs with you! Oh yeah, I've seen that before during the Welcome Party! Here, they're similar to mine!"

Kenji looked straight at Zoroaster. "What do you mean?"

"Because, I saw the two studs in your chin. And they're same as mine!" said Zoroaster and he raised his shirt to show the two studs under his belly button.

"Y-YOU??!" Kenji's eyes suddenly widened. "YOU!!!"

"Hm? What?"

Reinhardt hurriedly moved closer to the two and was also shocked by what he saw on Zoroaster. "Wait! Those studs with you... D-Don't tell me..."

Zoroaster wondered. "Hm? Why are you both so shocked after you saw my studs similar to yours?"

Reinhardt moved next to Kenji, and even Genji. "H-Hey, you are also one of our missing siblings!" Genji quickly pointed at Zoroaster.

"Hm?!"

When the three had proven Zoroaster's two studs, they suddenly felt joy. They proved that Zoroaster really was one of their siblings, and Reinhardt was the first one who hugged him. "Bro... Because of what you said, the truth has finally revealed... You are Zoroaster Foster, son of Alex Foster who was once the leader of DDE! I can't believe that my long-time friend is actually my own little brother!"

While as for Zoroaster. "Oh... R-Really?"

Dark Maximillian was now flying in the forest when he came across the Expland jet that was now on its way towards the DDE base. The Explands saw the dark version of Kenji and they immediately went to the Hydra to tell him about what they saw. When they returned, they carried the Hydra's massive stone head to show him the flying creature.

"IT'S MAXIMILLIAN!" the Hydra shouted out loud. "THERE HE IS! GET HIMMM!!!"

"Heh, it looks like something about him has changed a lot," said Neschar. Now he was back to his feet and was able to walk again. "He looks different now."

"WHAT ARE YOU WAITING FOR, YOU SLOTHS!" shouted the Hydra. "GET HIM WHILE HE HASN'T NOTICED US! HURRYYY!!!"

Their jet gained more speed to chase the clueless creature who was still in his peaceful flight. The Hydra's floating head was next to Neschar, and his body was left in the other dimension because of its gigantic size.

"CAPTURE HIM!"

A strong net came out of their jet and it captured Dark Maximillian. He fell downward, and he could not move his body which was covered by the net. As he fell on the forest grounds, the Explands came down from the jet. Neschar also followed, and they searched for Dark Maximillian.

Meanwhile, the dark creature was struggling inside the net and he had no idea to what just happened. "What's this? IGGHHH!!!"

He forcibly tried to break the net, but it was too strong. "Ihhgghhh! Who did this to me?!!"

"THERE HE IS!"

The Explands ran towards the trapped creature, and the first one who went closest to him was Neschar. He spoke. "Maximillian... We haven't seen each other for a long time..." and then he laughed.

The creature did not understand what Neschar said and he still forced his way out of the net. "What on earth..." said the creature as he grunted irritably. "WHO ARE YOU?!"

Neschar placed his boot on the creature's cheek. "Don't pretend anymore, Maximillian. I will not fail this time," and then, he pressed his foot a little harder on the creature's face. "You can't fool us even if you disguised yourself to conceal your identity!"

"Oh yeah!" an Expland agreed. "Even if you change your looks, we can still recognize you!"

"Maximillian..." called Neschar as he put his face closer to the creature's face. "Can I take your Holy element and give your dead body to our lord now?" and smiled.

"WHO ARE YOU, YOU INSOLENT SCUMS?!!"

Neschar drew out his sword. "Shut up! The moment that you die in front of us, your power will be mine!"

The creature cried out loud. "Arrrggghhh! No!!!"

"Wait a minute!" Neschar suddenly dropped his weapon after the creature cried and saw his long fangs. That was when he noticed that the creature had a tail.

"Sir!" called an Expland. "He has long fangs!"

And another Expland added. "And a long tail!"

"WAIT!" Neschar put his face closer to the creature again and observed him from head to toe. "His smell is different," he said as he backed away. "That is not Maximillian's exact smell, but..."

They were still looking at the creature when Neschar called an Expland to give him orders. "Call our lord and bring him here so he can see this immediately. Hurry!"

"Yes, sir!" said the Expland and he dashed towards the jet.

"Let me just ask you," said the creature. "What do you know about Maximillian, huh?"

"He's a Holy Wielder. But with your smell, you don't have the said element!" answered Neschar.

"Kggghhh... Remove this and free me if you don't want to get hurt!"

The Expland whom Neschar ordered came back with the head of the Hydra that was floating in the air. The Hydra's eyes glowed with joy when he saw the trapped creature.

"WHAT ARE YOU ALL WAITING FOR? TAKE THE HOLY ELEMENT AND KILL HIM NOWWW!!!"

"But our lord, Hydra," Neschar opposed. "Look at him closely. His smell is mixed with Maximillian's smell--"

The Hydra was in a hurry. "WELL, OBVIOUSLY HE HAS!"

"...But he doesn't have the Holy element!"

"WHATTTT?!! HOW DID THAT HAPPEN?"

The Hydra's head was hovering next to Neschar and he quickly went to the creature to observe him. Ten minutes had passed, the Hydra spoke again. "IT'S NOT HIM! BUT WHY DO YOU LOOK LIKE HIM? YOU FOOLED US! YOU FOOLED USSS!!!"

"What's this 'Holy' thing are you talking about and what do you need from me?" asked the creature angrily.

"The ultimate power of King Jethro's Holy Element is what the warriors in this world are fighting over," answered an Expland. "Maximillian possesses the Holy element which we need, because its power will serve as the cure so we can turn our lord back to his true form again."

"I don't care about what you need! Just free me! I do not know anything about that foolishness!"

"What a shame," Neschar smiled. "So you don't have any plan to acquire the only element that will help you rule over this world?"

The creature wondered. "What do you mean?"

"The groups of warriors that are long enemies of Explorers have one goal in mind, and that is to take the Holy element from Maximillian: Mercury, Expland, Humorian, Vanguard, Reminescence, and Pioneer... Because that is King Jethro's primary element which possesses strongest powers that no other elements nor magics can surpass."

The creature's eyes widened when he heard Pioneer. "What did you say? Pioneer? Even the Pioneers are seeking for that element?"

"Why? Do you have something to do with Pioneer, huh?"

The creature was forced to tell them his story from where he came from like what he told to the Pioneers. His story was not that long, but was detailed.

"So you're smart," Neschar chuckled, and the Explands joined in. The Hydra was still disappointed. "So you're like us who are excellent mimickers, but you're a Pioneer…"

"ENOUGH!" the creature went wild again. "Let me go! Before you all get hurt, you'll see!" and then he poured all his strength in order to escape the strong net.

Neschar deeply thought of something interesting, because he felt that he liked the creature.

"Okay… I'll release you if you agree with our deal. Why don't we join forces to capture the Explorers and take what we want. You'll come with us and help us get Maximillian. If we're successful, then both of us will take his element and we'll become the new Holy Wielders of this world!"

The creature did not answer.

"We'll go to the DDE mansion because it's most likely that the other elements can also be found there. If you're coming, I'm absolutely sure that you'll see Maximillian again and have your revenge. Then you'll take him… and bring him to us! Do you understand?"

The creature was forced to agree since he wanted to be free again. "Okay, I'll do it. Just don't include me in your other troubles. If it's Maximillian that you need!"

"So, you agree?" Neschar asked as he smirked. "That's a good plan, right?" and then he laughed. The Hydra was still silent beside him.

"Y-Yes…" the creature's tone was harsh. "I'll come!"

The UE boys were still outside the mansion and they were training, while the others got tired of waiting. "They're taking too long!" Claude complained irritably. "We have been waiting here for too long! Those Explands are like turtles!"

The weary boys were sitting beneath an acacia tree. They all got impatient as well.

"Oh come on! Did those evil mages mean to be so slow?" Tyrone also complained. "They made us go here then, nothing will happen?!" then he kicked a small rock. It flung far away.

The DDEs inside the mansion got impatient as well.

"What time will they arrive?" Aaron asked in boredom. "What if they were just threatening us. Then, they won't arrive!"

"They'll arrive, Aaron," answered Spencer. "If they said it, then they'll definitely do it. So we still need to be ready…"

Outside.

"It'll be like this," said Kenji. "Boys, I'm afraid that if we meet the Expland here and they start the attack, the DDEs might get involved. Why don't we go far away from here and wait in another place?"

"That idea of yours is good, Kenji," Zoroaster agreed. "But what if we won't come across them there or they go to different direction?"

"That's impossible bro," Kenji said as he smiled. "We'll still see them, and they'll see us. You know why? Because they're really after us, and…"

Maximus added to what Kenji said. "…And you are the one they really need."

Everyone agreed. "You're right about that Kenji," said Clio and he clapped. "Let's get far away from here so the mansion won't get involved in our possible battle. You see, they can still feel our presence wherever we are, right?"

With that, the UEs asked the DDE's permission to let them move a little farther from the base for its safety. Then, the boys went straight into the forest. They thought that it would be best for them to wait for the Expland there than to wait in the DDE base. When they got into the forest, they stopped.

They thought that the Expland was already there when they reached the forest… but they were wrong. Later, Lucky sat beneath a tree and Zoroaster followed.

While the boys waited for the Expland to come once more, they went back to train themselves again. Only three minutes had passed when Lucky's smartphone rang and he answered. "Hello?"

The boys were still in the middle of their training when Lucky stepped back in shock. "Come on Marion, why did you shock me? And you're yelling at me, eh?! Whaddya want?"

"Who's that?" Claude asked while he was chewing the bubble gum he brought.

"Who else? None other than Marion!"

"Ah…"

THE EXPLORERS

"What again?!" Lucky stood up as he was trying to listen to the other line. "Look, it's because you were still asleep when we left. And you called... What if we're in the middle of a fight right now? You're really too pesky!"

Lucky walked away from his friends while still talking to the phone. "Dang, whatever you say! It's up to you, if that's what you want to do. Move now if you're sure that you can go here by yourself!"

"Lucky, psst!" Jon chuckled when he heard that Lucky's voice was getting high-pitched, but Lucky did not pay him any attention.

"Yes, yes... Okay, hurry up because you're already too annoying now!" said Lucky as he gestured while walking back and forth. "Oh, Okay... Yes... We're not in the DDE mansion right now. Okay, bye. Take care!" and then he ended the call.

"Hey, Lucky," called Clio. "What's that kid's problem this time? It's a good thing that we haven't started yet."

"That brother of yours, he is always causing trouble in a wrong time," Lucky laughed. "Now that we're away from our base, he suddenly thought of coming along with us and go here."

Clio laughed. "Man, he'll take a long, long trip to get here. What else did he say?"

"Well, he has the guts... he said he'll catch up on us."

"C-Catch up? All by himself?"

"Well, I don't know about him. I should have given the phone to you so you would do the talking."

Clio turned to his back. "Hehehe... Who cares? I don't want to talk to him, you know?"

Lucky also turned to his back. "Hehehe! You're a good brother!"

The Expland was now getting closer to the DDE base and Dark Maximillian was with them. Later, the UE boys suddenly felt the Expland's presence approaching towards them from the distance.

"Let's get ready..." said Kenji as he readied himself for the war-. "Prepare yourself, Wielders. This is what you've been trained for... This battle is for our fallen leader and a friend. This is it!"

The Explands began to smile evilly when they also felt the strong presence of Explorers. "We have not reached the Explorers' base yet, but I can feel such strong presence close from here," said Neschar and he chuckled. "I see... They're here... In this forest, waiting for us..."

The dark creature answered. "I can even feel Maximillian's presence now…"

The two groups were silent, and they could still feel each other's presence that was getting stronger as the Explands approached. As the jet was getting closer and closer, the Explorers (and Maximus) already prepared themselves with their weapons ready in their hands!

55 THE KIDNAP

The Explands went closer and closer and the boys' senses became stronger. Kenji closed his eyes and spoke to himself. "Elijah… This is for you…" and then, Elijah's image suddenly appeared in his mind. "This is for you… We'll avenge your death, Elijah…"

"Oh, man…" Genji's head suddenly hurt. "G-Guys, it seems that we are about to face stronger enemies… Not like the ones we've faced before!"

"Ah!" Cyan quickly pointed above. "Look! Maybe those are the Explands!"

The UEs looked up. They saw the huge jet with the Expland's logo in the distance and it stopped nearly above them. "No doubt, those are Explands and they already saw us," said Jon. "They stopped."

"Let's all get ready!" said Kenji.

Meanwhile, the Explands were silent. Without a word, they took out a shooting weapon from their jet and it came out of the bottom. A machine gun!

"Oh no!" cried Lucky. "This is not good! Expland's first strike!"

Reinhardt cried as well. "TAKE COVER!!!"

The machine gun began to fire at them. The boys quickly took cover from rocks to big trees around them and they dodged every bullet that would hit them. The Expland did not cease fire on UEs while the bullets hit the trees and bushes around them.

Cyan was the first one to take revenge. "Windrunner!" he cried and the wind's direction shifted upwards. The direction of the bullets that came out of the machine gun also shifted, causing the bullets to hit one wing of the Expland's jet so they stopped.

"Yesss!"

"Good job, Cyan!" said Claude. "You're amazing!"

"'Coz I already learned!" Cyan boasted.

The boys waited for the Expland's next move and they still remained silent. Their jet's wing was now smoking.

"We should still be alert," said Kenji. "We still haven't memorized Expland's each move. I think they'll still mess with us…"

Jon pointed. "Oh no, looks like something else follows!"

The boys looked up again. After the machine gun, this time, the Explands sent a missile.

"O-Oh no!" shouted Tyrone. "RUNNN!!!"

The Explands released an air-to-surface missile from their jet. The missile flew and it chased the Explorers. "Let's all split up so it won't chase all of us at the same time!" Kenji shouted as he ran. "Dammit, they're cheaters!"

The boys split up, but the missile did not stop in chasing them. As the boys dispersed, the missile aimed for Kenji.

"KENJI!" cried Claude over Kenji. "IT'S CHASING YOU!"

The missile's flight was fast and Kenji was running very fast. He could not attack back because it might hit him to his death. He kept on running as fast as he could!

"*KUYA* KENJI!" cried Genji. "I'll take care of my brother! All of you, take care of the jet!"

"Dammit! DAMMIT!!!"

Kenji quickly thought of a tactic while he was running very fast. He let the missile chase him until he reached a perfect spot where there were tall trees close to each other. Because of the huge number of trees, the missile happened to hit there. It had a powerful explosion and Kenji jumped in great shock. Many trees were burned down and died.

The fires and smokes were all over the place when Kenji knelt due to extreme exhaustion. He gasped for air deeply in his sweaty face.

He rested for a bit as he was still gasping for air. He never realized that his twin followed him and saw him. "*Kuya!*" called Genji as he waved. "What happened? Are you okay?"

"*Kuya* Genji…" Kenji was still out of breath. "Wait… I'm so tired…"

"That's okay," Genji smiled. "Lucky and the others will take care of things there."

Kenji was still gasping for air. "W-Wait… Just a minute…"

"Out of everyone, the missile just chased you."

"Didn't I tell you all that I am the only one they need?"

"Because you are the Hydra's only cure so he can go back to his true form again."

Kenji nodded. "Yes…"

Meanwhile…

The group of UEs was now in battle against Explands. The other Explands came down the jet, but Neschar was not with them. The warriors fought fiercely with each other with their weapons and magics.

Reinhardt called Lucky even though he was in the middle of the fight. "Lucky, haven't you noticed that Neschar isn't here?!"

Lucky did not hear Reinhardt because he was busy with his opponent. And so as the others.

"It's not the right time to summon a Vrandolon!" cried Jon. "If we did that at the wrong time, we'll lose!"

Claude was the one who answered Reinhardt's question earlier. "Reinhardt! I kept on looking for him, but he's not here!"

"FIRE!" Jon shouted and his Expland opponent quickly dodged it. In turn, he was the one who attacked Jon.

During battle, the Explorers' eyes still looked for Neschar. They wanted a piece of Neschar to avenge the death of their one and only leader, Elijah!

"*Kuya* Kenji," Genji called his twin. "I think they need our help… What now? Can you stand?"

Kenji was still out of breath, but he forced himself to move. "Okay… We need to go back there, *kuya* Genji… Neschar is there… The one I will kill is there…"

Genji helped his twin to get up on his feet, but they suddenly heard a voice in a distance. "So you were here all along, Maximillian…"

The twins were shocked. "W-What…" Genji said. "That voice…"

"We haven't seen each other in a long time, you haven't changed…"

The whole place was foggy and the smoke from the burning trees was thick. The visibility was so low when the twins suddenly heard footsteps coming towards them.

"No doubt…" Kenji's eyes widened. "It's him…"

"What?" Genji asked as he rested his twin brother's arm on his shoulder. "Is it really him?"

Kenji had a bad look as he stared at the person coming towards them from the thick smoke. "What is this I'm feeling now? I-It's strange…" he said.

A stranger came closer and closer to the twins. The person who killed Elijah… "It is him!"

The person they waited for slowly came out of the smoke. The twins did not react as they glared towards Neschar, now in his different look. His hair was short, and he wore a creepy-looking mask all over his face. The twins suddenly recoiled in shock and disbelief. They had already beaten Neschar in their first fight!

Neschar was almost close to them and his whole body was now visible from the thick smoke.

"*Kuya…*" Kenji called his twin in whisper. "Let me be. He's here now," and he gently removed his arm that rested on Genji's shoulder.

"But, *kuya*!" Genji stopped him. "I can't leave you here!"

Kenji flicked Genji's left ear lightly. "Of course, you can't leave me here! What if something happens to me?"

Genji's face quickly blushed in embarrassment. "Oh… Y-Yeah, hehehe!"

Neschar was only a couple of meters away from the twins when they faced each other. Neschar spoke first. "What a pleasant surprise, Maximillian…"

Kenji slowly felt his anger again since he could not accept Neschar's resurrection. His body was shaking, due to intense anger when he remembered the scene where Neschar stabbed Elijah on his chest.

"*ELIJAAAAHHH!!!*"

"*Die now, you worthless Explorer! DIE!!!*" again, Neschar stabbed Elijah in the stomach three times during that fatal day.

Kenji wanted to crush Neschar now and kill him with full force!

"I really, really don't want to fail again this time, Maximillian…" said Neschar's as his whole body glowed by an aura. "Now is the right time of becoming the new Holy Wielder and your ruler! AHAHAHAHA!!!"

The twins glared intensely at Neschar, but Kenji was feeling in rage.

He gently moved his hand and took his weapon in his back. Genji also drew out his weapon.

Kenji grunted irritably as his hands shook more with anger. "Your laugh is so annoying… Curse you… YOU'RE SHAMELESSSS!!!" and then he dashed away from Genji and quickly attacked Neschar.

Neschar quickly dodged Kenji's first attack. "You're still slow, Maximillian. Is it obvious that you're becoming weaker now?!" then he laughed out loud again.

Genji attacked next as he also dashed towards Neschar. "SHUT UPPP!!!" he shouted as he cast his elemental-based magic, but Neschar quickly dodged again. In a flash, Neschar suddenly disappeared from the twins' sight!

"What!" Genji sprang back in surprise. "H-He dodged my lightning!"

Kenji looked up. "Above you!"

Neschar attacked from above. Good thing that the twins also dodged his first attack.

"Wow…" Neschar was amazed. "Are you two the so-called, Twins of Fate? I didn't think that both of you could dodge my first strike. Tsk…"

"SHUT UPPP!!!" Kenji was still in rage. "You killed one of our friends… You'll regret what you did! I'll make you suffer for this!!!" and then he performed a chain of attacks. "WHOOOAAAAHHH!!!"

"*Kuya!*"

Neschar drew out his long sword and retaliated at the same time he parried the blows.

"Do you think that you can kill me that easily?" he said and he quickly slashed the sword at Kenji. "TAKE THIS!"

"*KUYA!!!*"

Kenji quickly dodged Neschar's sword by moving to his right, but the tip of the sword sliced his left waist and it bled. He tripped and fell.

"Oh, no… No, Neschar!" Genji said angrily. "Dang it! Ha-yaaahhh!!!"

Neschar quickly turned to Genji. "YOU TOO!"

Neschar's sword slashed again and it also hit Genji's shoulder. He fell as well.

"Hehehe…" Neschar chuckled. "Is that all what you've got, Maximillian? If you surrender your powers in my hands now, then surely I will spare you and your brother's life…"

The blood was still coming out of Kenji's waist. He forced himself to stand.

"I'm telling you… The lives of your people will be the price if you still don't want to surrender…" Neschar added.

Kenji quickly got up on his feet and attacked again. "I TOLD YOU TO JUST SHUP UP!!!"

Neschar did not leave to where he was standing as Kenji was dashing towards him. The young man pointed his long sword out of the staff.

"STOP TALKING TO ME, YOU SCUM OF THE EARTH!!!" shouted Kenji and he forcefully stabbed Neschar's stomach.

"Yeah!" Genji's raised his fist happily even though he was still on his knees. "We won!"

Silence. Kenji's long sword still had penetrated Neschar's body and it went through his back. They were face to face.

But Neschar just smiled at Kenji, as the young man was still shaking in deep anger. Kenji's hands was still holding the sword's handle.

"Maximillian… You still don't want to surrender, huh?" asked Neschar.

Kenji's eyes widened in shock, even Genji.

"Brother, there's no blood coming out from the stab wound!" Genji shouted. "But how?!"

Kenji was panting, but the shock was seen in his eyes. Neschar did not feel any pain by the strong stab, even though the long sword went through his back.

Kenji added more force on the stab wound on Neschar's stomach, but still, Neschar just laughed out loud.

"Bwahaha… That's useless!!!" he said to Kenji. "For the innocent people's lives, surrender your element and your body right now!" and then, he forcefully kicked Kenji on the torso. The young man flung far away and he dropped his weapon. His back hit a big tree.

"No!" Genji attacked Neschar again to avenge his brother, but Neschar preceded his attack with a strong kick on the cheek. Genji's lip bled and he fell on the grass once again.

"GOOD-FOR-NOTHING, WE'RE JUST WASTING TIME HERE!" shouted Neschar very angrily.

The two were still on their knees when Neschar removed Kenji's sword that pierced his stomach. Then, he threw it on the grass. "I'm going to take you, Maximillian…" then he went closer to Kenji.

Genji opened his eyes and he forced himself to stand. "D-Don't… S-STOP!!!" then he ran towards Neschar and Neschar looked behind.

"Do you think that you can still stop me, you fool?!"

"NOOO!!!"

Genji dashed really fast that he almost reached Neschar. But suddenly, he stopped. He was shocked!

"Why don't you continue?" asked Neschar as he glared at Genji. "Are you afraid? Or are you going to surrender your brother to me now?"

Genji's whole body began to shake. "W-What's going on? W-Why did I stop? I-I can't move my body anymore. W-Why?"

Silence. Neschar was still looking straight at Genji and sighed. "Don't act stupid if you want to live!"

Genji's body was still shaking. "I really can't… m-move my body anymore!"

Neschar wondered as he looked at Genji who was no longer moving. "What are you saying?"

The tall grass behind Genji swayed like something was coming. They heard footsteps approaching them. Kenji turned to where he heard the footsteps. Later, a woman appeared from the thick grass.

"W-What?" Neschar was astounded. "A woman?"

The forest was still foggy when the woman spoke. "Good day, gentlemen…"

Genji still could not move when Neschar asked the woman in wonder. "And… who are you?"

Kenji was mum while looking directly at the woman. To him, the woman was familiar.

"I am Vedna, a Vanguard…"

"You!" Kenji remembered. There was a flash of memories that suddenly appeared in his mind about what happened to him with this Vanguard long time ago. *"She's the Vanguard woman who cast a black magic on me when I was a kid. And I slept for three years straight after Claude and I separated…"* he thought to himself.

"We're in the middle of a fight right now so just leave," said Neschar to the Vanguard.

"The person I need to see is here. And that's him!" Vedna pointed at Kenji. "He's the person that I just want to see."

Kenji and Genji were mum when Neschar spoke again. "I don't care! I also need him. Get away so you won't get hurt!"

The Vanguard woman smiled and did not pay him attention as she went straight to Kenji. "Kid... You still recognize me, right? You're a grown-up now..." then she put her hand on her hip.

Kenji looked at her intensely. "I think I do know you, but I'm still not sure..."

"I'm the Vanguard woman you've met long ago at the cursed town called Dakar!"

"D-Dakar!" Kenji quickly got up with his hand on his stomach. "It is really you!"

"Yes, it's me... the woman who cast a black magic on you when you were a child. You should be thankful that I let you live. Because if I didn't, then you would already have died with your nightmare, right?"

Kenji was more irritated. "I knew it... It was really you!"

The woman chuckled and spoke again. "Long time no see... You missed me, right?"

Neschar pointed at the woman angrily. "Hey, hold on for a second! You should also be thankful to me that the powers I possess now are wea--"

Vedna interrupted Neschar as she also spoke to him. "Do you really want this kid, Neschar?" then she pointed at Kenji. "The power you possess isn't weak. Maybe you're curious why this young man (Genji) cannot move, it is because I stopped him with my magic."

"Then I don't care! And how did you know my name, woman?!" asked Neschar angrily.

Vedna did not answer Neschar's question. "You are wanting to take the kid's (Kenji) power from him for a single purpose, am I right?"

Neschar shouted. "Shut up and leave! You're getting in the way. Stop wasting my time!!!"

"So do you really want that kid to go to you?" Vedna smiled. "If that's the case, then I'll help you."

Neschar did not answer. Vedna began to make a gesture as she cast a green magic on Kenji. The magic controlled Kenji's body, causing his body to stop so he also could no longer move like Genji.

"How about a trade? I will give you my power so you can acquire this ability to control this man in exchange of your power. And I assure to you that he'll be yours," she said to Neschar.

Neschar kind of liked the Vanguard's offer, but he was not yet convinced.

"Give me Maximillian first, and I'll surely give you my power, Vedna!" he said to Vedna.

"Agh!" Kenji grunted when his hands suddenly moved by themselves. "S-She can control my body… and my mind!" then he knelt. His vision was now spinning. "No… No…"

"History repeats itself, Maximillian…" said Vedna as she cast her black magic on Kenji again just like before. The twins could no longer fight anymore because of Vedna's ability of hypnosis.

"No…" Kenji vision slowly darkened as his eyes gently closed. "N-No…"

Neschar was amazed at what Vedna just did. She spoke. "He will lose consciousness again for a long time, Neschar… Like what I promised you earlier, he's all yours now."

Kenji still forced himself to open his eyes and fight, but his eyes were getting heavier as his vision continued to darken even more. He became fully unconscious, as he laid on the grass with his eyes closed.

"N-No… I don't want to…"

56 BLACK CURSE PART 1

The entire forest was damaged by the fight between the Explorers and Explands. The ground had full of holes from Claude's strong punches. Many trees were swept from Cyan's strong winds. The other wild plants were burned from Jon's fire, and much more.

"What we're doing now is just a big foolishness!" Lucky shouted during the battle. "We're wasting our energy, and it'll end up to nothing afterwards!"

The UEs became wounded from the fight. Cyan cast his magic when the white fog appeared. The fog scattered all over the forest which Cyan thickened.

"Lucky, what will you do?!" asked Reinhardt when he saw Lucky charged.

"I'll attack, HA-YAAAHHH!!!"

Zoroaster secretly wrecked the Expland's jet while the Explands were busy fighting the Explorers, without noticing his action because of the thick fog that scattered everywhere.

Later, the Explands only noticed that their jet was already destroyed and burned when the thick fog slowly disappeared. Zoroaster was standing there, next to the ruined jet.

"Whoa!" the Explands were shocked when they noticed their destroyed jet. "Our aircraft!"

"Idiots!" Claude laughed. "The Expland caught off guard!" then he

THE EXPLORERS

lifted his right fist and strongly punched the ground. The ground shook. "Let's finish this fight right now!!!"

Meanwhile.

There was a small jet that hovered above Neschar and he gently took Kenji who was unconscious. The mask was still on his face. He jumped upward towards the jet and left Genji all alone in the middle of the forest. There, he saw Dark Maximillian inside the jet.

"I knew that your plan to take Maximillian would be successful, that's why I told your lord to bring you your own jet here in order to escape," said Dark Maximillian.

As an answer, Neschar only nodded seriously.

Akira was late when he reached the forest and he was seen by Clio and the others. "Akira!" called Jon. "Leave this to us. We are just stopping these idiots from going into the DDE base! Please follow Kenji over there," and then he pointed his finger away in a distance.

"Is he still there?"

"Yes, he's with his twin. Hurry now, because they haven't returned here since earlier! They've been there for a long time, Akira!"

"Okay, I'm going there. Thanks!" said Akira and he quickly left.

Akira dashed in the middle of the forest going to where Jon pointed the direction. The fog was still thick, but his vision was sharp enough to see his way.

Akira ran straight for three minutes until he successfully found Genji under a tree. His shoulder was still bleeding. He was on his knees and was panting deeply.

Akira approached Genji and the young man saw him. "Genji! What happened? Where's Kenji?" he asked.

Genji shook his head with disappointment. "Tsk! We're too late, my twin is gone!" then he stooped down his head. "Neschar already took him away from me!" and then, he punched the grassy field with a sob.

Akira moved slightly away from Genji. "Enough with your cries! You're not a kid anymore (while Genji sniffed). Why didn't you follow Neschar?"

Genji was annoyed. "What?! If you only knew that I couldn't move my body because of the green magic by that Vanguard woman. I couldn't save my brother!"

Akira glared at Genji. "Hey, so what's the use of your power for being a Wielder if you acted nothing?"

"Hellooo??!" Genji was high-pitched. "Go and get cast by that stupid magic and see if you can!"

"That's enough!" Akira shouted as he looked away from Genji who was still shedding tears. His voice calmed. "Can you move your body now?"

"Ah, y-yes…" Genji answered as he slowly moved his hands. "I-It's gone…" and then he lifted his head.

"Tell me the last thing that happened, Genji…"

Genji lowered his head again. "It's just, uh… The last thing I saw is that they took my brother, that's all!"

Akira turned his head to his side when he saw footprints on the ground. "I think this will give us a clue for us to find your twin. I'm leaving," then he walked away.

"H-Hey, where are you going?"

"Of course, I am going to save your twin. And here's what you gonna do. Go back to your comrades and learn to use that element of yours while waiting for my return, okay? Help them stop the Explands from getting into your base, is that clear?"

Genji quickly got up on his feet. "And *kuya* Kenji?"

"I'll take care of your twin. I will make sure that I'll return to all of you with your twin, Genji."

"W-Wait, I am coming with you!"

"No way, just go back and save your base! I'll take care of Maximillian. I can handle this myself. Just go back and help your friends there, okay? Now go!"

"Akira…"

"Come on, man… I have to go before it's too late. Goodbye!" said Akira and he left Genji. He was already far away when Genji still looked at him until he was gone.

Genji followed what Akira said so he hurriedly went back to his friends. He ran fast and even jumped on the trees as he spoke to his mind. *"Akira… I know that you can do it… I trust you! Please return with my brother to us!"*

Neschar's small jet was in the air and Akira stood on top a mountain. The flying jet was in his sight. "No doubt. That's them," he said to himself. "It's a good thing that they haven't gotten far yet. I have a chance to catch upon them."

Akira jumped high on the trees as he quickly followed the jet. "Huh, why is it that their jet's flight is so slow? How many of them might be with Kenji?"

He was getting closer and closer to the flying jet. He kept on jumping on the trees as he was still chasing the jet.

"Hm?" Dark Maximillian turned to his back. "I am feeling a strong presence right now," he said. "It looks like someone is following us."

Neschar who was still on his mask also turned to his back. "Yes, I do feel that too. Someone is following us, but not an Explorer!"

The Hydra's head was with them. "HOW? AND WHO COULD THAT BE? STOP HIM BEFORE HE WILL RUIN OUR PLAN!"

Neschar looked intensely at Kenji who was laid down in front of him. He thought to himself. "What kind of black magic did that Vanguard woman cast on him?!" and then he turned to his back again. "Tsk, and who might that stupid person is following us?"

Dark Maximillian drew out a weapon that he got in the jet. "Let me be the one to stop him, whoever he might be. I'll go out."

The Hydra answered. "RIGHT, DO EVERYTHING IN YOUR POWER, DARK MAXIMILLIAN…"

"Excuse me," Dark Maximillian raised his brow. "Call me something else. From now on, I will be 'Maximo' and not Dark Maximillian anymore," and then, he opened the door's jet and jumped high. Afterwards, he opened his wings in the air and he flew away.

"AHAHAHAHA!" the Hydra laughed. "HE LOOKS RELIABLE!!!"

Meanwhile, Akira suddenly felt something strange while he was still chasing the jet. "W-What?"

He looked away. There, he saw Maximo flying towards him.

"What the--? Who is that?" he asked as he was still dashing and following the jet.

Maximo was getting close to him and he bared his long fangs. He hissed loudly. "Hyaaahhh!!!"

Akira quickly turned to the side and dodged Maximo's first attack. "Tsk! An Expland vampire!"

He continued to run very fast as Maximo was also chasing him.

"Can you please stop bothering me?!" said Akira annoyingly and he drew out his weapon. "If you don't, then I'll give you the cross!"

"I'll take your blood!" said Maximo as his mouth opened wide with a loud hiss. His arms could almost reach Akira when he saw the cross-shaped head of Akira's spear, but the cross did not frighten him. He continued to chase Akira.

Akira was shocked. "Huh?! Why aren't you afraid of the cross?" but then, he noticed something else. The sun was up and vampires were not supposed to stay outside.

The dark creature caught Akira and he coiled his long tail on Akira's neck. Then, he flew upward. Akira was choked. Both of them were in the air as Akira was forcibly removing the tail from his neck but it was too tight.

"Ahhh!!!" Akira shouted. Later on, he noticed the creature's stinger at the end of the tail. He suddenly remembered the time when he was in the UE mansion to talk to the Explorers when the Pioneers called him on the phone.

"What? He looks like Kenji now?! And then he left there? He transformed as Dark Maximillian, is that it?"

Akira observed the creature's face again. He really looked like Kenji!

"This means that Kenji really does have a look-alike now! That's why those people kept on blaming him! They mistook him for Dark Maximillian!"

"If that's the case, then that was the butterfly that sucked your blood, Kenji! He's Dark Maximillian."

Silence. Akira's eyes widened in big surprise!

"It is him... It is him!!!"

Maximo was still carrying him in the air when Akira raised his weapon. With the length of his spear, he was able to reach one of Maximo's wings. "Don't choke me anymore! Take this!" then he swung the blade of his spear to tear the wing. Maximo could not control the flight due to the damaged wing and Akira's weight. With that, they both fell downward into the forest, but the jet with Neschar and Kenji had gotten away. Akira never caught up with the jet that he chased.

Both of them were in a grassy field when they both stood up at the same time.

"I knew it," said Maximo with a smirk.

Akira smiled seriously. "Heh, thank you for stopping me. But I finally found the Pioneer's Wild Butterfly that transformed into a vampire now."

"You already called me a vampire, but you created me. So I won't hurt you, Pioneer!"

"I look at you as an enemy now, you monster… So, I can kill you now!"

Maximo smiled. "If that's the case, then I'll respect your decision. But because I came from you, I have no right to hurt you as a Pioneer… Even as a butterfly or a monster."

"Just tell me, where will you take Kenji, you monster?"

Maximo closed his eyes. "They are going to kill Maximillian in order for us to take his power and become the new possessors of his element."

Maximo's wing was self-healed and it went back to its strength. The dark creature only looked at Akira intensely. And then, he flew away until he disappeared in Akira's eyes. He left Akira alone.

"You cheater!" Akira shouted out loud after Maximo left him. "How come you only came to stop me in chasing your worthless jet?! Damn you!!!"

The Explands that were with the UEs already retreated when they saw their comrades had fallen one by one. Genji had returned to them.

"Cowards!" Zoroaster shouted as his voice echoed. "They have nothing else to do but to always escape the fight. COWARDS!!!"

Claude quickly approached Genji worriedly. "Hey, Genji! Where's Kenji now, huh?"

"He's gone, Claude, he's with the Expland now…" Genji said angrily.

Claude could no longer control his anger again so he cried out loud. "DAMN THESE EXPLANDS! BRING BACK KENJI TO US!!!" then he picked up a rock. "I'LL KICK YOUR ASSES WHEN I SEE YOU AGAIN!!!" then he threw it far away.

"But Akira told me earlier that he would return… with my twin brother!" said Genji and he stomped his feet.

"Though Akira said that he'd have Kenji in his return, we still shouldn't rely on him. Especially now that he's alone," said Maximus as he leaned on a tree. "What if the Explands gang up on him when he arrives there?"

Tyrone agreed. "He is right. Even if he tells you that he can save Kenji, his ego won't help him there, Genji!"

"I know!" Genji was annoyed. "Earlier, I told him that I wanted to come with him, but he didn't want me to! Where will we follow him now?"

The boys were in their deep thought about it. It was already sunset, until nighttime came.

In the Expland.

"WHY DOES MAXIMILLIAN LOOK LIKE HE'S DEAD? HE HASN'T WOKEN UP IN HOURS!" the Hydra asked angrily. "IS HE ALREADY DEAD FOR LIFE?"

Neschar was looking serious. "It might be, my lord. I even noticed that he still hasn't woken up…"

"HEHEHEH, THAT'S GOOD TO HEAR THEN. THAT VANGUARD IS AMAZING!" the Hydra laughed. "HURRY UP NESCHAR! STEAL HIS POWER, AND OFFER ME HIS DEAD BODY NOW! HURRYYY!!!"

Neschar was forced to agree. "Y-Yes, my lord…"

"FINALLY! FINALLY!!!"

They ritual had started. Neschar began to speak in his low voice as he was gesturing. "Olanihanike monarinuka…"

"I'LL BE ABLE TO MOVE AGAIN, I'LL BE ABLE TO MOVE FREELY AGAIN!!!"

Neschar slowly closed his eyes and he gently placed his palm on Kenji's chest. His palm shone.

"HERE IT COMES! HERE IT COMESSSS!!!"

The light on Neschar's palm grew stronger as he spoke. Neschar murmured. "Give it to me… the Holy Element… Come in my possession…"

"FINALLYYY!!!"

The secret room was now shaking. Neschar spoke again as he raised his hand. "Come, Holy Element! Come with me and be mine!!!"

The Explands turned their gaze away because they were blinded by the bright light the came out of Neschar's palm. The Hydra was overjoyed.

"A-HAHAHAHA! AHAHAHAHAHA!!!"

The light slowly disappeared. Silence. But after the ritual ended, it seemed that nothing happened.

"NESCHAR! WHAT HAPPENED NOW?" the Hydra wondered as he asked. "WHY CAN'T I STILL MOVE? WHY AM I STILL A STATUE? A STONE?!!"

Neschar wondered as well.

"NESCHAR! NESCHAR, WHY AREN'T YOU ANSWERING MY QUESTION?! NESCHAR!!!"

"Just wait a moment, my lord and I will repeat the ritual. I might have done something wrong earlier. Please calm down."

"HURRY UP!!!"

Again, Neschar placed his palm on Kenji's chest and spoke softly again. Slowly but surely. Then, the light lit up all over the place once again. The Hydra was delighted.

Afterwards, the light slowly faded again, but still, nothing happened. The Hydra became mad again.

"YOU'RE A FAILURE AGAIN, NESCHAR!" he shouted as the entire room shook strongly. "YOU'RE A FAILUREEE--"

"Please calm down, my lord! I didn't do anything wrong!" Neschar answered angrily. "I slowed it down, and I am sure that I didn't do anything wrong!"

"THEN WHY DID YOU FAIL?! I REALLY, REALLY WANT TO MOVE, COME ON!!!"

Neschar was fed up and he observed Kenji. "I have a feeling that his Holy Element is not following me. Because, as my palm lit up earlier, I felt different until…"

"NESCHAR!"

"I knew it!" Neschar was angered. "The Holy Crusade could restrain my power by itself but how did that happen? HOW? HOOWW?!!"

It looked like the Hydra had lost hope so he calmed himself down. "IT IS VERY UNEASY TO CONTROL THE HOLY ELEMENT WITH OUR POWERS AND ASK IT TO BECOME ITS POSSESSORS, ESPECIALLY THAT ITS TRUE WIELDER WAS THE ONE WHO PUNISHED ME!"

"How could that element still manage to stop me on its own? I can tell that Maximillian's body is dead… But how is it that he still has his powers?"

It was getting nighttime in the dark dimension. Neschar was deep in thought, as he observed Kenji who was now laying down on the floor of a room. Only he and Kenji were in a room. "It's really pissing me off… What kind of curse is this?" he asked himself.

Silence. Later, he turned to his back and walked back and forth. "Why? Why?"

He was still in his deep thoughts when he did not realize that Kenji's eyes slowly opened. Then, the young man slowly got up his back from the floor. Neschar, who had his back turned, had not noticed him while he was still walking around.

Kenji suddenly cried. "Wait! Where am I?! Who brought me here?!"

"What on earth--!" Neschar was shocked when he heard Kenji's voice and quickly turned to him. "MAXIMILLIAN, YOU??!"

"What do you mean by me? Where am I, Neschar? Where did you bring me again this time?!"

Neschar stepped back in great surprise. "You lousy kid!" then he stomped in anger. "YOU'RE STILL ALIVE!!!"

Kenji tried to escape, but Neschar used the green magic that Vedna gave to him. Kenji could not move his body again.

"Why did you live, Maximillian? Why?! Weren't you already dead?!" Neschar asked unbelievably.

Kenji still could not move his body. "What are you talking about? You're still not sick of capturing me!"

"Be quiet!" Neschar shouted. "You were already dead! Your heart was not beating anymore and we tried to take the Holy element from you. But your stupid element was preventing me to do so!"

"It was King Jethro..." said Kenji to himself. "Right... King Jethro is still here with me everywhere I go... He's still very alive in our hearts and protecting me all the time..." then he smiled.

Neschar became angrier. "I always end up looking like a fool in front of our lord! He's always telling me how much of a failure I am! I am always hearing it from him many times!" then he strongly kicked a wooden chair and it fell.

"Neschar, it's because you're a loser!" Kenji taunted.

Neschar did not answer back to Kenji's remark. Instead, he left Kenji in the room. He opened the door and slammed it with a bang. The young man still could not move his body.

After thirty minutes, Kenji was able to move again. "Wow, the green magic that stopped me already disappeared," he said.

The room's door opened again and Neschar entered. He was calm and not angry anymore. Kenji noticed him and he tried to anger Neschar again.

"Neschar, how about if I whip your ass now to prove you how feeble you really are?!"

Neschar did not answer to his taunt. He quickly approached the young man and put an arm around his shoulders.

"Maximillian... You still don't know me fully yet so listen to this... If you want to avenge Elijah..."

Kenji's eyes suddenly widened when Neschar mentioned Elijah's name. Neschar continued. "Elijah and I have known each other for long, Maximillian… It's true. Didn't he tell you something about our little secret yet?"

The young man was mum when Neschar whispered to his ear. "I will tell you something about him… Elijah was the former leader of Expland!"

57 BLACK CURSE PART 2

Kenji's eyes widened when he heard from Neschar about Elijah's past. He was still mum. "*Elijah was the former leader of Expland...*" Neschar's soft voice kept on echoing in the young man's mind over and over again... "*Elijah was the former leader of Expland!*"

"But Elijah decided to turn his back on our group, when our lord became a statue after King Jethro punished him because of his failure and betrayal... I know you won't believe me, but it's true!"

Kenji looked in wonder and disbelief. "Who failed?"

"Why, Elijah precisely! When he was our leader, our Hydra treated him like his special son. The Hydra loved him so much that almost everything he asked for was always being granted by him!"

Kenji was still mum as he listened. "His leadership in Expland back then was great, but the only reason why he decided to become an Explorer was because of King Jethro. Since King Jethro punished our lord, he spared Elijah's life and offered him to leave our group and join the Explorers in order to become a Wielder too."

"What were you when Elijah was your leader?" asked the young man.

"I was just a member of Expland back then, that almost every day I just followed Elijah's orders!"

Kenji stooped down his head. "If that's so, why did you kill your former leader?"

Neschar became irritated. "What kind of question is that?! He doesn't belong to our family anymore! He's our enemy now and he betrayed us, especially our Hydra lord! He abandoned us and joined the king who punished our lord. So he deserved to be killed!"

Kenji was still in disbelief about Elijah's history as the former Expland. His head was still stooped down. "Elijah…"

"Forget about Elijah, Maximillian. He's nothing but a piece of dead meat! Now that you learn his past from me, you know that he became your enemy once!"

Kenji's eyes began to shed tears and sobbed.

"I'll be able to take your Holy element someday soon, Maximillian… Remember that!" and then, Neschar turned away from Kenji and left him again in the room. "Stay here, kid! There's something I need to do! Troublesome element! So stubborn!"

Kenji was still shedding tears when Neschar shouted again. "I'll return Maximillian, you'll see!" then he slammed the door with a bang.

The young man wiped his eyes and stopped himself from crying. He slowly stood up when he remembered his friends again. He worried about them.

Meanwhile…

The boys were back to the DDE base again to check everyone in the mansion as well as the Sacred Items. They were safe. Marion was already there, and he arrived the DDE base all by himself. As a welcome, Lucky and Clio scolded the young warrior who just arrived.

"Marion, you really dared to come here by yourself though you're too young to do that!" said Clio as he scolded Marion. "Don't you know how far this is?!"

Marion blushed at the unexpected humiliation and he hated to be scolded in front of Explorers again. So he got mad.

"PLEASE *KUYA*, NOT HERE, OKAY?!!" Marion shouted at Clio with his blushing face. "Stop humiliating me in front of everybody!"

"It's because we're just worried about you," said Lucky with a hand on his waist. "How did you get here?"

"OF COURSE! I USED A MINI-JET!"

"So you know how to fly a jet, huh?" Zoroaster was in disbelief.

"That kid has a personal jet," said Shingue. "It was a gift from Elijah on his birthday. You wouldn't have thought, that kid is one of Elijah's favorite!"

Marion blushed again.

"Okay, but why did you arrive just now?" Clio's tone was calm now. "If you did bring your jet, then you should have been here since earlier."

"Because, I SLOWED my speed!" Marion answered, still with his blushing face. "I'm not an expert pilot yet. That's why!"

"By the way, Elbert!" Spencer called a Messenger. The Messenger approached and saluted. "Any news?"

"Sir Briant, there were no Explands that entered our base, not even one."

"How about the Sacred Items?"

"Sir, they are all safe."

"Did you check the whole mansion again?"

"Yes, sir!"

"Excellent," then Spencer turned to the UEs and Zoroaster. "Any reports?"

Reinhardt explained and recounted what happened. "Sir, the Explands have escaped and they took Kenji. We haven't heard anything from them yet…"

"How did they capture Maximillian?"

Genji answered with dissatisfaction. "A Vanguard woman named Vedna helped Neschar capture my twin, but Akira arrived--"

Spencer's eyes widened. "Akira? Who's that?!"

Isagani answered. "He's Augustus Sawyer of Pioneer."

"I believe he's also an Element Wielder, right?"

Everyone nodded.

"But he's still a Pioneer, right?"

Everyone nodded again.

Spencer faced Genji. "And what did that troublesome kid do this time when he arrived?"

Genji stooped down his head. "He said he'd take care of my twin. I wanted to come with him, but he didn't want me to. I'm not sure of what he promised."

"You shouldn't believe in him Genji," said Claude. "Even if he took our side, he's still a Pioneer."

Genji did not react when Spencer scratched his chin. "How will we recover Maximillian? The Expland did not leave us their trails."

Back to Expland.

Kenji was still in his prison as he played with a stick he was holding. He was slumped on the floor as he broke the stick into pieces and threw them away.

"I have the black magic again," Kenji said softly. "The…"

He waited for nothing and got totally impatient until three in the morning came. He stood up, and then, he felt a sudden, severe dizziness.

Kenji touched his forehead as his dizziness worsened. Neschar had not returned yet. "Ugh… I-I'm feeling woozy…" and he fell on his knees. "W-What's happening… W-Why?"

He forced himself to get up, but he couldn't. Slowly, his vision darkened again and he could no longer speak. He heard an eerie sound. Afterwards, he slowly closed his eyes.

Back to DDE.

It was already late at night when everyone slept. The UEs slept together in a room with Zoroaster, Maximus, and Marion.

Back to Kenji again…

The young man heard a low voice from afar so he slowly opened his eyes.

"W-What's… that?" he said.

"Kenji… Kenji… Maximillian…"

Kenji got up and observed the whole place. It was totally pitch dark! He could not see anything.

"Maximillian…"

"W-Wait… where am I? Where did that Expland take me again?!"

"Maximillian…"

The young man stopped. "Huh? It seems like someone is calling me… It's so dark in here."

"Take a step closer, Maximillian…"

Kenji turned away and followed the voice. The voice spoke softly. "You're getting close, Maximillian. Come closer and closer…"

Kenji still followed the voice coming in a distance. As he walked, he was able to slowly see a light. A dot of light from afar. "There's a light over there!" he said and he ran. He quickly approached the light.

He was getting closer and closer to the light, and the call that he repeatedly heard became louder.

After a while, he reached the light. There, he saw King Jethro accompanied by the Holy White Phoenix. Both of them beamed a white light that made Kenji's eyes glitter.

"Ki… King Jethro and the lord White Phoenix…" the young man said with a husky voice and quickly knelt in front of them.

"Maximillian…" the god called to him softly. "I have something I want to say to you."

Kenji began to shed tears again when he felt ashamed before the god. "F-Forgive me, my lord…" and sobbed. "I-I failed you. I ruined your expectation as a Holy Wielder… P-Please f-forgive me…"

"You did nothing wrong, my son…" said King Jethro as he slowly touched Kenji's cheeks to wipe away his tears. "I'm not angry at you. You deserve to have my power in your hands…"

Kenji was still weeping. "B-But, my lord King Jethro…"

The Holy White Phoenix chirped softly when King Jethro spoke again. "Maximillian, I want to tell you that I'm always with you wherever you go, so I know everything what is happening around you."

Kenji sobbed.

"Get back on your feet again, my son. What I'm about to say to you is important."

Kenji quickly stood back on his feet when King Jethro spoke again. "Son, you are under the spell of the Black Curse by the black magic that is in you. That curse will not go away unless you'll find its cure."

"B-Black Curse?"

"That's right my son. The Black Curse is an unholy magic that affects and controls someone's life when hit. During morning, a person's soul is dead whereas at night he is the opposite. Which means Maximillian, you are dead during three in the morning until the sun sets at six in the evening. And, you are alive only at night."

"Does that mean… I am dead right now? But why does it seem like I'm alive?"

"You're dead right now, Maximillian. You're only a soul that is trapped in a dark world. Whenever you die, the Black Curse brings your soul to the dark world and will be trapped in here until you regain your life again."

Kenji lowered his head. "Now I know," he said sadly. "How will my friends know about this? How?"

The king god gently touched Kenji's head and answered. "Fear not, my child. I will help you. Leave it up to me so the other Element Wielders will know about your current state. Just fight and be strong. The curse will be removed from your body if you find the cure. Just believe in yourself."

"Lord Jethro…"

"I will call the souls of your friends in order to inform them about your current state. I will do it now, Maximillian," then, the god's eyes shone, and so as the bird.

Kenji was mum as he stared at the two. His eyes glittered once again with hope.

Meanwhile, at the Element Wielders…

"Warriors, please wake up…"

The boys slowly opened their eyes when Maximus noticed something. "W-Wait, what place is this? It's so dark!"

The boys observed the whole place as they looked around. "It's pitch dark! We might bump our heads or fall elsewhere!" Clio shouted. "Hey, I can't see anything!"

"Welcome to the world of dreams. There is something I want to tell to all of you…"

"That voice…" said Reinhardt as his eyes widened. "If I am not mistaken, King Jethro is the one speaking!"

"What did you say, *kuya* Reinhardt? Did you say it was King Jethro?" asked Zoroaster. "But why is this place too dark though he's a Holy God?"

"Lend me your ears, Element Wielders. This is about Maximillian…"

"Ah, Kenji!" Claude shouted. "Please tell us what happened to Kenji and I'll find him right away!"

King Jethro's voice spoke. He told them everything about Kenji and his curse, and even the dark place they were at now. "I took your souls in this dimension so I could inform you about your friend's current condition," he said.

"Oh no, then I'm having a nightmare!" Tyrone cried in fear. "I need to wake up now!"

"So that Vanguard woman cast the Black Curse on my brother!" Genji said angrily. "Now I know!"

"What can we do in order for us to see Kenji and stop his curse?" asked Zoroaster.

"I will do the best I can to help you all. I will give more power to your elements since there is an element that can take you to the secret dimension where the Expland is currently lurking."

"You mean to say… that you're going to take our souls to Expland now?"

"I will not be the one to take you there, but a Wielder who possesses the said element. The Giant Lyncis or Lynx is a Vrandolon that can bring your souls to the secret world of darkness which cannot be entered by common people. Its element is Darkness."

Everyone turned to Reinhardt. "R-Reinhardt, then it is you…" said Claude. "So you have the power to bring our souls to the secret dimension that cannot be entered by any human!"

Reinhardt spoke to the god in his serious voice. "I read everything about my power in the Element Book and I learned a lot. According to the book, before I can summon the Lyncis and tell him to bring our souls to the secret dimension of darkness, we should all be asleep."

Everyone looked at Reinhardt again. "Asleep?" asked Isagani in wonder. Then, King Jethro showed himself as he appeared before the boys.

"What do you mean by that?" asked Lucky. "Huh?"

"Reinhardt is right, my sons," King Jethro agreed as he smiled. "Because the Expland are now staying in their secret dimension, which they call it the 'Dark Doom'. That is one of the dimensions of the dark that no any human can enter except the dead. So in order for you to enter the said world is to use your souls. The Expland can still enter despite of their living existence because they are Dark Mages, and each and every one of them possesses black magics. And as for you all, except Reinhardt are no Dark Wielders. So instead, we will use your souls to enter into the dead state with the help of Reinhardt and the Lyncis," and then, King Jethro turned to Reinhardt. "Reinhardt, I order you to include your soul with them in going to the dark dimension instead of your real body."

Reinhardt was serious. "But… according to what I've also read in the book that using this power will also have a repercussion. Because if the Darkness Wielder makes a simple mistake in using the power, then it is possible that a soul travelling to the secret world of darkness will never return to its living state anymore… For life!"

Cyan suddenly felt fear. "T-That means, if we are all into a state of sleep and Reinhardt fails… Then it's possible that we can die by a nightmare! Oh dear!!!"

"It's not that easy, Reinhardt," said Zoroaster. "We're all dead if you make even just a slight mistake in using your power… Tsk, tsk…"

Clio pursed his lips. "If that happens then, where will our souls go if

Reinhardt fails, King Jethro?"

King Jethro closed his eyes. "Your souls will be trapped in the Underworld for a lifetime…"

The boys were frightened. "Oh no, Reinhardt!"

"So, what dimension are we at now, my dear lord?" asked Shingue in curiosity.

"This is just a dimension that was once created by my Holy Crusade. Worry not, it is safe. From now on, this will also serve as our secret world."

Tyrone smiled. "Like our secret base, right? But as what you've said, we should also be asleep."

"I shall call this world as 'Wielder's Dreams' from now on. I shall leave now, my dear sons… And Reinhardt?"

"Yes?"

"Learn your power well because your friends' lives will be in your hands. Bear in mind that only your souls can be entered there. So Reinhardt, I know it may be hard for you to accept and do this task… but, you need to endure it. Remember, your brother is also there!"

"Yes, my lord!"

"Always remember that I'm right here in your hearts. Good luck on your dark journey. I will do everything I can to help you all and guide you all with anything…" and then, King Jethro slowly disappeared before the boys' eyes.

"He's gone…" said Maximus. "He didn't even say goodbye to us."

"Do you know why?" asked Cyan. "Because he said that he would always be here in our hearts," then he pointed at his chest as he closed his eyes. "He will never disappear on us and he's always with us… That's why he didn't need to say goodbye…"

Everyone turned to Cyan. "C-Cyan… You really are a Valedictorian, nice speech!" Lucky laughed. "You're right, he's always here for all of us!" and then, they put their hands to their chests at the same time and closed their eyes with a smile.

"Thank you so much with your tireless guidance, King Jethro…"

It was already six in the morning. The alarm clock rang in the room. The boys got up on their beds at the same time. They were still in the DDE mansion.

Claude yawned first before he spoke. "Good morning to everyone. I had a great dream last night. We talked to King Jethro…"

"Huh?!" Zoroaster quickly got up after he heard Claude. "That was also my dream. He talked to all of us."

"Me too!" said Clio. "That was also my dream! You see, we were in Wielder's Dreams!"

"Hah, you know what? I also dreamed the same as yours!" said Lucky.

"Yes," said Shingue. "Me too."

Reinhardt spoke. "We were in Wielder's Dreams and King Jethro told us something about Kenji. He said that they were at a secret dimension of darkness!"

Then Genji added. "And brother, you said that your power is our only way towards the Explands."

"Wait, wait!" Marion shook his head in disbelief after hearing the boys' conversation. "Why do you all have the same dream? I also dreamed last night. Did you also dream about my dream?"

"What is your dream, huh?" asked Cyan.

"I dreamed that *kuya* Kenji bought me ice cream, *halo-halo* (Filipino desert), and *adobong baboy* (a pork marinated in a sauce of vinegar, soy sauce, and garlic, browned in oil)! Hmmmm…"

Tyrone laughed. "Our dream wasn't like that, Marion," then he turned to Reinhardt and nodded. "Me too, dudes. I dreamed the same as yours."

"Hmmm, it seems that I understand now," Jon was thinking. "King Jethro was the one who manipulated our dream. By using our dreams, he was able to speak to us and give us information."

"But I actually don't remember Kenji and Akira with us in our dream," said Claude.

Genji agreed. "Oh yeah, you're right. I wonder why?"

"It doesn't matter!" Reinhardt became serious again. "Anyhow, we already have an idea about what we must do," then he walked away from the boys. "I am going to eat for a bit, then I'll study. Okay, I'll go on ahead. See ya!"

The boys' suddenly worried again. "Oh yeah! We have a special mission to work on, right? R-Reinhardt, good luck on your studies!" said Lucky worriedly.

The boys' faces were now showing fear. Meanwhile, Marion wondered. "Huh??!"

58 REINHARDT'S FEAR

The UE boys were in the DDE hall with Marion, and the kid still pestered them. He was too persistent on asking about their dream.

Marion kept on asking Clio. "*Kuya* Clio, what did you guys really dream of, huh? Did you also eat *sinigang na baboy* (sour pork soup), huh?"

"No!" Clio shouted with anger. "No, okay?! We had a different dream from yours. You see, we had the same dream and it has nothing to do with your young age!"

"Whatever you say!" Marion stomped his foot. "Say it!"

"Be quiet, Marion!" but Clio was not really that angry. "Just train here or go to study."

"I don't want to study!" Marion stomped once again. "Studying stupidity has nothing to do with my life!"

"Then leave us here. Why did you even bother to go here? You're just disturbing us!!!" Clio walked away and he approached Lucky.

Marion still had a bad look towards his brother and fear was still on the boys' faces. They suddenly became silent.

Meanwhile...

Akira had returned to the DDE mansion, but the gate was well-guarded by the gatekeepers. He looked for the opening so he could enter the mansion unnoticed. He was about to jumped at the wall when one of the gate keepers saw him.

"Stop at once!!!" yelled the gatekeeper.

"You're strictly prohibited to enter here!" shouted a gatekeeper and he took out his weapon.

"Don't waste my time! The UE's allowing me to go into their base! But why not here? I'm an ally of your Element Wielders!"

"That's impossible, you're an enemy of the Explorers!"

"Then tell them, you idiots!" yelled Akira and he jumped high on top of the tall gate and got down on the other side. He was already inside when the gatekeepers moved away from him.

"Don't you even dare to go inside the mansion, or else you'll be punished!"

Akira only stuck his tongue out and then he rushed towards the mansion. "BLEEEHHH, CATCH ME!"

"HEEEEYYY! THERE'S AN ENEMY WHO GOT INSIDE!!!" shouted the gatekeepers and they chased Akira.

The boys were still at the hall when they heard indistinct commotions that came towards them. After, they saw Akira being chased by the DDE guards and came towards them. They noticed Kenji was not with him.

"AKIRA!" called Genji when Akira approached them and went to their back.

"Don't chase him!" Claude ordered the gatekeepers. "He's our ally, don't worry."

"But, sir!" a guard complained. "He's a Pioneer! And it's highly forbidden for him to enter…"

Tyrone answered. "Just leave us here and stand guard over the gate. You have nothing to worry about."

The guards were silent and were forced to leave. The boys quickly focused their attention on Akira, especially Genji and Claude. "Hey, you! Where's my brother now?!" asked Genji.

Akira felt embarrassed. "I-I know Genji, but I'm sorry because…"

"YOU SEE!" Genji stomped on the ground. "I knew it! I knew it!!!"

"Wa-wait a minute, take it easy, man…" Akira smiled. "It was already impossible for me to catch up and save your brother because they're in a different dimension now. Any living creature except the Dark Mages, is not allowed to enter the secret world… So, I can't go in there."

Claude calmed himself down. "And how did you know about that?"

Akira's snapped his finger. "In my dream obviously!"

"So that means, you also dreamt the same as our dream! But you weren't in our dream," said Tyrone.

"That's because my dream might be slightly different from yours, but the meaning is the same. But, did you know that Kenji appeared in my dream?"

"Did he say something about what happened to him?" asked Claude.

"Yes, he said that he was cursed. I could hear his voice shouting all over and he was asking for our help. He was in... Uh, I couldn't understand what that freakin' place was called."

Shiela and Aaron came over them when they saw Akira and made their encounter pose. "Hey, it's Akira!"

Akira only ignored the two. He continued. "That's all. I think you already know what I'm about to say to you, huh?"

"Anything else?" asked Shingue.

"Hey, where's Reinhardt?" Akira was looking around the hall. "Reinhardt is our only hope."

"He's currently mastering his power that he will use in our mission," Jon answered. "He has the book, the Element Book."

Akira put his hand over his chest. "I'm getting nervous actually. Reinhardt is getting scary."

"Don't ever frighten Reinhardt or we may never get back to our bodies alive!" Cyan answered hesitantly.

A few moments had passed and everyone was silent when Reinhardt came towards them. He was carrying the Element Book in his arms.

"How's it going, Reinhardt?" asked Cyan.

"I just read it a little. Learning the said power is not that hard, but I still need to take it very seriously."

"Well, you should," answered Claude.

Reinhardt put his hand on his chin when he noticed Akira, but he only ignored him as if he saw nothing. "I think, we should start our mission immediately later in the evening."

"WHAATTT??!" the boys all shouted at the same time.

"Stop scaring us Reinhardt and you haven't even mastered your power fully yet!" said Isagani in fear.

"We're in a hurry, right? So how about if I study fast and then later on we can start immediately? Hahaha!!!" Reinhardt answered as he scratched his head.

Shiela yanked Reinhardt's hair. "Hey, stop joking around, Reinhardt!"

"She's right, Reinhardt. Come on, study hard and do your best to master your power sooner!" said Lucky worriedly. "I still have a lot of dreams in life... And I need to get married and have a family first before I die!" he joked.

"I was just joking around to relieve your worries," Reinhardt laughed. "You all have nothing to worry about because I was serious to what I have said earlier. So I think that we can start this mission later tonight."

"Please, Reinhardt... D-Don't frighten us."

"I'm serious!"

"I know we're in a hurry Reinhardt, but our lives are at stake in this mission. So if you really want us to do this later tonight, then we're asking you to leave us now and study hard," said Akira. "Isn't it a Giant Lyncis that will take us to the dark world?"

Reinhardt walked away from them. "You're right, Akira. Okay... I'll go and study again. See you later."

"Right! Just keep on studying until your eyes bleed, NYA-HA-HA-HA-HA!!!" Lucky joked.

"LUCKY!!!" shouted everyone to Lucky in unison.

The UE boys were still standing in the middle of the hall with Akira. Meanwhile, Akira constantly observed the mansion with his mouth open. "Now I know how rich the Explorers really are," and he held his chin. "But I think the Pioneers are still smarter, hehehe..."

Shiela pulled one of Akira's ears. "You really are our enemy, Akira... You should be thankful that we still let you in even though Sir Briant doesn't know about this..."

And Aaron also pulled Akira's other ear. "It is forbidden to let a thick-skinned Pioneer get in our base. Sir Briant is very strict, and if he knew that you were here..."

Akira pushed the two away from him. "Okay, fine! I already know that, don't be so noisy!"

"SHHH!!!" everyone shushed Akira when they noticed that his voice got louder.

"You're the noisiest one here!" Shingue said.

"How about if we stay outside instead?" said Maximus as he walked away first. "It's safer to keep blabbering around outside."

The boys followed Maximus and they went outside with Akira. Shiela and Aaron did not follow their back. The boys stayed under the tree, which

THE EXPLORERS

was their favorite hangout, as they waited for Reinhardt.

Meanwhile, Reinhardt was inside a special DDE room which they called the "Blessing Room" to study his power privately. He was mastering the command lines to give orders to the Dark Giant Lynx. As he was memorizing the lines, he was eating his favorite *puto* (Philippine steamed rice cake). Though his face looked very serious to his studies, he was even feared.

Reinhardt was very quiet in reading the Element Book when someone arrived. The young missionary was distracted. It was Spencer Briant who entered the room and was approaching towards him. Again, he felt a little dissatisfaction because it seemed like the DDE leader would disturb him.

Just as he expected, Spencer went next to him and the DDE leader noticed the book he was reading. Reinhardt did not make any reaction when Spencer spoke first while looking at the book. "I have really seen the evidence now…"

Reinhardt was chewing when Spencer turned to him and asked. "Rain, what are you reading that you have to read here in this room all alone? Do you really prefer to read alone in an extremely quiet place, huh?"

Reinhardt continued his reading. As an answer, he only closed his eyes for a moment. And then, he continued to read. He swallowed the *puto* piece that he was eating.

Spencer just stared at him as he read. The DDE leader noticed that his face was sad. He sat next to him.

"Reinhardt…" Spencer called Reinhardt softly. "C-Can I bother you for just a moment? I just want to talk to you…"

Reinhardt remained mum and Spencer was still staring at him. The young man did not even glance at the DDE leader.

"Just tell me Reinhardt, if you don't want to then I'll just leave…"

The supreme leader of the Explorers was about to stand when Reinhardt finally answered. "I will listen…"

Spencer sat down again next to him. "Well then… I-It's about you and your brother's disappointment with me, will you still listen?"

Again, Reinhardt did not react when Spencer continued. Firstly, he tried to speak an unrelated topic to catch Reinhardt's look at his eyes. "You are a skilled member of UE, and you never disobeyed your orders and responsibilities. Do you know that you amazed me so much?"

Reinhardt, who was still mum, tried to focus his attentions to both

Spencer and the book. "I just wanted to ask forgiveness from both you and your brother... As well as with Zoroaster, because we even kept your father's identity from him for so long. I admit, it was all our fault, but what my wife have told you was right."

Reinhardt answered in his low, serious voice. "I already accepted everything, sir... We were late on the news. Everything was all my fault that I didn't save my father."

"Reinhardt, forgive me for that time because..."

Reinhardt lifted his head, but he was looking away. His voice was low. "I should be the one to ask you and madam's (Mrs. Briant) forgiveness, because I became rude to both of you during the Welcome Party..."

"No, Reinhardt. I fully understood how you feel that time, that's why I did my best to remain calm with respect towards you... But, I still want to ask for your forgiveness because we lied so much to you... That we kept on telling you that your father didn't want to show himself whenever you came here for just a visit."

Reinhardt felt a pinch of pain in his heart when Spencer mentioned their lies back then.

"I know you've put a lot of effort of coming here just to see your father who was already deceased... That's why I'm asking so much for your forgiveness..."

Reinhardt was already disturbed and he wanted to stop Spencer from talking to him, but he did not want to be rude. He had no right to resist the supreme leader of the Explorers. But he thought of something. He would just act to show his great disappointment to Spencer so the DDE leader would leave, and then he would be able to study again. A little snobbish maybe... Just a try.

"S-Sir..." Reinhardt called hesitantly when he turned his attention back to the book he was reading. "Please give me more time to think. My brother is in great danger and he's the only one that I'm thinking about. C-Can we talk again some other time? We have a special mission to work on and I am the only way in order for us to travel towards the secret world of Expland."

The DDE leader suddenly felt embarrassed after hearing Reinhardt's remark and not answering his request of forgiveness. He hesitated. "Oh, o-okay then... S-Sorry... I understand. So that's why you're here all alone."

Reinhardt answered. "I have been given a difficult task by King Jethro

THE EXPLORERS

to do a risky job along with my friends. I need plenty of time and privacy to learn my power. Thank you for your understanding..."

"A-Alright," Spencer nodded as he stood up. "Thank you for your time as well. I apologize again if I disturbed you," and then, he turned to his back as Reinhardt remained silent. He walked away and he opened the door very gently. "Good luck on your special mission," then, he gently closed the door.

When Spencer left the room, he leaned against the door when he began to feel that Reinhardt still had anger towards him until now. He thought that it would be difficult for the young man to forgive him. Later, he closed his eyes. He remembered back then when Reinhardt visited them just to see his father, but they lied by telling him that Alex was not in the DDE mansion:

"I only came here just to see my father, is he here?" Reinhardt said to the DDEs back then.

"Your father is not here," said a DDE. *"He went elsewhere..."*

"What time will he return?" Reinhardt asked. *"I came from faraway... from UE. I just wanted to see him and talk to him."*

Spencer's wife came and approached him with annoyance. *"Your father can't come home now! Just go home and do your work in your base!"*

"But I just finished my assignment today and came from a faraway place, ma'am," answered Reinhardt with respect. *"I'll just wait for my father here, until he gets back..."*

Then, Spencer arrived. He approached the two and he spoke. *"I just received a call from your father, lad... He said he can't go back right now because he needs to do something important elsewhere. It would be better if you go back home now and stop wasting our time anymore."*

Reinhardt stooped down his head in despair. *"Where did he go? I'll just go to him instead."*

Dianara got irritated by Reinhardt's peskiness so she shouted at him. *"Stop talking to us like we're friends! My husband just said that your father would not come back today! Go home, you're much an embarrassing Explorer!"*

Spencer opened his eyes after remembering that day he could no longer forget. "F-Forgive me, Reinhardt..." he said to himself, and then, he left the Blessing Room.

Back to Reinhardt. He was still studying the book as he took another *puto* in a paper bag he brought and chewed. He was uttering the lines quietly as he even stammered. He forced himself to learn his power as fast as he could so they could start their mission later tonight.

"Oh, geez... Come on!" Reinhardt scratched his head in annoyance. "I already forgot the other commands! It's sir's fault!" and then he chewed again and read the book.

He observed the photo of the Giant Lyncis on one page of the Element Book. Later, he spoke to himself worriedly. "Me and my friends' lives are at stake in my hands. I must not fail in this mission..."

Spencer returned to a room to where he came first before he visited Reinhardt. His wife was there, along with a number of Explorers. He approached his wife and went beside her. "I am feeling regret right now..." he said.

His wife turned to him in wonder. "Regret about what?"

"Didn't we lie to him back then? To Reinhardt?"

"I don't care about that anymore! Alex has been gone for a long time!"

Back to the boys...

"Here's what we'll gonna do," Lucky acted like he was the leader for now. "When we arrive at the dark dimension, let's do the same strategy again when we were at the Explands' palace. Those idiots are really good mimickers, though we already know their weakness!"

"While the rest of us will take care of Kenji," Akira added. "We need to split up into two groups again."

"Okay, I agree. Let's split ourselves into two groups," Zoroaster agreed. "Seven members each."

"When will we start?" Genji worried too much. "I'm starting to worry about *kuya* Reinhardt. He was forced to study hard for us to get into the dark world."

"Don't worry, Genji," Clio patted Genji's shoulder. "We've known your brother for a long time. He hasn't failed yet!"

"Because he's smart," Shingue said with a smile. "He's always courageous."

It was already afternoon when Reinhardt showed up again. The boys quickly approached the young man as if they were fans. Reinhardt was with Marion.

"How are you, Reinhardt?" Claude greeted first. "Do you know how to summon your Vrandolon now?"

Reinhardt scratched his head as he smiled. "Yes, I learned enough...

That's why I told you all that we could immediately start tonight."

"I know your mission now!" said Marion happily. "*Kuya* Reinhardt told me, hehehe…"

"What's the matter with you? You even managed to disturb Reinhardt in his studies!" Clio said annoyingly.

"Are you really sure about this?" asked Zoroaster to Reinhardt.

"The Giant Lyncis is afraid of the sun, so we can only do our mission at night. If we'd do it tomorrow night, it would be taking too long for us to wait," Reinhardt was serious. "Our time would be wasted."

"Do you already know what to do then?" asked Akira. "Decide well, Reinhardt. Because if we're going to do it tonight, then we need to be prepared and sleep early."

"We'll start later tonight," said Reinhardt as he nodded. "But before we sleep, we should have to say--"

"I don't want to say goodbye yet! I don't want to die!" Lucky shouted jokingly. "I still have a lot of dreams in life!"

"No Lucky, come on!" Reinhardt laughed. "What I mean is… before we start the mission, we will ask permission from the DDE to leave their base. It is because I don't want all of us to sleep here in the DDE mansion. We will tell the DDEs that we will do our mission somewhere away from them. And not to say 'goodbye'… for good!"

"We'll follow your orders if that's what you want, because you are our leader now," Maximus agreed. "But is there anything that we should bring for our mission later?"

"Only our souls will travel Maximus, so we can only bring our powers," answered Reinhardt as he scratched his head. "B-But you know what, guys? I-I think I want to take Marion with us during this mission, hahaha!"

Everyone looked straight at Reinhardt in disbelief. "WHAATTT!!!"

Marion got instantly pissed off. "Hey, guys what wrong with you? That's *kuya* Reinhardt's decision and we should respect that. I can be trusted! I hate you all (except Maximus)!" and stomped. "*Kuya* Reinhardt said that I should come along with you!"

Clio quickly complained. "But Reinhardt, why do we need to bring this little rat with us? You know how pesky and naughty that kid really is. You see, he'll just cause so much trouble with us during this mission. He's more on liability than asset!"

"Don't call me pesky, you idiot!" as usual, Marion said it.

Reinhardt laughed again. "Don't worry guys, I'll take care of it. I'll bring Marion with us because I have faith in him," and then, he stroked Marion's hair as he was staring at him with a smile. "We will start our mission tonight!"

"Yup, the show must go on!" Marion was very much happy and he jumped in excitement.

"Oh, come on…" the UE boys only sighed as they put a hand on their foreheads at the same time.

59 DARK MISSION

It was six in the evening passed when Kenji was revived. He was still in his room when Neschar returned. "Good evening to you, Maximillian… You're alive again, and I already know the curse inside your body…"

Kenji was annoyed. "How stupid, why you didn't offer me to your lord when I was dead?"

"Why? Are you giving up now, Maximillian? Didn't I tell you that your element itself was not cooperating in taking it from you?"

"I will never give up, Neschar. I just asked, you really don't have a brain!"

Neschar was pissed off again and he quickly strangled Kenji. "HAHAHA! You're stupid! No one is going to save you now! You're in another dimension and no one else can enter here and even your friends, except for the Dark Mages like us!"

He was still squeezing Kenji's neck and the young man could not breathe. Kenji's back was on the floor and Neschar was on top of him. As he was still being strangled, he strongly kicked Neschar's torso and freed himself. He quickly got up his back and coughed as he held his throat. "W-What? Why can't they enter here? What kind of dimension is this?"

"Only the Dark Mages can enter here because this is a part of the world of darkness, and this dimension serves as our alternate world! So, if your colleagues will have their guts to go here and rescue you, then they must be stone-dead! And they also make sure that their souls should end up here. But…" Neschar moved closer to Kenji. "…but if by chance they really do make it here, I will make sure that they will end up to their second death! Because I will take off their souls in their existence completely and I will disappear them for good. Do you know why?"

Kenji looked concerned. "W-Why?"

"Because their souls will be eaten by my Vrandolon as my welcome… which only human souls are his desire," then Neschar chuckled.

Kenji was shocked. He looked troubled even more.

"How about that? Do you think your companions will still able to save you, Maximillian?" asked Neschar and he laughed out loud. Kenji was getting into his nerves again.

Kenji's body was shaking again in an intense anger. Due to Neschar's overwhelming insults, Kenji quickly charged and punched him on the face as strong as he could. Though Neschar face was on his mask, he still felt the strong impact of the young man's punch and he stepped back.

"DAMN THIS STUPID RAT!" cried Neschar in pain. "MAXIMILLIAN!"

"You're all heartless!" Kenji shouted and he dashed towards Neschar again. "You're all merciless!!!" then he performed a chain of combos!

"DAAMMMNN!!!" Neschar quickly got up and pushed Kenji hard, but Kenji charged again and punched him over and over again. Kenji wanted to release all his anger!

"DON'T MESS WITH ME, MAXIMILLIAN! IF YOU REALLY WANT A FIGHT, THEN COME ON! GET ME!"

Kenji's glared at him in fierce way. His body was still shaking. He and Neschar faced each other.

"COME ON, MAXIMILLIAN!" Neschar said and he threw a black magic.

Kenji's whole body released a white aura by his Holy element like a force field. Their one-on-one combat started!

Meanwhile, at the boys…

"And where are you heading to do this dangerous mission of yours, huh? Reinhardt?" Spencer asked worriedly after learning that the boys decided to do the said mission elsewhere. "When will you all return?"

"We don't know, sir," answered Reinhardt and everyone was serious. "We won't promise that we will return sooner with all these UEs. Some of us will make it and while others will not. We know each and everyone of us how dangerous this mission is. But when we return, we will have my brother with us. Just stay here to watch over the Sacred Items from the other intruders."

"Please be careful... all of you," said Aaron. "Reinhardt, please do your best."

Silence. A moments later, Spencer nodded as he agreed to Reinhardt's plan. He was aware about the UE Wielders' special task. "Okay, be careful. Good luck," and then, he patted Reinhardt's shoulder.

"We're leaving!" said Claude and they walked away. They had Marion with them. They did not bring any weapons or other things with them except their smartphones. They waved at each other until they were far away from the DDE base.

"By the way, where's Akira now?" asked Zoroaster as they were walking in the middle of the night. "He told me that we would meet him in the forest before he left the mansion."

"Because he couldn't show himself to Sir Briant so *kuya* Reinhardt and I distanced him," added Genji. "While he's gone, he said that he would look for a good place for us to hide."

The entire surroundings were dark as the boys still walked while talking. Later, Lucky's phone suddenly rang and he answered. "Hello? Oh Akira, have you found a good place for us to hide?" then he turned on the speaker phone so everyone could hear.

"Yes, I've known this place for long and it's safe. There's a small cave here in the far right side of the forest. I'm here right now waiting for you all. Come over here now so we can start immediately."

Jon moved his face near Lucky's phone. "Hey Akira, make sure that there are no wild animals that could eat us there. Y-You know, like *tikbalangs* (a Philippine myth of the demon horse), wolves, or boars, or whatever..."

"Don't worry guys, I made an Element Barrier for us. I'm really sure that nothing will disturb us here."

"Akira! Remember, you're a Pioneer. We still don't trust you completely!" said Isagani.

"I'm very, very sure! Okay, I'll meet you all here, hurry!" said Akira and he ended the call. Afterwards, the boys ran hurriedly towards the forest.

Back to Expland.

The room where the battle between Kenji and Neschar was now

destroyed. Kenji's body was enveloped by the Holy Fire while Neschar held his sword on his hand. Both of them were panting as they glared at each other. Later, Neschar spoke with a gasp. "Maximillian, have you heard the tale about the legendary Twins of Fate believed by the gods and humans? Do you know that the said twins could be you and your twin brother?"

Kenji was still mad. "Enough talking! Let's fight!" then he teleported with his magic. Neschar was not afraid. Afterwards, Kenji came out from Neschar's back and was about to kick him, but Neschar got hold of his foot and threw him away. Neschar continued.

"You and your twin are believed to be the Twins of Fate. And even the Reminescence knew the said legend during your mother's time. Do you know that?"

"Shut your filthy mouth, you devil worm!" Kenji shouted and he disappeared again. He suddenly appeared from above. Neschar fought back, as he was still talking.

"It is said that the Twins of Fate have something to do with your world's fate. They believe that if the Twins of Fate are together in the horizon, then your cursed world will be vulnerable to apocalypse, and its existence will be gone for good. But the legend also said otherwise if the Twins of Fate are not together in the horizon!"

Kenji was still attacking Neschar. "I've heard that before, but that's only a myth! That's not entirely true! The lives of the people and the human world have long been in harm even without the Twins of Fate because of you!"

"But the apocalypse has not happened yet, right Maximillian?" said Neschar at the same time he quickly cast a green magic on Kenji, but Kenji countered it by casting the white magic. "The people's lives must be perished. You and your brother must come and reach the horizon together. Your world must suffer and burn to its complete ruin… and when the right time comes… it will be in its complete final destruction and we will make our own planet--"

Kenji was in rage. "Stop blabbering around, you're much of a noise!" and he quickly gestured to cast white magic on Neschar. Neschar was hit and he flung away, but he quickly got up again. He continued.

"Your world will burn, Maximillian! Your world must ruin and destroy!!!"

Their fierce fight continued. Kenji shouted on top of his voice. "I said

THE EXPLORERS

SHUP UP! The world will still continue its existence!"

"You worthless fool! You don't really know anything much, Maximillian! YOUR WORLD WILL BE DESTROYED!!!"

The boys arrived at the cave entrance where Akira was standing. It seemed that the night sky would rain. The boys entered the cave and they listened to Reinhardt's instructions before they would start their mission. "My dear colleagues, as much as possible we must stick together no matter what happens during this mission. Do not leave behind my back and always stay close to me. We are going to ride a huge Vrandolon which is the Giant Lyncis. According to the book, the Lyncis is very obedient in following orders, but he has an unpredictable behavior. If the Lyncis becomes moody, then it is likely that he won't follow the Darkness Wielder's orders."

"But what if he does?" asked Akira.

"It's only the first time that I'll meet Lyncis, Akira. So we must get to know each other first."

"Fine, just do your best. The first meeting always takes forever."

"Okay. Now that I've said everything we'll do during our travel, may I ask all of you to please lie down and close your eyes. Concentrate and never fear. Go on... Our positions should be in circle, because I am going to sit in the middle of everyone."

The boys followed what Reinhardt said and went next to each other. All of them held each other's hands. Afterwards, they laid down and gently closed their eyes. Then, Reinhardt slumped in the middle of everyone. The place was so peaceful and calm. Only the dropping sounds of water from the stalactites were ripping the quietness of the cave. As the dropping sounds continued, the eyes of the boys got heavier until they fell asleep. Reinhardt also closed his eyes and started saying the first line.

"*Lyncis, gawatanit atik... Lyncis, gawatanit atik...*"

The wind blew and it rained outside the cave. Everyone was quiet and relaxed. Reinhardt spoke again. "*Naggnikap om gna gawat ok. Sian gnok tipamul ak ta nihlad imak as noysnemid gn namilidak* (Listen to my call and come forward. Bring us all in the dark dimension!)*!*" and then, he gestured slowly but surely. Everyone was still quiet. As Reinhardt was still gesturing his hand, he felt his eyes become heavy. "*Adnah an gna gnima agm awululak... Sabamul ak an ta nihlad imak as noysnemid gn agm Expland* (Our souls are prepared. Deliver us to the dimension of the Expland!)*!*"

Reinhardt was getting sleepy when he felt a strange thing happening to him. "Arrrgghhh! W-What's this?! I feel like my soul is coming out!"

His chest shone as the Lyncis' soul came out from his body. It stared at him before it spoke with its monstrous voice. "*Waki ab gna gnika oma* (Are you my master?)*?*"

Reinhardt nodded weakly. "*Noyang, nasutuuni atik an nihlad gna gnima agm awululak nood as Expland, nahidnitniinan om* (Yes! Now I want you to take our souls to the secret dimension of Expland, do you understand?)*?*"

The Lyncis did not answer back and it moaned. His whole body lit up and he immediately called the souls of the boys. In an instant, the boys' souls came out from their bodies. Reinhardt clearly saw the scene in his heavy eyes!

The boys' souls spoke to Reinhardt but the young man could not hear them. There were no voices coming out in their mouths. "I can't hear them… Why is that?" Reinhardt asked himself.

"*Noyang ya waki naman oma* (Now's your turn, master)…" said the Lyncis as he approached Reinhardt and also absorbed his soul.

"AHHHH!" cried Reinhardt when his soul also went out from his own body. When the soul came out, his body fell down and went into the deep sleep.

"Reinhardt!" his friends as souls called him as they approached him. This time, Reinhardt could now hear their voices.

"We're souls now. Here in this cave we'll leave our corpse… I mean… remains… I-I mean… our bodies, hahaha!" Shingue joked.

"There's my body over there!" Marion pointed his finger at his body lied down on the ground below.

"Marion, you're busted! You're sucking your finger when you're asleep!" Lucky joked.

Marion reddened and feeling guilty. "No, I don't!"

"Only the souls can hear each other's voices, that's why I couldn't hear you all when I was still awake," said Reinhardt. "Let's go, it looks like the Giant Lyncis is getting impatient. We must leave."

"Let's go!" said Genji. "We will be riding the Giant Lyncis now so we can save my twin. *Kuya* Reinhardt, you ride first."

"Okay," Reinhardt nodded and he rode on the back of the Giant Lyncis first. "Let's go, we're in a hurry! Stay close to me!"

Everyone followed and they hurriedly rode the Lynx. "The Lyncis already knows where we're going so hold on tight," said Reinhardt. "Let's

THE EXPLORERS

go!"

For a moment, everyone looked at their bodies sleeping below in circle. "So this is called soul travel…" said Marion with a smile. "It looks fun, but it also seems scary…"

"See ya all later, sexy bodies," said Akira in a joke.

"Do our bodies already protected by the barrier?" asked Shingue to Akira.

"Yeah, but I'm still sure that our bodies are safe there… even without the barrier," answered Akira.

"Great! Or else when we return, only our bones will be left!"

The Giant Lyncis opened its mouth very wide. A black orb came out of its mouth. The orb became a wormhole, which was the portal towards the dark dimension.

"It looks like we will enter that hole," said Reinhardt.

The Lyncis quickly entered the wormhole with everyone on his back. When they entered the doorway, the portal slowly disappeared.

They were now travelling in a secret passage as everyone looked around to observe the creepy and dark surroundings.

"It's so dark here!" Marion suddenly shouted. "I can't see anything!"

Clio got irritated instantly. "Stop complaining, you insect! Why did you even come along with us?!!"

"I was just thinking if we were going the right way. The huge monster might be going in a wrong way and then we'll end up in a different world."

"That won't happen," answered Maximus in his serious voice. "He knows what he's doing, kid…"

"I'm not a kid anymore, PRINCE CHARMING!"

"I knew it!" said Clio angrily. "Now you're talking back! Why did you even comeeeee?!!"

"Don't be too noisy guys," said Reinhardt. "I'm not familiar with the Lyncis yet and he might get irritated by your noise. So please, remain silent…"

"Come on Reinhardt, why did you let this little rat to come along with us?"

Reinhardt quickly answered before Marion would answer. "Because that is what I want. I really want Marion to come along with us," then he secretly winked at Marion.

"You're irritating, Reinhardt. You're so irritatinngggg!!!"

Reinhardt laughed. "Alright, Clio. Would you like us to leave you here?"

"Noooo!!!"

Kenji and Neschar were still in a middle of the fight. The entire room was completely destroyed. The two were surrounded by Explands who were watching their fight.

"Sir Neschar," called an Expland. "Need a help?"

"Tsk," Neschar's clothes was already torn by Kenji's attack magics. He turned to his colleagues and answered. "My strength is better than his. It would be better if you all just leave us here."

"Hehehe..." the Explands laughed towards Kenji, who was just standing in front of Neschar. "He's funny. And later at dawn he'll die again. How pathetic!"

Neschar also joined the laughter. "HAHAHAHA!"

As for Kenji, he still remained silent and serious.

"I thought of a great idea, Neschar!" said an Expland. "Let's toy around with that kid and gang up on him!"

"Hmmm..." Neschar touched his chin. "Anyway, I'm getting a little tired now. Okay, I am leaving it up to you. Our lord might need me now. Play with him as much as you want before the time of his next death comes, HAHAHAHA!"

Everyone laughed. Kenji still remained silent as he looked at the Explands.

"I'll leave you here," said Neschar and he quickly pointed at Kenji. "Now, taste the Expland's wrath and die later!" and then he left the ruined room.

Now, Kenji was surrounded by fifteen Explands. He was still mum as he was panting heavily.

"Right, keep on panting kid. We'll make sure that your continuing breaths won't ever stop!" said an Expland and they all charged towards Kenji. Kenji flung away to the wall and strongly hit his back. The wall cracked because of the impact.

Kenji was hurt as he fell on his knees. He held his back, but he was followed by another Expland and kicked his waist!

"AAAHHHH!!!"

"Does it feel good, Maximillian?" said the Expland and he repeatedly kicked Kenji's waist, but Kenji took an advantage to grab his leg at his tenth kick. The young man caught his foot and he pushed it upward so he swung away. Afterwards, Kenji quickly stood up with difficulty, though it was obvious that his one leg was already injured.

"You're strong, huh?!" shouted another Expland. "You want more?" then they all laughed again.

Though Kenji was injured, he still managed to brag towards them. "I can still crush all of you at the same time!"

"You're arrogant, huh?!!" said another Expland. "We will make you taste the true pain from Expland!"

The Explands posed themselves for the attack. Then, the fight continued.

Meanwhile, the creature named Maximo remained in the human world and he did not go with Expland to their secret dimension. He was on top of a mountain and looked for an enemy. But, he was more wanting to see the Element Wielders and take their elements all by himself. "So much blood... So much pain... So much meat..." he said first as he hissed out loud. "I'm hungry!!!"

It was now raining hard at the UE base. Percy and Tadteo were in Kenji's room and were both gazing at the window. They thought about their master.

"I missh our mashter already..." Percy said sadly. "I wonder what they're doing right now? I hope they'll come home shooner, Tadteo... They've not been with ush for a long time..."

Tadteo also looked sad. "Me too, Percy..."

"I alwaysh pray for thish misshion to be accomplished shooner, Tadteo. I missh their noise sho much."

"Don't worry Percy, they will come back soon."

"I wonder when our mashter and the othersh will return?"

"Let's just pray that it would be soon, Percy..."

"I hope tomorrow... Maybe?" said Percy as he was about to cry when Tadteo noticed him.

"Why, Percy? What's the matter?"

"N-Nothing really, Tadteo," answered Percy and he licked his foot to wipe his right eye where the first tear fell.

"Hehehe... Isn't it because our master hasn't fed you for a long time, is it? Hahaha!"

And then, they turned back their gaze outside the window to wait for their master's return with the boys.

60 THE RESCUE PART 1

It was late at night and the Wielders were still in the middle of their journey towards the Expland's dimension. The Lyncis was calm and the boys were silent. "Are we getting close to the Expland's dimension?" Clio asked impatiently. "I'm looking forward to fighting with them."

Silence. Moments later, Claude answered. "So am I! I am getting impatient. I want to save Kenji now."

"Do you all think that the Explands know we're going to them?" asked Genji.

"I don't think so," Jon answered with his lips puckered. "They're no just ordinary humans."

Silence. But after a moment, the Lyncis suddenly spoke in a language that the boys could understand. "Wielders, we're getting close to the Expland's dimension. Prepare yourselves because I can feel their presence now!"

"Okay, but I don't feel any presence from the Explands," said Shingue while looking around.

"The Lyncis is able to feel any presence of a person from the farthest distance," answered Reinhardt. "According to what I read in our Element Book, the Lyncis has strong senses. Maybe we're getting close to them."

"Hold on tight, warriors of King Jethro," said the Lyncis. "We will all make a turn, or you all might fall."

Meanwhile, at the Expland.

A group of Explands was now wounded (by Kenji's magics) and lay sprawled on the ground. Kenji was breathing heavily as he also sprawled away from them. The other Explands were on their knees, and some of them forced themselves to stand.

The wounded young man could not stand anymore because of the injuries inflicted by the Explands. He was still panting heavily without any movements. Silence.

"Are we still going to play with that pitiful Holy Wielder?" asked an arrogant Expland. "He can't stand on his feet anymore. He's been wasting our time with this boring fight!"

The group observed Kenji, and the arrogant Expland limped heavily towards him. But, he stopped halfway and quickly looked above. "There's a presence coming from the outside!"

His colleagues also looked above. He continued. "I'm starting to feel a lot of strong presences nearing our dimension. They seem like… Maximillian's comrades!"

Meanwhile, at Neschar and the Hydra.

"The Wielders!" Neschar said angrily. "I can feel their strong presence approaching our dimension now!"

"DO YOU MEAN, JETHRO'S WIELDERS? THE EXPLORERS?!"

"Yes, my lord!"

"BUT HOW DID THEY MANAGE TO GET INSIDE THE PORTAL TOWARDS OUR DIMENSION OF DARKNESS? NO ONE ELSE KNOWS THE WAY HERE EXCEPT THE DARK MAGES, ISN'T THAT RIGHT?"

"Yes, but they have a Darkness Wielder. They'll take Maximillian from us… I'm sure of it!" said Neschar and he drew out his sword.

"HURRY UP! STOP THEM FROM ENTERING HERE!"

Neschar did not answer back and he just left the room hurriedly.

"KILL THOSE IDIOTS!!!"

Neschar hurriedly returned to his comrades in the ruined room and called out loud. "Everyone, hide Maximillian and stop the Explorers from entering here. Hurry up!"

The wounded Explands quickly carried Kenji and took him elsewhere to hide, while the others joined with Neschar. The other Explands went into the Sacred Room to protect the god statue inside. Now that the Explands were scattered:

THE EXPLORERS

"Boss," called the spiked-hair Expland guy to Neschar. "We outnumber the arriving enemies. I think they're just thirteen."

"Hehehe..." Neschar chuckled. "Those brats are gonna die sooner!"

Meanwhile...

"I can feel their presence now!" said Jon. "They're many!"

"It doesn't matter, what more important is that we're ready," said Reinhardt. "This is what we're going to do, we will split ourselves into groups to do your tasks. Lucky, Jon, Cyan, and Clio: you'll take care of the enemies. Tyrone, Maximus, and Akira: your team will go straight to the statue. Zoroaster, Shingue, and Marion... join and assist them for a while until I give you an order. Meanwhile, Genji, Claude, Isagani, and I will take care of Kenji, okay?"

Lucky and Akira looked at each other. "The plan that we had for the two groups was not followed. That's sucks..." said Lucky.

Isagani raised his hand. He seemed uncomfortable to come along with Reinhardt's team. "Rei, can I go with Maximus' team instead?"

"Whoa..." Reinhardt's eyes widened in surprise. "Hehehe, wasn't it because Tyrone's there with them? You two are really too difficult to get separated!"

"Maybe he has a crush on Tyrone!" Marion teased.

Isagani pinched Marion's ear hardly. "Hell, no!"

"Okay fine," Reinhardt agreed as he smiled. "No one's against your decision. You can always be with Tyrone and I won't separate you two ever again."

"Ayiiieee..." Marion teased once more. "Because they're already dating!"

"NO WAY, YOU IDIOT!!!"

Claude pointed at the distance. "I-I, uh... Guys, I can see the light of life... o-over there!"

The boys turned to where Claude was pointing. "*Kuya* Claude, where is it?" asked Marion.

Silence. Their journey continued. Moments later, the Lyncis spoke. "We're here in their secret territory now. Do you see that glowing circle below us? All of you must jump over there in order to reach the Expland's place."

The boys became serious again as they listened quietly. The Lyncis continued. "Everyone, get yourselves ready... When I say 'jump', then you must jump immediately, is that clear?"

The boys nodded. "Yes!"

They were getting closer as the opening got wider and they could clearly see it from the darkness. The dark Vrandolon slowed down in its flight. "I can't get closer to it anymore as I've reached my limit. When you accomplish your mission, call me at once... and I'll be there," said the Lyncis.

Akira asked. "How will you know that we're calling you?"

"I'll will hear the call. Master Reinhardt knows how to summon me again."

The Lyncis stopped in its flight. He spoke again. "I can only go up to here," he said. "I hope that you will all succeed... Now jump!"

They boys held each other's hands and looked down as they gulped. They counted in unison. "One, two, threeee!!!"

The boys all jumped together still with their hands held with each other. Now they were diving down to the Expland's portal in circular motion. The Lyncis quickly went back inside Reinhardt's body, who was still diving in the air.

"They're here!" shouted an Expland. "They aren't thirteen, but they're fourteen!"

The portal opened wider and the boys successfully got inside their secret territory. As they entered, they quickly performed their first attack.

"Attack!!!"

The boys had no any weapons in hand but they still managed to fight the Explands with courage.

"BOYS!" called Reinhardt out loud. "The groups!"

Everyone formed their assigned groups. In the meantime, Genji, Claude, and Reinhardt sneaked away from the battle in order to find Kenji. With the help of Lucky's team, the group distracted the Explands so they would not notice the three UEs who had already escaped from them!

The three hurriedly ran away from the fight. Still, no one noticed them and they continued in their search for Kenji. They forcefully opened each door of all the rooms they could find, but Kenji was not in each rooms. The three only realized how huge this dimension was!

"It's impossible that Kenji's not in here, Rain," Claude told Reinhardt. "This creepy place is just big and they hid your brother somewhere here."

"You're right, Claude..." answered Reinhardt. "They will never show

THE EXPLORERS

Kenji to us, but I'm sure he's around here somewhere!"

"I don't feel any presence of my twin brother here," Genji said sadly. "This dimension looks like a maze because of its huge size!"

They continued in their search. "The size is nothing, Genji," said Reinhardt. "It's big, but the Explands are few! Still, I'm afraid were outnumbered!"

The other groups of Wielders were still in the middle of their aggressive battle against Expland. The Explands did not mimic anymore since the Explorers already knew their weakness.

Tyrone, Maximus, and Akira also separated from Lucky's team in order to find the Hydra and to check if Kenji was there. The three of them explored the dimension when suddenly, they ran into a group of incoming Explands in the hallway and they attacked.

"Ambush!" shouted Tyrone. "There's six of them!"

They had a two-on-one fight. The fight was aggressive and fierce.

Maximus quickly gestured his hands when a gigantic wave of water suddenly poured all over the hallway towards the six Explands. The huge waves washed away the six Explands causing it to destroy a part of the dimension.

"Let's go!" said Akira. "Just leave those fools. Kenji must be somewhere else!"

The three dashed away. Lucky's group were still fighting the Explands near the entrance. "Look, these evil rats can't copy us anymore because Prince Maximus already revealed their trick's weakness!" said Isagani.

"Tell us where you're all hiding Kenji, now!" Lucky said angrily.

"Then, I must say that your friend is dead now, HAAAYAAAHHHH!!!" said an Expland.

Akira's team continued in their search and so as Reinhardt's group. While wandering around the dimension, the two groups never thought that they would run into each other.

"Hey, dudes!" Genji called playfully. "Where did you come from?"

"Oh, geez... It looks like we just running in circles," answered Akira.

"Maybe there's a hidden passageway in here," said Maximus. "But I think we already traveled the whole area!"

"And, I noticed that Neschar isn't here. I'm positively sure that he's with Kenji!" said Reinhardt.

"Claude," called Akira and he touched the wall. "This area isn't destroyed yet. Can you use your strength in destroying this wall? Maybe Maximus is right. Maybe there's a hidden passageway here."

"Get away from there, Akira…" said Claude and he readied his right fist. "I'll try."

Claude only took a while to get ready. The five boys just watched him. Later, Isagani arrived next and he approached Tyrone. "Oh yeah, I was supposed to be with your group, Tyrone!" he said.

"HIYAAAHHH!!!" Claude punched the wall with full force. The two groups were impressed because the wall was destroyed easily by his single punch.

"The wall has nothing in it," said Akira. "Let's all split up again."

Tyrone patted Claude's shoulder. "But you have to do that again!"

The two groups separated again. After a few minutes, the Wielders had completely destroyed each of the walls. Until without expecting it, the group of Maximus had finally found the Hydra's Sacred Room!

"The Hydra!" shouted Isagani, then there was a strong quake all over the area.

"YOU WILL NEVER EVER GET CLOSE TO ME!!!" shouted the Hydra as his stony eyes lit in red. The laser beams suddenly came out from his eyes.

A laser beam quickly hit Akira's right arm and his sleeve was torn. It smoked by the beam's heat.

"How pitiful," said Isagani. "He has nothing else he could do but to only shoot lasers! Fine, then this is for you!" he cast his elemental-based magic.

The Hydra continued to shoot lasers as Isagani's magic hit his stony body.

"YOU'RE ALL TOO MUCHHH!!!"

"Take this!" shouted Maximus as he released the water and soaked the Hydra's eyes. The snake-god stopped shooting, and his eyes began to smoke.

"UUUGGGHHH!!!"

"Where did Neschar hide Kenji?" asked Akira.

"HEHEHEH…" the Hydra chuckled evilly. "I CANNOT TELL YOU WHERE HE IS NOW!"

"Whatever you say, or else we will destroy you for good!"

"IF THAT'S THE CASE, THEN TRY!"

THE EXPLORERS

The entire room began to wobble when a giant cell fell from above and trapped the boys. Afterwards, the Explands came in from above. Then, they jumped towards the Hydra to guard him.

"A trap!" shouted Akira. "We're trapped!"

The Explands were about to do their attack when the Hydra stopped them. "HOLD YOUR SEA HORSES! I AM ABOUT TO SHOW THEM SOMETHING INTERESTING!!!"

The boys were looking confused when the Hydra laughed. A while later, Neschar suddenly appeared before them!

"NESCHAAARRR!!!"

"You're all so lucky for being our first visitors in this secret dimension," said Neschar and he snapped his fingers. Suddenly, Kenji appeared next to him! He was unconscious.

"KENJIIII!!!"

"You're even so lucky that you were all able to enter here with the help of your Darkness Wielder! But now, I am going to destroy you all!"

"I don't understand..." said Isagani worriedly. "How did Kenji get in here if he's not a soul?"

Neschar looked angered. "Because Maximillian is being possessed by a black magic," then he turned to his back. "So let's finish this nightmare of yours now, Jethro's Wielders," and he snapped his fingers again. A creepy-looking skull suddenly appeared next to him and he spoke again. "This is Dark Skull, one of my dark Vrandolons that likes to feed souls of the dead. How about if I take him to his meal today? I guess he has a great appetite for your souls, hasn't he? Hahaha!"

"Uh-oh..." Tyrone suddenly shook in fear. "This nightmare of mine will be over..."

The Dark Skull went wild after seeing his meal before him. He seemed to be really hungry and he wanted to eat them right away.

"I'll set you free... my Dark Skull," said Neschar as he freed the Vrandolon. The spirit skull slowly moved towards the four with its mouth wide open in order to suck his dinner.

"This can't be, AHHHH!" shouted the four as they were now being absorbed by the Vrandolon.

They forced themselves to get away from the skull when Isagani quickly gestured his hands. Afterwards, a sharp light quickly came out of his whole body.

"AHHH!" shouted the Explands who were blinded by the sharp light. Even the Dark Skull recoiled in fear!

The sharp light came out through the damaged walls that instantly caught Reinhardt and his group's attention. They stopped running as Reinhardt pointed his finger at the distant light. "That's the sign that the good is fighting against evil. I think the good is telling us to go there! Neschar and Kenji might be hiding in there!" he said.

"AHHHH!!!!" the Explands still shouted out loud. Isagani emitted so much light around his body that even the three boys were dazzled by the sharp light. The light covered the entire room as the screams continued.

The walls of the Sacred Room gradually smoked and gave way by the intense light, and that's when Reinhardt and the others found them. The Explands were still blinded by the light, but a little while, Isagani stopped.

The Light Wielder was quickly weakened when his body suddenly collapsed, but Tyrone caught him in his back. Akira and Maximus slowly opened their eyes. As the Explands also opened their eyes, they saw that the Dark Skull was now wiggling violently because of so much fear of the light. The skull emitted smokes as he was slowly burning. The cell gradually melted.

Neschar returned his Vrandolon as he looked intensely at Akira and the boys.

"Let's go, Wielders!" said Akira and they charged towards Neschar. Unfortunately, Neschar was protected by the shield he cast with Kenji and the Hydra. The boys could not hit him with their chain of attacks.

Again, Maximus released a huge wave of water that washed away the Explands, except for Neschar, Kenji, and the Hydra who were inside the shield. The Hydra gave an order.

"NESCHAR! USE YOUR STRONGEST POWER NOW, HURRY UP! PROVE TO ME THAT YOU CAN DESTROY THEM ALL AT ONCE!!!"

Neschar followed the Hydra's order and he was about to use his strongest power. But, Kenji regained consciousness and he quickly strangled Neschar from the back, causing him to fail his attempt!

"It's Kenji!" Isagani shouted out loud while in the middle of the fight.

"LEAVE ME ALONE, MAXIMILLIAN!" shouted Neschar who was choked. He elbowed Kenji with full force but the young man still did not let go.

THE EXPLORERS

The two were still struggling with each other causing the shield to disappear. Neschar strongly elbowed Kenji again and freed himself. And then, they both cast their attack magics at the same time as the magics collided in the air with each other!

The wounded boys were on their knees after absorbing so much attacks from the Explands. They forced themselves to stand, but the Explands seemed that they would attack again.

"Maximus, Akira, and Isagani!" Tyrone shouted. "They're coming. Watch out!"

The Explands began to charge towards them when someone shouted in the distance.

"EARTH!!!"

The ceiling suddenly cracked as the huge rocks fell on the Explands who were running and they crushed. Claude, Genji, and Reinhardt came from above.

"TA-DAAA!" Claude made an intro. "THREE BLIND MICE TO THE RESCUE!"

61 THE RESCUE PART 2

"What on earth!"

"T-Three blind mice to the rescue?" Akira laughed.

"Hey guys, welcome!" shouted Tyrone.

The newcomers all looked at Kenji and Neschar who were still fighting.

"My twin brother!" shouted Genji, then he approached Neschar.

"Not yet, Gen!" restrained Reinhardt.

"AH!" shouted Genji when the Hydra suddenly shot a beam at him when he came close to the two.

The Explands made sure that the UEs would not get close to Kenji so they charged again.

Reinhardt and Claude were next to each other when Reinhardt whispered to Claude:

"Claude, you won't be noticed by the enemies in the middle of this fight, so I'll leave Kenji up to you…"

"Huh? Why not Genji? He's faster than me."

Both of them turned to Neschar when he strongly punched Kenji.

"KENJI!" they shouted. A fresh blood flowed in Kenji's lips and he fell down on the cracked floor.

Claude looked at his right fist intensely which was gloved.

"Claude, let's destroy this whole place together with your unique strength!" said Reinhardt to Claude.

THE EXPLORERS

Akira summoned a Vrandolon that was a fox-type monster. "Vulpecula!"

Claude still looked at his right fist intensely.

Reinhardt shouted. "CLAUDE! This chaos will end if we destroy them and this dimension together! Use your full strength as strong as you can when we get Kenji back."

Claude closed his eyes seriously. "Okay…"

Reinhardt smiled and nodded. "Okay, can you do it right now?"

"No… I need more time to charge first because I am going to pour my whole strength into my right fist."

"CRATERIS!"

"VELA!"

"O-Okay Claude, we'll protect you! Stay behind us and we will cover you. While we're in the middle of the fight, charge your fist immediately as fast as you can!" said Reinhardt.

Claude nodded. "Roger that. I'll give everyone a go signal when I'm ready to blow!"

"Okay, Claude!"

Claude moved away from Reinhardt. Reinhardt joined the fight while Claude was away from everyone. While in the middle of the aggressive fight, Claude started to gesture his hands. And then, a green aura gradually came out of his whole body.

The Hydra saw him when his body was now covered with the green aura. "OH NO! THE EARTHFALL, HE IS GOING TO DESTROY OUR DIMENSION!!!"

The Earth Wielder was serious and concentrating as he collected all his strength into his right fist. "CLAUDE IS NOW CHARGING!" shouted Isagani.

"STOP HIIIMMMM!!!" shouted the Hydra and the Explands charged towards Claude.

The UEs saw the advancing Expland. "Guys, we must protect Claude!" said Reinhardt. "Don't let the enemies get past us! Move!!!"

The boys hurriedly covered Claude, while Kenji and Neschar still fought without noticing they got further away from the Hydra.

Claude was still behind the boys as he concentrated very deeply. "There are so many Explands!" Maximus shouted. "Claude won't be easily defended against their number!"

"My brother!" Genji pointed at his twin as he approached to rescue him. Kenji and Neschar fought in the air (mid-air combat) as Genji summoned a Vrandolon. "Serpentis!"

A giant "serpent monster" appeared and it quickly attacked Neschar. When Neschar was hit, both he and Kenji fell in the air, but Genji caught his twin at the bottom.

"*Kuya* Genji…"

"Genji has my brother now!" shouted Reinhardt. "We need to get out of here fast!"

"But Claude isn't finished yet!" said Tyrone.

Reinhardt quickly turned to Claude and thought. "Claude, what now? Isn't it done yet?"

"REINHARDT, BEHIND YOU!" shouted Maximus and he quickly approached Reinhardt in order to defend him, but he was hit by the black magic from an Expland. He fell.

Reinhardt quickly turned behind, but the another Expland strongly kicked him in the back. He flung away and he fell down.

"Reinhardt!"

The remaining Wielders still covered Claude. The Earth Wielder was still deeply concentrating. "Claude, will that take longer still?" Akira said to himself. He positioned himself ready to defend Claude at all cost while looking at the Explands before him.

"ATTAACCCKKK!!!" shouted the Hydra and the Explands charged again.

The enemies were close to them when Lucky's group had finally arrived and also made an intro. "TA-DAAA! THREE BLIND PIGS TO THE RESCUE!!!"

"Lucky, Clio, Jon!" Akira called happily.

"Sorry we're late…" said Lucky.

Kenji slowly opened his eyes and he noticed that Genji stared at him, but there was an Expland who jumped from above to stab Genji at the back. Kenji turned above. "*KUYA* GENJI, BEHIND YOU!!!"

"What--!" Genji quickly turned around, but he just saw the Expland already lying on the ground. Marion's group arrived next.

"Zoroaster, Marion, and Shingue!" called Maximus.

"PLUS THREE MORE HANDSOME CARABAOS TO THE RESCUE… TA-DAAAAHHH!!!"

Everyone was overjoyed because they were now complete. Maximus and the others covered Claude again, who was still charging. "For the newcomers, we need to protect Claude because he is about to destroy their territory now!" said Reinhardt to the two groups.

The newcomers turned to Claude, who had now a stronger aura that came out of his whole body.

"Our victory is in *kuya* Claude's hands!" Marion shouted with joy.

Shingue helped the twins to stand on their feet. "Kenji and Genji… the Twins of Fate…"

Genji was confused. "Shingue… What did you say?"

Shingue suddenly blushed. "Ah… Ahm… N-Nevermind about it!"

"DON'T LET THAT EARTH WIELDER DESTROY OUR TERRITORY!!!" shouted the Hydra. "WHAT ARE YOU ALL WAITING FOR?! DESTROY THEM ALL, IDIOTS!!!"

The fight continued as Genji joined the battle. Kenji, who was now standing with difficulty, observed the unconscious Neschar who was sprawled in a corner. Afterwards, he turned his gaze towards the Hydra with a very angry look in his face!

"WHAT ARE YOU LOOKING AT, MAXIMILLIAN?!" asked the Hydra as he noticed Kenji's glare at him. "YOU'RE SO PERSISTENT! DIE ALL OF YOU… DIEEE!!!"

"Claude, will that take more time? Come on, man!" shouted the UEs while in the fight.

"STOP DEFENDING YOURSELF ANYMORE! YOU WILL ALL STILL FAIL IN THE END AND THE WORLD OF MEN WILL FALL!!!" shouted the Hydra at Kenji.

"HA-YAAAHHH!!!"

"Ahhhhh!!!"

"Horologium!"

"…AND REMEMBER THIS: WHATEVER YOU DO, YOU'LL STILL BE MINE NO MATTER WHAT HAPPENS… MAXIMILLIAN!!!"

"CLAUDE!!!"

"Um!"

Finally, Claude opened his eyes. The whole ground was now shaking. He shouted out loud so the boys could hear. "GOOO!!!"

The Wielders quickly turned to Claude.

"Reinhardt!" again, Claude shouted. "THE LYNCIS, HURRY UPPP!!!"

The Hydra was shocked. "WHAT THE--!"

Reinhardt quickly summoned the Giant Lyncis. "*LYNCIS, GAWATANIT ATIK* (Lyncis, I call upon your name!)*!!!*"

The dark giant monster came out from Reinhardt's body. The quake became stronger when the ground felt the great power coming from Claude's strength. "Everyone, get close to Reinhardt!" shouted Lucky out loud.

"Ride on the Lyncis, hurry!" called Reinhardt and the boys quickly jumped towards the dark Vrandolon. The quake got even stronger. And then, Claude's eyes lit up in green.

"NOOO!!!" shouted the Hydra.

"Lord Hydra…" called Kenji to the Hydra in his soft voice as he glared at him intensely. "Also remember this… If we're both going to die, King Jethro will still never forgive you. No matter what happens, you will still die as a stone… And he will erase your existence, for good!"

"EAAAAARTHFAAAAAAAAALLL!!!" Claude shouted out loud and he forcefully punched the earth with his right fist full of veins. Because of the strong impact, the whole floor cracked all over and was immediately destroyed. The huge rocks fell from above and crushed the motionless Explands.

"The rocks!" shouted Marion as he pointed at the rocks above them.

Afterwards, Lucky quickly cast his shield magic to protect themselves from the falling rocks. Everyone had already ridden on the Lyncis' back, except for Kenji and Claude.

The Expland's dimension continued to its destruction. The cracks kept on tearing all over the place. "YOU WILL ALL PAY FOR THISSS!!!" shouted the Hydra. "BY THE NEXT TIME WE SEE EACH OTHER AGAIN, YOU'LL BE MINE! MY ONLY CURE, MAXIMILLIAN!!!"

"That won't ever happen…" answered Kenji as an insult. "The next time we see each other again, we will offer both you and Neschar's dead bodies to the darkness so you'll be trapped to your second deaths forever!!!"

"SHUT UP, YOU INSOLENT FOOL!!!" shouted the Hydra as he started to shoot lasers, but he was unaware that Claude was already behind him. The Earth Wielder quickly punched the lord statue's back with all his might so he was destroyed, crumbled, and crushed into pieces!

"Claude!" Kenji called happily.

Claude winked at him. "Let's go, Kenji!" and then they came close to the Lyncis while the whole place was still shaking. "This whole place is about to destroy! We need to get out of here now!" he continued.

Both of them rode on the Lyncis, when the boys greeted Kenji with joy. "Hey, Kenji! How are you now? We missed ya so much!"

The whole area continued to crumble and the Lyncis immediately flew away. The portal, which was the exit from the Expland's dimension suddenly appeared. They hurriedly entered the portal as they returned to the dark secret passage again. Slowly, the portal closed as they passed thru it.

They were now in the wormhole of the dark world when Lucky removed the shield that protected them. "The white magic is consuming much of my energy... So I have to put it away... I can't take any chances..." he said.

Suddenly, there was a violent quake as everyone heard a loud rumble. "W-What's that?" asked Tyrone as he looked around. "We're already outside the Expland's place, aren't we? I see nothing, but I suddenly heard a rumble."

"I'm afraid that this dimension has been affected by the strong impact of my blow earlier..." said Claude worriedly. "I think this place will be destroyed next!!!"

"O-Oh no!" shouted Lucky. "We need to get away from here before it's completely destroyed!"

"Everyone, hold on tight!" said the Lyncis and it flew very fast.

"WHOOOAAAA!!!" shouted everyone.

Clio quickly pointed at the distance behind them. They noticed a part of the wormhole that began to crack and the crack quickly crawled towards them. It crumbled strong.

"It's coming, HURRYYY!!!"

The Lyncis flew as fast as it could, so they could escape the wormhole before it destroyed. Afterwards, the other side of the dark dimension that was also affected began to crumble as well, and then it exploded with great force. The explosion was so strong that its strong impact traveled so quickly and pushed the flying Lyncis with the boys. Everyone flung away and got separated from each other.

"AHHH!!!"

Everyone was now falling down along with debris from the strong explosion. The boys tried to dodge every rocks, boulders, and debris that were crossing their path as they fell into nothing. Due to zero visibility by the total darkness, some of the debris hit the boys.

"Goddamit! Damn!!!" shouted Zoroaster while they were still destroying the debris with their magics as they fell downward.

The Giant Lyncis was the first one who fell to the bottom and got badly injured. Unfortunately, a huge rock fell on his head so he lost consciousness. The boys were the next ones to fall to the bottom. But before they reached the bottom, Maximus released great volumes of water and it quickly splashed to the bottom. Then, the boys fell into the water and they sank to the bottom so they would not be hit by the falling big rocks.

A few minutes had passed when the explosion ended. Everyone swam back to the surface of the water with Marion as they gasped. Silence.

"It's over…" Tyrone said with a low voice. "Our nightmare is finally over…"

Everyone looked above. It was still pitch dark.

"Only the top part of this dimension was destroyed because it's close to the Expland's territory," said Claude to the boys. "So, how is everyone? Are you all okay?"

The boys were open-mouthed especially Lucky. Claude laughed. "Hehehe. It looks like Lucky and the others were traumatized!"

"Where are we now?" asked Jon.

"We're still here in the dimension of darkness," answered Reinhardt.

"Are we still not in our bodies, huh?"

"We haven't returned yet…"

"I want to go home now!"

"Don't worry, Jon. We are going home."

The boys were still in shock when Maximus spoke to them. "The important is that Kenji is with us now," and he peered around. "Now, where is our Lyncis?"

The boys already had forgotten about the Giant Lyncis when Reinhardt also looked around. "Oh right! Where is the Lyncis?!"

"Over there!" Marion pointed when he saw the dark Vrandolon away from them. "He's floating on the water!"

The boys saw the Lyncis in the distance with wounds all over its body. They all swam together towards the Vrandolon, and Reinhardt was the first one to approach him. He carefully observed the monster.

"The Lyncis has deep wounds…" said Reinhardt while touching the deep wounds in the head and different parts of the Lyncis' body. "We need a healer here. Who among you here is the healer?"

"I'll try," Kenji volunteered as he approached the Lyncis and used his healing power. He tried, but to no avail.

"What's wrong?" asked Isagani. "Is it because he's a Holy Wielder and he's going to heal a dark monster? Or because Kenji isn't a healer?"

Everyone just observed Kenji to what he was doing. Kenji tried again, but still, no effect. He tried again for one last time, but it was really useless. Until, he leaned on Genji's side who still floating in the water.

"G-Guys…" Kenji called harshly. "Later before sunrise I will lose my life again… I'm getting weaker again…"

"We already know that, Kenji. King Jethro told us," answered Clio. "You see, we talked to him in our dream."

Kenji closed his eyes. "Is that so? Can you all promise me that when I come back to life again, then we are back in the human world? Back in our world…"

Reinhardt and Zoroaster approached the twins. "We promise you… And we also promise you that we will remove the black curse in your body…" and they caressed Kenji's hair.

Silence. Moments later, Lucky spoke. "Maybe Kenji isn't a healer. We need to get out of here, now."

"Or maybe Kenji couldn't use his Holy Cure anymore since he's weakening," added Akira.

"Why don't you try, Akira?" said Jon. "Your power is almost the same to Kenji's though you're a Crusader."

"Okay, I'll try," Akira nodded and he swam close to the Lyncis. "I am still mastering my element, and I still haven't mastered the use of my known cure. But, I'll still try."

Akira gently touched the Lyncis' body and he concentrated. His palm glowed white. "*Kuya* Akira also has healing powers!" Marion said happily. "Finally, we'll be able to go back home now!"

Akira continued to heal the Lyncis while both his palms lit up. Slowly, his power was able to heal the Lyncis' wounds.

"Keep it up, Akira! That's right!" the boys cheered for Akira.

The Giant Lyncis was now fully-healed and it gained consciousness. Everyone shouted and jumped with joy as they splashed the water on to each other's faces.

"So you're the healer, Akira!" said Lucky with joy.

"Uh… Yeah… R-Right, hehehe!" said Akira as he scratched his head.

The boys quickly approached him (except for Maximus) in playful way and lifted their hands. "Heal us as well, please!"

"H-Hey, you!" Akira shook his head. "You're all in your dead state already. You all no longer need my cure!" and then they all laughed.

"It's time to go home now," Genji told his twin. Kenji was still leaning on him. "When we get back to our base, we will all take a long, long rest."

"I know…" Kenji said as he smiled. "Then, the curse will disappear in my body for good…"

"We'll just look for the Vanguard lady named Vedna and ask her for the cure…"

"Just promise me that when I wake up tomorrow, we have already returned to our world again…"

"We can go home now. No need to go to sleep, hehehe!"

Reinhardt approached the Giant Lyncis to give an order but he noticed that the monster was getting wild. "Giant Lyncis, take us back to our world now…" he ordered.

The Lyncis still went wild. The boys also noticed the Vrandolon and they stopped playing around with each other.

"What is his problem, Rain?" asked Cyan.

The Lyncis was still restless when Reinhardt tried to stop him. "Lyncis, what's the problem?" he also asked.

"Uh-oh…" suddenly, the boys became worried. "It looks like we won't be going home today…"

"Reinhardt…" Shingue called worriedly. "Ask him what his problem, please…"

"Come on, Lyncis… What's the matter?!" asked Reinhardt who was now looking concerned. "Damn it! Just as I expect… he is getting moody now!"

"This doesn't look good…" said the twins. The boys were still looking at the restless Lyncis.

"Tsk! Lyncis, come on?!" Reinhardt was losing his patience. "If we ever did something wrong to you then we're sorry. But for the meantime, I order you to take us back to our world and to our own bodies right now!"

"Yup, and go wild again some other time!" said Tyrone as an insult.

"Don't be the pain in my ass!"

The Lyncis heard Tyrone's negative remark towards him causing him to become more restless.

"Tyrone!!!" shouted Claude who was also concerned. "You're even insulting him!"

"LYNCIIIISSSS!!!" Reinhardt shouted irritably.

The Lyncis did not listen and he quickly returned inside Reinhardt's body. Silence.

"Hurry Reinhardt, call him again," Clio said worriedly.

"*Lyncis… Gawatanit atik… Gawatanit atik,*" called Reinhardt, but the Lyncis did not listen to his call. He was dumbfounded.

"W-What's wrong, Reinhardt?" asked Lucky. "What happened? Call him again."

Reinhardt tried again, but the Lyncis did not respond.

"Reinhardt?"

"………………………"

"D-Don't tell us…"

Reinhardt spoke worriedly. "O-Oh no… The Lyncis doesn't want to obey me anymore!!!"

62 UH-OHHH…

Silence.

The boys were stumped. All of them had their mouths opened, but were all speechless. Clio was unaware that he already drooled.

Everyone was looking at Reinhardt with concern. They were all waiting for his next move, but even Reinhardt was dumbfounded. They could not think of anything else to do next.

What happened? Reinhardt thought to himself. *Why did the Lyncis disobey me? What did I do wrong?*

Maximus could not take the lengthy silence anymore. He swam towards Reinhardt and asked. "How are you sure that the dark Vrandolon doesn't want to obey you anymore, huh? You're his Wielder, aren't you?"

Reinhardt did not answer. Up to that moment, he was still deep in thought.

"So it's hard to be a Dark Wielder," Lucky said sadly.

Everyone still looked at Reinhardt. Moments later, Marion also moved over Reinhardt and caught his attention. "*Kuya* Reinhardt, hurry… Summon the monster so we can all go home now."

Reinhardt looked at Marion, and he only answered with a smile. He stroked the kid's hair gently.

"Please… *kuya* Reinhardt?"

Reinhardt still smiled at him. "Okay, I'll do it again," and afterwards, Marion was able to smile again.

THE EXPLORERS

The boys distanced from Reinhardt. Reinhardt closed his eyes again and he concentrated. He once again summoned for the Lyncis but there was still no response.

"Please, *kuya* Reinhardt..." Zoroaster prayed.

Reinhardt repeatedly called the Lyncis by force but it did not want to obey his call. He was now feeling disappointed.

Maximus decided to remove the water all over the place. As the water subsided, the boys sat on one side. Marion continued to tap Reinhardt's shoulder.

"Come on, *kuya* Reinhardt... Force him to obey you again..." he said.

Clio quickly pulled Marion in annoyance. "Get away from there. Can't you see you keep on pestering him?!"

Silence. Everyone still looked at Reinhardt.

"Reinhardt, how is it? Still nothing?" asked Jon.

Reinhardt shook his head. Then, he just sat down in disappointment.

"Man..." Isagani sat too. "I'm so much worried now..."

While as for Marion. Even at his tendered age, he feared that they would not be able to return to the world of the living anymore. Moments later, he could no longer stop his fear when he suddenly cried out loud.

"WAAAAAHHHH! WAAAAHAHAHAHA!!!"

Everyone turned to Marion when they heard his cry. Clio hugged his brother to give comfort.

"Reinhardt, what about now? Won't we be able to return to our bodies again? We've been trapped here for long!" Tyrone said annoyingly. "What kind of Vrandolon is that thing?!"

"When you read the Element Book, have you read another way if ever the Lyncis won't obey you anymore, huh?" asked Akira. "Maybe there's another way."

"If there is, then I already have done it, right?" Reinhardt answered with a frown.

Marion was still in the middle of his crying. "WAAHH!!!"

"Call it again, Rei," said Tyrone.

"It still won't obey."

"Try it again."

"Later..."

After a moment, Tyrone sat down irritably. "Dammit, I'm getting impatient! DO IT AGAIN, RAIN!!!"

"I'll do it again later…"

Tyrone was forced to stand up again and walked away from his companions. Marion still cried.

It was 1:55am when Reinhardt tried to call the Lyncis again, but still, no response. Marion was not crying anymore, but he still sobbed. While as for Tyrone, he was just walking back and forth as he became more and more impatient.

"It's almost 2am…" Kenji said with a low voice. "My life will only last an hour…"

"Don't worry Kenji," said Claude. "We will return to our world soon. And, we will do our best to find its cure."

Kenji just smiled as an answer.

The Wielders talked to each other while they were resting. Tyrone still walked back and forth away from them.

Reinhardt tried to summon the Lyncis again, but still, no response. This time, he gone mad. "Tsk… Come on!"

Tyrone had completely lost his patience so he quickly approached Reinhardt angrily.

"What kind of Wielder are you?!" he shouted at Reinhardt and asked. "You're his master, why on earth can't you control your own element?!!"

Reinhardt suddenly felt anger towards Tyrone, but he already knew Tyrone's real personality! The cranky, bad-tempered guy!

Reinhardt did not answer to Tyrone's question, so Shingue spoke instead. "Tyrone… Relax, man…"

"SHUT UP!"

Shingue was shocked. Everyone turned to Tyrone.

"Maybe Reinhardt isn't deserving enough to be an Element Wielder, right? What now?! Will we all just stay here for life?!!"

Reinhardt took a deep breath. "Tyrone… please…"

"What?!"

"I'm sorry… I'm not that fully skilled in handling my element yet."

"Oh, come on! We've been here for long and up to now you're still not doing anything. Are you an asshole?"

Reinhardt was annoyed. "I did it just now, didn't I? And I kept on trying in everything I could!"

"Do it again and again until your stupid Vrandolon gets pissed off and listens to you!"

"Tyrone, I already did it so many times, didn't I?"

"If you're really that smart, then you should know a lot of other ways!"

Isagani stopped Tyrone. "Tyrone, that's enough…"

"Shut up, Isagani! All of you, shut your mouths! It's just me and Reinhardt are talking here!"

"Okay, please calm down now… I'll do it again," said Reinhardt and he did it, but nothing happened.

"OH, COME ON!" Tyrone shouted and stomped very angrily. "I really, really hate to say this to you Rain, but the whole truth is… You're not deserving to be the Dark Wielder!"

Reinhardt's brothers were hurt by Tyrone's remark, but Reinhardt himself acted that he heard nothing. That kind of remark did not matter to him. He knew Tyrone's usual attitude since then!

Kenji spoke to Tyrone to defend his brother. "Tyrone, I thought you've changed now. Please… think of every words first before you say it, is that okay?"

"And what will I think about, huh?! I knew I was right, so I told your brother that he's not deserving to be the Dark Wielder, understand?"

"Tyrone, use your head!" but Kenji was calm. "Tyrone… I am going to ask you something. But before that, we all know that *kuya* Reinhardt's role as a Dark Wielder isn't that easy. All of us did not want this to happen, and so as *kuya* Reinhardt. My brother knows that his job is tough, but despite of any difficulties he is facing, still he never gives up… We all know that there's a way, but right now we still can't figure out yet. Tyrone, each of us possesses different kinds of elements. Our roles as the chosen Element Wielders aren't the same and so as our abilities, but our powers have their equal strength!"

Tyrone laughed and answered rudely. "I am not convinced. He is not really deserving!"

"Tyrone, King Jethro would never choose *kuya* Reinhardt to be the Wielder of Darkness if he's not deserving--"

"Yeah, yeah… Whatever," Tyrone interrupted Kenji rudely. "You talk too much (Claude was also losing his patience towards him). So, what were you going to ask me??!"

Kenji hesitated by Tyrone's rudeness. "W-Well… thank you for listening and for your attention, Mr. Federlein. You still treat me the same. Now that I'm the leader of UE, you are still rude to me. I won't forget the day when you said that you could greatly outweigh my element. That was also the day when you argued with Elijah when he was still alive! And that was the very first time I'd seen your true color!"

"I SAID, WHAT'S YOUR QUESTION NOW?! YOU TALK TOO MUCH!"

Claude quickly rushed over as he wanted to attack Tyrone, but Akira restrained him. "Don't do it Claude, everything will be alright…" he said.

"Thank you for your interruption…"

"GEEZ, I'M LOSING MUCH OF MY PATIENCE ALREADY! WHAT THE HELL IS YOUR QUESTION NOW?!!"

Kenji closed his eyes. He remained calm towards Tyrone. "Fine…. First, do you desire to possess the Darkness Element?"

Tyrone quickly answered. "Of course! I would even want to possess all of your elements!"

"Second, do you deserve this to happen if you were the Dark Wielder?"

"No! If I was the Dark Wielder, all of us would already have gotten home since earlier without failure!"

"Oh, really? So, you really think that you are more deserving to be the Dark Wielder?"

Tyrone suddenly became silent, but after a while he answered again. "YES!"

"If that's the case, if you think that you're more deserving and *kuya* Reinhardt isn't… Then why weren't you chosen by King Jethro to become the Dark Wielder?"

Tyrone was stopped.

"What now? Are you tongue-tied, Tyrone?"

Everyone quietly listened to Kenji. Tyrone answered.

"He did not choose me because… He didn't see me!"

Kenji suddenly became frank. The nerve!

"You're COMPLETELY wrong about that, Tyrone. Do you know why? Because you're too much of a pride! First of all, if you were the Dark Wielder, maybe at this time you're still not make it to reach the dark dimension. And what worst maybe, is that we would all be stuck in this world because of your stubbornness. Am I right?"

"Hell, no!"

"Yes, I am ABSOLUTELY right, Tyrone! That's what would have

happened for sure. You know why? Because you are so aggressive! You're too arrogant! Your pride is so high that we can't even reach it! You are lacking patience, you're too grumpy! If you became the Dark Wielder Tyrone, maybe from the very beginning of this mission you're already arguing with the Lyncis! And since the Lyncis is also moody as you are… a hundred percent, all of you wouldn't have any hope in getting to this dimension in order to save me! When King Jethro chose each and everyone of us as his Element Wielders, that was not a mistake. He entrusted us his powers depending upon our capacities and attitudes. Failure is not an option in this quest because lasting peace and eternity are what at stake in this battle. Personal satisfaction has no room in this mission. Remember, this is for King Jethro and to the survival of all human species who may continue to rebuild our own world. That is the only world we got."

"Why are you judging me as a bad person now, huh?!"

"Tyrone, I have seen you like that for so many times. You already acted like that towards me from the start. And now that I'm the leader, you are still treating me the same. Not only to me, but also to all of them (the UEs) and Elijah."

"I'm scared… WAHAHAHAAAAA!!!" Marion cried again.

Kenji glanced at Marion and turned back his gaze towards Tyrone. "If that is really your true color, Tyrone… I'm telling you this now… You won't be able to handle the Lyncis."

"WHAT?!!"

Kenji shook his head. "I'm sorry…"

"No way! And what did that dark element see in Reinhardt?"

"Your attitude is far more different than *kuya* Reinhardt's, Tyrone… Everyone knows that, even me."

Zoroaster agreed. "I agree with Kenji, Tyrone. Maybe in the beginning, we might already have failed our mission if you are our Dark Wielder with that kind of attitude."

And Maximus added. "For a short period of time that I stayed with your company, now I just learn who you really are."

"It's not that we're not on your side, Tyrone. We're just saying that Kenji was true," said Clio. "Maybe that's the reason why King Jethro chose Reinhardt instead of you or me because he saw something with Reinhardt. You see, being a Dark Wielder has much of a tough job, but Reinhardt can still handle the job because of his positive attitude… So please, can you stop this argument now? You're just wasting your time, your voice, and your remaining patience!"

Tyrone turned to his back and walked away from them very angrily. "You're all on your own! If Reinhardt still won't make a move then we will stay here for life!" then he walked farther and farther away. "Stupid Lyncis! Go to hell!!!"

"See?" said Reinhardt as he turned to Tyrone in the distance. "Now you are arguing with the Lyncis though you're not the Dark Wielder."

"GET LOST, REINHARDT!"

Silence. Until, 2:45 in the early morning came. "Only fifteen minutes have left," Kenji said in his low voice. "We're all still here… *Kuya* Reinhardt, try to summon Lyncis again!"

"Alright Kenji," Reinhardt nodded and he stood back to his feet again. He concentrated. Tyrone was still away from them. "I hope everything will be alright, my boys…" he said.

But there was still no response.

Reinhardt sat down again looking confused. "I really do not understand what is going on… I am so confused."

Everyone was mum and deep in thought. As deep as Marion's eyes from crying.

"I think I need help from King Jethro now," said Reinhardt.

"But how will we call King Jethro?" asked Jon.

Reinhardt lowered his head sadly. He did not answer.

Kenji forced himself to stand. "I will call him!"

The boys were surprised. "Huh?"

The Holy Wielder concentrated and his whole body began to light up in white. "I suddenly remembered that all of you here are in the dead state except me. So, leave this up to me!"

Kenji gently lifted his hands when the light around his body lit up all over the place. Moments later, the boys felt the cold air that gently touched through their ghostly face. Afterwards, the light gradually disappeared. King Jethro appeared with the Holy White Phoenix before them. The Holy White Phoenix was Kenji's Vrandolon.

Everyone slowly knelt down before the god as a sign of respect. Tyrone quickly went next to them and also knelt.

"Good evening to you all," greeted King Jethro. "I'm glad that you were all able to rescue your friend. And now…"

Reinhardt quickly spoke to the god hesitantly. "I-I wasn't able to make the Giant Lyncis obey me, my lord… I knew I never made a mistake nor made him upset towards me. B-But--"

King Jethro closed his eyes. "I understand your concern my son, but the Lynx will never disobey you for life. He is very obedient and respectful towards his master. Reinhardt, my Darkness element chose you because of your good deeds. Having this kind of element is tough because of its role, but the element sees that you can handle it and you are perfect to become its beholder (Tyrone was unconvinced). Summon the Lyncis one more time."

"I have done that in countless times, but he still did not pay me attention. We have been here for a long time."

Claude whispered to Lucky, who was just next to him. He was touching his stomach. "Lucky, why am I not hungry?"

"Because, we're just souls remember?" Lucky answered.

"Oh, right… Gosh, I miss my favorite *kare-kare* (Philippine beef stew with peanuts)…"

"Is there another way for us to return home other than the Lyncis, my dear lord?" asked Isagani.

"Alright," said the king god as he smiled. "I will help you all."

The boys' faces were now showing gladness as they all smiled wide with joy.

"But, my dear lord," said Reinhardt. "Even if we call him, he still won't listen to our call. Believe me."

"Don't worry anymore. You don't need to call the Lynx anymore. I can talk to him for you."

The boys were curious. King Jethro smiled. "I know that you cannot understand, but no worries…"

The boys happily agreed when King Jethro ask Reinhardt to come before him. "Come closer to me, Reinhardt."

Reinhardt went closer to the god and faced him. King Jethro gently raised his right palm and placed it on Reinhardt's chest. He closed his eyes and whispered a language that everyone could not understand.

Everyone just watched in silence. A while later, the Lyncis suddenly came out of Reinhardt's chest. Everyone jumped in joy, as the other boys hugged with each other.

The Dark Lyncis looked fine when he approached King Jethro as the god stroked his fur. As they faced each other, the god whispered to him with the language that the boys still could not understand.

Afterwards, the Lyncis turned to the boys. "You can all ride him now," King Jethro said with a smile. "I was able to tame him. Next time, be careful."

Everyone knelt in front of him again with joy. "Thank you so much for your great help, my dear lord!"

King Jethro smiled. "You're always welcome, my sons. I won't be long… Until next time… Goodbye," and then, he slowly disappeared. The White Phoenix went back to Kenji's body, as the young man lost his consciousness.

Cyan looked at his ghostly watch. "So that's why… It's exactly three in the morning now…"

Genji carried his twin when Akira asked the boys to leave now. "Hurry, let's all ride," and afterwards, they all rode on the Lyncis' back. The Giant Lyncis started to fly upwards, which was led by Reinhardt.

They were now traveling back to their world. Everyone was silent, but they were overjoyed. Even Marion smiled, though his eyes were still swollen.

"I don't want this to happen ever again…" said Zoroaster while they traveled. "Be thankful if you weren't the Darkness Wielder…"

"But I never feel any regrets. And I won't ever give up…" said Reinhardt.

Finally, they had safely returned back to their world again. The portal slowly appeared in the cave where they left their bodies. Everyone came out of the dark portal and the Lyncis returned to Reinhardt's body. The boys were overjoyed because they had finally returned.

"Yohoo! We have all returned!" said the boys very happily. "We'll be able to go home and take a long, long rest!"

Claude approached Reinhardt, who was now peering around right after they arrived the cave. "Hey, what's the matter, Rain? Return our souls to our bodies now."

"Uh… Oh…" said Reinhardt as he was biting his finger. "G-Guys, have noticed something fishy here?!"

"Huh?" everyone stopped. "What is it again?"

Reinhardt pointed below the cave. "E-Everyone, look below…"

"WAAAAAAHHHHH!" everyone was so shocked when they noticed

that their bodies were no longer in the cave anymore. They felt as if the sky would fall to their heads due to their intense shock. Marion burst into tears again.

"OUR BODIES… THEY'RE ALL MISSING!!!"

63 BIG PROBLEM

Silence.

Everyone was mum with their faces looked very concerned, while they observed the cave with nothing in it.

Marion was crying out loud when Zoroaster called his brother and asked. "*Kuya* Reinhardt, maybe we got into the wrong cave, you think?"

Reinhardt was confused. "I know that this is the right cave…"

"Then, the bodies should be here!"

Tyrone suddenly became irritated again. After he argued with Reinhardt and Kenji, this time, Akira was next.

"AKIRAAAAA!!!"

"Tyrone… Please not me…"

"We thought that you cast a barrier here, huh?!!"

"I-I did, but I don't know why--"

Everybody turned to Akira with an angry look on their faces. Akira noticed. "W-Why are you all looking at me like that, huh? You're all glaring at me!"

Claude quickly confronted him. "Akira, you are really untrustworthy. We thought that this place was safe here?"

Akira did not know what to say. "Claude, everyone, please listen to me… I'm absolutely sure that it's safe here. Wild animals are rarely found in this place or even none. Me and my colleagues have known this place for long--"

THE EXPLORERS

"Oh, whoh... wait... wait..." Tyrone stopped Akira. "I knew it! You Pioneers made a plan of taking our bodies away from here, huh?!!!"

Akira quickly shook his head. "N-No! That's not it... The Pioneers have nothing to do with this!"

"Admit it!" Clio was also angry.

"Everyone, please listen to me! Do you think that a Deity Wielder would do such a betrayal behind your back?! I can't be a Deity Wielder if I would just fool you all and lie!"

"No--"

"Guys, Akira's right," Reinhardt agreed. "He may be our enemy, but he cannot deceive us. He did nothing wrong."

"But Reinhardt," said Jon. "Even if he's a Deity Wielder, he can still fool us!"

"And he said that he cast a barrier here, but why did our bodies disappear? He fooled us!" Isagani was frightened.

"When you say 'barrier', then our bodies should still be protected whatever happens in here up to now," said Lucky. "What if our bodies were already eaten by wild animals passing here?"

"No way, don't say that!" Marion cried even more.

Even Akira was in confusion. He did not know what to explain to the angry boys. He thought deeply to himself: *What is going on now? Why does everyone think of me as the bad guy now? I really do not understand why our bodies disappeared in here!*

"The animals would not attack our bodies here," said Reinhardt. "It's almost sunrise. Blaming and shouting will not help our problem. The much better thing to do is to look for our bodies instead."

"But we have no idea where those are..." said Genji.

"Do you think we can easily find our missing bodies in this place so huge, Reinhardt?" asked Maximus calmly.

Reinhardt scratched his head in annoyance. "W-Well... I even don't know what else to do now!"

Tyrone repeatedly pointed at Akira very angrily. "This is all your fault! You will pay for this, traitor!!!"

"Fine, let's just look for our corpses instead!" Lucky still joked though he was serious. "So how about this time? Should we split up?"

"No, we cannot split up. We will find them together," said Reinhardt.

They were about to leave the cave when Claude stopped the boys.

"Wait! What about Kenji? He can't come with us!"

Everybody turned their gaze at Kenji, who was lying on the ground and sleeping. "I can't touch him anymore," said Genji as he tried to touch his twin over and over again, but his hands went through the twin's body. "Why is that? A while earlier, he was leaning on me!"

"It's because we have returned to the human world in living state," said Reinhardt. "Later, he'll regain consciousness again and I'm sure that he won't be able to hear us. Because, he's the only one here who is not in dead state among us."

"I'm afraid he won't hear our call if we fail to find our bodies before he become conscious again at six in the evening," Jon said sadly.

"Okay, so what will we do now, huh?" Maximus was becoming impatient. "Kenji has no idea about what's happening to us here anymore. He cannot help us."

"We can't leave *kuya* Kenji here…" said Genji. "I don't want him to disappear too when we get back here."

"And I don't want to trust SOMEONE over there anymore!" Tyrone shouted as he hinted at Akira. "He's a traitor! An untrustworthy Element Wielder!"

Akira was hurt by Tyrone's remark, but he only hid his feelings from everyone. "I will stay here…" he said uncomfortably. "Kenji and I will be left here. I'll watch over him."

"There you go again!" Claude pointed at Akira annoyingly. "We won't believe you anymore! I'll be the one who stays here."

"You know what, I am thinking of something," said Genji worriedly. "When *kuya* Kenji wakes up again later, I'm afraid he might not see us since we're just souls. If there's someone of us who will be staying here, *kuya* Kenji might not notice him too and then he'll suddenly leave and go somewhere else."

Lucky went beside Kenji and sighed. "Haaayy… Problem… Another one big problem…"

"Don't worry, guys," Reinhardt encouraged the boys. "Kenji will surely notice us because I remember when you all turned to souls first, I could see you all."

"But you knew that we were here back then," said Zoroaster.

"Kenji also knows this, alright? Okay, I am going to ask two people to stay here and look over him. Who will be the two?"

THE EXPLORERS

"Me!" said Claude for sure. "You can leave this up to me alone!"

"You also can stay with Akira, Claude," Zoroaster said with a smile. "So there will be at least two bodyguards!"

Akira suddenly changed his mind. "Nah, I'm coming with you all. Reinhardt have more knowledge about this, so when Kenji regains consciousness later, he can explain."

"But I just said that he wouldn't hear me even if I would explain to him! Pfff…" said Reinhardt as he shook his head. "Anyway, fine… Claude and I will guard him here. Now listen to me, everyone. Always stay close together and don't ever split up, is that clear?"

Everyone nodded.

"Another thing: if ever the nighttime comes and all of you still haven't found our bodies, please return here immediately before six in the evening, okay?"

"Okay!"

"I hope you will succeed, take care."

The boys were about to leave when Lucky spoke. "Reinhardt, Claude, take care also. Watch over Kenji!"

"We'll be here…" said Claude as he waved.

"See you all later!" and the boys left, until they disappeared from Claude and Reinhardt's sight.

"Reinhardt, how can you be sure that Akira has nothing to do with this, huh?" so Claude still was not convinced.

"Because he was also involved in this incident, right?"

Claude lowered his head. "I hope that our friends will succeed in searching for our bodies, Rain… I want to be alive again."

The boys were now searching for their bodies in the middle of the thick verdant forest. It was 3:45am when Clio noticed something as he looked around. "Hey, I don't see any signs of wild animals here. Not even foot prints."

"I already told you earlier, didn't I? Animals are rarely found here in this forest," said Akira and sighed. "Man…"

"Or maybe, the Pioneers really took our bodies and they turned it into their dinner by now!" Tyrone joked with an insult.

Akira sighed again. "Geez…" and scratched his head. "Whatever…"

"And we have no idea where our bodies went," Marion said as he sobbed. "It'll be so hard to find them!"

They observed the entire forest around them. "Are there any people living near here?" asked Shingue in wonder. "I'm afraid the people will see us as ghosts when they see us around."

"Let's go, let's walk again!" said Lucky.

The boys continued to wander around the forest. The trees and grass were so thick that suddenly frightened the boys.

"It's scary here... so creepy!" said Marion looking frightened while he was hugging Tyrone.

They suddenly heard a wolf cry howling in a distance when Cyan jumped in surprise.

"Whoa! What's that?" Cyan asked looking scared.

"Oh, come on, Mr. Valedictorian. It's just a wolf!" Jon said with a laugh.

Cyan was shaking in fear. "Eeee!" and he hugged Akira.

"W-Why? What's wrong, man?" Akira asked looking confused.

Again, they continued to walk when the wolf cried again in the distance. "A-WOOOOO!"

"I-I don't want to hear wolf cries!" said Cyan and he moved behind Akira.

"Hey, enough with the pleasantries, Cyan. You're scaring us!" said Akira as he removed both of Cyan's hands that clutched his back.

"Think of it as a toy horn," Isagani encouraged.

"Could we continue this some other time, huh?"

"Come on, Cyan! Let go of me!"

They still walked closer together, but they all stopped when something moved in the grass. "W-What's that?!" asked Genji looking scared.

A grasshopper suddenly came out of the grass and quickly jumped through Isagani's ghostly forehead. Isagani was super shocked before the others and he ran away fast.

"ISAGANI, WHERE ARE YOU GOING??!" said Lucky after seeing Isagani dashing away from them.

"Cyan, get away from my back!" said Akira as he was still struggling to free himself from Cyan's grip.

The boys ran hurriedly to follow Isagani without realizing that they were getting close to where the wolf cry came. When they got into the wolves' nest, they ran into the pack of wolves.

"WHOOOOAAAAAHAHAHAHAHAAAA!!!" shouted everyone,

THE EXPLORERS

especially Cyan!

Their goofy search continued until seven in the morning. The sun was already up. Claude and Reinhardt looked at the sun. "Wow, it's already morning. The boys haven't returned yet," Claude said worriedly and he looked at Kenji. "Where do you think they are now, Reinhardt?"

"They're still searching, Claude…"

"It's getting longer than I expected. Then later, it will be nighttime again…"

The boys were already dead tired in searching for their bodies almost everywhere. Akira was still in deep thought of how their bodies disappeared though they were all protected by his Elemental Barrier.

"I really can't understand how that happened," Akira was still confused as he was walking back and forth while the boys were resting. "Damn it, how?"

"Think well, Akira. And if we're still unable to find the bodies then we're all finished!" Tyrone was still really angry at him.

Akira was silent while thinking very deeply. Later, he spoke. "Everyone, stay here. I'll look for them myself."

"Did you hear Reinhardt's instruction earlier?" Tyrone asked annoyingly.

"I know, but you stay here. I'll return immediately, okay?"

"And where will you go?" asked Marion.

"I know some other places where the Pioneers often go. I'll look for the bodies there."

"And then after that, you will not come back to us!" Tyrone said annoyingly.

"It's up to you if you keep on judging me over and over again, Tyrone!" said Akira irritably. "Whether you'll believe me or not, I'll return here immediately!"

"Okay, Akira. We're keeping your words," said Cyan.

"Alright, see you all guys later! I'll be in stealth mode now," said Akira and he left. He quickly disappeared from the boys' sight.

It was already twelve noon and the boys still had not yet returned. Reinhardt became worried this time as he turned to Claude. "Where do you think they are now, Claude? Hmm, they're taking too long!"

"Heh, good thing that we no longer need to eat even if we wait for long," Claude jokingly said.

The food was not the thing in Reinhardt's thoughts right now. He did not answer to Claude's joke.

Three in the afternoon…

"AKIRAAAAAA!!!" shouted Genji that suddenly surprised the silent boys. "You're fooling us again! You're taking too long!"

"That's what I was saying," said Lucky annoyingly. "Maybe, Akira already has found his body and then he went back to Pioneer with our bodies!"

"Let's kill Akira when we see him!" said Jon though he knew they were still in dead state.

The boys had no idea about Akira's hardship in searching for their missing bodies. He was in the middle of his search when he ran into Maximo somewhere in the forest unexpectedly. The Deity Wielder had seen all of their bodies lying next to this blood-sucking creature!

"I smell the sweet scent of all your blood…" said Maximo in his low voice while looking at the bodies. Akira was mum as he was posing for a fight in front of him. He tried to speak, but Maximo could not hear him. He even noticed that the bodies looked okay and did not show any signs from Maximo's advantage.

Akira was still mum and he knew it was useless if he spoke. So, he used his mental telepathy to ask the creature how he saw and took their bodies though they were protected by the barrier. Maximo answered to his mind. "Thanks to the Pioneers. I acquired the ability from their experiment to remove the barrier from you. Augustus Sawyer, prove to me that these bodies are really that worthy to be the true warriors and protectors of the entire universe. I can feel such powerful strengths these bodies possess as if they can destroy the pure evilness in this world…"

Akira still remained silent. He just listened to the creature's words while watching out for the bodies that lay on the grass. "I've heard about the Twins of Fate from Explands when they still existed in this world, Augustus. I guess they were right, the world of men will fall into apocalypse if the Twins of Fate will meet in the horizon!"

Akira was shocked when the creature just flew away while he laughed out loud evilly. He left Akira alone with the bodies.

"He's gone," Akira said happily. "Good thing that he didn't do anything bad with our bodies…" then he stroked his chin as he thought. "Hmmm… but what did he mean by the 'Twins of Fate' and the

THE EXPLORERS

apocalypse? Tsk, well anyway... I have our corpses now, yeehaaaw!!!"

Akira gladly summoned his Vrandolon which was the White Unicorn. He commanded the Vrandolon to immediately call the boys who still waited for him for a very long time. The White Unicorn quickly obeyed and it left Akira who was guarding their bodies.

Everyone was overjoyed when they received such good news from the White Unicorn and they quickly followed the Vrandolon back to Akira.

"Akira!" Jon called happily as he approached. "We're here to kill you now!"

"Going back to our bodies wasn't going to be as easy as we thought," said Zoroaster with a smile. "Oh, by the way, how did you find these, huh?"

Akira told them everything that happened during his search, and even everything what Maximo said about the apocalypse. The boys wondered at first, but later on they ignored about the apocalypse.

"We need to call Reinhardt now so we can return to our bodies right away," said Clio. "Isagani and I will go back to the cave. All of you, stay here."

"Would you all look at that Marion's corpse," Lucky joked as he was pointing at Marion's body. "Until now, he's still sucking his finger, hahaha!!!"

The boys laughed together (except Maximus and Marion) by Lucky's jest. Clio and Isagani ran back to the cave for fifteen minutes and they told Claude and Reinhardt everything about their search. The two were overjoyed. Afterwards, Reinhardt went with them and left Claude in the cave to look after Kenji.

"Oh, what a relief... Finally, resting time!" said Claude as he was still overjoyed.

When Reinhardt, Clio, and Isagani went back to the boys, Reinhardt immediately used his unique power to return themselves into their bodies. They successfully went back to their living state, and Reinhardt carried Claude's body and they all returned to the cave. Then, Reinhardt also returned Claude's soul to his own body. The Earth Wielder felt a great joy when he was able to touch Kenji again.

Finally, their mission was accomplished. The boys were much eager to go back to DDE base again to tell the Explorers about the success of their mission. And also, to take their full rest after their long and unforgettable journey...

64 HOME

It was five in the afternoon when the boys returned to the DDE base. Reinhardt was carrying Kenji in his arms. It was not obvious that the boys had difficulty in accomplishing their mission since their bodies were all clean and had no any wounds, not even a single scratch. When they arrived at the DDE's entrance gate, Akira thought to say goodbye to them for a while.

"Okay, 'till we meet again next time, boys…" said Akira as he waved happily. "Sorry about the incident and the delay earlier in the morning…"

"Apology not accepted!" said Lucky jokingly. "Who cares, you're reckless!"

Isagani smiled as he also joked. "Now is the time to be friends again, Akira! From what we have seen and from the way you cared about us, there's no doubt that you are the true Wielder. From now on, we're buddies!"

Akira smiled looking wondered. "R-Really, huh?"

"It doesn't matter," said Reinhardt with a smile. "Anyway, thank you for your effort in finding our bodies… And, thanks for your protection--"

"But they all disappeared," said Marion. "But it's a good thing he found it!"

The boys' stomachs began to growl one by one. Clio laughed. "Wow, now I'm feeling hungry! I am getting excited to eat again and take a long rest!"

"Yeah, it's time to eat again!" Zoroaster agreed.

"I hope that the Explands are completely gone now, because Claude destroyed the Hydra and so as their dimension," said Tyrone. "I hope so…"

"For sure, the Hydra is already gone now because we saw him shattered into pieces by Claude's blow. But I also hope that Neschar is gone too," said Akira. "By the way, we have an hour left before Kenji will be revived again."

Everyone turned their gaze at the unconscious Kenji who was being carried by Reinhardt.

"Oh right," said Claude. "Why don't you come back here later? While we're resting, we will think of a way to remove the black curse from Kenji's body."

"Can we consult King Jethro again?" asked Jon.

"It depends," answered Genji. "In our dreams, maybe!"

Akira thought about Maximo. "Hmmm, it's not yet over. The evil creature named Maximo is still alive!"

"Hmpt, let's think about that some other time!" Tyrone said impatiently. "Come on, let's get inside," and then he turned to his back. "Now scram, Akira!"

"Okay," said Akira as he smiled. "Until next time, bye!"

"Bye!" said the boys and Akira left the base. Afterwards, Shiela and Aaron came first to greet the boys before the DDEs when they entered the mansion.

"Reinhardt!" Shiela hugged Reinhardt, even though he still carried Kenji in his arms. "How are you? Where did you all come from? You've been gone for a long time!"

"That's Kenji, how is he?" asked Aaron after he noticed Kenji with so much wounds around his body. "He looks like he fought hard by looking at his wounds!"

"Please, can we talk later?" Claude asked as he wanted to rest immediately. "We're dead tired already."

"R-Rest, why?"

"And, I'm hungry!" added Marion.

Reinhardt spoke to Shiela. "Shiela, please take us to your available room so we can rest. Kenji is slightly heavy in my arms."

"We understand," answered Shiela. "Okay, I'll take you all. Come with me!"

Shiela led the boys to one of their vacant rooms. As they walked, Clio looked for the DDE leader. "By the way Shiela, where's Sir Spencer Briant?"

"He's not here right now. He and his team left for a while. They're doing their assignment."

"And you guys stayed here?"

"Yes, they've been gone for a long time."

They entered at a vacant room when Reinhardt thanked Shiela. "Thanks Shiela. Um, I don't want to be rude, but… can you also give us our privacy here for a while?"

"O-Oh, okay…" Shiela said sadly. "But I'll visit you all later, okay?"

"Sorry, but thanks…"

"No, it's alright. See you all later!" said Shiela as she waved and gently closed the door.

The boys leaned against the walls of the room.

"Hmmmm… finally," Isagani laid down on the carpet as he rested. "Rest time…"

Reinhardt gently laid Kenji on the bed. Later, they heard their stomachs growling out loud again. They looked at each other with a smile on their faces.

"Isagani, cook something!" Lucky ordered. "I'm hungry…"

Isagani was still laying down on the carpet. "And I'm still tired… I'm feeling lazy to cook right now."

"How about you, Tyrone?"

"Come on, Lucky! So am I!" said Tyrone.

"Hmmm, do you think the DDEs have already prepared some foods downstairs?" Cyan asked.

It was already 5:30pm when Shiela returned and she was with her husband, Kato. She greeted the boys. "Hello! How are you, now? Are you all alright in here?"

"Here they are!" Marion said happily and spoke to her frankly. "Hey, we're all hungry. You have some foods already prepared?"

Clio pinched Marion irritably. "Hey, you don't have manners! You can ask her nicely!"

"Oh, so the boys are hungry," said Shiela as she chuckled sweetly. "We have foods available in the main hall. The DDEs ate their lunch before they

THE EXPLORERS

left."

"That's great!" said the boys and they got back on their feet again excitedly.

Everyone went out of the room when Shiela noticed Kenji who was still lying on the bed. "Oh, how about Kenji? Hasn't he eaten yet?" she asked.

"He's sleeping," said Genji. "He'll catch up later."

"I'll wake him."

"N-No, don't," stopped Reinhardt. "He'll catch up later, don't worry."

"Hmmm," Kato observed Kenji as he touched his chin in wonder. "Is he really alright?"

"Of course."

"He's too tired…"

Tyrone stomped impatiently. "Hurry up! I'm hungryyy!!!"

"Oh yes, okay lets go," said Shiela and they gently closed the door. "Follow us."

The boys followed the couple as they went to the fancy dining hall. The delicious leftover snacks were still served. Due to their starvation, the boys (except for Maximus) hurriedly ran to the table and goofily raced ahead of each other to take the leftovers and eat.

Aaron watched everyone as they were snatching the foods and laughed. "Man, you're all so hungry for years! If Mr. & Mrs. Briant were here, they would kick you out of this mansion!"

A few moments later, the boys calmed themselves. They still ate at the dining table decently while Shiela, Kato, and Aaron were watching them. Later, Aaron looked for Kenji.

"By the way, where's Kenji?" he said.

"He's upstairs, they said he was asleep," answered Kato.

Aaron stood on his seat. "Should I wake him?"

Reinhardt stopped him. "Don't wake him, Aaron. He'll go down later."

"But he'll be left behind."

"It's alright," answered Genji as he ate. "He knows what to do."

"But where did you all go? We know that you did a sort of special mission, but where?"

Tyrone laughed as he was chewing. "None of your business!"

Aaron shrugged his shoulders. "Okay, but where did you find Kenji?"

Tyrone answered again. "In Aaron's heart!"

"Whatever you say, idiot!" Aaron said as he stomped irritably and everyone laughed.

It was six in the evening when the boys still ate at the dining table. They already had forgotten about Kenji as they were goofing around with the three DDEs.

"Isagani, taste this *biko* (sticky rice cake)!" Clio called Isagani.

"What are you eating, Zoroaster?" asked Claude.

"It's *leche flan* (Filipino custard), Mr. Eyebrow!"

"You're all so greedy," Shiela laughed. "You've eaten much already!"

"By the way, we have some *lechon baboy* (Philippine suckling pig) leftovers here," said Aaron as he served the said food. "Eat this. It was so much so we weren't able to eat all of it."

"That pig's gonna be in big, big trouble!" said Jon at the same time he took a chopping knife and goofily chopped off the meat. "A-TSA-TSA-TSA-AAAA!!!" everyone laughed.

Moments later, Shiela stood on her seat to get something from their fancy bar and spoke to the boys. "Oh, by the way... Since you've accomplished your mission and the Explands are finally defeated, why don't we celebrate a happy toast party today?" then she brought out a big bottle of red wine and placed it on the table.

"There's the exciting part!" Lucky jumped in joy. "Time to drink wine!"

Aaron helped Shiela to take the drinking glasses from the bar and gave it to the boys one by one. They put down the extra glasses on the table.

Reinhardt did not want to drink wine but he would try to taste it. Everyone filled their glasses with wine one by one, and then, they raised the glasses together at the same time.

Shiela spoke first in their toast party as her glass of wine was raised in the air. "For your accomplished mission!"

Everyone shouted. "TOAST!" and everyone drink their glass of wine at the same time.

Reinhardt and Maximus both coughed the wine out since they were not used to drink alcohol. Everyone heard their cough at the same time and they laughed out loud.

"That's okay, dudes," Jon laughed. "Learn to get used to it from now on!"

THE EXPLORERS

When they finished their first glass of wine, they filled up their glasses again for the second time and raised them to continue their toast celebration. This time, Reinhardt spoke:

"For our *(ahem!)*..." he coughed first. "F-For our victory against the Expland!"

Their glasses were still raised. Reinhardt added:

"...And also for our success in rescuing my brother, Kenji!"

"TOAST!" everyone shouted and they drank together. That's when they suddenly remembered Kenji as they also coughed out their drinks.

Claude quickly looked at his watch. "It's 6:10pm already! Maybe Kenji's awake now!"

"Oh yeah, we almost forgot to include Kenji in our toast celebration," said Shiela still holding her glass. "Let's wake him up!"

"I'll go upstairs," said Claude. "I'll check on him."

"Okay."

Claude was just about to leave the room when someone spoke coming from the dark archway in the hallway. "Don't bother, I'm here now..."

Everyone stopped. They saw Kenji coming out from a dark archway with Akira, who was now in the DDE mansion to take a visit and join with their celebration.

"Kenji! Akira!" everyone called the two newcomers happily as they looked at them with a wide smile on their faces.

Kenji smiled sweetly for everyone as his answer. Both he and Akira approached their friends when the boys patted their shoulders and their backs.

"Akira, we're so glad you came back!" Claude said happily to Akira. "And you even got inside the mansion again, hahaha!"

"Of course, attendance is a must. I don't wanna miss out the Wielder's celebration today!" Akira said happily.

Claude turned to Kenji next. "Kenji, how are you? Are you alright?"

Kenji smiled as he answered. "Of course..." and then he gently took an extra glass from the table. "Now we're all complete, do you all mind if I lead the celebration this time?"

Everyone smiled. Afterwards, Kenji also poured the wine into his glass and raised it with a sweet smile on his face. He asked. "Toast?"

Akira also took a glass and filled it with wine. Then he also raised his glass next to Kenji.

Everyone raised their glasses again when Kenji was the last one who led the celebration and spoke. "For the Explorers ultimate success!!!"

Everybody answered with a shout. "TOAST!" but instead, they splashed their wine in the air and at the same time they also jumped high in the air together!

- THE END -

BONUS CHAPTER: EXTRAS

Bonus Endings:

The Toast Party Ending

Everyone was having fun with their toast party inside the DDE mansion and both Kenji and Akira were with them. Afterwards, the two of them also ate the leftovers, and Kenji had six plates of food! Everybody laughed as they teased the greedy young man and their celebration continued.

It was passed seven in the evening when the DDEs returned to the mansion after today's assignment. Everyone was unaware of the DDE's return as they still partied inside the dining hall. When Sir Spencer and his wife entered the dining hall to take their dinner, everyone suddenly stopped and were surprised to their unexpected arrival. Shiela and Aaron immediately approached the two and they apologized, but Spencer was not angry. The boys were mum when Spencer told them that the entire DDE heard about their success in defeating Expland and rescuing Kenji. With that, the DDEs decided to join in on the Element Wielder's happy toast party inside the mansion!

Reinhardt's Ending

Since the boys did an exceptional performance and successfully accomplished their special mission, Spencer Briant of DDE decided to give them a great recognition and reward. Although Akira was non-Explorer, Spencer also included him in the acceptance of the reward, because he could see Akira's truthful loyalty towards his Wielder companions despite of being a Pioneer. A week had passed after the Toast Party, the UE Wielders had decided to return back home to the UE base.

Back in the UE mansion, the UEs were back to their everyday routine as they trained and rested within a month straight. Out of nowhere, Kenji received an emergency call from DDE. He called for all of the Element Wielders to go to the DDE mansion for an important announcement from Spencer Briant. The boys were able to go, but Kenji could not come because of the black curse that was still inside him. When the boys arrived at the DDE base, Spencer immediately looked for Reinhardt and talked to him face to face. Spencer once again apologized with all of his heart to Reinhardt for all the lies they told him in the past. Reinhardt could not hold his feelings anymore as he cried when he remembered his bitter past. But then, he immediately forgave Spencer. The two shook hands and hugged with each other with the smile on their faces.

After their private conversation, Spencer quickly called all the UE Element Wielders to listen to his announcement. In the middle of his announcement, he mentioned about his sooner retirement and Reinhardt's great potential of becoming the DDE leader. Then, he quickly announced the good news that the UE Element Wielders (including Kenji) were promoted to DDE rank. The boys were overjoyed with such good news and they hugged with each other. Then, Spencer happily approached Reinhardt and told him that he would be the next DDE Leader of the entire Explorer Family. At first, the young man declined his offer, but Spencer insisted and told that he had the potential and he was deserving to become the new Supreme Leader. Afterwards, Reinhardt happily thanked Spencer, and the DDE Leader declared to everybody that Reinhardt would be their next "Superior Leader of the Explorers Organization (DDE Leader)"!

After Spencer's formal retirement, Reinhardt, as the new DDE leader made his new rules and regulations to the three Explorer classes. Also, he

THE EXPLORERS

gave Akira's permission to enter the DDE base anytime he wanted to.

The Wild Butterfly Ending

Akira was currently on his way back to Pioneer when he unexpectedly ran into Maximo once again. But surprisingly, Akira noticed that Maximo had turned back to his original form as a Wild Butterfly again. The young man wondered how that happened, but the butterfly only said that it was caused by a strange mystery from Kenji's blood that flowed in his body. He mentioned that the young man's blood suddenly reacted in his body and gave him a mysterious warning, causing him to turn back to his original form again as a butterfly… Akira asked about the mystery, but the butterfly did not answer. Later, the Wild Butterfly laughed as it flew away from Akira to find a new victim and look for more of its hidden unique abilities!

The Water Bearer Prince's Ending

His name was Prince Maximus, a loner prince who was the only son of King Maximus X in the Reminescence family. The Reminescence discovered that he became cursed in his young age when a mysterious spirit possessed in his body and planned to kill his own father. The king learned about it so he punished his son by imprisoning him in a sealed room since childhood. When the curse left the prince's body, he became a "Waterbearer".

Maximus gained unique powers from the time he was healed by the curse. With that, he had the ability to control, talk, and summon the water. Whenever he was worshipping the water in their palace, he would play his flute and the water would dance before him. It became the prince's common routine everytime he was freed from his imprisonment by his father. His powers remained in himself until his present age.

When he arrived at Explorers, the Wielders discovered that he had a power of water and gave them an idea that he was probably the chosen Water Wielder by King Jethro. The prince had been staying with them for longer time, and yet, the Explorers' thought about his mystery was not yet answered.

The boys only learned Maximus' true personality from King Jethro in their dream after they all promoted to DDE. The god told them that Maximus was his first chosen Wielder of Water element and confessed that he was the one who possessed in the prince's body to kill his father and leave Reminescence.

Printed in Great Britain
by Amazon